THE CRYSTAL HEIR

BOOKS BY BRENDAN NOBLE

The Realm Reachers:
The Crimson Court
The Crystal Heir

Realm Reacher Novellas:
The Amber Dame
Crystal & Blood

The Frostmarked Chronicles:
A Dagger in the Winds
The Trials of Ascension
The Daughters of the Earth
The Deathless Sons
The Shards of the Moon

Frostmarked Tales:
The Rider in the Night
The Lady of Rolika

The Prism Files:
The Fractured Prism
Crimson Reigns
Pridefall
White Crown

For Breana,
Twins.
One journalist. One fantasy novelist.
Both writers. Both archers.

AUTHOR NOTE: TRIGGER WARNING

The Crystal Heir contains elements that may be triggers or traumatic to some readers, so please proceed with caution if any of the below are so for you. I have done my best to treat these serious topics carefully and with respect.

- Mental illness
- Suicidal thoughts
- Death
- Mass murder
- Torture
- Mention of attempted sexual assault

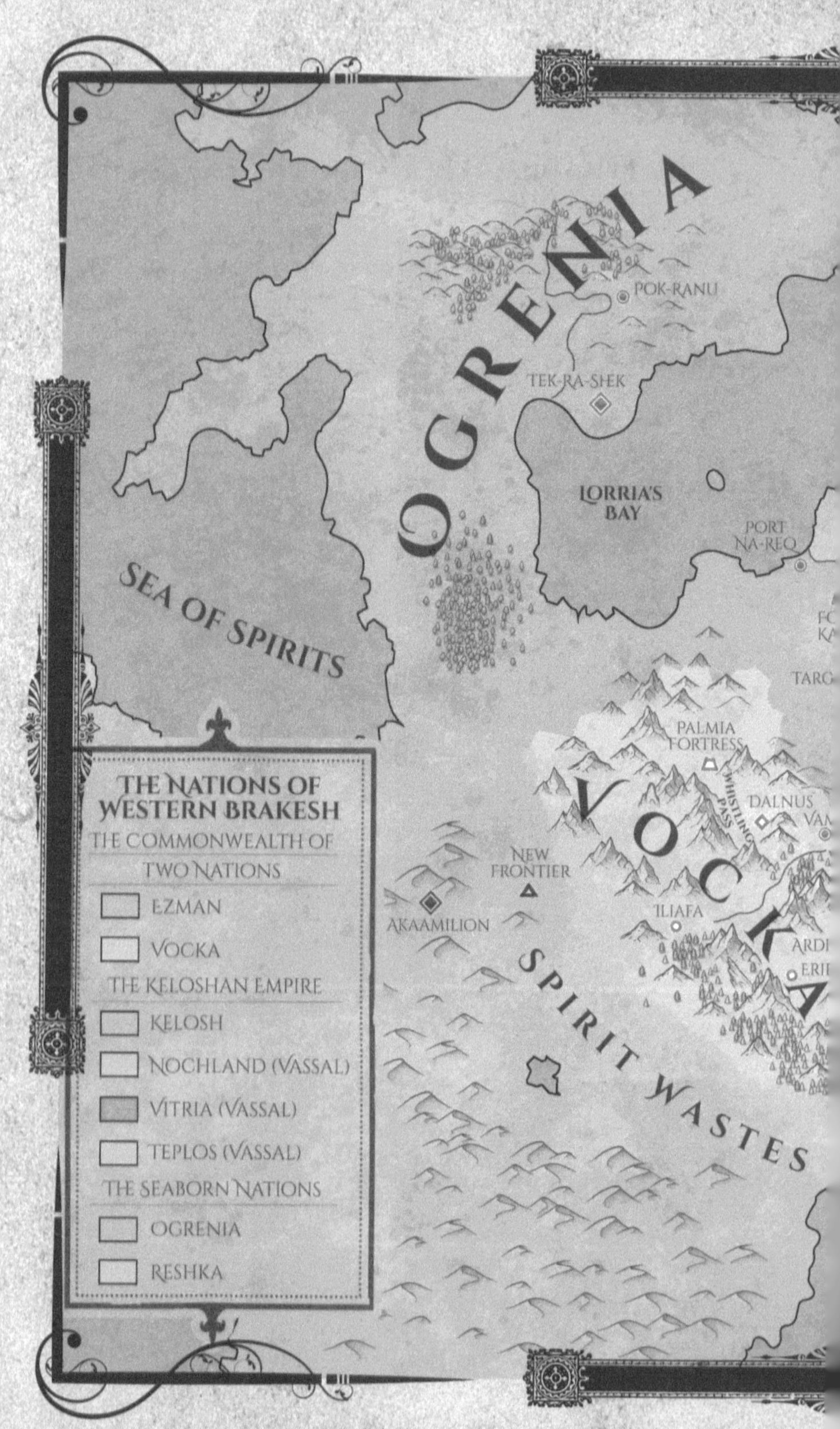
OGRENIA
POK-RANU
TEK-RA-SHEK
LORRIA'S BAY
PORT NA-REQ
SEA OF SPIRITS
FO KA
TARG
PALMIA FORTRESS
VOCKA
WHISTLING PASS
DALNUS
VAN
NEW FRONTIER
AKAAMILION
ILIAFA
ARDI ERIB
SPIRIT WASTES

THE NATIONS OF WESTERN BRAKESH
THE COMMONWEALTH OF TWO NATIONS
EZMAN
VOCKA
THE KELOSHAN EMPIRE
KELOSH
NOCHLAND (VASSAL)
VITRIA (VASSAL)
TEPLOS (VASSAL)
THE SEABORN NATIONS
OGRENIA
RESHKA

VITRIAN SEA
VITRIA
ISLE OF BALAN
KELOSH
ORIOKSTAK
LITIANITAN
OCHLAND
ZAKINIV
A RIVER
KALASTOK
ANUKIT
LOST BROTHERS' FORTS
ZMAN
TEPLO
REXANIV
FORT HARIZAK
RAVIAK FOREST
GIAMIVIK
JAANIIK
UVANESS
TYSTOK
NIMASTOK
RESHKAN COLONIES
GULF OF NIMAZ
NIMAA FORTRESS
LOONAANII CHANNEL
RESHKA
ESHKANAA

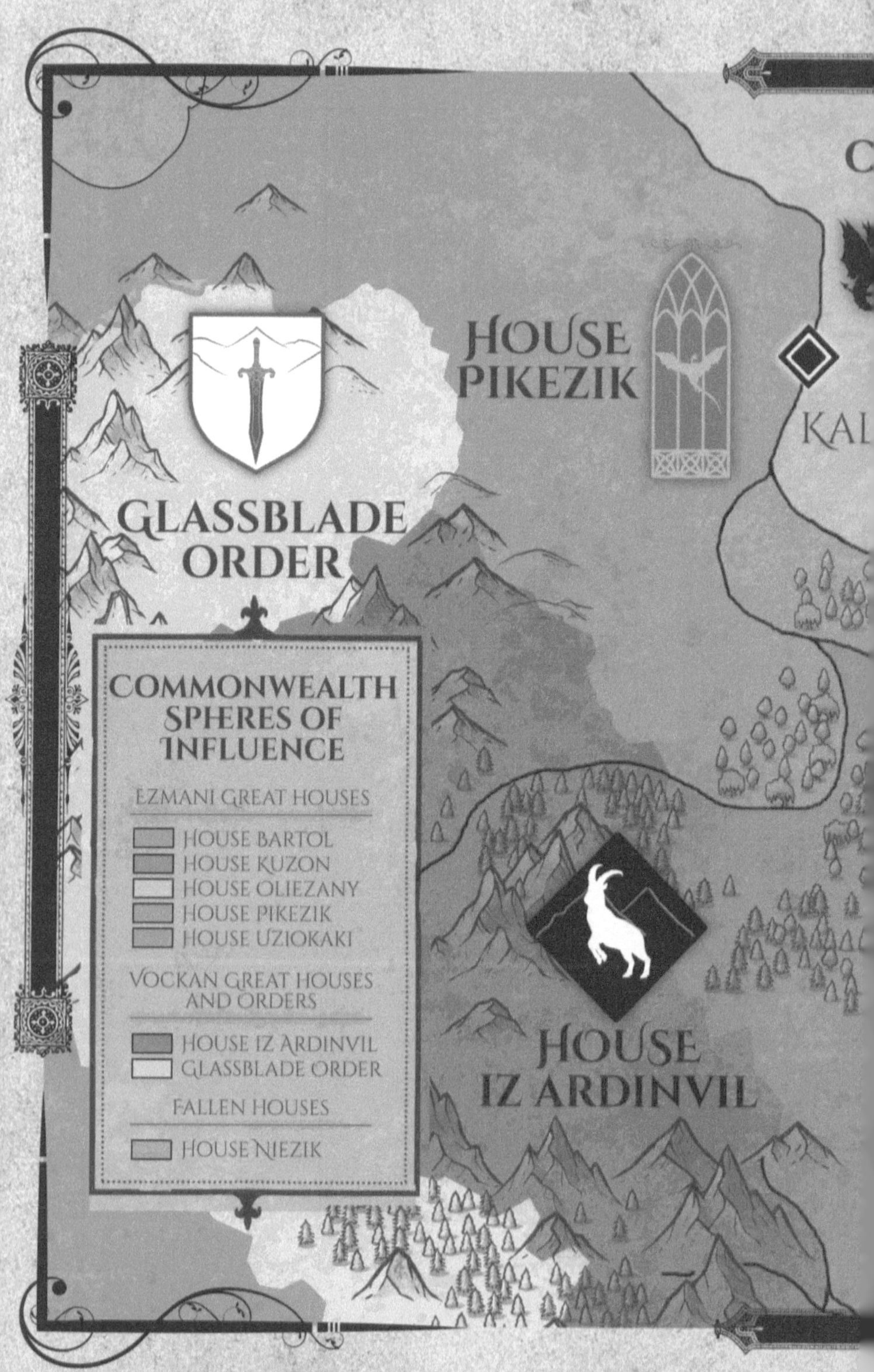

GLASSBLADE ORDER
HOUSE PIKEZIK
KAL
HOUSE IZ ARDINVIL
COMMONWEALTH SPHERES OF INFLUENCE
EZMANI GREAT HOUSES
HOUSE BARTOL
HOUSE KUZON
HOUSE OLIEZANY
HOUSE PIKEZIK
HOUSE UZIOKAKI
VOCKAN GREAT HOUSES AND ORDERS
HOUSE IZ ARDINVIL
GLASSBLADE ORDER
FALLEN HOUSES
HOUSE NIEZIK

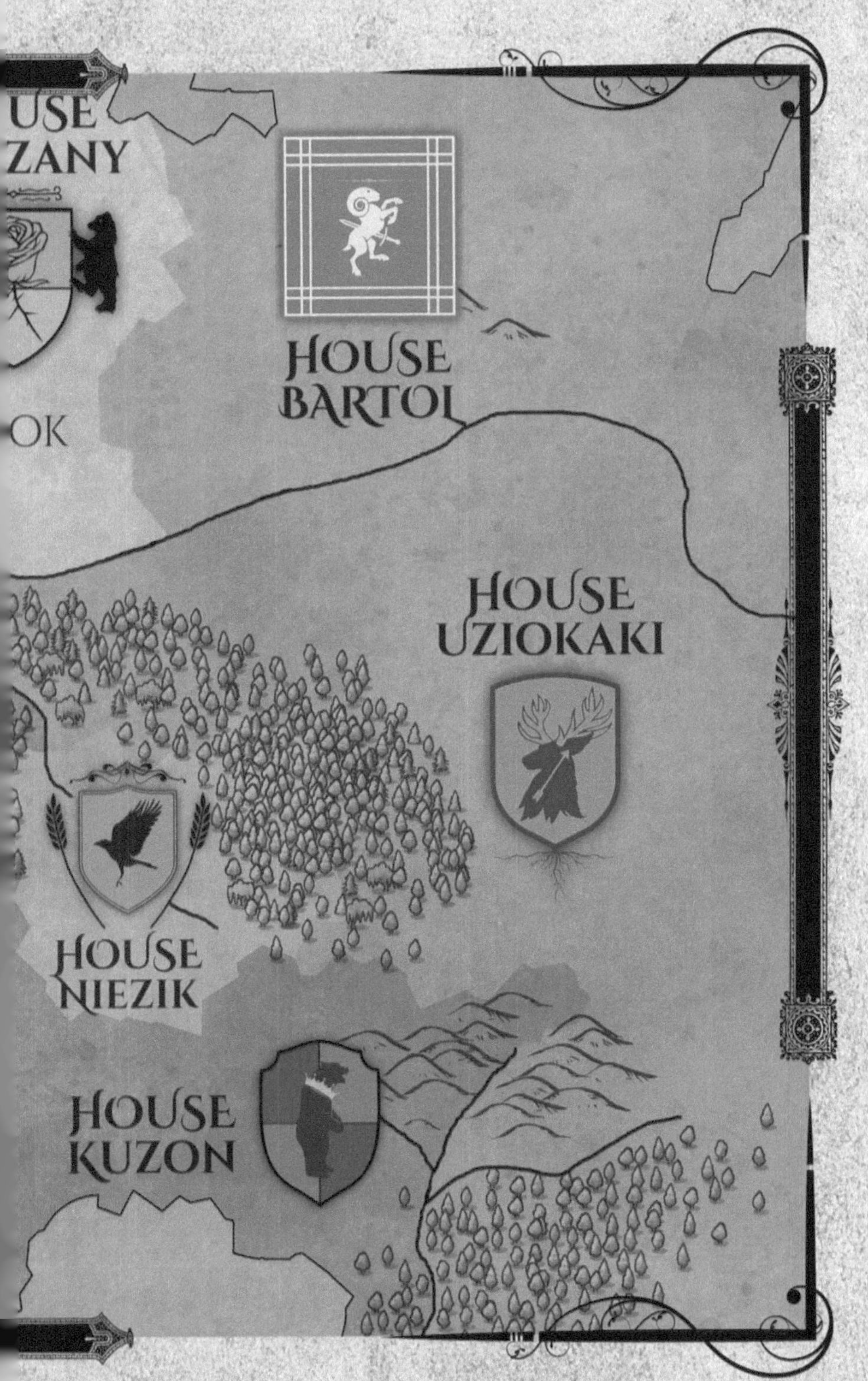

USE
ZANY
OK
HOUSE
BARTOL
HOUSE
UZIOKAKI
HOUSE
NIEZIK
HOUSE
KUZON

THE CITY OF KALASTOK
PARZINA CAFE
CRIN
NEX'S APARTMENT
SHADOW REACHER TOWER
KING'S BRIDGE REACHER TOWER
SHADOW QUARTER
ASHES OF DAWN MAIN SAFEHOUSE
ABANDONED HOMELESS ENCAMPMENT
KING'S BRIDGE
INDUSTRIAL DISTRICT
BEG AVE
KALA RIVER
IRON ALLEY PUB
INDUSTRIAL REACHER TOWER
NEW BEGIN BRID

N DISTRICT
BURIED TEMPLE
KALASTOK COLLEGE
UNIVERSITY DISTRICT
KEZIK STATE
CRYSTAL PALACE
CRYSTAL REACHER TOWER
FALIA'S HOUSE
NORTHERN MARKET
KALASTOK ARENA
HAXON'S HALL
DRIFTERS' QUARTER
NORTH MARKET REACHER TOWER
IZ VAMIUSTOK TOWNHOUSE
TEXTILE ALLEY
OLD MARKET REACHER TOWER
ET DISTRICT
ENCE
OLD MARKET CLOCKTOWER
LAZIK STREET TAVERN
Y
OLIEZANY BRIDGE REACHER TOWER

The Wars of Crimsons and Spirits
Territory as of the 100th Day of Everdark, 791 Post-Awakening
Flags & Sigils mark known Army Locations/Movements
UTIANITAN
Occupied N
NA-REQ
Ogrenian Hegemony
FORT KALA
Ezmani 3rd Army
KALASTOK
TARGEER
Crims
Glassblade Order
PALMIA FORTESS
Tiuz's Rebels
DALNUS
VAMIUSTOK
FORT HARIZAK
Radais's Expedition
VAMIA MINES
iz Ardinvil
ILIAFA
TYSTO
ARDINVIL
Harizak Confederat
ERIENFAR
Vanashel

Keloshan Empire
Reshkan Colonies
ORIAKSTAK
ZAKINIV
Ezman
Eqmani 1st Army
Eqmani 2nd Army
Grand Keloshan Army
Keloshan Reclaimers
LOST BROTHERS' FORTS
NUKIT
Bartol
Olieqann
REXANIV
Uqiokaki
GIAMIVIK
RAVIAK FOREST
Kuqon
MASTOK
shan
rators
land
Factions
HARIZAK CONFEDERATION
CRIMSON COURT & ALLIES
KELOSH | BLADES | VANASHEL
?
Legend
NATIONAL CAPITAL
REGIONAL CAPITAL
MAJOR CITY
MINOR CITY
BORDER
LINE OF CONTROL
ARMY (SIGILS/FLAGS)
ARMY MOVEMENT

THE CRYSTAL REALMS

Realm	Reacher Power	Color
Air	Summon and control air/wind	Sky Blue
Body	Heal and strengthen bodies	Blood Red
Dark	Summon complete darkness and see within it	Black
Death	Kill target's body and spirit	Purple
Earth	Manipulate earth, alter metals, call earthquakes	Brown
Fire	Summon and control fire	Orange
Force	Call force fields and blasts of energy (or smaller pushes)	Bright Red
Life	Create plants and encourage their growth/Grant life energy to a target who is near death	Green
Light	Summon pure light and see through blindness	Yellow
Mind	Manipulate a target's thoughts	Pink
Possibility	Alter odds & appearances Summon objects	Rainbow
Shadow	Summon shadows and see through them	Dark Gray
Spirit	Repel spirits or guide them	Silver
Truth	Compel target to speak the truth/Mend broken inorganic objects	White
Water	Summon and control water	Navy Blue

HOUSE EMBLEMS

NIEZIK*

UZIOKAKI

BARTOL

OLIEZANY

KUZON

PIKEZIK

IZ ARDINVIL

IZ VAMIUSTOK*

*Not Great Houses. Included for reference

FLAGS OF WESTERN BRAKESH

THE KINGDOM
OF EZMAN (CRIMSON)

THE CONFEDERATION
OF HARIZAK

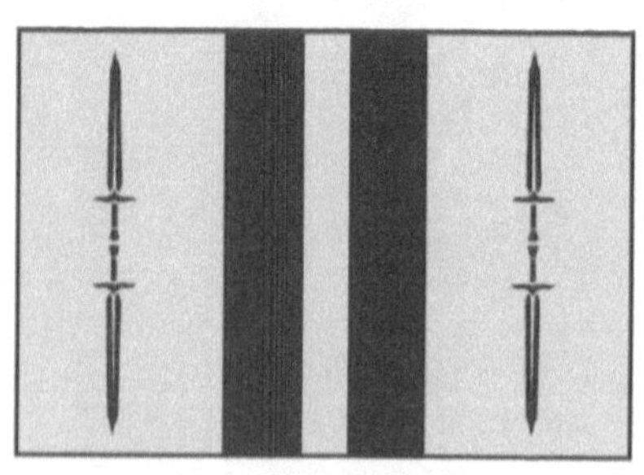

THE KELOSHAN
EMPIRE

THE OGRENIAN
HEGEMONY

THE KINGDOM
OF RESHKA

THE MERCHANT REPUBLIC
OF NOCHLAND

THE CRYSTAL BRIGADE'S RECORDS OF RELEVANT NAMES

Records valid as of final day of Everdark, 791 Post-Awakening. Classified by the Crimson King. Annotated by Tzena Oliezany.

Bakeekek – Name taken by first breathless from Kariazan Pikezik's experiments in the Spirit Wastes. Leader of the "Sands of Salesh" spirit faction. Mind Reacher/Bound One. *Notes: Kariazan, you ignorant fool. Create breathless Reachers, then die on us. We must learn more.*

Bess (pseudonym) – Female lowborn of unknown bloodline. Boss of the Murder Mitts gang. *Notes: Eliminate. Keep out of range of fists.*

Borys Kuzon – Male Ezmani scion. Patriarch of House Kuzon, sixth of spirit. Life Reacher. *Notes: Joined the Confederation. Eliminate.*

Carelias iz Vamiustok – Female Vockan (Ezmani scion blood). Sister to Sania. Aunt of Zinarus. Body Reacher. *Notes: Known radical. Allow her to live. Those like her inspire discontent in their own ranks.*

Chatik Bartol (Formerly Pikezik) – Male Ezmani scion. Crimson. King of Ezman. Patriarch of House Bartol. Dark/Unity-Crystal Reacher. Second son of late Jazuk Bartol the Fourth. Aliases: "King in the Dark" & "Crimson King." *Notes: All hail. We actually did it, my dear.*

Crax (pseudonym) – Male Ezman (may be scion, unconfirmed). Boss of Crax's Folly gang. *Notes: Figure out if he is a scion. If so, exploit.*

Etal iz Noshok – Male Vockan (Ezmani scion blood). Professor at Kalastok College. Force Reacher. *Notes: Execute. No cure can be found.*

Gregorzon Niezik – Male Ezmani scion. Contested patriarch of House Niezik. Son of Leonit, brother to Katarzyna. Fire Reacher. *Notes: You, young one, have immense potential*

Hazat Tozki – Male Ezmani scion. Son of Crimson Fantil Tozki. Spirit Reacher. *Notes: Let him join the Brigade. He could be more than Fantil.*

Iktaros ik Vamiustok – Male Vockan lowborn. Cavalry officer. Served under Tiuz Hazeko. *Notes: Eliminate Tiuz's former soldiers.*

Ivalat iz Ardinvil – Male Vockan (Ezmani scion blood). Patriarch of House iz Ardinvil, second of spirit. Father of Manalias. Spirit Reacher. *Notes: In custody. To be used when the time is right.*

Jazuk Bartol – Male Ezmani scion. Former king of the Commonwealth of Two Nations. Father of Lakuzk and Chatik. Grandfather of Nikoza. Spirit Reacher. *Notes: Deceased. Now our real work begins.*

Jolzena Kaerz – Female Ezmani scion. Crimson. Twin sister to Vanzearik. Force Reacher. *Notes: Disloyal, but she will serve her purpose.*

Katarzyna (Kasia) Niezik – Female Ezmani scion. Contested matriarch of House Niezik. Daughter of Leonit. Sister to Gregorzon. Axiom Bound. Former Death Reacher. Aliases: "Amber Dame" & "Death's Daughter." *Notes: Threat to the Cause. Find & eliminate.*

Lazan Karianam – Male Ezmani scion. Body Reacher. *Notes: Affiliations with supreme defender Radais and K. Niezik. Can keni buy his loyalty?*

Lilita Pikezik – Female Ezmani scion. Matriarch of House Pikezik, third of spirit. Spirit Reacher. *Notes: We must find her and the children.*

Lok-Tag Rekta – Male Ogrenian lowborn. Boss of the Glass Teeth gang. *Notes: We need him to keep the Kala clear. Negotiate or dump him in it.*

Manalias iz Ardinvil – Spirit-shifted Female Ezmani scion. Heir of House iz Ardinvil, third of spirit. Fire Reacher. *Notes: Rebel. Eliminate.*

Nex (pseudonym) – Genderless Ogrenian lowborn with traces of scion blood. Unregistered Possibility Reacher. Aliases: Naniana-Li, Ariaxa, Tarak-Nan. Wanted for theft, gambling fraud & espionage with Ogrenian agents. *Notes: Keep an eye on them. Could be trouble.*

Nikoza Bartol – Female Ezmani scion. Former heir of House Bartol. Granddaughter of late Jazuk Bartol the Fourth. Niece of Chatik Bartol. Water Reacher. *Notes: Protect at all costs.*

Otterzon Oliezany – Male Ezmani scion. New patriarch of House Oliezany, ninth of spirit. Son of Gornioz Oliezany the Eighth. Spirit Reacher. *Notes: You may be patriarch, Cousin, but you are but a puppet.*

Paras ik Lierasa – Male Vockan lowborn. Alchemist in west Kalastok. *Notes: Deceased. Katarzyna lied, but we have rectified the situation.*

Polina ik Aniaka – Female half-Vockan, half-Reshkan lowborn. Glassblade commander. *Notes: Never trust Reshkans. Even half corrupts.*

Qaraza Uziokaki – Female Ezmani scion. Crimson. New matriarch of House Uziokaki, second of spirit. Minister of war & rural affairs. Spirit Reacher. *Notes: If we lose these wars, she will receive my dagger first.*

Radais ik Erienfar – Male Vockan lowborn. New Glassblade supreme defender. *Notes: Affiliated with K. Niezik. Watch. May be useful.*

Razamat Uziokaki – Male Vockan lowborn. Commander. Spirit Reacher. *Notes: Lost duel to K. Niezik. Let him prove himself worthy.*

Rakekeaa – Rumored Sands of Salesh breathless commander. Shadow Reacher/Bound One. *Notes: If the spirits already have armies…*

Sania iz Vamiustok - Female Vockan (Ezmani scion blood). Matriarch of House iz Vamiustok. Sister to Carelias. Mother to Zinarus. Former lover of Uzrin Ioniz. Light Reacher. *Notes: Use her if the son refuses to cooperate. Zinarus is too honorable to let his mother suffer.*

Tairanik ik Oraikus – Male Vockan lowborn. Glassblade commander. *Notes: Reports say he values tradition. Could we set him against Radais?*

Tazper Janka – Male Ezmani scion. Footman of Katarzyna Niezik. No known Reaching. *Notes: Eliminate. Revealed all he knows already.*

Tiuz Hazeko – Male Ezmani scion. Field Marshal of the Harizak Confederation. Spirit Reacher. *Notes: Eliminate. He threatens the Cause.*

Tzena Oliezany – Female Ezmani scion. Minister of crime. Captain of Crystal Brigade. Cousin to Otterzon Oliezany. Shadow Reacher. *Notes: How far we have come…*

Uzrin Ioniz – Male Ezmani scion. Crimson. New patriarch of House Ioniz. Truth Reacher. *Notes: Why is Chatik trusting him? Of all our allies…*

Vanzearik Kaerz – Male Ezmani scion. Crimson. Twin brother to Jolzena. Spirit Reacher. *Notes: The twin is disloyal. This one is far more.*

Vinnia (surname unknown) – Female half-Vockan, half-Reshkan lowborn. *Notes: Rumored to be connected to Nex.*

Wanusa ik Iliafa – Female Vockan lowborn. Glassblade warrior. *Notes: Apprentice to supreme defender. Naïve. Useful?*

Yaakiin Tinaanuuk – Male Reshkan scion. Former King of the Commonwealth of Two Nations. Fourth of spirit. Spirit Reacher. *Notes: Deceased. It feels like ages ago.*

Zinarus iz Vamiustok – Male half-Vockan, half-Ezmani scion. Heir of House iz Vamiustok. Bastard son of Uzrin Ioniz. Truth Reacher. *Notes: Accomplice to K. Niezik. Seize assets. Get rid of Uzrin's spawn.*

Notes on Spirits

From Kalastok College's archives.

Inheritance Rituals: A practice conducted in various forms across the Spirit realm of Zekiaz, it is limited to the Commonwealth of Two Nation's great houses. The process involves the house head (also called a magnate), their heir, the heir's newborn child, and a Spirit Reacher. The heir uses a specialized blade to kill the magnate, releasing their spirit and allowing the Reacher to guide it into the newborn. When done correctly, the child will gain the spirit's experiences when they themselves touch the Spirit Crystal and become a Reacher.

Types of Spirits

Drifters/Pure Spirits: The most basic form of spirit birthed from the Spirit Crystal itself. A spirit must inhabit a child within twenty hours (one day) of birth, or the child will become an empty husk. Drifters are harmless, and it is believed they endure through passive spirit energy emitted by the Spirit Crystal.

Awakened: First appearing during the Awakening nearly eight hundred years ago, it is not known how the awakened were created. Theories suggest that a drifter was infused with Life Reaching, thus requiring the "awakened" spirit to devour other spirits to endure. Glass and Spirit Reachers are the only known ways to repel or kill awakened.

Breathless: This newest form of spirit only recently emerged due to the studies of the Crimson Court's Kariazan Pikezik. It is believed they were created by infusing Mind Reaching with an awakened, granting them both sentience to tame their aggressiveness, but we are not yet aware of what energy allows them to endure.

Bound Ones: This is the word the breathless use for the Realm Reachers among them. It is not known whether they are limited by the First Law of Reaching, or if they endure Realm Taint at all.

Acknowledgements

There is not much that can match the joy of creating something you love, and I am so grateful for the incredible support of those who helped make *The Crystal Heir* happen. An author crafts the story. The process of publishing a project like this, though, is not one I can complete alone.

My thanks begin with my editor, Kavin Narke at Space Mage Press for providing crucial checks to help me take another step with this book. An amazing amazing team of beta readers both returning and new were also incredible with reading early copies of this monstrous book. With their help, I've managed to refine the lacking storylines and ensure the best moments could truly shine. Those beta readers were (in alphabetical order): Aldchad, Andrea W. N., Ann D., Brandon S., Crystal D., Drew G., Felicia, Filipa R., Hannah S., Jessica J., Jo-Ann C., K.B. Diaz, L. Cawkins, Lizz T., Lynda W., Nick F., Rebecca C., Ryan W., SAM K., Spencer W., and a few more anonymous Reachers. *The Crystal Heir* was a collaborative effort because of all of your feedback, and I cannot thank them enough for diving into such a massive novel in its unrefined form.

After the success of *The Crimson Court*'s Kickstarter, I wanted to truly take the art for this second book to the next level. Kateryna Vitkovksa continued her work on the series with the beautiful cover art of Nikoza Water Reaching, the mirrored hardcover art with Nex, and the interior landscape art of a certain purple realm (hint hint). I brought in new artists as well with Eddie Yorke and Alhin Row. Book one had many portraits, so Eddie's dynamic work on the action art pieces of Zinarus, Kasia, the Crimson King, and Radais & Wanusa brought incredible new depth and expressions of the magic in the Crystal Realms. I wanted to expand on our portraits with more full color too, and Alhin's portraits of Kasia and Nikoza had me falling out of my chair. I must also thank Deranged Doctor Design for their final text and formatting work for the book's cover!

It was an incredible honor to work with such amazing illustrators.

Truly, I hope you enjoy seeing all these artists' illustrations as much as I enjoyed collaborating with them. Their artwork brings these books to life, and I am excited for more creations in the future!

We also have expanded into audiobooks for this series, so I want to express my gratitude to Ellie Gossage for her passion as narrator. She had to do over *one hundred voices* for each of these books. That is amazing, and there is something special about hearing her literally grant voices to these characters.

These projects are a huge time commitment, and I am so thankful for my wife, Andrea, and her support. She is my first reader and first to give feedback on any designs. That means you can credit for anything that looks good! If it was not for her being willing to hear my rambling thoughts about these books as well, I probably would lose my mind (in addition to all the hair I already lost making these books haha).

Lastly, before all the awesome Kickstarter backers who made this book happen, I want to thank my author friends in our "Tuesday Tribe" group. They were the ones who convinced me to do Kickstarter in the first place, and they are such incredible touch points for feedback and questions. I would not be where I am as an author and publisher if it were not for their help.

Now, it none of the rest of this could happen without the support of readers, and I have been overwhelmed with the enthusiasm of the Kickstarter backers for this series. I was not sure how a sequel book would go, so it going above and beyond the first in funding was incredible. Thank you all for your support and trust. We are building these stories together! Here are all those backers:

A Vogel

Adam Maynard Myers

Adam Nemo

Adrian McAuliffe

ALB

Aldchad

Alex Joyner

Alex Laemmle

Alexandra Corrsin

Anders Sørensen

Andrew Barnett

Anja Peerdeman

Anna Liang

Annie Kavanagh

April Ayton

Arwyn Cunningham

Ash Monogue

Ashley Byrd

Bill Kong

Billye Herndon

Boris Bunschoten
Brandon Simmons
Breana Noble
Bryan "Dorkasuarus" Ballard
C.Niehot
Caitlyn Price
Camithril
Carissa Boehmer
Cat Parker
Cathy McLoughlin
Chantelle-Emma Hilton
Charles E. Norton III
Chase McGlinchey
Chelsea Harper
Cheyenne Thompson
Chris Brimmage
Christie Silvers
Christopher Bernardo
Christopher Wesselstam
Claire Jarvis
Cody L. Allen
Connor Barrett
Cortney Babcock
D.J. Desmond
Danielle "Dandelion" Riccardi
Danielle Anderson
Danny O
David Holzborn
David L
David Oliver Kling
Dawn Marie
Drew Gohmann
Drosfix
Elivin Mendez
Emma Adams
Eric Vilbert
Erik Cieslewicz
Erika McCorkle
Ethan L
Flemming
Franchesca Caram
George Lundie
Georgina Nicholls
Gianna Christopher
Heather Cooper
Heiko Koenig
Holly Hansen
Hugo Essink
Ian Bannon
Ike
In loving memory of Basil Martin
Iris Juylyenne
Irma Thompson
Jairo Rosado

Jamie & Thaila Cook
Jamie Lindsell
Jan B
Jennifer Saldana
Jessica Johnson DVM
Joe Barros
Joe Rixman
John Idlor
Jon M
Jon Marino
Jonathan Hamm
Jordie Polly
Jose Vicab
JP Rindfleisch IX
Julie Drucker
K M
K.V. Sentinel
Kallen Frieling
Karin Holt
Karrie C
Kassie H
Kate Stuppy
Katherine Leslie
Katherine Malloy
Katrina G
Keith Dolan
Kelli and Joshua Luebke
Kelly Hogue
Kelsey Stenberg
Kimberly Sudbrink
Kirsten
Kjalar Odins
Kupo
Leslie
Liza Clarke
Lora Cawkins
Lorin Francell
Lou Dakin
Lukas
M. H. Woodscourt
Madeline Cawkins
Madge Watson
Magnus S. M. Johannessen
Maira O.
Marcellin FROSCHAUER
Matt Godec
Matt R
Matthea W. Ross
Matthew Miller
Melinda Kucsera
Merle Schlanke
Michael B Mitchell
Michael Johnson
Michelle Sanchez

michikogail cooh
Mike Dubost
Mike Vance
Misti Jorges
Morgan G.
Nancy Richey
Nathan Daleness
Nathaniel
Nguyen Tran
Nicholas Paynter
Nick Fragosa
Nicolas Kubacki
Nicole Sanders
Paul Staples
Poischeltier
PunkARTchick "Ruthenia"
Qavee
Quinn Giguiere
Rachel
Raúl Aguilar López
Rebecca Chappell
Ricardo Monascal
Ringmaster
Robert Brown
Rosalina Night
Rumen Ganev
Ryan H.
Ryan Wearmouth
Sara Lawson
SaraBeth Roberson
Sarah-Jane Baird
Sean Gray
Shanon M. Brown
Sharon Karpierz
Simon Grant
SnapDragon Esq
Spencer Wright
Starr Z. Davies
Stephanie Fischer
Sunny Side Dice
Tamara Hart Heiner
Tanya Semmons
Tanya Young
Terry Mitchell Hulett
Tetiana Kocherhan
The Tinsleys
Trevor Jerome
Trevor Roelfs
Tyler Cheek
Valerie A. Sizemore
Vanessa Mohr
Victoria P
Vid Lenarcic
Walter E. Alvarez Jr

Warren McColgan
Wendy Martinez
Xiomara Reyes
Zeb Berryman

THE STORY SO FAR

Nearly thirteen years ago in the Spirit realm of Zekiaz, a seemingly rogue spirit broke into the mansion of Leonit Niezik and assassinated him in the presence of his young daughter, Kasia. Years later, Kasia discovers that her father had left her a list of names of those who had conspired to kill him, followed by the name of an organization she has hunted ever since: the Crimson Court.

Kasia uses her magical Death Reaching to kill those associated with the Crimson Court. But this power comes at a heavy cost, as her inability to control it leads to the death of her lover, Aliax, and a dozen bystanders. Those she has killed through her Reaching now haunt her as her investigation leads her to Kalastok, the capital of the Commonwealth of Two Nations.

Far to the west, Radais of the spirit-hunting Glassblade Order discovers the strange death of a noble scion deep in the uninhabited Spirit Wastes. Deadly awakened spirits appear to be growing more dangerous, and he believes the deceased scion knows why. His former lover and the leader of the Glassblades, Miv, orders him to go to Kalastok to seek aid from the capital's scions. Except when he arrives, he finds Kasia is the only influential scion willing to listen.

Kasia ingratiates herself in Kalastok society and politics, all while seeking the magnate Sazilz Uziokaki, whom she believes to be a Crimson leader. Her efforts grow more difficult, though, when awakened spirits attack the city, forcing her to reveal her illegal Death Reaching as she works with Radais to stop them. She also discovers her family's valuable amber can be used to capture spirits.

Soon after, Sazilz Uziokaki invites her to a gala at the mansion of the great house Oliezany, whose patriarch she suspects is also Crimson. When she arrives, she connects with a half-Ezmani, half-Vockan scion by the name of Zinarus iz Vamiustok. Unbeknownst to her, he was recently accosted by a Dark Reacher robed in red, who forced him to sell his family's valuable sand mines (used for creating spirit-resistant glass). Their shared skepticism, and perhaps attraction, lead him to aid her in her infiltration of House Oliezany.

That infiltration allows Kasia to discover that same Dark Reacher threatening Sazilz, whose life the Reacher offers her as a gift. The Reacher claims Sazilz ordered her father's death, not the Crimson Court, and that Kasia could be useful to the organization. Kasia Death Reaches and kills Sazilz, pretending to join the Crimsons to discover the true leader's identity.

To further her pursuit, Kasia allies with Nex from the slums of Kalastok. Nex is a Possibility Reacher who is searching for a cure to the Spirit Plague that has infected their lover. They are skilled at following people on rooftops, and with their help, Kasia infiltrates the Crimsons further until she receives an invitation to officially join the organization.

She is taken to a remote manor, where the Crimson Court gathers to open a portal to a sixteenth realm at the center of the other Crystal Realms. The Dark Reacher calls it the Axiom, and with Kasia's Death Reaching, they finally have the final Reacher required to open the portal. The Dark Reacher reveals himself as Chatik Pikezik, the second son of King Jazuk, and claims his goal is for the noble scions of Ezman to conquer the entire realm of Zekiaz.

When Chatik successfully opens the portal to the Axiom with Kasia's help, she follows him, entering a strange realm where gravity is shifted. He is furious at her betrayal and shoots her. The bullet destroys the crystal Reacher talon on her finger, effectively removing her powers and nearly killing her until a strange force in the Axiom saves her.

The force claims that Chatik stole an artifact called the Unity Crystal, granting him abilities from across all the realms. It is dangerous and must be returned for the stability of the Crystal Realms to be maintained. Kasia agrees to take back the Unity Crystal in return for the ability to Axiom Reach, allowing her to create a portal back to Kalastok.

In Kasia's absence, Zinarus and Nex join with Princess Nikoza Bartol, the granddaughter of King Jazuk, who helps them work with Professor Etal iz Noshok to find a cure for the Spirit Plague. They learn that spirit-capturing amber is also an essential part of the cure, and together, they gather spirits for Etal to use in his potion.

The Crimson Court captures Kasia's trusted footman, Tazper, after her betrayal and forces him to reveal her past murders. Upon her return to Kalastok, she is now a wanted criminal and teleports without direction in order to escape.

Meanwhile, Radais and his Glassblade allies travel into the Spirit Wastes to investigate the strange awakened spirits further. He is accompanied by a young initiate, Wanusa, and a Body Reacher, Lazan, whom he grows close to after coordinated spirits ambush the Glassblades and capture Miv.

A group of spirits called the Saleshi soon rescues the Glassblades and reveals that they are sentient spirits created by the Crimson Court. The Crimsons invented the Spirit Plague to test the process of creating awakened and turning them into "breathless" spirits with controllable minds. Along the way, the Crimsons sought to create Bound Ones—spirits that could Reach into other realms. The spirit bound to the Mind realm broke free, creating the reclusive Saleshi faction of spirits. Another group of free breathless and Bound Ones called the Vanashel seek instead to destroy humanity. They kidnapped Miv during their initial raid, and Radais swears to save her.

Kasia's misguided portal sends her to perceived safety with Radais, who reveals the Crimson Court's schemes to her. She realizes the plague and breathless spirits are how the Crimsons killed her father and how they intend to stage a coup. With Radais's evidence in hand, she returns to Zinarus and pleads with him to expose the Crimsons in front of the Chamber of Scions. He reluctantly does so after some romantic persuasion on her part, but Princess Nikoza refuses to aid his efforts, trying to protect her family against conspiracy.

When Chatik seeks to convince the Chamber of Scions to depose

King Jazuk peacefully due to his perceived weakness against the invading Keloshan Empire, Zinarus's evidence exposes Chatik as part of the Crimsons' conspiracy. Chatik calls upon the crystalline dragon behind the throne to kill the king, then summons an army of breathless. With the help of his Crimson allies, spirits, and the Unity Crystal, he forces the entire Chamber to make him king.

Kasia attempts to intervene to stop the coup, but even her new Axiom Reaching is not enough to stop Chatik's overwhelming power. She instead desperately tries to teleport both herself and Zinarus to safety. She's overused her power, though, and Realm Taint causes the portal to send them somewhere far from her intended destination.

All the while, a riot consumes Kalastok as the poor lowborn rebel against the government's war conscription and inability to stop the plague. Nex has a cure for their lover, but not for everyone, and the riots lead to mass burning across the city. Princess Nikoza, seeing her mistake to not aid Zinarus, uses her Water Reaching to save a family from the fires in one of Kalastok's poorer districts.

In the ashes of the coup and riot, a famous general named Tiuz Hazeko receives a gift from a mysterious benefactor: a gun capable of shooting glass bullets to kill spirits. He swears to defend the Commonwealth against those who seek its destruction.

THE CRYSTAL HEIR

BRENDAN NOBLE

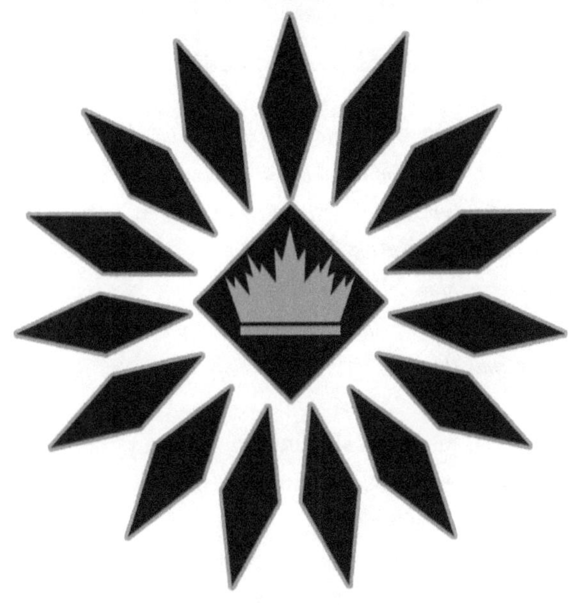

PROLOGUE – THE CRYSTAL'S COST

"It is better to have wielded great power and been slain for it than to wither in irrelevance, knowing you have accomplished nothing." – Queen Caztroma Pikezik the Fourth, uniter of the tribes of Ezman

I am dying.

Those words stung like the fury of a thousand hornets beneath the quill of the Crimson King. He wrote them in the safety of the Crystal Palace's walls, far from rebels and assassins, but he could not flee from the truth. To do so was cowardice, and Chatik Bartol the First was anything but a coward.

The Axiom was all we hoped for, unlocking the greatest power Zekiaz has seen since the Awakening, if not in its entire history. I have channeled the Essence of gods, but I am a mere mortal. I knew there would be risks.

That is why I have you.

I worry not for my legacy nor my crown. The Crimson Cause goes beyond my own vendettas and wills. It is the hope for Ezman, of all of Zekiaz. It is the key to defeating our foes and regaining the glory we lost through weaklings such as Yaakiin and my father. With me or without, the Crimson Court shall not fall.

In the time I have left, I lay the foundations of an empire that shall outlast

us both, but I am nothing more than its creator. You shall rise from my ashes. You shall take the remnants of my spirit and create a new religion, a new truth.

There is no god. There is no Crystal Mother. There is only the Unity Crystal and the one who speaks for it: the Crystal Heir.

All others are nothing. No army. No technology. No politicians. They are irrelevant. All that matters is the Unity Crystal and channeling it to the betterment of Ezman and the scion race. Beyond my life, the Crimson Cause must endure.

Chatik paused, his hand shaking so violently that ink splattered across the page. He gripped it with his other and cursed. Had he become an invalid so quickly?

The spasms refused to relent, forcing him to set the quill aside before it ruined the whole letter. He sat back in his cushioned wooden chair and stared up at the ceiling of the study in his chambers. As the newly declared king by the Chamber of Scions, more marble and glass filled his rooms than every lowborn house in the Commonwealth of Two Nations. The Crystal Palace was a tribute to something greater. It deserved more than the likes of Jazuk and his Reshkan-born predecessor.

Chatik should have been the king to fulfill such glory. Fate had other plans, but he had accounted for every possibility... except for that bitch Katarzyna Niezik.

Without Lord Zinarus iz Vamiustok's objections at her bidding, Chatik would have taken power with ease. Instead, the half-blood's words had ignited an uprising within the Commonwealth as the Keloshan Empire's troops flooded across the eastern border. The Crimsons would crush both, but he feared the cost. The visions, hunger, weakness, and chill were too much after his coup. Realm Taint inflicted all who pushed beyond the limits of the First Law of Reaching. With the Unity Crystal in his grasp, he had broken it more often than he could count.

It was apparent now that his body and mind would fail him before long. Instead of years to nurture his Crystal Heir into fully believing the Crimson Cause, he would have a few seasons at most, making the entire plot susceptible to their foes.

THE CRYSTAL HEIR

All the more reason why the Crimson Court must be maintained, he told himself, grabbing the Unity Crystal and rising with some effort. *Our knowledge and foresight will ensure the Crystal Heir can continue what I have begun.*

"Are you well, my lord?" his manservant said from along the wall. A silver veil shimmered over the lowborn's face, matching his suit with its shirt's collar upturned so high it framed the veil to his ears. Only a blood red cravat pierced the sea of spirit gray.

Chatik collected himself and fixed his posture against all protestations of his body. People needed strength in the aftermath of the Crimson Coup, and he could not be seen as Tainted. Fear and Mind Reaching alike would hold the scions and lowborn in line for a time. Some in the Chamber, though, would demand that he earned their confidence.

So the king straightened his crimson suit, streaked with elements of black down the arms to match the current stylings of the aristocrats, and waved off the servant. "No, I am fine." He caught himself before offering an explanation which a lowborn servant did not deserve.

The manservant bowed. Chatik did not know his name, as he had created the Crimson Court's established code of veiled, nameless lowborn to ensure they knew their place. Only the greater scions had inherited the ability to Realm Reach through the Spirit Crystal, and only they could build the world that the Spirit realm of Zekiaz must become. Lowborn could not feel the realms at their fingers. They were just as their class implied—lowly beings to be commanded.

Chatik left his chambers to enter a marble hall lined with glasswork designs upon its walls and pilasters. Veiled servants stood at attention by each embedded column, bowing their heads as he passed. He gave them not even a glance, focusing instead on the woman waiting by the double doors at the hall's end.

The quarter-year everdark still suffocated the world beyond the windows, but Lady Tzena Oliezany's eyes shone like the great light of the dawn. Dressed in a high-collared dress of crimson that shimmered with golden designs, she resembled a queen more than a courtier. Crystal Mother knew she had the ambition to become one.

"Where is she?" Chatik muttered to Tzena as the servants opened the doors to the next hall.

She followed at his side, her footsteps like thunder rolling across his skull. Why did everything echo in this damned place, even with the Ezmani red rugs lining the floors? Or had his Taint merely made his mind vulnerable?

"It appears," Tzena began, a hint of nerves in her voice, "that Lady Lilita slipped away overnight with the help of her Pikezik mercenaries and a few minor scions. The trail runs cold there, as of now, as it seems she placed her bribes well. No one has revealed much, but my agents within the city—and Qaraza's beyond—are working tirelessly to find both her and your children."

Chatik held his hands behind his back as they ascended the stairs. The Unity Crystal was rough, uneven in his grasp, but holding it gave him confidence amid chaotic times.

His wife had fled after the coup. He had expected such betrayal, as Lilita had been far too prideful to resort to such dire means to get rid of King Jazuk, but his loyal guards were supposed to ensure she could not take his three children. They were all gone. Unacceptable! Though they were not to be the Crystal Heir, his son and two daughters would be the last remnants of his blood upon this realm. He had abandoned the Pikezik name to regain control of his birth house, House Bartol, but he would not abandon his children.

"Uzrin's Truth Reachers will loosen their tongues or cut them out," he replied. "However, that will not be enough. We must rebuild the Crystal Brigade and mold it in our image. Can I trust you to lead them and uproot dissent within Kalastok?"

"Gladly," Tzena said with a pleased smile. "There will be many, but there is no grievance among the scions that balls, wine, glass, and brothels cannot solve. As for the lowborn, well…" She balled her gloved hand into a fist. "They will require further persuasion."

Her lips parted for a moment to continue, then fell back together.

Like all great house scions, she was well-trained to hide her worries, but Chatik noticed the hesitation and stopped at the landing.

"Who else fled?" he whispered, softly taking her arm. "I had hoped my actions had frightened the house heads into submission, but something tells me you are about to say otherwise."

Her mouth formed a narrow line. "Your dear wife was not the only great house leader with deep enough pockets to slip free. We both know Borys Kuzon was one of Jazuk's most trusted allies, and it seems House Bartol's own servants aided in his escape. Though Ivalat iz Ardinvil tried the same, he lacked such connections." She tilted up her chin. "Uzrin's interrogators are working on Ivalat at this very moment. His family, however, is problematic. If Lilita intends to rebel as we lose houses Kuzon and iz Ardinvil—"

"Then the entire west falls from our control, yes," Chatik interrupted, biting his cheek. This was far from ideal, but a few rebel houses could hardly compare to the Commonwealth army which now fell into Crimson hands. If his plans with the controllable breathless spirits succeeded, a few thousand lowborn soldiers lost in a civil war would not hurt their efforts. In fact, it could accelerate them. "By the Mother, how did our guards miss a man as large as a carriage? Borys could be seen from halfway across Ezman!"

"I cannot say that I have an answer, but I will hasten to find one."

He huffed and released her, then offered her his arm. They continued up the stairs together, and his chest tightened knowing what awaited them at the top. Only a day ago, much of Kalastok's Market District and western city had burned during the idiotic lowborn uprising against conscription. It was up to him to quell the unrest. The spirits would be quite helpful with that, but *guided* unrest had its uses as well.

Glass doors greeted them on the next floor along with a group of guards clad in red. Most had also worn Vockan white before the coup, but the Crimson Court held no concern for Ezman's western brother. Vocka had neither Reachers nor access to the Spirit Crystal. At best, it was a vassal state, not an equal in the so-called Commonwealth of Two Nations.

Chatik nodded at the guards—who thumped their chests in salute—then passed through the doors as a pair of lowborn servants opened them to reveal a balcony overlooking Kalastok. Darkness swallowed what lay beyond, only broken by gas lamps hissing along the walls on either side of the door.

"It is about time our Crimson King graced us with his presence," Uzrin Ioniz said, lingering in the shadowed corner with a burned down cigar smoldering in his grasp. The silver-haired Truth Reacher had risen swiftly in status. Once an estranged Ioniz cousin too insignificant to have a Body Reacher fix his still bent nose, he had found a seat in the Chamber of Scions and now stood as a member of the Crimsons' inner circle. Unfortunately, the actions of his bastard son, Zinarus, remained a nuisance Chatik would have to address.

"You forget yourself, Uzrin," another woman mused from across the balcony, a glass of wine dangling from her gloved fingers. "The King in the Dark has stepped into the light and enlightens us with his presence."

Like Tzena, Qaraza the Second—newly ascended matriarch of House Uziokaki—had dressed for a ball more than a meeting of collaborators. Her elaborate gown had a collar high and tight enough to appear as if it were choking her, but beneath, a slit cut from sternum to navel, exposing just enough of her pale-gray Ezmani skin to tickle a man's imagination. Uzrin stared at that slit like it were a canyon.

Chatik sighed as he examined the three Crimsons who were to be his closest confidants. Tzena and Uzrin had proved themselves incredibly useful over the years in preparation for the coup, and Qaraza's whispers had ensured her father, Sazilz, had fallen into Chatik's trap with Katarzyna Niezik. He needed each of them if his plans were to succeed.

"It is not you three who require enlightenment," he said, stepping to the far railing and surveying the city beyond. "But them."

Kalastok's Reacher towers rose over the eastern Crimson and Market districts like great blades driven from underground. Light Reachers from their peaks cast searchlights over any remaining insurgents, allowing Spirit Reachers to direct the hundreds of breathless spirits where to strike.

It had taken over a decade to perfect the process of granting minds to spirits, then controlling them. Pride filled Chatik watching his creations work. No longer would mindless, ravenous awakened haunt their people. The Crimson Court had tamed the creatures who had destroyed civilization over eight hundred years prior, and through the creation of the breathless, had created an army that even the Keloshan Empire could not face.

"The lowborn have sought to destroy what scions have built," he said. "We must show them how they have strayed, and we must ensure all efforts—scion and lowborn alike—are directed toward the glory of Ezman. Only then may we revel in our accomplishments."

Uzrin pushed off from the railing, taking another puff of his cigar and not bothering to blow the smoke away from anyone's face. "You will be pleased to hear that all the newspapers are printing *our* truth of King Jazuk's cowardice. The people already saw him as weak. With the Crimson Coup complete, we must ensure they see us as their saviors against threats within and without."

"We will need more to convince them," Chatik replied as he stared over the dim western Shadow Quarter and the homeless encampment of Beg Ave beside the Kala River. "Tzena's new, loyal Crystal Brigade will round up the insurgents and send them against Kelosh to buy us time, but to do that, we must uproot their leaders. That is where your interrogators will come in." He turned back to face Qaraza. "What have you heard of my niece, Nikoza? Has she been found?"

She gave him a wry smile. "Tzena is handling operations within the city. The focus of my hunters has been finding great house magnates and other members of the Chamber who fled, including Katarzyna and the iz Vamiustok heir who disappeared into that portal. As far as we know, they have not joined Tiuz Hazeko's retreat toward Fort Harizak."

"Keep working. If the rebels have enough time to organize, then there will be many who flock to their cause." He held out a fist. "We must not let a civil war inhibit our operations against Kelosh."

Tzena nodded. "Of course, my king. As for the matter of Princess Nikoza, we have not found her yet, but she was seen running toward the Drifters' Quarter. She is an eager girl. Perhaps she believed her Water Reaching could somehow protect the lowborn there from the fires?" She stepped closer, once again placing a hand on his arm. "May I ask why you are so focused on her?"

"Do not concern yourself with that," Chatik snapped, voices from his newfound Taint stabbing at the back of his mind. But he calmed when he met her gaze. They had followed him this far. For this to work, his conspirators needed to know the truth.

He pulled away to stand in the middle of them as he raised the Unity Crystal. All fifteen of the Crystal Realms within his grasp, tempting him with their power… and their Taint. "The crystal's cost is beyond what I had imagined. Realm Taint grips me, and I fear that before the seasons complete their next rotation, the Crystal Heir must be ready."

"You believe her to be worthy?" Qaraza asked, taking a casual sip of her wine as if his Taint were no real news. Spirits, did he look that bad already? "She is popular, but she hardly believes in the Cause."

"Nikoza is not yet aware of our plans," he said, "but she is loved by many and can be guided with the power I now hold." He glanced around him at his gathered allies, each eyeing the Unity Crystal. "You all have proven your worth. Show me you desire the Cause more than this crystal, and I shall consider you as the true lords of this realm when the time is right."

Uzrin thumped his chest. "For the King in the Dark! For the Crimson Cause!"

"For Ezman!" Qaraza said as she raised her glass.

Tzena met Chatik's gaze and held out her talon, sending shadows over Chatik's face. She drew closer to him and finished barely louder than a whisper. "For the Crimson heart."

FROM ASH

"It is not enough for a ruler to merely wish to aid all their subjects. They must walk among them, breathe their stench and feel their toil. Only then can one truly understand how to ease their suffering." – Riata-Kanon Nav, Sea Castellan of the Ogrenian Spirit Coast

A bitter chill. A drought that crept across the skin. A deep, unquenchable thirst.

Thud.

Princess Nikoza Bartol shot awake to find herself entangled in a thin woolen blanket. Ash filled her mouth, forcing her to cough as she tried to wipe the bleariness from her eyes. She was in a small, dim room, and wind whistled through the rotted shutters along the near wall. It ran across her skin and made her shiver as a woman came into focus.

"Sorry, ma'am," the middle-aged woman said, stumbling over her words. She was lowborn based on her murmured tone, pinkish skin, and ruffled brunette curls in the light of her lantern. "I didn't mean to startle you."

"Where…"

Nikoza patted herself down. She still wore her frock coat,

combining Ezmani red and Vockan white designs as a show of unity, but the lavish silk and woolen exterior were now covered with cinders. Dear Mother below, that *smell* could choke a hog!

The woman set some clothes on a small dresser before straightening her skirt and sitting on the end of Nikoza's bed. It was far shorter and narrower than any Nikoza had slept in before, but as she studied this woman's round cheeks and button nose, she could not help but feel she had received a generous gift.

The woman gave a nervous, yet motherly smile with her hands clasped in her lap. "I am Falia, and you are in my family's apartment in the Drifters' Quarter. Kix from across the street brought you here last night with his wife and daughter. Said you're a Reacher and that you saved their lives."

Nikoza set her bare feet on the wooden floor, a fresh shiver striking her from the frigid planks. Of course, their floors would lack Fire Reachers to heat them, and the chill jolted her drowsy mind. The previous night had seemed like a nightmare, but had it been true? She had run into the flames with her Water Reaching and pulled a mother and daughter free? Spirits, there had been so many fires.

"They are well, then?" she asked, her voice raspy, and Falia hurried to grab a clay cup of water from the nightstand, handing it to her. Nikoza drank it greedily, but it did little to satiate her parched throat.

"As well as you could be after losing your home. Whole block nearly burned, but you doused enough of the flames to give the bucket brigade a chance. Probably saved a dozen townhouses at least, my husband said."

Nikoza set aside the cup and lowered her head. It swam from exhaustion as she studied her Reacher talon of silver-gray Spirit Crystal. Glimmering in the dim light, a part of her soared at the memory of the power she had held amid the flames. Reaching so often in a short span of time had a cost, though, and she had no doubts that Realm Taint explained much of her dehydration.

"I should have been more prepared," she breathed. "A trained Water Reacher would have done more than endure Realm Taint for two people when the fires threatened many more lives."

Falia paced to the room's center. "Forgive me, ma'am, but most scions wouldn't have blinked at our suffering. You risked your life for us." She pursed her lips. "Kix didn't catch your name."

Nikoza's chest tightened as she forced herself to rise, blood rushing from her head. "I am Princess Nikoza Bartol, granddaughter of King Jazuk Bartol the Fourth and heir to the house."

Falia froze, all the color draining from her rosy cheeks. She babbled an inaudible reply before making a sound somewhere between a frightened cat and a crow. Nikoza wavered, unsure whether to rush to her aid or pretend it had been a joke, but Falia soon recovered her wits, bowing her head.

"What have we done to earn your help, your highness? We are but laborers!"

Nikoza rubbed her talon, wishing for gloves to veil it, as was traditional among scions. "Why do you believe that makes you of any less worth? Is it not your labors that allow the great houses to endure? Is it not you who lack the protections afforded to the richest in the Crimson and Market districts?"

"The king sent you, then?" Falia asked with a glance at Nikoza before averting her gaze again.

"I came out of my own will alone."

Nikoza crossed the room and gave Falia a soft smile. For the first time, she felt worthy of Falia's honor. Last night had not been about birthright or bloodlines, but her desire to use the Crystal Mother's gifts to aid those who bore the most vulnerable spirits. She could do more, though, and she promised herself that her work had only begun. That meant she needed to strengthen her Reaching, whether through Kalastok College or further practical usage.

Falia stepped back, holding an arm across her torso. "I apologize. We have no better clothing to match someone of your repute, but I figured you would want something not soaked with smoke." She fled to the door before Nikoza could insist that all was well. "Please, join us for breakfast when you are dressed. It is the least we can offer as thanks."

Then she left, and Nikoza let out a long breath. Her shoulders sagged, heavy as she allowed herself to abandon her royal presentations. What punishments would greet her when she returned to the palace? What had happened to the rest of the city after the riots?

She deposited her coat on the dresser and peeled off her sweaty dress. Falia had left her a wash basin, but though she cleaned the soot from her skin, it could not match the glory of a warm bath. Ash had dug deep into her pores. She yearned to scrub away the grime, memories, and Taint, but she was not naïve enough to believe she could so easily escape the consequences of her actions.

Falia's gifted attire was too short and wide, making Nikoza feel as if she were wearing a blanket more than a dress. Such a gift, though, was significant from a lowborn family. She reminded herself of that as she draped her dirtied clothes over her arm and left the room.

Beyond, a lantern-lit hall held three closed doors before opening into a small joined kitchen and dining room. Falia hurried about with a pan, coal fumes spewing out of the stove as she deposited eggs and somewhat charred beans onto the table's plates. Nine of them. There were only four rickety wooden chairs and a three-legged stool around the table, though, and the people crowded throughout the rest of the room stared hungrily at the food.

The man from last night, whom Falia had called Kix, started at Nikoza's appearance and removed a flat cap. Frayed strands of fabric sprouted from it like a garden, but he clutched it as if it were a prized heirloom. "Princess Nikoza, I… er."

"You saved our lives," his wife said beside him, visibly shaking as her daughter clung to her leg. "Why us?" Her voice cracked. "Why us, when there were so many others?"

Nikoza held a hand to her breast and considered the question. "I heard you needed help, so I tried the best I could. It seems the Crystal Mother guided me to you."

"And abandoned the rest of the fuckin' Drifters' Quarter," Kix muttered. "Where were the other Reachers?"

Falia yelped and waved her pan like a mighty blade. "Not in my house! Not in the presence of a *princess*, Kix."

The five children who were scattered throughout the room's

nooks and crannies giggled at the chiding, but Nikoza stepped forward through it. Hands held behind her back, she straightened her posture as her grandfather had taught her.

"I abhor the scions' treatment of the lowborn," she said. "You were abandoned by the government and great houses, and no matter how fervently I insist to King Jazuk that things must change, my words fall on deaf ears."

"Well, they're deaf as all shit now," another wrinkled man said, entering the apartment from a door at the far end of the room. His slicked back hair seemed like a creeping shadow in the dim light, and Nikoza assumed him to be Falia's husband based on her rolled eyes. "Just heard the news. King's dead."

Nikoza's heart stopped. She fell back into the wall, her mind descending into a violent headache. "I left him…"

"Crystal Mother have mercy," Falia called out, throwing the pan onto the brick stove. "Entyn! Our guest is Princess Nikoza!"

"What… What happened?" Nikoza asked Entyn. "How could this be true?" The words tumbled out before she could comprehend the situation. Her grandfather, dead. She was House Bartol's matriarch now, but that hardly felt important compared to the fallout to come.

Entyn draped his coat over the back of the furthest chair and slumped into it, rubbing his temples. "Awakened attacked the protestors. Whole damned sky was full of the bastards, and rumor has it, the Reachers and watchmen were helping them. They must've killed the king while they were at it."

Nikoza threw her frock coat over her shoulders without slipping her arms through. There was no time. "I must be off. Thank you for the hospitality and clothes, Falia. I will ensure you are compensated for them, but if my grandfather is…"

The last word failed in her throat. Gossip spread as quickly as the last night's fires, and the further one was from the source, the further they were from the truth. She clung to that hope as she rushed to the door.

"Princess?" Falia called after her with a plate in hand. "Please, Princess!"

But Nikoza was already tearing down the stairs, the smell of soot and rotting wood suffocating her. Did the lowborn always have to endure such stenches, or had the fires simply swallowed the poorer districts?

She hoped for answers as she threw open the townhouse's front door and stepped onto the ash-covered streets of the eastern Drifters' Quarter. The gas lamps lining the street were extinguished. Usually lit by Fire Reachers to banish the everdark come morning, their absence created an eerie darkness that seemed to grasp at Nikoza. Only a few scattered groups of lantern-wielding lowborn revealed the devastation left by the rioters' inferno.

Those lowborn gave Nikoza a sidelong glance as she passed before returning to their conversations. With the endless, pure darkness above, she had little to navigate with besides the Reacher towers dotting the eastern sections of Kalastok. The Light Reachers within sent beams of searchlight through the city itself instead of above. Had Entyn been right? Were they not worried about the spirits, focusing entirely on the lowborn who resisted the conscription instead?

Her stomach churned. The timing of this all had been too fortuitous. Just hours before, Professor Etal iz Noshok and Paras ik Lierasa had successfully found a cure for the Spirit Plague with the help of Nikoza, Lord Zinarus iz Vamiustok, and a prickly lowborn named Nex.

Zinarus had accused her uncle, Chatik Pikezik, of creating the disease through a secretive organization called the Crimson Court. It all seemed so far-fetched, but if Jazuk had been killed on the same night that spirits spawned by the plague swept over the city, it was awfully convenient for Chatik. He had despised Jazuk's decision to not surrender to the traditional great house Inheritance Ritual and grant Nikoza his spirit at birth. Now, Jazuk's death would offer a chance for Chatik to seize influence over the Chamber of Scions and House Bartol.

Heavy footsteps tore her from her thoughts as she turned onto one of the six main roads leading to the Crystal Palace. The palace's gold-tipped spires and illuminated walls of glass and marble loomed over the dark city, and beneath it, the patrolling squad of red-clad watchmen resembled ants more than men. To Nikoza, though, they were a welcome familiarity.

She rushed to the nearest of them, but they spooked, raising their muskets. "Halt, in the name of the king!"

"I am the king's granddaughter," Nikoza proclaimed with her chin raised.

She doubted her words immediately. If King Jazuk had been assassinated, was there already a new king? Royal elections usually took entire seasons, but that assumed there would be elections at all. Her return would be a convenient trap for her grandfather's foes.

One of the watchmen pushed forward, shoving down her compatriots' guns. "Princess Nikoza, you must come with us at once! The streets are not safe after the riots."

Is the palace? Nikoza thought, but gave them a relieved smile. "Of course. I assisted in the efforts to fight the flames and found myself overwhelmed."

"Follow us," the watchman instructed. "Your Uncle Chatik has half the city watch searching for you, and he will be glad to know you are safe."

They formed a box around her before heading toward the Crimson District. The usually bustling main road was quiet, only patrols and a few stray people hurrying this way and that. It sent a shiver down Nikoza's spine, and it grew worse as she caught a glimpse of the spirits swirling through the lanternlight above.

Not the meandering of harmless drifters, but the sharp jolts of awakened.

"Spirits!" she exclaimed, cowering back into the rear guard. "Those are awakened."

"Worry not," the watchman said as he ushered her along. "They are tamed breathless, sweeping the city for rebels." A few of the other watchmen, though, offered nervous glances at the spirits.

Nikoza held a palm to her throbbing head. Commanded spirits, her grandfather's death, and now rebels? What was this strange world she had emerged into? These watchmen did not appear interested in a conversation about such questions, so she tightened her coat and continued into the lamplit Crimson District.

The home of the scion elites showed no obvious wounds from the fires. Signs of the change lurked beneath the surface, though. While neither smoke nor awakened filled the sky here, the wide streets and gardens were empty of their usual promenading couples and conspiring politicians. Only the Crystal Palace's dull glow exposed the king's crystalline dragon swooping overhead instead of perching atop the spires in its watch.

Swarms of guards covered the entryways to the palace itself, their eyes weary. They parted for Nikoza's escort, but averted their gazes when she looked in their directions. One even pressed two fingers to his lips before extending toward her in a blessing.

He is dead, then.

Their solemn expressions revealed what Nikoza already knew deep in her heart. She had walked into the flames and emerged to find that her life would never be the same. Could staying in the palace have saved her grandfather, or would she have been caught in the chaos?

Scions of the Chamber gathered in the main halls, whispering and sparing Nikoza only nervous glances. Most gave a wide berth to the Crystal Mother's statue in the center, but Nikoza approached it. She knelt and touched the fragment of Spirit Crystal at the statue's base, then pressed her fingers to her lips as she whispered a prayer.

"Let Grandfather's spirit be free from compulsion, dear Mother. In his absence, please guide us from this strife."

One of the watchmen tapped her shoulder. "Princess, King Chatik awaits you in the Chamber of Scions."

She swallowed her fear the best she could and rose, arm held across her chest. The double diamond emblem of the Commonwealth of Two Nations marked the Chamber's doors. On most days when Nikoza had followed Jazuk into the palace, the rounded room was raucous with debate, but it was silent now as servants wearing odd silvery gray veils opened the doors.

Chatik awaited her within.

Her uncle paced before the throne with his hands clasped behind him. Black stripes cut down his suit of deep crimson, and his slicked back hair matched the silver glint in his eye at Nikoza's entrance. Wrinkles crossed his brow along with speckled aging spots that had not been there the last time she'd seen him.

Two spirits hovered on either side of the Spirit Crystal pit that surrounded the throne. Placid, they showed no reaction to Nikoza descending the stairs, but the ball in her chest told her they were not simple drifters.

"Welcome, my dear niece." Chatik's voice echoed across the marble and glass. "Come, we have much to discuss."

OF SEA AND SICK

"All the world began as an ocean. So, too, will it end as one." – Rorik-Tin Santin, the crystal-eyed prophet

Kasia Niezik's entire body revolted as she awoke in an unfamiliar room. Everything rocked beyond her bleary eyes, sending tied-up sacks sliding over the small room's floor and into her. The air was impossibly humid against her skin, but her throat was so dry that it hurt to swallow.

Something shifted behind her.

She jolted to turn and face whatever it was, but only managed to painfully twist her shoulder. Seated on the cold floor, which seemed to be made from some kind of interlocking shells, her arms were bound to a wooden pillar. The rope was green and slimy, and she winced as it rubbed against her reddened wrists.

Where in the realms am I?

Last she remembered, she had shifted gravity in the Chamber of Scions to escape Chatik and the Crimson Court's coup against King Jazuk. She had pleaded for Zinarus to follow, but only Aliax and the Realm Tainted spirits of those she killed greeted her on the bright, sandy island she'd fallen onto. That same Taint now haunted her stomach and pounding mind.

"Kasia?" a familiar, gentle voice asked from behind her. "Are you awake?"

An acidic stench stung Kasia's nose as she craned her neck to look over her shoulder. That earned her sight of a flash of auburn hair and purple fabric, and a smirk tugged at her lips knowing Zinarus was with her. It vanished at the realization that she had dragged him into further danger.

"I am," she replied, leaning her head and its matted, ashen locks back against the pole. Spirits, the Taint had struck her hard this time. "Are you real or just a specter of my mind?"

"If I say I am here and real, would that convince you?" he asked. "Or could a ghost of Realm Taint say the same?"

She cursed to herself and surveyed the rest of the room as her vision adjusted. "Where in the wastes are we?"

A bone lantern swung overhead with the constant motion. Its dim light revealed strange blue lines that ran across the walls—also resembling massive sea shells—and a closed door that lacked even the tiniest crack beneath it. A few dozen sacks lay scattered around them, now close enough to touch, and instead of leather or wool, their surfaces resembled that of a frog's skin. Zinarus grunted as one skidded into his mechanical leg with a *clang*.

"I am not all that experienced with the sea," he replied, "but I believe we are in the hull of a ship. Not long after I followed you through the portal out of the Chamber, a vessel unlike any I have ever seen emerged from the waters. There were these creatures…" He paused and shook his head, laughing at himself. "You will think me insane when I say it, but they were like enormous crustaceans. Their ship launched these heavy nets over us. Though I tried to cut us free, they threatened me with harpoons and shark-tooth swords before dragging us in here."

She scoffed and scooted around the pole until they were next to each other. This was insane, but being near him gave her some sense of normality. "A ghost could not have spun up such fantasies. You're telling me we were taken hostage by *crab people*?"

"That appears to be the case, yes." He made a horrid noise,

clutching his stomach. "Oh, by the Mother, this rocking is going to be the end of me."

That explained the smell. The front of his suit and shirt were stained with day-old vomit, and his usually deep gray face was nearly as green as their bindings. If the situation were not so horrible, she might have laughed, but she shared his queasiness.

"I am guessing you saw the great light on the island too?" Kasia asked. "This cannot be Zekiaz."

Claustrophobia struck her at that realization. She was far from her world, her domain, and a tight ball formed in her stomach. Wherever they were, she needed to escape and figure out a way to stop Chatik before it was too late.

Zinarus leaned his head back into the pole, mirroring her. It was by far the least formal she had ever seen him, and despite his misery, there was something unusually cordial about his posture. "That Axiom Reaching of yours is quite the power. Perhaps, however, you pushed yourself beyond your limits."

That, she already knew. Her fingers traced the golden Axiom Crystal wrapping itself around her bound hand and up her forearm. It followed the burn scars caused by her brother Gregorzon's Fire Reaching years before, and in mere days, the crystal had grown another half-a-foot. Death's Taint was all too familiar. Had this misdirected portal been the cost of Axiom Taint?

"I could not let him kill you," she admitted, leaning into him as she remembered Chatik wielding the Unity Crystal, purple Death wisps circling the King in the Dark's hand.

"There were so many others who never had the chance..." Zinarus sniffled, but could not wipe his nose with his hands bound. "How did it all fall apart so quickly?"

"I—"

A loud *whoosh* came from beyond the door. The blue lines running across the wall pulsed, and navy-blue vapors drifted over them until the sound ceased moments later.

Kasia tensed, wishing she could grab her father's revolver—stashed in her coat's interior pocket—but the bindings were tight.

Leonit had taught her how to break free of glove-less handcuffs by dislocating her thumb. That was not an ideal solution. Her left hand was uncovered, so she could probably summon an Axiom portal if they could get off this pole.

Another series of thumps and rattles came from behind the door before it swung open with a heavy creak. What stood beyond was unlike any person or spirit Kasia had ever laid eyes on.

A shelled creature with four pairs of orange-red legs and a horizontal, rounded torso scuttled into the room. Sopping wet, it wore a pair of tubular glass spectacles over its eye stalks, and bright yellow scales wrapped around the carapace behind its stout head. Kasia had not spent much time on the seafront. This creature was in all manners of possible description, though, a giant crab with fish-scale armor. Three more followed, wearing similar uniforms as they righted the toppled sacks with one claw and wielded obsidian-tipped harpoons in their other.

"Tell me I am living a nightmare," Kasia mumbled in her confusion.

Zinarus drew a shaky breath. "I fear not. They have entered before, but you were unconscious for the last few days."

One of the crabs jabbed its harpoon at him, then ran its free claw down the ridges along its carapace to make a kind of rapid clicking. The lead one, bearing no weapon, side-stepped to its aggressive ally and tapped its claws together. Another series of clicking followed from each of them, but eventually, the warrior retracted the harpoon. The leader took its place and stared down at Zinarus.

"Is he the captain?" Kasia asked. "Can we force him to let us go?"

But Zinarus just sat rigid, flicking his gaze from the lead crab to the obsidian blade and forcing a smile. Kasia highly doubted such a motion meant anything to a creature without visible teeth. After a moment, though, the lead crab ran its claws together slowly, the clicks sounding less agitated.

So Zinarus bowed his head. "Act cordial," he whispered to Kasia. "I have been trying to ingratiate myself with them."

Ever the politician.

She copied his bow despite doubting that the crabs would understand. At least their captors did not seem interested in killing them immediately. That hopefully could buy her time to reach for her pistol, but she found it strange that the crabs had left her with a lethal weapon. They were aquatic creatures. Would they be familiar with firearms?

The lead crab—whom she decided to call Clacky—repeated its communication at Zinarus. When he didn't reply, it pointed a claw at Kasia and ran the other across its leg, as if to ask, "What about her?"

"I am Lady Katarzyna Niezik," she told it, assuming it couldn't hurt. "We did not mean to fall onto your island."

Spirits, she felt ridiculous speaking slowly, as if it were a child, but it felt more reasonable than any other idea she had. With her hands bound, she could not attempt to mimic the crabs' communication by tapping their body.

Clacky tilted to one side and then the other. It ran a claw over its spectacles, which were coated with condensation, but its claw was far from dry. When that fruitless endeavor was complete, it tapped its claws twice together in front of it, then prodded its carapace again. Some part of her hoped it had understood and was trying to introduce itself.

"It did the same motion when I told it who I was before," Zinarus said. "Perhaps that is its name." He mimicked the clicking, creating a sound that was nowhere close to Clacky's name.

Clacky rubbed its claws together. Its legs tapped anxiously, so Kasia nudged Zinarus. "It is probably best not to try and speak their language. You could have cursed it or something."

Whatever he had said apparently was clearly wrong, because Clacky signaled to the rest of the warriors. They surrounded the bound pair. Kasia averted her gaze and awaited a killing blow, but instead, one of the crabs reached down and clipped her bindings, freeing her. She took advantage and tried to grab her gun.

A harpoon struck, stopping just short of her neck. The closest crab's free claw chittered away against its carapace as Clacky studied Kasia. She muttered under her breath and leaned back. So close…

"Was that the wisest decision?" Zinarus asked as he rubbed his wrists. "We are at their mercy."

She nodded toward his Truth Reacher talon and snapped, "Your Reaching could stop them for long enough! Give me even a moment, and I can open a portal."

He shrugged. "I have already tried. My talon no longer glows, and it appears my connection to the Spirit Crystal does not extend into this realm. Besides, I cannot compel more than one person to answer my questions at a time. They would not understand them anyway."

Before Kasia could reply, the warriors dragged them to their feet. Their claws dug into her skin, but she just bit her cheek and allowed the crabs to lead her into a hall, then a wider room full of puddles. Shells composed its walls and floors too, and basket-like containers sat atop rows of upright pillars throughout the space. Sand filled each. She could see little more, though, with only a few bone lanterns dangling above.

The ship swayed as they passed between two of the baskets, sending Kasia stumbling into one and knocking it from its pillar. Chittering came from slightly smaller crabs gathered nearby. Mockery or scorn? Clacky gave a sharp response either way, quieting them.

"Perhaps we are not so different," Kasia wondered aloud to Zinarus. "Commanders tell others what to do, and youth break protocol."

He was not so amused. "Are you not worried about where they are taking us?"

"Of course I am!"

As they entered another hall, she took the chance to try Reaching. Strands like a web usually met her when she focused on teleporting to a location or person, but no answer came now. The Axiom Crystal along her hand and arm was dull, just like Zinarus's Spirit Crystal talon. That deepened the pit in her stomach. Were they trapped in this realm?

They entered another chamber with a set of stairs heading up, toward what appeared to be daylight. Kasia's heart skipped a beat at the thought of getting out of the ship, but a sight across the room drew her attention.

The lines that ran along the walls and ceilings met at a pulsing, deep blue crystal on the far wall. It hummed, and the air tremored when they passed by.

"Did you see that crystal?" Kasia asked over her shoulder, climbing the difficult stairs whose construction had obviously not been meant for humans.

Zinarus's mechanical knee screeched after so long without maintenance. He exhaled sharply, and his steps turned to heavy thuds with no handrail to lean on.

"Could it be this realm's version of our Spirit Crystal?" he asked, stopping to take a break. "It resembles the color of Water Reaching, and every room beyond the hold was still dripping. Perhaps it is used to control the crabs' environment within the ship and to help it move? If the Axiom is the core of the Crystal Realms, could your Axiom Crystal connect to another crystal somehow?"

Fascination glinted in his eye and banished his exhaustion for but a moment. The warriors urged them onward with more chittering, but Kasia glanced at the crystal and the lines running from it one last time. It gave her hope. But hope had betrayed her before.

They emerged into sunlight obscured by an endless sky of rolling clouds. Ahead, the sea seemed to stretch just as far, waves crashing against the ship. The light was enough now to reveal that many of the shells composing the ship resembled barnacles. A small hole opened at the top of them to allow feather-like arms to reach into the air, and Kasia shuddered at the thought of one grabbing hold of her leg.

It was nothing compared to what lay ashore.

Kasia froze as the crabs tried to drag her toward the gangplank that led to a rocky isle. Waves lapped at jagged rocks and towering cliffs to either side, but ahead, a stairway of wooden planks cut through them. And the creatures standing at the stairs' base were no crabs.

"By the Mother below," Zinarus said, shielding his eyes as he studied the dozen figures of flesh and bone. "What are other humans doing here?"

THE TILTED THRONE

"Legend has it that the Ezmani throne was crafted with one leg purposely shorter than the others. It sits surrounded by the Spirit Crystal pit and the Chamber's scions, and that stunted leg ensures the monarch never feels too comfortable." – An excerpt from *The Commonwealth from an Outsider's View*

Blood and scorched marble stained the once glorious Chamber of Scions.

Just days before, Nikoza never could have imagined combat in these hallowed halls, but it was clear there had been a coup within the very heart of the palace. King Jazuk was dead. What did his second son intend with the ashes that remained?

"You must have many questions," Chatik said from before the throne, craning his neck to look back at her as she crossed the narrow path over the Spirit Crystal pit.

The pit loomed on either side and threatened to swallow her whole with one misstep. Would she fall into the Crystal Mother's embrace or face damnation as a spirit controlled by Chatik and his Crimson Court? Boths options frightened her, so she clasped her hands before her as she knelt with her head bowed.

"I do not know where to begin."

Chatik waved a hand. "Rise, Nikoza. We cannot have you kneeling like a commoner."

So she did, her heart aching as she stopped at her former place beside the throne. Jazuk had asked her to join him at the Chamber's center more often in recent hundred-hours—the unit used to measure five twenty-hour days. It had been an honor, but also a responsibility.

One she had so badly failed.

Chatik turned back toward her, and she noticed then that another woman lurked in the shadows behind the upper rows of benches. Tzena Oliezany, Lord Gornioz's niece, if she remembered correctly.

"Let me begin with a question, then," Chatik said. "What were you thinking, running off into the Drifters' Quarter during a riot?"

Nikoza laid a gloveless hand on the throne's armrest, cold beneath her skin. Tears stung her eyes, but she held them back. Now was not the time for grief.

"There were fires," she whispered, her voice echoing across the stone and glass. "None of the emergency Water Reachers rushed to stop them, so I decided to."

He stepped to her and lightly rested his hands on her shoulders. "That was a brave thing, but you are an inexperienced Reacher and lucky to have not been injured. The riots consumed much of the city outside the Crimson District. If something had happened to you, I never could have forgiven myself."

"Is it true?" she asked with a hand held across her body. "Is Grandfather dead?"

His eyes hardened for a moment before he pulled her into a hug. It was unwelcomed, and his pungent cologne struck her like a blow to the face. "A tragedy befell us all last night. My father refused to see reason when considering action against Kelosh, and I was forced to challenge his rule for all our sakes."

He released her, but stood too close for comfort. Pink Mind Reacher wisps emanated from him, curling around her. "This war threatens all we know, Nikoza. If we fail, the Keloshans would have every scion head sliced at the neck."

The knot in her back loosened, her distrust slipping away, as those Mind wisps plunged into her. Chatik had protected her against her grandfather's fury before. Why would he lie to her now?

"Why are these spirits here?" She glanced at one before staring at her feet. "The watchmen said they are somehow tamed, yet I have never heard of such a thing before."

"The greatest advancements happen away from the light," Chatik replied, pacing away with his chin tilted up at the vaulted ceiling. The pink wisps faded, but his Mind Reaching lingered like fingers pressing deep into Nikoza's thoughts until she had no conscious memory of the Reaching at all. "Zekiaz gifted us spirits through the Crystal Mother. Now, with the help of dear friends and allies, we have uncovered the key to granting minds to those spirits, allowing our Reachers to command them. These are called breathless."

"Your allies: the Crimson Court," Nikoza said without a thought. She clasped a hand over her mouth. What had compelled her to blurt out that she knew of such an organization? For a moment, she prayed Chatik had not noticed, but his grin dashed that hope.

"So, you have been doing your own investigations. That is little surprise. My father and Professor iz Noshok both saw your potential, and so do we." He gestured to the empty seats. "I wish for you to serve in the Chamber of Scions as one of the representatives for House Bartol's lands around Anukit. It is time you stepped beyond the king's shadow and held your own voice."

Her heart jumped, but the joy of finally sitting in the Chamber herself faded at the deeper meaning behind his comment. "A representative?" she asked. "I was Jazuk's heir, so should I not be named House Bartol's matriarch?"

"Under normal circumstances, yes," he said. "However, Lady Lilita has betrayed me, so by necessity, I have renounced my allegiance to House Pikezik and taken up the Bartol name again. Jazuk broke tradition when he refused to conduct the Inheritance Ritual upon your birth. Therefore, when my elder brother died during your mother's pregnancy, his true line of succession never passed to you. I am Jazuk's oldest remaining child, making me Jazuk's heir and now the patriarch of House Bartol."

Her breaths caught as she considered the ramifications of this all. Some doubt lingered within her, but it faded quickly against the Mind Reaching she had forgotten, allowing his complicated explanations to seem obvious. Still, so much had happened so quickly. She wished to leap back in time and warn her grandfather, but of all the powers in the Crystal Realms, no one could alter time's inevitable flow.

"You shall be king, then?" she asked with folktales of the mythical King in the Dark creeping into her thoughts. Chatik was a Dark Reacher, yes, but he meant well, did he not? "If I am not a princess or an heir anymore, what does that make me?"

"The gathered scion representatives of the Chamber have elected me king, indeed." He glanced toward Tzena, then returned his gaze to her. "As for your role, you are my niece and shall remain an integral part of House Bartol. You have shown a desire to do more for the people of this city, and I believe we have the perfect opportunity for you to do so."

Tzena descended the steps toward the pit, wearing a finely cut dress that could only have come from House Bartol's most experienced dressmakers. The Oliezanys could afford much, but their businesses focused on armaments and mechanical watches, not the elaborate stylings of the day. Nikoza noted that she should bury a prayer later for her house's workers in the likely burned areas around Textile Alley.

"With much of the old Crystal Brigade lost in the conflict between the Crimson Court and King Jazuk," Tzena said, "it has become my duty to rebuild Kalastok's elite protectors with fresh spirits—so to speak. You are an inexperienced Water Reacher, but you hold immense potential and care for Kalastok. Join us as a sergeant, leading a squad of recruits from across Ezman who will help us mend the damage done to this great city."

That gave her pause. Did he wish for her to become an enforcer and spy for the Crimson Court? The Crystal Brigade had earned their infamous reputation as Reacher hunters, silencing dissidents and the worst of the lowborn gangs. A warm contentment sought to smother her worries, yet these remained.

"I must apologize," she said, head bowed, "but I do not believe I am well-suited for the Crystal Brigade. Their methods—"

"Are brutal, yes," Chatik interrupted as he offered a sharp smile. "Will you work with me to change the corruption of our past leaders? I do not need you to be brutal. I need you to act as an insightful, powerful bridge between the palace and its subjects. Smother fires if you wish. Bring aid. Research this horrific Spirit Plague or any other scientific mysteries. You will have the crown's resources behind your projects."

His arguments made sense. Why would she oppose an opportunity to receive the Reacher training she desired and further her connections with Kalastok? Though she had wanted it to be at the college, this was her chance to collaborate with other young Reachers.

"Our crystal talons are what elevate us to greatness," Chatik said. "The Crimson Court seeks to foster those bonds and protect Ezman through them, and soon, you shall join our ranks too. First, you must learn to wield your influence."

"That begins with your first mission with the Crystal Brigade," Tzena said as she stopped at the pit's rim.

"What is it?" she asked, eagerness and apprehension stirring within her.

Tzena's shoulders dropped, but light glinted in her golden eyes. "Our glorious capital was ravaged by those who are undeserving of the Crystal Mother's grace. Your actions prove how deeply you care for our people, no matter their status, and we believe they would find immense relief if you were to lead a delivery of supplies to those who suffer in the Market District and western city."

Nikoza's jaw dropped, but she quickly shook off the shock. "Oh, yes! I had hoped for exactly that. Though there are many areas that suffered, the Industrial District and Shadow Quarter surely will have the least available resources to rebuild." She hesitated. "Is it safe? I hear there are gangs west of the Kala River, and with the rebels…"

"The situation remains unstable, so you would of course receive an armed escort," Chatik said before nodding toward the spirits. "If matters escalate, our commanded breathless will be present to ensure your safety. We cannot allow the Industrial District to fall into savage hands when we need its factories more than ever against the Keloshan Empire."

"I will do my duty to the people and nation," she said with a curt bow.

Why did this all feel so easy? The great weight she had felt at the news of her grandfather's death was but a fleeting memory, and only the dryness in her mouth and faint throbbing in the back of her head reminded her she had endured Realm Taint at all. Everything had changed overnight, but she found comfort knowing Chatik would guide her and the Commonwealth through it.

He squeezed her hand before stepping aside and waving toward Tzena. "I knew you would rise to face this challenge. As we are still working to secure the Market District around our house's residency in Textile Alley, I insist you reside here for a time. Lady Tzena will take you to your quarters and instruct you further on the delivery."

"Thank you, Uncle."

"No, dear Nikoza," his voice boomed across the Chamber. "Thank you for the role you shall play in rebuilding our battered nation."

CLIFFS, CRABS, AND CRYSTALS

"To some among the gentry, the concept of being bound is enticing. To most, it's a bloody nightmare." – Jack Himolox, lowborn writer

A dozen humans studied Kasia and Zinarus from the cliffside shore. Kasia knew she should be relieved seeing someone who wasn't a giant crab, but threats lingered in these strangers' eyes.

Clacky took the lead, its fish scale armor rattling away as it crossed the gangplank. The islanders showed no surprise, so this must have been a usual meeting of some kind. Still, they carried spears and bows with arrows nocked.

A woman with sandy blonde hair rested one foot on the plank, wearing a feathered headband and clothes crafted from the fanned leaves of the island's trees. She had frog-like webs between her fingers and three strange slits along each side of her neck. When Clacky stopped before her, her tone in an unfamiliar language was sharp.

"Do the crabs believe we belong to these people?" Zinarus asked from beside Kasia. "We clearly do not have those *things*—or gills, perhaps—on our necks, and I fail to recognize a single word the woman has said."

Clacky made a few harsh motions toward the woman, rubbing its claws over its torso and legs.

—

Water

We must be grateful for the Water realm's nourishing element, but to focus merely on such things is foolish. Water holds immense power. Imagine the energy we may unlock through a Reacher. If we were not so narrow-minded, could we not unlock unlimited energy through Reachers and their propulsion of Water — far beyond a mere water wheel? Why burn coal or gas that choke our skies when Water gifts us a cleaner alternative?

Water itself is also an excellent tool for hybridization! Imagine steam power through Fire and Water Reachers alike. Or vibrant rain when it is joined with the powers of Air and Life?

For too long, we have viewed the realms and their powers as purely independent, but our very world was crafted from those realms intersecting. Let us look beyond. To create, not just destroy.

"Whatever is happening here," Kasia replied, "it is not a friendly interaction. Be ready for anything. Facing the tide might be better than what these people have prepared for us."

Zinarus swallowed hard and glanced over the ship's edge. Waves crashed against the ship and cliffs, covering them with a roar frighteningly similar to the crystal dragon's. "This… er… This may not be the best time to confess that I cannot swim."

A twinge of regret struck her chest. Of course he couldn't with a leg made of steel, brass, and mechanical gears. "The waves would likely kill us anyway," she admitted, not helping either of their nerves.

Clacky and the woman finished their argument, and the crab leader signaled to its allies, who urged Kasia onward with a prod from the obsidian harpoons. By the Mother, those things were sharp. A trickle of blood ran down her spine from a single touch, only adding to her frustrations.

The gangplank was narrow and unsteady. She had to slow more than once to keep from falling, and some foolish part of her wished to risk the waves despite the obvious power they held. Nature's forces could be brutal. After years of seeking vengeance against her father's murderers, though, she knew full well that people were capable of far worse than breaking her bones against the rocks.

But she just bit her cheek and continued to the gangplank's end, meeting the woman's gaze with a glare of her own. Men armored with strips of bark stood ready behind her. Woven beards stretched down their chins, and one man's held vibrant chunks of what appeared to be more Water Crystal. If he was a Reacher, she had never seen one like this before. That woman's look, though, Kasia knew well.

She held power greater than any weapon.

With a single barked word to her warriors, the woman stopped Kasia's progress as spears and arrows aimed toward her throat. Clacky seemed to object, but the woman ignored it.

She stepped toe-to-toe with Kasia. Though her head barely reached Kasia's chin, she was far more muscular. Those gills flared across her neck as she muttered something. When she received no reply, she smacked Kasia with the back of her hand and repeated the order.

Kasia staggered back, holding her throbbing cheek, but the crabs gripped her coat and held her in place. What did this woman want from her?

"I am Katarzyna Niezik," she said as she gestured to herself. "Touch me again, and I will make you wish I still had my Death Reaching."

Zinarus protested from her side, but she paid him no heed. Neither did the woman. She only cocked her head and looked Kasia up and down for a long minute. Then she spun away and gave her warriors another order.

Clacky seemed to understand, because it signaled to the other crabs, who forced Kasia to stumble onward once again. Realm Taint swam in her mind as she glanced back at the water one more time. It reminded her of Leonit's tapestries depicting the storming Vitrian Sea, and she yearned for a single drink. Dehydration was as potent as any Taint, her head spinning worse by the second as they climbed the stairs cutting into the cliffs.

The thick air was suffocating. Even with the sun hidden behind the clouds, sweat soon covered her skin and stuck her unruly hair to her face, but she trudged onward with obsidian threatening her when she slowed.

Oh, how she wished for her Death Reaching. She would have gladly traded worsened Taint for escaping this misery, but shadowy figures draped in purple wisps haunted her peripherals, their whispers ensuring her mind found no silence. Perhaps that alternative was not as inviting as it seemed.

She blinked hard and stared only at the steps ahead. She had problems aplenty without the ghosts of her past murders returning. Aliax had threatened her on that sandy island, and time would tell whether her gunshot had truly gotten rid of him. It had not been her first attempt to slay his lingering spirit. Likely, it wouldn't be the last. There was no escaping her sins, and as she pondered the Axiom Crystal creeping up her left arm with every Reach, she knew her Taint would only deepen.

What insanity-ridden fool would she become?

Mercifully, the climb ended to reveal to a windblown island of scattered stones, trees with fan-like leaves, and ruffled plants that leaned away from the gales. Those same winds struck Kasia as she left the steep cliffs' protection, sending goosebumps up her arms. More people gathered here in similar clothing to the human woman. Only a few warriors held weapons, and many dragged fishing nets or carried baskets made of carved bone.

The entire island crested at a ridge, which appeared to be their destination. They passed wooden and shell doors to buildings built into earthen mounds. Shallow trenches ran down the slope in front of each, and no doors faced the wind.

"This construction is fascinating," Zinarus huffed from behind her. "They seek shelter from the rains despite likely being able to breathe underwater with those gills. Imagine what we could learn from cultures in these other realms if we were not so embroiled in our own wars."

His words were ragged. This climb had been a struggle for her, but without his cane, it must have been brutal as his mechanical leg screeched for oil. When Kasia glanced back, pitying him, his face was as red as his hair.

"You are barely walking, yet you admire the architecture of our captors?" she quipped. His fascination loosened the tension in her gut a little—a reminder that she was not alone.

He smirked, still surveying the village as a puff of steam escaped his knee. "How can you not when no one else from Zekiaz has ever experienced such a place? Regizald would have loved to see this."

His smile slipped away at the mention of his old footman, slain by Chatik in his manipulations for House iz Vamiustok's sand mines. They shared that mourning. So many had already died. When this was all over, would their names just be another footnote, lost to history?

Kasia sucked in a sharp breath. No, like with her father, Regizald would live on in Zinarus's memories. They would find vengeance together, and Chatik could no longer hide beneath Reacher darkness.

She gasped as they crested the ridge to reveal the expansive ocean and dark clouds dumping rain and lightning over it. They were dry for now, but based on the gusts, that would soon end.

The villagers noticed the rain's approach too, hastening about to deposit their items within the mound buildings. None, though, stayed inside for long, as they gathered around Kasia and Zinarus as the warriors shoved the pair to their knees. Clacky continued its conversation with the lead woman. She crossed her arms, eyes narrow, but after a minute, she ran one hand slowly over the other—a gesture which Clacky mirrored with its claws.

"Looks like they figured out some kind of deal," Kasia told Zinarus. She studied the weight of her coat and where Leonit's revolver rested within it, itching to fight her way out. The crabs' harpoons were still close, but if she caught the warriors at the right moment, none of their weapons could match a gun. "Do you have any weapons?"

The woman approached with an obsidian knife before Zinarus could reply. He winced, trying to pull away, but the crabs held him in position as she snatched his wrist and ran her thumb across his fingers. Her own fingers' fleshy webs flared in the motion. They looked so *wrong*, like a monster's digits more than a human's.

The feeling of disgust must have been mutual, because the woman threw Zinarus's arm aside, then drove her dagger into his sick-covered shirt and ripped it off. Leaving him thoroughly bare chested, she stepped back to study him.

Kasia cursed the jealousy that struck her. It was such a stupid feeling, but it only deepened when the woman nodded to one of the other villagers, who exchanged some type of stone currency with Clacky. Spirits, were they being *ransomed?* That thought made her sick, but it didn't stop her from noticing that Zinarus was more built than she had expected, his arms muscled from jousting and relying on his cane. Though he held more fat than a lowborn soldier, he was no lazy scion lord.

"Well, Lord Zinarus," she muttered. "It seems you have passed inspection."

Her lip curled as the woman moved to do the same to her. For a moment, she considered pulling the gun, but that knife was far too close for comfort. So, instead, she slid off her coat to place the hidden gun's pocket just beneath her hand. The woman raised a brow, but did not seem to consider it suspicious.

"Unhand her!" Zinarus demanded as the woman grabbed Kasia by the neck and tilted up her chin, examining her teeth and gill-less neck. "She is a scion lady!"

The woman released Kasia with a savage glance at Zinarus, then jabbed the knife into the matriarch's dress just above the navel and began to cut. A shout stopped her.

Zinarus leaped with his good leg, a jagged piece of brass flashing in his hand. His copper eyes burned as he tackled the woman. The move caught her off guard, and her knife skidded out of her grasp as he pressed the shard to her throat.

"Let us go!" he shouted for all to hear.

With the warriors of both species distracted, Kasia took the chance to draw her gun. The humans hesitated with their apparent leader at risk. The crabs didn't.

Neither did she.

Gunpowder stung her nose as two bullets ripped through a warrior crab. It had been a heartbeat away from stabbing Zinarus. Too close. Its allies fled at the sight of their comrade dropping amid a seeping pool of blue-gray blood.

Clacky made a harsh rattling sound barely audible over the gunshot-induced ringing in Kasia's ears. The human warriors' cried echoed up the slope, and she need not understand their language to understand. Anguish, shock. These people had no understanding of her gun. They didn't know what to do with Zinarus and her turning the tide so quickly.

A harsh reality clutched her chest, though—Zinarus was not a killer. He'd tackled the woman to protect Kasia, but now that he had the advantage, she saw how his hand trembled. From fear or his curse?

"Do you want him to be a murderer?" Aliax's haunting voice echoed in her mind. *"Do you want to destroy him too?"*

The shadowed form of her late lover wove through the cowering warriors as she rose, pointing the gun at each one that looked ready to pounce. She had not thought this through, but the time for plans was long past. Surviving and escaping were all that mattered now.

"We need to get back to that Water Crystal," she told Zinarus. "Can you walk and hold her hostage?"

The woman scowled up at him. Her muscles coiled like a striking viper, and if she countered Zinarus, Kasia doubted he would slice her neck before she bested him.

"This piece is unfortunately essential to my leg's operation," he replied, not taking his gaze off the woman. "It was the only one I could remove quickly, and when I saw her threatening your—"

"There is no time for those worries," she insisted as the islanders gathered again. "I'm going to sweep toward you and help you walk. If any of them try to chase us, then I'll shoot them first."

His eyes darted to her, then back to the woman. "We are not even sure that Water Crystal will work! How many bullets do you have?"

"Not enough."

"Kasia…"

The warriors shuffled closer, but they weren't the greatest threat. She fired first at the one with the crystal-woven beard as Brown Reacher wisps rose around him. Her aim had improved since her duel with Razamat years ago over the forest's amber, and her bullet plunged into his collarbone. Though not perfect, it was plenty lethal.

The downed woman took advantage of the distraction, flipping Zinarus in a swift maneuver and slamming her palm into his nose. Blood gushed from it, but Kasia was there before she could strike again.

"Do not fucking touch him!"

Kasia slammed the butt of her revolver into the woman's temple with a *crack*. Their leader's collapse spurred an outburst from both the warriors and the gathered villagers. Many turned to flee as Kasia threw Zinarus's arm over her shoulder, hauling him to his feet and waving her gun like a madwoman. Aliax watched curiously from the ridge with the others she'd killed with her Death Reaching.

"Do what is necessary, Katarzyna," Sazilz Uziokaki urged from among them. "Mercy will only inspire resistance."

Kasia cursed as Clacky and his two remaining allies scampered down the slope with the villagers. They would reach the ship first, then leave with the Water Crystal she badly needed, but shooting each would empty her revolver. That assumed she even hit each moving target.

She fired anyway, the recoil sending a jolt up her arm as the first bullet ripped through a warrior crab's body. It stumbled and tried to crawl onward. Clacky slowed to help, but that just opened it to another bullet.

Which flew wide.

"Shit!" Kasia swung her gun back around as the islanders surrounded her. She had only managed to drag Zinarus a few strides away from the woman, who staggered back to her feet with her warriors' help. All while the crabs escaped.

They were trapped. With only a single bullet and Zinarus's shard of brass to fight with, there was nothing they could do against so many warriors, but these people didn't know her revolver's limits. To them, it could be magic or some advanced technology far beyond their understanding. That gave her a crucial advantage. Except she'd forgotten these humans had their own ranged weapons.

Sharp pain struck behind her shoulder, forcing her to lower her gun. A warrior took his chance. He leaped toward them and stabbed his spear straight for Kasia's scalp until a harsh whistle split the chaos.

The man stopped, nose wrinkled, before backing away with his head bowed. Kasia slumped to her knees. She had been shot thrice before, and that familiar, deep ache was undeniable. These people had no guns, so from the weight, she assumed it had to be an arrow embedded into her back.

Shuffled footsteps approached as a sharp gust threatened to throw her onto her side. The air cooled, and lightning snapped at the far end of the isle, illuminating an elderly woman with a necklace of bright fish scales beneath her gills.

"Let us try diplomacy, as I suggested before," Zinarus whispered, kneeling beside Kasia and ensuring she didn't collapse. "I fear a single bullet will not mend this situation."

The elder held out her arms and sang from deep in her throat. Ethereal humming answered from the other villagers, and reluctantly, they returned to their mound homes. Only the blonde woman whom Zinarus had tackled remained, along with archers perched across the ridge. Kasia glared at them for shooting her, but when the singing ceased, the elder woman used her cane to draw a line from her to the foreign pair. Then she waved for them to follow.

Kasia glanced at Zinarus. "We could use this chance to run."

"And take more arrows to the back?" He gave her shoulder a worried look. "You are already wounded, and it would be better if we do not resemble fletched peacocks when we escape."

She scowled, but another jab in her back interrupted any reply. The blonde woman had recovered her obsidian dagger. From the tone of her voice, her patience had run dry.

"Maybe you were right about diplomacy," Kasia said through gritted teeth. "But not everyone got the message."

She stood, helping Zinarus. Her head spun from both Taint and her shoulder's pain, but meeting with this elder was their only option now. Could they have done so without killing so many of their captors? A twinge of guilt struck her as she glanced at the dead man with the crystals in his beard. Deep crimson blood pooled around him, exactly like that of any man from Zekiaz.

These people had been purchasing them for some reason. She had deserved the right to fight back, yet staring down at that man…

Another jab of the obsidian dagger into her spine urged her onward. It ignited the pain in her shoulder too, and talking was preferable to more arrows. She clutched that thought as they hobbled toward the elder's home, hoping for some way out.

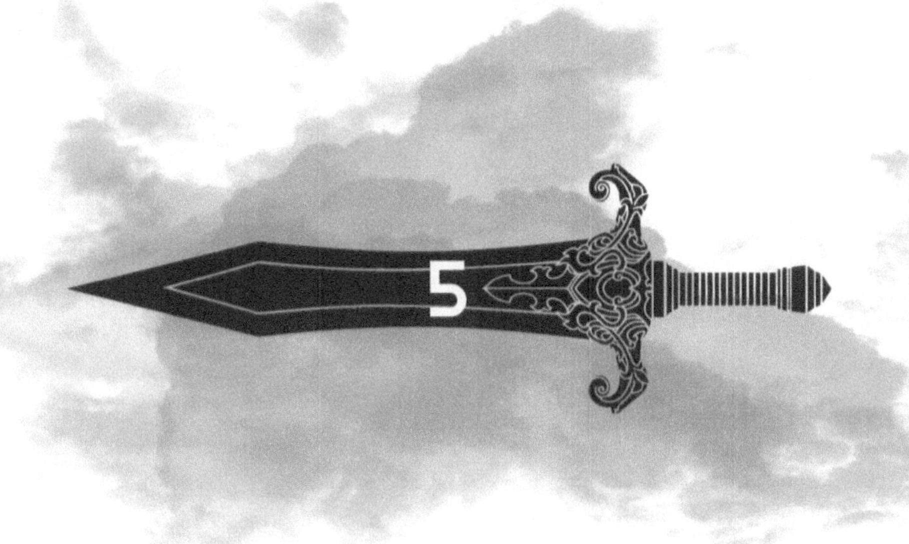

THE NEW DEFENDER

"A shepherd protects his flock from koilee and povniks. A lord protects his domain from scheming rivals. A king protects his nation from expansive empires. But a supreme defender protects all the world from the spirits beyond. In this, they are Zekiaz's shepherd, and we are all sheep, ripe for the wolves." —
Arminas ik Dalnus, Vockan Whisperer

The distant torchlight of Palmia Fortress ignited a new drive in Radais's heart as he crested a ridge on his trusty ibex, Vuk. Home, or at least the closest he would ever get.

"C'mon, boy," he said, patting Vuk's neck. "Almost there."

The ibex bleated back before plodding onward. Master Radais ik Erienfar of the Glassblade Order had taken this trail plenty enough for even Vuk to recognize its winding path. Cutting west through the Vockan Mountains, it was the Order's main route to the western wastelands and the ravenous spirits within.

Except they had found more than dangerous awakened in those Wastes. Radais had left Palmia a few hundred-hours before with a Reacher and ten Glassblades, including Supreme Defender Miv herself, but returned having lost most of those warriors. Miv had become a breathless herself, and her final instructions were for him to lead the Glassblades.

He was no commander. Her words, though, marked a promise. She'd been his leader, and before that, his lover. From her to his father and all those who'd fallen on his expedition, he had failed so many, but he swore he would not fail this.

"It feels as if we return to another world," Lazan said from the mount beside him, their lanterns casting a shadow over his face. "By the Crystal Mother, I am glad for it."

Radais could only nod. He'd been distrustful of the Ezmani Body Reacher at first, when Katarzyna Niezik had hired him to help Radais's father, but Lazan had proven himself a worthy ally and companion. With his sharp chin now covered in scion gray stubble and his once trimmed hair curling over his ears, he was looking more like an adventuring Glassblade each day.

Palmia's mountain valley was indeed a different world from the one of the spirits, drawn in detail throughout Radais's sketchbook. Living, thinking spirits called breathless now inhabited the Wastes. The Saleshi of Akaamilion had aided their expedition and fended off the aggressive Vanashel spirits who'd killed Miv, but Radais had a feeling in his gut those rogue spirits weren't finished.

All breathless seemed to despise the Crimson Court who had created them through torturous experimentation. The Vanashel, though, sought to destroy all who lived.

"I will miss the Spirit Wastes, actually," young Wanusa said, pushing her ibex into a trot and splitting the two men. "There is so much to discover out there, and I can't help but feel we only uncovered a slice of it."

Radais glanced at the eager girl. With dark Vockan skin and long hair like the fortress's flames, she reminded him of Miv at a younger age. Miv had trusted him with Wanusa on her first journey as an initiate, and since Miv had become breathless among the Saleshi, it was his responsibility now to keep Wanusa safe. It was a dangerous time to be a Glassblade. That made it all the more important he trained her well.

"Not all secrets are for us to know," he told her as they rounded another switchback, snow skidding over the edge and his breaths fogging the frigid mountain air. "Zekiaz belongs to the purest of spirits, and we are merely warriors against the corrupted among them."

She rolled her eyes. "Master, you sketch them and the Wastes daily! A warrior can be more than just a brute with a blade. We need not all be Mhanain."

"Watch it, lass," the bald, wrinkled archer muttered from behind. "Would hate for an arrow to slip off my bowstring."

Wanusa opened her mouth to reply, but a stern hand from Radais stopped her. "We have had a long journey and are all rightly exhausted. Let's save the bickering for after a warm meal and bath."

"Aye, *Supreme Defender*," Mhanain mocked, only deepening the ache in Radais's heart.

He'd spent every moment since Miv's death and rebirth dreading what it meant to lead the Order. Most Glassblade masters were far older than him, and Miv had been the youngest supreme defender before. How could she believe he had the experience to guide the Glassblades into the uncertain future? The Ephemeral Slaughter and recent surge of awakened caused by the Spirit Plague had left them weakened and dispersed. Somehow, he was supposed to rebuild an order that had already been crumbling for a century without the Commonwealth's aid.

Palmia's belltower rang for the twelfth hour of the realm's twenty-hour day as they reached its bustling dirt streets. More people than normal mulled about with tools, supplies, and ibex-pulled wagons full of ore, but many peeked out from snow-covered tents that lined the buildings.

"Who are all these people?" Wanusa asked, reining in her ibex.

Radais studied their unkempt hair and ragged clothes that were far from enough in this chill. "Refugees. There must've been more awakened attacks while we were gone."

"Or perhaps the Vanashel," Lazan added.

Radais wished not to consider that possibility, but he shared Lazan's worry. Vockan villagers eyed the Glassblades and shied away. Usually they would flock to a band of Glassblades in thanks or awe, but these gave frightened glances. Gargas, the blacksmith, would know why.

They found him at his usual place before the forge, fiddling with his hair tie and frowning at passersby from his stool. His brow rose at Radais's approach. "Ah, the master returns. Where's the rest of you lot?"

Radais held a fist over his heart. "They are with the spirits now. May they bless those who remain."

"Huh." Gargas threw down the tie onto the leather apron draping over his lap. His scarred lip twitched. "All you so-called warriors do is fucking die nowadays, you know that? Got people camping here from all over Vocka after the attacks. All of 'em tell the same story." He pointed at Radais. "Glassblades ride in all tall with their fancy armor, just to fall like the rest."

"We discovered that an Ezmani group called the Crimson Court created spirits with minds, called breathless," Radais replied. "One faction of the breathless, the Vanashel, wants to destroy humans. The Order wasn't ready for this, but I will figure out how to defend the villages."

Gargas shook his head. "It's the bloody Second Awakening. Gonna need more than you and a Body Reacher to stop this."

Without a solution to that, Radais bowed his head. "Then we will need every hand wielding a blade. Ever considered switching to glasswork?"

"Yeah, and you ever thought about swinging around a musket?" Gargas rose and snatched his stool. "It ain't that easy, kid."

Radais sighed watching the old man go. He hadn't meant his comment like that, but he understood how hard it was to break from habits. The Glassblades needed him now, and he still didn't want to lead. Even if all of Vocka could use Gargas's weapons to fight breathless and awakened, he would not change his ways.

They passed through the rest of the village before crossing the bridge to Palmia Fortress. Its walls of glass and stone steeled Radais's resolve—a reminder of the Glassblades' valiant defense during the Awakening. This fortress had been a beacon for all who lived.

He would make it so again. For Miv. For his father. And for those he fought to protect.

"Master Radais!" one of the archers on watch exclaimed, surveying the approaching group. "We have awaited your return, but where is the supreme defender?"

Radais lifted his chin against all his wallowing sorrow. Hope was thin, and they needed to see him as strong. "She fell in the Spirit Wastes. We have discovered a threat greater than any we've seen. Open the gates, and call for all who remain to gather in the muster yard in an hour."

The archers' shock froze them before one finally signaled for the gate to open. Radais couldn't blame them. It had not been long since Miv's appointment to supreme defender, and losing two in such a short span would hit morale hard. A voice in the back of his head said he should be gentler about breaking the news, but they were trained warriors. No matter the peril, they would face it with blades drawn.

Mhanain, Lazan, and Wanusa went to the barracks to wash up and change, leaving Radais to drop the ibexes at the stable, then head toward the commanders' hall. Miv had left commanders Tairanik and Polina in her stead. It was highly unusual for a master to be appointed directly to supreme defender, and he doubted they would take it well.

At the far southern end of the fortress, the commanders' hall was no grand building compared to the others. Its walls were simple stone, and the only markings that truly differentiated it were a pair of banners beside the door, bearing the Glassblade sigil of a glass sword beneath a mountain. It was a reminder that they sought not to be heroes, but protectors.

Tairanik stood over a circular table with a map of Vocka and the Wastes stretched across it. Flickering lamps hung overhead, but only cast a dim glow over the aged commander. He was shorter than most Vockans and far wider than a trained warrior should have been. Bent over, he barely reached Radais's shoulder as his blue jacket lined with glass epaulets and buttons—two of which were missing—strained to keep shut over his protruding belly.

"What is it?" he asked, not looking away from the map at Radais's entry.

Radais held a fist to his chest and bowed. "Commander Tairanik, I am here to report back on my mission to the Spirit Wastes."

Tairanik appeared to either not notice or care about Miv's absence. "Come, then. There are greater concerns to discuss as well."

"Unfortunately, sir," Radais began, "I doubt there are greater concerns than the ones I bring."

Pacing to the opposite side of the table, he explained what had happened in the Wastes, but left out the location of Akaamilion to hold his promise to Bakeekek, the Saleshi leader they called the First One. The tenuous relationship they had forged could be easily broken. The Vanashel were already dangerous enough with the Saleshi acting as friends.

Tairanik followed their path with his finger as Radais told the story. Stone figurines marked the known locations of Glassblade groups and awakened attacks across the region, and he placed a cluster of spirits around New Frontier at the mention of breathless there. His eyes were wide, but his hands remained still. That was, until Radais mentioned the breathless Bound Ones.

"If you didn't have other witnesses, I'd call you insane," Tairanik muttered. He rapped his knuckles against the table. "Spiritdamned awakened that can think, talk, plan, and now *Reach*? And Miv thought you should lead? Awfully convenient, considering your past."

"I am aware of my… affiliation… with the former supreme defender," Radais replied, standing firm with his hands held behind him like a soldier. "Warrior Mhanain and Initiate Wanusa will confirm her orders."

The commander sneered. "We don't promote commanders because they slept with the supreme defender!"

Radais slammed his fist into the table. He regretted it instantly, but he was not about to let Miv be mocked like this. "Do you question her honor? Our relationship ended long ago, and I was as surprised as anyone that she chose me. She despised me, Tairanik. I do not desire the position, but I refuse to deny her final command." Straightening his posture, he took a long breath to calm himself. "Now, where is Commander Polina, and what is this important concern you spoke of?"

They glared across the room at one another. Only the crackling of the lamps' candles broke the silence until Tairanik pursed his lips and rounded the table to Radais, pulling a letter from the pouch at his belt.

"An alpine accentor arrived with this just yesterday. Ezmani never send birds as messengers, so we knew it must be urgent if they sent one to us."

Radais eyed the letter, then took it carefully with his gauntleted hand. A cut seal of a jumping ibex marked it. "House iz Ardinvil is not Ezmani, but I'm surprised they would write after ignoring my requests in Kalastok."

Tairanik crossed his arms. "Calling those bastards Vockans is like calling an awakened a pure spirit."

That statement held political connotations that Radais would rather not consider, so he opened the letter.

Supreme Defender Miv of the Glassblade Order,

I regret to inform you that the Commonwealth has descended into civil war. By the orders of Lord Chatik Pikezik, a group of rogue scions have assassinated King Jazuk Bartol the Fourth and filled the skies with spirits under their command.

Kalastok has fallen.

The renowned commander Tiuz Hazeko has taken up arms against this corrupt coup and is organizing a rebellion called the Confederation of Harizak, based at the fortress sharing its name. With the Keloshan Empire's invasion in the east and the rising awakened threats, we must unite in these trying times. It pains me to say that my father, Patriarch Ivalat iz Ardinvil the Second, has not been seen or heard from since he announced his decision to join with the Confederation. I fear the worst for him.

As the acting head of House iz Ardinvil, I will be calling upon our mercenaries to aid the rebellion, and as our foes command spirits, I humbly request aid from the Glassblade Order. The Crimson Court seeks to erase Vocka from the Commonwealth. Let us ensure they regret that decision until the end of their miserable lives.

May the pure prevail,

Lady Manalias iz Ardinvil the Third, Heir

Radais set down the letter and ran an armored hand over his now sweaty brow. He'd only heard stories of previous confederations, which were traditionally used by Ezmani scions to revolt against an unpopular monarch. Usually, it ended in negotiations before too much blood was spilled. All signs now pointed toward a greater conflict.

It was a bad time for civil war. The Commonwealth needed to be focused against their foes of both spirit and blood, not divided among themselves, but Kasia's warnings in Akaamilion hung with him. This Crimson Court had to be behind it. There would be no aid from Ezman against the Vanashel, and now, this rebel Confederation of Harizak requested Glassblade aid when their numbers were at their thinnest.

So much for that meal and bath…

"I have called everyone to the muster yard already," he said, steadying himself. "I'd expected to speak about the Vanashel, but it seems we have yet another problem."

Tairanik nodded. "As I said, I do not favor House iz Ardinvil, but we will have to pick a side. What do you suggest we do, Supreme Defender?" Those last words held all the power of a man swallowing his tongue, but Radais ignored that.

"We will do what our order was created to do," he replied, studying each piece on the map. "By the bidding of the pure spirits, we will slay the corrupted awakened and these Vanashel. We will protect the people from the spirits. House iz Ardinvil denied my requests to be heard in Kalastok, and now, I shall leave the damned politics to them and the rest of the rich scions."

OF ASH AND SPIRIT

"Let the scions have their coups and courts, balls and battles. It matters not who rules or who wields the blade. They're all the same, and when the fires have faded, it's the poor trapped in the fucking ashes." – An excerpt from *The Dawnrise Manifesto* by Evit Paxian

Smoke curled over the smoldering remains of Kalastok, stinging Nex's nostrils as they ripped off another bite of charred jerky. It was disgusting, but food was as rare as scions west of the Kala River.

The Spirit Plague quarantine had already stifled its limited supplies. Now, days after the Crimson Coup, you could get stabbed for looking like you had bread in your pocket. Who could blame them? Desperate people did desperate things to survive.

Nex scowled at the Crimsons' breathless spirits circling in the everdark above. The Shadow Quarter and Industrial District had few lights beyond what scattered torches or candles people could find, and gangs had hoarded those quickly. In this season of darkness, a flicker of light cost more than a hundred-hour of rent.

The scions didn't care. They cowered in their glass-trimmed homes while the spirits picked off lowborn one-by-one, leaving the rest to starve or fall to the Spirit Plague. Only Kasia Niezik's offered funds had ensured Nex could help the struggling, but no amount of keni could buy supplies when there was nothing left.

So Nex would fight.

They clambered off the top of the warehouse they'd used as a perch in recent days. Much of the southern sections of Kalastok had burned in the revolt, and even here in the northwestern Shadow Quarter, ash traced each of their steps. Crimson watchmen would follow those they found suspicious. But the breathless were the real threat.

A group of kids scampered up to Nex with hands extended as they crossed Iron Alley. The old pub was shut, a dim lantern by its door making the kids little more than shadows. Their faces were gaunt, their fingers bones, so Nex tossed them what remained of their jerky. It was shit, and they deserved more. But the kids devoured it as if it were the finest meal.

"Don't stay out too long," Nex told them. "Those spirits are hunting us. Got glass?"

Each shook their head, so Nex reached into their pocket and pulled out a few glass daggers. They were nothing more than impure shards bound to a poorly carved handle. But splinters were better than becoming a husk when a breathless or awakened sucked your spirit from your body.

"Take these and scram," they said.

The kids obeyed, and Nex went on their way with their wide-brimmed hat tugged low and their hands tucked into their duster's pockets. Iron Alley had once been full of workers and scion enforcers for them to con for their keni. Now, it was empty except for the wind. And spirits lurked in those gusts.

Nex clutched another glass dagger in their pocket, eyeing the shadows. Gunfire and breathless had killed hundreds during the lowborn revolt, and every day since, fewer lowborn returned to the hideouts Nex had organized with others around Beg Ave.

They had enough to worry about without the gangs, but whether it was the Murder Mitts, Crax's Folly, or the Glass Teeth, everyone wanted territory in the chaos. Nex had paid the gangs off to protect their friends and the refugees whose homes had burned. Peace wouldn't last. And while Nex had managed to keep old King Jazuk's watchmen happy with a few keni to cross the Kala, these Crimsons had proven they weren't interested. The west side wasn't just a quarantine zone anymore. It was a damned prison.

There were too many factions, too many guns, too many spirits, and too many starving people. The west side had burned. If things continued like this, it would explode.

A chill ran down Nex's spine as they reached a side alley. It cut north, toward the few warehouses and tenements Nex protected, but they kept going east. That chill was too familiar. Their fogged breaths and hairs raised on their arms could only mean one thing, and it made them grip that glass dagger even tighter.

Breathless.

"Fuck off," Nex spat at the fiend as it entered the light of a nearby torch. Awakened took indistinct forms, but Crimson-controlled breathless resembled shadowy humans. This bastard fit the bill.

Nex brandished their dagger, swiping toward the spirit. "I said go away!"

But it just drew closer as whispers circled overhead. They didn't need to understand the words to know it was that strange language only breathless used. Either they were deciding whether to attack, or they were planning how. Nex sure as shit wasn't staying to find out.

They lunged at the one before them. It tried to dodge, but their dagger stuck true. Purer than the one they'd given the kids, it tore a hole right through the spirit's misty form. And when it sent misty tendrils to steal Nex's spirit, they drew out a bead of amber in their other hand.

The breathless shrieked, but the amber caught its tendrils. In just a few beats of Nex's rapid heart, the bead had consumed it entirely.

Capturing one breathless didn't silence the others, so Nex darted down another alley, silently thanking Kasia Niezik for letting them steal a few beads of spirit-capturing amber. They hadn't figured out if the breathless could report to the Crimsons yet. If they could, then Nex couldn't afford for them to expose where their friends were hiding. It meant taking a longer route, but it was worth it to keep Vinnia and the others alive.

Spirit whispers stalked them for what felt like an eternity. What were the things waiting for? Nex could surprise one, but they were no Glassblade.

Gunshots rang out somewhere along the riverbank. Glass Teeth territory. When a second volley followed, the whispers faded until Nex was alone in the dark. Or as alone as one could be in the over-crowded Industrial District. There was always someone lurking around a corner or in a window above, and Nex wasn't used to being the target rather than the hunter.

They weren't about to complain about the breathless retreating, though, so they hurried deeper into the Shadow Quarter and stopped before a boarded-up warehouse. No visible light split through the shutters, and the roof looked ready to cave in. Any watchman would think it abandoned.

That made it perfect for Nex's uses.

Instead of knocking on the decrepit door, they tapped on the shutter to the right twice, then coughed. A few seconds passed before the door flung open to reveal a muscled Reshkan man wearing a tattered shirt that ended in strips above his stomach. He held no light, but Nex would recognize anywhere his curled black hair and cheeky face, the color of duskfall leaves.

"It's me, Jiinaan," they whispered, casting a glance over their shoulder.

"Ha!" he exclaimed, stepping back and holding the door for them. "Don't need word from Nex. Could smell miles ago."

Nex was still working with Jiinaan on his Ezmani speech, but he was exactly what they needed in times like this. While they were short, quick, and could pretend to be almost anyone, Jiinaan could knock a watchman out in a single punch—then kill the asshole with the next one. He was constantly annoyed he couldn't punch spirits. That didn't stop him from dual-wielding glass daggers like a ber-serker from Keloshan folktales.

The first floor of the warehouse was empty except for a few toppled crates and an infestation of rats that made the place reek. Neither of them winced at the stench as they headed toward a pile of boxes in the back. Jiinaan set each aside with the delicate care of a mother swaddling her child, revealing a trap door, and Nex didn't wait for him before yanking it open.

"Tough one," Jiinaan noted. "Nex hurt back, not careful."

Nex grunted and set the trap door down to avoid making a loud noise. Their back did hurt from hauling the stubborn door, but there was no way in the Wastes they were going to tell him that. Instead, they just swung onto the ladder heading down with Jiinaan a few steps behind.

Light finally greeted them at the bottom as they entered the warehouse's old storage room for its illegal goods. Flashsmoke, a drug infamous for causing hallucinations after a single puff, had filled the place days ago. The gangs had hidden those stashes quickly after the riots, and from the grumbles around Nex's safehouses, the price was higher than ever. No one could afford food or lodgings. But flashsmoke could make you forget your problems for a few minutes. In this awful pit, Nex couldn't blame those seeking its release.

Over a hundred people crowded into the cramped quarters. Cloaks and blankets for makeshift beds were laid out so tightly at night that there was hardly anywhere to step, and even with people rolling them up during the day, Nex had to squeeze through.

People's faces turned to a smile when they caught sight of Nex, despite the horrid state of their living. Why? Nex hadn't done anything but throw away Kasia's money to gangs for food, guns, and the most impure glass you could imagine. They couldn't protect this safehouse and the others for forever. Spirits, they could barely convince themself to get up and face this shit every day.

Catching sight of Vinnia pushed back that dread pooling in their chest. Their half-Vockan, half-Reshkan lover sat on a stool in the corner. Her fingers worked on a pair of knitted mittens, and her eyes were alight as she spoke with an elderly Ezmani woman on the stool across from her.

Half the forlorn people here wore something of Vinnia's creation: whether gloves, scarves, or hats. Neither she nor Nex had slept much recently. They'd admitted their love for each other when Nex had cured her of the Spirit Plague with Etal iz Noshok's potion, but they'd spent every day since worrying about everyone else. Spirits, Nex so badly wanted to curl up in her arms on their old bed. Even one meant for a single person was better than this.

"We all thought we'd die during the last wars too," the old woman told Vinnia, practically shouting over the base murmur in the small space. "Then Commander Tiuz gave us hope!"

"He's a scion," Nex said before kissing Vinnia, then leaning on the wall beside her. "They don't care about us. That's why he fled with all his rich friends."

The woman wagged a finger. "You just wait. Tiuz is organizing a rebellion against these motherforsaken Crimsons! He can't do that with those breathless flying about like winged koilee."

"I'd prefer koilee," Nex muttered. "You can shoot a beast in the face. Those things…"

Their voice trailed away as they felt the amber bead in their pocket, one of the many they'd used in recent days to catch breathless. Each use made the breathless resist the small beads more, and Nex wondered whether a larger piece would be more effective. Unfortunately, they hadn't stolen any larger ones from Kasia. Where was the Amber Dame when they needed her most?

Vinnia stopped her knitting and glanced up at Nex. Her eyes were wet from tears. "We have one day of rations, maybe two. Jiinaan had to break up a fight over a slice of bread earlier, and a few people decided they'd rather risk the streets than be here."

Nex removed their hat, tracing its brim. One day gave them time, but the city was bone dry west of the Kala. They'd have to cross one of the bridges.

"What about Spirit Plague cures?" they asked. Etal had cured the disease that turned people into spirits with Paras the alchemist's help, but only a few vials had made it out of Kalastok College before everything went to shit. With the bridges locked down even worse than before, they had no way to get more.

Vinnia just held her hands to her face. "What are we going to do, Nexie?"

Nex stomped their foot back into the wall. They watched all the people in this room and thought about those beyond. Crimson watchmen and spirits haunted the west side, and gangs destroyed it from within. They weren't going to stop it by hiding in this hovel.

"We're going to fight back." They looked to Jiinaan. "Tell people to gather all the glass and amber they've got. No more stupid trinkets. We need weapons."

Vinnia threw down her hands. "People need those trinkets for hope! Some pray with them."

But Nex kicked off the wall and slid their hat back on, tugging it down over their left eye. "No Crystal Mother is going to save us, and neither are any 'pure' spirits. It's up to us."

"Where are you going?" Vinnia asked as Nex headed toward the ladder. "You just got back."

That dread clutched their chest as they turned back to see Vinnia's pained expression. They hated this. Why couldn't they abandon this wretched city? Why did they have to care?

"I'm going to find the gangs. It's about time we started fighting the Crimsons instead of each other."

WHERE WATER DARE NOT FLOW

"Where power seeps from one realm to another, we find creation and change. However, were the barriers between realms to fall, Zekiaz would cease as we know it." – An excerpt from *The Convergence* by Professor Etal iz Noshok

Rain pounded the windswept isle moments after Zinarus hobbled into the elder woman's earthen home with Kasia's help. By the Mother below, the matriarch had an arrow sticking out her back, yet *he* was the one who needed aid.

It pained him to admit that he was truly a disaster. The crustacean sailors had given them neither food nor water for days on their fascinating ship, and blood still trickled from his nose, dripping onto his bare torso. His attack against the blonde woman had been hasty; he recognized that. She had been moments from stripping Kasia in front of a crowd, however, and he could not tolerate that. It was another question entirely whether he could have actually slit her throat.

Zinarus glanced at Kasia as they knelt in a rounded chamber with a door on either side and a pit of sand in the center. Heat rushed to his cheeks at her torn open dress. He couldn't help but feel exposed with his shirt off as well, the fight and humid air coating his skin in sweat.

But he forced himself to focus on that arrow in Kasia's back. Were these people going to just let her endure it?

As if hearing his thoughts, the elder woman waved a webbed hand, and one of the men positioned around the pit approached Kasia. They had taken her revolver, and the blonde woman held an obsidian dagger to her back in case she dared try anything. Zinarus prayed she didn't. They had agitated these people enough. Yes, they had seemed interested in purchasing them both for some reason, but his greatest concern for the moment was not dying.

Water Crystal chunks patterned the man's light beard, just like the Reacher Kasia had shot. He examined her wound as she gritted her teeth.

"What is a Water Reacher going to do?" she muttered to Zinarus.

He studied the Reacher, who placed a hand beside the embedded arrow's shaft. "Just as not all who bear Spirit Crystal Reach into Zekiaz, perhaps these people can Reach into other realms as well."

She had no chance to reply, as the man yanked the arrow free from her back. Enough blood followed that Zinarus clenched his fists and steeled himself for a fight. But Kasia's hand found his, squeezing until he worried his bones would break. She was tougher than nearly every scion he had ever met, and her scream pierced straight through his heart.

"Pulling out the arrow fixes nothing if you do not—" Zinarus stopped as deep red wisps swirled around the man's hands, plunging into the wound.

He had seen Body Reachers work many times, but it always astounded him how each strand of muscle or skin wove back together like a finely crafted tapestry. And she was the most beautiful tapestry of them all. Some would call it a gruesome thought. His Truth Reaching offered mending of inanimate objects, though, in a similar, yet far less intricate process, and one could not deny the wonder that was creation—whether body, tool, or art.

Kasia's breaths soon slowed. She leaned into Zinarus, shuddering before giving him a silent look, as if asking whether she was alright.

"He healed you," Zinarus breathed, holding her. He exchanged nods with the man as he returned to his position around the sand pit. "You are well."

"But he can't fix my head," she mumbled. "Why did she bring us here and heal me?"

Zinarus raised his gaze to the elder woman. "I believe we are about to find out."

The elder sat cross-legged across the pit and dragged the end of her cane through the sand. With her free hand, she tapped her chest. "Bentun."

"Zinarus," he replied, mimicking the gesture. Kasia was still tense and her eyes distant, so he touched her arm. "Kasia."

Bentun stuck out her tongue and pressed her index finger to it, then held her finger in the air. A greeting or honoring, perhaps? So Zinarus copied her again, but his tongue was so dry that his finger was no wetter than before. He tried to mime a drinking motion to ask for water. Spirits knew they had plenty of it.

Yet again, Bentun waved to one of the gathered people and gave her some instruction. The woman, who had Water Crystals dangling from piercings across her nose, hurried past. She returned moments later with two bowls that seemed to be made from joined sea shells. It was an unusual vessel for drinking, but Zinarus bowed his head anyway and accepted them.

"You must drink," he told Kasia, raising a bowl to her lips. "Realm Taint is deep, but caring for your body will inevitably help your mind."

She straightened her posture after the first few sips and took the bowl for herself. Her hair draped over her shoulders in a mangled mess, and her skin had lost its scion gray, falling pale. A fury burned deep in his core, but he forced himself to remember that the crustaceans had starved them, not these people. Though the blonde woman had been far from kind, Bentun had given him no reason to distrust her.

Relief came as he drank the cool water slowly, then set the bowl aside to meet Bentun's gaze. His leg whirred to adjust to his posture, but between the piece he had torn free and its lack of greased gears, it creaked without any real progress.

Bentun's gills twitched at the sound, but she shifted to focus on the sand. She guided her cane through it like a trained artist would a brush across a canvas. First, she drew waves surrounding an island topped with the wide-leafed trees, then a line toward Kasia and him. When she had reached as far as her cane could, she stopped and waved at the pit's end.

Zinarus hesitated, studying her drawing. Was she asking them to add to it or simply understand who her people were? It gave no more information than he had already inferred, though, so he glanced at Kasia.

"She wants us to show where we're from," she said as she clutched her Axiom Crystal hand. Fifteen golden lines met at a ring in her palm's center, and her eyes flicked from it to Bentun. "Does she know we came from another realm?"

"A line can mean many things," he replied. "However, it is quite obvious we are not from their island or anywhere else they are familiar with. If you are feeling better, then perhaps you should draw our realm. I cannot move well with my leg, and—"

"You wish for me to be the one embarrassed by my horrid artistic work," she quipped, rising with a slight wobble.

Her eyes darted toward an empty spot, and her lips parted for a moment before she slammed them shut. Had she seen her former lover, Aliax, again? It was hard for Zinarus not to feel a twinge of jealousy at that thought. They had only shared a single kiss before Chatik's coup, but the heart rarely carried the mind's logic.

Kasia grabbed a stick that sat alongside the pit and began to draw. The waves and island had been an obvious choice for Bentun, but Zinarus wondered how Kasia would show Zekiaz and the Commonwealth. Their realm had mountains, rivers, forests, and fields alike, and sand was hardly an easy medium to depict ethereal spirits with indistinct forms.

But Kasia opted instead to draw buildings and a crude dragon on the tip of what must have been the Crystal Palace. It was by all means a poor re-creation. The dragon being a monster was clear enough, though, and when she drew the spirits, they were floating angry faces that made her laugh at herself.

"I hate you for making me do this," she said with a glance back at him. Her eyes held the storms of the overcast sky, but a smirk tugged at her lips.

He bowed. "And I am ever grateful for your artistic abilities."

"How am I supposed to show us arriving here?" She tilted her head back, staring at the ceiling. "Spirits, I can barely think with this headache."

"Perhaps the simplest idea would be a circle between the two realms, then an arrow going through it? If you want to complete your masterpiece, then you could even show us heading through the portal."

Bentun watched Kasia work with interest and occasionally whispered something to a bearded Reacher beside her. Her expression exposed neither annoyance nor any joy, making it difficult for Zinarus to plan. What did she want from them? Were they supposed to be purchased slaves who'd become more than the islanders expected?

When Kasia finished, Zinarus gestured for her to give the greeting. "It is best to show her respect. Our lives are in her hands for now, and she is the only one who seems interested in caring for us."

Kasia wrinkled her nose, but touched her finger to her tongue and held it up. That drew a chuckle from Bentun.

"Wonderful," Kasia muttered. "Now she thinks I am a fool."

Zinarus shrugged. "She believes we are strange. Given the circumstances, that makes perfect sense."

The Reachers around the sandpit stepped back when Bentun waved her hand. Slowly, she rounded it to Kasia with her cane tucked under her arm. Despite appearing to be an aged woman, she moved with surprising agility, but perhaps the cane was merely a tool for the sand drawings or even something else. This was an entirely different realm. Whatever assumptions he had brought from Zekiaz did not apply here.

Bentun held out her left hand as she approached Kasia, then tapped all over it. Kasia furrowed her brow, so Bentun pointed to Kasia's drawn portal.

"She knows about your Axiom Crystal," Zinarus said. "Or, at least, she thinks it is related."

Kasia held up her crystal-wrapped hand with a side-eye at Zinarus. "This?" she asked the elder.

The golden crystal glimmered, even drained. It contrasted harshly with the sight of her missing index finger, and Zinarus tensed knowing Chatik had shot her. A scarred line over her left ear showed where the bullet had skimmed—inches from tragedy. He refused to accept how close she had come to death. She may have lost her talon, but she was still Death's Daughter. It could never steal her.

Bentun snatched Kasia's hand and prodded at her crystal and missing finger. Though Kasia sneered, she did not pull back as Bentun reported what she saw to the Reachers. All research on Reaching in the Commonwealth was done by scions. Obviously, Bentun was their leader, but it was strange that she herself did not appear to have any Water Crystal on her person. Did these islanders not value Reachers as highly?

Bentun released Kasia, looking between the realm jumpers before holding out an open hand to each of them. She said a single word, then pointed back toward the drawn circle.

Kasia furrowed her brow. "Go? You are letting us go?"

The sand shifted as brown wisps circled around another Reacher, pulling back the sand to reveal a deeper bowl at the pit's center. Within it pulsed a deep blue crystal the size of a jouster's shield.

Hope swelled in Zinarus's chest as Bentun grabbed Kasia's wrist and guided her around to the clear side of the pit. They stepped in, and she gestured for Kasia to touch the Water Crystal. Zinarus staggered on his one good leg, the other stuck half-bent. Was this it? Could they finally return home after days trapped in this realm?

Light surged into Kasia's Axiom Crystal the moment she touched the Water one. Her eyes widened, and the Water Crystal dimmed the brighter hers became. The gathered Reachers shifted uncomfortably, but Bentun's glare met the blonde woman when she charged past Zinarus to protest. The two debated for a moment, the younger's tanned cheeks turning red. In the end, she stormed out. Thunder and rain pounded through the opened door for but a second before it slammed shut.

All that remained was the hum of magic. It filled the pulsing crystal across Kasia's hand and forearm now, leaving only a faint light within the Water Crystal.

She looked to Zinarus when she rose. "I feel the Axiom's web again." Disbelief replaced the cut in her voice, and she smiled. "We can leave this horrid place."

"Why is she doing this?" Zinarus asked as he hobbled toward them.

Bentun seemed to understand the question, because she held a webbed hand over her heart again, then pointed to the ground. Once Zinarus joined them, she pointed to Kasia and him before gesturing toward Kasia's drawing.

"She belongs here," he tried to translate, "but we belong in Zekiaz. By the Crystal Mother, how does she understand all of this?"

Kasia shook her head. "Maybe others like us have visited before, or maybe she merely wants to get rid of us before I shoot someone else."

"The other woman would much rather we stay and take a beating, I gather, but Bentun is right. We do not belong here."

He glanced about at the earthen home and longed to further understand these people, their culture, and the intelligent crustaceans who inhabited their waters. There was depth to the realms that he had never considered before. He feared he would never see these wondrous places again.

One of the island warriors approached and offered Kasia her revolver. He held it as if it were a piece of rubbish, but Zinarus could not blame him. To these islanders, gunpowder probably resembled a curse more than any known weapon. That gun had killed this man's allies, maybe friends. Of course he would despise it.

Kasia deposited it back into her coat's inner pocket. "Ready to return?"

Zinarus wobbled, throwing his arm over her shoulder to catch himself. He covered his bare torso with his other arm and chuckled. "Wherever our destination, can it have some clothes? I feel quite exposed."

"We are returning to Tystok, where I intended to go in the first place before this whole escapade," she said as her eyes scanned him up and down. Though she obviously tried to hide it, she grinned. "I quite prefer you like this, but if you insist on finding another shirt, that can be arranged."

His face was suddenly aflame. After her initial rejection in his carriage, she had now kissed him without warning and given him a solitary compliment. Was she merely flirting, or did she share his affection? He did not know, but he was grateful that these islanders couldn't understand what they were saying.

"To Tystok, then," his voice squeaked.

Bentun moved aside as Kasia held out her crystal hand. Light flared across it in a swirl of golden threads, her eyes reflecting the glow until one snapped taught in her palm. She snatched it, and the remaining wisps burst into a portal at the pit's edge.

Near darkness lay on the other side. Lamps along a stone wall barely pierced the everdark to reveal a gate of steel and glass, and beyond, a mansion rose—the infamous home of the fallen House Niezik. An entire realm away.

"Come, Lord Zinarus," Kasia said, helping him hobble to the portal. "Let us see how my dear brother has fared in my absence."

CALLS FOR AID

"All the realm pleads for my aid when I have but one sword." – Carnion ik Tanion, former supreme defender of the Glassblade Order

Radais stood on the elevated platform overlooking Palmia Fortress's sparring yard. There once would have been hundreds of masters and warriors dressed in training garb and shining glass armor, but before him now were little more than sixty experienced Glassblades. Miv had sent far more out into the villages already. That had only left them dispersed, vulnerable against the threats they faced.

The letters he'd received in recent days only confirmed the issue.

Villages across western Vocka had all requested additional Glassblade support, reporting overwhelming awakened attacks. Radais had replied with his knowledge that these were organized breathless under the Vanashel's command, but informing them didn't fix the problem.

Civil war had begun in Ezman. Here, they faced a war between man and corrupted spirit with only a small fraction of an army. Tairanik and Polina had launched an unprecedented search for recruits while Radais was in the Wastes, but the fifty or so new initiates would have to learn on the march. It was unfair, but what choice did they have?

"They are not ready," Commander Polina insisted from Radais's side.

Tall, even for a Vockan, she had all the bulk of the strongest warrior despite being in her mid-fifties, and her voice still held its bite. Her half-Reshkan blood had given her a rounder face and dirty blonde hair that appeared burnt along the sides. It was rare for a Glassblade to not be entirely Vockan, but no one dared comment on her lineage. She had flogged enough initiates to make sure of that.

"None of us are," Radais replied, studying the initiates as they sparred with their instructors. Wanusa was among them for now, but that would change today. "This threat is unlike anything the Order has ever seen. We need every blade we have. If there are more Vanashel than we saw, then even that may not be enough."

"Then we should muster our forces here," she insisted. "Palmia is the most defensible location in the entirety of Brakesh against the awakened or these accursed breathless!"

Tairanik climbed the steps to join them. Wearing a collared officer's jacket like theirs, he hadn't matched Polina's fitness into his later years, and it fit him tightly in all the wrong ways. "Recalling our dispersed forces would eliminate what little trust we have among the villages. It also assumes they wouldn't just go around us."

Radais winced at an initiate taking a wooden training flail to the face. Instructors dual wielded ones with many striking heads to mimic a spirit's tendrils, and it was a far different style of combat compared to typical swordsmanship. Even those trained with blades or spears would struggle as they adapted to Glassblade ways.

"Tairanik is right," he said. "Trust in the Order is low already. Our mission is not merely to hide in our fortress and survive, but to protect the people. The Vanashel are not awakened. They will seek to slay all the living they can to draw us out, then ambush us on their terms."

"You propose marching to meet them?" Polina said, brow raised. "That is… That is suicidal if what you've said is true."

Radais crossed his arms. "It's what Miv would do. We are Glassblades. We will face the corrupted spirits, and our armor will protect us."

He poured all the confidence he lacked into his words. Odds against them or not, they needed to believe success was possible. Miv had once told him that defeat was only certain when one entered the battle expecting it, so he would focus on the goal and how to achieve it.

"We have recovered our fallen brethren's armor and blades," Tairanik said. There was an unusual hesitation in his voice, but he'd at least stopped challenging Radais's command over recent days. "It is tradition for a Glassblade to lie upon the pyre with their sword, but the glaziers cannot keep up with this surge of initiates. If you insist on marching to war against these Vanashel, they must have true swords."

That explained the hesitation. All Glassblades knew the honor of a funeral, melting the sword in the fallen warrior's wake to be re-forged later. The Order's fallen deserved better, but it would truly be suicide to force initiates to fight with only knives or glass-tipped spears. He could not allow that.

"Distribute the blades to initiates," Radais replied, "but ensure each knows who wielded it before them. Before we leave, they are all to go into the mountains with the blade and grant an offering to the spirits. Let that honor the fallen."

Tairanik held a fist over his heart and bowed. "Yes, Supreme Defender."

"What about their armor?" Polina asked. "Awakened can be manipulated to strike at just the breastplate for initiates, but these breathless will target their unarmored limbs and heads."

"Then freely distribute the armor from our fallen," Radais said with another glance at the initiates. Spirits, there were so many of them. Would such an inexperienced force be worse than a smaller group of masters and warriors?

Tairanik stomped his boot. "That would break nearly a millennium of Glassblade tradition! We have reused blades before, but initiates have always earned their armor as they become warriors. To defy that..."

"Every person who made their way here faced the attacks happening all over Vocka," Polina replied with her eyes like daggers at Tairanik. "They crossed mountains in the everdark to join us. It would be ridiculous to haul armor for them on the journey, only gifting it when they earn it. More would perish through our insolence than those who gain through tradition."

"It would bolster our strength as well," Radais added. "A fully armored initiate is one a warrior or master need not watch constantly in battle. Wanusa would've benefited from it on our expedition."

Polina nodded. "Then it will be done. Come, Tairanik. There is much—"

A fluttering alpine accentor interrupted her. The small bird had a gray head and brown streaks across its back and underbelly, and its kind were the trained messengers of the Vockans through the mountains. As Tairanik had expressed with the iz Ardinvil letter, it was rare for those with Ezmani leanings to rely on them instead of traditional couriers. This one, though, held a letter wrapped around its leg bearing an unfamiliar sigil.

Radais thanked the bird with a gentle pat on its head before handing it to Palmia's accenteer—their keeper and trainer of the little birds—who rushed up to them at the sight of the letter.

"Do you recognize this sigil?" Radais asked the commanders, but found only shaken heads. Strange. They had received many communications in recent days regarding the chaos in Ezman and Vocka alike. Most had been from familiar Vockan contacts.

He sliced open the seal with his iron dagger and studied its contents, far shorter than Manalias iz Ardinvil's:

Supreme Defender of the glorious Glassblade Order,

You must know well by now of the Commonwealth's coup at the hands of the Crimson Court. Honorable people from across our nation, regardless of birth, are rallying at Fort Harizak, near the confluence of the Ty and Vamia rivers. Our foes command the spirits, and your blades would be of great use. Join us, I plea.

Sincerely,

Tiuz Hazeko

Field Marshal of the Confederation of Harizak

Radais crumpled the letter, grinding his teeth. "Half the damn realm wants our help."

"Who was it this time?" Tairanik asked.

"Tiuz Hazeko himself," Radais replied. He had already made his decision to face the Vanashel, ignoring the war in the east. But denying a direct request from the Commonwealth's most famous general? He so badly wished to spend a few days on leave after the expedition to draw the mountains and the new initiates. Instead, every problem in Zekiaz was apparently his to solve.

Oh, Miv, I judged you too harshly. This burden must be how you punish me.

He looked over the eastern wall, the mountains covered by the everdark beyond. Dawnrise would come soon, but it wouldn't bring its usual hope. "It's another request for aid from that Confederation of his."

Tairanik scoffed. "Those never go well."

"It would win us favors with the Ezmani," Polina countered. "Even a small band would cover an infantry flank."

"Ahh!" Radais shouted, slamming his fists into the railing at the platform's edge. He heaved with each breath as the pressure mounted on him. Why did he bother to accept this role?

The training Glassblades stared at him when he raised his head. Warriors and masters smirked at the outburst, but initiates stood wide-eyed. Radais's shoulders sagged, and he turned back to the commanders with regret stirring in his chest.

"I don't want to make this decision," he admitted. "No matter what I do, I am condemning someone to death, and I don't even know who or how many."

Polina smacked him on the arm hard enough he swore it would bruise. "It's the supreme defender's responsibility. You took the job, so you make the decision."

"What would you do?" he asked them, forcing himself to take a long breath. "I ignored Manalias's plea, but you have far greater experience than me. Miv gave me this position. That doesn't mean I can do it alone."

Tairanik huffed. "You were right to leave those bastards. Kalastok has ignored us. Why should we slay their spirits for them?"

"My first inclination is to agree," Polina said, but pointed to a few warriors. "That being said, we have a squad of warriors who come from Ezman. They're Vockan by blood, but they'd fight damn hard for their homes."

"The Spirit Plague has been creating thousands of awakened for those Crimsons to turn into breathless," Tairanik said. "A few men with glass swords won't change that."

Radais examined the warriors Polina had pointed out. They were good, trained Glassblades and would be missed if they went east, but he remembered his family. His brother despised him for leaving. His father may have died because of it. There was enough sacrifice as a Glassblade without being forced to completely abandon one's home.

"Give them a choice," he said. "If they choose to leave, they will do so as Glassblades, not deserters."

The commanders thumped their chests, so Radais departed, waving for Wanusa. She'd been eyeing him during her drills and broke away at the signal. A girlish smile conquered her face.

"Supreme Defender," she said with a fist over her glass breastplate. "Is it time for the ceremony?"

He mirrored her smile and patted her on the shoulder. "It is. Ditch that silly wooden thing and grab your true sword. Soon, you'll be the newest Glassblade warrior."

She did so with all the haste of a hungry ibex at supper. The greatsword fit her height, and though she had a narrow build, the sixteen-year-old had gained serious muscle during their expedition. Radais took pride in that. Their first encounters had made him believe she was an overeager rule-follower, but she had proven her grit.

They headed out the gate and up the winding switchbacks hidden beneath a foot of snow behind the fortress. All trained Glassblades knew the Initiate's Path well, though. It marked the moment when their efforts had paid off, and when they would finally be a true member of the Order.

A nervy silence hung over them, only pierced by the whistling of the gales through the peaks high above. Those mountains were far beyond the light of their lanterns, but Radais had drawn them enough times to have each crevice memorized. He'd sparred Miv countless times with them looming in the background. His favorite season was duskfall as the setting northern sun made them resemble a crown of gold.

He chose not to break Wanusa's focus. It was natural for an initiate to worry about this moment, but this was nothing but a formality after all she had accomplished. In a single season, she'd faced more fearsome foes in the Spirit Wastes than some warriors did in a lifetime.

Snowfall greeted them as they reached a crest. He didn't wear his armor, and his exposed face stung, but it was almost gentle compared to the Wastes' ashen sand. Stopping atop the crest, he breathed in the alpine air and stared down at the fortress below.

"Why do we take up the blade of glass?" he asked Wanusa, as Miv had once asked him.

She stopped beside him, sword sheathed on her back and her shoulders stiff in a soldier's stance. Some things never changed. "Glassblades are the protectors of pure spirits and people threatened by awakened—now breathless too."

He nodded. "That is what you're taught to say, yes, but why do *you* want to become a warrior? You told me in the Wastes that you ran from your family after a fight, and that you wanted to protect those at civilization's edge."

"I want to see what no one else has," she replied, each word shaky before she raised her chin again. "There is so much even the Glassblades don't know about the spirits. Of course, I want to slay awakened and the Vanashel, but more than that, I want to understand what they truly are. An awakened stole half my brother Inrius's spirit not long before I left. It changed him, and I want to know why the awakened attack us. Why did they first emerge? How do they experience the world? Why can even they become Bound Ones and Reach, while pure-blooded Vockans cannot?"

"A scholar's path," he noted.

She furrowed her brow at him. "You have your sketches. Why can't I wonder about the spirits?"

"My comment was not meant to be a criticism." He held his hand over his heart. "It is important that being a warrior is about more than slaying spirits. We carry our blades, but we are more than them. Our interests and desires are what keep us whole when times are dark."

"Like with your father and Miv."

"Yes." He winced and cleared his throat. "You have shown your will to discover and learn about the spirits. We need that these days. Now, kneel." She cocked her head, but he grabbed her shoulder and pushed her to her knees. "This is where all Glassblades complete their initiation, and it's best to not do so with questioning glances."

She pursed her lips, then nodded. "Yes, Mas… I mean, Supreme Defender."

"Don't worry. I was far more nervous than you when it was my time. Miv damn near threatened to throw me off this ledge."

He stared longingly down at the fortress with its torches and lanterns ablaze, giving it the appearance of a bastion against the darkness and spirits alike. Twenty years had passed since he knelt here. What had he accomplished in that time?

Wanusa shifted, tearing Radais from his thoughts. He drew her sword from her back and held its flat over her head. "Wanusa ik Iliafa, do you swear your life and efforts to the Glassblade Order?"

"I do," she whispered, then raised her voice. "I do."

He lowered the sword to rest its edge on her shoulder. "Will you uphold the pure of spirit, defend the living of spirit, and slay the corrupted of spirit?"

"I will."

He moved the sword to her other shoulder. "Will you wield this blade only to protect, never to harm?"

"I will."

Radais pulled back the sword and stepped away. Pride filled his chest looking down at her. They had met only a few hundred-hours before, but in that time, he'd come to see her as his responsibility. Miv had seen something in her, and so did he. It was up to him to help her reach that potential.

"Then rise, Warrior Wanusa," he declared, his voice echoing through the mountains. "Take your blade, your helm, and your armor. Now and forever, you shall be a member of the Glassblade Order."

The Scouring Scion

Kelosh? The Confederation? Trust our Crimson King!

ISSUE NO. 139   EVERY SCION'S FIRST READ   105TH OF EVERDARK, 791 PA

Don't you love dawnrise? Light blooming in the south. Nature stretching its limbs. Oh, and the blood of fallen soldiers watering the ground as thoroughly as the Ephemeral Storms!

Weak King Jazuk the Fourth led us into this war against the wretched Keloshan Empire, and every weeping parent in Ezman knows he caused their child's death. It is because of his failures that our glorious nation remains divided against this foe. Luckily, we have a *true* king now in Chatik Bartol the First to face enemies both abroad and within our own borders.

In these days of great uncertainty, we must trust the Crimson King and his Court to make right his predecessors' errors. Pledge your spirit and body alike to ensuring Ezman stands! Every laborer. Every farmer. Every conscript. Every Reacher. All our efforts support our king's restoration efforts, and we must not fail! - Continued on A4

LADY NIKOZA BARTOL FACES THE FLAMES ALONE

Our princess becomes a hero in Kalastok's most dire hour! When the fires started by vicious rebels burned the Market District and spread east, Lady Nikoza Bartol could not watch her people suffer. The darling of a Water Reacher risked life and spirit to rescue a desperate mother and daughter from the flames. Read on for an onlooker's harrowing account of the rescue! - Continued on A2

SLIM FIM'S SLIM COLUMN

You know what Slim Fim hates more than anything else? Liars! And this here city is full of them.

I was playing cards in a tavern when an Ogrenian walks in with a hat tugged over their eye. They're a cheat! Don't trust Naniana-Li! So many lost keni...

LAMP LURKER'S CHATTER

All lurkers are thoroughly disappointed that Tiuz Hazeko would betray us in such a manner. The silver wolf had so many admirers, but we must turn our attentions to another newly arrived bachelor: Lord Gregorzon Niezik, brother of Death's Daughter herself!

DAILY SPIRIT READ

Be lively dawnrise girls, and follow the spirits both within and above. Adorn oneself with silver, and wear not the glass which harms both our spirits and our breathless friends.

THE VELVET FIST

"Many wise rulers have found that a stern rule is best hidden behind a face claiming a gentler touch." – An excerpt from *A Neo-Piorakan Guide to Governance*

Crowds swelled across Kalastok's streets as Nikoza rode amid her supply train. Wearing a well-fit Crystal Brigade uniform with glass bracers and a tall cap, she held tight to the reins, eyeing the throngs pressed against her guards on either side. Desperation filled their eyes in the dim light of the gas lamps, and she took heart that she could do something to help.

Watchmen across the supply train unloaded boxes of collected food and basic materials for people to rebuild their burned homes and businesses. Their shouted orders were lost amid the cacophony, but there was only so much they could give. So far, the caravan had only supplied the Drifters' Quarter and now the Market District. People here were more affluent than those in the convoy's destination west of the river. At this rate, though, the crowd would overwhelm Nikoza's guards before they ever reached the Kala.

"We must continue onward," she told the watchman driving the cart ahead of her. "If we remain here, the scions and richest lowborn will take all the supplies."

People grabbed onto the cart's wheels and the banners on its sides. The Crimson Court's sigil of a red diamond surrounded by fifteen others hung alongside House Bartol's of a slain ram. Nikoza held a hand over her mouth as people tore away the banners. Some among them had scion gray skin and hair, but they acted like animals!

"What do you think I can do?" the driver called back to her. "We'd have to shoot 'em to get moving again."

That would not do. Chatik had sent her to bring relief, not cause more strife, but the crowd shouted at her from so deep that many were just shadows in the everdark. Some claimed the Crimson King failed to stop the Keloshan Empire's rapid advance in the east. Others called Chatik a usurper. Most simply cried out for help.

Was that not what she was doing? As Tzena Oliezany trained her, Nikoza had personally Water Reached to ensure these jugs contained the freshest water, and the Crimsons' new government had quickly secured food to feed thousands.

A stray doubt about Chatik's intentions slipped into her mind, but it was swept away. Katarzyna Niezik had tried to convince her that Chatik had created the Spirit Plague to kill innocents and create an army. The Niezik matriarch, though, was a murderer and deceiver. After days of watching Chatik do everything he could to protect his people, all Nikoza knew was that he, Tzena, Qaraza, and Uzrin together were far more effective than her grandfather's council had ever been. They were acting swiftly to counter Kelosh and Lord Tiuz Hazeko's rebellious Confederation of Harizak. Lowborn had ravaged Kalastok, but the Crimsons were gracious, protecting the city with the breathless spirits and sending aid.

"I will clear a path," she declared.

Sitting tall on her steed, she saw ahead to the front of the supply train. The crowd blocked any way forward. So she threw off her long left glove and Reached into the realm of Water. Realm Taint had left her mouth dry and her body feeling as if she endured the everbright heat, but Tzena's coaching granted her a confidence she had never possessed before.

Blue wisps burst from her hands. An experienced Water Reacher could cause great waves or part entire lakes, but it took all her focus just to summon two small walls of water to push back the crowd a few feet. Though she told herself she was just being gentle, she lacked the skill to put much force into it if she had tried. The caravan drivers saw the clearing regardless.

They charged forward as watchmen leaped back onto the supply wagons. Nikoza could only hold the water walls for a few seconds with a single Reach. The crowd pressed against the waves, and horror would follow if she failed to stop them.

So she bit her cheek and Reached again to keep the mass of people from stumbling into the convoy's path. Taint struck her again, threatening to break her grip on her power. She held for just long enough, though, and as she passed, the crowd called out to her both in thanks and desperation.

Will this make any difference? she asked herself.

Nikoza clung closer to her horse's neck when they broke free from the crowd, Taint's dehydration dragging her exhausted mind. Every time she blinked, she saw people clinging to the supply wagons with hope in their eyes. *Her* supply wagons. Hope in *her*. But she was only one person. Perhaps she could have devoted House Bartol's resources into rebuilding if Chatik had allowed her to become matriarch, but he had foreseen another purpose for her. It was up to her to fulfill it.

They passed westward down a street just south of Textile Alley, where her family's townhouse and businesses were based. From what she saw, the fires had scarred many of the buildings, but House Bartol's mercenaries had protected the townhouse itself. She longed for that familiar home. Living under Chatik's guidance in the Crystal Palace made her feel so distant from her family and the city.

Another rider galloped up to her. Dressed in deep red and gold, the watchman saluted her by thumping his chest. "Lady Nikoza," he said, referring to her no longer as a princess now that Jazuk was dead. "We do not believe it is safe to continue."

Nikoza raised her brow. "We must be more careful than we were in the Market District. However, we also cannot allow this aid to go to waste. Let us be swift on the west side, depositing the crates and jugs with only a brief stop."

"It will be a risk," he said. "You are exposed, and there are many who are discontent in the Industrial District and Shadow Quarter."

She just adjusted her glass Crystal Brigade bracers as Chatik's voice echoed in her head. The Crystal Mother commanded her to aid the masses, so she would aid them, even if they could not put aside their savage ways. "Then do what you must to protect me. We cannot let the western city fall into ruin because of cowardice."

Her voice trembled with every word, but the watchmen bowed his head and rode off, barking orders. With him gone, Nikoza rubbed her temples. It was ridiculous to endure Taint for such little Reaching. She needed to do more—both with her Reaching and her influence.

"I am not finished," she whispered to the Crystal Mother, hoping her goddess would hear as her caravan crossed the brick bridge. "Not in the slightest."

NEX GLARED OVER THE KALA RIVER from the dark western shore. Perched atop a lookout point in the southern Industrial District, they had a perfect view of the line of wagons heading over the New Beginnings Bridge.

So the Crimson Court trapped the lowborn west of the river, just to come parading in like heroes with soldiers guarding supplies? Whoever had thought of that idea had bolts for brains. Those rich assholes didn't know what starvation could make people do.

This would go poorly, so Nex climbed down to ensure they got closer to the action. Their people had to get the aid before the gangs snatched it. Nex had given up a lot of keni for a truce between their protected areas and the other gangs, but a meeting between all the gangs was taking more time to organize. To fight back, Nex needed all of them.

A few heads peeked out from shuttered windows to see what all the commotion was about. Gunshots were common west of the Kala. Nowadays, horses and wagons were not, and this many of them made a racket.

Nex found an open spot on New Beginnings Ave, better known among lowborn as Beg Ave, which ran along the Kala River. The bridge sharing its name wasn't far, and they had to cover their eyes as the convoy's lanterns split the everdark. Spiritdamned Crimsons had more light on those wagons than were left on the entire west side.

As if a hundred watchmen weren't enough, Nex flinched seeing the breathless circle over the supply wagons. That flinch turned to a yelp when a hand fell on their back.

Nex prepared to punch whoever it was in the jaw, only to hesitate at the sight of Jiinaan's wide smile. "Found Nex," he exclaimed over his shoulder. "Knew that hat."

Another familiar face appeared in the growing crowd. Old man Jax wore a floppy hat which draped over his ears, and his tin cup rattled away as if he were sitting and waiting for donations in the homeless encampment. "Caught word of these shenanigans after you left," he said with his rotten teeth glinting in the lanternlight. "Sore eyes, this sight. Been a long time since a princess crossed the Kala."

Nex shook their head at his continued failure to understand what a *sight for sore eyes* was, but then paused. "Wait, did you just say 'princess'?"

Jax pointed toward a single rider near the caravan's front. A young woman with silvery-blonde hair and purple eyes sat tall upon the tallest horse Nex had ever seen. Most of them around the west side were half-lame things pulling carts until they fell over and died, but this steed stepped high like a performer.

"Something's not right," they muttered, standing on their toes to get a better view as soldiers unceremoniously dumped crates of food, supplies, and water jugs off the carts. Nikoza had been stiff when Nex had seen her before, but she seemed torn, visibly shaking now.

They turned to Jiinaan. "Think you can clear the crowd for me? I've gotta get to the princess."

The brute tugged down on his shirt, which still revealed his hairy stomach. "I push, but need help."

"I can distract some folk," Jax said with a grin and a shake of his cup. "The people listen to Jax."

The pair headed straight into the crowd without further questions. Nex wondered if it was some strange loyalty or whether they enjoyed messing with all the people. Either way, Nex charged through the alley the two opened for them.

People rushed the crates the watchmen threw from the wagons. Fist fights started around the closest ones, but the watchmen didn't care, worrying only about pushing the crates free. Many cracked in the resulting tumbles. Water jugs poured out over bread, and people trampled vegetables and fruits underfoot to get to the more expensive building materials. Some tried to shove Nex out of the way, but they Reached into the realm of Possibility.

Wisps of every color swirled around Nex's hand as they drew upon Possibility's luck. It gave them a sense of what could happen next, allowing them to duck and dodge strikes and foresee where Nikoza would be in a few heartbeats. A mounted guard separated her from Nex, but the princess's gaze shot to them when they called for her.

"Nex?" Nikoza asked, gasping. She reeled her horse about to the shock of her guards. "Nex! We must speak. Let them through."

A watchman leaped from the nearest wagon with her musket pointed at Nex. "Get away from the princess, now!"

Nex ignored her. "I know Nikoza," they snapped, trying to duck behind the mounted guard. A hand caught them. "I told you—"

"No touch Nex!" Jiinaan's voice boomed through the noise. His fist struck true against the watchman's cheek, sending her sprawling and spurring more to jump from their wagons.

"Enough!" Nikoza pleaded. "Allow Nex through."

But the watchmen ignored her, raising guns toward Jiinaan and Jax, who had appeared beside the half-Reshkan with his tin cup banging into another watchman's head. The pair backed away as Nikoza's guard dragged Nex off. Nex kicked and spat, but the watchmen threw them to Jax's feet as a shot rang out.

Blood splattered over Nex's face as they stared up at their allies. Jax's cup slipped from his grasp, and it clattered to the street where he'd begged for years. He clutched his chest and tried to speak, but only a gurgle came out. As he fell, only Jiinaan's muscled arms stopped him from striking the pavement.

Nex glared at Nikoza, but the watchmen guided her away. She shouted something, a strange fierceness in her eyes as she met Nex's gaze. They wanted to believe she called for a Body Reacher, but the surge of watchmen pushing back the crowd said otherwise.

What had happened to that girl?

Nikoza had claimed she wanted to talk to Nex only moments before her guards had shot Jax. Supplies surrounded the princess, but so did rifles and spirits, who swept overhead now. People scrambled everywhere to grab what supplies they could before darting to safety.

Nex couldn't bring themself to grip their amber or glass. All they could do was stare up at the bloody hole in Jax's chest and that damn cup lying in the muck beside them. They'd asked for his help, and now the old man was dead. He'd never hurt anyone, giving up all his extra keni so the homeless of Beg Ave could afford a meal or another hundred-hour of rent. Scions all slept in their warm houses and soft beds while Jax froze on a bedroll beneath sheets of scrap metal. Fuck them all. He'd been better than any of those rich assholes.

And he'd been far better than Nex.

"We go now!" Jiinaan demanded, grabbing at Nex with his spare hand. He threw Jax over his shoulder as they staggered to their feet. "Bring Jax home."

"He's dead!" Nex spat with a glance at the supply crates. Little was left, but they hoped their other allies had managed to recover *something* from this mess.

Jiinaan nodded. "We'll give him honor and release his spirit."

"Fine." Nex gritted their teeth, but he had a point. Funeral rites were the least Jax deserved. "Lead the way."

So they ran through the remaining crowd. Screams echoed among them as breathless dove at those bearing pistols or any other visible weapons. Nex hoped Jax's blood covering their face and coat wouldn't draw the spirits' attention, but one soon circled through nearby torchlight, eyeing them with its strange humanlike head cocked.

Nex growled and pulled their glass dagger, shoving their hat into Jiinaan's chest. They weren't going to capture this breathless. No, these bastards had killed one of Nex's only friends, and each Crimson, man or spirit, would suffer for it.

"Don't!" Jiinaan appealed, but it was too late. Nex charged.

Tendrils shot from the breathless. They encircled Nex as Possibility's remaining luck showed them where each would be a moment before it struck. Nex dodged the blows and screamed in fury, jabbing the dagger straight into the spirit's torso. It relented and tried to flee, but Nex slashed again and again.

Glass tore the spirit's body to ribbons. Its smoky form dissolved as its tendrils tried to grasp at Nex in one last strike. But Nex cut through them until nothing remained.

Sweat dripped cold down their brow, sticking their raven black hair to their skin and smearing Jax's blood. The area had cleared, and Nex stood in a circle of spirit dust with their heavy breaths joining the gales. Cries rang out in the distance. Here, though, there was only the light of a single torch and a young, heartbroken lowborn who'd lost their friend.

Nex kicked away the spirit dust and shoved their dagger into their coat pocket. Stomping back to Jiinaan, they snatched their wide-brimmed hat from him and pulled it down over their face. Usually, it was to hide their identity. This time, though, they sought to hide their tears.

"C'mon," they muttered. "There'll be more of 'em, and I'm not dying tonight. Got too many people to kill."

BLOOD AND BETRAYAL

'It is a horrid thing to be betrayed by one's ally. It is worse still to be betrayed by one's kin, but if history has taught us anything, it is that those who share blood tend to cause it to flow.' – Votzan Evonska, former grand secretary of the Commonwealth of Two Nations

The everdark greeted Kasia like a snowball to the face. She stumbled from her portal and landed before the gates of House Niezik's manor in Tystok, Zinarus hanging over her shoulder as his mechanical leg screeched.

Her own legs wavered, and she dropped to her knees beside him. Another Reach into the Axiom. It had come far after the last, ensuring she did not worsen her Taint, but carrying a second person through the portal deepened the pit in her stomach. Just touching her power now spurred Aliax, Sazilz, Parqiz, and all the others she'd killed with Death Reaching to torment her. Reality and her Taint merged in her mind. For all she knew, Zinarus could've been a figment of her imagination too.

No, she told herself. He was real. He had to be.

People cried out from across the street, and heavy footfalls announced the arrival of guards beneath the gas lamps. Kasia drew a long breath. For once, those with guns were allies. The Chamber of Scions had marked her for execution, but she was still matriarch of this house.

"Identify yourself!" one of the guards shouted, wearing a deep amber uniform. He didn't raise his gun yet, but his hands tightened around it.

Kasia gave a silent glance to Zinarus to ensure he would be alright. When he nodded, she brushed herself off and rose. A light snowfall struck her as she did, her nose tingling from the frigid flakes. Spirits, she probably looked out of sorts enough for her own servants not to recognize her.

"I am Lady Katarzyna, matriarch of this house," she declared as she tightened her coat to cover the slice in her dress. Zinarus was not so lucky with his bare torso. "I bring with me Lord Zinarus, heir to House iz Vamiustok. We were attacked and must hasten inside."

The guard's jaw dropped. He swapped glances with the other guard, who waved for the gate to open a crack before slipping through at a full sprint. Kasia tensed and prepared to Reach if things got violent. Had word of her condemnation made it here so quickly?

"Apologies, Lady Katarzyna," the remaining guard said as he raised his musket, hands shaking. "There were accusations…"

"Which were all true," an all too familiar voice said.

Aliax drifted between them with a wagged finger. He looked far more real than ever, each gust blowing snow over his chestnut hair as if he weren't a long dead specter.

"Accusations spread by Lord Chatik Pikezik," she spat. More of the dead spirits' voices joined Aliax's, and it took all her focus not to scream at them. "He assassinated King Jazuk Bartol the Fourth and usurped the throne for the Crimson Court! He conspired with Sazilz Uziokaki to kill my father!"

The guard's eyes were like saucers. "Just stay there until Lord Gregorzon emerges."

"*He* is not the magnate of this house!" she roared as a crowd of onlookers gathered around them. Oh, what a sight they were. A shirtless lord and a matriarch covered in blood, rumors of her being Death's Daughter hanging in their minds.

"Lady Kasia!"

A stumbling man emerged from the mansion gardens and slipped through the half-open gates. Dressed in a woolen coat and flat cap, Tazper looked more like a courier than her footman, but the loose cravat twisted slightly beneath his formal shirt confirmed it was him.

Pink filled Tazper's cheeks as he stopped before them with his hands on his knees. Unlike the scions of greater houses, his skin was pale more than gray, and he resembled a young swine more than a man when flustered. Some house heads would find that annoying, but to Kasia, it was endearing. Tazper would do anything for her, no matter how much he regretted it afterward.

He looked from Kasia to shirtless Zinarus with his jaw ajar. Without another thought, he ripped off his coat and threw it over the purple lord, helping him up as more guards emerged from the mansion gates. Gregorzon followed in their wake.

"This is your brother, I presume?" Zinarus asked, thanking Tazper before sticking his arms through the coat's sleeves. It was far too short for his long Vockan frame, but Kasia had no time for amusement as she turned to face Gregorzon.

"It is," she whispered, then raised her voice. "Gregorzon, dear brother, why do you leave your matriarch waiting before the gates at gunpoint?"

Gregorzon's face remained expressionless. Four years younger, he carried her same tight eyes—hazel instead of blue-gray—and their familial, ghastly narrow torso. He wore his ashen gray hair slicked back, and both his shirt and jacket collars were popped to frame his jawline. Red and black replaced his usual dull clothes, including fanciful gloves that covered his talon for now. Kasia's forearm itched at the thought of his flames.

"One can never be too careful these days," he said. "Rumors of Death Reachers abound."

Kasia gritted her teeth, studying his attire. Could he be a Crimson? He had always been affiliated with the nationalists, and that red shirt seemed to proclaim it. It was a popular color among Ezmani scions, but a knowing look filled his eyes. A challenge.

"There are greater issues at play than a power which I no longer have," she countered, displaying her crystalline hand and its missing index finger. "Lord Chatik Pikezik made sure of that."

"While I must express my condolences for the loss of your talon," Gregorzon said as he raised his voice for the crowd, "I cannot claim to be disappointed. After all, your Reaching killed your lover, Aliax Exusix, and a dozen other innocent people who discovered you. It… *You* would have killed our mother too, if I had not intervened."

Gasps spread across the crowd. They backed further from Kasia, and she realized that she recognized many among them—the families and friends of those she had killed. This was a small portion of Tystok. By midday tomorrow, though, all in the town will have heard.

"Perhaps it is best for us to make a retreat," Zinarus told her. "Your brother has taken command of your estate's guards, and with these accusations against you, there is little to stand on."

He no longer leaned against her, but his flinch at the mention of her kills was obvious. Affection still filled his eyes. Why? Tazper's Reacher-induced confession in the Chamber had revealed her worst secrets. This man of honor should despise her, not seek to court her!

She averted her gaze and considered Gregorzon's final statement. Their infirm mother, Yazia, despised her, but Kasia had not tried to kill her.

"I admit the result of my inexperienced Reaching," she said to the crowd. "Aliax and I sought a safe place where I could learn to control my power and not hurt others, but we were chased down, threatened. They called me a whore for pursuing a lowborn man, bearing torches to burn me alive."

Aliax and the other peasant ghosts joined their families in the crowd. No longer surrounded by Death's purple wisps, they looked indistinguishable from the living, and Kasia focused on Aliax and his mother, whom they had confided in many times. She had welcomed Kasia when others would have questioned the matriarch's intentions with her lowborn son. Now, though, her lip twitched.

"I did not wish for their deaths when they wished for mine," Kasia continued with guilt trying to choke her. "But I was young, inexperienced. It is not enough of an excuse, I know, and I see every one of them when I close my eyes. In recent years, I have tried to better the lives of their families. You deserved the truth, though, and I was too afraid to give it."

Tears streamed down the face of Aliax's mother. Kasia couldn't find her own with fear and exhaustion overwhelming her. Realm Taint hadn't relented, and when voices answered her speech, she could not tell which ones were true and which were her imagination.

"Murderer!" a man shouted. "You took everything from us."

Another lobbed a rock, which struck her arm hard enough to bruise. "She deserves to burn!"

"But she's trying to help fix it."

"It was an accident! They threatened her."

The crowd devolved into more arguments, and through it all, Gregorzon stood with the lamplight giving his face a fiery glow. He signaled to a guard, and a single musket shot into the air silenced the lowborn. "All that leaves your lips, Sister, are false accusations and desperate excuses. Perhaps this was a mere accident wrought by fear, but our mother's infirmity stems from your wretched power as well. I watched your talon dig into her skin as she fell ill!"

"Liar!" Kasia spat, drawing her pistol before she could think otherwise. "This revolver was our father's, and you dishonor him with every action you take, hurling these falsities at me to divert from Chatik's crimes. Is he your ally, Brother? Do you fraternize with those who brought our house to ruin and assassinated both King Jazuk and King Yaakiin?"

The guards tensed at her holding the pistol, so Zinarus hobbled forward with Tazper's help and extended his taloned hand. "I am a Reacher of the realm of Truth. Let me settle such a claim." He stood as straight as he could with his mechanical leg still twisted and im- mobile. "Lord Gregorzon, will you speak such accusations beneath Truth's power?"

Kasia grinned. Perhaps Zinarus had more bite to him than she had expected. Gregorzon would fail, and he would be forced to admit his affiliations with the Crimsons.

"Of course I will," Gregorzon replied, striding toward them and rolling up his sleeve. "What I have to say is important for our people to hear."

Kasia swapped glances with Zinarus. What was her arrogant, foolish brother doing? Did he not know what agony he would endure if he dared attempt a lie? Tazper's raised brow expressed his own shock, and that only made her chest tighten further.

White wisps circled Zinarus's hand as he Reached without issue now that they had returned to Zekiaz. "Let only the Truth be spoken," he said, taking her brother's exposed arm.

Gregorzon spasmed as the wisps shot into his skin. Teeth bared, he glared at Kasia. "Ask your questions."

"Admit it," she replied. "I had nothing to do with Mother's infirmity. You struck me with your flames out of the same inexperience that I struggled with."

Gregorzon scoffed and shut his eyes. "Mother protected your failures, but you were too selfish to understand. When she forced you to admit what you were and what damage your power had done, you cornered her. Even now, I remember those lines of purple spreading through her veins. I heard your shouting and rushed into the room. My Fire Reaching forced you to release her, but you claimed you had done nothing." Returning his gaze to her, he sneered. "Lady Yazia has been in this state ever since—not dead, but not completely alive either."

"No..."

Kasia stepped back, her heart racing. He was *lying*! She remembered that night clearly, and though she had argued with her mother, she hadn't Reached to kill her. It was impossible. But the Truth Reaching said otherwise.

She grabbed Zinarus's shoulder with all formality slipping from her voice. "Your Reaching failed. This is not true! I swear it upon my father's life and my honor." When Zinarus could only offer incoherent mumbles, she turned back to her brother instead. "These are

Chatik's lies, aren't they? You are a member of the Crimson Court! You conspire with those who killed our father."

"King Chatik Bartol does not need me to speak lies," he replied before stepping back and removing Zinarus's hand from his arm. "I require no compulsion to admit my affiliation with the Crimson Court. King Jazuk and King Yaakiin before him failed to secure our nation. We shall do so through the spirits of our lands."

"You are traitors," Kasia insisted.

Gregorzon wagged a gloved finger. "We are patriots. The Keloshan Empire far exceeds us in industrial production and advanced weaponry, so we must utilize our Reachers against them. Because of the Crimson Court's research, we will soon no longer have to fear any awakened. They shall become breathless who follow our every command, and no weapon which Kelosh wields will defeat us then."

"How many in Tystok have fallen to the Spirit Plague which the Crimson Court created?" Kasia said, waving toward the raucous crowd as she regained her noble tone. "You scorn me for an accident which I have sought to mend while you slaughter innocents who become instruments in your faction's games. Decry my sins all you wish. The Crimson Court is a scourge, and so are you!"

She turned to the guards. They wavered, looking between the Niezik siblings with their guns lowered. "Many of you have served me for years, and some of you I recognize from our amber expedition into Raviak Forest. You know my will. You know my desire to rebuild our lands and bring better lives for the people who rely on us. Would you rather serve a man who cares not for his people, or the Amber Dame, who fought back the Uziokaki to claim amber?" She raised her hand to emphasize her point. "Amber which can protect one from spirits by capturing them within the stone?"

"Lady Katarzyna has spoken!" an authoritative voice called out.

Artaxan, chief scout of that very amber expedition, emerged from the lowborn ranks. His duster was lined with dark fur from a dangerous koilee, and he donned a felt hat that was more bullet holes than felt. Of course he wasn't hiding from his ranger reputation. In the years since she'd last seen him, he had grown a curling black handlebar moustache, and the lines above his brow had deepened to canyons.

"You heard me," he barked at the guards. "Lower the damn muskets before there's more bloodshed than this civil war's about to bring."

Remarkably, the scouts who'd served under him complied. The rest followed, leaving none to threaten Kasia.

Gregorzon gawked at them. "What is this? You are sworn to this house, to Ezman! Katarzyna is a fugitive from justice."

"It seems problems run deeper in this family than I thought," Artaxan said, stopping beside Kasia with a subtle nod. "I returned from my hunts when I got word of this Crimson Court, but I didn't expect Lady Katarzyna to be preparing for another duel. By the Mother, let's settle this without Reaching or guns. Get the Vockan lad a shirt and Lady Katarzyna a dress that isn't bloodstained."

Some in the crowd exchanged unsteady glances as the guards moved to take the scions inside. They had just been told the siblings warring for House Niezik were a murderer and a traitor. Times were uncertain enough without the house who owned much of Tystok and the surrounding villages falling once again, so Kasia turned back and grabbed Zinarus's taloned hand.

Remnant white wisps bore into her skin, forcing her to bite her cheek. Deception would get her nowhere, and she needed to earn back her people's trust.

"Beneath a Truth Reacher's power, I swear that I will do what I can to fix what I have broken," she told them, especially focusing on Aliax's mother. "As I no longer bear Death, I will seek to reduce its lasting sting."

No agony came, so she released a sigh. Her intention, at least, was true. All she could do was hope her people saw the depth in those words.

The guards approached to guide her inside until Artaxan held out a hand for them to stop. "I will handle her myself. Come, Kasia. Let's be done with this mess."

She bowed in thanks before passing through the gates with Zinarus's hand still in hers. Doubts lingered about her past, but for now, she pushed them away as plans stewed in her mind. "Listen to me carefully," she whispered to the purple lord, "and when we enter the mansion, do exactly as I say."

HALF-AN-HOUR LATER, THEY GATHERED in the drawing room at the rear of the Niezik mansion. Kasia's handmaiden, Kikania, and the house nurse, Uliusa, had scrambled to find her an appropriate dress that would both make her impressive to Zinarus—their idea, not hers—but not too obtrusive in the face of Gregorzon's challenge. She had taken most of her finest clothes with her to Kalastok. Those were likely a lost cause along with thousands of keni of other possessions, so she focused on the slim, sky-blue dress that she wore now.

It would be her armor for tonight's battle.

She tugged her sleeve over her scarred forearm as Gregorzon entered with an entourage of minor scions, only some whom she recognized. The break had given her time to consider the situation, devour some much-needed sustenance, and recover from her Taint. Death's specters had not vanished, but what bothered her more was the doubt that now surrounded her memory. Gregorzon had revealed that she tried to kill their mother. How did she remember a completely different truth?

"You Crimsons quite enjoy running in little packs, like rats," she quipped, settling on her settee and attempting to appear as feminine as possible. Gregorzon needed to believe he had the upper hand for her plan to work.

Her brother took his position on a wingback chair in the far opposite corner. His three allies mulled about, leaning against the fireplace or taking seats of their own. Dear Mother, they looked like squirrels who'd found an acorn and now couldn't figure out what to do with it. Their presence was a good sign, though. If he was relying on local minor scions for his entourage, it meant Chatik either hadn't expected her to return to Tystok, or he lacked assets this far from the capital. She could use that.

"Is that what we have come to?" Gregorzon asked. "Petty insults?"

Kasia stroked her gloved left hand. It felt confining after Reaching so often in recent days, but those same Reaches had severely Tainted her. Besides, this was not a conflict which her magic could solve.

Nearly every Niezik guard had abandoned the gate and was now posted either around the drawing room's walls or its doorways. Once Zinarus returned with Artaxan and Tazper, it would become more cramped than any time in recent memory. Was this what it took to bring people into House Niezik? Civil and familial war?

"This became petty when you betrayed me," she insisted, letting a bite slip onto her tongue. "Tell me, what did you hope to accomplish by airing your grievances like soiled laundry before the masses?"

Gregorzon clutched his armrests. "If we are being honest, dear Sister, then I regret not ordering the guard to strike you down immediately. King Chatik would have rewarded me greatly."

"He is king already?" she asked. "I am not surprised the King in the Dark acted with such haste. It took little time for his dragon to fling King Jazuk into the Spirit Crystal's pit. The poor old man lacked even the chance to resist, but that is the intent of a dagger in the back."

"Why are you here, Katarzyna?" he replied. "You lack the forces to resist the Crimsons, and House Uziokaki will not hesitate like I did. Not after what you did to Lord Razamat in Raviak Forest."

She furrowed her brow. "I am here because I survived a coup and sought safety in my estate. Though you have always been a thorn in my side, I did not foresee you stooping so low as to lick Chatik's boot. What did they offer you? Power? The hand of Lady Qaraza Uziokaki herself? She is a new matriarch and will surely need a spouse, so why wouldn't the Crimsons seek to end our feud by making Leonit's house irrelevant?"

Footsteps announced the arrival of the men, as Gregorzon was simply pretending to be more than a mere boy. Artaxan entered first, nodding to the guards before crossing his arms. "You two have yet to shoot each other. That is a start."

Kasia's mind drifted to the revolver tucked away in her handbag beside her. She had fired all but a single bullet in the Water Realm, but that was all it would take to end this. Irregular footfalls tore her from those dark thoughts.

"To continue, we require more than mere unwillingness to kill," Zinarus said as he entered with Tazper's help.

Kasia wanted to reply, but her words caught at the sight of him. Without his usual purple and gold wardrobe to choose from, he wore a simple cutaway jacket meant for a rural rider and a ruffled shirt from stylings two decades before. His cravat carried exotic colors splitting through its white. It originated from beyond Brakesh to the nations across Zekiaz's oceans—and it had been one of Leonit's favorites.

Kasia's fingers traced her lips, assaulted by memories of her father standing in that doorway over a decade before with Reshkan chocolates for her. Leonit had often been a serious man. With the sweets, though, he'd flared that cravat and declared the Dance of Dawn celebration had arrived early. Oh, how she missed dancing in his arms with no worries of the world beyond their mansion.

"Lady Katarzyna, are you well?" Zinarus asked, stepping away from Tazper with the help of an old wooden cane. Leonit's clothes were short with the half-Vockan's height, but it only served as another reminder that they were borrowed from the dead.

Unbidden tears had welled in her eyes. She wiped them off with a handkerchief. She had meant for Gregorzon to feel he had the advantage, not weep before him. "Yes, thank you. That outfit was one that my father used to wear, and it just brought back memories."

His cheeks burned as bright as his auburn hair, which he ran his hand through. "Oh, my. I did not mean to offend, my lady. If you would prefer I find another…"

"Sit," she said, patting the place next to her on the settee. It was armless and low-backed—a woman's seat—but having him beside her would ensure she didn't do something she would regret. "My brother and I have yet to delve into discussions about our house's future."

He bowed his head and did as commanded. Behind him, Tazper slipped out the door, an embarrassed look across his face at dressing her suitor like Leonit. It was truly a minor error, but Kasia had learned long ago that her footman wore his heart on his face rather than his sleeve.

"There is nothing to discuss," one of Gregorzon's lackeys insisted.

Kasia ignored him. "I will allow you to run off to your patron," she told her brother. "If only to inform Chatik that I am not finished with him."

"You said it yourself," Gregorzon replied, crossing his legs and pulling a cigar out of a drawer beside him. The lackey struck a match and lit the cigar's end. "You are no longer a Death Reacher. What threat could you pose to him and the Crimson Court?"

She looked to Zinarus to see if he had any insights, but he remained silent... and all the way on the other side of the settee. By the Crystal Mother, did he wish to be with her or not?

"Why would I tell you what threat I hold?" she asked. "Talon or not, I will avenge our father."

Artaxan paced between them. "Before you two bicker further, you should think about your guards. I commanded most of them once, and I consider myself reasonable."

"You stood by my side as we secured amber for this house and enriched our entire region," Kasia said.

He nodded. "I also know better than most what you are capable of, and how Death Reacher Taint devours you like a koilee would a doe."

"That is precisely why she must be detained and brought to Kalastok," Gregorzon said. "She does not remember harming Mother, so what if there are others?"

Kasia retreated into the settee's corner. So many specters watched her from the room's shadows, making the room even tighter, but knowing her memory had betrayed her was more frightening than even

Aliax. That moment with her mother had been years ago, far before the worst of her Taint. Was it twisting her mind further even now?

"The matter of Lady Katarzyna's mind is for doctors or Reachers of the relevant realms to examine," Zinarus said, not looking at her. "House Niezik's governance, meanwhile, is a legal dispute, but as she was found guilty of murder without the chance to defend her actions, it appears hasty to declare that she is no longer matriarch. Furthermore, Lord Gregorzon's own affiliations with an organization who assassinated the elected king could illegitimize his tentative claim as well."

One of Gregorzon's lackeys chuckled. "Just because you speak many words, it doesn't mean they have any meaning."

"She has no defense," Gregorzon said with a puff of his cigar, further startling Kasia as embers flared at its end.

"An act of self-defense is in itself a legal defense," Zinarus replied, then paused. "So is insanity."

All her fear burned away. "WHAT?" She shot to her feet so fast that her head felt as if it were floating. When she caught her balance, she glared at Zinarus. He was supposed to be helping her, not labeling her as mad! "I am not insane!"

"Are you sure?" Aliax asked, sitting on the settee's edge and stroking her hair. "Is it normal to see the dead as if they were among the living? Is it normal to destroy all those who you hold dear?"

The ghost of Parqiz Uziokaki rounded the willow wood pianoforte with his stomach protruding and his blond hair like a wet dog's. "I see why Sazilz never attended events within this mansion. What a dreary place compared to our grand estate."

Gregorzon said something, but it was drowned out by the specters' chattering. She couldn't keep track of it all. Even when she shut her eyes, Aliax's hands graced her head and back. All her instincts told her to lash out, to force him away, but that would only prove her madness. It was *not* true. She was sane!

"My sanity is not the question," she muttered, throwing a dismissive hand in Gregorzon's direction. Someone else had been talking—at least she thought it was one of the real people—but they silenced at her voice. "I am, by all rights, still matriarch of House Niezik. Go to your Crimson King and have him declare otherwise, but until that time, this estate and all property of House Niezik is mine. I will allow you a carriage to flee to your friends in Kalastok. Anything more, and you'll have to duel me for it."

"Kasia, I am not calling you insane," Zinarus said as he reached for her hand, only for her to pull it away. "Please, if you would just listen."

"I am done listening," she snapped. "I must act for myself and my house."

Artaxan groaned and ran his fingers through his mustache. "Not another duel. My heart nearly gave out during the last one."

"A game, then," she said, drawing her pistol from her handbag. "Father said this revolver was the last of the pirate known as Stormrider, so let us resolve this like the privateer kings of the Vitrian Sea."

Gregorzon shook his head. "We are certainly not playing pirate's demise."

"Kasia…" Zinarus warned. "Do not attempt something that you cannot step back from."

But she held the revolver out for him to take. "You are a man of honor, Lord Zinarus. This is the last remaining bullet in this gun. Please place it in a chamber at random so that none of us may see."

The pair shared a look, and she silently pleaded for him to do so. There was a time for affable diplomacy. This, though, was not it. She knew what it would take to beat her brother, and Zinarus needed to play his part.

"Very well," he said with a nervous twitch of his lip. "I will do as you say for the sake of fairness." His hand trembled as he plucked the bullet free, then turned away. Once it was placed in another chamber, he spun the cylinder and waited for it to stop before returning the gun to Kasia with a courteous bow. "All I ask is that you are careful, my lady."

She winked at him. "Am I ever not?" Without waiting to see his reaction, she snapped her attention back to Gregorzon. "As I requested the competition, I will go first," she said, holding the gun to her temple—the one Chatik's bullet had skimmed in the Axiom. A scar still marked it, and no hair had grown in its place. "Play the game, or leave."

Gregorzon looked to Artaxan for aid, but the scout just shrugged. "It's legal in Ogrenia. I fail to see why we cannot honor it here."

"Savages," Gregorzon muttered before snuffing out his cigar and rising with his chin high. "Fine, then. Let us play your ridiculous game, Katarzyna."

He acted confident, for now. So Kasia spun the revolver's cylinder and cocked back the hammer. She took a sharp breath, then pulled the trigger.

Click.

She grinned and held out the revolver for Artaxan to bring to Gregorzon. Reluctantly, he transferred it, and Gregorzon's hand trembled as he raised the gun.

"Mother is upstairs. If she knew of this, she would scream until our ears rang, all because you destroyed her."

"You have convinced yourself of lies," Kasia replied, not allowing herself to glance at Aliax's smirking form. "That is how you escaped the Truth Reaching."

Gregorzon gave a patronizing look. "I only hope a bullet grants your lost mind rest."

Click.

He exhaled sharply before stepping forward and handing her the revolver. Pity almost seemed to fill his eyes, but she ignored it as she pressed the gun to her head. Gregorzon showing care was more ridiculous than her seeing the dead. Part of her wished to further contest that she was sane, but in truth, she knew this proved otherwise. What lady in her right mind challenged her brother to a game where one person inevitably died? There was a reason only pirates ever competed.

Click.

She passed the gun back to him without another word. None were required. They both knew there were six chambers, and that meant half were gone. The odds of a live round increased with every pull of the trigger.

"Why did Chatik choose you?" Kasia asked as Gregorzon raised the revolver, but kept the barrel's end far from his skin. "You have yet to say why you betrayed both Father's legacy and me."

"What reason do I need but service of my country?" he replied. "We are doomed to fall without the breathless spirits, and the Crimson Court is the only group willing to do what is necessary to ensure we survive."

Click.

He took a sharp breath at the realization of what that meant. Two rounds remained, but Kasia's shot would reveal the result. If she died… Well, that was obvious enough of an ending. But if she found another empty chamber, then Gregorzon's defeat was inevitable.

Kasia's heart thumped as she took back the revolver, thinking of all it must have seen during Stormrider's ventures through the great Vitrian Sea. How many had stared down its barrel and met their fates? Would she join them?

Zinarus pushed himself to his feet as she pressed the gun to her temple. It was cold, and a shiver ran down her spine. A thrill came with it. Just days ago, she had held Death at her fingertips. Now, she was at its mercy.

"Kasia, please," Zinarus pled, balancing on one leg and snatching at her free hand. "I do not wish to see you meet a horrible end. You are not insane, even if Taint manipulated your mind during your argument with Lady Yazia. The mistake of a single moment need not beget further errors."

She drew a long breath. "This is no error."

Then she pulled the trigger.

A STRANGE KIND OF FAMILY

"To the scions, gangs are just violent thugs. But to the urban lowborn, it's a bond thicker than blood. We protect each other by bullet, kena, and tongue, and if you interfere with my family, you'll never see yours again." – Crax of the Shadow Quarter

Sweat coated Nex's brow beneath their wide-brimmed hat, tugged down to cover their left eye. For once, they didn't need it to hide their face. Just a single candle hung from a chain above, and all four figures seated at the table were little more than shadow.

Except for their hands.

The hulking woman across from Nex drummed her fingers against the cracked and peeling wood. Bold, as nails protruded from the table's surface in enough ways that its craftsman must've been a lunatic. But Bess's hands were more scar than skin anyway. The only smooth part of them were the brass knuckles rounding each finger, and even those were splattered with old blood.

"You got us here," the boss of the Murder Mitts said with the cracked voice of a heavy smoker. "Talk."

Subtle rainbow wisps swirled around Nex's crystal ring as they examined the gang leaders. For the first time in years, the bosses of the Murder Mitts, Crax's Folly, and the Glass Teeth were in the same room—and not trying to kill each other. At least, not yet. The bribes to get them here had taken all but the last of Nex's keni from Kasia, so from here on out, the Possibility Reacher would need the magical kind of persuasion.

"The Crimson Court is manipulating us," Nex began, pulling on Possibility's luck. "We all saw that bitch of a princess march down the west side with supplies, just to dump them and shoot at us. Their breathless spirits cut us down. Their Spirit Plague makes us into their undead slaves. And if we don't unite against them, they'll slaughter every one of us."

The man to their right spat on the table, striking in the center of the hook that replaced his missing hand. "United with these arse-holes? I'd rather kneel before Chatik with my cock loose."

"Eloquent as always, Lok-Tag," Crax replied in his aged voice. Though lowborn, the boss of Crax's Folly wore leather gloves over his hands, and many on the west side whispered that he was a Reacher of some kind. None could agree on which realm. "Your fishers starve because blood and shit poisons the river, but you'd shoot old Crax first."

"Ain't no one shooting west siders," Nex insisted.

They allowed their accent to slip into a native Ezmani lowborn's instead of their usual mix of Ogrenian like Lok-Tag. Sounding like a foreigner wouldn't help.

"How you 'xpect to kill breathless?" Lok-Tag replied. "Not enough glass west of the Kala."

Nex rolled their eyes. "I'm not stupid. You're all hoarding glass and food and clean water. Can't blame you with all the shit going on, but you'll run out eventually. Then, those Crimson bastards will come for you."

"Ha!" Bess exclaimed. "Let them try."

"You're supposed to protect your people," Nex muttered. "Sure, you steal and hold the best shit for yourselves, but your gangs are nothing if the west siders make them nothing. They'll realize real soon what you have. Think brass knuckles and your thugs with guns will stop 'em?"

"Pretend I'm interested," Crax replied with a disarming wave toward the other bosses. His skin almost appeared scion gray, and Nex bit their cheek. Was he a fake or a scion who wanted to help for once? "What are you offering?"

Nex thumped the table. "I've got a cure for the plague and a new way to fight breathless."

"You control a cure, but accuse us of hoarding food?" Bess mused, leaning forward to reveal her squared jaw and wide nose. You didn't call Bess ugly to her face, but damn, Nex saw why people told her anyway. "Wheat grows a mile west, but nobody can cure the plague!"

"Help me, and I'll help you," Nex said. "We all hate the scions. The Crimsons are the worst of them, and they want us divided."

"What?" Lok-Tag asked. "You take glass and food? We get a cure and weapons against spirits?"

Nex nodded. "And I want guns. Once my allies can protect ourselves, then I can trust you won't shoot us in the back."

"You have my promise," Crax said with a bow. "These *allies* of yours concern me, however. What are your goals with them, Nex?"

"You ever heard of Evit Paxian?" they asked, recalling a small booklet their father had carried around before his death. "*The Dawnrise Manifesto?*"

Lok-Tag leaned forward and dragged his hook of bent scraps across the table, clanking against each protruding nail. "Paper rubbish."

"I'm calling us the Ashes of Dawn," Nex said as that hook drew closer to their hands than was comfortable. They considered pulling them back, but that would look weak. In front of the gangs, weakness would mean death. "I don't care about territory or profit. Those Crimsons killed Jax from Beg Ave, and their fucking plague almost took my girl! I want to shatter their glass houses and tear them from their cashmere sheets."

"Where's the cure?" Bess asked.

Nex flipped open their empty hands. "Etal, that professor at the college, made it with Paras. The alchemist faked his death, and I know

you've heard the cure works. We don't have more of it because of the lockdowns. But I can get to Etal. Just need guns to shoot our way across the river."

Bess leaned back and huffed, arms crossed. "Fine, but last I heard, they got that old man locked up tight. This must be why."

"Doesn't matter," Nex said. "We'll break him out."

"And the weapon against spirits?"

Nex flared their nostrils. "You in? I'm not telling you shit if I don't have your word."

"Yeah, I'll give you what you want." Bess rapped her brass knuckles against the table. "That is, *if* you're not a lying piece of shit. We all know your record in the gambling halls."

Lok-Tag lunged and dug his hook into the table between Nex's spread fingers. "Don't lie, little Nex," he hissed. "I'll give glass, but bullets follow witches with crystal rings. Might hit your girl too."

Nex drew in a sharp breath, considering the bosses' threats. They'd make Nex suffer if they didn't receive a cure and amber to fight the breathless, but Nex didn't know how to break Etal out of prison—or if Paras was even alive. Nor did they have all of Kasia's amber reserves in Kalastok. They'd used their allies in the new Ashes of Dawn to round up any amber on the west side they could find, but it wasn't enough. They needed to get into House Niezik's mansion. That meant crossing the Kala to get both amber and the cure. Risky, but if Lok-Tag threatened Vinnia, Nex would do whatever it took to get over that damn river.

"Give me what I want," Nex said, "and I'll get you the weapon and the cure. Swear it."

Bess shrugged, but when Lok-Tag retracted his hook and nodded, she did too. "This better be good."

Nex pulled a bead of amber from their duster's pocket. Two spirits' gray bodies floated within it, not still, but not moving with any noticeable speed. "Amber catches the spirits," they said, setting it on the table. "Gets weaker with each use, especially small pieces, but even the breathless can't fight it."

Crax snatched the bead. "Do they escape if the amber shatters?"

"Dunno, but I wouldn't try it."

"This explains you buying up all of it," Lok-Tag said, leaning forward enough for his glass fangs to glint in the candlelight. "Shoulda saw it sooner, but I doubt you've got enough to fight the breathless anyway."

Nex gave a knowing grin. "Don't worry. You'll get your share as long as I get mine." They pulled a few empty beads from their pockets and rolled one to each boss. "Take these as a first token. Once I've got the guns, glass, and food, I know where to get the rest."

"The Ashes of Dawn," Crax hummed, snatching his piece and rising. "Let us see if you prove your worth."

Bess glared at Nex. "Better work, or I'll bury your nose in your skull."

Only Lok-Tag stood without a word. He rolled the bead between his fingers, then tapped it with his hook. This must've satisfied him, because he tucked it away and turned into the darkness.

"Mysterious bastard," Bess grumbled, but she soon followed.

That left Crax.

"You really a Reacher?" Nex asked him, wriggling their crystal ring. "Sure would help to have another on our side."

Crax raised his brows. His eyes beneath them were a dull gray, like drifting smoke. "Who said that you and I are on the same side?" He stood slowly and buttoned shut his high-collared frock coat. "Be careful. This Crimson Court has friends in every nook of the Commonwealth, and though you're not part of my family, I'd rather not see you turned into a husk."

They didn't know whether to consider that a threat or a genuine worry, so they just nodded. "Thanks."

"I doubt you will thank me when all this has passed."

A BULLET FOR MY VALENTINE

"When you've got a gun, try to aim it away from you." – Quickshot Miko

Zinarus leaned so heavily on his old borrowed cane that it creaked. By the Mother below, he shook as Kasia raised that blasted revolver to her temple and dropped its hammer for the third time. His fingers twisted around themselves, remembering the feeling of placing the lead bullet in the revolver's secret chamber—only accessible with the flip of a hidden switch. Kasia claimed it had been the infamous Stormrider's key to winning every game of pirate's demise.

Deception of the highest degree. It made Zinarus's stomach churn.

"Kasia, please," he said in as desperate a voice as he could manage. Sweat beaded on his brow, but he hoped Gregorzon thought it to be from nerves about this game, not the act Kasia had him playing. "I do not wish to see you meet a horrible end. You are not insane, even if Taint manipulated your mind during your argument with Lady Yazia. The mistake of a single moment need not beget further errors."

Her bloodshot eyes fell on him. Though his accusations of insanity had been Kasia's idea, part of him meant the claim. Taint had affected her mind, but he had yet to grasp truly how much.

"This is no error," she replied before pulling the trigger.

The resulting *click* was barely audible, but it spurred a gasp from Gregorzon. He stepped back, shaking his head. "You cheated!"

Her mouth formed a narrow line until its ends flicked up. "Would you like to test that hypothesis?" She offered him the pistol, slyly running her thumb along the switch to activate the secret chamber. "You may take your final turn if that is your preference."

"Those are the established rules," the scout, Artaxan, added. He held his bullet-riddled hat over his chest. "Concede with honor."

Gregorzon looked to his gathered allies for advice, but from their appearances, they were minor scions who were unfamiliar with disputes between the houses. Most scions were from families that held either little land or none at all. Though they possessed all the same rights as more significant scions and could Reach if they paid for a talon, Zinarus's mother had often claimed they reeked of desperate ambition. Like leeches, they clung to scions whom they believed could grant them the prestige they desired.

Kasia advanced at her brother's hesitation, pulling away from Zinarus's grasp and waving the gun before Gregorzon's face. "You have always been a coward. Go and tell Chatik of your failures. Let him know how you fled."

"By participating in this competition," Zinarus added, "you both agreed to it as the legal judgment of control over House Niezik. Refrain from further violence, Lord Gregorzon, or you will find yourself a criminal and an outcast."

Gregorzon's grabbed at his talon-hand glove until Kasia raised the gun to his forehead. For once, the game was true. He would die if she pulled the trigger.

"Your flames have tasted my flesh once, Brother," she snapped. "I have no intentions of ever enduring them again."

Gregorzon stepped back, looking from the revolver to the guards stationed around the room. Each now aimed their muskets at him. Artaxan stood among it all with an open hand raised, but he showed no pleasure at commanding them.

"I have served House Niezik for many years," he said, "and I am not afraid to defend its honor. Make yourself scarce, Lord Gregorzon. You have been shown plenty of patience considering your betrayal."

The younger Niezik scowled, but gave the slightest bow of his head before storming out with a wave toward his allies. Each shared their master's scorn, and Kasia kept the revolver raised until the final one's tailcoat struck the door on the way out. Tazper stepped into the room and slammed it behind them.

"That was quite the event, was it not?" he asked with a wide smile.

Kasia shoved her gun back into her handbag and shot Zinarus a look that made his heart stop. She had held the same one when the island woman tore away his shirt. It made him feel like some intricate art piece under intense study... or a slab of meat before a carnivore.

"It..." Zinarus squeaked before clearing his throat, his cheeks burning as bright as his hair. "It certainly was. You worried me, Lady Katarzyna, but I am relieved this strange duel did not end with your untimely demise."

Amusement flashed across her eyes before vanishing to a scion's formality. Artaxan did not know of their ruse, and the scout seemed to value honor. It pained Zinarus greatly to cooperate in Kasia's deception, but if Gregorzon was a Crimson, he was part of the organization that had killed Zinarus's close friend and servant, Regizald, and stolen his family's sand mines to control the glass market. Necessity sometimes outweighed sensibilities. This had been one of those *rare* moments, and it still made him sick to his stomach.

"The game is called pirate's demise for a reason," Kasia said. "Gregorzon's claim was difficult to contest, so severe measures were necessary."

Artaxan waved away the guards. "Return to your posts. I wish to speak to the scions alone." When Kasia nodded her approval, they departed, and Artaxan folded his arms the moment they were gone. "You rigged the game, didn't you?"

Heat rushed to Zinarus's cheeks again, and he wobbled on the cane, stumbling into the settee's edge.

But Kasia just moved to help him sit. No apparent panic crossed her face, and he wondered whether there was something he was missing. "You know me too well, Artaxan," she said, facing down the scout. All the fuss had undone her hair above her scarred temple, and its strands dangled loosely over her cheek in unruly curls. "We hid the bullet in the secret chamber of Stormrider's revolver. Razamat Uziokaki was much harder to fool than my cowardly brother, however, and I am pleased this particular confrontation did not require me to be shot."

"Do you mean to say that you have been shot by someone other than Chatik?" Zinarus asked. After all he'd seen of the Amber Dame, he should not have been surprised, but with her *everything* was a surprise.

"A story for another time," she replied, her eyes snapping to some unseen target before returning to Artaxan. "I hope you both see that this was necessary, and though I tricked my brother, I have no such intentions with the people of Tystok. To make amends, I must seek out the families of those whom I harmed and ensure they never bear a burden again."

"That will not be easy," Tazper replied from the door. "Even my family questioned me for staying with you when I returned. If Gregorzon were not a member of the Crimson Court, then the lowborn and minor houses alike may have sought to hang you themselves."

Zinarus winced at that, but Kasia nodded. "I appreciate your candor," she said.

Artaxan took the wingback chair that Gregorzon had vacated, grabbing the smoldering cigar and taking a puff. "If you've shown me anything, Lady Katarzyna, it is that you have more willpower than any man in all of Brakesh. I know little about this so-called Crimson Court, but they killed Leonit, so there's nothing more I need to know. Others will agree, and you've earned the loyalties of many in recent years." He waved around the cigar like a spear, and Kasia shied away from it with a hand over her scarred forearm. "This whole Death Reacher business will shake some. Others, though, will march with you to war."

"War?" Zinarus asked. "Do you mean with the Keloshan Empire?"

"They're a problem for another day," Artaxan said. "The real war is the one splitting the Commonwealth in half. Commander Tiuz Hazeko has gathered scions and lowborn in rebellion against the Crimson Court. They're calling themselves the Confederation of Harizak after the fort where they've made their base. It's about halfway between here and Kalastok, right at the intersection of the Ty and Vamia rivers."

A ruckus came from the hall outside before Kasia could reply. Zinarus prepared to remove his talon-hand glove if necessary, but neither Kasia nor Tazper showed any concern. She looked to him with a sigh. "That is just my mother. I have no doubt that she is throwing a fit with me sending Gregorzon away. Though I would sincerely love for her to leave with him, she is the sister of Lord Borys Kuzon, and plenty of magnates are furious with me already."

Good, Zinarus thought. *She still has enough sense not to make every powerful scion her foe.*

Kasia removed her left glove to reveal her crystal-wrapped hand and its missing index finger. "Much has happened since we saw each other last, Artaxan. I am no longer a Death Reacher, but I managed to discover Chatik Pikezik's… or *Bartol's*… plans for the Crimsons before they attempted to depose King Jazuk without a fight. Zinarus alone challenged their attempt in the Chamber of Scions, giving us this chance to resist them."

Artaxan laughed. "This Chatik fella is the head of the Crimsons, then? Never heard of him."

"I forget how few people know of all the factions in Kalastok," Zinarus replied, drumming his fingers. His own house would be caught in this civil war too. "You seem of the more informed sort, so it is an important reminder that our politics are a distant thought for most people. It will take some convincing for laborers and farmers to join us in opposing the Crimsons."

"They need not care who rules within the Crystal Palace," Kasia said, straightening her bodice before scowling at an empty section of the room, where he assumed she saw a specter. He would have to investigate her Realm Taint when they were alone. "However, when they learn that it is the Crimsons who control the breathless and the Spirit Plague, they will desire vengeance against those who killed their families."

"Many want the same against you," Artaxan challenged with another wave of his cigar.

She stomped toward him and shoved the cigar into the ashtray, snuffing it out. "Unlike Chatik, I regret the innocent deaths I have caused."

"Keni do not fill empty beds. They will say that you took their husbands and wives, and now, you demand they march to war against the usurper king in Kalastok while Kelosh invades. More death from Death's Daughter."

Kasia pondered for a moment, crossing the room, then fixing her gaze back on Artaxan. "I will not send anyone against their will. All will be compensated, but they need someone to lead them. I am no general."

"Even divided," Artaxan replied, "we could raise two thousand soldiers from House Niezik's territory in a short time. That is far more than I have ever commanded."

"All generals must begin somewhere," Zinarus said, wondering about Tiuz's plans at Fort Harizak. His friend would not act with undue haste if he did not believe he could gather a coalition, but confederations were rarely successful unless called by the greatest houses. "Then I must return to Vamiustok to raise my own forces as well. Our two houses alone cannot supply the soldiers needed to confront Chatik's armies. If I can recapture my family's sand mines, though, we will gain access to both amber and glass, and both will be great tools for the Confederation against the breathless."

Kasia nodded before returning her attention to Artaxan. "I need your help to assure confidence among the ranks. Many know and trust your leadership, and having that core group will ensure they cannot be turned against us by Gregorzon or anyone else."

"Aye," the scout said, rising and offering her his hand to shake. "I'll do it. But *my* command will be law among the soldiers, understand? No Niezik surprises unless I approve them first."

She shook it. "We have a deal. Tazper, ensure he has all he needs."

Artaxan threw on his hat before nodding to the footman. "Then I'll be off. There's little time, and it's no small task recruiting such a force."

As Tazper showed him out, Zinarus closed his eyes and pictured the Commonwealth's many factions. Kelosh marched in the east, threatening House Bartol and House Uziokaki. Kasia had uncovered that the Crimsons wanted Sazilz Uziokaki out of the way for Qaraza to take control of the house. That meant at least one major Crimson was under threat.

The status of House Bartol was less clear. Princess Nikoza had been King Jazuk's heir to the house. Chatik himself, though, was Jazuk's second son and could attempt to seize control of his birth house. Nikoza would be in danger either way, and despite her unwillingness to help Zinarus present his evidence against Chatik, he hoped she was safe. There were few pure of heart among Kalastok's elite. He still believed she was one of them.

"We are entering strange and dangerous times," he said, raising his gaze to Kasia, whose eyes lingered on the cigar's drifting smoke. "I fear that no good will come from this, but I must return home to warn my mother and prepare."

She held an arm across her torso, still not looking at him. By the Mother, he so badly wished to stand and embrace her, but his knee refused to budge. A gaping hole opened in his chest. Would she even want him to?

"Stay," she said, her voice meeker than he'd ever heard it. "Just for a few days. I can send a courier through a portal so Lady Sania is made aware of the situation and can prepare herself. For now, I could use your level-headed demeanor with the families of those whom I killed, and there are also a few more than capable workshops in Tystok where you could mend your leg." She hesitated before offering him a solemn smile. "Thank you for damaging it to protect me. I'm sorry it has limited your mobility."

With a bow, he hid his uncertainty. "As long as my mother is aware of the situation, then I will stay and do what I can to comfort the grieving."

He gritted his teeth and forced himself to rise with his cane. His good leg was badly sore from holding his weight, but he did his best not to let it show. Strength was an ideal Kasia seemed to hold in high regard, so he would foster it within himself.

"Is that all, my lady?" he asked, not knowing what he hoped for in response. There were so many ramifications to consider after recent days. From life in other realms to the Crimson Coup, nothing would ever be the same. Most of his thoughts had once been engaged with jousts in the Kalastok Arena and how to establish House iz Vamiustok in the Chamber, but now, those were distant considerations.

Kasia bit her lip. Her eyes bore into him, and a silly thought in the back of his mind questioned whether she could read his very spirit.

"What would you do if you had wronged so many people and tarnished your reputation?"

His leg pain wormed its way into his thoughts as he hobbled forward with his knee's mechanisms stinging him with hot steam. "A wise writer once said that the most grievous wounds within us never truly heal. As long as they are tended to, they may scar instead of festering as we grow around them, learning to live with the pain. It does not mean accepting that the wound was just, only that it has become part of who we are."

"Wise words indeed." Her shoulders sagged, and she turned toward the door, her true emotions hidden by what he assumed was two decades of practice. "Come, Lord Zinarus. Tazper is otherwise occupied, so let me show you to your guest chambers. We both deserve a rest."

THE CRIMSON CAUSE

"Firstly, and most importantly, a Crimson must hold sacred their bond to Zekiaz. In truth, it is the only holy force in the Crystal Realms. It reminds us why we are greater than the unbound, and why we must ascend above them." – An excerpt from *The Crimson Cause*

Humid gales pushed back Nikoza's hair as she leaned over the half-wall surrounding the roof of the Crystal Palace. Her eyes ached from pouring over Crystal Brigade reports and Chamber of Scion proposals, so she had left them on the desk to let Kalastok's sounds and scents surround her.

Peace. There were no gunshots or screams for the first time since the riots, and smoke no longer smothered the eastern half of the city. Fresh aromas from the palace gardens and the bustling of the Crimson District's vendors were badly needed reminders of life before this chaos. Oh, how badly she wished for that peace to last.

Chatik had promised Nikoza a way forward after the awful end to her supply caravan's trip through the Market and Industrial districts. She had indeed brought some aid to the suffering, but had caused immense strife in the process.

Memories of soldiers shooting into the lowborn stole her moment

of tranquility. So many desperate faces. So many crying out to her for help. Nex had been among them, but the watchmen had refused Nikoza's demands that Nex be let through. It was all unnecessary.

Nex's furious face filled her mind as she opened her eyes and stared over the Kala River. They were the vengeful type and would surely blame Nikoza for what had happened, but one conversation could have changed that. Instead, breathless and watchmen patrolled the western city as if it were a prison. Earth Reachers and laborers had brought the factories back into working condition through force alone, and Chatik had demanded that weapons be ready to send against Kelosh.

"I need your guidance more now than ever, Grandfather," she whispered into the darkness.

Jazuk had spent many nights up here with her, wondering about the realm and its struggles. He was gone. Only she and the crystal dragon remained, but it no longer felt like her secret confidant now that she knew its true loyalties lay with Chatik.

The creature's silvery-gray scales glinted in the palace's lamplight. Gold-tipped spires stretched above it, but here, both she and it could see all of Kalastok, from the defenses encircling the city to farmlands beyond. It should have been a shining city for all. Instead, much of it remained in ashes, and with civil war brewing due to the traitorous commander, Tiuz Hazeko, rebuilding felt a distant wish.

Breathless spirits hung overhead. For now, they were still, but Nikoza shied back from the wall at the sight of them. Though Chatik had persuaded her of much, she did not enjoy being guarded by the silent figures. If they could be commanded, why could they not communicate?

"Ah, the maids told me I might find you here," a woman said from behind her.

Nikoza painted a smile over her sorrow and turned to meet Tzena Oliezany, captain of the Crystal Brigade. It was strange for a mere cousin of the new Oliezany patriarch, Otterzik the Ninth, to take such an important position, but Chatik insisted that he needed people he could trust. Gornioz Oliezany's betrayal had caused his death.

For a time, Otterzik would have to be watched closely in case he followed in his father's footsteps.

The politics of it all made Nikoza's head spin, so she focused on curtsying to Tzena. Her dress was robust with a hoop skirt and many layers of petticoats to keep away the cold. Though not the best for mobility, it reminded her she was still a lady of the Chamber, not just a sergeant of the Crystal Brigade.

"I am surprised that you are here instead of in the Reachers' hall," Tzena said, gloved hands held behind her back. Her own attire was far more confined, and Nikoza could not help but notice that it put her form on display. For who? "We were to train your Water Reaching tonight, were we not?"

Nikoza's eyes widened as she checked her pocket watch. It ticked away, signaling fifteen minutes past the time when she had agreed to meet Tzena.

"Please forgive me," she pled with a hand over her heart. "I got lost in my work for my house in the Chamber of Scions, and with the preparations for how to further aid the struggling areas…" She straightened her posture. "No excuses justify it. You do not deserve to have your time wasted."

Tzena drew nearer and took Nikoza's free hand. "As I have sought to rise to the position I now hold, I understand completely how great a weight this must be for one as young as you. We may delay the lesson, should you desire."

"No!" Nikoza blurted before catching herself. "My grandfather had always insisted becoming a powerful Reacher was secondary to my other responsibilities, but recent hundred-hours have proven otherwise. I wish to be an asset more than a liability when there is danger."

Her counterpart grinned, and Nikoza's breaths caught at that. Was this a test? "Very well," Tzena said, stepping back and removing her talon-hand glove. "Let us begin."

"Should I not change into more appropriate attire?"

"When our enemies come for you, you must be ready no matter your attire," Tzena replied, her golden eyes alight. "Now, Reach. The Reachers' hall offers nothing we cannot accomplish here."

Tzena approached the nearest gas lamp and opened its latch. Its *hiss* pierced the quiet night, stirring the dragon to gaze down at them with interest.

"Lady Tzena?" Nikoza asked. "What are you doing?"

The Oliezany dangled her glove over the flame at the lamp's center. Nikoza called out for her to stop, but it was too late. The glove caught fire, and instead of attempting to douse its rapidly spreading flames, Tzena tossed it straight at Nikoza.

Nikoza yelped, Reaching in her panic. Deep blue answered as she threw up her arms to protect herself from the glove. It struck her elbow a moment later before flopping to the ground with a sound resembling a wet rag, and when Nikoza dropped her arms, she found her front was just as drenched.

Her maids would not be pleased.

Tzena, though, gave a slow, exaggerated clap. "Instinctual Reaching is an important skill. To avoid Realm Taint, however, you must learn not to burn an entire Reach with one burst. An experienced Reacher can manipulate their realm for minutes if they taper their usage." She studied Nikoza as she approached, then crouched to grab her glove. "I have trained you for a few days now, but have yet to ask: Have you felt Taint yet?"

"I have, twice," Nikoza replied. Chatik had told her to trust Tzena fully, and if she was to learn, Tzena needed to know what she had done. "During the riots, I rescued a mother and her daughter from a burning townhouse, but it took three Reaches in a short span. I tried to hold them for longer. The flames overwhelmed me, though." She traced her wet dress, blushing at how it clung to her skin. "The second time was during the first supply caravan, when the people would have been crushed by the wagons had I not held them back."

"Do you feel the inherent dehydration?"

Nikoza nodded. It was fainter than in the direct aftermath, but even now, she was more sluggish. No amount of water could cure her dry tongue either. "My Realm Taint is not as severe as that described in textbooks, but I cannot deny that there have been some lingering effects."

"That is normal," Tzena said, raising her own talon. "My Taint from the realm of Shadows is less straightforward than your own, but all Reachers will endure some amount after a time. There is a reason most of our elder statesmen are actually quite inexperienced with a talon."

"And that is?" Nikoza asked. It was a question she had held herself, but Jazuk was tight lipped about.

Tzena stepped closer and lifted up Nikoza's chin with her taloned finger. "Dear girl, all power has a price, and some are unwilling to pay. Whether it be magic, wealth, or influence, one must always surrender some part of themselves in exchange for what they desire. Never forget that."

Nikoza thought back to Chatik's diminished condition. She had hoped it to be merely a sickness, but he looked worse with each passing day. "What cost has my uncle endured?"

The talon slipped from her chin as Tzena's lip twitched. She held that exposed hand to her breast, closing it into a loose fist. "Everything." She spun away and headed toward the stairs, stopping with a hand on the doorframe. "Anything more, he must tell you, as King Chatik has given every ounce of his mind and spirit to protecting Ezman."

CHATIK SUMMONED NIKOZA TO THE PALACE GARDENS the following day. A glorious place in dawnrise, death consumed it now as the final rains of everdark drizzled over them. Not true death, Nikoza considered, as she traced a leafless bush whose branch stretched toward her skirts like a grasping hand.

Did it yearn for her aid too?

Like this bush, she reminded herself that Kalastok would be reborn from the ashes come the dawnrise season. The thought almost carried Chatik's exact words and tone, repeating until it wove into the fiber of her being. Not even Jazuk's wisest teachings had buried so deep into her spirit, and she awaited Chatik's lesson eagerly as his pink Mind Reaching erased itself from her perception.

"Lady Tzena tells me you have progressed well," her uncle said as they walked beneath an umbrella held by a servant.

His tailcoat drifted in the gusts behind him, the spare droplets off each end resembling blood against the coat's crimson trimmings. As she feared, he no longer moved with a younger man's smooth gate, and his silver eyes seemed to wander between statements.

"She has?" Nikoza asked, her hands clasped before her and an elaborate Bartol hat deflecting the wind from her unblemished face. She took the chance to enjoy the scent of rain meeting the earth compared to Kalastok's endless stone and brick. Why could she not train out here instead? "We had another lesson only this morning, and though the strength of my summoned water is increasing, I struggled yet again to maintain my Reach."

He coughed into his arm, then extended it toward the bare plants. "A garden such as this was not planted in a day. It required time, dedication, and direction. Even more, it requires maintenance and constant care to not become overgrown or infected by unwanted specimens. You are young, but unlike many scions your age, you desire to seek your potential instead of wasting away as a lustful fool."

"A representative of the Chamber has no such time for distractions," she said, repeating Jazuk's instructions. "Neither does a sergeant of the Crystal Brigade."

"Yet a young lady of the court should pursue a match to procreate and continue the Inheritance Rituals." He stopped and examined a dark flower that bloomed despite no light reaching its petals. "You see? Even in the darkest days, beauty persists in Zekiaz, and so must we. Lust is a distraction, indeed. Matchmaking, however, is an essential role for any influential scion."

Her fingers dug into her skirts. "This sounds like the prelude to an arranged marriage, and per your decision, I am not a matriarch. There is no such need for the Inheritance Ritual."

"It is nothing of the sort," he assured her, offering her his arm as they continued on. "As to the Inheritance Rituals, let me just say that the old ways restricted the true power of near immortality to just the heads of the great houses. Should not all Crimson scions have the chance for their spirits to live forever, passed to their descendants for all of time?"

"The tradition allows for the most experienced to retain their wisdom through generations," she replied. "Would expanding the practice to all willing scions be more effective? Even the lowborn could do so if provided a Spirit Reacher. Imagine the gains of knowledge…"

Chatik waved toward the western Shadow Quarter, its streets dim. "We must be careful who we offer power to. This season's events have shown what the misguided masses are capable of." His expression softened. "This time is one of great opportunity for you. We have invited many eligible bachelors to join the Crystal Brigade's ranks, and their houses could make great allies for our own."

Nikoza found herself stiff. She was not repulsed by the concept of a relationship for her house's gain—it was all but expected for great house scions—but how could she seek love and marriage when the Commonwealth tore itself asunder?

"Is this truly a legitimate use of our resources and time?" she asked. "Uncle, we are at war, and if the whispers I hear are true, Lord Tiuz Hazeko has formed a confederation against us! What shall the lowborn and mercantile scions think when they see me gallivanting instead of bringing further aid?"

He gave a conceding wave. "That is why this invitation serves multiple purposes. Our transfer of power and now this war have led to a great depletion of the Crystal Brigade's ranks, so these invited scions shall train to fill those holes. You are a sergeant, and by overseeing this new era for the watchmen, you will become ingratiated with many young men and women who may be of particular interest."

Her worries faded beneath his subtle Reaching. The chance to speak with suitors did intrigue her, after all, and so did this chance to alter the Crystal Brigade's troublesome practices of the past.

Chatik released her and gestured toward the peak of the Crystal Palace. The dragon was gone from it, likely sent away to war, and the towers felt empty without the majestic creature. "You have begun your journey toward joining the Crimson Court, but you must take these opportunities to prove yourself as an influential prospect. There is another Chamber meeting this afternoon. I suggest that, during it, you make a proposal which you believe shall benefit Ezman. Perhaps one which we have discussed?"

She raised her chin. Yes, she had considered this, and it pleased her to know she could make a difference. "May I propose a resolution to construct Reacher towers on the west side? It would be an attempt to bridge our divide, protecting both the great houses' factories and the vulnerable people who live there. Especially as the Spirit Plague persists, it would be useful to have Spirit Reachers close to ensure the awakened do not continue to strike."

"And Mind Reachers to create breathless from those awakened," he added with a sharp nod. "Yes, this is exactly the kind of thinking we must pursue."

She took a long breath and glanced east, toward Kalastok College. For so long, it had been her dream to study there, but that chance felt as if it had slipped between her fingers.

"May I ask…" She said as one lingering doubt wriggled in the back of her mind. "What has become of Professor Etal iz Noshok? I was to be his apprentice, and with my help, he developed a cure for the Spirit Plague. We must distribute it to all who suffer. Why has this not happened?"

The shadows grew long over Chatik's face as he turned from the lamplight. "Professor iz Noshok instructed me during my time at Kalastok College, and I am certain his misguided research caused this disease in the first place. We have arrested him and secured his research. From what we have read, it confirms that he never found a cure, but sought to influence you through this supposed apprenticeship."

"That…"

Nikoza cocked her head, memories warring within her. She had collected spirits in amber with Zinarus and Nex, bringing the lowborn thief a cure for their lover. Had it failed? And what of Etal's claims about Chatik and the Crimson Court? Chatik had not mentioned the alchemist, Paras ik Lierasa, either, but he had been essential to the cure's creation. Except, other memories smothered those. They revealed the scientists as dangerous deceivers.

Chatik's Mind wisps deepened within Nikoza as they headed back toward the palace. All around her, the limbs of each plant and tree seemed to stretch toward her. But it was magic, not branches that pierced her mind and tore away her thoughts while Chatik spoke about his goals for the Crimson Court and the nation. Those goals became hers, suffocating any memories that dared claim her uncle's guilt.

"This is the Cause of any member of the Crimson Court," he finally said, stopping her at the base of the palace's southern entryway. Columns of marble trimmed in glass rose around them. Once, Vockan white had joined the Ezmani red, but now, the rain made the whole palace bleed only crimson. "Defend Ezman at all costs, and ensure its scions ascend to glory."

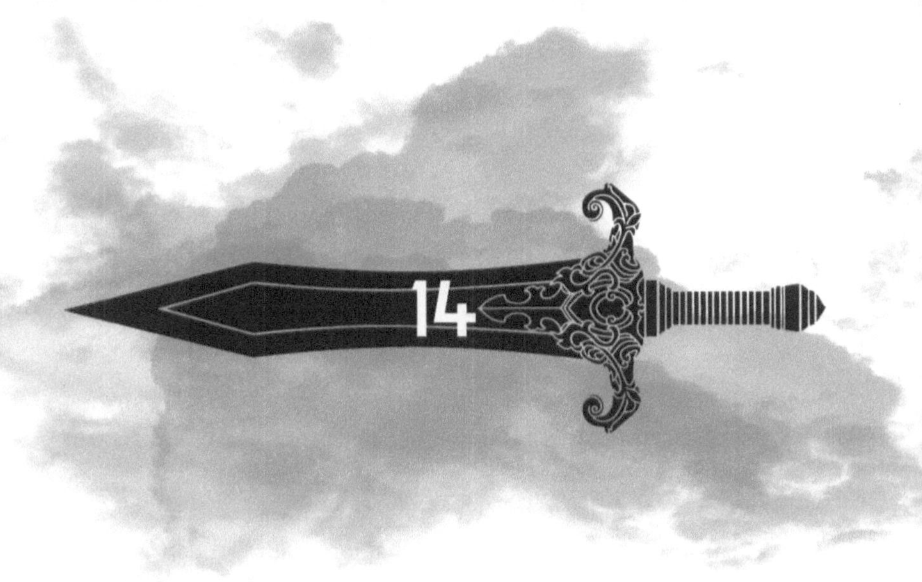

THE WHISTLING PASS

"I would rather die a husk, having fought by my brothers and sisters of the Order, than live having fought alone." – Erenius ik Talianfor, former Supreme Defender of the Glassblade Order

Vuk bleated beneath Radais as they crested a great ridge, only for their lanterns to reveal yet another narrow pass ahead. The Glassblade leaned forward to pat his trusty ibex's neck. "We will rest in Dalnus, boy. Just a few more miles." The capital of Vocka was far from Kalastok's tight alleys and expansive industry, but it held their allies and the Whispering spirit shamans. Hopefully, they would offer some aid against the Vanashel.

"I feel like you said that three hours ago," Wanusa complained, leaning back in her saddle and staring into the everdark sky. Not a single light pierced it. Even on the ground, a hundred Glassblade lanterns could only reveal what lay a dozen strides ahead.

Radais chuckled and pushed Vuk on. The rest of the Glassblades—experienced and initiates both—followed, and their groans were not lost to him. They had ridden hard since leaving Palmia Fortress. Making it to Palmia through the mountains was any initiate's first test before they even joined, but none of it compared to his expedition's desperate days in the Spirit Wastes. It would take them time before they were used to an adventuring Glassblade's life.

Crags threatened their descent between two mountains and into the Whistling Pass, but Vuk navigated them without hesitation. It gave Radais a far more comfortable ride than those who'd yet to bond with their mounts. His legs ached, and if he was this sore, then the others had to be far worse.

"We will make camp at the next clearing," he announced over his shoulder.

Tairanik and Polina were positioned strategically to relay any orders, and the Glassblades all sat higher once they heard. Radais had considered leaving one of the two commanders behind with the skeleton crew at Palmia Fortress. They had proven that he needed their insights, though. Even as a master, he had not seen as much as them, and it was a waste to leave two of his most valuable assets behind when they faced the unknown.

While the other ibexes struggled, Polina's practically leaped down the slope until she drew up beside Radais. Her glass armor was flawless, her helmet almost blinding in even this dim light. Radais could not claim the same.

"It's a risk to stop near the Whistling Pass," she warned.

"Do you intend to clarify why?" he replied, scanning for awakened or breathless, but seeing none.

Polina sneered beneath her helm. "You and I both know that old stories hold some truth. There's a miner's tale that claims spirits haunt the western peak here. I am surprised you haven't heard it."

"I'm from Erienfar in the south. Never had many reasons to—"

Radais snatched his glass sword from his scabbard and turned about on Vuk. It was silent beyond the ibexes' hoof falls and the clanking of glass armor, but he could have sworn he'd heard breathless voices—like whispered chattering. He was no Taint-inflicted Reacher. The Spirit Wastes had levied a heavy cost on a Glassblade's mind, though, and he winced at all the people staring at him like he was some madman.

"Do you not draw your blade when your commander does so?" he barked at the nearest of them. They swapped glances, but did as he said with a shake of his head. That only made him angrier.

Polina had her sword already out, but her expression lacked confidence. "Seems you do believe in old tales, then."

"The breathless speak," he insisted, searching for those who'd been on his expedition. Inexperienced on an ibex, Lazan was caught somewhere further back with the archer, Mhanain, but Wanusa hopped eagerly between the commanders.

"He's not lying," she said. "I didn't hear them this time, but I trust the supreme defender."

Polina looked from her to Radais, then nodded. "Then we shall keep our blades at the ready, specifically focused on the southern peaks. Vanashel or not, we'll face the spirits here."

She waved the rest of the convoy on, leaving him with Wanusa as the others passed with eyes averted. Only Lazan stopped, and he looked mighty relieved at the break. Or was it excitement at rejoining Radais?

"I am confident of it now," he said. "I prefer the flatlands. Even Lady Katarzyna did not make me endure such torment during our time in Raviak Forest."

"Vockan roads are a heavy burden," Radais replied, pulling his gaze from surveillance to the Reacher. The few strands of scion silver hair which stuck out from beneath his woolen cap were so covered in snow they were nearly white. His gray cheeks were horribly wind-burned, and he shivered beneath that noble smile. "I wish I could make it a lighter one for both you and my Glassblades."

Lazan gazed ahead at the departing lanterns. He still wore an Ez-mani high-collared frock coat, refusing to take any armor Radais of-fered, claiming it was out of respect for the Order. "I fear it is not my approval you must seek, but theirs. They whisper of your 'youth-ful inexperience.' If you ask me, that commander who cannot keep his buttons or straps aligned, Tairanik, seems to be the source."

Wanusa crossed her arms with a huff, but the motion caused a horrific screeching noise as her glass bracers scraped against her breastplate. "Sorry! I'm still getting used to a warrior's full armor, but Tairanik's had *decades* to do so. Miv never let him get away with that when she was in charge."

"You're saying I must be stricter to earn their respect?" Radais asked, blade resting on his shoulder. "I'd hoped a lighter touch would make up for my inexperience."

"We are warriors!" Wanusa said. "There's times for listening and times for keeping order. At least, that's what Miv always said."

So Radais grabbed the reins with his free hand and nodded to them both. "I don't wish to lead exactly as she did, but you're right. I cannot have a commander challenging my orders."

Lazan grabbed Radais's arm before he could push Vuk into a trot. Streaks of red wound through the air around them, and Lazan smiled proudly as they pushed into the Glassblade's skin. "A little strength can go a long way, my friend."

That burst of Body Reaching dulled Radais's soreness and even the anxieties panging his chest, and when he finally caught the end of the Glassblade convoy, he rode taller. Armor made it hard to tell which of his warriors were which. He soon spotted Commander Tairanik chuckling with a few grizzled masters, though, their laughter fading at the sound of his approach.

Spirits, Lazan was right. Even the initiates looked at him mockingly here, despite Tairanik appearing like he'd strapped his armor on still half-drunk from the night before! That was unacceptable, but Radais reminded himself he was not Miv.

"Commander." He held a fist over his chest to honor another warrior, not bow in submission. "Your group looks as organized as if I'd let an ibex lead them. Double file!"

His voice echoed through the mountains, and though the cold air had his throat aching, he reveled in the power behind it. The warriors obeyed at once as he rode beside the elder commander. Still, they eyed his blade in doubt there was any real threat here.

"This pass holds tales of awakened strikes," he declared to them. "They may just be old stories, but a Glassblade remains at the ready. Masters and warriors, pair up with an initiate. The Vanashel will find the most vulnerable and strike them first. Let them see that none of us stand alone."

He spoke without thought, but the words were natural. They were what it meant to be a Glassblade, trained to protect one's siblings in arms. Wanusa was his to oversee, yes, but so were the other hundred whom he led. This wasn't just about his role as a master anymore.

"You give a stern reminder, Supreme Defender," Tairanik said, matching Radais's fist over his chest. "Sometimes, I forget the simple things after spending so long in that fortress."

"I cannot see the entire convoy," Radais replied. "The rear guard's lives are yours, and I expect you to act like it. That starts with making sure your armor is in the right condition. Talk to the quartermaster, or we'll have initiates thinking that's how they're supposed to look."

Tairanik's expression soured. "So, there's some of that bitch in you after all."

Radais grabbed the commander's arm and nearly yanked him from his ibex. This fury was unusual for him when sober, but his nerves were at their ends. "Miv was far from perfect, but we respect our dead, got it?"

He hadn't told anyone outside the expedition that Miv had become a breathless in Akaamilion. There were some secrets better kept from blabbering warriors. Get one drunk, and they'd tell half of Vocka everything the Glassblades knew. Radais's experience losing his letter in Kalastok had proven even he wasn't above that.

"Aye," the commander muttered, so Radais released him. They were about to the other side of the pass already. They could relax beyond the site of the stories' supposed attack zone.

"I expect to see two orderly lines when I check in again," Radais insisted. "Can't have… Damn it!"

He spun about at the sound of voices suddenly filling the air. A moment before, there'd been nothing, but smoky figures shot into the lanternlight now with spirit tendrils grasping for gaps in warriors' armor.

Radais scanned the line to see Wanusa and Lazan still catching up. He tried to hurry toward them, but a breathless bearing the yard-long fangs of a monstrous koilee blocked his path.

So he bit his cheek and charged. Lanterns extinguished every which way as spirits doused their flames, but their glass swords refracted the remaining light into dozens of scattered rainbows. An unearthly scene amid savage spirits.

Except these breathless were not their mindless awakened siblings. They followed tactics, keeping to pairs, and another flanked Radais as he tried to slice through the first. Its tendrils struck his pauldron. The glass held, sending it back with a shriek, but the blow had been a true force. Though not enough to shatter his armor, it was a reminder that he wasn't invulnerable.

Radais stabbed through the reeling spirit with ease before turning to the other. It tried to dive past his blade, but as its tendrils targeted his unguarded armpit, an arrow shot straight through its core.

Mhanain whooped from a few rows of Glassblades away. Few warriors could fire effectively from ibexback, but he rose on his stirrups and loosed each arrow with all the glee of a child with his first wooden sword. Radais raised a fist in thanks, then urged Vuk through the gap the archer had opened. More breathless swarmed everywhere. This many Glassblades in one place ensured they found more glass than flesh, but a few scattered cries echoed through the pass.

One came from Lazan.

Three breathless surrounded Wanusa and the Body Reacher, not granting them any chance to rejoin with the larger group. Wanusa rode confidently with her blade flashing, but her new armor slowed her strikes. The breathless took advantage. While she was distracted with two, the third's tendrils struck Lazan.

Why didn't you take that armor?

Radais burst onto the scene at full gallop. Lazan's glass dagger had cut through a few of the tendrils, but these breathless were more resistant than awakened to such small weapons. The life was draining from the Reacher's eyes. He had seconds left as the breathless devoured his spirit. Radais put a stop to it.

The breathless's form held some strange substance beyond an awakened's, but his pure glass sword cut through it with ease. Sweat clung to Radais's skin as he passed the spirit, flipping back his two-handed blade to stab behind him. His target had already begun to dissolve, but that wasn't enough of a punishment. Breathless were sentient. They knew they were killers, and for threatening to take Lazan, Radais's burning heart demanded that this monster suffer for it.

With the spirit evaporating around him and Wanusa finishing the others, he turned back to check on Lazan. The gray-skinned scion rightly looked as if he'd seen a ghost.

"You okay?" he asked, grabbing the Reacher's arm.

Lazan flexed and closed his taloned hand, a glazed-over look in his eyes. "That… That was quite unlike anything I have ever felt." He glanced around. "Are the others gone?"

"No!" Wanusa shouted a moment before a winged beast crashed into her. She tumbled to the ground, and her shattered helm sent glass scattering over the snow.

Above, a Vanashel breathless held a dragon's form. Armored in a strange earthen plate, the ground rose into its clawed hands to create a massive war pick. Its tendrils struck at Wanusa's exposed head as it raised the pick to slam its sharp point into her breastplate.

Glass would do nothing to stop it.

Radais roared as Vuk lunged at the dragon. The ibex knew better than to think his horns could pierce spirits, but his move gave Radais the chance to throw himself over Wanusa with his blade raised. The pick met its edge with a horrifying *crack*, and a fracture split across the glass.

"Embodied Supreme Defender," the dragon hissed. An Earth Bound One based on its Reaching, its voice carried a gruesome shrill as the very ground shook beneath Vuk's hooves. "Blood spills. Free your spirit."

Radais's arms strained against the Bound One's strength, but the panic entangling his stomach was far worse. He wasn't trained to face a spirit wielding a metal weapon. Those tendrils still tried to strike out at Wanusa as he was occupied with the war pick, and more aimed for the chink in his own armor.

He hastened a glance down to see if Wanusa could strike from beneath. She appeared dazed, trying to roll away, but only managing to do so slowly. And his blade's fracture only expanded.

"Why do you want to kill us?" he asked the Bound One. "What are the Vanashel?"

"Home," it replied. "Ours!"

Earthen spears shot from the earth, one striking Vuk and the other impaling Radais in the gap between the front and back of his breastplate. He cried out, but threw his left arm under the flat of his blade to hold it against the pick's force. That sharp point was inches from his face. He forced himself to think only of protecting himself and Wanusa from that, instead of the agony consuming his side.

"Perish!" the Bound One screeched.

Vuk collapsed against the spear impaling him. The shift threw Radais off balance, and his blade fell from his grasp. He swiped desperately to grab it, but without Vuk, he dangled from the other spear's end, its point digging deeper into him.

His sword shattered as it struck the icy ground. Radais's heart broke with it, and tears stung his eyes as he grabbed desperately at the earthen spear to pull himself free. It was no use. His weight only pulled him further onto it, and the Bound One slammed its mighty pick into his breastplate, splintering it in a single blow.

Radais opened his mouth to call for help or even beg for mercy. He only managed a squeak, staring in horror at the blood pouring from his wound. The pain should've been worse. But he was numb, a calmness spreading through him as the Bound One readied its final strike.

A shout came first.

Glass struck the Bound One's earthen plate as an ibex leaped over Radais. Its rider was stout, his armor dirtied and cracked in more places than one. His blade, though, was as pristine and clear as an everbright sky, refracting the light of Radais's fallen lantern into a rainbow that formed a strange contrast to the crimson pooling beneath him.

"Get back, vermin!" Tairanik exclaimed, swiping again at the Bound One.

His sword's glass didn't crack like it should've against such stone armor. Instead, its edge cut into it as if it were a skin-like membrane before the armor repelled the strike. Radais's dying mind couldn't comprehend why that was, but the thunder of hooves made it plenty clear Tairanik hadn't come alone.

The Bound One reeled back at the oncoming Glassblades' charge, facing a hail of arrows from Mhanain and the few other archers. "Suffer," it spat at Radais. "Not finished."

Then it fled into the everdark. The Glassblades' lanterns only lit a small area, and Radais wanted to command them to stay alert in case the Bound One returned. He couldn't. Staying conscious took all his strength. The deep throbbing that his mind tried to numb made him wish to fade away, but another of his mind's instincts told him that death lay beyond. To close his eyes was to accept its embrace.

As he stared down at Wanusa and the scion man approaching at a trot, he told himself he wasn't done. He had failed so often. But he did not regret throwing himself in front of that Bound One's war pick. In the span of a couple minutes, he'd saved Lazan and Wanusa. His friends. His family. Those he loved…

He didn't really know what it meant to have a family whom he loved, and who loved him. Around these new companions, though, there was a comforting warmth. It silenced his personal anxieties and replaced them with worries for the safety of his loved ones. That was messy, but with his head drifting back and his energy fading with his lost blood, he much preferred the mess to his lonely searching for a place to belong.

Lazan laid his taloned hand on him, but Radais tensed. No, he shouldn't be first. Vuk had fallen beneath him. A warrior trained to manage a wound for some time, but the poor ibex would bleed out quickly.

"Vuk…" he muttered, coughing up blood.

Though a reply came, he couldn't understand it. Sounds were distant and scattered. What light he could perceive grew brighter until it turned blinding, and against his better instincts, he closed his eyes to protect them. A warmth enveloped him. It banished the chill and everdark stretching over the sky, replacing it with the gentle contentment of lying in Miv's arms all those years ago.

Safe.

A Leg Up

"There are many a scion man who would vie for the Amber Dame's hand. There are not many, however, who would likely survive the encounter." – Yoxan Kiutok, *The Ty River Herald*, three hundred-hours after the discovery of amber in Raviak Forest

"It is not the most organized, nor the most numerous army," Artaxan said, leading Kasia through the training fields he'd cleared for their recruits in the days after her arrival. He still wore his heavy duster and shot-through hat, but he looked far more natural here than in a scion house's drawing room. "Recruitment from the outer villages of Niezik lands has gone well, though, and our numbers should double. Expect two thousand in all by the time we must march. More should join along the way."

Gunpowder and smoke stung Kasia's nose as they passed the fires used to light the firing lines. Men and women alike saluted at her, then fired horribly at the targets twenty strides away.

"They appear inexperienced," she said, arms crossed. She wore a long, fur-lined coat with her hair pulled up beneath her koilee fur hat to protect from the wicked wind. Among the lowborn, she looked horribly out of place, and their curious glances sent pin pricks across her mind.

Another round of cracks signaled a volley, most peppering the hill beyond the targets. Artaxan wriggled his jaw and ordered them to reload their black powder muskets. Then he grabbed one of the guns from the rack.

"We haven't traded much with House Oliezany in the last decade, so we lack modern rifles. These muskets we have scrounged together are hardly up to military grade nowadays."

She dug her heel into the snow. "That is not ideal, but we have no time to import more from Reshka or Ogrenia. Even my teleportation would not allow us to bring enough without worsening my Realm Taint."

"Yes, about that." He glanced over his shoulder and stepped closer, not wincing at the next volley. Kasia's ears rang, but she showed no outward evidence of the pain. These recruits needed to believe she wasn't some craven scion. "Your brother left, but his accusations remain."

"What of them? I have met with most of the impacted families to express my apologies. They will want for nothing for generations to come."

A musketman reloaded nearby, his face turning to Aliax's as he shoved the ramrod down the barrel. "What about my ma?" he asked. "I bet she's been crying every night since Gregorzon told the truth."

"I will see her tonight," she promised. "That conversation…" She caught herself, realizing she spoke to a specter no one else could see.

Artaxan rubbed the back of his neck and waved for the musketman to continue. When Kasia looked at the man again, he was a stranger with a heavy beard and wavy black hair. Nothing like Aliax.

"You've gotten worse since the duel with Razamat two years ago," the scout said. "Still remember your outbursts then. The men thought you were damn insane, but I kept them in line. Though those meetings with your victims' families have helped cool some tempers, I cannot promise they are enough."

She snatched his arm and led him away. "You want me to leave again, do you not?"

"I do. Enough are convinced to fight by the Crimson Court's use of these breathless and creation of the Spirit Plague. The money you're offering for any who sign up is useful too, of course, but your active presence complicates matters."

Disgust overcame her. Not at the people's reaction, but at the situation. She could unite people in hatred against the Crimsons, yet they wanted nothing to do with her besides payment? Spirits, Tystok had worshipped her above even the Crystal Mother after she had secured Raviak Forest's amber! All it had taken was Gregorzon's treachery to turn those very people against her. It was offensive, demeaning.

But she wasn't too stupid to understand. Despite Tystok being the most populous town in the region, it barely held twenty thousand people, and like much of Ezman, House Niezik's territory was largely made up of scattered villages and hamlets. Everyone knew someone she had killed, or at least knew of them. Gossip spread quickly, and questions would linger about who she could kill next as long as she remained with her forces.

"Then I will consider leaving with Lord Zinarus to recruit in Vamiustok," she replied once she'd thoroughly beaten her ego to a pulp. It didn't take much, considering the recent days. She had only hung onto control of her house through deception, and even now, that grasp was tenuous at best.

Artaxan nodded. "Good. I will organize the rest of the mercenary company from here and lead them to Fort Harizak in the north. It's hardly an army, so we'd better hope General Hazeko has arranged significant forces to arrive from elsewhere. If not…" He stomped his foot. "Best not think of it."

Giving him her thanks, Kasia departed toward her carriage. She had a few hours until her meeting with Aliax's mother, and she needed to speak to Zinarus first. His calm demeanor had made the previous conversations with victims' families far smoother than they should have been. He'd also plainly stated he would not question her further until she was ready, but that trust could only last so long. With them about to encounter her dead lover's mother, she feared stretching it too far.

Every volley from the trainees worsened the ringing in her ears, but she welcomed the noise. The specters haunting her no longer appeared with Death's purple vapors, and their chatter never ceased now. Those shots gave her a piece of reality to cling to. Something beyond her Realm-Tainted mind.

But her victims' spirits weren't the worst of it. Deeper, another voice challenged her every move—her own. Except it was unruly, almost sinister as it appealed to her darkest desires.

"We should not have allowed Gregorzon to go free," the Taint whispered in her head. *"He will aid Chatik. He will burn us again!"*

Kasia held her scarred forearm, the Axiom Crystal running up it only worsening the discomfort. Every night, she told herself Gregorzon had lied to the lowborn to turn them against her, but he'd passed Zinarus's Truth Reaching. Had she truly tried to kill their mother? Had she lost control and endured Gregorzon's wrath as the result?

"He apologized before," she muttered, turning her head away from a squad of female recruits so they wouldn't see her talking to herself. "I did not try to kill Mother."

"Do you want to know the truth?" the other her replied. *"Do you want to know the extent of our corruption? How deep Taint has buried its roots within us?"*

She clenched her fists. "There is no *us*. Get out of my fucking head!"

Even Aliax passed her a nervous glance as Tazper appeared beside her carriage. Sazilz Uziokaki and the other specters followed in her wake like some gruesome funeral procession, each telling the living of her crimes. Only she could hear the specters, but every spirit, every scar, she had locked away in her past was now free for all to know. Part of her wanted to flee the judgment to come.

Another part wished to send it all to ruin.

"Is all well?" Tazper asked at her approach, covering her with an umbrella.

She raised a hand to her brow to find it dripping. Snow whirled around them, sending the ends of her coat whipping at her heels as her cheeks turned red from cold and shock. Her fur hat had kept the worst of the sudden blizzard from soaking her hair, but how had she not noticed the storm's arrival? Moments before, even the wind had felt still.

"Yes," she lied.

They hurried to the carriage, and he helped her step into it before clambering in behind her. A heavy layer of snow covered his wide-brimmed hat, which he removed and set on his lap. He allowed it to melt as he studied Kasia with the carriage's lantern making his gray eyes appear aflame.

"Apologies, my lady, but I do not believe you." He yelped as she kicked at him in response. "Thank you for confirming my suspicions."

"I could send you crawling back to your family without a talon or a coat on your back," she quipped.

He swiped a bunch of the snow over her with a wry smile. "Oh, really? Well, *my lady*, should I pack my bags then?"

Most scion ladies would have been furious at their footman for saying such a thing, but she laughed. She badly needed it. Recent hundred-hours had her trapped in the worst recesses of her mind. Any reminder of life's joys was another reason other than revenge to keep going, but it failed quickly against the weight of what lay ahead.

"Aliax would hate who I've become," she said, staring out the window. "All of this scheming and vengeance was exactly what he didn't want for me."

"He was never all that fond of me," Tazper replied as they hit a rock in the dirt road that nearly knocked him from his seat. "Whenever he saw you, though, I could have sworn he became a different man. He knew your power, but he didn't fear it, didn't fear *you*."

Kasia rejected a wave of memories that would only pull her deeper into her melancholy. Six years had not healed the scars, but as Zinarus had said days before, she wondered if they ever would. Today would hopefully offer some closure. To cauterize the wound, though, she needed to leap into the flames.

"Fear may have saved him," she said, fighting the crack in her voice.

Tazper leaned forward. "Aliax loved you. Though you might choose not to believe this, you were worthy of that love, and you still are."

"Tell that to his mother."

"I say this as your friend, Kasia," he said with a smile, but pain lingered in his eyes. "Do not allow a moment's mistake to define you. Continue your attempts to show your regret and aid the grieving. In time, they will see you as I do."

She raised her brow. "And how do you see me? After years of service, I have failed to secure you a Reacher talon. You have been tortured on my behalf, forced to lie and endure people's scorn for serving me."

Dirt roads turned to cobblestone, rumbling away as he tugged on his wool coat and crossed his legs. "I shared with you already that I consider you my closest friend, but that means I worry for you all the more. You have pushed me far beyond my comfort. I see, however, why you do so, and I would not have the confidence in myself and my ability to interact with scions if it were not for this position."

"You should not need to endure coal's pressure to be forged into a diamond." She closed her crystal-webbed fist. "That makes what I am about to ask of you even more difficult."

He swallowed. "What must I do?"

"Chatik controls Kalastok, and as long as I am here or in Vami-ustok, I know nothing of what is happening there. The Crimson Coup has ensured my connections are few. Nex, however, may be an asset with whatever resistance exists in the city."

"You wish to teleport me there?"

She bit her lip, already regretting the horror she was about to send him into. "I do. While I would rather go with you, I would draw unneeded attention with the Crimsons' price on my head. Nex only knows a few of us, and Crystal Mother knows Kikania would get eaten alive."

Tazper considered that for a long time until they pulled to a stop outside a blacksmith's shop on the northern edge of Tystok. In recent days, Zinarus had taken to it in hopes of fixing his mechanical leg and conducting other experiments. What those experiments were, however, Kasia had no idea of, because he had suddenly gotten all sorts of shy when she asked. He let her hold her own secrets for now. The least she could do was allow him to do the same.

"Think about it, at least," Kasia said, sliding to the door before Tazper could shake himself from his daze. "I will be sending you with enough keni to fund a small army of your own, and I expect you to use some of it to acquire a Spirit Crystal ring."

His eyes widened further. "But… That… That is illegal!"

She tapped him lightly on the cheek. "Please, never change. You remind me that not all the world is as corrupted as me."

Then she stepped into the blizzard, the winds buffeting her, but she embraced that pain. It was something other than sorrow. Other than numbness. The gales screamed louder than her Tainted mind could speak, and for a long moment, she allowed the storm to consume her before Tazper arrived, fumbling with the umbrella.

She waited for it to open before advancing toward the smithy. It was more for Tazper's sake than her own. Over the years, she had found her friend would break down if she didn't allow him to actually do his job, and clumsy Tazper was far more preferable than crisis-of-confidence Tazper.

The umbrella protected her for the mere ten strides to the door. Tazper would take another minute to shut the umbrella again, so assuming she had appeased him enough, she sent him back to the carriage. Her conversation with Zinarus would be difficult enough with only one nervous man in the room. When the footman was gone with only minor protestations, she pushed open the creaky door.

Smoke billowed over her as she stepped across the threshold. The smithy was a soot-covered world apart, its heat melting the snow before Kasia took her first breath of the dry air. Her second was stifled by the sight inside.

Zinarus half-sat on a stool and leaned over a workbench before the roaring stone forge as he worked on his mechanical leg. On his head rested a contraption with all kinds of metal arms extending from it. Tools hung on each end, and he replaced the ones he was holding with another from the arms with a ferocity she'd never seen in him before.

He was also bare-chested. His drenched shirt sprawled over another bench nearby, and more sweat covered him as he bared his teeth.

"Get in the damn hole!" he muttered under his breath before throwing aside a tweezer-looking instrument and grabbing a hammer. Without hesitation, he slammed it into the leg's mechanics, sending sparks showering over him.

Kasia's heart skipped a beat at those sparks. Not because they'd caught his pants aflame, but because this man before her was an entirely different one from the tepid politician trying to climb Kalastok's ladder of prestige. Mother below, where had *this* Zinarus been when they faced Chatik?

She tore herself from her trance at the realization he was in fact burning. Rushing to him, she threw off her soaked coat and batted away the flames that now covered his thigh. He'd apparently not noticed until her approach, and his chest rose and fell like an athlete who had just finished a long run.

"Katarzyna?" He coughed from the forge's fumes and stumbled off the stool, sending his strange helmet of tools crashing to the floor. He nearly followed until Kasia caught him. "What in the realms are you doing here?"

She smiled wryly as she helped him back onto his seat. He reeked of coal smoke and sweat, and his normally groomed hair stuck flat to his head. With his attention away from his work, though, his rage turned to the shock of a child who had been caught sneaking sweets. Embarrassment flared his kind cheeks as bright as his Vockan hair, and his eyes burned like molten copper.

"I thought we could discuss how to approach my conversation with Aliax's mother, but…" She paused, realizing she still held him close to her, and stepped back. Luckily, windburn had already reddened her own cheeks, so he wouldn't know the difference. Would he? "I did not realize quite how frustrating your work could be. Where are the laborers? Could they not aid you?"

Lips pursed, he turned to snatch his shirt, throwing his toned arms into his sleeves. He tried to button it shut, but when his shaking hands made it impossible, he puffed up his cheeks and tilted back his head. She'd thought jousting had given him his strength. Had his tinkering required such heavy labor all the time?

"There were others for the first couple of days," he said to the ceiling. "They called me a fool to try such craftsmanship, and when I demanded the materials too… forcefully… they left." His face resembled a man who'd been impaled in the arena, not simply had an outburst. That drew Kasia's smile wider.

"Lord Zinarus iz Vamiustok, heir to his house, has a temper? I would have bet on a lame horse before suspecting such a thing."

"If I remember correctly, you did bet on a lame horse during our competition," he replied, contorting his face into an abstract painting more than a smile. "By the Mother, I apologize. I should not have presented myself to you in this way. Nor should I have tormented your town's workers." He glanced around, then pointed toward a chair tucked into the opposite corner. "I would pull you up a chair, but I am rather single-legged at the moment."

Kasia grabbed the chair and dragged it over in an exaggerated fashion to grant him some relief from his embarrassment. Though she enjoyed seeing him flustered, she had no desire to torment him. At least, not more than necessary.

Aliax wasn't so kind. He lingered behind Zinarus, prodding the mechanical leg with one of the tools. "I admit, the scion seems smart," he said. "But him liking you this much makes me doubt that. Doesn't he understand being close to you is a death sentence?"

Zinarus caught her looking over his shoulder, but didn't comment on it. Instead, he leaned forward on his bench and ran his fingers through his messy hair. "You need not warn me of the complications that will surely come tonight. If you and Aliax were lovers, then I assume you had a relationship with his mother as well."

That gave her pause before she could sit. Her shoulders sagged, her fingers digging into the splinters on the chair's back. "Do you ever wish you could switch positions with someone?"

"Of course," he replied, his formal tone shifting as he studied her. "Who doesn't envy those who are wealthier, comelier, or those who are not bastards, trapped in an accursed form that shrivels around them?" He stared down at his hands. They still shook, despite his apparent calm now.

"I never wished to trade places with the living," Kasia whispered. She couldn't say it any louder. It was as if she needed to pry the words from so deep within her that they lost their volume by the time they escaped her lips. "Only the dead: my father, then Aliax. Leonit would have known how to combat the Crimsons with his friends in the Children of Zekiaz, but I cannot even figure out what the Children want, let alone who they are. Aliax…" She bit her cheek, a tear slipping down it. "Fuck it. I can't do this."

She turned away, but couldn't bring herself to take a single step toward the door. "Talk to his mother for me, please."

No reply came for a long time. Her chest ached for each second she held her breath, that damned forge spewing smoke and making her burned arm sting. Images of her mother flashed before her. Yazia's screams and accusations. The hatred in her eyes. And the resentment bursting from her own chest.

Kasia's fingers dug so deep into the chair that its splinters tore through both glove and skin. She squeezed shut her eyes, refusing to remember. Lies! All of it!

"Kasia," Zinarus prodded before raising his voice. "Kasia! Your hand is bleeding."

She forced her eyes open to see that the visions were gone, replaced by a room full of the dead. Oafish Parqiz Uziokaki took her chair, and he laughed up at her. "If you are just going to stand there, girl, why don't you grab me a drink? Or would you rather sit on my lap?"

He's not real. She told herself. *Just sit in the fucking chair.*

But when she moved to do so, she smelled his disgusting odor, felt her leg strike his. Her stomach churned at the thought of sitting on his lap. It didn't matter that she knew Parqiz wasn't truly there. Every one of her senses told her he was, so she sucked in a breath and circled toward the workbench where Zinarus's coat lay.

"Talk to me," she told the purple lord, focusing on where his unbuttoned shirt didn't cover. His torso was not muscled like his arms, but it was a far more appealing sight than the haunting dead.

"About what?" he asked with concern creeping into his voice. "Kasia, are—"

She growled and leaned onto the spare workbench with a shaky breath. "About anything! Please, just drown out the other voices."

That must have sent enough of a message, because he cleared his throat and laid a hand on the stump of his missing leg. "I realize now that you have revealed your darkest secrets, whether willingly or not, but I have not been so honest with you." He spoke quicker than normal, as if he worried the words would vanish. "Whatever your feelings for me or lack thereof, if we are to be partners in this expedition against the Crimson Court, you deserve to know the truth about my leg."

His pantleg covered the stump, but Kasia's gaze drifted to it anyway. Some macabre part of her wondered what it looked like apart from his mechanical one. Did it ache like her scar and what remained of her index finger? Did he wake in the middle of the night, wondering what his life would be like if his body were different?

She forced herself to meet his gaze again, his hooded eyes seeming to carry the weight of Zekiaz within them. "You owe me nothing," she said. "Since we met, I have brought you only torture, half-truths, and death. You held your dream of the Kalastok Arena for mere hundred-hours before you lost it in my schemes."

"As far as I am aware, the deed is still in my family's name," he replied with a horrid attempt to hide his discomfort. "The arena, however, is not the point right now. I do owe you the truth, as though you insist on claiming otherwise, you have brought me into a war for justice. Sacrifice is inevitable when we face corruption at the core of our nation. Your actions have inspired bravery I did not know I had within me, and for that, I am eternally grateful."

Kasia took a long, hard blink to shut out the specters' voices and focus on Zinarus. His words oozed with that high-brow approach he so loved to take, but there was something deeper within them. It required her full attention.

"My leg was amputated before I ever had the chance to walk," he continued with his head dropping and his hands pressed together before him. "My leg was numb, irresponsive at times, and Body Reachers could do nothing to heal me. A rare disease of the blood, my mother claimed. In truth, though, no one has found the true ailment that inflicts me, and they claimed without evidence that the amputation would rid me of its effects."

He rested his hand on the mechanical leg. A longing filled his eyes, and he fiddled with a loose gear as he spoke. "Recent seasons have proven them wrong. My hands have begun to shake at random, the needles I had once felt in my leg extending to them. That in itself would be just a minor worry of nerves, but I have moments where I feel too weak to stand, or when my muscles refuse to answer."

Kasia sucked in a sharp breath, the fear evident on his face a far too familiar friend for her. That same dread sunk deeper with every new voice she heard in her head. But she had earned her affliction. Zinarus's only sin had been his birth. Did he deserve to carry her sins too… or even suffer the wrath of them as Aliax had?

"My mind is slipping away, and your body betrays you," she replied with a weight growing on her shoulders. Strangely, it made her crave his embrace even more, a longing to rekindle the ashes of herself. "What a pair we are."

He placed a hand over his heart. "I would not blame you if you wished to leave me behind. This quest for vengeance of yours will inevitably place you in more grave danger, and my body already froze during the fight in the Water Realm. That could happen again. And if my ailment were to stop me from protecting you, I—"

He didn't have the chance to finish, as she stormed across the forge and kissed him. Pressing herself onto his lap, it wasn't a lady's gentle invitation for a suitor to court her, but one filled with the passion and pain they shared. Heat washed over her—both the forge's and the burning in her heart for something real, not ruined by the specters of her mind.

The momentum of the kiss nearly sent them toppling, so she shifted to sit against the workbench. Even separated, they held each other so close that she could see nothing more than his bright eyes. She met them with a stern look.

"Don't you fucking tell me to leave you for dead. Every minute of the last few days has been the consequence of death I've lived through or caused. I am done with that shit, you understand?"

When he gave an exasperated nod, she gripped his shirt until she held her fist over his heart. Its beat was rapid against her skin. "Good. Now, how bad is it?"

"Wha…" He winced. "I don't understand."

She shoved that fist harder into his chest. "How bad is this curse of yours according to the Body Reachers and doctors? Is it something that will get worse?"

"To be honest, I do not know. Each year seems to bring more stubbornness or shakiness to my muscles, but my spirit does not feel as if it wishes to flee my failing form. Time, though, is not my greatest concern." His hold on her loosened, and he dropped his gaze to his mechanical leg. "There must be others like me who endure this ailment or similar without the resources or technology to aid them. If I can solve this riddle, or at least provide relief for them, then the time I have left will have been worth it."

She kissed him again, catching him off guard. Spirits, how did he care so much about everyone but himself? "Then we *will* solve it."

He huffed as he rubbed the back of his neck. The motion couldn't hide the smile tugging at his lips. "If only it were so simple. There is little time for such pursuits during war."

Pulling away, she ran her fingers across his cheek. It was cruel to tempt him like this after he had admitted his fondness for her, but fear broke through at the ease of being with him. Aliax's decayed face flashed before her when she blinked. As she grappled with her own ailment and doubts about her past, could she truly allow herself to love again, putting Zinarus at risk?

"We cured the Spirit Plague," she said with more confidence than she felt, "and we shall do the same for you."

But her Taint replied in her mind, *He makes us vulnerable, weak. Cut him free like he wishes, and we can pursue Chatik alone.*

"Finish your leg," she told him, retreating. "Then join me at the estate when you are ready. Aliax's mother is not a patient woman, so ensure you wash up quickly. We can talk about everything else another time."

A PROMISE BOUND IN INK AND AMBER

"The fool's contract is verbal. The scion's is scribed in ink. The king's is sealed in blood." – Chatik Bartol the First, king of Ezman

Zinarus felt as if he had tumbled off a horse. Every muscle in his body tensed, and his chest ached with haggard breaths. The forge's wafting heat only made gripping his instruments more difficult, which was not ideal when he required absolute precision.

He stared through a small lens at the end of one of his mobile toolkit's arms. To those who were not craftsmen, the metal hat-like device resembled a monstrosity, but it ensured one always had the tool they needed within reach. Unfortunately, he had borrowed this one from the lowborn who managed the smithy, and its lens had some of the most contaminated glass he'd ever had the misfortune of staring through.

"Not everyone can afford pure glass," he mumbled aloud to himself. Still, it made him wonder how Kasia's laborers could work with any precision using such horrid tools.

The thought of her only made him tense further, sending a tiny screw into some hidden crevice. He cursed and sat back on his stool. It was difficult to manage his balance while working on the leg, as his late servant, Regizald had always helped him in his townhouse in Kalastok. Still, he had managed by himself before. Why was this so different?

It was a ridiculous question. Of course, the difference was that he'd been practically attacked by Kasia in their second kiss. This one had lasted *far* longer than the first, and he had been no more prepared for the quick third one. She had heard he was cursed by some horrid ailment, yet still decided to make romantic advances.

By the Crystal Mother, why did she always do that when she thought he may die? Not that those advances were unwelcomed. Just confusing.

With a replacement for the dropped screw and a few additional tweaks, he soon had his mechanical leg in what he believed was a functional form. He would ensure it returned to full efficiency when he returned to his family's estate in Vamiustok. For now, this would have to do.

He had an angry mother to calm.

Kasia's arrival and then retreat had come like a whirlwind that left him breathless, but he was grateful she was gone for this part. Even he did not quite enjoy looking at the stump at the end of his amputated leg. To make matters worse, there was always a chance the leg would fail in one of a dozen ways. Grease, gears, and fittings could all slip, and he was embarrassed enough already after admitting so much to her. It was better he faced this hill alone.

The mechanical leg latched onto his amputated one with a combination of latches that allowed him to tighten its cushioned top. Once snug, he locked it into place and flipped the switches to activate the knee and, lesser-so, the ankle. Such joints were tricky to perfect, and he still had a long way to go before he did so. These prototypes, though, had massively improved his mobility in the years since he implemented segments of Ogrenian designs.

With the leg attached, he drew a long breath. The moment of truth. He lowered himself onto his legs, leaning heavily on the workbench until he was confident. Then he let go.

Gears whirred, and a puff of white smoke signaled the tiny implanted power source had ignited. A faint clicking in the ankle alerted him to a few misaligned elements, but they seemed functional for the moment. He checked his pocket watch. It would have to be enough, since they were to meet with Aliax's mother, Paxalia, in just over an hour.

It was barely enough time for him to call the carriage Kasia had let him borrow and then clean up. Adventurers talked about nose blindness during their expeditions, but Zinarus was fully aware of his stench. Why had Kasia decided approaching him in this condition was for the best?

He sighed and threw on his coat. Like the others he had borrowed from House Niezik, it was Leonit's and of a dated style, but he dared not complain. The real discomfort came from the way Kasia flinched at the sight of him wearing her father's clothes. She tried to hide it. Except her skill at that had faded in recent days, and between her failed memories and the Tainted voices that haunted her, he could not help but be concerned.

His leg clicked away as he closed up the forge and headed into the frigid everdark. The worst of the blizzard had passed, but in its wake, a knee-high mound of snow blocked his way back to the road. Tystok lacked the Air and Fire Reachers to keep away the heaviest storms and clear the streets. No carriage would make it through this.

Seems I must test my leg more than expected.

Letting out a foggy huff, he stomped his cane into the snow and lumbered onward. The wind struck him immediately, blustering his sweat-soaked hair that would surely freeze before long. Having only dressed for a short carriage ride, he was woefully unprepared for the mile walk back, and he found himself once again grateful for Kasia's absence. She would think him an absolute fool for...

A figure interrupted him halfway to what resembled the road. Tazper, from the look of his wide-brimmed hat and woolen gray coat with half its collar up and the other half down. For a minor house scion, he dressed quite well, but spirits, the lad always failed at the finer details. That didn't matter now, though. With Zinarus's leg already starting to ache, the footman was as beautiful a sight as the Crystal Mother herself.

"Lord Zinarus!" Tazper called out, hurrying to him and offering his arm. "The carriage is not far. Lady Katarzyna sent me to fetch you."

So she did know he was ill-prepared. It was what it was—and Zinarus was too cold to be embarrassed—so he took the footman's arm and followed him to the carriage. Beyond it, at least a hundred lowborn laborers shoveled away enough of the snow for them to pass.

Zinarus whistled. "Must your lady summon an army to relieve me?"

"Oh, believe me," Tazper said, opening the carriage and helping Zinarus into it. "She is quite smitten at sending us to your aid."

Of course she was, but Zinarus was not too prideful to take that aid. He settled onto one bench as Tazper took the spot across from him. The carriage rolled on immediately while he studied the footman, who tapped his foot and stared out the window of impure glass.

"It is improper for me to ask this," Zinarus said, "but what is your opinion of Lady Katarzyna's worsening Realm Taint?"

Tazper's foot only tapped faster. "I… er… She has struggled with hearing Aliax's voice for a long time, but with the dead spirits following her now, she has become more erratic." He wrinkled his nose at that word. "Sorry, I did not mean it that harshly. It is simply that—"

"I understand," Zinarus said. "You care for her, and even in the short time I have known her, the shift is apparent."

"It seems you care for her as well?" Tazper said, shifting to a question halfway through. He glanced at Zinarus before averting his gaze. "My apologies if that is none of my business."

Zinarus just chuckled. "It is beyond my understanding what my situation with her is, but yes, I do care for her. That is why I asked your opinion. You have known her far longer, and with me leaving for Vamiustok, it is my hope you can help me ensure she does not go without support."

"It is ironic, then, that you will be the one by her side. Not me."

"I beg your pardon?" Zinarus furrowed his brow. "She has told me nothing of this."

Tazper straightened his cravat, still not fixing his collar. "I do admit my surprise at you not discussing it, considering her time in the smithy with you, but that is not my business." He coughed into his hand to hide his grin. "While I am to be sent to Kalastok to meet with our lowborn associate, Nex, and understand the Crimsons' hold on the city, she will join you by teleporting to Vamiustok. It seems Commander Artaxan believes she is a distraction to recruitment."

The knot in Zinarus's chest loosened, but his heartbeat hammered his mind. She would come to Vamiustok with him? What would his mother think after the letters they had exchanged about the Amber Dame? Sania had seen Kasia as a risky yet powerful ally, but the coup and revelations about Kasia's past had so much in upheaval.

Those questions, however, could not dampen his excitement to continue journeying with her. Whatever his struggles with his health, she was crucial in his fight for justice against the Crimson Court who'd killed Regizald and stolen his family's sand mines. She had revealed his foes, provided the amber to help him cure the Spirit Plague, and shown him an entire other realm. There was no one like her. That was frightening, but so too, was it invigorating.

They soon crawled through the mansion gates, and once they stopped, Tazper helped him climb the stairs to his guest room. Kasia's voice carried from her chambers down the hall. Zinarus kept moving, though, not wishing to violate her privacy. The meeting ahead would be plenty tense, and she deserved the chance to prepare for it however she pleased.

A wash basin was already awaiting him within the bedroom, so he sent Tazper on his way and removed his mechanical leg again. It had worked remarkably well considering his repairs lacked Regizald and his usual toolset. He had improved on Ogrenian designs by implementing some water resistance, but immersing it in a bath was not wise.

Though an annoying process, he managed to climb into the tub and clean himself while keeping an eye on his ticking watch. Returning to the mansion had taken far longer than he had expected.

So he rushed, choosing a gray jacket and trousers along with a humble woolen frock coat to avoid appearing ostentatious. These conversations only stirred up new mourning among the lowborn families. They did not need to see scions striding into their homes in rich clothes and claiming their money could mend the wounds of the past. Especially with his Vockan hair and darker gray skin, Zinarus drew enough unwanted attention, but his role was merely to ensure all remained calm.

The mechanical clicking of his leg echoed through the mansion as Tazper returned to help him climb down the stairs. Kasia awaited him in the foyer, its decorative glass windows proclaiming House Niezik's old ambitions to be named among the great ones. She had opted for a high-collared dress of muted blacks and grays that lacked her usual flashes of amber jewelry and embroidery. It made her resemble a woman called Death's Daughter more than one seeking to make amends.

Zinarus held back that worry. The look in her eye was not a matriarch's determination, but that of a frightened cat. She did not need to raise her hackles for him to take that as plenty of a warning.

"You hardly resemble the man I saw in that workshop," she said, likely trying to cover her worry behind a quip. He allowed that to pass too.

"Clothes make not a man," he replied. "But send him through the everdark's expanse with neither flame nor crystal, and you shall see the true essence of his spirit."

Her eyes narrowed. "Careful, Lord Zinarus. Quoting a Keloshan like Bartigost during a time of war could put you in dire straits."

"In times like these, I fear we are all caught in the riptide, my lady."

He took her arm, and they headed out into the darkness together, the lanternlight revealing gardens that were far from their glory. Little thrived in the everdark. These, though, showed brambles that had not been trimmed since the duskfall season at least. Was that due to Gregorzon's management or Kasia's focus elsewhere?

Neither of them spoke again until the carriage was on its way. The streets were still full of shoveling laborers, but mercifully, the snow had ceased. With dawnrise soon approaching, these blizzards would only get worse until the great light's return. The following rainstorms would nourish the farmers' lands and allow the dawnrise planting to begin before the everbright droughts. Zinarus pitied the lowborn who had to endure the worst of the snow in the meantime. Some of the laborers were young enough that their shovels were nearly as tall as them.

"I had expected you to employ more Reachers," he said, sitting across from her and hoping to provide some distraction from what was to come. "Especially with so much labor draining into mercenary recruitment."

She bit her lip and watched the laborers as the carriage passed. "It was not until our discovery of amber that we had sufficient funds to maintain our holdings, let alone fund a significant number of Reachers. Before recently, many villages lacked even a single Spirit Reacher, but I have at least changed that. The streets are another matter entirely. Our farmers are often in search of extra keni apart from the growing and harvesting seasons, so though the work is strenuous, they are well compensated." She gave him a challenging look. "I am not Gornioz Oliezany."

Holding no desire to counter that challenge, he nodded. "Tazper tells me as well that you are to join me in Vamiustok."

"Yes," she said through clenched teeth. "That was not for him to share, but as he has revealed it, I do intend to come with you. My presence here is still controversial. Despite my attempts to cool tempers, recruitment would be better if I were to leave and rejoin with them at the Confederation's Fort Harizak later. I considered going to Kalastok myself to meet with Nex, but I would draw too much attention." She clenched her fists in her lap. "Apparently, all is better off without my presence."

"I do not agree with that appraisement of the situation," he insisted.

"Oh really?" She rolled her eyes, the bite returning to her voice. "What *appraisement* do you have then? The Crimsons control the Commonwealth and the Unity Crystal, our nation faces invasion from a superior force, the Spirit Plague still rages with Chatik likely smothering the cure, and each death from it grants them another spirit to turn into a breathless. Not to mention my being wanted for execution and half my people despising me for my errors."

Her quick breaths filled the carriage as they rumbled their way onto dirt roads. The snow crunched beneath the wheels, slowing them, and Zinarus's nervous glance at his watch revealed they would be late.

"None of that is false," he admitted, crossing his mechanical leg over his good one. "Perhaps, however, your focus should be on what assets you have, not what you lack."

A scoff answered him. "We face the Crimsons and their great house allies with a few thousand lowborn soldiers and a handful of Reachers."

"And yet, a few hundred-hours ago, we had neither the identity of the Crimson Court's leader nor allies in the fight against them. You are the reason I could stand and interrupt Chatik's attempt to depose Jazuk without resistance." He leaned forward and met her gaze. "Yes, this civil war is hardly ideal, but the alternative would have been far worse. We have allies. And I dare say we have each other's desire for justice."

She hesitated, then nodded, the pain evident in her eyes—like cracks across a frozen sea. "I realize that I wasted my chance to prepare you for this meeting with Paxalia. We will be arriving later than arranged, so she will be rightly aggrieved. I..." Her eyes shot to something unseen, then back to him. "I do not know what she will say, but you know full well that my emotions run deep here. It would be unfair of me to ask you of anything more than you have given. So all I will ask is this: No matter what happens, ensure she receives this."

She pulled out a rolled piece of parchment and handed it to him. A single sheet, it was a quick read, and he sat back in shock when he was finished.

"You are granting her a ten percent stake in your amber mines?" He took a moment to comprehend the scale of such a transfer. "You must realize that will mean your house surrendering millions of keni over the years, especially as word spreads of amber's ability to entrap awakened and breathless. Aliax's family will likely become the richest lowborn in all the Commonwealth."

They pulled to a stop, and Kasia reached for the door. "I know, and even that is not enough. Just do this for me. Then, I promise I will aid you however I can in Vamiustok."

"You need not promise anything," he replied, softly catching her arm. "This piece of parchment proves your resolve, your heart, more than any words ever could. It is my honor to deliver it."

"Then let us do this and leave at least one ghost in my past."

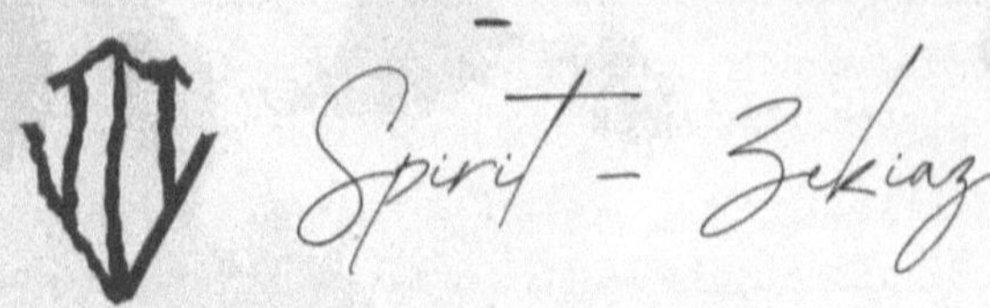

Spirit - Zekiaz

The Spirit realm is one familiar to all who reside in our lands. Yet that very fact makes us overlook Zekiaz's potential so often. The awakened scourge did not emerge from nothing. All beings are combinations of the realms' Essences. Spirits and mortals alike are no different. Give a spirit life, and it will seek to consume.

I conceive of the potential for spirits not who attempt to destroy us, but who hold our same sentience. What could we learn from those who are inherently bound to the Spirit Crystal? But sentience allows control... I fear what some may do with such power.

The most powerful among us live many lives because of the Inheritance Rituals. Spirits and our Reachers make such things possible for anyone given a room of the purest glass. I cannot help but wonder what our realm would be like if all great scholars held such extended lives as well. So much knowledge is lost to death. Must these abilities remain with only the richest of the houses?

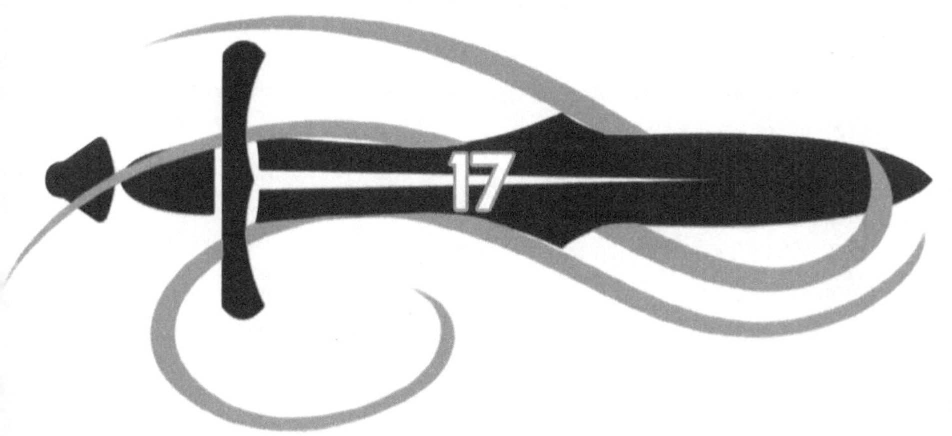

THE WHISPERERS OF DALNUS

"If the Glassblades are our army against the awakened scourge, then the Whisperers are our song to quell their rage," – Orionus ik Dalnus, former scribe of the Vockan Nation

"Dalnus is just over the ridge," Commander Polina shouted over the Glassblade lines. "Keep in formation! Let them see our order has not fallen from its glory."

Wanusa ik Iliafa rode beside Lazan on her sleek chestnut ibex, Ereniany, and followed close behind the Glassblades ahead. She had never stepped foot in the Vockan capital of Dalnus before. Stories called it nothing more than a mountaintop village for politicians and shamans to bicker over how to fend off spirits or the greater nations. With Vocka uniting with Ezman, Kalastok had taken the vast majority of the city's importance, so what remained?

Her excitement to see the city gave way to her heavy heart as they passed the terraced farmlands across the mountains of Dalnus's outskirts. Memories of the battle in the Whistling Pass haunted her. She'd been slow to return to the rest of the convoy after talking with Radais, and now, the supreme defender was slumped over the back of an ibex whose rider had died in the attack.

She clenched her gauntleted fist over her breastplate. Glass clinked against glass—armor built to fend off awakened and their lethal tendrils, not breathless wielding solid weapons. That Earth Bound One had cut right through them like they were nothing, and if Tairanik hadn't arrived with reinforcements when he did, Radais would've been dead. All while Wanusa was too stunned to act.

It had taken her less than a hundred-hour to shatter her helmet and fail her master. On that mountain over Palmia, she'd sworn her life to the Glassblade Order and her siblings in arms. What use was she if she couldn't fight when she was needed most?

"From Kalastok to Akaamilion," Lazan said, his eyes swollen and his scion gray cheeks red from the cold. "Now Palmia to Dalnus. Where shall our spirit-cursed travels take us next?"

His words were absent their usual wonder, a sentiment she shared. Even the dreary, blizzard-draped mountain passes between Palmia and Dalnus had brought a serene beauty far different from that of the Spirit Wastes. That attack, though… Wanusa twitched remembering the first Vanashel ambush on their western expedition, when they had lost Supreme Defender Miv and so many others. The Glassblades' numbers and organization had prevented such slaughter this time, but the mere thought of that Bound One made Wanusa question all she'd devoted herself to.

There had to be a way to defeat the Vanashel's Bound Ones, and she promised herself she would find it. For Radais and for the six Glassblades who'd died in the attack. They might have been alive if she'd been prepared, if she'd stayed in formation.

"We'll go wherever the Vanashel haunt," she finally replied to Lazan, raising her chin and tightening her grip on the reins. "They are corrupted, evil, and we'll put an end to them."

Lazan tugged down a floppy fur hat over his ears. "Such fire of youth. Share some of that determination with an old scion, won't you?"

"You aren't *that* old," she said. At least, she thought he wasn't. Lazan had never actually told her his age, but if Radais was thirty-five, then the scion couldn't have been more than forty based on the faint wrinkles across his brow.

"I am older than your mere sixteen years," he said with a sigh that sent fog rolling before them. "Realm Taint makes it feel as if I have lived far more. Healing Radais and that ibex of his took far too much from me."

He left it there, but Wanusa knew he'd Reached more to heal other wounded. Instead of a quick rest of the journey, they had taken days to near Dalnus. Lazan looked worse with each day of it. The Reaches obviously had something to do with his weariness, but though Wanusa was young, she wasn't blind. Radais had a bond with the scion, leaving tension between them so thick that she could've cut it with her sword. That dread Lazan held was the fear of almost losing a loved one.

Wanusa knew it well.

A glimmer of hope filled her as they crested the ridge to see flickering lights filling the valley ahead. Conifers broke much of the view, but the sacred Peak of the Sheptasa rose like an open hand held toward the empty skies. Torches lined the pathway to the peaks resembling the hand's fingers, and a few shamans in heavy robes knelt there with arms extended. Their Whispering song hummed through the trees' needles like a gentle breeze that took Wanusa's breath away.

"I have never beheld such a sight," Lazan said, watching the shamans.

"They are called Sheptasa," Wanusa replied, "or Whisperers in more common tongue. I've only heard stories of them. Our village elders said they speak to spirits and can lull even awakened to rest with their songs."

Lazan's lips parted, as if he'd suddenly remembered. "Ah, yes. I remember hearing of the shamans who led the Vockan Nation before it joined with Ezman. Considering I have not heard news of them since, I doubt their power has remained when compared to that of House iz Ardinvil."

Wanusa considered that. Yes, House iz Ardinvil and other scion houses of mixed Vockan and Ezmani blood now wielded influence over the mountains, but was true power not with those who could protect their people? If the Whisperers could calm awakened, could they do the same to breathless? The last Vanashel attack had shown that Glassblade tactics were not infallible, and they would need all the allies they could get.

She pulled out Radais's sketchpad and flipped open to a free page, grinning at the countless drawings of Lazan from recent hundred-hours. The Body Reacher had endured Taint to save Radais's life *and* Vuk's because he knew what the ibex meant to Radais. The two men just needed to talk about their feelings, or the rest of their travels were only going to get more awkward.

She drew the Peak of the Sheptasa as they rode into the valley. The peak never disappeared behind the trees, offering a sign of hope no matter where you were in Dalnus. Spirits hung around it, and though she assumed they were drifters, those legends made her wonder whether there were placid awakened among them too.

Commander Tairanik rode down the line with his fading red hair flattened badly from wearing his helmet. He raised that helm as he barked orders, "Keep yourselves sightly! Looks like the iz Ardinvil mercenaries are here, and I won't have them thinking we're lesser."

The usually ill-dressed commander had cleaned up his dirtied armor and commander's jacket, or at least had ordered someone else to. Radais's last action before the battle had been to chew out Tairanik and ensure the Glassblades' lines remained orderly. If he hadn't, the slaughter could've been even worse. Maybe Tairanik had caught on to that point too.

"How fares our supreme defender?" Tairanik said, lowering his voice as he slowed beside Lazan and Wanusa. "Politics isn't my friend, and even in Dalnus, there's nothing but politics."

Wanusa held her fist over her chest and bowed her head. "Commander, he is—"

"I wasn't asking you," he muttered before pointing to Lazan. "You, Body Reacher, what's his status?"

Lazan resembled a sheep staring down a rider, a lost look in his eye. But from the fists clenched around his reins, there was something else there. "As Warrior Wanusa intended to tell you, Supreme Defender Radais has recovered physically, but even with a Body Reacher's aid, exhaustion comes from such extensive healing. Should he need to be woken, you may do so. Know, however, that he will be sluggish for quite some time."

Wanusa raised her brow at his tone. Conceit had oozed from every syllable, and though Lazan had always spoken more like a scion than any Glassblade, this level of formality was new. Was he trying to defend her?

"Wake him," Tairanik ordered.

Then he left without another word, his ibex kicking a cloud of snow over them in his wake. Wanusa sneered. She was only a warrior, but she so badly wished she had been the one to tell him off. The man was a commander, yet he was afraid of talking with some mercenaries and shamans? How irresponsible.

Lazan slowed and laid a hand on Radais's shoulder. "Radais? It is time to wake."

He seemed a different man than just seconds before, but his actions remained stoic as pulled back and ran his fingers through his ever-growing silver beard. She knew better than to believe his display of indifference. From what Miv had taught her, even minor scions were trained to hide their emotions out of fear of rivals exploiting such vulnerabilities.

Her heart ached knowing what Lazan felt, yet didn't express. Both he and Radais had become mentors for her. She wanted them to be happy, but amid a war with the Vanashel as the Crimson Court commanded other breathless, there were so many greater forces at play.

"They broke it," Radais mumbled, his eyes fluttering. "Rock… Glass."

Wanusa waved at him. "As eloquent as a poet."

He shot up and his gaze darted around as he grabbed at his saddlebags to draw his blade. Except it wasn't there. Along with his breastplate and one of his pauldrons, his blade had shattered against the Earth Bound One's massive war pick. To surrender his sword was a great sacrifice for any Glassblade to make, and it had saved her life. How could she ever make it up to him?

"Have calm, dear warrior," Lazan said, once again resting a hand on Radais. "The Vanashel are gone, and you are safe with us in Dalnus."

"Where is Vuk?" Radais demanded. "Tell me he is alright!"

Wanusa nodded back to the ibex, who lazily trotted up to Radais and bleated. "He's been slow since the battle, but Lazan mended both of your wounds." She winked at the scion. "He won't admit it, but he took Realm Taint to help you two and others. Even some of the masters were calling him a hero, asking why we've never used Body Reachers before."

Radais scratched Vuk under his chin and smiled. His motions were still slow, his eyes baggy and red, but he showed no other remnants of the injury that had nearly killed him. "You saved him?" he asked Lazan with his lips remaining parted. "But your Taint… You told me it killed you slowly with overuse."

"That was not a lie," Lazan said as they passed grazing goats, sheep, and even cows. Conifers gave way to cultivars that would bear fruit come dawnrise and everbright. For now, though, they were bare, and it felt like their branches were awakened tendrils grasping at the passing Glassblades.

With a sorrowful smile, Radais clasped Lazan's hand with both of his. His armor was with the glassmaster to be repaired, but even weary and unarmored, he looked twice the scion's size. "I cannot repay you enough. By the pure spirits, I swear, I am in your debt."

"And I am in yours," Wanusa told him. She kept the riding posture Miv had taught her, but bowed her head slightly. "The wounds you took were to protect me when you have dozens of other warriors."

"I dragged you into this mess and left your family exposed to the Vanashel in Iliafa," he replied. "It is the least I could do."

Lazan chuckled and reached across to grab Wanusa's hand too. "As Warrior Wanusa slayed the breathless that threatened me as well, it appears that we have quite the triangle of debt. Let us agree to be free of that guilt, yes?"

"You hear that, Vuk?" Radais asked the ibex. "You won't owe the greedy scion a kena!"

Wanusa laughed and tapped one of Vuk's curved horns. "Technically, he said *triangle*, so Vuk might still owe him."

"He stood over you too, remember?"

"Then perhaps I owe him some treats after all." She reached into her pack, taking a handful of dried apples and feeding some to Ereniany and the rest to Vuk. Both ibexes lapped them up like they'd never eaten in their lives, and that excitement helped dull her heartache. "I think he accepts the thanks."

Radais let go of Lazan and stretched out his back. There were enough audible pops to make Wanusa worry for him, but relief crossed his face. "Vuk is not the picky sort. How long was I out? My mouth feels like a damned desert, and the rest of me isn't much better."

"It has been two nights and almost three days," Wanusa replied, handing him her canteen, which he downed. "At least that's what Lazan's watch said."

The scion raised a brow at her. "So you have been studying my watch, huh?"

"I have never worn one before. We don't have any in Vocka, besides that tiny clock they have on the Palmia belltower."

"That makes it a clocktower," Radais protested, surveying the Glassblades ahead before turning his attention to the Peak of the Sheptasa, slack jawed. "You didn't wake me until we were basically *in* Dalnus, then? Did Tairanik throw a fit at my absence yet?"

Wanusa grimaced. "He is the reason we woke you. The iz Ardinvil mercenaries are ahead, and he expects you to handle the politics."

"I'd rather fight that Earth Bound One again than face politicians." He straightened his seat on his saddle. "The last time I was here, I didn't say a word while Miv talked. This must be her vengeance. I'll be back. Make sure Vuk doesn't wander off before then."

But Wanusa grabbed him before he could leave. "Please, let me come too. Miv wanted me to learn in every way I could, and if I'm to follow in her footsteps, I need to learn to handle both politicians and the whisperers."

"She is just curious about the shamans," Lazan said with a wry smile and a glance that said it was revenge for exposing him earlier. "It is probably for the best that you do not go alone, however, and she is much milder mannered than most of your other warriors."

"He's right!" Wanusa exclaimed. "Would you rather bring Mhanain?"

Radais held a palm to his forehead and shook his head. "Fine, you may come. Just give me my sketchpad back."

Her cheeks burned as she flipped the book shut and returned it to him, along with his charcoal. "I was trying to draw the peak and Whisperers, but I'm far worse than you."

Carefully avoiding his sketches of Lazan, he peeked at hers and gave a single nod, then threw the book into his saddlebag. "You understand perspective better than most beginners. I'll teach you in time, but that will have to be after this. Come, let us join the commanders before Tairanik starts a fight."

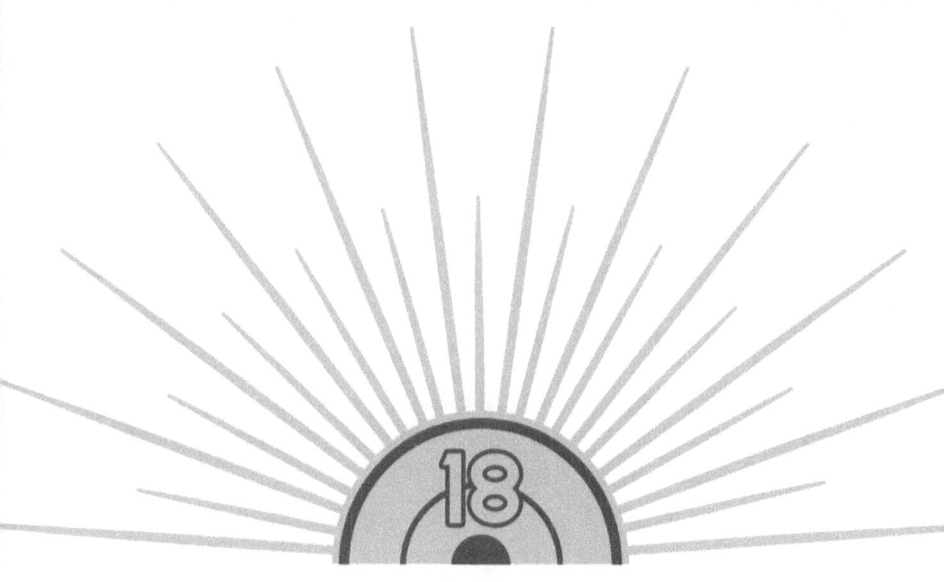

THE FACES OF ASH

"There are two faces one holds: the public and the private. The more aligned these are, the more whole the person becomes. To stray from who we are is to deny the spirit granted to us by our Mother below." – Bridgezet Tarizon, former anointed sister of the Buried Temple

"How do I look?" Nex asked, turning about in front of Vinnia. They wore a fine woolen coat over a businessman's jacket and trousers. Rich enough to pass as a middle-class lowborn from the market district, but draw any real attention.

Vinnia looked them up and down in the dim light of an oil lantern. Crax and his crew had traded Nex's Ashes of Dawn the lanterns as part of their deal, and having a steady supply of light made a crucial difference for morale. Wasn't easy to keep people happy when they couldn't see where they ate, where they slept, and where they shat.

"You look lovely," Vinnia said before adjusting how the coat sat on Nex's shoulders. When she stepped back again, she crossed her arms and nodded sharply. "Like a merchant if I ever saw one."

Nex took some pride in that, but couldn't deny the irony of dressing like this while lurking in the corner of an abandoned warehouse.

They were just doing what was necessary to get across the Kala River. The Crimsons had the damn things locked down tighter than ever since Nikoza's pretend aid convoy, so Nex had decided to pose as one of the managers overseeing a shipment of weapons.

"Glad it convinced you, but now I gotta convince the guards," they said.

Vinnia stepped closer and held a hand to their cheek. "You look... different. Beyond the clothes. Like your jaw tightened." She glanced down at Nex's Possibility Reacher ring. "Please tell me that doesn't have something to do with your Reaching?"

Nex shook their head. "None of us are eating right. Lost some cheek fat, that's all."

"Alright," Vinnia replied before kissing them. "Just be safe, okay? I can't settle when you're gone, and with everyone relying on us..."

Nex kissed her back before turning away and popping up their collar like many of the scions did. They hated lying to Vinnia, but she'd get concerned if she found out Nex had altered their appearance with Possibility Reaching. Rumors were common about such abilities, and with them playing so many roles, they figured it was worth the shot. If Vin noticed, it meant the change was real—but temporary. Nex needed to move fast before the alteration sapped their Reach.

"I'll be fine," they said. "Not my first time across the river, and it damn sure won't be my last."

Once Vinnia had climbed back into the hidden Ashes of Dawn safehouse below, Nex grabbed the lantern and headed out into the streets of the Shadow Quarter. Spirits skirted along the edges of the light. It was impossible to tell if they were breathless or drifters, so Nex dimmed the lantern to calm their nerves. With their free hand, they gripped a bead of amber with two spirits already within it. Such a small piece was incredibly weak at that point, but they needed to conserve their supply. The gangs were clamoring for the Ashes of Dawn to fulfill their end of the bargain.

That started today.

The old clocktower in the southern Market District chimed for the thirteenth hour as Nex traversed the snow-covered streets. It rose halfway up their shin with dawnrise's approach bringing its usual blizzards. East Kalastok had Air Reachers to keep the storms at bay or turn them to rain, but that only sent more of it tumbling over the west side. Part of Nex wondered if the scions wanted that. Lowborn couldn't revolt if they were too busy shoveling just to get out of their apartment or whatever hole they'd hidden in.

The air was frigid, fogging Nex's breaths before them. Streaks of firelight danced over the Kala beyond. A layer of ice should've covered its surface, but on duty Fire and Water Reachers constantly kept the river open for trade ships and fishermen to pass. Bastards. Nex could've just walked right across the ice if they'd let it freeze.

But that wasn't an option, so they turned south, toward the screams that echoed through the city.

Most of the Industrial District was still ashes. At its heart, though, were the great house factories that fueled the Crimsons' war against Kelosh and rebels, both lowborn and scions. Reacher light illuminated those expansive factories that had *remarkably* been spared from the worst flames. Everyone knew the houses' Water Reachers had rushed to protect only their properties during the riot, and they'd quickly rebuilt the sections damaged by the inferno. All while the rest of the lowborn rotted.

Scions always had enforcers guarding the factories, but they'd used to just be lowborn brutes. Now, Light Reachers scanned from the rooftops. Snipers stood at the ready nearby, and Nex had no doubt other Reachers lurked elsewhere, waiting for the gangs to try something stupid.

Except all the gangs had connections in the factories. For example, Bess's Murder Mitts had a mole in one of House Oliezany's gunsmiths, and they'd let slip the location of a transfer along with a name Nex could use: Witten Kalinov.

That cover had given Nex inspiration for their altered appearance. They were pretending to be a man, so a stronger jawline and paler Ezmani lowborn skin were a start. It had taken them days just to get the slightest bits of those changes right. Especially without any pure glass mirrors, that was difficult, but Jiinaan had been happy to provide blunt feedback.

Nex could feel their last Reach beginning to fade as they approached the rendezvous point they'd set with Jiinaan. At Bess's insistence, Nex had sent him to help the Murder Mitts "deal with" the true Witten Kalinov. The gang's name—inspired by the brass knuckles they all wore—left little to the imagination with how they intended to do that dealing, and Jiinaan beamed as Nex rounded a corner and found him leaning against a half-collapsed wall.

"Take it you got rid of him, then?" they asked, glancing around to ensure no one could overhear.

Jiinaan cracked his knuckles. "Sinking down, down. River ate him like cobbler."

"Cobbler?"

He imitated eating, and a hint of longing seemed to creep into his eyes. "Dessert from fruit and cake. You'd like."

"I'll take your word for it." Nex winced as Reacher light swung toward them, then tarried away. In it, they'd caught glimpses of the breathless watching from above. "None of the spirits saw you, right?" He shook his head, so Nex patted him on his elbow—practically as high as their chin. "Get back to our territory. Don't want them offing you after what they did to Jax."

"Don't die," he replied, smacking Nex on the shoulder hard enough to send them stumbling into the wall. "And don't fall."

"Thanks…"

Nex collected themself as Jiinaan disappeared with each of his steps like a bull's in the snow. Stealth and brute force were two different skills. Jiinaan couldn't keep quiet, and Nex couldn't knock a fucker out with a single punch. That's why they needed the Ashes of Dawn. After so long working by themself, Nex wasn't used to relying on others, but they weren't going to beat the Crimsons alone.

This part, though, was all on them.

Nex tugged down on their felt cap as they drew the attention of the guards above. A hovering ball of Reacher light drifted closer, revealing a pair of approaching guards in gray uniforms trimmed with House Oliezany's favored pink.

"Stop right there!" one called out. "This area is for workers and approved traders only. State your business or go back the way you came."

"I am Witten Kalinov," Nex replied, raising their gloved hands and doing their best to imitate the countless merchantmen they'd swindled in gambling halls. "On the orders of House Oliezany, I am to oversee the transfer of a rifle and musket shipment across the river." They checked an open-faced watch they'd stolen. It was badly broken, but the guards couldn't see that. "They will be disappointed if they were to hear about you holding me up."

The guards whispered to each other, and one retreated while the other kept her hand up. "Sorry Master Kalinov, but we must confirm with the records that you are on the schedule. Protocol and all that shit."

Nex gave a conciliatory smile. "Of course."

The ends of their lips twitched as the breathless drew closer. Three of them circled through the Reacher light in their shadowy forms. Whispers hovered among them, but none made an aggressive move. Nex figured breathless commonly followed the merchants coming into the guarded areas around the factories, so the Possibility Reacher kept their mouth shut.

Time passed slowly, but they didn't need a working watch to know they had just seconds before their Reaching failed. Bones creaked and snapped together in their jaw in a process that was more uncomfortable than painful. Worse was their itching skin as it changed back to its usual mid-tone brown.

The process wasn't immediate, but those breathless would notice soon enough. So too, would the guards once they could clearly see that Nex was no Ezmani man. Nex needed to Reach again.

And accept the Taint that followed.

Faking a cough, they turned away and threw their left arm over their face. Wisps of every color rose from the slit in their glove as their crystal ring tremored. They urged those wisps to disappear quickly, and only took another breath when their face began to change back.

Realm Taint struck like a punch to their gut, nausea washing over them. Nex held up their chin just to keep from vomiting as they stared down the remaining guard. The breathless, though, escalated their strange whispers.

"Are you sick?" the guard asked. "We can't have the plague around here."

Nex tensed. What was it that the old men always said? "It was just a tickle in my throat," they replied. "Nothing to be worried about."

They looked around for the other guard. What was taking so long? Bess's mole had claimed Witten was expected at this time, so unless the actual Witten's corpse had somehow been found already, there shouldn't have been any disruption. Instinct told them to check for escape routes. There were a couple alleys, but with the breathless so close and a rifleman staring them down on the nearby roof, fleeing wasn't an appealing option. So they waited.

Footsteps approached from behind the guard just when Nex's nerves were at their ends. The figure who emerged wasn't the returning guard, but a stern-looking bald man wearing suspenders and a worn duster over worker's clothes. He waved Nex toward him with one aggressive stroke.

"C'mon then. Not gonna get these guns to the front with you standing there."

Nex exhaled a long breath, checked that their hair was still hidden under their cap, and followed. In theory, getting in was the hardest part. From here, they just needed to pretend to inspect the crates now and hop on a wagon. Easy.

The man offered Nex a handshake, his third finger missing from the ungloved hand. "Name's Ulren. I'm the foreman on this shift for the rifle line. Got a solid load of 'em this round. Lord Otterzik will be pleased."

"Very good," they replied without a clue of who this Otterzik was. Magnates came and went without any real difference to the low-born. Great houses' weird Inheritance Rituals gave them another name with the same damn spirit of an asshole to guide them. Otterzik was probably the tenth or so rebirth of this Oliezany patriarch's spirit.

Ulren nearly crushed Nex's hand when they shook, but his expression softened when he let go. "You've got a workman's hand. Were you a laborer before?"

"Everyone starts somewhere," Nex said.

"Huh, good lad. Need more like you that know our work ain't like signing papers."

He led Nex past the guards and onto the main road that ran along the line of factories. His stride was quick, but had a bit of a stagger. A true worker who'd done his time and taken his scars for it. Unlike the Oliezany scions who owned Kalastok's gunsmiths, this lowborn man wasn't Nex's enemy. Just the opposite. He'd endured the west side's shit for decades to become a foreman, all in hopes of a slightly better life than the average laborer's.

A convoy of covered wagons awaited them. Oliezany guards rode on every side with guns shouldered, and they saluted at Nex's approach. Was Nex supposed to salute back? They'd never imitated someone of such importance before, so they just nodded, which seemed passable.

Ulren walked Nex between the wagons, ordering a pair of laborers to crack open a crate for inspection. Inside were guns if Nex had ever seen them. Besides that, they could barely tell a rifle from a musket, but they pretended to give their approval.

"These are finely made," they said, thumping Ulren's arm in the way men did. "They'll put quite a few bullets through Keloshan skulls for certain."

Ulren chuckled. "Aye, they will. Best grooved barrels south of Ogrenia, but spiritdamned expensive. If we could keep up with these, the front would be going far better. Most of the shipment is smoothbarreled muskets. Far less accurate, but a third of the cost. Those can't match Keloshan infantry in the slightest."

"It's that bad?" Nex asked. News of the war's progress hadn't slipped through to the west side, and if Kelosh stomped the Crimsons' armies, they'd uproot one master just to find another.

"You haven't heard?" Ulren huffed and waved for the laborers to close the crate again. "Our half of the Lost Brothers' Forts fell in a couple days. Kelosh took Rexaniv already and is damn near to Anukit in the north. The king won't be happy that his birth house's home is about to fall."

Nex didn't know much about geography, but they knew Anukit was in the northeast and not all that close to the border. Things were about to get a lot worse soon if Kelosh kept advancing like that. Until then, the Crimsons' focus on the war would hopefully keep their attention off Nex's little gang of rebels.

"My work has me stuck in my office too often," Nex said. "If the war proceeds this poorly, though, it makes these guns all the more important. Let's get going."

Ulren nodded toward a wagon in the middle of the column. "You're to sit there. The guards are worried about violence after the princess's arrival, and we can't have you getting shot."

"That would be unfortunate, yes."

They climbed onto the front of the wagon Ulren had signaled to, and luckily, its driver showed no interest in Nex. The guards, too, were focused on the perimeter as the convoy rolled on. It just needed to stay that way until they crossed the southern Oliezany Bridge.

Either Reachers or laborers had cleared the roads of the southern Industrial District, making their passage far easier than Nex's trudge through the snow. Heads peaked out from doors when they passed beyond the security cordon, and Nex knew more would be watching from shuttered windows and dark alleyways. This shipment wasn't Nex's. Still, they found themself suddenly feeling as if they were under far closer watch now than within the cordon.

Do they always feel like prey under vultures' gazes? Nex wondered.

Most of these guards and wagon drivers were lowborn too, but they were the ones threatened by the gangs' attacks, not the scions themselves. If anyone resembled a scion in the convoy, it was Nex. They hoped the bosses had called off their thugs at Nex's warning. Unfortunately, thugs were known for brawn more than brains, so Nex kept an eye out for any threats.

None came besides some drunkard wandering into their path. The guards shouted for him to get out of the way, and when he didn't, they signaled to a Reacher on a nearby building. A breathless shot toward the drunkard.

He was far too slow, and the spirit killed him in a single strike. Except, instead of tearing his spirit from his body and devouring it like an awakened would, it let his spirit float free. Nex shuddered at that. The Crimsons would make him one of their breathless slaves, all because he'd been too scammered to understand what he was doing.

Nex forced themself not to glance down at the man's husk, his mind trapped inside with no spirit to guide it. A merchant wouldn't care, right? Witten Kalinov dealt in guns, so what was another dead body to him?

They soon rumbled over the Oliezany Bridge, its stone forming windows in its high walls with metal bars crossing each. The Kala's flow crashed against the supports below, and Nex shivered at the memory of tumbling with Kasia into it. That hadn't been their best plan ever. Both of them had survived, though, so it wasn't their worst either.

None of the crimson-garbed soldiers interrupted them now. The Oliezany guards handled the documents, and they were quickly waved on until the watchmen spotted Nex, whose heart shot into their throat.

One of the watchmen approached, but then tipped his hat in greeting. "Good day, sir. Make sure those weapons get to the front lines, you hear? Our brothers will need them."

"I'll do my best," Nex replied with a tug on their own cap.

The rich were treated so much differently. Watchmen met people like Nex with a raised gun, no matter what they were wearing. But pretend you were a well-off businessman, and suddenly they *tipped their hats*?

Assholes.

Nex hid their discontent and focused instead on the Water Reachers on the eastern shore. How they weaved their wisps of magic made it look like an art more than Nex's less refined technique. The Reachers worked as one, sending away a thin section of ice that had formed near the river's center, but a woman further down the coast struggled to keep the same consistency.

That bitch!

Nikoza Bartol wore a high-collared coat as a woman directed her from behind. Reacher light illuminated their luxurious clothes and made Nikoza's silvery-blonde hair almost blinding from a hundred yards away. Probably within range of one of the rifles in the wagons, Nex considered. They could avenge Jax and make her pay for mocking the west side with ruined aid.

But that would be suicide, and Nex needed to make it back to Vinnia and the Ashes of Dawn. Amber was their goal today, not vengeance. Two-for-one would be advantageous, but a tight feeling in their gut told them there was something else going on with Nikoza. Her losing her head would ensure they never found out what.

House Oliezany's barracks awaited them on the far side of the bridge. Dozens of the mercenaries watched there, but it was the same place where the house's guards would switch out with their more established soldiers, then begin the trek east.

Nex needed to make their escape during that exchange before anyone noticed they didn't belong. Their Reach wouldn't last much longer, and they couldn't do it again. The last one already had them feeling sick to their stomach, a heavy dread threatening to fix them to their seat. They'd had no chance to research realms and their Taints. Possibility's had crept up on them more than once, though, and they knew that horrible stasis well.

The exchange happened like organized lightning. Guards saluted and broke off, immediately replaced by soldiers whose mounts carried heavy bags and black powder horns. Any chance to leave went with that speed.

Taint not only slowed Nex, but made the world faster around them. They'd barely shifted one leg over the wagon's edge by the time the whole process was complete. Soon, the wagons would head out of the city and off to the east, and Nex would be trapped with nowhere to go. They needed off this thing now.

So they did something incredibly stupid.

"Spirits, my coat!" they exclaimed, pretending they'd gotten caught in a wheel as they tumbled off the side. The move sent them sprawling into melted snow and the muck beneath. Exactly as they'd hoped.

An officer called for a halt as the carriage driver scrambled to help Nex up. "Is all well, Master Kalinov?"

"Does all look well?" Nex exclaimed, throwing up their arms. "Because you can't drive straight, my clothes are ruined, and I simply cannot continue on like this. Tell the house that they must send someone else in my place!"

It took all their will not to giggle at the driver's stunned expression, but he just held his round-top felt hat over his heart and nodded rapidly. "Yes, yes. Of course, we shall find someone else. Let me ensure you find someplace wa—"

Nex pushed him away and staggered back to their feet. "You've done plenty enough. Leave me be, won't you?"

The soldiers failed to hide their expressions, many of them snickering at the exchange before Nex shot them a glare. Each silenced immediately, and Nex pretended to hobble off like they intended to head home and find a bath to avoid hypothermia. The fall had turned them frigid. Here, though, the wind was calmer with the Reacher towers' protections, so if they could get to Kasia's old townhouse, The Confluence, they would be fine.

Multiple more Oliezany servants tried to rush to Nex's aid as they passed onto the road, heading north. Nex waved them off until there were no more pleading voices. They forced themself not to look back for another minute, confirming the servants and soldiers were just shadows in the lamplight.

"Almost there," they told themself with a slow breath.

Oil was precious, so with the Market District's gas lamps to light the way, they extinguished their lantern and hung it from their belt. A faint smoke lingered. Some claimed to enjoy the stench of oil lanterns, but Nex puffed out their cheeks to stop from vomiting as it met their Taint's nausea.

People went about their days almost like normal here. Many buildings had burned and others showed scorch marks, but those left standing were open for business, just with more private guards than usual. Crimson watchmen patrolled more than the great house mercenaries, though, and plenty of breathless lingered at the peak of the lamplight. Watching.

Why hadn't the Crimson Court sent their spirits to the front if the war was going so badly? Was silencing dissent more important than ensuring they didn't all die? Considering everyone who died became one of those spirits, maybe that was what they wanted…

Nex reached The Confluence a few minutes later and rounded it to the back. They didn't have a key, but to get out undetected hundred-hours before, they'd leaped from the second floor's balcony. That meant they could get back in the same way, and the lack of light at the townhouse's rear provided them plenty of cover. It also made it incredibly difficult to identify handholds.

Possibility Reaching would've made the climb a lot easier, but accepting more Taint wasn't something any Reacher did lightly. The initial sluggishness had faltered. Still, Taint had begun to build up in Nex already, and they did not want to be stuck like some statue as the world sped past them.

They hauled themself up the brick exterior one step at a time. Buildings with worse craftsmanship were easier due to inconsistencies, but The Confluence suffered none of that. So Nex threw their gloves into their bag and gripped the seams until their fingers screamed.

Relief filled them when they grabbed hold of the balcony's bannisters. If it had been on the third floor, they doubted whether their Taint-sickened body would've made it, and their shoulders ached by the time they leaped over the ledge. Blood trickled from their fingers, but they weren't concerned about leaving a trace. The Crimsons had probably already looted the place for evidence about Death's Daughter.

But Kasia had been practically dripping with amber. Either a stash of it or some amber-trimmed clothes had to be around somewhere. The Crimsons must've had higher priorities than searching through the belongings of a scion who was probably dead.

The balcony door was unlocked, so Nex re-lit their lamp and headed down the hall to the study.

Well-furnished with high-backed chairs, sofas lined with velvet, and enough books to make the place reek of paper, this hardly looked like the home of a fallen house. Nor did it appear to have been ransacked at all. Besides some papers strewn about on the desk, the place was as tidy as any other time Nex had been in it.

They half-considered finding a way to move the Ashes of Dawn in. There was plenty more space here than the warehouse basements they were hiding in now, but that many people would draw attention. Not considering the difficulty getting them across the river.

Nex threw away those thoughts and searched the papers on the desk for any hint of an amber warehouse in the city or anything else that might be useful. Nothing there was, so they tore open drawers and threw anything that looked promising into a pile. It made a racket, but no one was around to hear it. Better to move quick in case someone saw the light inside and got curious.

This would've been much easier if Nex had been more than street literate. Most of the papers meant nothing to them, forcing them to focus on ones that had addresses on them. A list of Niezik assets in Kalastok was a start.

A *thud* came from downstairs, followed by footsteps.

Nex cursed, grabbing the most useful papers and shoving them haphazardly into their bag. Their bloodied fingers streaked across the ink, but that was the least of their concerns. Someone was climbing the stairs, and they would clearly see Nex if they left the study.

Another stairwell spiraled up from the study, though, heading into the darkness beyond their lantern. They had no idea where it went, but that didn't matter. It was an escape.

They extinguished the lantern as they bounded up the stairs, stumbling at the top and falling into some weird fabric on the curved wall. On their way up, they'd spotted the circular gap in the floor on this level. It allowed them to look down into the study, where lanternlight crept into the room.

A feminine figure in heavy robes walked to the room's center. Nex tried to crane their head to see the person's face, but some kind of bird mask covered it. They found themself holding their breath. Goosebumps ran up their arms, the air holding an unnatural chill beyond even that of the everdark, and it only grew worse when the figure tilted her head to stare straight at Nex.

"Come down, Nex, and let us speak about your Ashes of Dawn."

RAVEN'S BLIGHT

"It is fitting that the Amber Dame has taken the raven as House Niezik's new sigil. After all, a flock of them is referred to as an 'unkindness'." – Qaraza Uziokaki the Second, matriarch of House Uziokaki

Snow fell in fluffy chunks the day after Kasia's meeting with Paxalia and the rest of Aliax's family. It was a gentle, almost joyous precipitation that heralded that dawnrise was near, but joy was nowhere to be found among the ball of emotions strangling her chest.

Her hand trembled as she plucked a cigar from her father's old box and lit it with a match. The smoke made her cough when she took a puff, but she returned quickly for another. Of the Reshkan variety, this cigar was popular for its light hallucinogenic effects. Smoking it was probably irresponsible when she was set to leave with Zinarus for Vamiustok in the morning. But she saw the dead already, so what could hallucinations do to hurt her?

"A lot," Aliax replied, settling alongside her on one of the stone half-walls surrounding her mansion's garden beds. Nothing was in bloom, but neither was her mood. "Visions don't go well with in-sanity."

Kasia eyed him. The conversation with his family had not gone as poorly as she expected, mostly consisting of her apologizing, them yelling at her, and then Zinarus handing over the documents which sealed them as part owners of her amber mines. She had left immediately afterward to not pressure them into thanking her, but their sobbing haunted her wake.

With that memory stuck in her head, she decided she had seen enough of Aliax's family this hundred-hour, so she stood and paced through the gardens. She breathed heavily of her cigar smoke as she went. Anything was better than the constant reminder of her failures.

Specters awaited her around every corner, though, turning the gardens into a maze of undead. Those, she could flee, but her Tainted voice joined them.

"We will never break free from this torment unless we seek our vengeance," it said in her mind. *"While Chatik rules on the throne, we rely on honorable fools and common lowborn! Teleport to him and strike when he is unprepared. Turn his allies against him."*

"He will see me coming," she replied, stopping beneath an oak and leaning against it. "The Unity Crystal allowed him to heal from even a Death Bolt. What could I possibly do to him that's worse than that?"

Her head throbbed, so she covered her eyes with a hand. The lanterns hanging from the trees and wire lines strung between the beds gave the gardens an elegant aura. By the Mother, though, they sent dots through her vision.

"Exactly what he did to you," the Taint said. *"Destroy all he holds dear."*

The idea inspired Kasia, but she had realized in recent days that she knew far less about Chatik than he knew about her. Besides that he had an eldest son and two younger daughters with Lilita Pikezik the Third, she did not know whom he loved or whom she'd even be able to threaten. Most of the Crimsons would be expendable to a man like him. Were some not? Tzena, perhaps? Or the magnates whom he had formed alliances with?

Her Taint offered no reply.

For days, she had wanted that voice gone, but she found herself missing it as she took another puff. The cigar tasted horrid. It wasn't like she had much to compare it to, but if this passed as a high-class smoke, why did anyone bother with the cheap stuff?

No specters lingered when she opened her eyes and tilted her head back against the tree's trunk. Snow fell over her ashen hair, tied in an up-do with strands dangling over her ears. She probably should've worn a hat and a coat heavier than her belted one of Reshkan inspirations. Those southerners enjoyed displaying their collarbones, so it cut downward instead of protecting the neck like high-collared Ezmani designs. But it fit loosely, and on a day when Realm Taint and guilt threatened to strangle her, the last thing she wanted was a coat to do the same.

The snow burned cold against her skin. Except it no longer appeared as snow, but flaking embers which drifted through the haze. They caught against her clothes, forcing her to bat them away as it grew heavier and heavier. Smoke choked her. Her scarred forearm seared.

She rushed away from the tree with her arms protecting her face. Without destination or view of what lay ahead of her, she burst through the smoke, stumbling over bushes and garden bed walls. But the embers followed. They carried Gregorzon's mocking tone, and she found no relief when she sought the mansion's protection.

Her coat burned as she stumbled through the front doors. Though the embers no longer fell, smoke filled the halls. It stung her eyes and sent tears streaming down her cheeks as her mother's voice called out for her.

"You have ruined everything!" Yazia screeched from down the hall.

Kasia rushed after it. "Mother?"

Yazia had screamed often during her time of infirmity, but this was different, visceral. It held a life that she had lacked in recent years, growing ever louder as Kasia threw open every door on her way. The rooms beyond were distorted from the ones she knew. Overly large furniture filled one as vines of vibrant hues crept over the walls of another. This had to be a dream or hallucination, but it was all too real.

She found Yazia in a sitting room far from where it should have been. Free from the haze, it resembled the aging arrangement it had held years before Kasia secured her house's amber. A fire roared in the hearth, amplifying the fury in Yazia's eyes.

"Mother?" Kasia asked, batting away the last of her own flames. "What is wrong?"

Yazia scoffed and threw out an arm. "Do not ask if you are ignorant of your murders, girl! What were you thinking, testing Death Reaching with that lowborn scum?"

"Aliax was not scum."

"It matters little, now that he is a mere corpse, empty of life and spirit alike." Yazia advanced, snatching Kasia's wrist and throwing off her left glove to reveal her missing index finger. A stub marked where her talon had once been, but her mother acted as if nothing had changed. "If I had my way, I would slice off this spiritdamned talon and bury it as penance for our house's sins. What else could excuse a dozen murders?"

Kasia tried to pull away, but Yazia's grip tightened. "It was an accident!" Kasia pled, the words pouring unbidden from her. "They threatened me."

"Foolish child!" Yazia smacked her with a backhand, sending her reeling. "You have led us into ruin, and now you stain our name with the mark of death. A thousand people shall threaten you in your little matriarchal life, Katarzyna. Will you kill them all?"

"If they intend to kill me first, then yes."

Grabbing her again, Yazia dragged her toward the fire and forced her to stare into the flames. "Your brother wields fire, yet *he* can control his fury. Why must you be insolent just because you favored your father over me?"

Kasia bared her teeth. "He elevated us among the great houses and helped run the entire Commonwealth, yet it was him who cared for me, taught me. Where were you when he died? Asleep in a separate bed chamber! You never loved him, and you never loved me!"

"Katarzyna…"

"Do not call me that!" Kasia spun away from her grasp, her exposed left hand extended. The fire's heat burned through her thoughts until only hatred remained. This woman was not her mother, but an old crone who'd rather let her daughter die than teach her how to Reach safely.

Purple flickered at the edge of her vision. Tendrils of it rose from her every breath, pooling in her hand as Yazia staggered back.

"What are you doing?" her mother spat. "I protected you from the masses! No one whispers about your murders because I covered the evidence and bribed those who spoke against you. Your power is horrid, but you are my daughter!"

Kasia lunged forward and grabbed her arm, the wisps of purple surrounding them both now. "Liar! You have always hated me, blaming me for Father's death. Gregorzon has always been your favorite, and I'm sure you would love for him to take my place at the house's head."

Only a choked reply came, Yazia's eyes widening as the purple plunged into her skin at the forearm. Decay consumed it. Like a flood, Death's power swept through her veins until the door flung open.

"Stop this!" Gregorzon shouted amid the hall's swirling haze, the embers setting his silver hair ablaze as an inferno enveloped his taloned hand.

Kasia had no chance to appeal. The flames surged from his hand and the hearth, forcing her to release Yazia and throw up her arms in defense. Blinding light flashed behind her closed eyes, and agony rushed across her left forearm.

She screamed, collapsing to the floor as Gregorzon rushed their mother from the room. Of course he did. They both despised Kasia like they had Leonit, and now they would leave her to suffer alone.

A force struck her chest. Frost suddenly replaced flames, and Kasia spat out the taste of snow filling her mouth.

What in the wastes just happened?

She shivered and raised her head to see that she lay face down in the snow. Twigs and old, cracked seeds covered her, brambles stabbing her every time she tried to move. Something else, though, kept pricking at her ear.

Slowly, she worked her way up to her knees. A flapping answered along with a loud series of *gwah, gwah* noises.

A black bird dropped to the ground, its head cocked. Feathers the color of rich amber puffed up across its chest as it repeated the noise louder and hopped around her, apparently offended at her lack of response.

"I haven't seen one of you outside Raviak Forest," she said extending a finger toward it, but pulled back when the raven pecked at it.

Amber-throated ravens like this one had practically led the way to the place where Kasia's scouts first discovered reserves of amber within the forest. On the border of Uziokaki territory, she had earned her title of the Amber Dame by dueling Razamat Uziokaki and refusing to surrender, despite being shot multiple times. Those ravens had inspired her to take them as House Niezik's new sigil. Sadly, none had followed her from Raviak Forest.

Until now.

The raven hopped closer and pecked at her coat's amber cufflink. When it failed to pull the gem free, it repeated its frustration and clicked until she chuckled.

"Do you know who you're threatening?" she asked it, remembering her mother's words in the hallucination. Or at least, that's what she thought it had been. The exchange too closely matched Gregorzon's description of how she'd received her burn to be mere imagination, though, and she much preferred the raven's distraction to confronting what that meant.

Ignoring her question, the raven hopped to her other cuff and tried that one instead. It was dark in what she assumed was a garden bed she must have stumbled into, but the shift revealed the mangled state of the bird's left wing.

"What happened to you?" she pondered without any real reply.

The scouts during the amber expedition had claimed ravens were intelligent and cunning, but this one appeared like a determined brute, trying at that cuff until it gave a resigned *click*.

"Fine, you can have it."

The raven hopped back at her move to remove the cufflink. She rolled her eyes, but continued, setting the amber piece wrapped in metal before the raven as if it were some gift to a king. Apparently, the raven approved, because it skittered forward and plucked the amber piece into its beak. It was small for a raven, likely juvenile based on her limited knowledge of them.

She expected it to leave immediately with its prize, but it instead hopped around one of the nearest bushes before returning. It stared at her with eyes of a dull violet and ruffled its one good wing.

"You cannot fly, can you?"

It replied in its odd, off-beat *caw*-ing, then took a few hops away. Once again, though, it didn't flee, and instead shook its tail feather as it hopped once more. Did it want her to follow?

Pain ran up her scarred arm each time she closed her eyes or dared to look away from the raven. This was a ridiculous waste of time when she should have been preparing for their trip to Vamiustok, but she feared the specters and memories that waited outside this garden bed. For a few precious moments, this was her escape. She intended to hold onto it.

So she rose into a crouch, trying not to frighten the raven, and stepped toward it. It made a few clicking noises and then scurried off into the shadows. She cursed. In one movement, she had managed to lose track of it already, but as she considered leaving the garden before anyone saw her acting like a fool, the raven emerged with a half-decayed mouse in its beak. It darted to Kasia and deposited the carcass at her feet, then made its strange *gwah* sound.

She smirked. Was this a gift of some kind? "Thank you, I guess..."

The carcass smelled horrid, so she pivoted around it, toward the bush the raven had first disappeared behind. It had wanted her amber. Did it hoard other trinkets here? Since the raven made no move to protect the bush, she kept going until a small arrangement of objects appeared beneath the brambles.

"You're quite the little thief," she said, catching sight of at least one House Niezik pin—likely a guard's—along with a smattering of amber beads and a single kena bill trapped under the heavier objects.

"Gwah!" the raven exclaimed as it hopped over to the

arrangement and pecked at one of the twigs beneath the trinkets. A failed nest, perhaps?

"A better thief than a builder, then." Just like her. After experiencing a memory so ugly that she'd forgotten it, the hole in her chest felt a little smaller near the bird. She crept closer and poked at the sticks, receiving a cocked head in response. "You're not going to survive long without wings or a real nest."

I'm going to regret this.

She plucked off her other cufflink and offered it to the raven, holding out her arm so that it could leap upon it. "You can have all the amber bits you want if you come with me. People have a knack of falling dead around me, but you aren't a person, so you will probably be safe."

Her left glove was gone, probably lost somewhere in her smoke-induced hallucination, and the raven picked at the Axiom Crystal upon it before grabbing the amber in its beak. She pulled back her sleeve in hopes of luring it further with the Axiom crystal. The little bastard had another idea.

Sharp pain forced her to recoil as its beak grabbed hold of her stubbed index finger. The jolt spooked it, and it hopped free, running its beak over its damaged wing. Then it hopped closer again.

"Don't do that," Kasia muttered. "I gave you amber, remember?"

. The raven lifted its head, as if proudly displaying that very fact. When she held out her hand for it again, it hurried onto her forearm. Slowly, she closed her fist to prevent it from attacking. It showed no reaction, so she stood and finally left the isolated world of the garden bed.

Zinarus awaited her.

"Kasia?" The purple lord looked at her like she were an awakened. He wore a much heavier coat lined with furs over Leonit's borrowed clothes, his pants barely reaching the middle of his calves. "The guards told me to look for you in the gardens, and I was worried when I heard rustling in the bushes. By the Mother below, is that a raven?"

Her cheeks burned as she hastened a glance at her clothes. Soaked, covered in dirt, and misaligned enough to expose her entire shoulder instead of just the collarbone—not what the Reshkan designers had intended.

"I had gone for a walk to clear my mind when this raven approached me, asking for my cufflinks. It was injured, and when I gave it one of them, it hopped over to its nest to show me."

"Likely a female then," he noted, rubbing his chin. It was unusually stubbled. "Amber-throated ones are quite rare, I hear."

She scoffed. "I'm standing like a snow-covered fool in a garden bed, and you are worried about the bird's sex?"

"Believe me, I already worry about you too much." His eyes widened. "Not your se… err… never mind that. Our butler in Vamiustok has a bit of a birding obsession, so I endured many a story about them. He would have been jealous of you holding such a unique one." He smiled at the creature, but it couldn't hide how his bright cheeks now matched the few strands of auburn hair tucking out from beneath his cap. "Do you intend to keep her?"

"I honestly had not thought that far ahead," she replied, letting him get away with his verbal slip. The raven, meanwhile, appeared perfectly content to stare at Zinarus's mechanical leg from her arm. "Bringing an injured bird to war is not the best idea, I imagine."

He shrugged and pulled a quarter-kena coin from his pocket. The raven clicked away at the sight of it, and he chuckled as it… *she*… shifted the amber cufflink in her beak, then took the coin. "Keloshan commanders are known to bring hounds with them, so I see little reason you could not bring a bird, should you so choose. It would require far fewer rations than most other pets. Besides, our butler could examine it. He is no Reacher, but perhaps he can decide whether the wing will repair itself in time."

"For a jouster and a politician who claims honor and justice above all else," she mused, "you so often wear your spirit upon your sleeve."

"It is better to remind ourselves in dire times like these that we are more than mere husks, lost and empty."

Her shoulders sagged. "Emptiness would allow me to forget all I've done."

"Forgetting even our worst actions would mean changing who we have grown to become." With a gentle smile, he touched her free hand with the back of his. "For all your flaws, I am proud to know the woman you are now. I fear the girl who fled her sins would not have surrendered a significant portion of her wealth to Aliax's family." He reached into his coat's pocket and plucked out an extinguished cigar, soaked with snow. "I would, however, recommend not engaging with Reshkan mindsap."

"What are you talking about?" She snatched the cigar and held it between them. "This was my father's. It's a Reshkan cigar, but nothing as strong as mindsap."

He ran his thumb across the palm of his hand. "Is that why you were stumbling through the garden beds, shouting at what sounded like your mother?"

"Fuck off," she snapped, her patience gone in an instant.

Without another look at him, she climbed over the bed's half-wall and headed toward the mansion, her whole body burning despite the cold. The conversation had been going so well. Why had he been so intent on ruining it with accusations?

And why did he have to be right?

Her fury drove her straight into the study for reasons she couldn't explain. The raven didn't leave, so she set it down on the haataamaash game table by the fireplace while she settled on the chair her father had always taken. Lately, she found herself stuck in his positions far more than her own. Trapped between factions as secrets abounded—even his. She still had his empty purple book stuffed in her back, its lock bearing the old Piorakan word for *seek*, but was no closer to uncovering why it had been so important to him.

"What would you do, Father?" she asked as the raven pecked at the board's red spy. "Should I strike straight at Chatik's heart, or work with this rebellious Confederation of Harizak?"

Leonit would have found alliances, both public and secret. He'd always known when to plunge the dagger into a rival's back—likely how he'd risen to become the minister of glass in the first place—but also when to conspire with others. Kasia had spent too much time as a lone hunter. But as her father had always said, even wolves hunt in packs.

She eyed the raven. "My scouts say you're intelligent."

Taking the spy piece, she held it before the raven's beak. The bird deposited its amber and coin before accepting the spy as an offering. Though not Kasia's intent, she chuckled and let it happen, daring to stroke the raven's head. It accepted, and that only drew her smile wider against the faint pain still haunting her arm. The truth was a problem for another day. Like her little raven insisted, she needed to play the spy's game, and a spy knew when to twist the truth to their will.

"You're smart enough to pick your own name, then," she told the raven, stroking down its puffed neck of amber. "You shall be Spitza, the one who whispers."

THE PROFESSOR'S PERIL

"The only greater threat than rebellion to a ruler is knowledge," – Etal iz Noshok, professor of forces and spirits at Kalastok College

Nex froze as they gawked down at the masked woman in The Confluence's study below. Kasia had mentioned some strange group called the Children of Zekiaz who wore masks like this, but how had this woman known Nex was here? Was she following them?

A quick glance around the dark upper room revealed no obvious escape, so they conceded and headed down the spiral staircase. But concession didn't mean surrender. They gripped the glass dagger in their coat pocket, wishing they'd risked sneaking a pistol through the Oliezany checkpoint.

"Wise choice," the woman said as she watched Nex's descent. "We see much potential in you, and I would have hated to end your life before you fulfilled it."

Veiled threats meant a scion, likely a Reacher too. Without knowing what kind, though, Nex couldn't anticipate her actions as they stopped at the bottom step. "What do you want?"

"Cooperation." The woman swept her hand toward the two

opposing sofas to the room's side. "Let us sit instead of glaring each other down like carnivores."

"Carni-what?"

The woman laughed, covering her mouth, but her lanternlight revealed her teeth weren't chipped or badly stained. *Definitely* a scion. She took a seat on the furthest sofa and crossed her legs. "My hands are gloved, Nex, and as such, I pose no danger to you. If anything, that crystal ring of yours is far more of a threat."

Nex curled their lip. "How'd you find me? How do you know about the Ashes of Dawn?"

"We have taken great interest in you and your partnership with Lady Katarzyna Niezik. Many secrets exist among the lowborn west of the river, and like those whispers dancing through the halls of the Crystal Palace, well placed keni can turn those embers to wildfires."

"The fuck are you talking about?" Nex rounded the room until the scion's back was to them. They only needed a few more strides to get to the door, and that would give them time to flee before the woman could Reach. "I'm just trying to get amber to protect suffering people. If you're one of those Children of Zekiaz Kasia talked about, do you know where she hid it?"

The woman finally stood, accepting that Nex wouldn't join her. "Indeed, I am a daughter among the Children, and there is much we may offer you, should you remain cordial."

Nex crossed their arms. "You want a trade? Fine. Stop wasting my time and tell me what you want."

"Direct, efficient. Such an approach is why the Children have sent me to you with this offer." She clasped her hands behind her and raised her chin in that annoying way scions always did before they manipulated you. Nex had seen it a thousand times, and it made them sneer. "You know of Professor Etal iz Noshok and his cure for the Spirit Plague, do you not?"

"Yeah. What about him?"

The daughter sighed. "Though not a member of our organization, he is a great asset to us. The Crimson Court has captured both him and the alchemist, Paras ik Lierasa. They killed the latter in secret, as the people already believed him dead after Lady Katarzyna's deception, and they are planning Professor iz Noshok's public execution in two days' time. It is our belief that they intend to blame him for the Spirit Plague and decry his cure as a falsity."

A smirk replaced Nex's sneer. "You want the Ashes of Dawn to free him—that's spiritdamned risky. What do we get in return?" Sure, they already wanted to free him, but this scion didn't need to know that.

"We do not wish for you to free him from the palace dungeons," the daughter said, her tone turning amused. "Instead, you shall interrupt the execution itself in the northern market. We wish for you to make it a vibrant display of resistance, after which we shall use Etal's knowledge to flood the Commonwealth with cures for the plague. Without him, however, we do not have access to the cure's formula, and the plague will only continue to spread and grow the Crimson Court's breathless army."

"I'm still not hearing what I get in return."

The daughter advanced, lips drawn to a narrow line. "You shall have all the amber and glass your rebels need, along with the cure to protect your people and all others who endure the Spirit Plague. Should you agree to one additional task, an up-front payment will be delivered to your hidden warehouses this very eve. Clean food and water will be among the supplies, and I am certain you will find us far more agreeable than the greedy gangs."

Nex rocked back. This was the kind of offer that was too good to be true, but they were tempted anyway. Even with the gangs' help, food was scarce, and Nex owed them both amber and the cure. Failing that would probably mean the end of the Ashes of Dawn and their own life. Not that freeing the professor from under the noses of a bunch of Reachers would be easy.

"We'll rescue Etal," they replied after a few moments. "But I need the exact time and anything you know about the Crimsons' guards."

The daughter nodded slowly. "You shall have it."

"Then what's this extra task?"

Stepping forward again, the daughter practically pinned Nex

against the far bookshelf, a grin flicking across her lips. She raised her gloved left hand. "I wish to examine your spirit."

Nex drew their blade and jabbed its point between her ribs. "What game are you playing, scion?"

"None of this is a game," the daughter whispered. "The Children of Zekiaz seek what is best for all who reside in our realm, and we carry this responsibility with great reverence."

"What's that have to do with my spirit?"

She gave a knowing smile. "Most spirits have lived many lives, forgetting their pasts when they become drifters, yet elements of their wills follow them into us. As a Spirit Seer, I seek to understand how our pasts connect us to the fate of the realms." With a single finger, she guided away Nex's dagger. "Your aura speaks of one whose spirit found them not long after the spirit's previous life ended. Such a thing is rare."

Nex suddenly felt as if they were being prodded like a butcher examining a cow. What did that even mean, that their spirit had found them quickly? "It won't hurt, right?"

"You shall feel no pain." The daughter advanced again. "Allow me to do this for but a moment, and you shall have your aid."

"Fine," Nex muttered, slamming shut their eyes. "Do it."

A warmth washed over them as the daughter laid her hand on their chest, but she didn't remove her glove. Nothing else followed except for an uncomfortable silence, so Nex cracked an eye. Gray wisps swarmed them in greater numbers than they'd ever seen from a Spirit Reacher. A strange glow rose from the daughter's collar, but compared to the silver consuming the daughter's entire eyes, it was almost dull.

Then it was over. The daughter stepped back, the light vanishing as her eyes returned to normal. Her absence left a frigid hold on Nex's core that stole their breath, and they raised a hand to their racing heart.

"What did you see?" they asked.

"You knowing the result was not part of our deal," she replied without a readable expression beneath the mask. "Focus your mind upon rescuing Professor iz Noshok, and when you return to your safe house, you will find I am true to my word."

Nex shook their head, but relented once again. "Fine. Just give me the details quickly. I don't have 'til dawnrise."

GLASS BRACERS OF THE CRYSTAL BRIGADE COVERED Nikoza's elaborate coat's sleeves as she channeled her Water Reaching from the bank of the Kala River. Under Tzena Oliezany's tutelage, she had improved with each day, but the other Water and Fire Reachers kept back the Kala's ice with far more efficiency. They resembled skilled weavers while she was too busy getting tangled in the threads.

"Your instincts are consistent," Tzena noted from beside her in a tight-fitting coat, "and you are managing to temper how quickly you expend a Reach. You are, however, failing to maintain focus on your intent."

"I want to send away the ice and turn it to water," Nikoza replied, a cold sweat dripping from her brow. Though Tzena had been careful not to Taint her further, her mouth remained dry, and that sweat felt as if she were losing precious water amid a desert.

Tzena adjusted her elbow. "That is too vague. Focus your intent, and you focus your power. *How* do you intend to banish the ice?"

"My aim is to energize its elements so that it may shift from solid to liquid."

"Precisely. The Fire Reachers must do so indirectly," Tzena said with a wave in the direction of the flaming tendrils which danced over the river. Most of the ice was gone by now… except in front of Nikoza. "You command the power of the Water realm, so you must change water itself, not what is around it. Use the rest of your Reach to do so."

Nikoza drew back her shoulders and took a long breath, slowly raising her hands. A few deep blue wisps danced at her fingertips in wait of her command, but she looked to the ice beyond them.

Energize and shift to water, she told that chunk of ice over and over in her mind.

Then she threw out her arms and plunged her will into her magic. She held her breath as the wisps shot toward the ice with more vigor than they had shown at any time during their sessions so far. That was a good sign, and she clung to that hope as the ice melted.

"I did it," she whispered to herself, but her Reach was not finished.

Instead of merely melting, the water began to bubble around the last bits of ice. She tried to command it to stop, but she couldn't without Reaching again and risking Taint. So she just held a hand over her mouth, gasping as the ice disappeared into a haze of water vapor.

Tzena chuckled to herself. "Though you were perhaps a little over-ambitious, you completed the task. That is enough for today, but I believe the king requires you for the Chamber meeting."

"Of course," Nikoza said, stiffening.

Chatik had told her of his plan to invite young bachelors to join her in the Crystal Brigade, and the thought of them being potential suitors was a distraction from her efforts. She already had plenty to handle between her training, dealing with the Chamber, and planning how the Crystal Brigade might aid the less fortunate. How was she to find a spouse amid it all?

Tzena went her own way as Nikoza returned to her carriage. Out of the corner of her eye, she caught a convoy from the Industrial District waiting near the Oliezany barracks. Such shipments were bound for the front and usually departed quickly, but this one lingered as mercenaries argued with a man who Nikoza recognized from the distant cousins of the Oliezany family. She worried about Chatik's focus on the war more than his people. Her work would not matter, though, if Kalastok fell to a foreign empire.

Gas lamps lined the streets as her carriage wound its way toward the Crystal Palace. Snow fell heavily in the little light across the river, but here, it resembled little more than a few stray willow catkins during dawnrise's bloom.

Tonight, the Chamber of Scions would vote on her proposal to extend the Reacher towers' protections to the western city. It was her first proposal, but surely not her last. Chatik had assured her that it would pass, but that was not the issue that had her bouncing her foot. As he was a scion, Etal iz Noshok's execution required approval by the Chamber. Her muddled memories of helping Etal had her doubting what was true. She trusted Chatik, though, and he said this was necessary.

Members of the Chamber gave her curious looks as she passed into the palace's main hall and touched the silver stone at the foot of the Crystal Mother's statue. Pressing her fingers to her lips afterward, she whispered a prayer.

"Guide us toward your will. Let us find peace and solutions for all which ails us."

She had buried dozens of similar prayers in the aftermath of the Crimson Court's ascendancy. Her uncle had calmed her nerves, but the deeper she pressed into the depths of Kalastok's new elites, it felt as if a serpent constricted ever tighter around her heart. Instinct was a primal base that Jazuk had taught her to ignore. Still, she could not help but wonder if something was missing inside her.

When she continued toward the Chamber itself, she became acutely aware of the fact she was wearing Crystal Brigade bracers still. Her fine clothes were an armor of their own, but her glass bracers gave her authority.

She held her chin high as she took her seat among the scion representatives. Where there had once been opposing factions, none had spoken against the Crimson King's propositions since the riots. It was unity that Nikoza had never seen in the Chamber, but she could not ignore that three magnates were no longer in Kalastok: Borys Kuzon the Sixth, Ivalat iz Ardinvil the Second, and Chatik's own wife, Lilita Pikezik the Third.

"It is a pleasure to see you, Lady Nikoza," Otterzik Oliezany the Ninth said from near the front of the seats, tearing her from her thoughts. "Will you not join me for the vote?"

Nikoza smiled sweetly. The new Oliezany patriarch matched Gornioz's height, but had a portly build that cushioned his square face. With short gray hair, he held a classic appearance that mirrored his coat, its collar popped enough to skim his trimmed beard.

"Of course, Lord Otterzik," she replied, curtsying.

From her seat beside the Oliezany patriarch, she surveyed the Chamber and its members. The pit down to the Spirit Chamber encircled the throne before them, only broken by a narrow passage to the throne's platform. At its center, Chatik traced the throne's golden edge as he conversed with his three most trusted council members: Tzena, Qaraza Uziokaki, and Uzrin Ioniz. Breathless spirits guarded them from above.

"Your uncle is a fascinating man," Otterzik said as he crossed his legs. "It must be strange for you to one day be the heir of House Bartol, and the next for him to take it."

"My uncle has always been a Bartol by blood," she said, smothering a stray irritation. Was it because he questioned Chatik's intentions, or because he was right? "After King Jazuk's unwillingness to complete the Inheritance Ritual, it is right for Chatik to lead both our nation and our house. I am resigned to my new purpose."

Otterzik gave the slightest smile. "Is that why he treats you like his daughter, then? Why he appoints you as a nearly untrained Reacher to a sergeant within the Crystal Brigade? Come now, Nikoza. He shows you favor, and you best make use of it before he is replaced by a king who does not share your blood."

Nikoza stiffened as Tzena whispered something in Chatik's ear, followed by his gaze flicking to his niece. It was unreadable, and she wondered whether he was proud of her progress.

"Our king's loyalty is to the Commonwealth," Nikoza whispered to Otterzik as Chatik called the Chamber to order. "As is my own. Divided houses will only pull our nation deeper into disunity."

No reply came, so Nikoza turned her attention to the Chamber's duties. Formalities passed slowly, but she showed no boredom, reminding herself that those traditions kept the nation from crumbling completely. Still, she was grateful when Chatik's council stepped into their reports on the situation internally and on the warfront.

Uzrin Ioniz, minister of national unity, stepped onto the pathway before the throne. With his gray hair slicked back and his stubborn nose bent, he resembled an unusual mix of politician and soldier.

House Ioniz was not among the great ones, but they had the heavily grayed skin of elite scions and aspired constantly to earn a glass room to complete the Inheritance Ritual. Uzrin's extramarital affairs with Lady Sania iz Vamiustok surely had not helped matters.

"You have of course seen the success of the breathless in ensuring we do not repeat the problems of our earlier conscription efforts," he said. "Resistance has remained minimal among the lowborn within Kalastok and beyond, but we must continue to show that the Crimson Court is beneficial for all of Ezman. For this, we have appointed Lady Nikoza Bartol and many other promising young Reachers to the Crystal Brigade. Sergeant Nikoza shall guide this once secretive force's efforts to instead bring relief."

Nikoza swallowed at the realization that all two hundred representatives were watching her. It was one thing to stand behind Jazuk as he confronted the Chamber. Now, she wasn't the innocent princess, but the Crimsons' favored prospect. She was only eighteen, and she felt their skepticism like a great weight upon her shoulders.

Yet none contested her appointment.

Under Jazuk's reign, the Chamber had descended into contention on every issue, but there was only silence now. It gave her an eerie feeling. Was that fear in their gazes, or focus on the greater issues the Commonwealth faced?

"I will do all I can," she finally told both Uzrin and all the Chamber. "Let the Crystal Brigade represent our desire to protect all our people, no matter their birth."

A few grumbles came from nearby, but a wave from Chatik silenced them. Uzrin waited for the prime minister to step back before continuing, "And that desire we shall uphold. The lowborn are the backbone of our production in the factories, fueled by Fire, Earth, Body, and Air Reachers to ensure they are more productive than ever. That production shall ensure we win this war and show Tiuz Hazeko's rebels that they must join us, not defy us."

Uzrin cleared his throat and fixed his posture, but he couldn't fake formality. His shoulders were too far back, his chin caught-halfway between clean-shaven and intentionally stubbled—a man out of place, holding the Chamber's attention against his will.

"That work begins tonight with her first proposal." Once again, he nodded to Nikoza. "My lady, would you care to explain?"

She rose with her hands clasped before her. *You can do this. Speak just as you heard the representatives do a hundred times.*

"Ladies and Gentlemen of the Chamber of Scions," she said, her voice beginning with a squeak before falling into a more confident rhythm. "I am honored to address you this evening with my first proposal, both as a representative from House Bartol's lands around Anukit and as a sergeant of the Crystal Brigade." She paused, drawing a sharp breath. "During my attempt to bring aid to those west of the Kala River, I saw their desperation and fear. They have endured the Spirit Plague more than any of us, and they still face attacks from awakened and gangs, both who prey upon the vulnerable. I seek to change this through the construction of Reacher towers within the Industrial District and Shadow Quarter. Though we must maintain the sequestration of the west side for security and health purposes, let us ensure they are not without protection during this difficult period."

The intent of the words was her own, but as she sat, trading nods with Chatik, a bitter taste filled her mouth. She wanted to attribute it to the dehydration of her Taint. Her gut, though, screamed that she needed to look deeper.

There was no such time, as Chatik called for a vote. Not a single voice rose in defiance. Nikoza chose to hold that as a point of pride, believing that she would bring some relief to the suffering of the west side. Maybe she could even find Nex and work with them to organize where the Reachers were needed most.

Uzrin soon finished his report and ceded the space before the throne to Qaraza Uziokaki the Second, minister of war and rural affairs. She had recently ascended to become matriarch of her house, but she was twice Nikoza's age, holding far more confidence in her eased smile. While Uzrin had looked far out of place, she wore a gown of crimson and black with the elegance of a queen, a ruby ringed in glass gracing her collar.

"We must admit that we face one external war and stand at the brink of an internal one, if our efforts fail," Qaraza said. "Proposals such as Lady Nikoza's will aid with Kalastok's woes, but the vast majority of our populace resides in dispersed villages. They shall hear of the Crimson Court through second-hand knowledge and the lies of traitors. Therefore, while our armies face Kelosh in the east, we are dedicating our breathless spirits and elite forces to confront our internal foes before they organize against us."

She swept her gaze across the representatives, and as Nikoza followed it, she caught sight of an unfamiliar man. Some scions came and went from the Chamber, but she knew nearly all of them. This man was unlike most. Dressed in a knee-length patterned fur coat of rural stylings over a shirt with amber buttons, he held a presence that she had only felt around one person.

Katarzyna Niezik.

Nikoza pursed her lips, drawing a hand back to her chest. Could Katarzyna's brother have come in her absence? Was he an ally or a foe? And could he be a Death Reacher like her?

Those were thoughts for later, so she pulled herself back to Qaraza's report. She had missed a bit of it, but it was clear the situation was far from ideal. Even less ideal was her answer to Nikoza's ponderings about the missing magnates.

"Many of you may wonder about significant members of this Chamber who are no longer among us," Qaraza said, her face growing stern. She spun quickly with her finger waving like a pistol. "Borys Kuzon and Ivalat iz Ardinvil—though he remains in hiding—have announced their treasonous intentions, tearing away much of our western lands. This is why we must act swiftly. *This* is why we must utilize our breathless spirits to finish this petty civil war before it begins."

A chorus of stomping feet met her from throughout the hall. No proposal was needed, but it signaled the scions' approval of the war effort. Nikoza, though, held silent doubts about the breathless being used as weapons. The spirits of the dead were sacred to the Crystal Mother. What would become of Zekiaz's children if all her spirits perished before they found a newborn child?

Chatik's cough interrupted her again. Her uncle lumbered

forward, his eyes sunken and dark, as he stopped at Qaraza's side. He looked as if he had lost significant weight in just the last hundred-hour, and his usually well-fit Bartol suit enveloped him like a heavy blanket.

"I cannot allow Lady Qaraza to ignore my former house's ills," he said with the Air Reachers along the pit's rim carrying his weak voice throughout the room. Pink wisps swirled from his right hand, gripping some sort of stone, but Nikoza found herself unbothered by that as he continued, "My now former wife, the Lady Lilita Pikezik, has suffered a mental break and fled into hiding, taking our children in the process. You would be just in fearing whether this may split my loyalties, but I assure you, my loyalty is to House Bartol, our proud nation of Ezman, and the Crimson Court. Lady Lilita will be apprehended. Justice will and must be done."

Nikoza's jaw nearly dropped, but those pink wisps drifted into her and the other scions. It smothered her shock, swept away her questions. Surely, Chatik had a reason for telling neither her nor the Chamber of this sooner. She had wondered about her aunt's absence in recent days, but many had shuttered themselves in their houses until all was calm again. This, though, was far from what she had expected.

Chatik's Mind Reaching told her it was expected. Her uncle was loyal to his nation, and he would bring his former house into line soon. The children Lilita had taken were Chatik's too; any father would rightly worry for their safety.

Nikoza's head grew light, the room seeming to fade for a few blinks before snapping back to normal. The wisps were gone along with her ponderings. Tzena, not Chatik, stood before the throne with her arms raised. As minister of crime, she touted the number of gang members and rebel leaders the city watch had apprehended with the help of house mercenaries. None of the names she mentioned were Nex, much to Nikoza's relief, but that feeling faded to confusion when Tzena thanked them for supporting the proposal to execute Professor Etal iz Noshok for creating the Spirit Plague and false cures.

When had they voted?

She looked about to see if anyone else was confused, but no one questioned Tzena as Chatik called the assembly to a close. Otterzik noticed her confusion, taking her arm.

"Are you well, my lady? I would say that it looks as if you have seen a spirit, but they are all too common these days."

Patting his gloved hand with a nervous laugh, Nikoza nodded. "Yes, of course. It just felt as if an hour passed in a blink."

He chuckled as he rose. "Wait until you reach my age. Time's passing is a gift, and we should be glad that Reacher magic does not allow us to alter it. I shall not waste more of your time, however, as I am sure you have much to prepare for between Professor iz Noshok's execution and these new Reacher towers west of the Kala. Fascinating times these are." His face grew heavy. "I do wish that my father would be here to guide me through it."

"Lord Gornioz was a fine statesman," Nikoza said, half-telling the truth. The late Oliezany patriarch had been quite successful as an influential politician, but he had been a thorn in her side when it came to swaying Jazuk. "I am sure you shall walk well in his footsteps, especially given the experience of the spirit you bear."

"You humble me." He bowed, then waved her on. "Go, go. I cannot allow myself to draw the ire of our king for making you linger on such grief."

She gave him a parting curtsy and headed up the stairs. Eyes watched her from everywhere, but she found herself focused on the breathless swirling over the Spirit Crystal pit. They would execute the rebels, just as she and the Crystal Brigade would execute Etal. There was so much death, but two fingers held to her lips, she prayed to the holy Mother below that her efforts led to peace in the end.

THE DALNUS QUESTION

"Call not to the spirits unless you yearn to listen to their reply." – Mariana ik Ardinvil, Vockan Whisperer

Smoke stung Radais's nose as he joined Wanusa and Commander Tairanik outside a rounded stone building near the city's southern edge. Whisperers formed a ring around its entirety, holding bowls of smoldering shrubs that made most passersby keep their distance. The Ezmani knew the shrub as climber's bane for its thorns which punished an adventurer's misplaced hand, but among the Vockans, it was the protector of the high places where pure spirits lingered.

"Find peace in the incense of the talilus flower," the female Whisperer said from before them. She wore heavy robes, and threaded mountain stones wound through her red hair like ash through a crackling flame. Though an elder, she stood proud without the slightest sign of weakness. "While its thorns prick those who threaten the mountains, it blesses those who commune with the spirits."

Radais dismounted and bowed his head, spurring Wanusa to do the same. "Thank you for honoring us. I am Supreme Defender Radais ik Erienfar, and this is Warrior Wanusa ik Iliafa. Looks like you've already met Tairanik."

"The talilus smoke is not to honor you, Supreme Defender, but to hide your glass from the pure ones."

Tairanik leaned over from his ibex and whispered, "I told you this Mariana would be trouble. She's even from Ardinvil, but won't recognize the house's command over Dalnus." He turned about. "While you deal with her, Polina and I will find enough beds for our men."

Just the thought of politics made Radais want to find the nearest tavern and camp over a mug of beer until they were ready to leave. He'd brought the Glassblades here to address the attacks with House iz Ardinvil and the other Vockan politicians, but Dalnus was mainly useful as a resupply and information gathering stop on their way through the mountains. The Vanashel obviously knew where the Glassblade forces were. He hoped Dalnus's leaders would help him find the Vanashel in turn, and if the Whisperers could actually tame spirits, he'd take all the help he could get.

Wanusa stepped forward while Radais considered his problem. She removed her helm—taken from a fallen warrior after her own shattered—and placed it on the ground before the Whisperer whom Tairanik had called Mariana. "I will remove all my armor if you wish. To respect both you and the purest spirits, I do not wish to taint your holy place."

Nearby, a squad of iz Ardinvil mercenaries scoffed, but they silenced at a glare from Radais. All had been quiet between the Whisperers and mercenaries when he'd arrived. He doubted it had been so a few minutes before.

"It is not our intention to disrespect your traditions," Radais added, returning his attention to Mariana and taking a step back to appear cordial. He'd not had the chance to retrieve his armor, but his commander's uniform had glass strewn about it.

"Did House iz Ardinvil send you?" Mariana asked with a distrustful glance toward the mercenaries. "They cannot frighten us with musket balls and swords of glass."

Radais crossed his arms. "I am the supreme defender of the Glassblade Order. We do not answer to any house's commands, but the call of Vocka's people. An organization of aggressive spirits called the Vanashel threaten us all, and we are here to find a way to solve it."

"The breathless, yes. We have read the letters." A warmth entered her eyes for the first time, and her shoulders lost their defiance. "Come, let us speak, but you alone may enter."

Wanusa opened her mouth to protest, but Radais silenced her with a raised hand. This was his duty, not hers. He would not have a chance at information ruined because of pride.

"Keep an eye on the mercenaries," he told her instead. "House iz Ardinvil has never closed their fist around the Vockan regional government completely, but with civil war looming, they will seek to pounce here as well."

"Yes, Mast… I mean, Supreme Defender," she stammered, fist held over her heart.

Mariana led him inside with the other Whisperers remaining to protect the entrance. Men and women both, they all wore similar attire, yet he noticed as the smoke dissipated that each robe held unique silver designs across the upper chest and neck. Mariana's had spirals overlapping themselves at random, but the room beyond drew Radais's attention before he could identify any consistent pattern.

A single round room filled the building. Its floor was terraced, rising to points where sculptures depicted strange beings like the forms breathless took. He admired the first of them and considered how long it must have taken to etch each small crevice in its geometric head, human-like hands, and wispy body. Every medium had its merits, but compared to his charcoal sketches, it was hard not to be jealous of the immense skill on display in this room. That feeling faded to sorrow at the realization of how few would ever see them.

"How did your sculptors know what breathless look like?" he asked as he neared the second piece. Depicting a spirit with fangs and sharp quills like the koilee of the Ezmani wilds, it sent a shiver down his spine.

Mariana set down her bowl of talilus incense on a stone pillar at the room's center. Its smoke curled through the still air, but in less concentration, Radais recognized its sweet scent that calmed his nerves. The shaman's look was far less pleasant.

"Your order would have known about the spirits' potentials if you listened to them instead of simply slicing down awakened."

Radais grabbed his sketchbook from his bag and held it out to her. The book included his most intimate sketches, but it also proved his fascination with the spirits beyond killing them. Little did she know, Wanusa was the true student of spirits, and he'd just inherited his recent understanding from her.

"You may look through my sketches if you think we do nothing but swing blades," he said. "I spoke with the first breathless on my expedition and learned about the culture of the Saleshi, a reclusive group of them. They are not the ones we've considered pure, but we don't strike them down as monsters."

Curiosity filled Mariana's gaze. She lowered her head respectfully as she took the sketchbook, understanding the vulnerability he'd offered. Letting it go was difficult enough, so he turned away to examine the statues.

He had no desire to hear the Whisperer's reactions to his sketches. Wanusa had doubtless seen that Lazan had become his muse of late, and the last thing he needed was a shaman using his feelings against him. Miv had made it clear that the supreme defender's personal bonds were a vulnerability for the Order as a whole.

Mariana spent a long time flipping through the sketchbook as Radais examined the other statues. Unlike the rest of the Commonwealth, there wasn't a single shard of glass among them. Each was made of a different base stone, whether marble or quartz, but bore signature touches that implied a single sculptor had created them all. Immense patience would've been required to sculpt even one, and there were seven in total. What was a master artisan doing to lock their work away among Dalnus's Whisperers instead of spreading it across the entire continent of Brakesh?

Eventually, Mariana gently closed his sketchbook and placed her hand over it. She said something quieter than he could hear, then handed it back over. "Your spirit inspires you, Supreme Defender.

Follow its call, or that armor you bear will grow heavy enough to crush your very core."

His brow wrinkled, and though he tried to put the book away, he found himself staring down at it instead. "Desires often don't meet the world's needs."

But she approached and lightly held his arm. "Do not assume that people reveal their needs for all to see. The arts reveal what is deeper within us, sometimes even deeper than what we are ready to accept. You manage to capture that with only charcoal and paper far better than painters who wield every color imaginable."

"Then why hide masterpieces within a room like this?" he asked. "Tens of thousands live in Dalnus. Show them the truth of spirits."

"Says the man who hides his works within a book," Mariana replied, "growing nervous as an old woman examines them."

"That is—"

She released him and turned to the nearest statue, its burnt orange and gray colorations implying it was made from raw ironstone— commonly mined in the Vockan Mountains for Ezmani industry. "There is no reason to worry of my judgment. You desire to defeat the Vanashel spirits, but to do so, you must know what they desire in turn."

Radais considered Bakeekek and Rakekeaa's warnings in the Spirit Wastes. "The Saleshi breathless protected us, and they claimed the Vanashel intended to destroy humans. To them, we are the 'embodied ones.' "

"It is clear they intend to slaughter us freely," she said. "Slaughter is rarely a desire in itself, however. What we must discover is *why* they are so intent on killing us."

"You've listened to them, then?" he asked.

As if reading his skepticism, she shot him a glare. "Do not question methods which originated before the rise of old Piorak millennia ago. Whether drifter, awakened, or breathless, we whisper to the spirits and hear their replies. We have known about the breathless who Reach for years."

"The Saleshi called them Bound Ones."

"Yes, and we tried to tell you Glassblades as such." She shook her head. "Supreme Defender Miv—may her spirit find eternal peace—must have ignored our claims."

Radais winced at the mention of Miv. She was dead in a way, but seeing her rise as the breathless spirit called Ataakanan had given him some relief. Mariana would likely consider it an afront to spirits' purity, however, so he avoided the topic.

"Miv was bitter toward Sheptasa, yes. I won't stain your holy place by repeating her words." He sighed, looking from the statue to Mariana. "What do you know about them that we've yet to discover?"

"In truth, very little," she said, giving a surprisingly joyful smile. "Your willingness to accept that the Glassblades are not the only source of wisdom on the spirits, though, is reassuring. What we have heard from your encounter with these Saleshi is far more than we have learned about breathless, but our learnings cover different topics. Spirits calmed by our songs often reveal aspects of their past lives and limited insights into their current existences. Pure spirits seem to desire Spirit Crystal."

Radais nodded. "The Saleshi confirmed that. Instead of food and water, they need the power of the Spirit Crystal, and the more evolved spirits need more than drifters."

"A cycle of life, breathed through by the very spirit at our world's core." She traced one of the spirals on her robes. "Only when the spirits spoke of complex, present desires did we realize the breathless existed at all. Awakened have life's vigor and must feed upon humans' and animals' spirits to maintain it, but breathless hold greater understanding. Though their need for Spirit Essence is deeper, most see that they need not kill living beings, but instead grow closer to the Spirit Crystal itself. I assume these are the ones who became Saleshi."

"That makes sense, since they…" He caught himself before he revealed too much about the Saleshi's secrets. Bakeekek had trusted him, and he would not so easily betray it. "Since they did not pursue humans, that is. What did the Vanashel reveal?"

Mariana furrowed her brow, but did not contest his slip. "They are much more like awakened: ravenous, starving. To the Bound Ones who lead them, drifters, awakened, breathless, and humans alike are resources to feed upon or manipulate. There is more about them we've yet to understand. They keep repeating a single word, *dragon.*"

That word sent stabbing pain straight through the wound he'd suffered in their battle with the Earth Bound One. Though healed, it screamed as if it were fresh, and he stumbled into the base of the statue.

"We have seen Bound Ones take the form of dragons," he said through gritted teeth. "One in the Whistling Pass attacked me, and when I asked why, it said something about home being theirs. Some of the spirits with the Vanashel were awakened too, but the breathless seem to be able to command them."

"Like slaves."

"It would seem so."

She looked him up and down. "You need rest, but I will consider what you have said."

Her pity forced him to right himself, fists clenched. "You still haven't told me how to fight them!"

"I told you that I would consider it," she muttered. "Not all answers come as simply as a sword to an awakened's core. Return to me tomorrow, once you have met with the iz Ardinvil representative. Those half scions are incompetent, but I cannot deny their influence. All of Vocka must know of the threat we face if the information we've shared is true."

"Then I will do that," he replied with a quick bow. "Thank you for your cooperation. We are better for your teachings, and I will quiet any mockery of your Sheptasa within my ranks."

He turned to leave, but her voice caught him at the door. "Supreme Defender, tell the eager girl to discard her armor with your warriors and return to me. I wish to speak with her."

"Warrior Wanusa is a smart young woman," he replied. "She is the first of us to realize that drifters need Spirit Crystal, and that saved my life when Vanashel awakened attacked us the first time. What do you want from her?"

"That is for her to know. If she decides to confer with you, then that is her choice alone."

Miv would have smashed a statue at that disrespect, but Radais just nodded. There was an unspoken understanding between them. Tradition dictated that the Whisperers often acted in secret, and though it was strange for them to call upon a common Glassblade warrior, he saw no harm in building rapport. Perhaps Wanusa could learn the parts that Mariana was unwilling to reveal to him.

"Let our cooperation bring our spirits closer," he finally said.

She pressed a hand to her heart. "And let greater understanding bring us closer to the spirits."

WHERE THE SANDS MEET THE SHORE

"All the sands flee to the river, then the sea. So is the end of our bodies when we perish, but our spirits shall soar to the heights of the great light." – Everanitus iz Vamiustok, first patriarch of House iz Vamiustok

Taint seized Kasia as she stepped from her Axiom portal and found her legs trapped in a sandy riverbank. Snow fell heavy upon her hat and shoulders, but that was far from her greatest concern.

The horrid punishment for her past Reaching twisted her stomach. Voices of the dead echoed in her mind, turning to screams until her handmaiden, Kikania, stumbled into her side with a yelp.

"Watch yourself," Kasia said over the sound of the voices. "I would rather not enter a noble estate covered head-to-toe in sand."

"So-Sorry," the slight girl replied. Half-a-foot shorter than Kasia, Kikania seemed to be swallowed up by the sand, her pale Ezmani-lowborn cheeks bright red in the light of Kasia's lantern. "I thought it would be easier the second time, but I feel as if my mind is soup."

Zinarus chuckled from beside them, his cane steadying him as his mechanical leg clicked away. Surprisingly, he looked delighted to have his pants ruined. "Perhaps the effects worsen with the number of people who come through the portal." He glanced at Spitza upon Kasia's shoulder. "I am unsure whether ravens count in that strain."

Neither did she, but as heaved for each breath with her hands on her knees, she regretted bringing two others and a raven with her. It had been easier to send Tazper to Kalastok that morning. This, though, had caused Realm Taint with a single Reach. Surely, it had to do with the numbers she'd brought through the portal, and she did not need to look to know the Axiom Crystal had crept further up her forearm.

Spitza helped matters by pecking at Kasia's ear and *gwah*-ing loud enough to make it ring. Her instinct was to swat the bird away, but she was still earning the troublesome little raven's trust. It made Kasia wonder if this was how annoying she'd been to Yazia growing up.

"I obviously did not target your estate well enough," she said to Zinarus, trying to pry herself from the sand and toward the rocks ahead. Tainted voices, though, told her to drown in the river instead of finding solid ground.

"Join us," they whispered with each word echoing in her mind. *"Fall into Death."*

But Zinarus, bless his spirit, just smiled with all the warmth of his fiery hair. "Worry not. We have found the Vamia River, so Vamiustok cannot be far. Once we find a waypoint, I can lead us to my family's estate." His smile turned slack jawed as Kasia's lanternlight fell upon her face. "By the Mother, are you well? Did we not leave enough time between your Reaches?"

She gritted her teeth and trudged onward with Kikania. "I swear, all you ask me is whether I am well. No, I am not, but your well wishes and buried prayers will not change that."

It had not escaped her that, before teleporting here, her last real words to him had been to *fuck off*, yet here the purple lord was, acting as if nothing had happened. That mindsap cigar and increasingly worse Taint had her tumbling into the insanity they had pretended to show Gregorzon. Zinarus did not deserve to endure that.

"Let us continue then," he replied, gaze averted.

He led them toward a rocky ledge as Kikania kept close by her side. "We both know he is fond of you, my lady," she whispered. "Do you really wish to push him away when he has already learned the worst of your secrets?"

Spitza clicked thrice, as if echoing the maid's insistence, and Kasia stroked the bird's head while clenching her teeth. Little wounded her as much as being wrong, but nothing was so straightforward. Relationships created vulnerabilities. For years, she had done everything she could to limit both. It felt now as if she were forming a new bond every day for Chatik and his allies to exploit.

Their shoes squished against the hard ground as Zinarus grabbed hold of a willow's exposed roots and hauled himself onto the ledge. He leaned his cane against the trunk, then offered the women his hand. "Let me take your lantern. It will make the climb easier."

Kasia complied and took his hand. His grip was firm, pulling her up before she had even leveraged her foot on the rock. The momentum carried her straight into him, and for a few long moments, they lingered there with a thousand unsaid words hanging beneath the willow's boughs. So many of them filled Kasia's mind that they silenced the voices of the dead. Why could only he banish them?

Spitza pecking at his nose spurred Kasia to nod down to Kikania. "You should probably help her too, but I won't take kindly to you holding her this close."

"It appears that Spitza does not like me in your proximity either," he quipped.

She scratched the raven's chest. "Good bird."

Zinarus gave her an amused look before stepping back to the ledge and offering Kikania his aid. "Thank you for your patience. Your lady was being unduly distracting."

Kasia scoffed at that jest, but took it. His temperament was too infectious to not improve her mood. It hurt to admit, but she needed it. Even with a swirling head, a nauseous stomach, and a cursed mind, the Taint's offer of drowning in the Vamia River no longer felt preferable to enduring.

She recovered her lantern and Zinarus's cane once Kikania had clambered up. Both her and Kasia's dresses were ruined from the knee down, freezing from the cold and moving like rigid boards more than flowing skirts. Unfortunately, they could only bring through the portal what they could carry in their packs, and that meant relying on House iz Vamiustok for spare clothing until they reunited with the Niezik forces at Fort Harizak.

That wasn't ideal, as her attire was her armor. Often, her dresses—or trousers at strategic times—were meant to prod her enemies or draw attention from potential allies. She had chosen a heavy woolen blanket scarf clasped with amber over a simpler dress to appeal to the Vockan sensibilities of Zinarus's mother. At least it fared better than her usual Ezmani finery would have.

A glance at Zinarus's too-short pants, though, made worries about her own attire feel petty. He had handled wearing her father's old clothes with humility, and he surely wished to return to his noble fineries.

She bowed her head and returned his cane. "I must say that you have quite ruined my father's clothes."

"Oh, yes," he stammered, attempting to brush off the sand, but she caught his arm.

"I jest. It seems being near you is the only thing quieting my mind."

He pursed his lips and studied her with his thumb tracing the curved top of his cane. "Aliax is here, then? Sazilz?"

"Surprisingly, no," she replied.

The woods within the lanternlight were empty besides snow and the rustling of the branches. A single drifter slipped in-between a pair of trees, but showed no interest in the trio before vanishing into the everdark.

"The voices are still in my head, though, and I can barely form a thought without them suggesting that I join the dead." She noticed his panic and shook her head. "Do not look at me like that. My struggle is plenty irritating, but I have felt a spirit's peace once already. At least until I've avenged my father, I have no intentions of doing so again."

She started through the woods in hopes of finding a road, forcing Zinarus to match her pace with some effort. He kept an eye on her as he tried to hide his concern. Deceit was hardly his skill, though, and she could practically hear the gears in his mind echoing those of his leg.

"Would you prefer my voice to theirs, then?" he offered a minute later, speaking fast enough for his words to tumble over each other. "There are a number of topics I am sure we could discuss…"

Kikania jumped on the opportunity before Kasia could rebuke him for such a simple solution to her deepening insanity. "Why don't you tell us about Vamiustok? I have of course heard of it, but know next to nothing about it, besides it being by the river it's named after."

As if understanding their plan to distract Kasia, the specter of Sazilz Uziokaki appeared beside her suddenly, tugging on his elaborate high-collared coat and scowling at the weather. "A Vockan city bearing an Ezmani name. It is appalling. Why do we allow these fire-haired lowborn to mix with our blood and accept the Crystal Mother's power? If she rejected them, why should we not?"

Kasia scowled, trying to ignore him, but Spitza croaked and climbed around her back to the shoulder further from Sazilz. Had the raven seen him? It was a ridiculous thought, and Zinarus's hand on Kasia's back interrupted any further consideration.

"You see them now, do you not?" he asked. "I have noticed how your eyes dart away, if only for a moment."

"You wound me," she muttered, failing to sound joking. "I thought I had hidden it better than that."

"You likely succeeded with most. When you do not have outbursts, your distractions are more subtle, but I simply know what to look for." He followed her gaze to Sazilz. "Is it Aliax?"

"It is not." She pushed onward, staring at her feet. That did little to quiet the voices, even if she couldn't see their source. "You are quite obsessed with him, you know. Perhaps he should haunt you instead."

Zinarus opened his mouth to reply, but the sound of a horse-drawn wagon interrupted him. They swapped glances. Assuming he could not run, Kasia rushed ahead. Any chance at a ride to the city was better than trudging through the snow on foot.

She stumbled onto a half-cleared trail barely wide enough for a carriage to pass. Trees arched over it like looming giants, lit by the two lanterns dangling off the front of the approaching covered wagon. One with four massive horses barreling down upon her.

"Stop!" she called out.

The horses spooked at her sudden appearance, practically skidding to a stop amid the icy ground as the wagon's swinging lanterns sent shadows shifting around them. Behind, the lowborn Ezmani driver stood and grabbed the musket at his side.

"I don't have nothing worth stealing," he shouted, as if ensuring some hiding ambushers could hear from the woods. A short man with a commoner's flat cap and woolen coat, his hands shook as he primed the gun and hoisted it to his shoulder. Kasia doubted he had much experience with it, but even such a dated musket was effective from this range.

Spitza squawked back, but Kasia waved for the bird to be silent. "My friends and I lost our way. We were seeking Vamiustok, but the snowfall covered the path."

Something snapped near the tree line as Zinarus and Kikania peeked from it. The man jumped at the sound, and the resulting shot sent Kasia's ears ringing. She staggered back, every muscle frozen as memories of falling through the Axiom consumed her mind. The pain, the loss of her talon. A spirit's form replacing her own.

Spitza's screeching tore Kasia back to reality. The raven pecked at her face, flapping her wings as if to tell her mistress she was being ridiculous. When Kasia looked to her companions, she found why.

"Zinarus!"

She sprinted to the wounded lord so quickly that Spitza had to claw into her shoulder to hold on. Slumped into Kikania's arms, blood soaked his clothes over his stomach, and his eyes fluttered as he stared into the sky.

"I… I think he shot me," Zinarus stammered.

"Quite the insightful one," Sazilz's specter said from the nearby shadows. A devious grin pulled back his cheeks so far that it looked as if his face would split from joy. "You were better off without the half-blood anyway."

Kasia muttered a curse in the specter's direction before clutching Zinarus's trembling hand. He gripped her too, but though he was weak, the musket ball had not struck his heart. They had time still.

She glared at the wagon driver. "You just shot the heir to House iz Vamiustok! There better be a spiritdamned Body Reacher close, or you'll be joining the spirits before he does."

"Oh Mother…" The man dropped the gun and fell back onto his seat. His face turned ghastly pale. "I thought yous were raiders!"

"How far are we from Vamiustok?" Kasia insisted.

The man glanced at Zinarus. "We're a ways west. About two days' walk."

"Just kill him!" Kasia's Tainted voice hissed in her head. *"You know he'll die without a Reacher."*

She drew her pistol from her coat's inner pocket, aiming it at the driver as she advanced on the wagon. "Then it looks like you're taking us. You had better hope that Lady Sania is forgiving for you attempting to assassinate her son."

But the man's hand crept back toward his gun. "Won't make it in time for a Body Reacher."

"KILL HIM!" the voices demanded.

Kasia pulled the trigger, sending a bullet ripping through the man's extended hand. He cried out and clutched his bloodied, mangled hand. "Why? Why? I was just protecting myself. I was—"

But Kasia was already mounting the wagon. She snatched the musket and threw it onto the ore lumped in its bed. "It appears you are in need of a Body Reacher too, good sir." With a wave for Kikania to help Zinarus to the wagon, she held her father's revolver to the driver's head. "Seems best that we arrive within a day, then, or that hand of yours will be like that for life."

The man needed no further inspiration. Leaping from the wagon, he helped Kikania half-carry, half-drag Zinarus and set him on the driver's bench. Blood pooled around him.

Kasia cursed her lack of medical knowledge, but knew to cover the wound at least. She threw off her coat and tore off her dress sleeves, tying them together and wrapping them around Zinarus's bleeding stomach as makeshift gauze. Kikania gawked at her mistress like she were some monster. But the dress was ruined anyway, and it if kept Zinarus alive long enough for them to get to Vamiustok in time, then so be it.

"Keep your eyes open," Kasia told him, pressing her lips to his temple. "I'm not done with you yet, Zinarus iz Vamiustok."

There was only room for two up front. She certainly could not drive a wagon, so she climbed into the covered back with Kikania. The ore was bright yellow in the lanternlight and smelled horribly of rotten eggs, but that and the stones jabbing through her clothes were the least of her concerns. Her allies were few. Those she could truly trust were fewer. She needed Zinarus to live, and though the voices haunting her mind wished for her to continue without him, she couldn't.

Whether she liked it or not, watching that auburn-haired bastard bleed made her heart bleed with him. He had professed his fondness for her despite all she'd done, and she damn well wouldn't let him get the last word.

"Hurry," she commanded the driver. "For all our sakes."

ILIAFA'S CALL

"Love is the death of one duty and the birth of another." – Reshkan proverb

Radais paced before the roaring bonfire at Dalnus's heart. Glassblades joined with the civilians for a dance to both celebrate the warriors' arrival and honor the purest of the spirits. He had never enjoyed dancing, but he partook heavily of the offered beer, emptying one last mug before wiping his mouth.

Where is she? he asked himself.

While he'd met with House iz Ardinvil's envoys, Wanusa had stayed back with Mariana and the Whisperers to discuss spirits knew what. The scions had demanded his Glassblades protect their assets against spirits. Ivalat iz Ardinvil planned to rebel against Kalastok's rule as long as Chatik sat on the throne, but they cared only for power, not Vocka's protection against the Vanashel. The Whisperers were the only ones who could help him now.

It made no sense to him how the shamans could calm awakened and breathless with mere words. Sure, the breathless had minds and could be reasoned with, but Mariana had claimed to have spoken with Vanashel breathless, maybe even Bound Ones. They wanted to slaughter the living. He didn't believe for a second that it was only to feed upon humans' Spirit Essence—whatever that meant.

Lazan emerged from the dancers, swaying on his feet and echoing their song with his long coat flapping in the gales. Snow pattered his shoulders, but he made no effort to avoid it as he held two mugs of his own. One he passed to Radais before taking a ginger sip from the other.

"You resemble a statue more than a man, my incredibly tall friend."

"Hmph." Radais took a swig from his new mug and handed the empty one to a nearby initiate. The roaring blaze showered them in sparks, but he didn't back away, admiring instead how it made the Body Reacher's silver hair shimmer like molten glass. "I'm worried about Wanusa."

With a hiccup, Lazan threw his arm over Radais's shoulder, but he was only of average height for an Ezman, far too short to reach all the way around. "The girl will be fine."

"She has been gone for hours," Radais muttered. He regretted the bite in his voice, but he couldn't help it. He'd never been a happy drunk.

"With the spiritual leaders of your people, yes?"

He shrugged. "Not exactly, but they were once."

Lazan chuckled and drank sloppily, leaving some beer to trickle down his stubbled chin. An unbidden urge told Radais to clean it with his own lips, but he just shook his head and looked away as the Reacher spoke. "Are you worried they are bestowing all the lessons of the world upon your ward? Can she not learn from the wisdom of women and men your elder? We have both seen how she desires to learn more about the spirits than merely fighting them."

"I want the same. We need to learn from them."

"You want to know about them and their secrets, yes," Lazan corrected, "but she wants to truly connect with their very being. There is a wonder in the lass's eyes that being among the Glassblades cannot tame, and you should know better than any that clipping her wings won't make her remain in the nest."

Radais furrowed his brow. "You think I'm afraid of her leaving?"

"I think you are afraid of being alone." Lazan patted Radais's chest over the heart. "Miv practically hated your guts, but you near killed us all trying to save her. Almost killed yourself too rushing to Wanusa and my aid back there in the Whistling Pass. A shame. I had them handled."

"Did you, now?" Radais asked, a smirk splitting his well-worn melancholy. "Are you telling me you'd rather me leave you be next time?"

Lazan rocked his head back and forth. The motion knocked him off balance, and Radais had to catch his coat to stop him from stumbling into the fire. "One's a fool if they reject aid, especially when it comes from a muscled, flame-haired man who's damned good with his blade." His eyes flicked downward at the statement's end.

Radais's whole face burned as he hid his embarrassment behind a drink. Were they flirting right now? Spirits, he was not in the mood for this, but Lazan made it difficult to be upset around him. A big change from his initial irritation with the scion.

"You're not, you know," Lazan said, stepping right up to Radais and smiling nervously up at him. "Alone, that is. I doubt Wanusa is going anywhere—she looks at you like some kind of hero—but even if she does leave, you will have me. It has been two motherforsaken years since I have felt like myself. After Katarzyna's duel in Raviak Forest forced my Reaching too far…" He shook his head at himself. "The Taint doesn't seem so damned oppressive when you are around."

The drumming of Radais's heart silenced his rationality as he raised his mug to his lips, but found it empty. How much had he drunk this night? His gaze fell to Lazan's eyes of golden gray before he could even consider a number, so instead of thinking, he slipped his fingers between the Reacher's. Then Lazan's lips greeted his in an embrace that warmed his heart more than any fire ever could.

It was a swift kiss, and Lazan glanced around to see if anyone had noticed. If they had, they were being quiet about it. So, Radais realized, did they need to be. He was the supreme defender and on a mission.

"We can't do this here," he told Lazan, their cheeks brushing as they swayed to the song. "But I doubt there's many Glassblades in the inn right about now. They reserved me a room with a bed big enough to fit a herd of ibex. How's that sound compared to a bedroll?"

Lazan stepped back and used his taloned finger to trace Radais's jawline. Its crystal was trapped beneath his glove, but its point sent a thrill down the Glassblade's spine. "Lead the way, Supreme Defender."

COLD SWEAT CLUNG TO WANUSA'S BROW as she hurried from the Whisperers' temple, throwing on her glass armor. Its rattling dulled her thoughts, but she needed that. They raced faster than a diving spirit.

What in the realms had she gotten herself into?

Singing and the sharp smell of smoke met her near Dalnus's city center. Most of the higher ranked Glassblades, her included, had rooms in the inns, leaving the initiates to camp outside. Radais had told her to find him in his once her meeting with Mariana was done. That meeting had come as a shock and taken far longer than she'd expected, but the hour didn't matter. She needed to talk to him *now*.

Old training partners called for her to join their revelry as she hurried toward the inn. Normally, a good laugh and dance were far more appealing than Glassblade business, as people often revealed more about themselves during such times. Not tonight. There was no question what her mission was now.

She hastened a glance around to ensure Radais wasn't among the celebrations. Her mentor often drank heavily, but if he'd partaken, it seemed he had already retired. More surprising was Lazan's absence. He adored every chance he could get to study Vockan culture.

Wanusa shrugged and pushed open the inn's door. They would swap stories about the songs later, then.

A burly woman greeted her inside the inn. Dressed in a Vockan blanket scarf and trousers with multiple overlapping layers, she resembled a boxer than an innkeeper, so Wanusa bit back her hurry as she addressed the woman.

"Hello, ma'am. I'm looking for Supreme Defender Radais's room. Urgent Glassblade business."

The woman looked her up and down, arms crossed. She huffed. "Figures. I'd be more shocked if someone dressed like that wasn't one of your kind."

Wanusa rapped her gauntlets against the wooden desk. A ledger lay behind it, likely holding the information she needed. "Yes, of course. Can you please tell me which room he is in?"

"All your folk are out there." The innkeeper threw out an expressive arm. "Take off your armor and join them, or you'll be wearing it the rest of your life."

Wanusa groaned. She didn't have time for this. "It is not such a bad thing."

"That is your choice." The innkeeper clicked her tongue and flipped through the ledger, occasionally glancing up at Wanusa. It felt like forever, but she eventually slammed her finger down on one line and then slid the ledger to the side. "Room twenty-three. It's on the second floor, turn—"

Wanusa was already charging up the stairs. By the spirits, why did people act like she was just some girl? She was a Glassblade warrior! The Order had saved Zekiaz from the Awakening, and they were the only ones apparently interested in stopping what appeared to be a second one. The least they deserved was a little respect.

The stairs creaked beneath the weight of Wanusa and her armor. She was still getting used to it, and her muscles were sore most days. Miv had always said soreness meant strength in the end, though, and with what lay ahead, she would need all her strength and more.

Two halls split away from the top of the stairs. She realized then that the innkeeper's instructions may have been useful if she'd bothered to listen for a moment longer. Such rude haste was unlike her, but nothing was like what it was supposed to be anymore. The Commonwealth warred with itself, a strange organization controlled spirits, and a faction of breathless sought to kill all humans as some kind of vengeance. This was not what she'd anticipated when she joined the Order.

But she was here now, and when she glanced down the right of the two halls, she noticed odd numbers. That was indication enough.

She quickly found the room labeled twenty-three, the iron numbers nailed to the door rusted and chipped at their ends. The door itself bore multiple gouges, and scorch marks across the hall's carpet implied its torches had slipped free at least once. She huffed. Had Vocka fallen so far under Commonwealth rule that its capital could not maintain a decent inn?

Wanusa raised her hand to knock, but a *thud* from behind the door stopped her.

"Radais?" she asked.

Another sound came, then silence. She tensed and reached for a steel dagger at her side. Her sword would shatter against the walls in these tight quarters, and an attacker here was more likely a person than a spirit. A city as big as Dalnus had iz Vamiustok or another scion house's Spirit Reachers at the ready, even in Vocka.

No one answered, so she pushed on the door to find it unlatched. Assuming that either meant someone had broken in, or Radais had left it open to visitors, she stepped inside.

And immediately regretted it.

So much skin was on display. Both Vockan black and scion gray were pressed together in a puzzle that took Wanusa's beleaguered brain far too long to understand. Lazan was in Radais's bed, and from the look of it, she had interrupted quite the passionate display.

"Oh…" she mumbled, backing out and throwing the door shut, as if the extra force would take what she'd seen. And it had been *a lot*.

That cold sweat returned as she trudged down the hall. She had no particular destination in mind, but moving helped her think of anything besides Radais's bare bottom and the other bits she'd had no desire to see. By no means did she disapprove of them together. In fact, she had all but encouraged it. That didn't mean she wanted to see her mentors having sex when she so badly needed to tell them about her conversation with Mariana.

Oh, that…

The reminder drew her to a stop at the corner, where the hall bent to reveal another series of rooms. She was a warrior now, so one was probably hers. Finding out which would require asking the innkeeper, though, and that thought was unappealing enough to make her consider sleeping under the everdark instead. Worse was the truth she'd fled when she left the Whisperers' temple.

"They're dead," she finally admitted, each cold breath stinging her throat as she fell into the wall. A warrior shouldn't weep. She knew that, but she did anyway. "I'm sorry, Inrius. I failed you again."

Rapid footsteps pounded toward her. She cursed silently, then wiped her face and spun to meet them.

Radais had thrown on a loose-fit pair of trousers and his commander's jacket. It was half-buttoned, revealing most of his chest and the sweat covering it, but from the sweet smell rising from him, he'd bathed since their arrival. Wanusa didn't even want to consider how bad she stunk from days in heavy armor.

"Wanusa, I…" he began before his panic shifted to concern, his arms embracing her. "What has happened? What did the Whisperers do to you?"

She buried her head into his shoulder as the tears rushed from her. Oh, how she wanted to be strong, but all her efforts had been silently for one boy. The little brother she'd failed to protect years ago. The one who'd lost half his spirit before she could drive away the awakened as a child, and whose suffering their parents blamed on her. She'd sworn to protect as a Glassblade, but if Mariana was right, then Inrius was already gone.

"What does it mean if only half your spirit remains when you die?" she asked, clutching onto his coat as softer footsteps signaled Lazan's approach.

Radais held on tighter. "I don't understand."

"Mariana told me the Vanashel attacked my home." She looked up at Lazan with her vision blurred by tears. "Iliafa is gone, and they took what remained of my brother's spirit."

"I am so sorry, little one," the Reacher replied, laying a hand on her cheek.

But her lip curled, and she pried herself from Radais's grasp. "I don't need pity. Inrius died because I failed to protect him *again*!"

"Slow down," Radais said. "Start with what Mariana told you, and let's go from there."

Wanusa took a long, haggard breath, fists clenching and unclenching at her sides. Fury and sorrow alike filled her. She let those feelings dance in her chest until she collected the strength to meet his gaze. "The Whisperers know so much more than they told you. They discovered that the Vanashel hunted my family, punishing me for helping you at the ruins of New Frontier. All of Iliafa is dead. Because of me!"

Radais tried to comfort her again, but she gritted her teeth and pushed on. "There's more. One of the Whisperers read my spirit, and she said that I must learn from them."

"What does that mean?" Radais asked.

She shook her head. "I don't know, but Mariana insisted on coming with us... teaching me to become a Whisperer. We must go west to Iliafa. The Whisperers claim the Vanashel did this to send a message and to mark the point of battle on a place where spirits linger. They're luring us there to face us, but apparently, something on the way holds our key to ending this."

Lazan patted Radais on the shoulder and stepped to his side. Fear lingered in his eyes. "Then that is what we must do. If these Vanashel are striking at our families, Erienfar and wherever in the wastes Mhanain is from are at risk. I am from far to the east, but I worry for your relatives."

"You trust the Whisperers?" Radais asked Wanusa after considering that for a moment. "You agree with this path?"

She forced herself to stand up straighter and meet his gaze. He'd made her a warrior, and though everything in her chest made her want to curl up in a ball, she reminded herself why she'd taken up the blade. Why she sought to understand the corrupted spirits. Inrius was not the only one who suffered, and she would not stop until she found a way to bring them peace, in this life or their spirit one.

"I do," she said. "And if defeating the Vanashel takes me becoming a Whisperer, then so be it."

The Wars of Crimsons and Spirits
TERRITORY AS OF THE 1ST DAY
OF DAWNRISE, 791 POST-AWAKENING
FLAGS & SIGILS MARK KNOWN
ARMY LOCATIONS/MOVEMENTS
LITANITAN
Occupied N
NA-REQ
Crimson E
FORT KALA
Ogrenian Hegemony
KALASTOK
Pikezik
TARGEER
PALMIA FORTESS
Ezmani 3rd Army
Glassblade Order
DALNUS
VAMIUSTOK
FORT HARIZAK
Rebel Army
Vanashel Ambush
Glassblades
VAMIA MINES
TYS
ILIAFA
Harizak Confeder
ARDINVIL
ERIENFAR
Vanashel

Keloshan Empire
ORIAKSTAK
shan
...ators
...and
...and
...orre
ZAKINIV
Bartol
Grand Keloshan Army
UKIT
1st
LOST BROTHERS' FORTS
Oliezany
REXANIV
Ezmani 2nd Army
Keloshan Reclaimers
GIAMIVIK
Uziokaki
AVIAK FOREST
ASTOK
Reshkan Colonies
Factions
HARIZAK CONFEDERATION
CRIMSON COURT & ALLIES
KELOSH | BLADES | VANASHEL
Legend
NATIONAL CAPITAL
REGIONAL CAPITAL
MAJOR CITY
MINOR CITY
BORDER
LINE OF CONTROL
ARMY (SIGILS/FLAGS)
ARMY MOVEMENT

OFF WITH HIS HEAD

"When Ogrenians invented the guillotine to be quicker with their executions, we Keloshans banned it immediately. Why let one's enemies die so quickly? If they deserved it, then let them swing from their neck for a good long while. A slow death is something beautiful when they know there's no escape." – Barginon Tarianik, the Butcher of Teplos

Dawnrise came the morning of Etal's execution. Just a sliver of light, since the sun had yet to rise above the horizon, but it made the southern sky bleed as Nex walked along the Kala's bank with their hands stuffed in their duster's pocket.

Kalastok's streets would match it by day's end.

"You're sure of this plan?" Vinnia asked beside Nex, her arm wound with theirs. "If it goes wrong…"

Nex clicked their tongue. "It'll go wrong. Bound to. You don't just walk into a square guarded by Reachers and soldiers and expect it to go cleanly. But it doesn't need to."

A pair of breathless hurried overhead, their wisps barely visible in the lanternlight. Nex hadn't wanted to bring any light to draw attention, but when Vinnia insisted upon something this much, they relented. There were faces you just didn't say no to.

Vinnia stopped and picked a stone from beside the water. She rolled it in her palm, checking its smoothness with her thumb. "So you aren't worried then?" she asked once the spirits were gone.

"Of course not."

That didn't please Vinnia, but shouting from the Industrial District interrupted her protestations. Apparently, the scions had decided the west side was worthy of a two Reacher towers now, and an Air Reacher had dropped one of the stones that he'd been raising to the level of the builders. It lay in pieces between a pair of red-faced workers. They were lowborn based on their pale Ezmani skin and darker hair, and they were letting the Air Reacher know exactly how they felt about his failure.

Vinnia pursed her lips. "Everyone is always fighting. Maybe some Reachers will help keep the peace once they're built."

"Fat chance," Nex muttered, grabbing a stone of their own. It was jagged and uneven, and when they tried to skip it, it landed in the river with a *thwomp*. Then it sank. "The Crimsons act like they care, but we were starving until the Children of Zekiaz helped us. Those Reacher towers are to control us, not protect us."

Vinnia shrugged and threw her stone. It flew far more evenly than Nex's, skipping three times before disappearing beneath the current. No pleasure crossed her face, though. "Rumor has it that Princess Nikoza proposed it. If she's like you said before, I don't think she would try to hurt us."

"She's a scion."

"Who helped save my life," Vinnia replied, taking Nex's hands. She studied her lover with a pained expression. "You might not fear, but I do. Nexie, I can't lose you."

Nex swallowed. It wasn't true that they didn't fear. In fact, Nex feared more now that they had revealed their love for each other, but they couldn't find the words to admit it. Vinnia used every moment to help those in the Ashes of Dawn who couldn't feed themselves or afford warm clothes. The last thing she needed was to know that Nex spent their nights staring at the ceiling of the warehouse basement, thinking of every way a mistake could get them all killed.

So they kissed her instead, taking her in their arms and spinning until they both nearly tumbled into the Kala. Vinnia stepped back with a hand over her mouth to cover a giggle. Her rich skin glowed almost gold in the lanternlight, and her cheeks flushed to match the rose of her lips.

"We should be more careful," she insisted.

Nex wrapped an arm around her waist and led her back toward the Ashes of Dawn's territory. They tugged down on their wide-brimmed hat to shadow their face. Some of the workers near the half-built tower had noticed them, though, and they whistled in the couple's direction.

"Don't do anything rash," Vinnia whispered to Nex, feeling them tense. "They have Reachers."

But Nex's free hand slipped to the pistol in their duster's pocket. Guns had never been their specialty, as it was much easier to bat their eyes and trick scions out of their money than threatening them. That didn't mean Nex doubted the effectiveness of a bullet to the head. Just that the clean-up afterward would be more of a mess than was worth it.

That wasn't why Nex released the gun, gripping a chunk of amber delivered by the Children of Zekiaz instead. Those men were ass-holes, but besides the couple of Reachers, they were lowborn ass-holes. A swift kick to their groins was probably in order, sure. Bullets were scarce among the Ashes of Dawn, though, and Nex was saving theirs for the Crimson bastards keeping the Spirit Plague cure from the sick.

Watchmen patrolled the main streets, so the pair kept to the side alleys as they worked their way northwest. Lowborn workers whis-tling at them was one thing. Men in uniform could do far worse, and Nex had no intentions of letting any of them lay a finger on Vinnia.

Gangs watched those alleys outside the few blocks Nex had claimed for the Ashes of Dawn. Nex knew well the chalk markings or purposely stacked refuse that signaled which gang ruled each area, but their deal with the bosses meant they needn't worry about it for once. The makeshift patch on their shoulder—a rising sun splitting through scion gray—showed them as a member of the Ashes. Vinnia and the other seamstresses had been busy making patches for every-one to keep them safe from at least the gangs. It made them look damn near like a united group.

They neared the Ashes' main warehouse without issue, checking over their shoulders for breathless and watchmen along the way. None followed them, but a sight stopped them across the street from the warehouse.

Footprints.

A pair of them headed down the street and straight through the warehouse door. Members of the Ashes of Dawn knew better than to leave their tracks uncovered, and these might well have been glinting like a glass medallion in everbright. Lowborn entered the west side's many abandoned buildings all the time, but on the day Nex would rescue Etal from execution, they didn't need this attention on their safehouse.

With a signal to Vinnia, they both drew their pistols. The gangs had provided plenty enough for most of the Ashes to carry a gun of some kind, even with ammunition limited. Nex hated that Vinnia had to. She should've been in the safety of the warehouse basement, using her dexterous fingers to sew gloves and patches, not to pull a trigger.

A light snowfall drifted over Nex as they crept to the footprints. Whoever's shoe it was, it had little tread and obviously wasn't made for heavy work. Most likely a scion's then, or a shoe the Ashes had stolen from one. Nex covered the tracks either way, then approached the door.

Vinnia held out the lantern to illuminate the cracked door, and Nex peeked inside with their gun raised. They dared not enter, not if an ambush awaited them.

Footfalls echoed inside. A figure loomed in the room's center, his hands stuffed into the pockets of his woolen coat and his fur-lined cap sitting crooked on his head. He spun around at the sight of the lanternlight and surrendered.

"Please, do not shoot!" he stammered.

Nex lowered the gun as Vinnia held out the lantern to reveal the man's face. Clean-shaven with pale skin only stained slightly by scion gray, his eyes were misty, and Nex damn-well wondered if he was about to cry.

"Tazper?" they asked, stepping toward him with a brow raised. "What in the wastes are you doing here?"

NIKOZA STOOD ON THE SOUTHERN PALACE STEPS and stared down at her gloved hands, contemplating what she was about to do. Gloves usually restricted a Reacher's power, but in recent days, her house's master seamstresses had crafted ones for the Crystal Brigade which perfectly aligned with their talons. Patterns of embedded rubies across the other fingers flashed bright Bartol red in greater light. In the dim glow of dawnrise's arrival, they seemed to bleed crimson.

"Chin up, dear child," Tzena Oliezany whispered from beside her. "This is your first public action leading a squad of the Crystal Brigade, so let it be one of unbridled confidence."

So Nikoza straightened her posture, glancing about at the gathered watchmen and Reachers as Tzena ensured all were in order. Among those closest to Nikoza stood the young scion man she had spotted in the Chamber during the execution vote. In the days since, she had learned her instincts were correct. That beguiling face was just like his sister's.

"Do you understand your assignment, Gregorzon?" she asked the Niezik who had been cast out by Katarzyna. He had called her a traitor and claimed to now be the rightful patriarch of his house—a claim which Chatik and Tzena had reiterated—so Nikoza had found pity for him. Even if his rural fashion was horribly out of style.

Luckily, as matriarch of House Bartol, she had been able to convince Chatik to provide the Crystal Brigade with uniforms more befitting of powerful scions. Each Reacher now wore a long, high-collared crimson coat, belted at the waist. Embroidery ran along it in the color of the Reacher's associated realm to form images related to their abilities. For Nikoza, those were deep blue waves, while

Gregorzon's burnt-orange stitching depicted the curling tendrils of fire.

"I will watch for any riflemen on rooftops," Gregorzon confirmed, clenching his taloned hand into a fist. "As our king commands, none will interrupt the proceedings."

Nikoza nodded, then repeated the question to the other three Reachers under her command.

"I know we are supposed to order the breathless to watch the crowd," Vanzearik muttered from beside Gregorzon, stepping closer so that Tzena and the other Crimson officials couldn't hear, "but those things still give me the chills. Mother says we can trust them, sure. That does not mean it feels right."

Jolzena scoffed and smacked him on the back. "This is why Father sent you here instead of the warfront. Kelosh would eat you alive, Brother."

In their mid-twenties, Vanzearik and Jolzena Kaerz were twins from a middling but aspirational house whose parents Chatik assured her were loyal Crimsons. Being twins did not mean they were anything alike, though. Vanzearik was a squat Spirit Reacher with a shaved head, his features sharp. His twin, meanwhile, was a tall Force Reacher with a full figure and eyes so white her pupils seemed to be floating alone.

"Remember, he sent you too," Vanzearik replied with his scion gray cheeks flushed.

Jolzena threw out her arms. "Because someone needs to ensure you do not bring us all to shame!"

"The only shame originates in your bickering," the squad's second Spirit Reacher said from the formation's rear, stepping between them with strands of silver curling through his brown eyes. Lord Hazat Tozki was maybe two or three years older than Nikoza, and he had a boyish smile plastered across his well-groomed face. "Mess this up, and I am sure Tzena would happily have you working those towers west of the Kala."

Nikoza nodded to him before wrinkling her nose at the twins. "Hazat is correct. We are to be orderly, unified, and attentive for the entire ceremony. Professor Etal iz Noshok betrayed us all by creating the Spirit Plague. We cannot allow his clandestine allies to set him free."

"You're sounding like Tzena more every day," Jolzena said, but stepped back from her brother and rejoined their formation.

Nikoza tilted up her chin. She couldn't deny the twinge she felt whenever Etal was mentioned, as if her memories warred within her, but Chatik had given her orders for a reason. The professor had created the Spirit Plague. He deserved execution.

"Is it such a bad thing to resemble a minister of the king's council?" she said. "Besides, you have not confirmed whether you understand your orders."

The Force Reacher wriggled her jaw. "I'm to cover the dignitaries east of the guillotine with a forcefield if there is any trouble."

A horn blared out before Nikoza could reply, so she turned back to the front of her squad and stood at attention. Four other Crystal Brigade squads like Nikoza's gathered on the palace steps around them. Each had instructions to protect a cardinal direction around the guillotine or the execution platform itself when they arrived in the square at the northern edge of the Market District. Until then, they were to wait for the procession of watchmen taking Etal from the dungeons.

Nikoza shifted nervously. The parade to the market was a traditional display for executions. War and the Crimson Coup had depleted the Crystal Brigade's ranks, though, and not allowing them to take positions ahead of time put immense stress on Nikoza and her ill-trained Reachers.

But she trusted Chatik. He always had a plan, and when he emerged at the procession's front, all the brigadesmen thumped their chests in salute.

"Your duties this eve are crucial to the security of Ezman," the Crimson King said, stopping at the top of the stairs with his hands clasped behind him. He wore an elaborate crimson tailcoat and a vest beneath patterned with gold—not glass, as he had no reason to fear spirits anymore. "We shall execute a traitor to our nation, and in doing so, begin the process of healing those affected by the Spirit Plague."

Tzena took his side with a crooked smile. As the minister of crime, she wore the Crystal Brigade uniform for herself as well, but golden designs joined the ones of deep Shadow Reacher gray across her coat. She stood incredibly close to Chatik, the backs of their hands touching until another horn blared.

Nikoza bit her lip at the sight of the guards leading old Etal, bound and gloved, through the doors. He wore little better than rags, but he appeared unharmed as he staggered down the steps. Truth Reaching left no mark, though. She had no doubt that Chatik had used the few remaining Truth Reachers in the capital to learn everything he could about the plague Etal created. Maybe, it would lead to an actual cure in the end.

Etal stared at his feet most of the descent, but looked up at Nikoza as he passed. Pity, not anger or fear, filled his gaze.

A force stuck Nikoza's chest in that moment. She lost her footing, nearly falling down the steps before Gregorzon caught her. Etal was gone by the time she collected herself, but that shock still hung over her.

I remember.

It was just flashes, but she saw the secret laboratory behind Etal's office. The alchemist, Paras ik Lierasa, had been there, asking her and Zinarus iz Vamiustok to retrieve spirits in amber. Nex had helped, and Nikoza had sent them a cure for their sick lover—a true cure.

The memory of the cure's vial stung cold in her hand as she forced herself to follow Etal down the stairs. Watchmen and Reachers surrounded him five layers deep in each direction. It was a ridiculous amount of security to contain an old man wearing prisoner gloves, but one glance back at Chatik told Nikoza he wasn't the threat.

Chatik watched the rooftops south of the Crimson District, his fist clutching the pulsing stone he always carried with him nowadays. In the aftermath of the coup, he had tried to hide it, but he held it like some prized bauble now. That confused Nikoza. He had never been the most materialistic of scion, let alone been interested in gemstones.

Wondering further about the stone would have to come later, though, as the procession headed down the road splitting the palace gardens. Dim dawnrise light met the gas lamps to illuminate them in a solemn glow.

Beyond, the crowds roared.

Nikoza flexed her hand in case she needed to Reach. Thousands of people crowded behind a thin line of watchmen clad in Ezmani crimson, the guillotine before the market's fountain looming over them like a storm cloud. Their shouts merged into a mass of unintelligible nonsense, but from the stones and bottles thrown at the approaching watchmen, she assumed they discontent about Etal's imminent demise. Her memories' sudden return had her uncertain whether they were wrong or not.

"Do not cower!" Tzena demanded, striding through the Reachers as mounted watchmen joined those at the cordon.

Nikoza led her squad to the left of the guillotine. Two buildings near the Crimson District's wall formed a natural chokepoint for the watchmen further north, so she headed due east and stepped up to a guard platform that allowed her to see over the cordon. Her breaths fled at the swell of people beyond. Half of Kalastok had to be there, all fighting to get a sight of the execution.

The ones before her pushed against the watchmen, shouting up at her.

"Reacher whore!"

"Murderer!"

"You kill our only hope!"

They flung stones and other discarded refuse at the Reachers. Most clattered at the base of the platform, but enough struck Nikoza that she was grateful for her reinforced glass bracers to deflect the projectiles.

Except the stones meant little compared to the absolute vile in the people's words. This was not the usual lowborn contempt against elite scions. These people *despised* her, and their bloodshot eyes screamed murder if the watchmen failed to hold them back. Before, she had doubted the Crystal Brigade's purpose, but it was clear now. Rage like this had left Kalastok half burned. Much of it still lay in ashes beyond this area, and Nikoza's chest ached knowing how little she had accomplished during the riots.

This time was different. She led a squad of Reachers, and they would keep the peace. Somehow…

Chatik and Tzena climbed the steps of the central execution platform as watchmen dragged Etal behind. Jeers echoed from the crowd at the sight of the professor, followed by another surge forward. Nikoza drew her pistol with her free hand and reminded her squad of their orders, but her demands were primarily to calm her nerves. The gun, too, was next to useless with her lack of experience.

Only the breathless guided by Hazat, Vanzearik, and the Crimsons' other Spirit Reachers spread across the towers did anything to abate the crowd's fury. A single lowborn slipped through the watchmen anyway. Unarmed, but throwing his arms about like a madman, he rushed toward Nikoza's platform.

A breathless got to him first.

The man lacked the chance to scream before the spirit's tendrils tore into him. Nikoza hadn't even raised her gun in her shock, and she trembled watching the breathless tear the man's spirit from his body. It had the same effect on the crowd, their anger shifting to fear as many tried to flee the breathless by pushing back against the tide. There were far too many people, though, and those up front found themselves trapped between the protestors and the watchmen.

Chatik's voice, carried by Air Reachers, echoed through the market square, but his words were lost to Nikoza as she stepped to the platform's edge. She still struggled to channel a Reach for longer periods. This would be her single available one for an hour, but her role was to stop anyone from interrupting the execution. If this crush continued, chaos would ensue.

So she Reached into the realm of Water. A cool, humid feeling washed over her as she turned the half-melted snow into a wall of water before the watchmen. Then she sent it through the crowd.

People staggered back against the wave crashing over them. She'd pushed it slowly enough to do no real harm, but in frigid temperatures, no one wanted to be soaked. Lowborn had little understanding of a Reacher's ability anyway, and many seemed terrified of the wave based on their cries.

She released her Reach a few seconds later to maintain a fragment of its power, but it had done its job. People no longer pressed against the watchmen. Many had turned to leave entirely, and few bothered to enter the sloppy mess of mushed snow where the crush had been.

Nikoza let herself smile as she lowered her hand and turned back to Chatik and Tzena to check if they'd seen her success. The sight that greeted her stole that excitement immediately.

The executioner had just pushed Etal to his knees. The professor's eyes were stern, but he gave no resistance as the executioner lowered his head into the guillotine, the steel blade glinting in the lamplight above. Chatik's eyes, though, were directed to the south.

Nikoza's heart sank as one of the two Crystal Brigade squads on the execution platform moved to reinforce the main crowd pushing from the Market District. Protestors threw torches and flaming bottles there, only to be struck down by breathless or musket fire from the mounted watchmen. Corpses of both lowborn and watchmen formed three bloodied rows before what remained of the cordon.

If that wasn't bad enough, the western squad was missing from their platform. They charged through the crowd with their breathless and cavalry leading the way. One of them shouted something, but it was impossible to hear through the chaos.

Until a blast shook the ground.

Fire and smoke poured from a half-burned building down a western alley. A horde of people rushed away, sending calamity through the crowd as gunfire echoed throughout the square.

Nikoza could do nothing as a bullet ripped through the executioner's head, allowing Etal to roll free from beneath the guillotine's blade. That was the final squad's concern, not hers. She ordered

Jolzena to throw up a forcefield to defend their nearby allies, but the blast had her ears ringing so loudly that she couldn't hear her own voice. She had to trust Jolzena knew what to do. This was what they had been trained for.

Except Nikoza had already used much of her Reaching. She was supposed to flood the area to clear civilians and reveal the attackers, but doing so with full effect would require another Reach and worsen her Realm Taint. With her lips permanently dry and thirst following her every moment, she focused on a protective wave, carrying away a few dozen panicked lowborn from the crossfire until her power ran out.

She looked to Gregorzon instead to see if he was targeting the gunmen. Orange wisps encircled him, the heat drawing sweat from her brow. He waited, and when another shot rang out from the south, he loosed a series of firebolts.

Her eyes followed the bolts to a rooftop, where a charred figure tumbled from the ledge. Even a corpse falling among the crowd could not stop the stampede away from the market. She should have been relieved that they fled the guillotine instead of rushing it, but instead, she felt every ounce of pain around her like a knife to her heart.

It is happening again…

She had sworn after her aid convoy to the Industrial District that she would not allow herself to cause such hurt. This was not her doing directly, yet she couldn't help but feel useless as more shots rang out from the south and west. All she had was a short-ranged pistol to stop them, unless she Reached again.

Gregorzon grabbed her before she could consider it further. "There is another shooter on that building. I have Reached twice already. If I must do so again—"

"You must not," Nikoza replied, pulling him behind the platform for cover. It was instinct alone, as any rational thought had fled her mind long ago. Only warring panic and determination remained. "Point him out, and I will target him myself."

The Fire Reacher nodded. When he leaped to his feet, she

followed, Reaching and aiming her power at the second-floor window of the building he pointed to. A woman knelt there with her musket resting on the sill. Sending a wave from the snow to knock her back would be impossible from that high, so Nikoza focused instead on summoning a burst of water from behind the shooter.

She dropped to a knee, winded, before she could see if she had succeeded. Dehydration's dizziness took hold. Her vision faded, and her tongue and lips dried until they numbed.

Gregorzon cheered as he pointed into the crowd. "There goes that lowborn scum!" He turned back. "Nikoza?"

She had already collapsed into someone's arms. Muscled, he wasn't the softest rescuer, but Nikoza cared not for comfort as she blinked up at the figure above her.

"Is all well, Sergeant?" Hazat asked, keeping one eye on her and another on the battle.

Nikoza coughed through her dry throat. Taint was horrible, but a deeper dread consumed her as she looked back toward that now empty window. "I killed her…"

She had barely ever hurt someone before, let alone kill them. The convoy slaughtering innocent lowborn in its push forward had been horrifying. This… This made her want to be sick. She was supposed to be helping the lowborn, but instead, she was throwing them from windows with her magic.

"You took down the sniper, so your kill kept our flank secure," Hazat said before wincing. "Though, I cannot say the same for the others."

He helped Nikoza stagger to her feet as another series of blasts rocked the city from the south and west. Plumes of smoke towered into the dim dawnrise sky, breathless circling them like a swarm of flies. How could they not find who was conducting these attacks?

Air Reaching carried Chatik's commands as he hovered above the guillotine's platform amid a torrent of Reacher wisps. Purple Death bolts shot from his left hand as the other crafted shimmering forcefields that deflected the bullets peppering him from each direction. The impossibility of it deepened Nikoza's dread. No one could

Reach into more than a single realm, but nearly every of the fifteen Reacher colors swirled about him in a dangerous array. Despite the show of power, though, the Crimson King looked ready to crumble.

Nikoza held a hand to her breast, breaths catching. All of it made sense now. Her uncle's rapid aging and moments of confusion weren't from the stress of stabilizing a nation on the brink of collapse. They were the result of him wielding enough power to take that control in the first place.

By the Mother below, what had she become a part of?

Motion out of the corner of her eye pulled her attention to the north. The Crimson District had been secured, but every Reacher, even the inexperienced dignitaries who so often relied on their Reacher servants, was focused on the onslaught from the other directions. No one watched the path from the palace, and a lone man carrying a rifle advanced down it.

"Uncle!" Nikoza cried out, rushing toward him. Her voice was lost in the noise, though, and Chatik's defenses covered only his front as the northern gunman stopped just over a hundred yards away and aimed.

She couldn't hear the resulting shot, but the puff of powder smoke signaled enough. Chatik gasped a moment later, his Reaches failing as he dropped before the guillotine.

Nikoza rushed toward him. It was completely against orders, but her flank meant nothing if Chatik died. He had proven that was the last thread preventing the Commonwealth from ripping apart. It mattered not that he had hidden this immense power from her. Without him, all Nikoza had worked for would fall to further ruin, and she could not let that happen.

The foolishness of her haste became apparent, though, when she climbed the platform to see deep red Body Reacher wisps circling Chatik. They matched the blood pooling around him, and she had seen Reacher healing enough to know that his wound would be sealed in seconds. Despite the shot being well timed to strike him down, it would do nothing but Taint him further in the end.

"Execute the prisoner!" Chatik exclaimed as she knelt beside him.

"The Unity Crystal will protect me, but if Etal escapes, he will further the Spirit Plague against our people."

So Nikoza rose and approached the kneeling professor who'd once invited her to be his assistant. Etal looked wrinkled and worn, his gaze heavy with time's burden. He had not tried to flee, and a pang of guilt clutched Nikoza as she stared down at the defenseless man. One person had lost their life at her hand already. Could she truly take another so soon?

"Why did you trick me?" she asked him, taking his arm, but not finding the strength to pull. "Why ask me to become your assistant, just to create a false cure?"

Etal gave a knowing smile. "Was it a false cure, or has Lord Chatik deceived you with his newfound power? Mind Reaching has a powerful sting. Look inside yourself and remember, dear girl, what we achieved together. Seek the truth!"

Nikoza's tongue caught on a reply, and someone joined her by the guillotine before she could gather her wits. They donned watchman's clothes. Except all the watchmen Nikoza had met wore well-fitted uniforms, their boots muddied at worst. This one's pants draped to the ground, and their belt was drawn so tight at their waist that their jacket wrinkled horribly.

"Excuse me," she protested. "Who are—"

The watchman's face entered the lamplight as they stepped forward. Nex of the Shadow Quarter grinned beneath their stolen watchman's helm, a pistol in their grasp. More suspicious guards swarmed from the Crimson District behind them and fired at Crystal Brigade and true watchmen alike. Amid it all, Nex held a smirk savage enough to make an awakened cower.

"You going to give me trouble, Princess?"

A GLORIOUS RETURN

"When the heir returns home, we shall blow our trumpets and hunt enough koilee for the richest furs to drape from his shoulders. All shall hear our glee."
– Harizak Kuzon the Third, former king of Ezman

This was not the trip home Zinarus had hoped for.

Blood covered his stomach and legs in a wash so thick it felt as if he were swimming in it. His eyes were heavy, his breaths labored. He had no idea how long had passed since the shooting, and he lacked even the strength to read his watch as he slumped in the front of that motherforsaken wagon.

Its ticking rang in his ears like some distant mockery of the time he had left. Stories claimed one felt death's grip before it arrived, a kind of premonition that only the most skilled Possibility Reachers held otherwise, but Zinarus was just cold and uncomfortable. Sure, his stomach was tight, and blood loss had his head spinning like the tops used by Vockan children. His spirit didn't *feel* ready to escape his mortal form.

One of the women shifted in the wagon's bed, full of reeking sulfur, and drew up beside him. Kasia, based on the flash of ashen hair and perfume which carried hints of Raviak Forest's famous black raspberries.

"Do you need water or anything else?" she asked him, laying a gentle hand on his shoulder.

Such a simple touch, but a web of relief crossed Zinarus's body from it. He closed his eyes and allowed her aroma and presence to replace the pain knotting in his stomach. His body knew the musket ball was still there. Like the palace guard swarming an invader, all his strength went to fighting the wound, but only a Body Reacher could mend him now.

"Water," he managed to croak. Even that single word sent another wave of agony over him, and he instinctively reached for her. When her hand met his, he clutched it as if it were the last thing anchoring him to life.

It may have been.

He heard her open her canteen, then felt it press against his lips. "You need to open your mouth to drink," she said.

As if to emphasize the point, Spitza hopped onto Zinarus's head and pecked at his unruly hair. The burst of pain opened his mouth, and Kasia immediately took the opportunity to drown him.

"No more!" Zinarus sputtered, half the water shooting down his windpipe.

Each cough only worsened his pain. It nearly knocked him unconscious, and Spitza cawed at him to stop his fit as Kasia smacked his back. Neither did anything to help. Like a fire spreading from his lungs straight up his face, tears streamed from his burning eyes for what seemed an eternity until he finally managed a clean breath.

Only hoof falls and the rattling of the wagon's wheels met his ears when his coughing ceased. He could see nothing, feel nothing beyond that tightness in his stomach. The flash of pain had left him numb, but a crazed cackle soon split his core.

"Zinarus?" Kasia asked, her voice strained as she took his arm. "I'm sorry. Do you need us to stop?"

Her sudden, deep concern made him laugh harder. Death's Daughter had killed dozens of people and struck fear into beings in two realms, but her shell lay broken because of his coughing fit! By the Crystal Mother below, what was happening to them?

Zinarus leaned back against the seat's wooden back and sucked in a long, painful breath. "I fear I am the one going mad this time, Lady Katarzyna. Please tell me we draw close to Vamiustok. If a sip of water almost kills me, I cannot fathom surviving the threat of an awakened or—Crystal Mother save us—a squad of breathless."

"Less than an hour now, my lord," the driver, who somehow happened to be both Zinarus's savior and attempted murderer, confirmed as they passed by a series of farms and pastures around Vamiustok's outlying villages. His shot hand was as gruesome as Zinarus's own wound, and he had not looked at any of them since they had set off. The poor man no doubt wondered if Zinarus's mother, Sania, would have him imprisoned, or worse. That was before one considered whether he'd ever heal his hand.

"Do not think of such spirits," Kikania squeaked from the back. "The Crimson Court has no reason to know we are here, so we are safe. Right, my lady?"

Kasia released him. The fear in her eyes deepened, and though she replaced it with a scion's stoic expression, he caught her gaze flicking to what he assumed to be one of her haunting specters. "Chatik will have seen Zinarus leave the Chamber of Scions through my portal. Likely, the Crimsons will believe House Vamiustok is an enemy and potential vulnerability, considering your proximity to the sand mines they seized from you. We must hope they have greater problems like Kelosh and Tiuz's Confederation of Harizak."

"My mother's people trust her," Zinarus replied, taking some relief in how close they were. They had to be nearing the end of the twenty-hour day since his shooting. A second late and Body Reaching would be useless. Only a surgeon could keep him alive then.

Spitza adjusted on top of his head, nestling down as if he were her nest. He had forgotten the raven was there, and the motion nearly sent him into another fit.

Kasia made a clicking noise and extended her hand toward Spitza, but she remained. A defiant *gwah, gwah* was her only reply, spurring a terrifying glare from Kasia, even if Zinarus knew it wasn't directed at him.

"Trust is important," Kasia muttered to both man and bird. "We cannot assume people's loyalties in times such as these, however, and whatever Body Reacher we find, you must be *certain* that they will seek to heal you."

"Carelias, my aunt," Zinarus replied. "She despises my mother, but used to keep our miners fit. She would never have agreed to work for House Oliezany. Driver, take us to the Glass Quarter, if you could."

The driver tightened his grip on the reins with his one good hand. "Roads are steep around there. Will be hard with the cart."

"That is alright. Do what—"

Kasia waved for Zinarus to be silent, then snatched the back of the driver's coat, pulling until he choked against the force. "You *will* take us where he says if you care about keeping your head."

"Kasia!" Zinarus spat. His face burned, but not from pain this time. "This man shot me out of surprise and fear. Your bullet in response went beyond justice already. Let us worsen neither his guilt nor his pain when he is clearly doing all he can to right his error."

She released the driver, who glanced at Zinarus out of the corner of his eye before giving a subtle nod. Zinarus needed no thanks, though. Their sudden appearance had upset this man's journey. He had surely not set off with the intention of shooting a random passerby, and his shock appeared genuine. Most people, lowborn or scion, had no desire to wound others.

They rode the rest of the way in relative silence, the pain creeping back into Zinarus's stomach as he kept pressure on the wound. Kasia's gauze had done its job, but was now soaked as blood flowed freely from his abdomen. The musket ball itself had likely not hit any vital organs. As they neared familiar territory, though, he worried he would perish from blood loss on Carelias's doorstep.

His vision faded to mere blurs, sounds like the gargled nonsense of swimmers underwater, by the time they passed from the outer farms into Vamiustok proper. Ironically, it was in this infirm state that he realized light pierced the southern horizon. It was a few mere copper rays, but dear Mother, it injected fresh vigor straight into Zinarus's veins.

"It is dawnrise," he mumbled through lips that were so numb they felt like boulders upon his face.

Kasia shifted from the sulfur pile and peeked out of the wagon again. Had she truly been so focused on him not to notice? He was thankful for it nonetheless, as each word she spoke pulled him from death's embrace. "So it seems. Assuming that makes today the first of dawnrise, yesterday was my twenty-fifth spiritday—twenty-five years since I became an accursed daughter of everdark. I am surprised Tazper failed to remind me as such, but I cannot blame him, as I have not been the most amicable friend as of late."

Spitza clicked as the wagon bobbled over stray stones, the slope ever-steepening. She flapped her wings, but the left one remained useless. Only when Kasia extended a hand to her once again did the bird chitter happily and return to her mistress's shoulder.

Oh, what he would have done to comfort Kasia like Spitza could. Her words weren't wrong, but neither were they right. Though she had been far from amicable in recent days, that had not made him less willing to be by her side. If anything, he realized now more than ever how much she needed to not be alone, as that pit of grief in her heart tore her apart piece-by-piece. Such pain never left, but it was better shared than buried away. Regizald had been his confidant. Now... Well, he needed Kasia just as much as she needed him.

"You... are... more," he stammered, his eyes rolling back. Though he wanted to congratulate her for finishing her twenty-fifth year and reassure her that he understood her struggles with her victims in Tystok, he had the strength for neither.

Shouting, either distant or near, rang out, but Zinarus couldn't raise his head to see. Time slipped past. One heartbeat, he was on that carriage bench. The next, his skin found the warmth of a house, firelight dancing behind his eyelids and the gentle sweetness of Vockan fire lilies tickling his nose.

He blinked up at a lamp hanging over him. Senses frayed, he tried to focus on one thing at a time, tracing the lines of what felt like wood beneath his fingers. A table perhaps? Some kind of cloth covered its center, but he found it wet near his torso.

"You must remain still," the voice of his Aunt Carelias said from above him before she muttered under her breath, "Why is it always the men who squirm?"

"Thank you," Zinarus breathed, but he doubted the words made it out before she stuck something between his teeth.

"It will be uncomfortable, but you will thank me when that courtly tongue of yours is not bitten off."

Zinarus tried to lift his head to scan the room. To no avail. All he could see was a flash of amber, followed by a smooth palm meeting his own.

"You will be fine," Kasia assured him. "Though you lost a lot of blood, we found your aunt while you were unconscious."

Carelias clicked her tongue. "Yes, yes. I will do what I must."

Then she raised a knife and cut straight through Zinarus's shirt, and he suddenly bit down on the stick in his mouth as she pressed her finger into the wound. No crimson wisps rose from her talon yet. What in the realms was she doing? Surgeons inspected the wound closely, but were Body Reachers not supposed to heal with ease?

"The ball is embedded inside him," she continued. "Lead is quite the poisonous metal, making removal and healing by magic alone a difficult task. A single Reach may do the trick, but it is better for me to surgically remove the ball first, then finish with Reaching."

Kasia grabbed her arm. "Lazan healed my bullet wounds with Reaching alone."

"Splendid for him, but I have no intentions of Tainting myself when I am a perfectly capable surgeon. The wound will heal well if you unhand me." The bite in his Carelias's voice called Zinarus back to his childhood. So many fights between her and his mother. There were few people who could match the Amber Dame's spite, but in this confrontation, Kasia backed down.

"Do what you must," she said. "Just save him."

"I intend to, but if you are queasy, you should step away."

Instead, Kasia held Zinarus's hand and squeezed as if her grip was all that kept him from death's door. A yelp from what sounded like Kikania followed, and the maid hurried off into another room as Zinarus bit harder on the stick in anticipation of the pain to come. This choice wasn't his. Even if he tried, there was little chance the women would listen to him in his delirious state, so he just closed his eyes, holding Kasia's hand and praying silently for it to be over quickly.

INCREDIBLE WARMTH AND SOFTNESS ENCOMPASSED ZINARUS when he next opened his eyes. A stray part of him wondered for a moment if he had died and passed into the Crystal Mother's embrace, but that thought faded at the familiar sight of his four-poster bed in House iz Vamiustok's estate.

He sat up, stretching to test his stomach. Remarkably, there was no pain at all. He laughed in relief as the bed's glass-imbued curtains scattered his chamber's firelight over him like the everbright through a decorative window. Those curtains protected the bed on each side as Sania's paranoid final defense against spirits. After all they had seen in recent hundred-hours, though, Zinarus was grateful for his mother's preparedness.

A realization struck him then: He was home.

Guilt followed. The trip from Kalastok to Vamiustok took about a hundred-hour and a half—longer when the roads were laden with snow—so with Zinarus's focus on business in the capital, he had not visited his family as often as he should have. It was safe to say Sania's letters made it clear she had not appreciated his absence, but everdark was the busiest time for the Chamber of Scions particularly because travel was difficult. Scion elites hunkered down beneath Kalastok's protective towers and conducted business until they could return to their remote estates for much of everbright.

Except dawnrise had come. Soon, neither Kelosh nor the Crimsons' armies would be as slowed by the ephemeral storms, and Zinarus feared the destruction to come. Nothing good came from war, especially for the most vulnerable.

Some discomfort returned to his stomach as he pushed open the curtains and swung his legs over the edge of the bed. There was no apparent mark when he lifted his shirt to check where the musket ball had been, but even Body Reaching couldn't fix the mind's instinct to believe one was still hurt. The projectile was gone, and he was healed. Unfortunately, though, his mechanical leg was missing.

He eyed the little bell hanging from the panel above the bed. Sania had installed it early in his life to ensure he was never trapped without his artificial leg—either his old peg one or the mechanical one he had constructed more recently. Her sentiment was pure, but a part of him ached each time he rang it. It was a reminder that, in many ways, he was not yet truly independent. Not until he could craft a perfect prosthetic for those like him and find a cure to this ailment.

That ache joined with his tight stomach as his old curse sent his hand trembling. He slowed his breaths, waiting for the shuddering to lessen before he could ring the bell and signal to his mother's servants. The ache only worsened at the thought of Regizald and how Zinarus had failed his friend and servant.

To distract himself from his dread, Zinarus studied the glass-lined furnishings of his bedroom. Demand for the sand from House iz Vamiustok's old mines to make glass had ensured their estate was far finer than his townhouse in Kalastok. The desk and wardrobes were crafted from red cedar and adorned with carvings of spirits, Glassblade, and the shamans known as Whisperers among the Vockans.

He smiled, remembering how he would stare at those carvings as a child. Carelias would sit across from him in the lush, curved-back chairs and tell stories. They all focused on heroes fighting for justice in an unjust world, and he would swing his good leg and his peg one while he imagined riding as a knight into battle.

"The greatest warriors for change must know when to don their armor," she had said, "and when they must set it aside to find peace. Progress does not arrive so easily, but it will never come if we do not know when to fight and when to talk."

Sania had never been pleased at Carelias's teachings. While his mother was an ambitious woman, seeking to make House iz Vamiustok the second Vockan one to ascend to the ranks of the great houses, his aunt was a radical. Zinarus had found himself somewhere between them, and it pained him how Sania saw that as a betrayal. After seeing how Gregorzon truly betrayed Kasia, he wondered what it took to have a united family.

A Vockan manservant soon arrived. A new one, based on his unfamiliarity, and Zinarus held to Kasia's warning about who to trust. It was an unspoken, but well known, truth that scion houses rarely conducted assassinations directly. A bribed or blackmailed servant made it much easier to deny responsibility.

So he went through the exercise of attaching his mechanical leg without speaking. It was disconcerting compared to his usual genial nature, but despite Kasia's flaws, she knew the world of deceit far better. That did not mean he needed to be rude.

"The ladies Sania and Katarzyna await you in the dining room," the manservant said, head bowed when Zinarus was finished. "Is there anything else, my lord?"

Zinarus stood to test the leg. It still clicked away at the ankle, but with his tools here, he would finally be able to mend it completely. "That is all…" He chuckled to himself. "My apologies, I failed to ask your name."

"Atticus ik Vamiustok, my lord," the boy replied without raising his head. Lowborn Vockans held the *ik* before their home city instead of a scion's *iz*, and most of the servants in the estate would share the surname, whether related or not. Such was Vockan tradition of valuing the community more than simply one's family.

Zinarus patted him on the shoulder and smiled. "Thank you, Atticus. Know that if I am quiet, it is not because of you, but because I lost my previous servant recently. He was a good friend."

"I'm sorry."

"As am I…" Zinarus sighed, taking the cane which Atticus offered. It was made from the same red cedar as the chamber's furniture with its head forming a swoop that ended at a sharp point. Though different than the cane he had lost while kidnapped by those strange Water Realm crustaceans, it would do well.

He began to sweat as he left his chambers and headed down the hall. Rugs were uncommon in Vockan estates, and his cane rang against the quartz floors, the swirls of white and gray broken by amethyst crystals that had inspired the house's iconic purple garbs. They still mined for these other minerals and crystals after losing the sand mines, but for nothing could match the value of pure, glass-worthy sand. Amber, though, challenged that notion.

A female servant opened the dining room door, allowing him to meet the gaze of the Amber Dame herself. Seated across from Sania at the long table, she wore a conspiring expression over a traditional Vockan shawl and woolen dress. That itself was hardly a surprise, but Zinarus's chest tightened knowing she had likely been questioned by his mother.

"It seems Lady Carelias acted with enough swiftness and skill," Kasia said as she rose with Sania. "Thank the Crystal Mother that her gifts could keep your body whole."

He narrowed his eyes. Was he dreaming? In what realm did Kasia appeal to religion, unless she was simply appealing to Sania's ideals?

His mother rushed toward him, her violet blanket scarf clasped with gold billowing behind her like an Ogrenian kite. Sania shared his sloping oval jaw and near non-existent eyebrows. Even she had a portion of Ezmani blood from the Commonwealth's formation and Vocka's most powerful families earning Reaching through the resulting marriages. Her skin, though, remained deep Vockan brown with her brighter hair tied up in a traditional fashion.

"My dear boy," she said as she took his face in her smooth hands. "How could you allow yourself to be put in so much danger?"

He held the back of her hands and guided them away, his cheeks burning. It was impossible not to see Kasia's wry smile out of the corner of his eyes. "There is far more danger than a cart driver with a musket, I fear. How much has Kasia told you?"

"Kasia?" Sania asked. Her voice resembled a serpent's hiss more than a mother's question, and Zinarus immediately regretted letting such an informal name slip. She no doubt had her suspicions already.

In mere seconds, he had all but confirmed them. "Lady Katarzyna was just beginning to explain the events of everdark. I must say, you have had quite the adventure, and I cannot wait to hear your side of the story."

The questioning squint of her eyes made all Zinarus's joy of home vanish, but there was no turning back now. To face the Crimsons, they needed both Kasia's army and whatever forces his house could muster. That meant convincing Sania that this was the right path.

"Of course, Mother," he said with a horribly faked smile. "There is so much to discuss."

FLAMES FROM THE ASHES

"Let the scions learn to eat dust, then become it." – An excerpt from *The Dawnrise Manifesto* by Evit Paxian

FIVE HOURS BEFORE ETAL'S EXECUTION

The Ashes of Dawn's safehouse buzzed with excitement upon Tazper's arrival. Too much. Nex was ready to crack some skulls to clear space for them to meet with the scion and their own lieutenants, but Vinnia managed to coax enough people into deliveries or other preparations first.

"You let a scion just hang around the safehouse?" Nex asked Jiinaan once they'd huddled in the back of the warehouse's underground storage. "He could've been anyone!"

Jiinaan looked to Vinnia for back-up, but she just raised her hands. "This one wasn't my choice," she said.

"You know you can trust me," Tazper appealed, standing among the trio of lowborn like a cat surrounded by hounds. "Kasia sent me, and as far as I am aware, she left you with a sizable amount of funds to help until she had more work for you."

Nex crossed their arms. "It's the only reason the Ashes' safehouses weren't eaten up by the gangs. That doesn't mean Jiinaan knew who you were."

"Hey," Jiinaan replied, the Reshkan's Ezmani still rough. "He didn't look like threat. I crack neck if he was." He mimed doing exactly that, which convinced Tazper to take half-a-step back.

"We are united against the Crimson Court, are we not?" Tazper asked, sweat pouring down his brow. "Consider me an envoy from House Niezik to aid your efforts against them in Kalastok, and if those fail, to lead you to safety among the rebels in the Confederation of Harizak. As I explained, Kasia had no desire to abandon the city, but the Crimson Coup made that impossible."

Nex curled their lip. "So she sends us a footman who can't even Reach and tells us to join up with the scion rebels if that's not enough? I'd rather eat my boot than help those assholes."

Vinnia yelped. "I *think* that Nex means to say—"

"I said exactly what I meant," Nex snapped. "We're a tool to Kasia, but I can't claim I didn't use her the same way to get the cure. It's effective. That doesn't mean I'm joining with another group of scions who locked us on the west side. They're just mad because they're not in charge now, and if we help them, nothing will change for us."

"Commander Tiuz, Lady Katarzyna, and Lord Zinarus are all dedicated to reform," Tazper said. "Fighting beside them would certainly help prove that even the lowborn of the western city deserve more rights than they have now."

Jiinaan shrugged. "Fair point he make."

"Fine." Nex closed on Tazper until they stood toe-to-toe. They were far shorter than the footman, but his lip quivered anyway. "You want us to trust you and the scions? Then you need to prove yourself to the Ashes."

"Nex, be careful," Vinnia said, taking her arm. "He is a friend if he comes from Kasia."

Nex gritted their teeth, but nodded as they stepped back. "You're right. We need our allies, but they're useless if we don't take advantage of them. Remember Etal, scion? He'll be executed in a few hours, and our plan to rescue him relies on distraction. That'll be a lot easier with you."

"Professor iz Noshok is to be executed?" Tazper asked. His voice remained exasperated, but he appeared calmer without Nex in his face. "What of his cure?"

"That's why we've got to stop them before they…" Nex ran their finger across their throat, making an exaggerated sound of a blade slicing through flesh. "The Spirit Plague ain't going anywhere until we rescue him. You in?"

"You have yet to tell me what this plan is."

Jiinaan cocked his head. "Yeah. What you want him do? I can handle."

"No offense, Jiinaan," Nex replied, "but you look as Reshkan as you are. There's no way they'd let you into the Crimson District." They turned their attention back to Tazper. "Think you can grab us a carriage if we get you to the east side?"

"A rental, perhaps," Tazper said, rubbing the back of his neck, "but that assumes the places Kasia told me about did not burn in the riots. How do you expect to get past the quarantine?"

Nex grinned and glanced at Jiinaan. "Sometimes, you need to crack some eggs and peel off the shell."

"I WOULD SAY YOU LOOK SILLY, but that is a vast understatement," Tazper said as Nex piled into his rented carriage with Jiinaan and the two biggest brutes that they could find in the Ashes of Dawn.

Nex stuck out their tongue. "It worked, didn't it?"

Each of them, besides Tazper, wore watchman uniforms that the Ashes of Dawn and other gangs had collected. Most of their agents spread throughout the protestors in the Market District had similar disguises as they hid barrels of gunpowder in abandoned buildings. It was risky, but those explosions were placed to not hurt anyone, just draw the Crystal Brigade's attention away from the guillotine itself.

"Crossing the Kala River when the entire city watch is focused on the northern market was hardly the riskiest part of your plan,"

Tazper said, fixing his gaze on Nex. "Are you certain of your escape route?"

Nex grinned back. "Don't worry, scion. I won't leave you to the hounds."

They weren't at all certain, but they had no intentions of letting Tazper know that. Getting into the Crimson District, distracting the Reachers, and grabbing Etal all came first. If that worked, then Nex would drag the professor out by his damned talon if they had to.

"Keep your head down," Nex told Jiinaan, following their own order as they rolled to a stop at the western-most entrance to the Crimson District.

A few watchmen patrolled, and they would notice a sand-skinned Reshkan man and a short Ogrenian whose uniform practically swallowed them whole. Nex wished they could've altered their appearance with Possibility Reaching, but for this to work, they would need that Reach for luck instead. They'd barely slipped by the bridge guards by throwing some powder over Jiinaan and Nex's faces to make them look like pale Ezmani. This would be a closer inspection, though, and Nex doubted it would hold up.

Jiinaan pulled down his watchman's helm, but it had only a small brim at its front, unlike the swooping one Nex often used to conceal their identity. They had to hope sitting him in the center, between the other two brutes, would be enough.

Nex bit their cheek as the watchmen opened the carriage door to peer inside. The driver had directed them to Tazper's side, and the footman gave a toothy smile that might have well announced they were hiding something.

"Hello!" he exclaimed far too gleefully. "The protestors were gathering on these watchmen's route, so I figured I would give them a bit of assistance on my way north."

The first watchman huffed and drew back. "Papers or talon? Can't let anyone in without proof they're a scion."

Tazper winced, but nodded, rifling through his bag to pull out a stamped piece of parchment. "This verifies that I am Tazper of House Janka."

"The name sounds familiar," the other watchwoman said from behind. "You with one of the great houses?"

"Not directly, no, but I do business in the Crimson District often. You may have seen me before."

Nex put a hand on their pistol's butt as the guards shared a whisper. The Possibility Reacher slowly nodded toward Jiinaan, just in case this went down poorly, and silently thanked Vinnia for insisting she stay in the safehouse with the rest of the Ashes. She didn't know how to fight, and Nex couldn't have handled worrying about her the whole time.

They so badly wanted to Reach, influencing the chances of Tazper's persuasion, but they held back. Wasting it now would likely ruin everything. The Children of Zekiaz were a mysterious organization with more resources than the Ashes of Dawn could dream of, and Nex preferred not failing their part of the deal, especially as it would doom all those impacted by the Spirit Plague.

The watchwoman turned to leave as the man returned the papers to Tazper. His expression was stern, but for now, he didn't make any threatening movements. "Be careful. The Crimson Court are shooting first lately, and they've got the whole Crystal Brigade in there."

"The Brigade has brought in new recruits?" Tazper's voice cracked. "That... That is wonderful."

With a chuckle, the guard slammed the door shut and waved them on. Nex didn't relax until they started rolling, and when they were out of sight of the guards, jabbed a finger into Tazper's chest. "You're nothing like Kasia. You know that?'

"There are few who can match her," he replied. His cheeks turned red as a poppy as he crossed his legs, the stress finally getting to him. "I am not skilled at deception, but luckily, my role is complete."

"About that..."

Nex nodded to Jiinaan again, and the Reshkan held out the rifle that had been sitting on his lap. It was the type the Oliezany foreman had called quality. They'd find out soon whether that was the truth, or if it was typical businessman bullshit, as they needed to accurately shoot Chatik Bartol to draw attention from Etal. That would allow their real advance.

Tazper gawked down at the gun, waving his hands. "There has been a mistake."

"You shoot," Jiinaan told the stunned scion. "Point. Pull trigger. Send bullet through head. Easy."

"I am not a rifleman!" Tazper replied as he cowered further from the gun until Nex lunged at him and threw their hand over his mouth.

"Half the Crimsons will hear if you keep it up. I'll Possibility Reach to help you hit Chatik, but it needs to be you." Nex threw a hand toward the other two brutes. "These two will pretend to capture you after you take the shot while me and Jiinaan handle the rest."

"Jiinaan and I," Tazper said.

Nex bopped him on the forehead. "I'm the one in charge here. There's no way you're going to grab Etal. One of those scions will probably recognize you if you try."

He wrinkled his nose and gave an exasperated sigh. "I meant your grammar, but that is irrelevant now." Tentatively, he took the rifle, holding it as if it were some disgusting slop his kid had found in the street. "As Possibility Reaching is not all that familiar to me, can you explain how it is supposed to help me shoot the Crimson King?"

"Simple. Like Jiinaan said, all you gotta do is aim and pull the trigger." Nex removed their glove and wriggled the Spirit Crystal ring on their index finger. "Possibility is a weird realm. It lets me change what kind of cards I have in my hands, mess with my appearance, and sometimes even pull a small object from nothing when I focus enough. But more importantly, Reaching makes me lucky. Seems to me that'll help us if I give some of that to you and some to me when we pull this off."

"Luck?" he muttered. Nex had seen the footman exasperated, but his anger was new. There was something adorable about it, like a little squirrel that was mad you stole its acorn. "Chatik wields the Unity Crystal and apparently every realm through it, and you intend for me to shoot him with *luck*?"

Nex sat back and pretended to think about that. They had no idea what a Unity Crystal was or why it mattered, so they just stroked their chin and failed to hold back a smirk. "Maybe you are like her after all."

"That is not what is relevant now! We are attempting what would be a dangerous, foolish maneuver against anyone else, but knowing that the Crimsons rebuilt the Crystal Brigade and have Chatik probably watching Etal makes this suicide. He can create a forcefield, Nex, then shoot a death bolt straight into each of us."

The carriage rolled to a stop outside the groomed trees of the western palace gardens. There was no going back, but Tazper might well have lit a bomb's fuse among them.

Nex balled their hands into fists in their lap. "Chatik can fucking Death Reach, and you didn't think to mention this sooner?"

"I did not know that you intended to have me, or anyone for that matter, shoot him." Tazper shook his head. "I want nothing to do with this."

"Unfortunate."

Nex cocked their gun and held it to his head, the other three Ashes of Dawn members following suit. They didn't want to do this, but Tazper was either an asset or a liability. It would be a lot more difficult without him. If he betrayed them, though, it would be impossible.

"Think," Jiinaan said. "Be smart."

Blasts from the south shook the carriage and only worsened Tazper's shaking. Distant screams followed, and Nex gritted their teeth with each second they wasted. It was now or never.

"Plan's started," they said as they pressed their pistol deeper into Tazper's temple. "You're either with us or against us."

"You will get us all killed!" the scion said. Sweat poured down his brow, but a familiar twitch in his eye convinced Nex to pull back their gun and wave off the others. Fury. These Crimsons had tortured him, and that hatred was exactly what the Ashes needed in him.

"Not if you keep that hand of yours steady," they said. "Make the shot, and you might save thousands from the Spirit Plague. Or you can let it run its course, handing all those awakened spirits to the Crimsons."

Tazper gripped the rifle and nodded as a deep chasm formed between his brows. Exactly the grit they were looking for. "I will do it for the innocents. We cannot allow the plague to burn through people who have done nothing wrong."

Nex threw open the door. "That's the spirit."

Everything from there passed like a blur. Once Tazper stumbled from the carriage, Nex grabbed his arm and Reached, sharing luck between the two of them. They'd only done it a couple times before and had no idea if it would be enough. It had to be, so they held onto that fact before nodding to Tazper and hurrying through the gardens with Jiinaan.

The pair soon arrived at the scene of the chaos, pretending to be reinforcements around the guillotine as the riotous crowd sparred with watchmen and Crystal Brigade Reachers. Some in the crowd were from the Ashes or other gangs, but Nex had seen the mob gathered around the guillotine in protest. The Crimson Court had hoped to make a scene of an apparent traitor. Instead, they'd yet again ignited the powder keg that was Kalastok's lowborn.

Nex shouted fake orders and forced people back from the western flank of the guillotine platform as they caught sight of Etal, curled in a ball. The Crystal Brigade had been upon another small platform here, but they'd abandoned it to chase down a second planned explosion that erupted in a burned building near the river. That gave Nex and Jiinaan a clear spot as Chatik rose above the guillotine with his Reaches whipping around like a damn magic blizzard.

Now Tazper just needed to do his job.

"C'mon," Nex muttered to themself as Jiinaan shoved back a group of rioters. "Take the shot."

From the rapid pace of their arrival, time slowed to a crawl. Gunshots rang out from the gangs' positioned snipers, and the Crystal Brigade replied in turn. They wore ridiculous red frock coats with colored threads that likely represented the realm they Reached, but even the scions in suits had removed their gloves. Took a lot for those lazy bastards to lift their taloned fingers.

Chatik flew above it all with what Nex assumed was Air Reaching, the exact forcefields Tazper had warned them about protecting his front. Purple bolts of pure Death shot from his hands and slammed into the chest of the nearest sniper.

Nex forced themself to watch the lowborn rebel shrivel and die. Whether from the Ashes of Dawn or not, these gunmen had volunteered to help rescue Etal. They knew what was on the line, and they were willing to give everything for it.

Guilt clutched Nex's chest. They'd put all these people at risk, just to rely on a scion. Sure, even scion Body Reachers couldn't cure the Spirit Plague, but Tazper didn't live among those suffering the most. He didn't know what the lowborn endured every single day. Had Nex made a mistake trusting him?

Just as Nex considered heading back to check what was taking so long, a gunshot rang out from the north. A single one, and Nex worried for a second it had been a watchman spotting Tazper.

Then Chatik dropped.

Nex grabbed Jiinaan and pulled him toward the platform, waving for the other hidden false watchmen to join them. "Time to go!"

Their heart pounded as they hurried through the lines of guards. Amid the chaos, few had the time to rush to Chatik's aid, but the one who did sent fury burning through Nex's veins.

Nikoza Bartol knelt beside Chatik in a Crystal Brigade uniform, her face and body unmarked despite the firefight, but tears welled in her eyes. Nex scoffed at that. The former princess wept for the tyrant who slaughtered thousands for an army of spirits, and now, she was a sergeant in the band of Reachers who exacted his every command. Hypocrite, just like all the rest.

Nex cocked their gun again as they climbed onto the guillotine's platform. Somehow, Nikoza had gotten to Etal first, standing over him with a pistol in one hand and her Water Reacher talon exposed on the other. That wouldn't do.

So Nex aimed their pistol at Nikoza as the Reacher turned to meet them. "You going to give me trouble, Princess?"

Nikoza's jaw hung ajar until she noticed Jiinaan approaching from the other side. She swung her talon toward him, keeping the pistol pointed at Nex. "What in the Mother's name are you doing, Nex? You are causing a massacre!"

There was a bite to her voice that Nex hadn't heard before. They liked it. It screamed of the pain, the sorrow, that every lowborn on the west side endured, and now, she had a taste of it too.

"I'm saving us from the Spirit Plague," Nex snapped. "Get out of the way!"

Nikoza's fierceness wavered, her gun lowering slightly. "The professor is a liar."

"No, Chatik is."

Nex burst toward Nikoza before she could raise her gun, then slammed the butt of their pistol into the scion's temple. She stumbled back, and Jiinaan scooped Etal into his arms as the Ashes of Dawn's false watchmen formed a defensive ring. The true guards were trapped.

Even shot, though, Chatik remained a threat. Nex caught sight of the deep red Body Reacher wisps healing his wounds as he stood with a wry smile. They needed to get out of here, but he could stop them with a point of a finger.

"For Jax!" Nex shouted as they fired a shot directly through the Crimson King's chest.

He barely flinched.

"Fucking Crimsons!" Nex leaped off the platform as Jiinaan did the same with Etal. A dozen more shots peppered Chatik behind, but the bastard barely winced as those red and Life Reacher green wisps surrounded him. Spirits, he looked like a walking corpse!

Though far from killing him, those shots forced Chatik to focus his Reaching on healing and defense. Nex didn't look back to check if Death Reacher purple had joined the other wisps. They couldn't do anything more except run.

Some of the other guards of the Crystal Brigade must've caught sight of their rescue, because firebolts shot overhead. The ground quaked too, rolling Nex's ankle when a fissure formed in the middle of the cobblestone. It devoured their foot and threatened to hold them there until another of the Ashes grabbed Nex's arm and tore them free. They stumbled onward on the injured ankle. All they needed was to reach the safety of the Crimson District's wall, then make their way back to the carriage.

This had always been the worst part of their plan. It relied entirely on luck and the chaos of the riot to split the Crimsons' forces, and Nex regretted not having more ideas as a firebolt struck their shoulder.

"Run, Nexie!" Jiinaan shouted back at them, using the pet-name Vinnia had for them. It would've annoyed them if it was anyone else, but you couldn't be mad at a big oaf like him.

But Nex could be plenty angry at the pain consuming their back. They gritted their teeth, pushing on until they staggered around the wall and into the palace gardens. It was ironic the district they'd so often hated gave them protection now, but they couldn't find the strength to laugh. They needed all of it to haul themself toward the carriage.

Straight into the rush of palace guards.

Cursing beneath their breath, Nex decided to continue their watchman act as the guards approached with a skeptical glance at Etal. "The rioters were about to seize the prisoner," Nex insisted before pointing back to the northern market. "Hurry, the king has been shot!"

The guards exchanged looks, nodded, and ran off. Nex wasn't sure if it was because of their Possibility Reaching or the chaos, but they patted their crystal ring in thanks as they hurried on. Jiinaan helped Etal into the carriage as the other Ashes of Dawn kept guard. Tazper was already inside. Spirits, they'd actually done it!

"WHAT ARE YOU DOING?"

The question reverberated through Nex's whole body, white wisps twisting around them and plunging into their skin. They fought on with all their strength, but a force demanded they answer. A Truth Reacher.

Jiinaan turned to interfere, but Nex threw out an arm with all the will they had left. "Go!"

The Reacher forced Nex to their knees as more watchmen rushed past. Jiinaan gave Nex a sorrowful look, then leaped onto the carriage. The driver had probably fled once he realized what was going on, so the Reshkan snapped the reins and sent the carriage rushing away before the watchmen could get a clear shot through the trees.

"It seems we have caught a rat," another Reacher said as Nex bit their tongue to keep from speaking. A Fire one based on his orange-trimmed uniform, he looked familiar, but Nex was sure they'd never met this asshole before.

The Truth Reacher shook her head and crouched before Nex as if they were some infant. "No, this is the one that grabbed Etal. I have heard about you, Nex, and I know you have more poison spines than a koilee." She grinned up at the Fire Reacher. "We lost Etal, but they're about to tell us every secret in that shithole west of the Kala."

WHISPERS OF THE WEST

"Follow the whispers deep within yourself. Hear their meaning. Your meaning. And find the way forward." – Reshkan proverb

Radais rode with a heavy heart as his Glassblades departed from Dalnus, leaving a few small groups behind to protect the capital and other vulnerable villages further south. Against Radais's instincts, Ardinvil was among them. House iz Ardinvil could afford its own estate, but its representatives had more than compensated the Glassblades with supplies for their march to Iliafa.

A crucial piece of that was steel swords capable of stopping a physical weapon. That Earth Bound One in the Whistling Pass had easily shattered Radais's blade and armor, and Radais had an inkling that wouldn't be their final confrontation. Both he and his warriors needed to be ready.

The supreme defender tested the weight of his new blade, slashing through the air as he led the rest of the army. It was heavier before, but he'd intended it to be so. Most of the warriors had simply taken up whatever cavalry or infantry swords that the iz Ardinvils could spare. Radais had gone for something more special.

"I have never seen anything quite like it," Lazan said from the other side of him.

Steel and glass alike glinted in the dim light of the arriving dawn-rise season. Ephemeral storms came more often than not during the season changes, but today had offered them a rare relief. Three days and nights in Dalnus had just barely given the city bladesmith and Order's glassmaster enough time to forge Radais a sword with one edge a blade of the finest steel and the other that of more familiar glass. The craftsmen insisted it could handle any weapon's blow, as long as Radais deflected it with the sleeve of steel that covered one of the sword's flats.

Radais wanted to be proud of the weapon he'd commissioned and now wielded. He couldn't. The weight of Wanusa's loss was too horrible, and it hurt twice as much because of his own failures to protect his family.

"A blade alone cannot stop the second Awakening," he told Lazan.

The scion nodded, letting the topic drop. They had barely spoken and definitely not been intimate since the night Wanusa discovered them. Radais regretted only his drunken forgetfulness to lock the door, but even that had allowed Wanusa could voice her grief. She deserved that much at least.

Vuk bleated beneath him as they crested a ridge, revealing the shadowed valley ahead. Dawnrise had offered some light, but the towering cliffs and mountains surrounding them ensured little of it reached them here. Radais had journeyed to Iliafa from Palmia during his last assignment. This route from Dalnus, though, was unfamiliar. The valley stretched like fingers through deep sand, and he would need to send scouts ahead to decide the best route.

He picked four groups of two experienced warriors and an initiate each to explore the most promising western paths. His instincts told him to send only more experienced warriors, as an initiate could slow them. But this was the most effective way for the recruits to learn. One didn't become a Glassblade master by marching in a column for miles.

Tairanik relayed Radais's orders to the gathered scouts before they set off. The old commander had stitched up his uniform and ordered his armor to be thoroughly polished in Dalnus. Radais allowed himself to take pride in that, as he'd pushed Tairanik to get his act together ahead of the battle in the Whistling Pass. Maybe he could make a difference for the better. When his gaze met Wanusa's solemn one among the warriors making camp, though, his confidence waned.

Polina nodded beside the other commanders. "Keep your wits about you, and return if you find a path too hazardous to continue. Any route that scouts cannot cross will be impossible for the full force."

"Do not engage any breathless either," Radais said. He wondered if he was a coward for it, but they'd lost enough people already. They couldn't defeat the Vanashel without an army to do so. "Rogue awakened are fair under normal protocol, but we don't know if the Vanashel have another ambush planned. Assume any impure spirit could be working with them."

Then he dismissed the scouts, turning back to make his tent, but instead, found Wanusa ordering a group of initiates to do it for him. He caught a few strange glances from them as he approached her.

"Let me guess," he said. "They know about my night with Lazan."

She'd have normally replied with a wry smile, but instead, just slumped her shoulders. "A few of them saw you two kiss in front of the fire. That wasn't necessarily the most indiscreet location if you ask me."

Radais scanned the camp for their resident Reacher, finding him at his makeshift medic station with blood-red Body Reacher wisps encircling him. "I want to pretend it was because of the beer."

"Don't try to lie to me." Wanusa unstrapped her armor and cracked her neck once it was free. The girl had bulked up a lot in the last season, resembling a grown woman more with every passing day. "You two are acting like you're teenagers in some forbidden romance. The warriors trust you, and everyone loves Lazan fixing their worst wounds without asking anything in return. They couldn't care less what you do in your tent, as long as we defeat these Vanashel in the end."

Another voice interrupted Radais before he could reply, "There is far more to the breathless and Bound Ones of the Vanashel than battle, dear child."

Radais scowled at Mariana eavesdropping on their conversation, but she had been among the Glassblades for days now. If the rumor about Lazan and him was that prevalent, she probably already knew. Still, a prominent Whisperer knowing his secrets wasn't reassuring.

"I want to understand the breathless," Wanusa replied, "but the Vanashel took my family, my brother. Inrius lost half his spirit to the awakened, and now he's gone. He didn't deserve this!"

Mariana drew in a long breath. "From what both you and the breathless have told us, it appears that the first of their kind did not deserve their treatment either. The Crimson Court turned innocents into test subjects and corrupted their spirits. These Vanashel blame us all for these sins. More than that, though, they see us as occupiers within their realm."

"Occupiers?" Radais asked. "Breathless didn't exist two decades ago. What claim do they think they have on Zekiaz?"

"Perhaps they see the purest spirits as their ancestors." Mariana extended her hand toward the few drifters hanging around the camp's edge. "As they are all our ancestors, they bind us to this land, but the Vanashel see our bodies as the same corruption of spirit that we see in them."

Wanusa tapped her foot. "The Saleshi feared us, so maybe the Vanashel do too. Just differently. While one faction hides in the mists of the Spirit Wastes, the other learns from our weapons and Reaching to defeat us—the very thing they fear."

"I'd say that is too logical for spirits," Radais said, "but I met Bakeekek. Even if it is more advanced than any other breathless, Rakekeaa implied the Vanashel were started from another group of those first Bound Ones. Could that Earth Reacher be one of them?"

Mariana smiled and rested a hand on Radais's armored forearm. "You see now why we must question our own thoughts and seek the spirits' desires, yes? They tell us much about themselves… and ourselves too."

"It doesn't change that they want to destroy us," Radais said.

Wanusa circled away, brow furrowed as she stared at her boots splitting the snow. "What if it does? They don't realize it, but their fear originates with the Crimson Court, not all of humanity. If we can show them that, maybe they will understand only the Crimsons are their true enemies."

"I wish it were so simple," Radais said. "You saw those things. Did they look ready to negotiate?"

Her gaze challenged him. "No, but neither did we."

Mariana released Radais, then took Wanusa's arm instead. Though her face remained the same stern one as she'd held ever since their first meeting in Dalnus, he could've sworn there was a hint of victory tugging at her lips. "This is why we believed Wanusa must learn the way of the Whisperers. Is she relieved of duty until your scouts return?"

"That is her decision," Radais replied with a nod to Wanusa. "It is your family who endured this first strike, and I won't force you to react a certain way. Do what you must. But do not stray far."

Wanusa thumped her chest and bowed. "Thank you, Supreme Defender."

She removed the rest of her armor per Mariana's wishes before departing with the shaman. With the weight on her heart, she showed no excitement at her new training, but Radais knew her well enough to see her anxious haste. Spirits knew he'd given himself no time to grieve his father, so if she needed to learn more in order to come to terms with Inrius's death, so be it.

The thought of his father pulled him to his sketchbook as he sat on a rock near the camp's eastern edge. From here, he could oversee the entire valley, watching the drifters dancing overhead and animals stirring beneath the bare trees. Life went on, even through the everdark and arrival of the Vanashel. Now, dawnrise enlightened the world.

He flipped the sketchbook open. The ephemeral snowfalls had made drawing difficult in recent hundred-hours, so he needed to take advantage of the clear day he had.

But flipping through the pages, he realized at no point during his journeys had he drawn his father—or anyone else in his family for that matter. It didn't surprise him that he'd ignored his spiteful brother and sister. Why not his parents, though? They hadn't approved of his art or his decision to join the Glassblades, but they had loved him.

That question invited a pain he had denied for so long. Alcohol could dull it, but it didn't fill the hole. Nothing could change that his mother had likely died from grief after he left for the Order, and he'd failed to bring Lazan to heal his father soon enough. He couldn't weep, not in front of all his Glassblades. Tears welled in his eyes regardless as he flipped to a new page and began to draw his father.

Lazan honed in on his distress like an alpine accentor delivering a letter. The Body Reacher still carried only a glass dagger to fend off spirits, but he now wore a steel cavalry blade at his hip. That long coat of his wasn't meant for blades, though, and it tufted up behind him like the bustles noblewomen wore in the Keloshan Empire.

"Ah, I had been worried not seeing that book out in recent days," he said, settling on the rock beside Radais, but not being accustomed to his steel blade, accidentally bumped him with the scabbard.

"Be careful where you stab that sword," Radais replied. "All of camp apparently knows how you used your other one."

Lazan grinned and crossed his legs once he finally managed to seat himself. "Do they? That would explain the looks I have been receiving of late, but it does not explain how closed off you've been." He nudged Radais's arm just soft enough not to interrupt his drawing. "Care to share your thoughts?"

Radais sketched his father's moustache, an arcing thing that stretched beyond his lips. Sorrow warred with his memories of bedding Lazan. How had things turned sour so quickly?

"It is hard to feel joy when I know Wanusa's pain," he admitted. "My mother, then my father, died because I left. I swore to guide

Wanusa, but the same has now happened to her family in the village I once protected. She needs to understand how to move forward." He set down the charcoal and shut his eyes. "How can I help her do that when I haven't moved on myself?"

Lazan's hand fell on his thigh, then tapped the sketch. "This is a start. Let yourself think of him, both the good and the bad."

"You don't talk much about your family," Radais said, opening his eyes and taking Lazan's hand. A few callouses had begun to form, and for once, Radais lamented the wear these travels were putting on the scion. "What would they think of you traveling with Vockan Glassblades?"

"That question bears a dull answer, I fear. House Karianam is a merchant house, and I have barely enough fingers to count my brothers and sisters, each of us another pair of hands around the shops in Niezik lands." He leaned into Radais. "Nothing horrible sent me on my journeys except Lady Katarzyna's call for Body Reachers on her expedition into Raviak Forest. The allure of finding amber, and quite the heavy payment, was enough to convince my family that it was worth it."

Radais remembered his stories about Kasia's duel in Raviak Forest and how she'd earned her title as the Amber Dame. "That is the origin of your Taint, then?"

Lazan released Radais's hand and slipped off his glove, allowing his silvery crystal talon to glint in the lanternlight. It was a majestic thing, and Radais made a mental note to draw the details of it later. Did all talons have the same structure? He'd never had the chance to examine them closely.

"All Realm Reachers endure some Taint when they first accept the crystal," Lazan said, "as we must learn the natural limits of our powers. It is not all that harmful until one pushes their power beyond a certain point."

Radais's heart sank at how casually he spoke about enduring a lifelong ailment. "Like you did to help Kasia win the duel."

The Reacher nodded. "She offered to massively increase my payment, so I strengthened her body, then healed her after Razamat

Uziokaki shot her twice in the duel. After he conceded honorably, not wishing to kill her, I Reached again to heal him. Two Reaches within an hour begins the Taint. A third had me shaking. My body felt like death for days, and though I recovered, I have endured further Taint since to earn my way. I feel my joints ache after every day of our journey. The Spirit Plague frightens me because of that. A couple initiates started showing symptoms after we left Dalnus, and if they're infected, there's not much I can do for them."

Yet more bad news. Radais felt little from it, as there were so many problems already. They would deal with them all in time… somehow.

"Then do what you must to protect yourself and the rest of the troop." He placed a hand on Lazan's back and pressed where it felt the tensest. It seemed to work, so he offered a conciliatory smile. "You saved my life and Vuk's in the Whistling Pass. Know that I don't expect you to push yourself so far for me."

Lazan sniffled from the cold, running his sleeve across his nose. "You say that as if you didn't charge into a squad of breathless by yourself to protect Wanusa and me."

"I would do it again."

"And I would take a thousand Reaches' worth of Realm Taint to keep you alive." Lazan laid his bare hand against Radais's cheek, the cold tip of his talon sending ice through his veins. "Though Wanusa may have had inopportune timing, know that my mind has never left that bed. I will not rush you, but when you are ready, I will accept your warmth eagerly in these frigid mountains. Send your spiteful brother to the Crystal. You are more than he could ever understand."

Then he rose, his talon tracing Radais's jaw before he returned to the infirmary. Radais watched him go without a breath in his lungs. Spirits, what was he doing?

He looked down at his father's sketch. It was far from perfect, but it was a beginning. Moving forward meant accepting the pain of the past, so he picked up his charcoal and went to work. Both on the sketch and on himself.

OH MOTHER

"As the Crystal Mother blesses her chosen scions with her gifts of Reaching, so too does a terrestrial mother grant her children blessings of her wisdom. That is, unless she's a bloody fool." – Jack Himolox, lowborn writer

It would be quite the under exaggeration to say that Kasia was pleased to see Zinarus in the doorway of House iz Vamiustok's dining room. His mother had been keen to discuss the events of everdark.

All of them.

The half-blooded lord averted his gaze after embracing Sania. She took the table's head, so he settled across from Kasia, finally giving her a look that asked whether his mother had crossed a line. She had, but Kasia was more than adept in the art of deflection and delay. They had managed to discuss little of substance beyond the war with Kelosh before Zinarus's arrival.

Focus had been difficult, though, with every other chair at the table occupied by the specters haunting her mind. Aliax took the chair beside Zinarus. His words haunted her as she fought to keep her attention on Zinarus.

"Chatik took your talon, but you don't need Reaching to ruin a partner… or a lover." Aliax clicked his tongue. "Was a bullet to his gut enough to get the point? You think you need your scion lord, but you'll destroy him in the process."

Kasia bit her cheek, crossing her legs and folding her hands politely over them. Sania expected her to lack poise, so she could not go shouting at specters. "Your mother keeps a well-run estate," she told Zinarus instead. "I see where you learned your skills in diplomacy and stewardship."

"I…" Zinarus babbled with his eyes shifting between confusion and fear. "Yes, of course. Mother has taught me well, and I can only wish that I will be a suitable patriarch when my time comes to take the role."

Sania waved a dismissive hand. "Enough with the pleasantries. Lady Katarzyna refused to answer most of my more pressing questions, and you will forgive me if I lack the patience to wait any longer. The Commonwealth is at war with Kelosh and potentially itself. You arrived on a sulfur wagon with a musket ball lodged in your stomach, and you brought neither a carriage nor attendants beyond a single Niezik handmaiden."

"Did you think a matriarch would not notice such an inconsistency?" Sazilz Uziokaki whispered from beside Kasia, his crooked old frame leaning over her seat and making her shift away.

She considered the questioning and Sazilz's interjection for far too long. They had opted to letter ahead via the Vockans' preferred alpine accentor birds instead of sending a courier through a portal, so no one knew of her Axiom Reaching besides her closest allies—and those who'd seen her flee the Chamber of Scions. For now, it needed to stay that way.

"Our arrival was indeed highly unorthodox," Zinarus said with a tug on his jacket. "We intended to travel light, as House Niezik has devoted much of their resources to assisting Lord Tiuz Hazeko and his Confederation of Harizak. It appears that was a mistake."

"How so?" Sania asked, leaning intently on the table.

His deep gray cheeks turned as bright as Vockan fire lilies. Spirits, this was bad. The man was the most honorable person she had ever met, and he would no doubt crumble under his mother's questioning.

"We are wanted by the Crimson Court for exposing the coup led by Lord Chatik Pikezik—now Bartol once again," he said. "Traveling without a significant force allowed us to be less noticeable, but the spirits they control, called breathless, found us and sent our carriage into a wreck."

"Congratulations," Aliax quipped with an exaggerated tap at the air between them. "You've made him a liar. What will be next?"

Zinarus's deception with his own mother shocked Kasia as well, and it took her a moment before she could manage a reply. "Lady Sania, your son was only shot because we were seeking help to take us the rest of the way here. If it had not been for his bravery, that musket ball may have struck me instead."

His jaw dropped, but Kasia merely gestured for him to shut his mouth. Not only was this meeting about securing House iz Vami-ustok's mercenaries for their war against the Crimsons, it was also her chance to ensure Zinarus stayed in good standing with his mother and matriarch. Losing those sand mines had been a signifi-cant blow to their fortunes, and the Kalastok Arena was a distant thought compared to their present problems. Aliax's doubts stirred within her. His boldness around her was quite attractive, though, and she would not dampen that now.

"Is that so?" Sania mused, glancing from Kasia to her son. She plucked a goblet of wine from the table and sipped daintily at it, like Kasia did when she pretended not to be sober. "That sounds nothing like my boy. Katarzyna, did you know the other lads around Vami-ustok called him a coward?"

Kasia did not have to look at Zinarus to notice his wince, and she clenched her fists under the table. It would be incredibly improper to strike a matriarch in her own mansion. That made it all the more tempting. "There is an old Ogrenian saying that my father used to love," she said as she met Sania's gaze. " 'Where the fool sees a cow-ard, history shall mark a strategist.' "

Yet again, Zinarus failed to hide his shock, and Kasia questioned her previous admiration of his deception. Their relationship was complicated. He had trusted her through her worst moments, though, and he needed to know she would do the same for him.

"That is an adorable sentiment," that horrible, Tainted version of Kasia's voice said, but for once, it wasn't in her mind.

A woman appeared in a puff of purple Death wisps behind Zinarus, running her talon across his temple. She held Kasia's features, hair, and build, but where scars marred Kasia's skin and exhaustion deepened her eyes, this Tainted version of her resembled a pristine marble statue more than a real person—perfection in every detail.

"Think about how vulnerable your dear Zinarus is," the Taint mused, "and how quickly Chatik can take him from us with that Unity Crystal. Is he worth risking all we have worked for?"

That struck straight at Kasia's heart, making her feel exposed in this tight room. The Crimsons had tortured Tazper, and they would do worse to Zinarus to disrupt her revenge. Leverage like that made all the difference.

She had left Sania's statement hanging for too long, so she leaned forward, mimicking the matriarch's assertive posture to hide her uncertainty. "No coward could have exposed the Crimson Court's coup with only a scrawled letter and a journal."

"Tell me," Sania replied. "Why do you so fervently defend my son? Can he not speak for himself?"

"I should question instead why you insist on demeaning your heir mere moments after he has recovered from his wounds and come to see you. Lord Zinarus shall inherit your house. Should he not have your full approval to carry on your legacy?"

Zinarus cleared his throat. "Perhaps we should refrain from arguing about my reputation when there are greater matters at hand."

"Listen to the flame-haired lord," her Tainted specter said, sitting on his armrest with a mocking smile. "Focus on our vengeance and not those who get in the way."

"Sania worries about her son," Aliax insisted. "You're a threat to him in her eyes, and she's right."

Kasia cursed under her breath as the specters kept taking her attention away from Sania. Her own reputation was ruined enough already without Sania thinking her insane, but even without the specters, she had stepped far beyond the bounds of a scion guest. A rebuke was inevitable.

But Sania's intensity vanished instead, replaced by a gentle smile. "I had wondered how many of the rumors about the Amber Dame were accurate." Her attention turned to Zinarus. "Though your affiliations surprise me, I am proud you have found allies who are willing to dig the trenches while you keep your nose clean. That is a lord's duty after all."

"You are not worried about the accusations against me?" Kasia asked, brow furrowed. Was Aliax wrong, or was this matriarch playing the verbal games that scions so often did?

"Quite the contrary. I had worried those accusations were exaggerated." Sania swirled her wine goblet, then took a long drink. "King Chatik is no fool. Neither are the others within this Crimson Court. They have planned for this moment, and we need those to face them in the light." She gestured to Zinarus, then looked back at Kasia, her smile turning wicked. "We also require those willing to wrestle them in the depths of the shadows."

Zinarus rapped his knuckles across the table as a door on the other side of the room opened to reveal servants carrying bowls of steaming soups. Mountain nuts and dried fruits adorned the plates beneath each bowl. Zinarus eyed them like the six-legged povnik scavengers of the Vockan Mountains would the scraps of a hunter's kill.

As they ate, the trio caught up on events from Kalastok and Vocka. Much of Vamiustok's problems meant little to Kasia, though, and the specters took the chance to pull her every direction.

"Ignore the Confederation and this half-blood," her Taint said. "The Crimson Court, Kelosh, and a dozen other factions could use him against us. We cannot be so exposed when we strike straight at Chatik's heart ourselves." She gestured at Kasia's crystal hand. "Use the Axiom and make Chatik regret ever bringing us into his confidence."

Aliax smiled in that cutting way that had once mirrored her worst impulses. "I know you. You need revenge, not some scion lord to pull your loyalties away from our home. Burn down the Crimsons' glass house. Let that fire torch the rest of the scion elites while you're at it. Zinarus won't do what's necessary to make that happen."

Slowly picking at her food, Kasia had to admit that burning down the Crimsons and the great houses' seats of power was an appealing prospect. Chatik wasn't her only foe. The Crimsons had infiltrated every part of an already corrupt system that did nothing to investigate her father's assassination. The Chamber of Scions had willingly voted for her execution. What did she care for the state of the Commonwealth when she was finished with her revenge?

The specters continued their bickering for some time. It made her head ache, then ring with their echoing voices, until one particular bit of iz Vamiustok family drama drew her attention.

"Your Aunt Carelias has been a menace during your absence," Sania told Zinarus, her geniality fading. "I had hoped you would speak to her and silence the mine strikes she inspires, but perhaps it would be better if you brought her to this Fort Harizak. Body Reachers are quite useful in war after all."

Zinarus set aside his spoon and dabbed his mouth clean. Even starving, he ate with the care of someone who believed all of scion society was watching, but two days without food had left his normally inviting face looking gaunt. "Carelias shares my concerns about the miners' working conditions. We may criticize the Ezmani houses for many things, but they provide Earth, Fire, and Air Reachers to ensure safety, not to mention the awakened attacks that are always prominent when we dig."

"It is a shame, then, that such Reachers would be a significant extra cost that may have been sustainable with our sand glass mines. Without them or this arena of yours, we are in a tight position."

"The mines do not matter," her Tainted specter hissed. "Vockans will not deliver us victory against when we require a precise strike."

"Why not take the mines back?" Kasia asked Sania, gripping the table's edge as she fought the specter's will. Leonit would have told her that strategy mattered to ensure options. "House Oliezany stole them through the Crimson Court's deception, and I know well that

Tzena will manipulate the new patriarch, Otterzon, now that Gornioz is dead. Why not strike while the Crimsons are focused on Kelosh and the Confederation?"

A light ignited in Sania's eyes, mirrored by the Tainted specter. "An excellent proposal."

"That would invite an armed response from our foes," Zinarus replied. "My apologies, but I do not believe we have just cause to assault Oliezany property. Whether through deception or not, I signed the paperwork and used the money from the sale."

"Told you," Aliax said. "He doesn't have what it takes, and he'll hate you for what you must do."

Kasia scoffed as a bead of nervous sweat trickled down her brow. *Hold it together.*

"A signature means nothing when it was scribed with a gun to your head," she said. "The Crimson Court declared war on us all the moment they launched their coup. Some chose to kneel before Chatik, but we have the chance to regain an essential resource. Between our two houses, we may form an alliance of amber and glass that negates their advantage."

Sania's expression soured at the mention of amber. "Your amber's effectiveness at capturing spirits will devalue our glass, which is unfortunate."

"This is not about profit!" Kasia snapped as her Tainted specter did the same. A savageness cut through their joined voices like a gash from a broken blade. "We must defeat the Crimson Court, and it does not matter what means we use. Take a share of my amber for all I care. If it funds your forces enough to help me face the Crimsons' armies, then so be it."

Sazilz clicked his tongue beside her. "So you surrender your amber to lowborn and Vockans, yet steal it from its rightful owners? House Uziokaki—"

"You have no claim," Kasia muttered back. "Raviak Forest is ours, and Razamat conceded it on your behalf."

"A false duel," Sazilz replied before fading into a purple mist. The rest of the specters besides her Tainted one followed, and Kasia swallowed as that haunting image of her lurked behind Sania.

The iz Vamiustok matriarch stared at Kasia as if she had thrown her food over herself. She hastened a glance at Zinarus, an obvious question lingering behind her lips: Is this woman as mad as they claim?

"My apologies," Kasia said, faking a smile and standing with her hands clasped before her. It was all she could do to stop from shaking. How had she lost her composure so easily in the end? "It has been quite the journey, so I should retire and allow the two of you to speak in private. Thank you, Lady Sania, for your hospitality."

She curtsied quickly and left before Zinarus had the chance to appeal. In mere moments, she'd gone from Sania calling her plan excellent to the matriarch thinking her insane. This Realm Taint wouldn't improve, so she needed a way to address it.

And she could only do that alone.

"Sania won't forget that," Aliax said, hurrying to follow her up the steps to her guest room. "Neither will he."

She stopped atop the mezzanine at the sound of Sania and Zinarus's voices heading down the hall. Lingering would be an intrusion, but her specters' doubts inspired her own. No servants were about, so she crouched out of sight as the pair's footsteps drummed across the stone floor.

"You should be more careful of your associations," Sania's voice echoed. "After that display, few would question that she is not in her right mind."

Mother and son passed into the visible area beneath the stairs, walking arm-in-arm. Zinarus's face remained as red as his hair, and with his hesitation to reply, they passed from the hall below before he said a word. A door to what Kasia assumed was the drawing room opened just at the edge of her sight. They were already in the room by the time Zinarus finally spoke, his words muffled. When he returned to the door to shut it, though, his voice was as clear as ever-bright: "…a spiteful woman whose bite carries deadly venom…"

Kasia froze with a hand on the banister. Her heart dropped into her stomach, fury burning the pit that remained. She had denied the greatest of her feelings for Zinarus, but standing there with his words hanging in the empty space between them, she realized how much she wanted to be with him. Against her instincts, she had let her heart open.

Then he had driven a dagger straight through it.

Footsteps alerted her to an approaching servant, so she forced herself to hurry down the hall to her room. Tears streamed down her cheeks as she passed the maid. The poor girl tried to ask if she needed anything, but Kasia just threw out an arm, knocking a stack of towels from her arms.

"I…" Kasia shut her eyes tight, trying to ignore her Tainted specter lurking behind the maid with an unnerving grin.

"Did I not tell you?" the specter said. "Did I not say we shouldn't get attached?"

"I know!" Kasia screamed back before charging through the specter. Their shoulders struck, but the pain just distracted from her heartache as the specter took her arm.

Aliax shrugged, leaning casually against the wall. "You don't need him. You never did when I'm still here."

"It is no use allying with those who despise us," her Tainted specter added. "Leave them and focus on the Crimsons, on Chatik! Show all who doubt us that we do not need armies to face our foes."

Kasia stewed with that thought for a moment before pushing on, the maid gawking at her as she passed. Some part of her deep down knew she should turn back and apologize, but she couldn't. Voices echoed in her head. Once, Zinarus had silenced them, but they were worse than ever now.

Kikania shot to her feet when Kasia rushed into her guest chambers. The handmaiden did not say a word, instead crossing the room to hug Kasia in a silent, caring way that was so unfamiliar to the matriarch. Everyone always wanted to speak their mind and tell her how to fix her problems, but in her friend's arms, she felt safe for a moment.

But she didn't want safety.

"Where is my revolver?" she asked, prying herself from Kikania's grip and snatching the coat which she had thrown over the settee.

Amber beads rattled across it as she threw it over her shoulders. Her hand came to rest in a pocket, the cold of a glass dagger biting her palm. Where she was going, she would surely need the blade.

"My lady?" the handmaiden squeaked. "Is all well?"

Kasia didn't reply. The Tainted voice was too loud, calling over and over for her to abandon Zinarus and face the Crimsons herself. It did not matter if she needed to fight alone. She would have her vengeance.

Her father's revolver lay aside a quill and paper on the desk. She considered leaving a note for Zinarus. Despite his rudeness, it would keep him informed of the situation, but he had made it clear there was no fondness there. So she retrieved the gun instead.

Spitza repeated her half-broken *gwah* from the cage in the room's corner. Zinarus's supposed bird expert of a butler had wrapped her injured wing, and the time away from Kasia had only made Spitza more determined to be with her mistress. Ravens signaled death. Did Spitza know what she intended to do?

"I'm going to face Chatik," she told Kikania as she opened the cage and allowed Spitza to hop on her shoulder. A strange clarity came with the raven's presence, but she'd made her choice. "Don't try to stop me."

Golden wisps surrounded her as she threw off her glove. Kikania's cries were distant, and somewhere beyond them, a torrent of footfalls rushed toward the room. None of it mattered. Her only focus was the Crimson King. Chatik Bartol had ordered her father's assassination, and she was done waiting for vengeance.

Gold shifted to swirling white and pink, the portal revealing a balcony and the dawnrise sky. A single figure clothed in crimson finery stood at the ledge.

Chatik.

Kasia pulled back her revolver's hammer as she gritted her teeth. Then, with her breath held and her blood as hot as lava, she raised the gun and stepped through the portal.

A dense, bitter aroma met her on the other side. Half-melted snow from the ephemeral storms blanketed Kalastok and stung her cheeks. The Crystal Palace towered over it, breathless circling in the Reacher light like vultures to a corpse, but not a soul besides Chatik lurked on the balcony.

Fog rolled from Kasia's lips as her finger tightened around the trigger. The revolver had no sights, so she closed one eye and aimed the barrel at Chatik's head, a task only made harder by Spitza pecking at her hair and the voices of a dozen specters' rattling her mind. With the Unity Crystal, he could survive a shot to the body, but one to the head would surely prevent him from having the chance to Reach. She just had to hit the target.

I hope you suffer.

The revolver snapped back, black powder smoke stinging her nose. Her ears' ringing swallowed both the specters calls and Spitza's cawing, and every muscle in her body tensed as the bullet pierced Chatik's skull.

She'd done it. With a single Reach, she had ended the Crimsons' leader.

But she didn't dare lower the gun. Deep red Body Reacher wisps had already formed from the blood, and green Life wisps soon joined them. The bastard was healing from a bullet to the head! So she rushed forward, firing into his brain thrice more.

Chatik slumped over the balcony's rail. The stone in his taloned hand pulsed brilliantly in every color of the realms, but his head was nothing but splattered gore and bone. He had to be dead. He must be dead! Yet the wisps stitched back flesh and brain, pushing her bullets from his skull and onto the balcony's marble floor.

Her heart turned to cannon fire, sweat pouring down her brow. Shouting echoed from behind her as she backed away. This wasn't right. How could he survive such a thing?

"Where are you, specter?" Kasia asked the suddenly absent voice in her head. "Send me into ruin and then leave! You bitch!"

Spitza squawked, alerting her to the now open door in the balcony's attached room. Guards flooded from it, calling for her to drop her gun as they raised their own, but she barely heard their voices. What did it matter if they shot her? She'd failed, and her few allies probably all thought the same as Zinarus. Listening to the screams of the dead had gotten her to this point. Now, she would join them.

She clenched her crystal-wrapped fist, Reaching as Chatik finished his healing. There was nothing she could do but flee. Where? Her scattered mind couldn't focus on anything but her impending death.

So she leaped over the side of the balcony and slammed her eyes shut, golden wisps bursting into a portal before her.

Take me anywhere else.

29

WASH AWAY THE BLOOD

"Blood stains deeper than the surface. Even when scrubbed away, the scars linger." – Zofia Iringiek, sister of the Buried Temple

Nikoza sat upon the edge of the throne's platform in the Chamber of Scions, her legs dangling over the abyss as she stared down at her ungloved hands. Dawnrise's dim light crept through the windows and cast shadows beneath the columns of decorative marble, crystal, and glass. Away from the debate and show of the Chamber sessions, she could've sworn she felt the Spirit Crystal far below reverberating in her talon. Calling to her.

What did the Crystal Mother say?

Buried prayers elicited no reply. Tears found no spiritual comfort. The sisters of the Buried Temple claimed their Mother below guided them through the everdark, everbright, and the seasons between. Dawnrise had come, yet she wandered deeper into the darkness than ever before.

I killed someone.

That single thought had stolen her sleep since Etal's escape with the aid of the rebels known as the Ashes of Dawn. Chatik believed Nex to be their leader. Though Nikoza doubted whether they were capable of such a thing, the Crimsons' Truth Reachers would find answers soon enough. They had asked for Nikoza's presence at the interrogations today, but she found herself trapped over the throne's pit.

Nex had apparently called out her name as the interrogators extracted the Ashes of Dawn's secrets. Both Jazuk and Tzena had explained that Truth Reaching took a heavy toll on its subjects when they refused to comply, so Nikoza had no doubts of her role. She would have to manipulate Nex into talking. For both Nex's safety and the Crimsons' ends.

Tzena's orders were clear: If Nex continued to fight the interrogators, the Truth Reachers would push Nex until they broke.

Dread burrowed so deep in Nikoza's chest that she feared tearing it free would leave nothing left. Despite Chatik's attempts to hide the Crimson Court's oppression of those speaking against them, it was clear to her now. *Something* had been altered in her memories about Etal and the Crimsons in general.

It was frightening enough knowing she had killed someone for the first time, but had her actions been justified against the rebels? Or were those people merely desperate for a cure to the Spirit Plague? Her memories were still fragments, but she had held a vial of a cure—or at least what Etal claimed was one—and delivered it to Nex. That much, she was sure of. Whether it had worked, though, she did not know.

Untangling what was the truth would be difficult. She would have answers from Chatik. First, she needed to talk to Nex and figure out what in the realms was going on.

The large double doors at the Chamber's rear opened, allowing a sliver of the main hall's lamplight to illuminate Nikoza for mere moments before they swung shut again. Footfalls echoed down the steps. She ignored them and imagined herself in the place of the crystal dragon that had curled around her grandfather's throne. Powerful, able to silence the most influential scions with a single roar. Bound to the Crystal Mother and her spirits.

But the dragon had flown to war, leaving only a lost Reacher in its wake. She had considered herself nothing more than a princess and ward to the king for so long. Always waiting for her time to step into power, yet never truly grasping what that meant. Now that she had lost her position as heir to House Bartol, she felt smaller than ever, and she feared that would never change.

"Sergeant Nikoza?" Gregorzon Niezik's voice echoed from behind her. It was a stern one, but there was genuine care in it, similar the layers of a complex dish, never sure what lay at the deepest level until one cut into it. Yes, he was quite like his sister.

"The interrogators need me, I am guessing?" she asked, tucking in one leg before pushing herself to her feet. She wore her crimson and navy-threaded Crystal Brigade uniform. Though of her own house's design, it felt like prison garb more than a symbol of honor.

Gregorzon wore the same, but his reassuring smile was a boy's, not that of a watchman. "Do you need time? I can come up with an excuse if so. The king, however, is growing restless with the interrogations, and you could gain favor if you manage a breakthrough."

Breaking Nex was the last thing she wanted. His sentiment, though, was welcomed as she slipped on her Reacher gloves. They fell perfectly around her talon, and she found herself wishing the rest of her life could align so well. "I am ready. If you have nothing else pressing, would you walk with me along the way?"

"Of course," he said with a sharp bow of his head.

Nikoza kept her distance from the throne as she crossed the Chamber with Gregorzon, unsure why she had asked him to come. His sister's presence had been scattered across Nikoza's muddled memories, and though Katarzyna hadn't been involved with Etal and Paras's cure, her amber had allowed them to capture the spirits used for its creation. Gregorzon had shown nothing but loyalty to the Crimsons since his arrival in Kalastok. That dedication was both admirable and worrying.

"Do you believe we erred by trying to execute Professor iz Noshok?" she asked as they ascended the stairs together.

He raised a brow. "Etal has lost his post. He is not a professor, and that is due solely to his schemes to slaughter the very innocents you have not ceased speaking about in recent days. Granting him a quick death was a mercy. One that the lowborn failed to recognize."

She had neither the strength nor the confidence to argue, so she silently waited for the servants to open the double doors. Twin diamond emblems of Ezmani red and Vockan white had once graced their surface, but the white one had been removed. It left the doors looking bare and misaligned.

"Though you have not been here long," she said, "have you noticed that my uncle refers to us as Ezman instead of the Commonwealth? We are still two united nations."

Once again, Gregorzon gave her a confused glance. "Is there something strange about referring to Ezman by its name? It has always been the greater half of the Commonwealth, and with House iz Ardinvil and the other relevant Vockan houses in open revolt, I hardly believe they deserve to be honored in these halls."

"Yet they are part of the Commonwealth nonetheless," she appealed. They headed down the hall, toward the stairs down to the deeper dungeons. Voices echoed well in the palace, so she had to tame her frustrations to keep every Crimson within it from hearing her complaints. "Chatik wishes to strengthen our nation. We cannot do that by slicing it down the middle."

"Ivalat and his allies fled when Kelosh knocked at our door. Tiuz, that traitorous general, saw a chance to seize power for his minor house, and he brought Borys Kuzon and Lilita Pikezik with him. It seems to me that it is the rebels who seek to slice the nation by driving a dagger straight into its spine."

She took his arm as they reached the steps down, stopping them halfway. "Tell me what you know of the Crimson Coup," she whispered. "The ministers have all evaded the full truth of it when I press them."

His lips parted, then slammed shut. "If they have not told you, I am certain there is a reason." He attempted to pull away, but she tightened her grip.

"So you do know…" She groaned. "Why does everyone treat me as if I am some fragile glass one moment, only to throw me into the Crystal Brigade's leadership the next? Please, Gregorzon. My grandfather was far from a perfect ruler or man, but I deserve to know why he died. I fail to believe it was because the scions suddenly were displeased with him."

"They were! Jazuk was a weak king!"

She shook him, then caught herself, realizing the unusual fury behind her actions. Fury, yes… That was it. She did trust Chatik, but that was why she was so frustrated with him. After all the faith she had placed in him, manipulation and half-truths were her reward.

"That stone Chatik holds," she said. "You saw him during the riot, how he could wield every realm at once. What if he used that same power to usurp my grandfather and force the scions of the Chamber to comply? My memories…" She hesitated. These were mere theories that sounded doubtful even as she spoke them, but that crack in her memories made her doubt others. "Why can I not remember events from the days before the coup?"

Voices echoed from the main hall, so Gregorzon drew close, his breaths as hot as the flames he wielded. "Be careful what you say. I grasp the purity in your words—and recent days have ignited my own concerns—but what you are accusing the king of is impossible." This time, he successfully pulled himself free and continued down the steps. "Come. The Truth Reachers are impatient."

They passed from brightly lit halls of marble to those of damp, ancient stonework with only dim lanterns to light the path. Gregorzon took one from a nearby hook and guided her through a winding series of turns. Having taken other rebel prisoners down in the riots' aftermath, she knew the way, but it always surprised her how easily one could get lost in a place like this. Most prisoners would be held for the long term in the city prison to the east. Chatik, though, had insisted all interrogations essential to the Crimson Cause took place within the palace itself.

Nikoza had so many questions about what exactly that Crimson Cause was beyond the uplifting of Ezman and the scions, but she had no time to ponder it further as they reached the interrogation chamber door. Made of heavy metal, it muffled the shouts from within.

"I will leave you to it, then," Gregorzon said before bowing swiftly. "If you need anything from me, I shall be in the Reachers' hall. Minister Tzena is convinced I am capable of more with further training."

She nodded back. "Thank you for your company, and your discretion."

"We are aligned in our desire to protect our nation, Sergeant. As for our concerns, let us discuss them when you are done with the rebel."

He left, so Nikoza turned her attention to the task ahead, fixing her coat—as if Nex would care. She doubted the odd Possibility Reacher had any trust for her. Even sending the cure to Nex had only earned glares during her aid convoy to the western city. Nex's rants had proven they had little care for any scion, and that clearly included Nikoza.

The shouts from the room ceased when she knocked on the door. Heavy footfalls approached, followed by a metallic screeching that made her wince. A brute of a man stood in the doorway, a wide moustache the only visible hair on him, and he wore a workman's garbs instead of any uniform.

"Chatik said you'd be here half-an-hour ago," he grumbled.

It was hard not to feel threatened in front of such a built man, but she tilted up her chin, remembering her position as a sergeant of the Crystal Brigade. This man had no right to speak to her like this. So she would imitate her grandfather's pride. "What is your name?"

His frown deepened as he crossed his arms across his broad chest. "Names are an asset in the Court."

"I am part of the Crimson Court," she replied, allowing conceit to slip into her voice. It felt wrong doing so, but her patience had run thin in recent days. "I am also a sergeant of the Crystal Brigade, so it would be in your interest to answer my question."

The man stepped out of the way. "If you were a true member, you would not need to say so."

Nikoza sneered, but passed him by without another word. This man was not her mission. The figure in the room's single chair was.

"Hello, Nex," she said, stopping before them and taking what she hoped to be a non-threatening stance. "When they first told me we had captured you, I failed to believe it."

The Ogrenian shifted forward. Even with their arms tied behind their chair, Nex grinned like they held a secret up their sleeve. "Takes no belief to know why you're here. Your papa dies, but you're a rich scion. When you fall, you fall up while the rest of us eat ash."

Nikoza spooked back as Nex spat at her feet. It was not a sergeant's move, and a second man on the far side of the room laughed.

"King Chatik has more trust in you than this," Uzrin Ioniz said. Dressed in a charcoal frock trimmed in crimson threading, his clothes looked far finer than his face. His bent nose made him resemble a half-finished portrait, and his hair was slicked back above cheeks that were far too jolly for his temperament.

A list of names in Etal's voice rang in the back of Nikoza's mind. It was a suppressed memory, as if splitting through a haze, but in his secret laboratory, he had explained who among his students were the most likely to have been the core members of the Crimson Court. Both Uzrin and Chatik's names had been on it.

She was surrounded by her uncle's loyalists here. That should have been a good thing, but a disconcerting feeling came over her. She gave an insincere smile to hide it.

"If you would like to help," she said, "then you may remain, but I did not descend into this dank dungeon for want of your mockery."

Hearing no reply, she crouched before Nex, still beyond reach, but close enough to study them. They appeared unharmed. Etal had as well, though, and the Truth Reachers would not be relying on her if they hadn't pushed Nex to near breaking. That didn't mean Nex had no fight left.

"It's funny," the Ogrenian said. "I actually thought for a minute that you wanted to help us, and everyone else did too. What a joke—the princess come to save the poor."

No mention of the cure, but that need not be said. Nex was smart enough to know the other two were Crimsons, and both already knew what Nikoza had done.

"I have not stopped doing exactly that since the day of the coup," she replied softly. "Whether dousing fires in the Drifters' Quarter, forcing my uncle to send aid to the lowborn, or calling for Reacher towers to protect the Industrial District and Shadow Quarter for the first time, I have always sought the best for the lowborn."

Nex cocked their head. "You mean the towers where they'll put the Reachers to watch us? Control us? The breathless swarming anyone who dared step out of line weren't enough for you?"

"Breathless?" Nikoza glanced at Uzrin, but his face offered no reaction. "They are simply there to protect people and stop the gangs from running rampant."

"We'd all have starved if it wasn't for the gangs!"

Nikoza reeled back as Nex nearly toppled the chair in their fury. "We provided food," she said, "but the rioters attacked our carts."

"You saw what you wanted to see," Nex snapped, their raven hair curling savagely over their face. It was slick with sweat, and their eyes were so bloodshot beneath that they resembled the Crimson Court's emblem of the Crystal Realms. Fifteen of them, except these were shattered. "They dumped the food and ruined it. They shot Jax because you called for me!"

The pain in their words struck straight at Nikoza's heart. "Who is… Who was Jax?"

Nex sat back, that hot fury cooling to sorrow. "Everyone west of the Kala knew him. Why would you? Scions have money, so you didn't need the keni he'd hand out, even when he had nothing. Scions aren't attacked by watchmen at random, so you don't need to know where the patrols are. The west side has a fuck ton of fists…" They sniffled, then scowled as they wiped their nose on their shoulder. "He was the spiritdamned heart. And you assholes shot him."

"I am sorry," Nikoza said, and she meant it. The Crimsons were not perfect. Beneath her uncertainty about her memories, though, she knew that she could do good through them.

Slowly, she reached out to embrace Nex, but they suddenly threw themself back and kicked. The blow landed, striking Nikoza's chest so heavily that her ribs cracked. Breathing turned difficult. Her throat felt empty with every gasp. And when she did find air, it sent her entire torso aflame as she tumbled back.

The Crimson brute lunged forward, a Truth Reacher talon suddenly flashing across his finger. White wisps followed. "Why must you continue to fight?" he demanded.

Nex froze. Not just still, but impossibly so, all but their eyes not moving even to twitch. Those eyes like copper, though, stared at Nikoza with unspeaking horror.

"Vi… Vin," they muttered through clenched teeth.

Uzrin laughed. "That is a name if I have ever heard one. A lead, and we have you to thank, *Sergeant.*"

"Not like this," Nikoza wheezed, clutching her ribs and stumbling back into the wall. She had barely been bruised in her life, let alone suffered a broken bone. It ignited something within her. Not anger or her deep sorrow, but a primal will to survive against the pain. By the Mother, it was intoxicating. "Release them from your power. I am not finished with them."

The brute looked to Uzrin, who waved for him to back away. "Be still, or admit the full truth," he commanded Nex with the last of his Reach before doing as Uzrin said.

Nex glared at Nikoza, but remained paralyzed beyond their face. "You know what happens when you pierce a heart?" their raspy, forced voice managed.

"The body falls still," Nikoza replied, "and releases a spirit."

Nex curled their lip. "How romantic. No! Pierce a heart, and blood flows."

"How do we mend what has been broken?"

"That's the thing…" Nex pushed back against the Reaching, leaning forward until their face contorted from the agony. Tears welled in their eyes, but not a single one graced their cheek. "You can't fix shattered glass when you're the ones holding the hammer."

Uzrin sighed. "This is a waste of time if you insist on ignoring the topic at hand. Our aim here is not to solve the problems of the western city, but to identify the rebel leaders and safehouses. The war effort relies on order in the homeland."

Nikoza met Nex's pained gaze with her own. Spirits, her chest hurt. "I beg of you, Nex. Tell them what they need to know. If you don't…"

"I'm not an idiot, *Princess*. I know what they'll do to me. You scions got Mind Reachers to poison our tongues and Truth Reachers to cut 'em clean out."

"They have not sent Mind Reachers to you," Nikoza insisted. "One can convince you of something, but they cannot force you to tell the truth."

Nex huffed and stopped fighting, allowing the Truth Reaching to force them back into the chair. "No, the Crimsons couldn't waste Mind Reaching on me. They're too busy using it on you."

"Enough!" the brute shouted.

He grabbed Nikoza's arm and dragged her out of the room before she could manage another word. Though she wanted to fight, her ribs sent stabbing pain through her body with every attempt, so she just collapsed in the hall as the brute slammed the door shut.

"She was talking," Nikoza said, barely able to raise her voice above her ragged breaths. "I just needed more time."

The brute threw out his arms. "Your job was to manipulate the bitch into talking, but instead, you let her manipulate you!"

"Them…"

"That's your problem." He knelt on one knee before her, his eyes the color of cold steel. "You are a sergeant of the Crystal Brigade. Caring that much about a damned rebel makes you unable to do what's necessary. We all saw you hesitate during the execution." He shoved his finger straight into her broken rib and grinned as she writhed from the pain. "Etal escaped because of you, so know that when we break the little boss of the Ashes of Dawn, it will be your fault."

Then he returned to the interrogation room, latching shut the door and leaving her with Nex's screams piercing the dungeons. The sound echoed through the halls and deep into Nikoza's skull. Her failure. Her responsibility.

"What have I done?" she asked herself as she once again stared down at her hands. They trembled, no matter how hard she fought to still them. But she was not strong enough. She had never been.

Footsteps approached, turning to a run. "Nikoza?" Gregorzon called out. The Fire Reacher skidded to a stop before her. His face was wild, his lips parted as he scanned her for some sign of her wounds.

"Why are you here?" she asked him weakly. "You were supposed to be training."

He averted his gaze, his thumb tracing his taloned finger. His gloves, like all that her house had designed for the Crystal Brigade, interwove perfectly with the talon to allow him to Reach, and his talon seemed to glint a fiery orange in the lanternlight. "I intended to do so, but when you expressed your worries… My apologies for breaking protocol. I just thought you may need help, and it seems I was right."

Nikoza pursed her lips. It had been so long since another person had shown such genuine care for her. A complex web of emotions stirred within her aching chest, but she had no will to address it in this horrid place.

"Nex kicked me," she admitted, trying to stand. The pain was too much, though, and she fell back into the wall. "I am sorry to burden you again, but could you help me climb to a Body Reacher?"

Without a reply, he interrupted her rise by sweeping his arms under her. Most scion men were far from fit, but he showed no strain as he carried her down the hall at a swift pace.

"I told you to aid me, not carry me," she appealed.

But he just charged onward. "You have done much for everyone else, my lady. For once, let someone do the same for you."

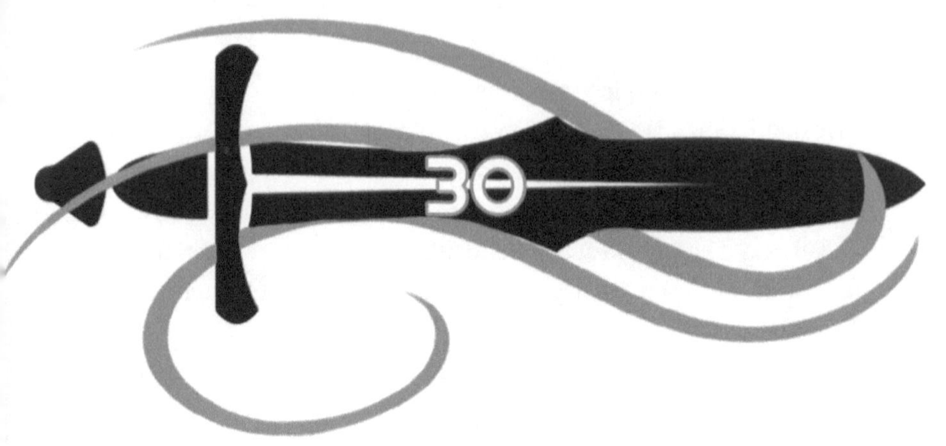

THE DEEPENING

"One's truest desires begin deep within. It takes bravery to merely accept them, let alone voice them as loudly as a whisper lost among breaths." – An excerpt from *The Fire Within*

Wanusa's cheeks stung atop the cliff overlooking the Glassblade camp. The winds howled, bringing blinding snow and ice that threatened to form icicles from her brow, but yet she stood. Watching.

"What are we waiting for?" she asked Mariana after what seemed an eternity. Usually, her armor provided an extra layer, but at the Whisperer's request, she had only her fur-lined coat now. Being un-armored when spirits were about made her feel naked.

Mariana cupped her hands around her mouth and whispered into the gales, "Come, children of the Crystal. Let us hear your words and join with you."

Join with them?

A shiver ran down Wanusa's spine. Mariana's voice carried an ethereal power unlike anything she'd ever felt, as if calling out to Wanusa's spirit as well as the wild ones. It gave her calm, and the drifters that had gathered over the camp answered in their meander-ing way.

"How do you do that?" Wanusa asked quietly to not scare the spirits.

Mariana held a hand to her breast and breathed in. "The Deepening binds us with the Spirit Crystal and all its children."

As if that clarifies things at all… Wanusa trusted her, though, so she waited for the drifters to draw nearer. Until one darted sharply toward them.

"Awakened!" she called, instinctively grabbing for her sword but finding only the steel one she'd acquired in Dalnus.

Mariana lightly touched her arm. "Stay your hand."

Wanusa tensed, but released the hilt of her blade. It would do nothing against an awakened anyway. Her Glassblade training, though, made her doubt the merits of defenselessness. There was seeking understanding, and then there was foolishness. Aggressive spirits had likely killed her entire family. It was difficult to want anything more than to send a blade through their shadowy forms.

But the awakened stopped before them, hovering within reach of her glass sword if she had held it. A strange voice rose from it. The breathless often spoken among themselves in an alien tongue, but she'd never heard awakened do so.

"What is it saying?" Wanusa asked.

Mariana stepped to the edge so that her toes hung over it. Like a child hoping to draw their parents' attention. "Spiritspeech is not a language of words, but a rhythm within the very Essence of their being. Through the Deepening, we alter the balance of the realms within us as well, allowing us to listen to those rhythms." She glanced over her shoulder at Wanusa. "To answer your question, however, it seeks to feed on Spirit Essence. Awakened are pure spirits who have been granted life. What is life's purpose if not to endure?"

Wanusa clenched her fists as drifters gathered around them. "It is corrupted."

"To view all things as black and white is to miss all the shades inbetween. Notice that it does not attack the pure spirits while I am here."

Mariana extended her hand to the awakened, showing no fear as the spirit's misty tendrils met her fingertips. The spirit language rose from her as a strange glow emanated from her chest. Silver wisps sprouted from her, and Wanusa backed away in horror as they joined with the awakened.

"You're feeding it from your own spirit," she said. "Why?"

As Mariana retreated from the ledge, the awakened did the same, disappearing into the dawnrise sky. The Whisperer smiled watching it leave. "It hungers no longer, so it will be docile for a time. While not seeking to feed, life endures in another way—the natural one."

"Is it a drifter now?"

"In its being, no, but while it is sated, it shall act as one. Perhaps it will grant itself to a newborn child." Mariana took Wanusa's hand. "Even the corrupted are born of the Spirit Crystal. If we may cure them of such corruption for a few days, is it not worth our efforts?"

Wanusa furrowed her brow. "But do you not lose your own spirit in the process?"

Mariana's smile faded, and she pulled Wanusa so close that their noses nearly touched. "If I am to tell you the secret of the Deepening, you must swear never to speak a word of it to one beyond the Whisperers or those seeking to become one of us. It is a secret bound by centuries."

"Not even Radais?" she asked, swallowing. Mariana's gaze was sharp enough to cut stone, and she felt as if her entire spirit were exposed to the Whisperer.

"The Glassblade Order seeks to eradicate all but the purest spirits. Some among their ranks have yet to accept that there are breathless who your supreme defender does not consider corrupted. To tell Radais is to open both him and us to immense danger." She pursed her lips. "If he proves himself, however, I may yet change my mind."

Wanusa's stomach churned as she stared down the cliff at the camp. Radais sat with his sketchbook atop a rock, far too peaceful for the leader of a mercenary order. He'd trusted her from the beginning, and it pained her to even consider hiding anything from him. If it could help her understand spirits better, though...

"I will do it," she finally said, "but I won't betray the Order."

Mariana nodded, patting the back of Wanusa's hand and backing away. She tucked her arms into her wide sleeves and tucked her chin in. "Nor do I ask you to. To become a Whisperer is like a scion touching the Spirit Crystal and becoming a Reacher. You do not join an official organization, but the process changes how you experience Zekiaz. Spirits are no longer wild animals whom we cannot bond. Instead, they become like a hound to a hunter. Allies, even companions."

She spoke again in Spiritspeech, summoning another set of silver wisps from herself until five drifters surrounded her. Except unlike most drifters, a spirit tendril bound each of them to Mariana's chest. Like a leash.

"You captured spirits?" Wanusa asked. She circled the tamed drifters and ran her fingers through their chilled, smoky forms. They gave no response. Why would they? After all, they were only drifters, but if they could use Spiritspeech, there had to be something substantial to them.

"Captured is an aggressive word that does not fit the heart of the Deepening," Mariana replied. "These spirits are not controlled by me—they are a part of me. All spirits in their deepest purpose seek to bind to the Essences of the other realms. Whisperers invite them to do so through ourselves and the elements that form us. By merely existing in Zekiaz, the pure drifters among them are replenished by the Spirit Crystal at our realm's core, so I may use fragments of their Essences to satiate awakened for a time."

She extended her arms, allowing the spirits to wrap around them like some sort of armor. "That is, however, only one of the many uses for the Deepening."

Wanusa sucked in a sharp breath. The ramifications of this were vast, far beyond the power of Spirit Reachers if Whisperers could truly bond with spirits. How had they kept their true abilities hidden for so long?

"The Deepening, then," Wanusa said. "It is a connection to the Spirit Crystal in some way, allowing you to bond with spirits?"

Mariana's expression turned heavy. She tilted her head toward the southern horizon, its dawnrise light granting her hair a pinkish hue compared to its usual red. "It is to surrender a portion of oneself to the Spirit Crystal in return for a pure shard of it. Not to Reach, but to remind one's spirit how to attune with the very language it was created to speak when it was born from the Crystal. When *we* were born from the Crystal. Because in the end, our spirit is the core of our being."

"Why do scions become Reachers when they touch the Spirit Crystal," Wanusa asked, raising her left hand, "but we cannot?"

Mariana gestured over the camp before facing the eastern lands. "Why do you believe that Vockans and lowborn Ezmani, Ogrenians, Reshkans, and Keloshans all cannot Reach? Why is scion skin tinted gray while others are a dozen other shades?"

Wanusa shifted uncomfortably. It was a question that weighed on all her people. No matter what they did, only those with scion blood could Reach, and Vockans could only acquire it by bearing children with scions of other nations. "I don't know. Radais and Miv said no one does."

"Yet I am not asking for the opinion of your supreme defenders. I am asking for yours."

So Wanusa raised her chin. "Ezmani scions claim it's because the Crystal Mother chose them, but Reachers aren't a religious order. Like you said, our spirits all came from the Spirit Crystal, and a scion's ability to Reach is passed down through generations. There must be an answer in their blood. An ancient group first held the power, so now their descendants have it too."

"Not just a warrior, indeed." Mariana dismissed her bound spirits, whose wisps burrowed into her again. Her lips formed a narrow line, but there was pride in her eyes. "There is an Essence within each of our cores, holding a rhythm. Once Deepened, you learn to sense the patterns. Vockans share one. Lowborn Ezmani another. Same for lowborn of other nationalities. Each Essence hums a different tune, but when you listen to a scion's core, no matter the ethnicity, you find the one that is shared among all spirits."

"Like the breathless Bound Ones," Wanusa replied. "If the spirits have the same Essence as scions, then both can Reach through the Spirit Crystal. That explains a lot."

Mariana nodded. "One does not need Zekiaz's rhythm in their core to communicate through the Spiritspeech. The existence of Spirit Essence's rhythm draws a question, however, about the origins of the other rhythms."

Wanusa's eyes widened as she remembered back to the city of Akaamilion and Rakekeaa's lantern. "The Spirit Crystal holds a rhythm, so what about crystals from other realms? The Saleshi held what they called Light Crystals. Spirits… Does that mean lowborn's Essences come from entire other realms? Vockans?"

"I have asked myself the same question, and though I have suspicions that each Essence corresponds to another of the Crystal Realms, I fear that I do not know."

Mariana nodded toward the path they had taken up, and they began their descent, the Whisperer deep in thought for a minute before she continued, "This has been my long-winded way of saying it is my desire for you to complete the Deepening. Despite my dislike of the Glassblade approach, I cannot deny that a warrior with the right mindset may be able to do far more with the Deepening than those following more orthodox Whisperer teachings. Listening to these Vanashel will not be enough."

"When can I do this?" Wanusa asked, hopping from a ledge before helping Mariana down the drop. "We are far from the Spirit Crystal reserves in Kalastok, and the Vanashel await us in Iliafa."

Mariana pointed over the western valley. "The spirits have told us of strange rhythms in the ranges between here and your village. At least one of them belongs to a Spirit Crystal, but there are more— including one which matches the Essence held by Vockans."

"This is the key you claimed could help us defeat the Vanashel?"

"It is my hope."

Wanusa caught her arm. There was something she wasn't saying. "Where are these rhythms coming from? Can you lead us to them?"

The Whisperer did not resist, simply dropping her head. "I know you are attached to the Glassblades, but we must travel without them for a time. Where we must go, you cannot bring an army."

"Radais will insist on coming with me. Even with your power, we will be vulnerable against Vanashel without allies."

"There shall come a time in which you must choose your own path, child," Mariana insisted. "Neither your supreme defender nor I can walk it for you."

Wanusa nodded, so they descended the rest of the way in silence. There was no clear path, and each step sent their legs burrowing deep into the snow. She was not all that fond of the hottest temperatures of everbright. The frost, though, was getting old, pricking at her skin beneath her pants.

She wrestled with worries of what lay ahead. Mariana hadn't revealed the full power of a Whisperer, yet it far surpassed anything Wanusa had ever seen. Glassblades were warriors, not Reachers capable of amazing magic. She had barely considered the possibility, but as it loomed before her, the thought of bonding spirits was tantalizing. With blade and magic alike, she could protect far more than any Glassblade otherwise. She could uncover truths about the realms and maybe find a way to bring back her brother, or at least mend his spirit.

I haven't given up yet, Inrius, she told him silently. *If you're out there, know that I'm coming.*

Mariana stepped away when they finally reached camp again. Half-a-dozen fires dotted the ridgeline, Glassblades gathering around them to either laugh or share their exhaustion. Some of the initiates called Wanusa to join them, but just like in Dalnus, she focused only on the supreme defender.

Radais still perched himself on that rock, sketchbook in hand and back hunched like a bird tucking in its wings. Not a good sign.

"I will leave you to discuss this with him alone," Mariana whispered before stepping away and drawing up her hood. "He is not well pleased with my presence, and this conversation will be difficult enough for you already."

Part of Wanusa wanted to fight for her to stay, but the Whisperer disappeared into her tent in a blink. That left only Radais and her. Easy, right?

"Supreme Defender?" Wanusa asked him, taking a soldier's stance to hide her nerves. "Do you have a moment?"

Radais's furrowed, focused brow loosened at the sight of Wanusa. Sorrow replaced it soon enough. "I always have time for you. What troubles you? Is it your brother?"

She sighed and took a long blink to clear her mind. "Is my worry that obvious?"

"Come, sit." He patted the rock next to him and set aside his sketchbook. From the glimpse she caught of it, he'd been drawing an older man who shared many of Radais's own features. His father or brother, perhaps? When she joined him, he held his hands in his lap and offered her a forced smile. "I know these days have been hard for you. After I lost my father—"

"This isn't about Inrius," she interrupted, pain shooting through her heart at the mention of his name. "At least, not directly."

His lips parted slightly, and he rested a hand on her shoulder. "Then what is it? You look like you're carrying the ibex instead of it carrying you."

Wanusa averted her gaze. She struck her heels against the rock to kick off the snow, and it showered beneath them in a shimmering dust. "Mariana has given me an offer."

"She wants you to leave the order, doesn't she?"

"Surprisingly, no." Wanusa glanced up at him, the fatherly care in his eyes unlike any she'd ever received from her now late parents. "She wants me to complete a ritual, becoming a Whisperer while remaining a Glassblade. Her abilities… I promised not to tell you all of it, but I think it could help me face the Vanashel and better understand the spirits."

He frowned. "Then why the hesitation? You have my support if you want to pursue this."

"That's the problem. Mariana says the key to defeating the Vanashel is in an area of the mountains ahead that the army cannot reach." She pointed toward the peaks to the west that Mariana had shown her. "The spirits told her of a Spirit Crystal and potentially others there. I need to go there to become a Whisperer."

"Others? Like the Light Crystals the Saleshi had?"

She nodded. "I think so, but Mariana wasn't sure."

He swiftly stood, scanning the camp as a commander's expression replaced his caring one. "Then Lazan and I are coming with you. Don't object. If this place, and the power it can grant you, can help us defeat the Vanashel, your mission cannot fail."

"I am a warrior and she is a Whisperer," Wanusa replied anyway, following him to her feet. "We can defend ourselves. Besides, Mariana doesn't want anyone else to come."

"You two alone can't survive against an ambush like we saw in the Whistling Pass." Radais caught sight of Tairanik and waved for him to join them before turning back to Wanusa. "The Vanashel may know of your mission's importance too. Breathless like that Earth Bound One will overwhelm even whatever magic she holds, and it is my responsibility to protect you now that Miv is a breathless."

Wanusa's eyes watered. "You... You want to protect me? Why? You are the supreme defender. All the Glassblades are your responsibility."

"That responsibility comes from my title, not my will." He sniffled suddenly, stifling it with a cracked laugh. "You have become like a daughter to me, Wanusa. I know what it's like to not have a real family by blood, and I don't want you to believe you are alone. If you'd rather I not come, then—"

He never finished, because she hugged him with enough force to nearly send him from his feet. Spirits, she felt so afraid hearing him admit that. She'd rarely, if ever, heard such care from her actual family, and knowing he'd risk himself and the rest of the army for her was a harrowing thought.

"What is this?" Tairanik asked, stomping his foot and standing at attention. "There are whispers about you diverting us at the whims of a shaman and a warrior you are far too attached to. Despite those we left behind, there are many villages that will be undefended because of your decisions. Villages that our warriors are from."

"If you disagree with the supreme defender's decision," Wanusa said, stepping back with her nose wrinkled, "then why didn't you voice it before?"

A smile tugged at the ends of Radais's lips, but he raised a hand for her to be silent. "Commander Tairanik may speak his mind. She is right, however, that you expressed no such doubts in Dalnus."

Tairanik huffed. He wriggled his shoulders in discontent, and Wanusa had to refrain from laughing at the thought he resembled an obese little shrew more than a commander. "I voice the rumors among our ranks, nothing more. Know that if we continue to listen to Whisperers more than strategic sense, you may lose the confidence of the warriors."

"Then it is good timing that I intend to leave for a few days," Radais replied.

The commander nearly jumped out of his boots. "You *what?*"

Radais failed to hide his grin this time as he nodded to Wanusa. "Tell him what we must do." The look in his eye, though, said not to reveal all of it.

"Of course." Wanusa straightened her back like Miv had always taught her. She was young, so she would face ridicule until she aged, but until then, she could ensure they didn't question her presentation. "Mariana the Whisperer has informed me that there is some kind of weapon in the mountains to the west. It'll help me become a Whisperer and combine my Glassblade training with their magic, granting us a new chance to combat the Vanashel."

"The location is remote enough that the army would struggle to reach it," Radais added. "Lazan and I will provide additional support to ensure they are not ambushed along the way."

Tairanik's frown deepened until his forehead turned to a washboard. "You would abandon your office to escort a single warrior and a shaman? Lazan is our only Body Reacher!"

"Warrior Wanusa has assured me this could shift the tide of battle." Radais crossed his arms, no longer shying away from the commander. "I will not risk our chances by leaving their expedition vulnerable, and like you said, the warriors are skeptical of the Whisperers, let alone an Ezmani Reacher. This will allow the rest of you to continue toward Iliafa until we catch back up. Lazan's abilities will grant us and our ibexes the endurance to do so quickly."

"You are leaving me in charge, then?"

"With Commander Polina," Radais said.

Tairanik glanced at Polina, who laughed and drank around a nearby fire with a group of initiates. One among them had the sandy skin and round cheeks of an Ogrenian, and a lowborn Ezmani stretched her legs behind with her light brunette hair loose over her shoulders. Though the Glassblades had no official restrictions against non-Vockans joining, most of the other warriors kept away from the foreigners. Wanusa smiled seeing Polina with them. The Glassblades fought for all the nations now, not just Vocka.

"With all due respect, Supreme Defender," Tairanik said, "Polina's disregard for tradition—"

Radais clapped him on the shoulder. "Ensures a balance between your decisions. Of course, that is an excellent insight. I'm sure the two of you will easily handle things with your decades of experience. Or did you have an objection?"

Wanusa snorted as Tairanik gritted his teeth. "Not at all," he muttered. "Thank you, Supreme Defender. We will begin once the scouts return."

"Good. Send an alpine accentor after us once you've chosen which to take."

Then Radais stepped away, waving for Wanusa to follow. She could practically feel Tairanik's glare on the back of her head, but that deepened her satisfaction. Soon, she would wield a greater understanding of spirits. And with Radais and Lazan at her side, the unknown wasn't quite as daunting.

"C'mon," he told her with a pat on the back. "Let's alert Lazan and prepare for our trek."

THE LOST CHILDREN

"There is no force comparable to a father whose child is threatened." – Barkas
the Boxer

King Chatik Bartol slipped out of yet another haze, voices echoing in the back of his mind and his body revolting against itself. All Realm Reachers feared the Taint, but none had suffered it as he did now. Katarzyna Niezik's assault had taken a great amount of Reaching to endure. The aftermath was like fifteen blades sinking ever deeper into his very spirit.

"My king, what are your orders?" Tzena Oliezany asked from among the arrayed Crystal Brigade before the throne.

Chatik raised his gaze to her. Each muscle in his neck twinged, but the effort was worth it. Tzena wore a fetching coat, more decorated than most of the Brigade, and he found himself staring at the strands of her lustrous silver hair which curled down her cheeks and high collar. He had not married for love. With Lilita gone, stealing away his three children, he longed deeply for it. And for Tzena.

He searched his memories for some knowledge of the conversation he had held with the Crystal Brigade in the minutes before this, but came up empty. Spirits, his mind had once been his advantage,

The opening salvos of war have not favored us. Today, the empire has breached our half of the Lost Brothers' Forts with cannon fire. Lady Qaraza, I must plead to you to send further Reacher reinforcements. Without them, we stand no chance against our foes' greater weaponry. While we focus on magic, they may strike us from greater distances than we can even conceive. Not to mention their sharpshooters picking off our musketmen one-by-one...

Do not interpret this criticism as disloyalty, but our strategy must be altered. Otherwise, I fear all the east shall fall before the Crimson Cause finds its completion.

- Field Marshall Korzin Uziokaki of the Ezmani Ist Army

allowing him to out plan his enemies and gain his kingship. But pressing so deeply on Nikoza and the other members of the Chamber had him losing his thoughts before they formed.

It is necessary, he reassured himself. *The Crystal Heir will be prepared.*

Tzena coughed. "My king?"

"Punish these Ashes of Dawn!" he spat, throwing out his arms. What decrepit limbs they were! Boils and sores covered every inch of him now, and he had taken to altering his appearance with Possibility Reaching to hide its horrid state. The voices told him his subjects mocked him when he turned away.

Tzena approached the throne. Stunning, but his eyes seared from the bright lanterns and the shadows seeping as deep as the everdark itself. Nothing was as it should have been.

Yet her touch against his ungloved hand was like the gentle waters of a child's first bath. Gentle, cleansing. It pulled him back into reality for long enough to recover his thoughts, but even then, Mind Taint slowly made him an imbecile. Why could he not remember all his plans?

He looked from Tzena to young Nikoza. He had held such high hopes for her to be a true Crystal Heir, but smothering her doubts had pushed him to the brink. She could still be molded into what they required. The true power, though, would remain with the Crimson Court as they sought to complete the Cause. This all would have been easier if that bastard Zinarus had not interrupted his attempt to depose Jazuk via a Chamber vote. The nation teetered on the edge of chaos while Keloshan armies ravaged the east.

But despite it all, the grand plan was working.

"We have pushed the Ashes' leader, Nex, to the edge of their mental faculties," Tzena whispered. "Should the Truth Reachers continue their interrogation, the prisoner will likely descend into madness, and that is of little use to us."

"Send Nikoza," he snapped.

His niece stepped forward, head held low. "I have attempted to convince Nex to comply, your highness, but they are disagreeable." She felt at her ribs. Gregorzon Niezik had reported Nex's attack to him, and warmth returned to her face as she glanced back at the Fire Reacher. He nodded, so she straightened her posture and continued, "In my opinion, we should not risk breaking them. We should instead release them and watch what they do, as they will likely reconnect with their associates. There—"

She slammed her mouth shut before she could finish the thought. From the sudden flush of her cheeks, it was not insignificant, so Chatik forced himself to rise and approach her. Every step was agony, further threatening to send him into another fit or haze, but he held his wits as he stopped before his niece. She would be his heir. Not just his hope, but all of Ezman's.

"The Crimson Cause calls us to assert the authority of the chosen scions over Ezman," he proclaimed, Mind Reaching to ensure all the Brigade were convinced of his ideals, "then spread our influence into every corner of Zekiaz. We are the protectors of this nation. We are the exemplary few, and we shall not allow lowborn miscreants to interrupt our plans. Do this as I have said. Show our people the glory of the Crimson Court and the chosen scions, and rid Kalastok of these fiendish rebels."

He waved for the Crystal Brigade to be gone, but beckoned Nikoza closer as his pink Mind magic burrowed deeper into her. His careful work on her was a silent duty, preparing her to be an asset—whether willingly or not. "You are a sergeant of the Crystal Brigade, a representative of our great house. At such a young age, you have become what so many scions aspire to be. So, when I ask this of you, I do it with the highest confidence."

"What do you wish me to do?" the girl asked with all the grace of a princess. But he did not need a princess. He needed an heir whose popularity was finely crafted among the scions and lowborn to create an icon—a reason for all of Ezman to devote their will toward the Crimson Cause.

"You are to prepare the way for our new, true cure," he said, pressing his words with the Reaching. "The towers you proposed for the western city will provide staging points for distribution, but as long as Etal iz Noshok is free, his false one shall permeate the most vulnerable sections of our population. Use what remains of Nex to your advantage, as the demise of their Ashes of Dawn will benefit all of Ezman. We must have unity, stability."

Her eyes widened. "Uncle… My king, is there no way to find peace? The lowborn rioted again when we sought to execute Professor iz Noshok—"

"Etal," Tzena corrected, "is no longer a professor."

Nikoza stiffened and raised her chin. "Regardless, inciting further violence will only further divide us. I will do as you ask, but I have seen their pain."

"You allowed Nex to free Etal in the first place," Tzena said. "It is only fair that you ensure he returns to our custody."

She put herself between Chatik and Nikoza, and though the king had no desire to let her take charge, a haze overtook him. His vision and mind alike clouded over. When his consciousness returned, he sat alone in the Chamber except for Tzena and Qaraza. The women discussed something in hushed voices, their gold and glass-trimmed dresses sharing his attire's crimson. It appeared like blood flowing down their ashen faces.

"Do not whisper before me!" he muttered, gripping the throne's armrests as it rocked upon its unsteady footing. Legends said it was built to ensure the king never felt steady over the Spirit Crystal pit. It was surely working. "My mind is fogged. What happened with Nikoza?"

"You Mind Reached over her and all the Crystal Brigade," Tzena replied. "It was impressive, but even your power has its limits. We layer deception upon deception with your niece, and her resistance to it grows. Soon, she will discover the loose threads and begin to untie the story we have woven."

Chatik stared at the spot where Nikoza had stood. She remained his hope to become Crystal Heir, as her heart for the nation was pure. Purity, however, was not ideal for a ruler who needed to make difficult choices, and that was why he needed the rest of his Crimsons.

Tzena stepped into his vision again, worry filling her eyes. "Despite the effectiveness of your abilities with the Unity Crystal, you fail to protect yourself from this horrid Taint. If we are to win this war, then we must project power from the very top."

Chatik huffed, rubbing his aching head. "My health is irrelevant. Our work prepares the way for the Crystal Heir. The people shall believe the Unity Crystal's power is hers, raising her above even the false goddess in their eyes. Now, what information has Qaraza brought?"

The Uziokaki matriarch stepped closer. "Your highness, I am pleased to say that we have identified your wife's hideout."

"Where?" He leaned forward, his fingernails scraping against the armrests. Lilita's absence had been a thorn in his side for too long, but if he could bring their children home, his bloodline would be secured beyond his life. And he could have his revenge. "Where did that bitch take my children?"

"Our spies claim they have joined Tiuz Hazeko's rebellion, but we have scoured Fort Harizak. Neither she nor the children are sequestered with his forces there." A grin crept across her face. "As you know, Lady Lilita cannot travel without a full entourage to support her rich tastes. Our recent economic woes and the civil war have caused a severing in trade routes throughout our nation's interior, but we have identified a particular estate that has been swarmed with deliveries in recent hundred-hours."

Chatik rose, but staggered until Tzena caught him. "Which house has assisted her deceit?"

Qaraza glanced at Tzena, who nodded. "My lord," Qaraza said. "Most of the minor houses within the territory of houses Pikezik, Kuzon, iz Ardinvil, and Niezik have joined the Confederation of Harizak. This particular estate is owned by an insignificant one: House Agronizak."

"We must make an example of those who betray us," Chatik insisted. Fury burned through Taint's malaise. He had waited too long for the Crimson Court's agents to uncover Lilita's location, but his target was in sight now. Soon, he would know his children were safe, even when his life waned. "Have every member of this House Agronizak hanged, drawn, and quartered. The guillotine is too kind an end."

"Our more clandestine methods have been more effective in the past," Tzena replied. "Further tightening our fist around scions will only make them despise us when it is them whom we are uplifting."

Chatik curled his lip. "Then conscript them all into the war. Force them to march against Kelosh on the front lines, then hunt down the rest of the traitors. Qaraza, this is your role from this point onward while Tzena deals with the rebels inside Kalastok."

"What of your family, then?" Qaraza asked. "Should we not bring them in? We could send the Crystal Brigade or a special detachment from the army to do so."

He hobbled between the women and down the narrow path before the throne. The Spirit Crystal below hummed through his Tainted mind, calling him to greatness, to complete the Crimson Cause. His life would be at its end soon enough. Taint ensured that. But his purpose was not yet complete. He needed a Crystal Heir, but he also needed to protect his bloodline, his blessed children.

"Focus on your assignments until I say otherwise," he finally replied, curling his fist around the Unity Crystal in his pocket. "My family divide does not relate to the Crimson Cause. It is my responsibility alone, and I will handle it from here."

Tzena caught him before he could hurry off. "If I may be so bold, you must not go alone. Let me come with you, if only to wait in the shadows in case Lilita springs a trap. My guess is that you intend on flying with that crystal's help, so it should not be difficult to bring me."

He looked her up and down. "You are armed, then?"

"I am the captain of the Crystal Brigade," she said with an amused grin. Pulling away her skirts, she revealed a holster strapped to her thigh, then dropped them back into position with a wink. "To find my other weapons, you would require a more thorough search."

Chatik cleared his throat, fighting the passion pooling in his chest. Marrying for convenience and influence had ensured he had not felt a loving woman's touch in over a decade. Tzena's intentions were likely for that same influence, but he could not deny that her advances had drawn his interest. Spirits, he looked like a leper beneath his Possibility Reaching. Of course a woman like her had no true desires for him.

Qaraza huffed from beside the throne and passed them by. "Enjoy your flirtations. *I* will return to my duties, saving us from Kelosh and sending the Third Army against the Confederation. We await your word, my king, on the arrival of the breathless."

"One cannot too quickly expose their greatest weapon," Chatik replied, thankful for the chance to focus on business. "Come, Tzena. Let us be rid of this mess my wife has caused."

DAWNRISE FELL UPON CHATIK'S FACE like the sweet smile of his daughters whenever he returned home. Their cheeks would be as red as poppies, their eagerness to hear his tales never-ending.

He had spent countless hours in the Crystal Palace since the coup. Flying now, even with the knowledge that it only deepened his Taint, was a freedom he so often lacked. The stress of his destination mattered not with the cool breeze across his face and the chattering of gulls following the rising sun in the south.

He'd thought he wanted to endure this mission alone, but as Tzena flew beside him with her hand clutching his hard enough to shatter a glass, he was glad to have company. Their relationship was a strange one. From passing, heartfelt moments during their time at Kalastok College under the tutelage of Etal iz Noshok to her aid during the Crimson Court's most trying times, she had always trusted his vision in the Cause. It had been clear for many years that trust went deeper than mere philosophical alignment.

Taint bled into his thoughts as his Air Reaching struggled to keep them aloft. They neared the place Qaraza had indicated. If they could just land close enough for a carriage to carry them the rest of the way to House Agronizak's estate, he would not have to endure further suffering. Air's Taint was plenty familiar to him already. He had no desire to lose his breaths until he suffocated.

"We will set down in Targeer," he said, nodding toward the

village below. "An approach via carriage will draw less concern than dropping upon their doorstep."

Tzena eyed him. "You cannot pretend this flight has not taken its toll on you. It takes little insight to guess you are avoiding further Taint, and it gains you little to attempt to deceive me. Have you heard the old homage which says to never hide your secrets when a Reacher of Shadows is near?"

"My breaths are fleeting," he admitted. "Perhaps that is worse around you than others, but it would be rather difficult to rescue my children while suffocating."

She gave no appeal, so they landed outside the village. Some in it had likely spotted them, but kooks and the elderly always claimed to have seen the impossible. By the time they had decided whether the story was true, Chatik and Tzena would have long since disappeared.

Muddied streets met his fine shoes but a minute later. This was the state of the rural parts of Ezman, far from Kalastok's cobblestone and gas lamps. Chatik reflected on the rumors of Kelosh's great machines which could bring materials across their nation and improve even the smallest village. Ezman has fallen behind. Reachers were capable of much. When they faltered to Taint, though, machines rolled onward. All the more reason why the Crimson Court required the breathless.

"This village resembles the Spirit Wastes more than the empire we once were," he said, scoffing down at his ruined shoe.

Tzena grinned. "Your opinion shall worsen when you realize that they lack our sewers, so what you are stepping in is as much fecal matter as mud."

He lacked the strength and will to react. Each ache of his body and stray thought stolen from his mind made him feel apart from himself, as if floating amid nothingness. But he clutched a shadowy thread tethering him to his corporeal form. Death would arrive on his terms, only when the Crystal Heir was ready.

Tzena caught him as he wavered, that grin fading to the deep sorrow of a child watching the spirit fade from their parent's eyes. What was to come was inevitable. Could he not enjoy the few pleasures he had left in the meantime?

"Are you certain you can handle this?" she asked.

Her words seemed to skip past, as if she were speaking twice as quickly as she was. Chatik shook his head to try and break the haze. Until it was the Crystal Heir's time, he had to manage. All of Ezman relied upon that fact.

So he nodded and labored onward until Tzena managed to flag down a carriage. It was shocking one was even available in a place such as this, but a few scions roamed the streets further from the village center. The houses here were wider brick buildings compared to the stonework or wooden ones he had spotted in clumps while flying overhead. Minor scions often lived in such outer residences. Far from estates, but also far from lowborn squalor.

The carriage ride passed in a blink, Chatik's muddled mind losing track of time's passage. Tzena spoke to him. Though he surely replied, the conversation's contents were lost to him, and he gave her a confused look when she moved to open the door.

"I confess I have forgotten whatever plan we had agreed upon," he said with each word plucking at his pride. "I intend to confront them directly and act with force if necessary."

She nodded. "All the while, no one will know I am here. Consider me nothing more than an observer unless events take an unfortunate turn."

He lightly touched her arm. His fingers trembled, but he knew not whether it was from fear of his feelings or from the Taint ravaging every muscle in his body. Perhaps both. "I have overlooked your value far too often during our years together. Forgive me."

"No forgiveness is necessary," she replied with her face revealing nothing of what lay beneath. "I was but a niece of Gornioz when we met. In the time since, you have elevated me to your left hand, granted me the influence I have always desired. There is…" Her voice trailed off before she cleared her throat. "Let us be done with your wife's treachery."

She helped him emerge from the carriage and step onto a row of planks forming the approach to House Agronizak's modest estate. The eager trees and shrubbery lining it had begun to sprout their first leaves, but the half-melted layer of snow covering their limbs made that a futile exercise for a few hundred-hours more. Chatik huffed at that. Were his own efforts against the empires and the corruption in his own nation any less futile?

No mercenaries greeted them as they headed toward the mansion's door. If you could call it a mansion. The squat building could have fit in its entirety within the Chamber of Scions, and its second story appeared to be only half the size of the first.

Lilita would feel trapped in a place like this. Chatik took no pleasure in that, however, as discomfort was little punishment for her betrayal. He'd pondered a thousand such punishments for her in the few hundred-hours since the Crimson Coup, but none had felt suitable.

Deep gray wisps circled Tzena, and she disappeared into the shadows cast by the southern dawnrise light. Alone, Chatik's shoulders drooped as he marched onward until he reached the door. His arm protested as he raised it to knock, and he did so far more lightly than he would have liked. But it was not a scion's place to pound a piece of wood in anger.

A startled manservant answered the door. "How may I..." He backed away. "King Chatik? What honor... Oh spirits..."

He turned to flee, but Chatik's Reach was faster. Purple snapped around his fingertips before shooting into the man's back. Death consumed him in seconds, but the Crimson King did not stay to watch.

The floorboards creaked underfoot as he worked his way through the house. Lilita would have heard the manservant's shout. He'd neither heard retreating footfalls nor seen movement in the darkness, and he Reached into the realm of Darkness to confirm as such. This brought no Taint, as his talon held its usual hourly charge separate from the power of the Unity Crystal. It did, however, bring his eye to a shifted rug in the corner of the drawing room.

Vigor filled him as he swept across it and threw aside the rug to reveal a trap door inset into the floor. Such doors were common in scion homes as glass-lined hiding holes in case an awakened somehow slipped into the house. With the Spirit Plague striking both lowborn and scions alike, they received more use now than ever.

Chatik shoved away his regret at failing to create a disease which spared scions. The Spirit Plague had gifted him thousands of awakened for his Mind and Spirit Reachers to mold into controllable breathless—an army which he would soon unleash. Suffering preceded any great victory.

The trap door swung open with surprising ease. Why would they not latch it?

Clutching the Unity Crystal, he prepared to Body Reach in case of a trap as he descended the ladder. His Dark Reaching exposed Tzena lurking behind him, ready to follow, and he took heart in knowing his back was covered. If he were Lilita, he would have done anything to distract or wound the intruder, if only to buy time to escape. Except the lack of a lock made that proposition unlikely.

Light flickered across the stone walls lined with imbued bits of glass when he reached the ladder's base. He shielded his eyes from the lamps, Taint making him far too sensitive to such dim glows. When his sight adjusted, he found rows of shelves filled with various boxes, sacks, and jugs lining the space—provisions in case of the exact situation Lilita had stumbled into.

A sharp smell pierced the musty, stale air. Gunpowder. Chatik's senses were charred, ghostly voices echoing and making every shift of the light seem like his absent wife's shadow, but he knew that acrid taste that pierced his tongue. He had spent his late teenage years among the soldiers in the last war against Kelosh. That time at war had given him another instinct to know when a gun was primed and ready to fire.

"Shoot me if you wish, dear Lilita," he called through the shelves, his shuffled steps echoing across the dust-covered floor. Another lantern hung over the central aisle, and his eyes watered as he forced himself not to look away. "It will be little more than an inconvenience for me, and we both know every round is precious in war. Why put a ball in your husband's skull when it could find a Keloshan's instead?"

His last words echoed through the tight space as Taint's haze stifled his perceptions. He could barely comprehend the four figures huddled at the far end of the row, their backs to the wall and the shelves blocking them from either side. No escape.

"Hello, children," he said, extending a hand toward the smallest three. Between eight and twelve, his children had yet to sprout to their full height, and he had no desire for them to see the blood that would inevitably flow between their parents. "Come, let me bring you back home. Back to the Crystal Palace where you deserve to live as little princes and princesses."

An unmistakable *click* silenced the noise in Chatik's mind. All fell still as the tallest figure raised her arm. Except the gun in Lilita's hand pointed not at him, but their son.

"Do not take another step," she warned, her words cutting through the haze until Chatik saw her and the children clearly. "I know what you want, and I will not hesitate to take it from you."

THE WORLD WHERE NO HEART BEATS

"I dream of sailing the other realms with anchors raised and cannons ablaze. Except Death's realm. That place must be a bloody nightmare." –
Stormrider, Nochlander pirate

A shattered plane of black stone stretched to the horizon as Kasia fell from her Axiom portal and landed straight on her face. The air was stale and still, inflaming her lungs and stinging her eyes. And when she screamed, her voice pierced it for what seemed a thousand miles beneath the dark sun.

I can't do it…

She'd shot him. Her four bullets had turned Chatik's head into a bloody mess, but the King in the Dark had healed as if she'd done nothing more than flick his ear. Experienced Body Reachers granted most elites near immortality until their Inheritance Rituals anyway. Now, the Unity Crystal had made Chatik invincible too.

Kasia's insides revolted as she collapsed onto the jagged ground, further Taint forcing her to expel the food she had eaten at the iz Vamiustok estate. Her two Reaches had come within a minute of each other, and her left forearm seared against the web of crystal creeping ever further up it. She had jumped halfway across the Commonwealth and then to wherever this place was.

A chill crept down her spine. Where *was* this place?

Spitza hopped around her, taking the shiniest of the black rocks in her beak and displaying it like a trophy. Kasia offered the raven her hand, and Spitza scrambled up to her shoulder as she stood. The skirts of her borrowed iz Vamiustok dress caught against a duller, jagged rock, but she gave it no care as they ripped. A creeping instinct told her to accept another round of Taint and leave this place. When she attempted to do so, though, she found no golden wisps at her fingertips.

She raised her left hand into the dim light emitted from the sun. The Axiom Crystal winding across it was dull instead of its usual radiant glow, just like it had been in the Water realm.

"Shit…" she muttered, closing her fist. Her missing index finger left a gap, and an aching hole in her heart echoed the two gunshots that had rang out before disaster: both Chatik's and her father's.

Why had she come here? Why had she dared to attack Chatik by herself when she knew the Unity Crystal could heal him?

Zinarus's cold words hung over her as an unbidden answer. "*…a spiteful woman whose bite carries deadly venom…*"

That phrase repeated in her mind as she picked a direction at random and started in it. She had let herself get attached, to consider the possibility of love, but it had been a child's wish. A cry for the care she'd lost with Leonit's death. For the loving caress she'd once had in Aliax's arms. Ridiculous. No one would love a Tainted, vengeful wretch like her, but she did not need them anyway. Attachments made her vulnerable, and Chatik would surely take advantage.

Why had she not killed him when she had the chance? Igniting her Death Reaching among the gathered Crimsons when he'd revealed himself could have ended their plot in an instant. They would likely have struck her with a dozen kinds of Reaching in response, but the Crimson Court's destruction would've been a worthy end to her life.

Instead, she had allowed the Crimsons take power. Zinarus's

appeals had failed to stop it, and she now lacked the Reaching she needed to kill the Crimsons and their breathless with a single point of her finger. Specters haunted her every waking moment, yet she was no closer to avenging her father.

So she wandered on in search of a crystal from this realm. The Water Crystal had allowed her to replenish her crystal hand before, and this was surely not Zekiaz. But where was it?

She focused on that question instead of her broken heart. Nothing from Zekiaz mattered until she got back to it. She would reunite with Kikania, then teleport to her house's marching army. Whatever came next, she'd figure out, but Zinarus had made it plenty clear that he didn't truly want her alliance. House Niezik would forge its own path without him or Tiuz's Confederation of Harizak.

Her legs grew weary before the horizon shifted in the slightest, her determination giving way to a dull emptiness that swallowed her chest. Where was she even going? There were neither hills, trees, nor a village to be seen. Just the sea of rock that sought to catch her ankle and tear her to her knees.

"You don't need to do this, you know," Aliax said, appearing from nothing beside her and poking his finger playfully at Spitza on her shoulder. He kept Kasia's stride with a wide-brimmed hat shielding his head and a duster clipping at his heels. Despite just emerging from the everdark, his skin was tanned and his cheeks spotted with sun freckles. "Leonit wouldn't want you to suffer."

She dragged her feet to a stop. Spirits, she was so tired. But sleep sounded like a horrid idea in this place, and Zinarus would inevitably fill her dreams. How could such a gentle face carry words as sharp as a blade?

"What else is there to do?" she asked before stumbling and falling into Aliax in her exhaustion.

He guided her head onto his lap as he sat cross-legged, her agony waning at his fingers stroking her hair. They traced the bullet scar at her temple before running across her neck with the perfect pressure to relieve her stress yet not cause pain.

Spitza followed him, pecking at Kasia's hair before displaying the shiny stone she had collected. Aliax chuckled at the raven and offered it another pat before replying to Kasia, "You must be joking. Even now, you are one of the richest, most influential people in the Commonwealth. Spend your time aiding your peasants and workers instead of chasing this obsession with revenge."

"They're hunting me," she replied, watching the strange dark sun set behind him. Her crystal-webbed fingers hung before it like a tree's drooping boughs in duskfall. How did the sun move so quickly in these other realms? Were their years just that short?

"You can teleport," he said. "Travel to another continent and start a new life. I could come with you, and between your amber and the Axiom Crystal on your hand, we could make it anywhere."

"You're dead," she tried to say, but her words caught as tears slipped from her eyes. The usual weight that came with that was absent. It was all distant, a notion of how she *should* hurt. That pain, that loss, sounded better than this emptiness, and even her heartache turned to some fading memory. Only the pleasure of his fingers gracing her hair and cheek broke through.

He extended an arm before them. "We could buy a ship—no, a fleet—and set sail across the Vitrian Sea. Challenge the privateer kings of Ogrenia. Explore the coasts of the Spirit Wastes where no one has dared to travel before."

Kasia allowed those impossible dreams to pass over her for a long while. They sounded so comforting, but there was no leaving the path she'd set upon. The Crimson Court had stolen everything from her. Surrendering now would make Leonit's life and death meaningless. It would mean the end of the house she had spent every waking moment rebuilding from the ashes, and Chatik would get away with all his treachery. She could not allow that.

Something cracked against the rocks nearby.

She spun to her feet, drawing her revolver and pulling back the hammer. It had only two bullets left, the others wasted on Chatik, but that was plenty to kill anyone messing with her now.

Except it wasn't a single attacker. At least a dozen decrepit, humanoid *things* shambled from the cracked landscape. Their bodies were naked, their eyes empty marble orbs as they gnashed broken teeth and surrounded her.

"Stay back!" she demanded, swinging the revolver at whichever of the creatures was the nearest at any moment. Spitza echoed the demand with her shiny rock waving like a soldier's blade and her one good wing extended to make her look larger.

But the creatures gave no care. One knocked away Kasia's arm as others grabbed hold of her. They reeked beyond belief from this close, but the stench was a familiar one. Death. It sent a shiver down her spine as a voice called out in a strange tongue, forcing the creatures to stop.

Another figure strode across the broken terrain with ease. Tall, with broad shoulders and a narrow torso, his body was only slightly less decayed than the creatures', but he was at least recognizable as a man. He wore a mask made of stitched together flesh which cut diagonally across his face to reveal his lips and the bottom of his nose. Raven black hair flowed above like a brewing storm, and his obsidian armor carried thunder as he approached, carrying a long, bloodied scythe.

"The Crystal-fucking-Mother never shows her face," Kasia muttered, meeting the man's gaze. Like his creatures, he had no pupils beneath that mask, and purple swam through the empty sea where they should have been. "But Death arrives the second I appear in his realm. Figures. It is what I deserve."

She should have been terrified. Instead, there was only that lingering numbness, accepting this horrible reality for what it was. Whether it was Zekiaz or the Death realm didn't matter. Everything was out to kill her, and maybe it was for the best if she was gone. Gregorzon's connections with the Crimsons would make House Niezik rich. Zinarus could find someone who wasn't Tainted with the ghosts of her murders. And Kelosh might finish off Chatik for her if she stayed out of the way.

So she stopped fighting as the creatures dragged her toward the man. Aliax, though, pulled at them, his eyes wild as Spitza pecked away at their mangled hands.

"You can't give up," he pled. "Not when you've come so far."

She scoffed. "What's the use? I can't Reach, and fighting all of them will accomplish nothing."

He let go of the creatures and turned his attention to the man, smiling smugly like he always did when he had an idea. "Look at his armor. Purple crystal!"

Most of the man and the landscape beyond him was a dull shade between everdark black and spirit silver, but the sun's strange setting light cast a shimmering glow over the lines of crystal crossing his breastplate. At its center pulsed a stone the size of her fist, embedded where his heart should've been. A Death Crystal?

A glimmer of hope split Kasia's shell, bringing waves of pain and regret with it. She tried with all her might to shove it away and forget all she'd endured, but her Axiom-wrapped hand hummed with excitement. It tingled up her forearm, as if eager to feed on the strength of another crystal again. That same desire poured into her spirit.

"Who are you?" she spat as the creatures forced Kasia to her knees before the man. It was a futile question, she knew that, but the fresh emotions had her mind swimming against the current, fighting for each breath of air. Desperation bred stupidity.

The man stomped his scythe, speaking a command, and his creatures backed away. Kasia laughed at that. Did she really look so harmless?

He proceeded to ask her a series of questions in his foreign language. Since she understood none of them, she stayed silent, eyeing that Death Crystal on his chest and considering whether she should dive at it and hope she could absorb its power. Failing that would mean her death, but her other option was to let this man—probably an undead one based on his appearance—do whatever he wanted to her. Not appealing in the slightest.

Curiosity about the other realms, though, kept her on her knees. Leonit had often said that patience reaped benefits, and she decided that unless the scythe man actively wanted to kill her, she could learn about the Death Realm while waiting for a better chance to strike.

The man furrowed his hairless brow. He ground his heel into the stone, lips pursed, then tapped his chest. "Valimor."

She smirked. Even here, some signals were universal.

"Kasia," she said, copying the motion.

Valimor did not acknowledge her name, but crossed his arms and circled her. It gave her the same unsettling feeling as the Water realm's humans seeking to take Zinarus and her as slaves. There was something else beneath those wispy eyes of his, though, and she never took her gaze off him. If he intended to kill her, she would not shy away.

But he did not raise his blade, and when he finished his circle, he held out his arm for her to take. She refused. Years of great house politics had made her plenty skeptical of apparent gifts.

"Touch the Death Crystal and get us out of here," Aliax said, his voice nervy. "This is not a place to linger. Believe the dead on this one."

That crystal was just at the edge of Kasia's reach now. All she needed to do was pretend to grab Valimor's arm and touch his chest instead, but she couldn't move. To follow Aliax's advice meant returning to the pain of Zekiaz and the weight she carried in her realm. This was a new place for her to discover. No one would really miss her anyway.

Valimor cocked his head at her refusal. His lips parted to ask a question, but they slammed shut again a moment later. Was Kasia not worth the effort, or did he realize she couldn't understand him anyway? Either way, he retracted his hand before nodding toward some place in the distance. Then he walked off.

Kasia clenched her fists, waiting for the creatures to drag her after him, but they just lumbered past. Purple flickered across their disgusting skin, stitched together like Valimor's mask. Death Reaching. She had lost her ability to call this realm's power, but if this man was a Death Reacher with Death's own crystal, could he help her get it back?

She would not let herself hope this time. No, hope was too deep, but faced with a choice between kneeling forever on that severed terrain or following Valimor, the latter was the logical answer. Logic had become foreign to many of her decisions. This, though, felt like the right moment for it, and as she rose, Aliax shifted into her Tainted specter. She nodded at Kasia's decision, offering a hand to keep her from falling in her exhaustion.

"He holds the power we need," her specter said in a savage, cutting version of her voice. "Learn from him, or take it from him. Imagine what power we could wield with beasts of Death like this at our command."

"Chatik commands an army of breathless who consume their victims' spirits," Kasia replied with her gaze fixed on the distant figure of Valimor and his minions. "What can breathless do against creatures without one?"

The specter brushed the sweaty hairs away from Kasia's cheek. "You did not see the truth in my guidance before, but now you understand. The Axiom has given us a key. To exact our revenge, we must use it to open the door."

BROKEN

"The irony of truth is that everyone has their own." – Era-Oniak Tal,
Ogrenian philosopher

Nex sat bound, broken, and delirious in a dim room. They couldn't remember the last time they'd eaten or drank. Spirits, they couldn't remember much of anything.

Blinking away the blur, they raised their head to find a woman sitting before them. She wore a high-collared, rich red coat with winding waves of blue across the torso, but to Nex's beleaguered mind, those waves just seemed to be reaching for her breasts. There wasn't much perfection where Nex was from (*where was that?*), but they could tell perfection when they saw it. From the woman's gentle smile to that grayish blonde hair swooping down her front and those radiant violet eyes, she was damn near as close as it got.

"What's someone like you doing in a place like this?" Nex asked, realizing yet again that they didn't know where they were. Just that they felt like they'd been thrown by a koilee and impaled on its spines.

The woman gave them a concerned look. "So they did push you to the threshold, then, but I hope not beyond. Perhaps it is deserved after that kick of yours broke my ribs, but I wish it had not ended this way."

Nex wanted demand answers, but when they tried to shout, their mind spun. They tried to shift instead, but their shackles bit into their arms and kept them held tight to the chair. Yeah, that had been stupid. But they *needed* to know what was happening to them. This woman had the answers.

"Who messed with my memory?" they asked, blinking hard as a middle-aged man with a bent nose flashed in their mind. "You? The bastard with a broken nose?"

Slowly, the woman nodded with her hands held before her. Not an interrogator's stance. The stance revealed a fancy glove that bordered her talon, probably allowing her to Reach even with the gloves that Ezmani scions were so obsessed with.

My ring!

Nex nearly broke their arm trying to feel for their finger. But they only needed to wriggle it to know that the familiar weight of their stolen crystal ring wasn't there. Those assholes had taken both their memory and their Possibility Reaching! It wouldn't do their captors much good, since bonded crystal couldn't be used by someone else, but it sure could keep Nex here.

"One of your interrogators was Uzrin Ioniz," the woman confirmed without any pleasure in it. "Do you remember the other one?"

Nex shook their head.

The woman sighed and traced her talon. "The bald, moustached one refused to tell even me his name, and if you cannot remember him, that was likely intentional." She looked up at Nex. "Based on your questioning, the same is true for your memories of me."

"I'd remember a face like yours." It was the type you either kissed or punched. Right now, Nex really wanted to do the latter.

"My name is Nikoza the First, representative of House Bartol and sergeant of the Crystal Brigade." Her eyes grew heavy as she crouched before Nex. "By the Mother, I did not wish this for you. I promise. When you kicked me, though, my Uncle Chatik did not hesitate to have you punished."

Nex scrunched their nose at the brutal strike that was Nikoza's perfume. Like overripe flowers burning in the everbright sun. She presented herself as if House Bartol and Crystal Brigade were important, but neither meant anything to Nex. A poking in the back of their head told them they'd once known, and distrust lingered at the thought of Nikoza's name. Beneath, there was just fog.

"I'd say sorry," Nex said, "but can't remember if you deserved it or not. If you're a sergeant or whatever, you probably did."

Nikoza winced, glancing over her shoulder. "I do not have long. Your Truth Reacher interrogators don't care much for your life at this point, but I heard whispers that you gave them some kind of information that they needed. What did you tell them, and was it the whole truth?"

Nex shrugged. "Ain't no lying to a Truth Reacher."

"Yet there are many forms of the truth to be given." Nikoza cleared the stray black hairs from Nex's face with a touch once again far too gentle for a sergeant. Was that some kind of half-truth? "Nex, despite all the animosity between us, I want to help you. I believe that you know something about my past and the Crimson Court's plans. Chatik is their leader, and it appears…" She sighed, her face twisting as if she fought with her own mind. "It appears he has interfered with my memories as well as yours. Please, I need you to try and remember."

Searching for any memories of a Crimson Court, Chatik, or even Nikoza just made Nex dizzy. They slumped back in their chair, nauseous. "Nothing."

Nikoza's expression soured. She suddenly grabbed Nex, shaking them until their teeth rattled like the marbles rich scion kids played with in the eastern alleys. Spirits, why could they remember that, but not anything important?

"We both need this!" Nikoza exclaimed. "Chatik is planning something for me and the whole country. It must have to do with Etal and the Spirit Plague, and you are here because you led the Ashes of Dawn to rescue him."

Nex stared, wide-eyed, up at the princess. That's right—this bitch was a princess! But that mention of the plague gave them another, more important name.

"Vin was sick," they whispered to themself.

"She was, and I have a faint memory of sending you back to the Shadow Quarter with a cure for her. Did it work?"

A deep pang struck Nex's chest. They struggled to breathe as images of a young flame-haired woman drowned them in emotions. Longing. Regret. Desperation. But neither recognition nor love—at least, not theirs.

"She…" Nex's voice cracked, tears stinging their eyes as they felt Vinnia's life waning in their arms. They'd almost lost her. Almost. "She's alive… I think. I remember the potion. It did something to help her."

Nikoza released them and sat back on her heels. "So it is true, then. Chatik lied to me. Etal and Paras created a cure, and the Crimsons wanted them dead for it. Why?"

"I don't know, but if you want my help, I can't do it strapped to this damn chair."

"Releasing you would draw attention that I don't know I can afford. Gregorzon…" She glanced over her shoulder at the heavy steel door across the room. There was only flickering torchlight in the room, and it made those violet eyes of hers burn like the duskfall horizon. "Give me a moment."

She rose and hurried toward the door until Nex called out after her, "Wait! You can't just leave me here."

Nikoza stopped with her hand on the door, then knocked twice. "I fear I have done so too many times already."

When the door opened, she slipped out. Was she going to talk to the person she'd called Gregorzon? That Z marked it as a scion's name, but that wasn't a surprise given the circumstances. Lowborn gangs didn't bother with theatrics when it came to interrogations. They just beat the shit out of you until you talked or lost the ability to.

The room offered no more answers, so Nex focused on what Nikoza had said. Who were these Crimsons and the Ashes of Dawn? She'd called Nex the leader of the Ashes, but how could they forget a group they were a significant member of? Then again, they had all but forgotten Vinnia before Nikoza's reminder. Names swam around their muddled head like eels which slipped away each time they reached for them. They'd never been much of a fisher—that much they remembered at least—but that's what the workers down by the docks always used to say.

Before they could remember anything all that useful, Nikoza returned with another scion, barely a man. This one was far from the perfection of his counterpart, with his patched stubble and early developing frown lines making him look both fifteen and thirty-five at the same time. Bright orange threads replaced Nikoza's blue on his coat, and his scion skin resembled smoke above a dying fire. He also looked incredibly familiar.

"Don't tell me I knew you too," Nex blurted out.

The man scoffed as Nikoza approached once again. Her pale-gray cheeks had reddened enough to match her uniform, and Nex took another look at the man to try and figure out how *this* man could possibly fluster her. "This is Gregorzon of House Niezik, and he has agreed to help us."

Nex furrowed their brow. "Why? He's a scion too, and there's always something in it for you."

"You would not believe I am doing this out of the kindness of my heart?" he asked.

"Scions don't have those, based on what little I remember."

He cast Nikoza a side-eye. "You are certain this is a good idea? The king—"

"I will face his wrath when he returns with his family," Nikoza interrupted, crossing her arms. Oh, there was definitely some type of spark between these two. Whether it was sweet or explosive, though, Nex couldn't tell. "If Nex knows about the Crimsons' involvement with the Spirit Plague, then that is what matters. They can ensure we deliver Etal's cure throughout Kalastok and the Commonwealth."

"There are better ways to find answers," he replied.

Nex stomped their foot. "You going to help me or not? I'll tell your Chamber or whoever that the Crimsons were involved. Just get me out of here."

Gregorzon guided Nikoza aside before circling Nex, his gaze

stern. "You are a rebel, so without a Truth Reacher of our own, we have no way to prove you are telling the truth. Just admit where Etal is, and we shall ensure he has a chance to clear his name. Otherwise, the other squads of the Crystal Brigade are sure to drag his corpse across the river based on the information you gave the Truth Reachers."

"You told me you don't know what I revealed," Nex said, eyeing Nikoza.

"We don't," she replied. "Gregorzon and I, though, are acting under the assumption that you revealed enough to them. They would have broken your mind completely otherwise."

Nex hesitated. "It gets worse than this? Shit. Don't you scions have enough without ruining all our lives?"

"Make your choice," Gregorzon insisted. "King Chatik could be back at any moment."

Choice? What choice did they have? If these two were right, then Nex was as good as a husk if they stayed here. The Truth Reachers would make sure of that. Working with Nikoza was their only real option, but that didn't mean telling her everything. Not that Nex knew enough to tell.

"Fine," they finally said before rattling their bindings. "But first, you need to unbind me and get my crystal ring back. I need it."

Gregorzon scoffed. "That is illeg—"

"So were Chatik's actions if all this is true," Nikoza said, holding his arm, her voice aflame with passion. "My grandfather's obsession with tradition led to his demise. To move forward, we must learn to adapt and partner with *all* our people."

He nodded. "I will distract the guards, then. Do what you must."

Nikoza opened her mouth to reply, but he left before she could do more than squeak in surprise. Nex grinned watching him go.

"Can't trust a guy like that."

"Most would say the same of you," Nikoza replied, rounding them and slicing the binds. "Luckily, though we have both forgotten much, I know you are the kind of person who carries a plot to its end. We both need answers, Nex, and to prove my goodwill, I will remind you of your reason for breaking my ribs."

Nex rubbed their wrists. They were raw from spirits knew how long in the bindings, and even the slightest touch earned them a jolt of pain. That didn't stop them from touching the wounds anyway. There was something all too human in the way people, whether low-born or scion, so often enjoyed reminding themselves of their pain.

"Why would you do that?" they asked.

Nikoza's breaths sent a curling fog between them as she neared the door, as if anticipating Nex's eventual lunge for it. "When I sought to bring aid to your people west of the river, the Crimsons' guards fought viciously against the desperate people and, as you told me not long ago, dumped the food and water in a display that may have been mockery. Or it may have been a further reason to divide us. Either way, you asked to speak to me, and I wished the same after our cooperation before. The guards refused to listen to me, killing your friend Jax in the process."

"Jax?" Nex stood, but only succeeded at wobbling before Nikoza caught them. That name sent a knife straight through their heart. That gunshot, the blood pouring from the old beggar's chest. A friend. A confidant. Dead, because Nikoza had been too gullible to see the Crimson Court's plans. "You killed him…"

"I did not," Nikoza breathed. Terror filled her eyes as she stared down at Nex. "There is blood on my hands, but just as Chatik has oppressed your people, I fear he has manipulated me. This is why I need you—to discover the truth. Let us ensure your friend's death is not but a statistic among many others."

"Chatik or whoever did this to us?" Nex muttered. "Then fuck him. The Crimsons killed Jax and tried to kill Vinnia with the Spirit Plague. I'll cut out his tongue and string him up on those damn towers you scions love. Let the awakened eat him alive."

Nikoza's nose flared. "You were angry at me proposing more of those in the west too. Chatik made me believe they would offer protection to your people and help him distribute a 'true' cure, but I must doubt all he tells me now. His plan must have to do with the breathless."

"Breathless?" Nex cursed under their breath. "Alright, you've got a lot to catch me up on."

"Can you walk?"

Nex tested their legs again—weak, but not collapsing this time. "I'll have to."

With a nod, Nikoza reached into her pocket and drew out a silver crystal ring. Something shifted in Nex at the sight of it, and they practically snatched the ring out of her fingers. "I have given you what you wanted," Nikoza said. "Tell me where Etal is, and I shall guide you to safety."

"I don't know," Nex muttered absently as they slipped the ring on. The fog remained in their mind, but it was as if they'd stepped from the icy river to firm earth. That alone released a dozen muscles across their torso.

But Nikoza looked at them as if they were an alien. "Did you never know, or do you simply not remember?"

"Hard to know what you don't know, ain't it?" They clenched and unclenched their left hand, that ring like a surge of energy within it. "Let me go, and I'll figure out who the Ashes of Dawn are and where they took Etal. If I lead them, they'll recognize me."

"How will you tell me of your discovery?"

Nex went up on their tip toes and patted the scion on her cheek. "I won't have to, because you're coming with me."

They started toward the door, only to find their arm torn back by Nikoza. "Are you mad?" she whispered. "The Crimsons will notice both of our disappearances and become suspicious."

"Tell them you were spying on me. Easy." Nex waved at her talon. "Besides, you're a Water Reacher. I'll need you to make sure I don't fall straight through the Kala's ice. That is... It's still everdark right?"

Nikoza's shock faded to a gentle smile. "Dawnrise has begun, but you remembered I was a Water Reacher. Perhaps that is a good sign."

"C'mon," Nex said, dragging her toward the door. "I need to get out of this spiritdamned room. Maybe I'll remember something actually important along the way."

DOMESTIC AFFAIRS

"International affairs create the greatest rulers. Domestic affairs kill them." –
Mataron Tongast, emperor of Kelosh

Chatik glared down the dim alleyway created by the storage shelves in House Agronizak's cellar. The woman at its end was familiar, but her expression was far from it.

"Calm down, my dear Lilita," he said, stepping slowly toward her and the three children at her side. Only their son and eldest, Bozumir, drew his focus. With Lilita's pistol pressed to the teenager's temple and the hammer drawn back, one flex of the matriarch's finger could steal his dear boy's life.

Lilita sneered and nodded at the gun. "I have my spies too. That crystal of yours reminded you of the First Law of Reaching, did it not? The Crimson King needs his heir, but Bozumir does not wish to come with you."

How did she know of his Taint? Perhaps it was obvious now, as his Possibility Reaching had dropped, but she spoke with the surety of a matriarch who held hidden assets. Traitors lurked in every government. Since the Crimson Coup, though, Chatik had spent incredible amounts of time and effort to purge all those not loyal to the Cause. The Crimsons could not rule without purity among their ranks, and if there was a single traitor feeding information to Lilita, it meant there were likely more.

He glanced at the children to judge their reactions, but veils made of glass chains hid all three of their faces. Were they afraid, eager to reunite to him? The Tainted voices swarming his mind reminded him that *she* had kidnapped his children. They loved him. They would want to return to Kalastok and take their roles as prince and princesses.

"Release them," he insisted, "and I will let you go free. We both know our marriage was one of political convenience, so let us be done with the charade. Take whatever funds you need to begin a life in some place far from here. Leave House Pikezik to Bozumir and you may endure with the knowledge your children are safe."

Lilita glanced down at the younger girls, barely tall enough to reach her hip, and ushered them closer with her free hand. "The only threat to their safety is you."

"Kill her," the voices told him in his mind. *"She dares use the children against us when our cause goes far beyond blood."*

"Beyond blood..." he whispered to himself, clutching the Unity Crystal and considering his options. His latent Dark Reaching alerted him to a movement in the shadows a row over, and he assumed it to be Tzena moving into position to aid him if necessary.

He put on his best concerned expression. Being a politician meant faking his care for many issues both scions and lowborn faced, and he believed it to be quite a good one.

"Which one of us holds a gun to our son's head?" he asked, shuffling forward. His efforts so far had taken a great toll on his body, and he hoped the lack of light would hide his visible tremble. "Please, Lilita, spare the children from our feud, or I will be forced to act."

Lilita cursed and swung the gun toward him, but he had expected it. Reaching into the realm of Truth with the Unity Crystal, white wisps burst from his hand.

"Why have you taken them?" his voice boomed before she could fire. "What was your plan?"

Her eyes widened, her lips parting as the wisps poured into her. Truth Reaching compelled her to answer, but as she fought, she dropped to her knees. The gun slipped from her fingers. A Spirit Reacher herself, she posed no threat now.

Paranoia gripped Chatik as he stepped past her. Truth's Taint. With each Reach, it made him question every movement, wondering whether Lilita could somehow break free from his Reaching and strike his flank. Had she laid another trap? He glanced at Tzena between the crates lining the shelves. Could she betray him too?

"Remove those veils," he told his children once he managed to pass his wife. Spirits, he was almost heaving! He could not go on like this, but now that Bozumir was safe, he wouldn't have to.

The two young girls did as he said, but Bozumir refused to move, stepping back into the far wall instead. When the lamplight revealed the girls' faces, Chatik realized why.

"You bitch!" he yelled, lashing out with his talon and scraping a bloody line across Lilita's cheek. "Where are our children? Where are *my* children?"

Before him were not his progeny, but two lowborn girls of similar height. He had not paid close enough attention to notice their pink-ish, Ezmani-lowborn skin. It was obvious now, and one glance at the cowering boy told him he was surely not Bozumir. Lilita had betrayed him already. That was unforgiveable, but he had walked straight into her deception. Her spies had outplayed his own, leaving him without his children.

"You will never find them," Lilita stammered through the compulsion as he Reached again to disperse her lies. His paranoia deepened further, twisting his thoughts against everyone he had ever known.

Purple wisps of Death enveloped him. They fed upon his fury and surged toward the fake children, killing them in an instant and leaving their decayed corpses to slump over the shelves. Their screams echoed. Those he heard, though, were not those of lowborn children, but his own.

"Did… Did they fear me?" he mumbled as the world became a haze. Madness sought to strangle him like an assassin's noose. He'd felt it far too often in recent hundred-hours, but he could not surrender now. He needed to know. "Did they wish to flee?"

"You are one of the most intelligent men I have ever met," Lilita replied, her eyes bloodshot. "Can you not comprehend why they would flee the man who conspired against the king and their mother alike?"

He turned and grabbed her by the throat. "Where are they? Tell me where you have taken my children!"

"I knew what you would do to me the moment I saw you wield such power during the coup." She glanced toward the dead children without a bit of visible regret. "Truth Reaching may pull all I know from my mind, but it cannot reveal what even I am not aware of."

Pain swelled within his chest. He released her, staggering back into the nearest shelf and collapsing as his body contested every breath.

"My lord!"

Tzena rushed from the shadows and scrambled to his side. Her hand was warm against his cheek, her breaths sweet, but the voices were stronger.

"We cannot trust her!" they told him. *"She knew of our plans. Perhaps she leaked them to all our enemies."*

"Was it you?" he asked through clenched teeth. "Did you expose my secrets to her?"

The Shadow Reacher stared back at him in shock. "Why would you suspect me of such a thing? Have I not been by your side every moment since our discoveries with Professor iz Noshok all those years ago? Have I not proven my loyalty whenever the others doubted our plans?"

He nodded toward Lilita, who still knelt as the compulsion slowly faded. "Then do what is required. Let us be done with this charade."

"Should we not take her back, interrogate her further?" Tzena asked. Her hand had drifted from his cheek, but the tips of her fingers lingered, like a last brush of the door before leaving home. "Perhaps she knows more of Tiuz Hazeko's rebellion."

Lilita laughed. "Your Crimson Court toppled Jazuk because he was weak. I am not a fool like him. My time has been spent in this lowly house, knowing you would find me long after our children were gone, so I chose to learn nothing that could aid you. Our mercenaries march to the Confederation's aid at Fort Harizak, but it is no secret their base is at the fort whose name they bear."

Tzena gave a solemn nod and drew her pistol. "Then you are right, my king. She is more of a liability alive than dead. If your children are truly gone, let us claim she locked herself in this place and killed both them and herself. There are others of House Pikezik who may seek command, but without her children, there is no direct line of inheritance… except to you." She grinned. "King of Ezman, overlord of Vocka, patriarch of House Bartol, and now, patriarch of House Pikezik as well. Who could dare challenge you?"

"You prove your worth yet again, Lady Tzena," Chatik replied, shuddering at the sight of the specters filling the cellar.

Most of the ghosts were recognizable rivals from his coup in the Chamber, but three smaller figures joined them now. Those hollow faces burned themselves into his memory like a branding iron as Tzena raised her pistol to Lilita's head. They were lowborn. Servants, tools to serve the chosen scions. Why, then, did something deep inside him squirm beneath their haunting gazes?

Tzena's gunshot cracked mere strides away. It could have been miles. A distant whistle on the winds that failed to pierce the haze Chatik wandered into with every passing breath. He had held the Taint at bay long enough to confront Lilita, but though he could delay the inevitable, he could not defeat it.

"We will require a carriage," he managed, his voice barely audible to himself. He could have been screaming or whispering, but it was all the same to him. "I cannot fly us back."

The haze consumed him before Tzena replied. There was no fighting it. All Reachers knew pushing beyond the natural bounds of their power resulted in Taint, and Chatik had long since left those limits behind. As he descended into the depths of his mind, tormented by specters, voices, and his failing body all the same, he reflected on the truth that he was likely the most powerful man in the empires of Brakesh, if not all of Zekiaz.

Perhaps, too, was he the most broken.

Aches of the Heart

"The deepest wounds are those of the heart, for not even the most skilled of Reachers can heal such pain." – An excerpt from *A Lover's Folly*

Zinarus collapsed in the doorway of Kasia's guest chambers. His cursed body trembled as a hot sweat poured down his brow and into his eyes. It felt as if the entire world were a top, and he was strapped to its center, powerless to stop its spinning.

"Why would she teleport away?" he asked absently, staring at the place where Kasia's maid, Kikania, had said the portal was. "What fit of passion would convince her to face Chatik by herself?"

Sania rested a gentle hand on his shoulder. "She was flustered during our meal, speaking nonsense that I must assume was some sort of Realm Taint if what you told me about her is true. A woman like that is a hammer. To her, all of Zekiaz is a nail to strike into place."

Zinarus placed his hand on hers and forced a genial smile to his face. It physically pained him to do so, but his time in the Chamber had given him years of practice hiding agony behind acceptance. "Quite the opposite, actually. Lady Katarzyna may appear like a blunt instrument at first, but beneath her unwavering determination, she has more guile than brawn. I was… well, *am*… fond of the way her mind approaches a problem."

"Then how do you explain this catastrophe?" his mother asked.

"I am more familiar with the complexities of my knee's mechanical elements than the emotions of women."

He glanced at the raven's birdcage in the corner. According to Sania, their bird-loving butler had inspected Spitza and found that her wing was permanently broken—something Zinarus was already pondering a solution for—but why would Kasia take a raven to her confrontation with Chatik? The man's Unity Crystal had repaired the damage of a Death bolt. Her attempt would surely be doomed, and a bird would do nothing to change that.

Only one explanation made sense, and it was exactly the one he feared most. He had heard hurried footsteps from the second floor when guiding his mother into the drawing room to talk in private. During their walk past the stairs, he had repeated how his absent father, Uzrin Ioniz, described Kasia when he visited Zinarus's booth in the Kalastok Arena.

"Lady Katarzyna is a spiteful woman whose bite carries deadly venom," Uzrin had spat. *"I care not that you are merely my bastard. Do not fraternize with that woman, or there shall be consequences for what remains of your pitiful house."*

If Kasia had heard such a thing out of context or without knowing who Zinarus quoted… By the Mother below, what had he done?

"Her emotions may be beyond my understanding," Zinarus continued. "Logic, however, leads me to believe that this was my fault. Mother, do you remember my quoting of Uzrin beneath the stairs?"

Sania rolled her eyes and paced across the room. "Eavesdropping never causes any good ends. If you had questions about whether she shared your fondness, it appears we have our answer."

"What do you mean by that?" he asked with a glance at Kikania, her neck as red as the hearth's flames. She had overheard plenty of his conversations with Kasia, and part of him hoped there was more the maid was not admitting.

"Must I say it?" Sania said, scoffing. She waved toward Kikania. "Girl, admit that your mistress favors my son."

Kikania squeaked before clearing her throat and replying, "Lady

Kasia's heart is a… complicated… thing, my lady. I cannot deny that she is emotionally tender so soon after addressing her guilt for the death of her former lover. If she overheard something, then yes, she may have acted rashly because of it."

"The path she has taken is not one I can follow," Zinarus said, working his way back to his feet. "That Axiom Crystal of hers could have taken her anywhere."

"Well, not *anywhere*…"

Zinarus gave the maid a stern look. "Please, tell me what you know. It does little good for her to challenge all the world alone."

"She mentioned going to face Chatik," Kikania said, shying away.

"Then she has truly gone where I cannot."

His heart felt as if it had dropped into his stomach, but he had to push on. Tiuz and the Confederation of Harizak needed his house's aid against the Crimson forces. The old cavalry commander had trusted Zinarus's plan to create a mercenary company in Kalastok, and more than that, had been a confidant and friend in the aftermath of Regizald's death. Zinarus could not abandon him to chase Kasia's whims. Though every fiber of his being wished to, he could not charge alone into the capital to save her. He just hoped the reckless move hadn't led to her demise.

"I will gather what mercenaries I can," he continued. "Mother, raise the rest of our forces who are willing to fight for an Ezman free of corruption and the Crimson Court's schemes. Have them meet me along the path east to Fort Harizak."

Sania raised her brow. "What do you intend to do? You are no commander."

He was also no fool. Her comment about him being called a coward in his youth had been a targeted strike, and he would not deny the fear swelling within him. What came next was a matter of duty and justice. In the face of those who had slain his friend and stolen his family's rightful assets, he would not falter.

"Perhaps not yet," Zinarus replied, straightening his back and holding his hands behind him like he had seen Tiuz do a hundred times. It was a leader's stance. One that conveyed responsibility and authority alike. "It appears that it is time to change that. By taking our sand mines, the Crimson Court has severed the Confederation's access to glass to face their armies of breathless. I intend to rectify the situation with a swift strike."

"That is a plan bearing great risk," she said.

Zinarus nodded. "This is civil war, Mother. I fear all our actions bear consequences far beyond what we are able to comprehend in any given moment. In this, however, I am confident. The Crimsons will not have a large force protecting mere mines, especially with their attention diverted to Kelosh's invasion and the Confederation." He took a sharp breath, gathering his confidence. "I will ensure Commander Tiuz Hazeko is aware of our plans, and in the meantime, I would appreciate you ensuring Kikania is taken care of until her lady returns."

Sania gripped the edge of one of the room's chairs. Her fingers' dark skin seemed to pale, her lip curling. "I am the lady of this house. It would suit you to remember as such. Lady Katarzyna may never return, and I shall not waste away caring for her handmaiden."

"Then you may run the estate as you wish," Zinarus said as he crossed the room to his mother and took her hands. He found no enjoyment in confronting her like this, but her conceit had been unwarranted. This was his chance to prove her and all those who doubted him wrong. "I will bring Kikania, hoping Kasia joins us on our march east. If you wish for this estate not to be burned by our enemies, then your efforts to gather our forces would be appreciated."

"You will have my support, but do not place us in a situation where we are crushed by greater powers. We both aspire to join the great houses. That is impossible if we are dead."

He kissed her hand before heading toward the door. "Then let us work to endure."

Kasia's chest heaved with every breath as the realm of

Death ascended beyond the shattered plains. The thin air whistled past her, carrying hissing laughter. She couldn't tell whether they were from her Tainted specters or some other force, and she shivered beneath the sight of Valimor's undead servants.

The Death Reacher—or whatever he was—paid her no heed. She assumed that the presence of his creatures was an indication that he either didn't want her to be attacked or to escape. The chances of the latter were high enough to frighten her.

But she had little choice. That web she felt when Axiom Reaching tickled her fingertips, haunting her. When she called out for it, though, no power answered, and a force struck her core like a mighty hammer. That feeling was far too familiar for her to try again. The last thing she needed while in the realm of Death was for its Taint to overtake her. That Taint had driven her to this place, and now, its power was her only hope of defeating Chatik.

She had long since lost track of time, but exhaustion had forced her to sleep twice already. Valimor had waited in the distance. Whether he rested too, she didn't know. Something was off about him, though, not fully human beneath that slicing mask of his. Neither of them had eaten or drunk since her arrival, and her throat was as dry as the rocks of the realm.

To make matters worse, blisters covered her feet, joining the sores from where the rough Vockan dress rubbed against her shoulders. That hatred of its wool turned to gratitude, though, as they passed through a sea of leafless, creeping brush with as many thorns as a vicious koilee. There were no other plants or animals around, and she began to wonder whether she was the only being truly alive within the realm.

Mercifully, they soon crested a peak and stared down into a valley filled by what appeared to be a settlement of some sort. Towering stone walls surrounded a series of buildings, all which formed a ring around a castle made of pure obsidian. The volcanic rock shimmered in the sun's grayish hue, and from its peaks emanated rays of purple that burst into the empty sky.

Valimor stopped on a ridge just below. He pointed toward the castle, then looked up at Kasia and held a finger over his lips.

"*Niek*, Kasia."

She stiffened at the command not to speak. Valimor had what she needed, though, so for now, she complied, copying the gesture to signal she understood. A smile cracked his stone-like demeanor, and he mimicked the gesture. Fool. Did he not realize what she was trying to say?

So she pursed her lips instead and raised her chin. Let him wonder. So long as she held secrets from him, perhaps she had something to trade as well.

If Valimor was intrigued, he didn't show it as he continued down the steep slope. Switchbacks had been built into its side. That usually represented a trade route of some kind, especially with so many buildings inevitably meaning some people were here, but they had encountered no other travelers.

Darkness fell as the sun disappeared over the horizon. It was as if the year's seasons passed in an instant with any warmth vanishing, leaving behind a dull chill that force Kasia to tuck her arms beneath her long blanket scarf. Vockans clearly knew how to dress for the mountains' harsh winds. Here, fashion meant nothing compared to survival.

Valimor and his undead creatures showed no recognition of the cold, and their empty groans followed her with an annoying consistency. They would've been of some use if they could silence the specters' voices.

They did not.

"So we are following the menacing masked undead into the castle of black rock," Aliax mused, striding beside her with his hands held before him and a smug smile on his face. "This isn't your best idea ever."

She raised her brow at him, but said nothing. Valimor hadn't told her why she needed to be quiet. In a realm like this, though, she wasn't going to break that command for the sake of a specter.

A worn trail led from the base of the mountain to the city's gates.

That wear allowed steadier footing compared to the broken pattern of the rocks before, but Kasia was too tired to notice. All she wanted was for the walk to end. Returning to Zekiaz was an entirely different mountain than the one she'd just climbed. For now, she would tolerate the company of her late lover and the necromancer who'd taken a keen interest in her. Except she found no enjoyment when the reek of burning flesh greeted them at the city gates.

No guards stood on the parapets. Nor were there artillery guns of any kind for siege defense. The only appearance of defensive weaponry at all were a series of spikes protruding from head height, and a sixth sense told Kasia those spears' tips were following her.

The gates drew open at Valimor's approach, but what lay beyond showed no further signs of life. Ancient oil lamps offered a harrowing visage of more undead creatures. Each held a spear in-hand, but beyond untarnished helms of a metal Kasia couldn't identify in the darkness, they wore no armor over their decaying bodies and tattered rags. A garrison like this implied some preparation for invasion. From where? She traveled for some time now, but had seen no evidence of other cities or even villages.

Valimor took one of the oil lamps, holding it gingerly as the guards followed Kasia's passing with turned heads. Their eyes remained empty and they reeked like rotten corpses. But she had the distinct sense that these were different than Valimor's lumbering creatures. They held a presence and had ticks in their movements. An itch or shift that signaled a sentient desire for comfort.

Kasia almost asked Valimor what they were, but quickly slammed her mouth shut. Those empty eyes were enough to strike fear into her heart. Yet they could not compare to the monstrosities lurking behind them.

Towering, fleshy creatures the size of an adult koilee stomped their way down the streets beyond the nearest buildings. Puss and a lumpy purple substance oozed from their joints, covering the stone behind in a horrid slime. They had nothing resembling a face. Eyes and gaping maws covered them instead, as if a dozen people had been sewn together to create each beast.

Kasia so badly didn't want to consider that possibility, but dried blood stained the trenches lining each street. The ground angled toward those trenches, and they were everywhere as Valimor led her past the patrolling monstrosities and through the city. This was the realm of Death. How much of it had these streets seen? And was her blood meant to flow here too?

Her specters joined the undead throughout the streets. Among them, Aliax knelt beside one of those trenches and examined the blood. "We don't belong here. I know I said to get away from Zinarus, but I didn't mean turning to this!"

"Progress requires great sacrifice," Sazilz replied in that boxy brown suit of his. It was always horrible, but in a place like this, it looked almost appealing. Almost.

"And their progress shall be our power," her Tainted specter said. She was dressed far more appropriately for this chilled darkness, with an Ezmani high-collared coat trailing down to her calves and her koilee fur hat covering her ears. Where fear filled Kasia's eyes, her specter carried unfettered determination. "We are no strangers to Death, and without it, we cannot hope to match Chatik."

Can we even match him with Death's power?

She shut her eyes at the realization she had referred to the specter and her as *we*. All of them were just manifestations of her Taint, nothing more. Then why were they more present than anyone who was real? Among undead who pulled carts and did other manual labor in jerky, unnatural motions, the specters seemed clearly alive.

That thought haunted her as they headed down a shallow slope toward the obsidian tower. Those trenches ran downhill beside them, so she kept her gaze on the pillars of purple shooting from its peak. Power emanated from it like the beating of a heart that echoed her own. Alluring, intoxicating, terrifying.

More than a dozen kinds of the decrepit, stitched-together undead passed them along the way. Most gave them little attention, but a few turned their heads—or whatever misshapen body part which held their pupil-less eyes—watching her until she disappeared between another set of buildings.

She peered into the slitted, glassless window of a smoke-smothered building. The stench of burnt flesh forced her to hold her breath as an oil lamp inside cast light over a mound of it on the ground. A shallow trench split from the street's deeper one and entered the building right by where that mound sat. Yet another mystery, but she decided that she had no desire to find this one's answer.

Valimor glanced over his shoulder to notice her stopping. He barked something in his language before waving for her to follow, and this time, he waited until she fell into stride beside him.

They soon crossed a stonework bridge over what appeared to be an empty mote. The bridge's lamps were far too dim to reveal any details of the mote's edge, but from the sight of the trenches ending where the mote began, her stomach churned thinking about how much blood they would need to fill it. Her Taint-induced nausea deepened, and she held her arms across herself just to keep herself stable. If talking would draw attention Valimor didn't want, vomiting surely would be no better.

The castle's thumping intensified to a dizzying extent as they stopped before its obsidian doors. Fortunately, the choking stench was fainter here, but her weakened constitution made even standing difficult. Taint, exhaustion, hunger, and disgust met, sending her stumbling until Valimor caught her.

The necromancer threw out an arm at his undead servants and gave them a series of orders. Despite their appearances, they held enough sentience to comply, pushing open the doors to reveal a foyer that was a realm away from the horror outside.

Kasia gasped at the decorative arches above. Oil lamps hung from them to illuminate gemstone artwork. They depicted a robed man confronting what appeared to be various kinds of beasts before traversing mountains like those Valimor had led her over. The back wall finished the tale with the man standing ahead of a crowd. He raised a staff tipped with a purple crystal and pointed it at a ruined city, emeralds across its castle cracked and surrendered to the purple—a castle that looked very much like the one they stood in now.

"Sadamar," Valimor said, pointing at the robed man.

A king, perhaps? The necromancer offered no clarification, so Kasia just lingered for a long moment, wondering what kind of man this Sadamar was and what city had been here before. In a game of haataamaash, there were those who favored the dragon, those who favored the knights, and those who favored the spy. None of her games against her father, though, had involved mindless undead creatures.

One of those creatures shoved Kasia after Valimor with a groan. She glared back at it and could've sworn there was a flicker of a smile across its warped mouth.

Maybe not so mindless…

There was no visible exit to the foyer except for a single door along the right wall. It bore the same symbol as those on the hung banners: two halves of an anatomically correct heart sewn together, blood dripping below. Where sigils in the Commonwealth often held crowns or weaponry, cracked rib bones lay beneath this sigil's heart.

Whoever this Sadamar was, he had an affinity for the macabre—that was certain.

Kasia thought Valimor would head toward that door, but he approached the final gemstone art piece instead. The necromancer muttered something under his breath, then drew his scythe across his hand and slammed his bleeding palm into the wall. Rubies in the art beneath it shifted to form another sewn heart beneath Sadamar's trailing cloak. The entire castle shook as Valimor's blood trickled over it to complete the sigil.

Cracks formed across the wall. Kasia staggered back from them, but the undead lurked behind, holding her in place as the wall slid aside to reveal rugged stone steps leading up. Valimor nodded to them before grabbing her arm and dragging her along.

She tried to fight back, but the necromancer was muscled, unwavering. He stared through his mask at her with those empty eyes jagged enough to slice a spirit. What she saw in them wasn't anger, but desperation.

"Kasia," he pleaded. Then he let go and held an arm out toward the stairs, bowing his head. "Sadamar."

That only made her hesitate more. She had expected anger, for him to force her to the feet of his king so that she could explain her presence here. This was far from that. Valimor did not breathe like a living man, but his motions and a nervous bite of his lip signaled far more than she'd learned about these undead by studying the city. Maybe his life was gone. But like that sigil, there was a heart of some kind within him.

So she nodded and climbed toward Sadamar. Valimor fell in behind, leaving the other undead creatures at the foot of the stairs. Being away from them lifted a weight from her shoulders, but it was a speck of amber when she carried a wagon-full.

The thought of amber made her instinctively slip her hand into her pocket, where she carried a few pure pieces she had forgotten about. A breathless had barged into House Niezik and killed her father. She'd not assumed House iz Vamiustok was any safer when the Crimsons were looking for her, and some part of her deep beneath the layers of numb exhaustion hoped that amber could impact the undead as it could the spirits of her realm.

The castle's thumping overwhelmed that hope. It grew deafening as she reached the top, swallowing her thoughts in a constant drum like those the villages far from Kalastok used during celebrations. This, though, was no celebration, and her blood ran cold as the sound warped into a voice that shook her to her core.

"Welcome, lifeborn," it said, "to the heart of Death."

THE CLIMB

"What are we if not spirits who have found flesh, sentience, and the breath of life? Some seek a greater meaning than the brilliant combination of the Crystal Realms' many elements, but I see glory in the very confluence of those elements: pure creation. From both Possibility and Truth we were born. Through Spirit and Mind do we aspire." – Erzik Niezik, former professor at the Seekers' Academy of Reentiioon

Radais whistled an old tune he'd once heard from his father during childhood. Old Paladus would adjust the pace as he chopped a tree or stirred the stew Radais's mother had left boiling over, always carrying the same beats, but shifting from the joyful flow of a birdsong to a landslide of notes that cascaded one after another. For hours, Radais would listen to him whistle. The only communication between them would be his father's waves in a general direction for his ax or for Radais to fetch something. No words were needed for such things.

On the eastern slope of yet another mountain, the wind's whistling swallowed Radais's own. Vuk stared over his shoulder, as if watching the sound disappear over the switchbacks and into the ravine below. A single bleat followed.

"Keep it up," Radais reassured him with a pat on the ibex's neck.

Vuk bleated again and threw his head side-to-side, nearly knocking Radais with his massive, curving horns. That spurred Radais to escalate his whistling. Just like his father.

"I'm surprised to hear you whistling when everything echoes up here," Wanusa said, glancing back at him from atop her ibex. They would normally ride double file, but they already sent loose snow and stones skidding over the edge. One misstep could have any of them falling with it. "You usually only do that when you're content."

Radais raised his brows. "What do you mean by that? It's just a song my father used to whistle."

Wanusa leaned over the safe side of her ibex and grinned back at Lazan behind them. "Do you want to tell him, or should I?"

"It does not surprise me that he was unaware of it," Lazan replied with a laugh. "After all, I hear it mostly when I am near, and we all know I can be quite the distraction for him."

Heat burned against Radais's cheeks, and he was grateful for his glass helmet to hide his embarrassment. "You speak about me as if I wasn't riding between you."

Lazan flung off his wide-brimmed leather hat and held it to his chest. It left his hair a mess, but Radais loved that rugged layer on the overly-groomed scion. "By the Crystal Mother, I failed to see you there, Supreme Defender. I mean, how could I have missed you in a hundred pounds of glass armor and with hair as radiant as the dawn-rise horizon. At least you are not obscured by the clouds!"

"Blah," Wanusa muttered. "Stop flirting. It probably attracts breathless."

Lazan swept his hat back onto his head. "Why, of course. Attraction is well known to take one's breath away."

Radais wished to crawl into his armor and pretend nothing had been said. While he shared Lazan's affections, he was not used to such open displays of it. Even his relationship with Miv had been hushed, secret affairs late in the night when no one would see him sneaking to her Chambers for a tumble, and she had hardly shown any public desire for him beyond those sexual encounters. By contrast, Lazan was giddy. Almost playful.

"Lazan is ridiculous," Wanusa said, shifting her gaze back to Radais as her expression grew serious, "but he's right about that whistling of yours. We're up on a frozen mountain, hunted by angry spirits as I mourn my family and village. You, though, deep down are just happy to be by him."

"I'm sorry," Radais replied, still trying to retreat into his turtle shell of armor. "I did not mean to mock your loss."

Wanusa held a fist to her chest. At Mariana's request, she'd not taken her armor on the journey, but had kept both her glass and steel blades. That left her with only a tunic beneath a fur coat whose hood she tugged over her reddened ears. "You of all people don't need to apologize to me. We both know loss. If it weren't for you, I'd have nothing real left, and you being happy reminds me that I can be too."

She smiled at the end, but it was a crooked, forced one. Radais knew the pain beneath it well. An experienced Glassblade like him was expected not to show it, keeping a firm and professional demeanor. Wanusa, though, was too young not to try and smile. He so badly wished to protect that part of her. She deserved to age at her own pace instead of being thrown head first into the Wastes and told to survive Zekiaz's brutalities alone.

"You're wrong about that, at least," he said, meeting her gaze. "The Glassblades are lucky to have a damn fine warrior like you. Didn't take me to notice that."

"Not everything is about the Glassblades," she replied. "Right?"

He huffed. "A season ago, I might have said everything was. Now... Well, you might have a point."

Behind, Lazan wiped the snow off his hat's brim and squinted into the storm. "Can any of you see Mariana? This blizzard has Wanusa looking more like a juvenile koilee than a Glassblade, so there is no way in the wastes I am able to see past her."

The hairs rose on the back of Radais's neck. Eyes narrow, he drew his modified blade, for now opting to hold it with the glass edge out. "Mariana?" he called out. "Where are you?"

An ibex's huffing rapidly approached from ahead until Mariana appeared with a stoic look in her walnut brown eyes. "Do all Glassblades panic when the snow covers their path?" she asked, her voice neither mocking nor accusatory. Void of any emotion, it stung cold against Radais's skin.

"I drew my blade out of instinct, that's all," Radais said. "Something felt odd about..."

His voice trailed off as the wind carried the familiar coppery smell of blood down the mountain. He pushed Vuk onward without another word, shouting for the others to stay behind him. Wanusa, though, followed at pace. She'd tied her long red hair into a warrior's tight braids to keep it from draping over her ibex, and her eyes were like daggers in the lanternlight.

"You have no armor," Radais insisted as the ground leveled off to reveal a plateau large enough for a dozen or so scouts to make camp on. "Stay behind me."

Wanusa opened her mouth to reply, but stopped as the horrid stench of gore washed over them. Three mangled corpses lay at the plateau's center, surrounded by six-legged beasts with fiery eyes and spines covering their backs. Knee-high, they were a mix of gray and browns that matched the mountain rocks, and blood dripped from their maws as they tore into the slain men.

"Povniks," Radais said, dismounting and turning his blade to expose the steel edge as he signaled for the others to stay back.

Povniks shared the poisonous spines of the eastern forests' ginormous koilee, but these were smaller pack animals. They were dangerous against a rider on ibexback due to their agility. Radais had faced worse, though, and it was easier to pick through them if they were all focused on him.

"They don't attack people," Wanusa said from behind, backing away with Vuk—thank the spirits. "Something is wrong!"

She would've been right under most circumstances, but any carnivore grew aggressive when hungry. Radais had seen it before when humans over-hunted the game in a southwestern village. An old Vockan saying claimed that when the hunter took all the meat, then nature ensured the hunter became the meat. Was that the case here?

Radais advanced slowly, hoping they would be frightened. Except the povniks acted as if he wasn't even there. They released a series of high-pitched yaps in the direction of the others instead until Radais was within striking distance.

"You're right," he shouted through the storm to Wanusa. "This isn't natural."

Standing before them now, he followed their gazes back toward the group. It made no sense. What about them had these animals so frightened? Then Lazan stepped aside, and the pieces fell into place.

Radais pointed his blade at Mariana. "What are you doing to them, Whisperer?"

"All creatures bear spirits, *Glassblade*," the elderly woman replied, riding forward with her chin raised. "Between the everdark and the surge of breathless and awakened alike, there has been little for these povniks to eat come dawnrise. I have listened to their hunger and led them to feast."

"On humans? What kind of monster are you?"

Mariana clicked her tongue. "I am no monster. These men were killed by spirits—spirits who these povniks feared. Their spines protect them from awakened, but they have noticed the breathless know how to strike at the unprotected parts of the povniks. I ridded them of the breathless, so they have chosen to follow us."

"You spoke to animals?" That alone seemed insane, let alone her revealing that povniks' spines somehow protected against spirits. How did no one else know this? He looked to Wanusa in hopes of some kind of answer. "Tell me this is lunacy."

Wanusa averted her gaze. "I don't know the full extent of Whisperer abilities, but it makes sense. If they can speak to free spirits, why wouldn't they be able to connect to those within us?"

"Are they enslaved?" Radais asked.

Mariana shook her head. "Not at all. There are some of their pack that chose to leave. These five are those that stayed, accepting my gifts while you tarried behind."

He studied them and the faint silver wisps circling them, then lowered his blade. There was logic to her claims, but he couldn't shake the disgust that churned in his gut. Reaching was unfamiliar enough to him still, and Lazan had proven its uses to aid. This was a strange power that did not sit well with him.

"Warn us next time," he said as he stepped to Mariana's ibex and patted its nose. "You put us all at risk by leaving the group and interfering with spirits. Don't claim I am ignorant when you refuse to tell me anything about your abilities or plans."

Mariana held a hand over her chest. It was ungloved, and matching silver wisps danced about each finger like the rejoicing Saleshi who rose from Akaamilion's pit. She bore no Reacher talon nor any other visible Spirit Crystal, so how was she doing this?

"There are many secrets of this realm that a brute with a blade should not know," she said.

Radais watched those wisps as he passed her, ensuring they didn't follow. "You influence the povniks' spirits. Can you do the same to people?"

"If only humans were so simple."

"Radais is more than a brute with a blade," Wanusa said from across the plateau. She clutched her coat tight around her, her once eager eyes narrowing. "Even as I learn from you, I learn from him too. There is more to Zekiaz than secrets, and we can't defeat the Vanashel if we keep bickering."

Radais whistled for Vuk, then swung himself onto the ibex's back. He caught Lazan's curious glance as he did. The Body Reacher had been quiet through the confrontation, but would no doubt express his opinions once he and Radais were alone again. Radais wished he wouldn't wait. As the only Realm Reacher among the group, he had far more arcane understanding than Glassblades, and Radais held some hope that Lazan knew what the Whisperer was doing to the povniks' spirits.

"We are not finished with this discussion," he said, "but every moment we waste is another for the Vanashel to terrorize whatever remains of Iliafa. How far to this weapon you claim will defeat the Vanashel?"

Mariana pushed her ibex into a walk up the next switchback, not a reply, but a song escaping her lips. It echoed the strange language both the Saleshi and Vanashel breathless had spoken, doing little to calm Radais's nerves. He kept a tight grip on his blade as the povniks took up the line's rear. None moved to strike, but Lazan's ibex bleated a complaint at the predators following them. It was one Radais shared.

To his credit, though, Vuk labored on in silence. He'd carried Radais countless miles in recent years, and these treks through the mountains were the exact reason why Vockans chose ibexes as mounts over horses. This terrain was too steep and uneven for horseback. Even on an ibex, Radais had to grip Vuk's flanks until his thighs were sore, but these mounts were bred specifically for their climbing skill and endurance through the slopes.

Radais offered Vuk a bit of his rations to give him energy until their next rest. They had spent days in these mountains already, and their mounts needed all the strength they could get. The next set of hungry predators were unlikely to be so friendly.

"Are you ready to tell me more about this weapon?" he asked Wanusa, who tarried behind him now.

Her head hung, and her forced smile barely pierced her rigid worry. "Mariana is taking us to a place where she says I can become a Whisperer. She called the process 'the Deepening,' but I don't think I'm even supposed to tell you that."

Radais chuckled through his frustration. "I can't believe Miv chose to train a rule follower. If you're going to be a Glassblade and a Whisperer, you'll need to know which rules to obey at which time. We're in times unlike any for centuries. Sometimes, the old texts can't prepare you for reality."

"Does that make it right?"

"I order you to tell me," he replied, trying not to sound too forceful. "There. Now it isn't some ethical question. Your position in the Order rests on your honesty."

She furrowed her brow. "Or does it rely on me believing you'd actually kick me out?"

"The girl's point is a fair one," Lazan said from close behind. Often quiet, but always listening. "We both know you will not expel her."

Radais tried to glare at him, but it came out far too soft. Spirits, he wasn't an angry enough man for this. "Just pretend I would. It makes all of this easier."

"Fine." Wanusa breathed out sharply, leaning to the side to ensure Mariana wasn't in earshot. "After completing the Deepening, Whisperers take spirits into themselves and can command them. Mariana only showed me parts of it, but I think it could be helpful against the Vanashel."

"So they do command them. Just like the Crimsons."

"Not exactly. It is more a bond, like they join with the Whisperer." She shifted uncomfortably, and Radais remembered that she was no older than sixteen. Such things were a heavy weight on her shoulders. "Whisperers can comprehend what Mariana called Spiritspeech—which is like a rhythmic vibration that matches the core Essence of spirits and scions—and they speak it to convince the spirits to bond with them. I don't understand it completely. Mariana used her bonded spirits' Essences to help calm an awakened for a time, though. That alone is a great power beyond even Spirit Reachers."

Radais considered that for a moment, much of it growing muddled in his thoughts. "Taming awakened is useful, but I doubt it would work against an entire Vanashel army. Is this the weapon Mariana spoke of?"

Wanusa just shrugged. "I should be able to fight them as a Whisperer if I can bond with spirits, but there was something else about the rhythms that are in people's core Essences. Scions' match the Spirit Crystal's pattern. Lowborn's and Vockans' are different, and she believes a power on this mountain matches the Vockan one."

"A crystal, like the Light one?" he asked, his breaths catching. What did this mean for the Vockans? Could it prove why scions were able to Reach while lowborn of any race were not?

"I think so," Wanusa said. "But I don't know what it means if it matches our Essence."

That unsettling feeling in Radais's stomach deepened. He suddenly felt the urge to stop their ride and vomit over the cliff's edge, but he held it in. Like him, Wanusa was worried, and she needed his reassurance. "Then we'll figure it out when we arrive. Mariana wasn't lying about secrets, but I don't understand why she and the Whisperers have hidden them."

"They fear the Glassblades. We're too zealous in our spirit slaying in their opinion."

Radais returned his attention to Mariana ahead. The storm separated them enough for their conversation to be private, but considering the Whisperer's power, he doubted even that. "Time will tell if they're right."

Hours passed at an excruciating pace based on Lazan's watch, but none of them spoke of the Whisperers' powers again. The weight of what lay ahead grew heavy enough without further considerations about Zekiaz and Vockans' places within it. They needed to focus on defeating the Vanashel and protecting the vulnerable Vockan villages. All else came second.

When Mariana raised her hand to signal a halt, Lazan slid out of his saddle without hesitation. Radais wanted to chuckle at his crablike walk as the Reacher tried to protect his worn and chafed thighs, but he couldn't muster the amusement through his anxiety. They were at the peak of one of the highest mountains in all of Vocka. Was this where Mariana had sensed these apparent rhythms?

"Please, by the grace of the Crystal Mother below, tell me this is our intended destination," Lazan said. "I do not know if my legs can muster another step of this."

Wanusa raised a brow at him. "You do realize that we're going back down at some point, right?"

He rolled his shoulders, spurring an audible *pop*. " 'At some point' implies the future. Therefore, I shall prefer it over immediate riding."

Mariana coughed. "If you two are finished, we have arrived at the point where we will conduct our rituals. Make your camp at the closest edge of the plateau, and do not follow me across until I tell you."

Then she disappeared into the blizzard, leaving only a few red strands peeking out from her hat as any indication of where she was. Even that was gone seconds later. They had no choice but to listen, but that same shiver ran down Radais's neck as the povniks passed.

"Keep your guard up," he ordered the others as he dismounted. "My gut says there's danger here."

Wanusa took Lazan's ibex and her own, leading them behind Radais as the scion muttered something under his breath. "Your instincts said we should worry about the povniks too, Master," she said.

Radais looked at the creatures out of the corner of his eye. Two had followed Mariana, but the other three lingered as the group unstrapped their bags from the ibexes. "I'm not sure they were wrong."

ACROSS THE FROZEN RIVER

"A scion only offers a hand to those below if it benefits them, and even with that offering, they never reach (or Reach magically) to ensure that effort actually helps." – An excerpt from *The Dawnrise Manifesto* by Evit Paxian

Nikoza had no idea what she was doing. Breaking a lowborn rebel out of the dungeons? Sneaking around in the shadows? Lying to her allies? That wasn't her.

Yet a sense of freedom overcame her as she pushed open the secret side entrance buried deep in the dungeons of the Crystal Palace. Drifters hung about, but from what she could see, breathless kept away. She gripped a glass dagger anyway and ensured Nex had another from their confiscated belongings. Kalastok had taught her well that true danger often lurked beyond sight.

"Why did I have so many of these?" Nex asked, holding up an amber bead as they hurried west through the Crimson District. The Kala River was close, but so were the Pikezik estate and nearest Reacher tower. Her uncle's loyalists would be everywhere.

"I *think* we used amber to capture spirits for Professor iz Noshok," Nikoza whispered back before taking their arm. "We are not clear yet, so I will still need to escort you as if you were my prisoner. Though I am certain you do not want that, know that I will release you the moment we near the river."

Nex stiffened, but didn't fight it. "Stop walking us through the lamplight. You want someone to notice who we are?"

"Right…"

Nikoza kept toward the shadows, but there were only expansive streets and gardens here, not the alleyways of the city's poorer segments. The best cover they could hope for was the trees further north, where they could cross along the ice without being questioned by any guards. They would be far enough from Reacher towers or the bridges' lights then if all went well. If it didn't… Well, she decided not to dwell on that.

They'd been whispering tidbits of missing memories since they left the interrogation chamber, hoping to gain a better understanding of what they faced. Nex had forgotten a frightening amount. Though there were gaps or altered segments of Nikoza's own memories, this Nex was nearly a different person altogether. Slightly more agreeable, and curious instead of explicitly obtrusive. Their appearance was altered too, as if their face had tightened, stiffening around their cheekbones.

"Let me Reach," Nex insisted as they turned north, only to find a squad of Crimson watchmen patrolling the only route that direction. "I can get us past!"

"That will only make us more conspicuous," Nikoza replied, gently guiding them to the west instead. Straight past the Pikezik estate. They would miss the most guarded front entrance, but her chest tightened knowing there would be more patrols.

Technically, Chatik had given her permission to do what was required to learn more about the Ashes of Dawn. This plan, though, had not been approved by others in the Crystal Brigade. She wasn't sure yet whether she intended to expose Nex and the Ashes or not, but any plan was beyond the watchmen's knowledge. She was acting outside the bounds of protocol, so they would be forced to assume she was a traitor helping Nex escape.

The largest trees in Kalastok lined the northern edge of the Pikezik estate. Beyond, the mansion's exterior of reflective glass displayed House Pikezik's dominance in the Commonwealth's glass industry. Hues of decorated reds and blues danced across its surface as smoothly as the most talented painter with their brush. And on its spires, dragons made of silver glass shimmered like the one who'd shared the palace rooftop with Nikoza so many times. Chatik had refused to directly say how her grandfather died. The dread clutching her made her wonder whether that once loyal dragon had shifted when commanded by the house who'd tamed it.

It was not dragons that threatened the fleeing pair now, though, but Pikezik guards clad in royal blue. They stood with rifles shouldered along the metal fence lining the estate, and more were surely around the corner by the main entrance. To make matters worse, breathless hovered above the lamps, guided by the Reachers in the tower a few hundred yards further west.

There was nowhere to hide.

Nex kicked back at Nikoza's shin. "Let me Reach!" they said far too loudly. "I've evaded the watch all my life."

The outburst drew the attention of the nearest breathless as Nikoza tried to hurry Nex toward the public gardens north of the street. Trees lined the Kala beyond it, and if they could get that far, they would be in the clear. Unfortunately, the breathless had other ideas.

The spirits hovered over the pair with their hushed language piercing the hiss of the nearest gas lamps. A few of the Pikezik guards noticed the disturbance and hurried over.

"What are breathless doing harassing a member of the Crystal Brigade?" the lead one asked, glancing from Nikoza's elaborate coat to Nex.

Nikoza straightened her posture and lifted her chin. As Jazuk had said a hundred times, act as if you belonged, and few would doubt you. "They are interrupting a *sergeant* of the Crystal Brigade, as a matter of fact. My mission is not to be questioned by mercenaries or spirits." She raised her voice for the last bit and shot a glare at the Reacher tower, hoping its inhabitants would understand her frustration.

One of the other guards wrinkled her nose. "That prisoner looks familiar. Aren't they the one—"

"Continue to question me," Nikoza snapped, putting on the face her grandfather had worn when challenged by his subordinates, "and

I will ensure you are all conscripted by the Crimson Court. Why waste away outside House Pikezik's estate when you can be our front line against the Keloshan Empire?"

The ferocity in her voice shocked her, but part of her liked seeing the arrogant mercenary guards cower. She had been seen as nothing more than a frail princess her entire life. Despite the Crystal Brigade's shortcomings, its uniform granted her authority, and she would need that to stop her nation from careening over the cliff.

"Yes… Yes, of course," the lead guard stammered before thumping his chest. "My apologies, Sergeant. Go on your way."

He waved for one of his guards to go tell the Reachers to back off, but a pair of familiar faces emerged from the shadows beneath the tower instead. Vanzearik Kaerz and Hazat Tozki wore the same Brigade coats with silver Spirit Reacher threading crossing the crimson fabric. Their expressions were far from matching, though. Vanzearik watched her with the wry smile of a cat cornering a mouse while Hazat looked as if he'd been attacked by an awakened.

Nikoza gave a silent prayer to the Crystal Mother. Both were members of her squad, so she should have remembered they were on tower duty today. So much for remaining anonymous…

"Sergeant Nikoza?" Vanzearik asked, scratching his bald head. "Why are you escorting the leader of the Ashes of Dawn away from the palace?"

Before Nikoza could reply, Hazat nudged his compatriot. "Sorry, Sergeant. I told Vanzearik to leave you be, but he insisted."

"Your initial intuition was correct," Nikoza told Hazat. "Do you remember when the Crimson King kept me after the briefing?" They both nodded. "Then know I am acting under his directive. If you have any respect for me, please tell no one that you saw us."

Hazat thumped his chest and bowed. "Of course, Sergeant. We should return to our duties anyway. The breathless need directing."

He nearly dragged Vanzearik away, but an idea popped into Nikoza's mind. "Wait," she said, waving them back. "Speaking of directing the breathless, there is something you could help with. We intend to cross the Kala north of the King's Bridge to avoid wandering eyes. If you could keep the breathless away from that section of the ice for a few minutes, I would appreciate it."

"That sounds easy enough," Hazat said with a tug on his tricorn hat. It did not match the Crystal Brigade's normal uniform, but brigadesmen were given more freedom than watchmen when it came to their accessories. Besides, it suited him.

"Captain Tzena will want to know about this," Vanzearik complained.

Hazat just grabbed him again. "She likely does already if the orders came from the king. Come, leave the sergeant to her duties, so we may return to our own."

Nikoza waited for them to be out of earshot before leading Nex through the gardens north of the street. The whole way, Nex held a wicked grin.

"You like this, don't you?" they asked.

"What in the realms are you talking about?" Nikoza replied, ducking down a side section of the gardens to avoid a strolling couple. "This is serious!"

Nex laughed. "You like being in charge. It's like… Shit, I don't really remember leading the Ashes, but I do remember liking it. People trust you. It's nice mattering for once."

Nikoza hesitated at the gardens' end, staring into the trees. A deep pit formed in her stomach, and she couldn't tell why. So she pushed Nex on. "My grandfather taught me to be a matriarch of the Chamber. I sought to help people, but to the scions, I was just a gentle princess with youthful ideals. Now, though I know Chatik is interfering with my thoughts, I have purpose. I am not a matriarch, but I am a sergeant. I can make a difference if I can figure out what is true and what is the Crimsons' propaganda."

"What do the Crimsons even want?" Nex asked as the rancid smell of the Kala struck them both like a needle straight to the nose. With most of the city's Reachers called to war, much of the filth tossed onto the streets was no longer filtered by magic, leaving it to rot horribly on the river and its banks.

Nikoza released them now that they were away from the guards.

All that remained was to cross the half-frozen river. That meant maintaining her Reach for longer than she had managed during Tzena's lessons, and she found melting ice far easier than freezing it.

A series of Fire and Water Reachers were conducting that melting upstream, the flames dancing across the river like during the galas held by the great houses. The war had postponed those, though, and this was one of the rare beautiful displays left of Reacher power in the city.

"My uncle keeps mentioning something called the Crimson Cause," she said as she approached the riverbank. "So many of my memories of it are fuzzy, so I imagine he was Mind Reaching whenever he spoke of it. From what I do remember, though, it calls for scion superiority over lowborn, claiming we are the Spirit Crystal's chosen."

Nex glanced down at their crystal ring. "What's that make me?"

"You must have scion blood if you can Reach." Nikoza raised her hand toward the river, but stopped before Reaching. Nex stared at her with their mouth agape. "Have you never considered this? No lowborn becomes a Reacher when they touch Spirit Crystal, and though it was not blessed by the Buried Temple, that ring of yours certainly counts."

"Maybe I did." Nex closed their fist and chuckled. "Would be dumb not to, but it doesn't feel like I ever realized that before. A lot of what you're saying is familiar, just caught in a cloud in my head. This is different."

Nikoza sympathized with not knowing where they belonged, but they needed to keep moving. So she Reached into the realm of Water and focused on what she wished the half-frozen river to become. Her power drew the heat from it and calmed the elements composing the water itself until it began to creak, the ice thickening.

"You are a Reacher either way," Nikoza said as sweat trickled down her brow, the heat she pulled from the ice hovering in the air around them instead. "Perhaps now would be a good moment to use that Possibility Reaching which you were eager to apply before."

Nex approached the ice. "Why?" Then they stepped upon it,

flinching as a few small fractures split across it. "Oh, because of that. How in the wastes did you become a sergeant?"

"Nepotism may have played a role."

They cocked their head. "Nepo-what? I forgot a lot, but I sure as shit never knew that one."

"It means my uncle decided I should receive favoritism," Nikoza rambled before thrusting her free arm toward the river. "Grant us a bit of that luck of yours, would you please?"

"Fine."

The pair locked arms as Nex's rainbow of wisps joined the deep blue ones still emanating from Nikoza's talon. Possibility Reaching's luck did not feel any different when it plunged into each of them. Nex seemed confident, though, so Nikoza pushed onward. Her Water Reach had been somewhat successful, but she felt how little of its strength remained. They had barely taken a few steps across the wide river. Each would only become more precarious as the last of her power sought to solidify their footing.

"Please tell me you have remembered where to find the Ashes of Dawn," Nikoza said to distract herself from the constantly thinning ice. "I would rather not spend the night wandering randomly through the western city until you find a friend."

Nex clung tighter to her. "Now's probably not a great time to admit I'm not good at swimming. Barely made it out when Kasia jumped with me—Hey! I remembered something."

"You jumped into the Kala with Lady Katarzyna?" Nikoza asked, letting herself laugh at the image of Death's Daughter leaping from a bridge with a lowborn. "What on Zekiaz led you to think that was a good idea?"

"I was helping her with something. Can't remember what."

Nikoza searched her memories with Etal and recalled the second scientist. An alchemist. "Was it to falsify Paras ik Lierasa's death? He helped develop the supposed cure, did he not?"

"Don't know," Nex said. "But she definitely faked his death. Almost drowned herself in booze afterward. Way more expensive than drowning in the Kala." They puffed out their cheeks. "Still not sure about the Ashes. I've got these images in my head when I think of the hideout, but it's just some random streets."

"Perhaps they may lead us there."

Nex yelped as their next step sent their foot through the ice, trapping it as the last of Nikoza's Reaching attempted to freeze the sudden gush of water. "We need to cross the damn river first!"

"Calm yourself," Nikoza said, taking their arm and pulling, but the ice held. They were just over halfway across. Her Reach had run out, and it would surely take another anyway to finish the journey. "I will free you with another Reach."

"Don't waste it!" Nex muttered before throwing themself out of the ice and falling into Nikoza in the process.

They tumbled onto an unsteady section. Cracks raced every which way as freezing water seeped through Nikoza's coat, but enough ice held for her to Reach. Taint struck her instantly, and along with her adrenaline, drew more force into the initial effort. The water around them froze over so thick that the resulting ice felt as solid as stone. It also left her with a Taint-sick stomach and only half her Reach's power.

"Your Possibility-induced luck may have just saved us," she said, clutching her chest as her lips grew drier, fatigue falling over her. Taint had yet to burrow deep within her, thank the Crystal Mother, but she felt horrid. "Except, I was going to Reach anyway to finish the ice across the river, so it was quite unnecessary."

Nex just shrugged and hauled themself back up as Nikoza did the same. The overly frozen ice was far slipperier than before, and they grabbed hold of each other to keep from falling.

"Wanted it to be a challenge, huh?" Nex quipped before noticing her sickly appearance. "Oh, you look like the river smells."

They threw Nikoza's arm over their shoulders as they continued on. Despite the lack of grip and Nikoza's limited remaining power, they made quicker progress than before. Even that first bit of practice had helped Nikoza find a balance in her magical freezing, and it allowed her to stretch the Reach to nearly the opposite bank. Her energy, though, waned. Realm Taint surely would have sent her stumbling into the unfrozen sections without Nex's aid.

She collapsed the moment her foot struck the muddied, rubbish-covered shore. It was disgusting, but for once, she didn't care about perfect appearances. She had hardly expected crossing the Kala to be so difficult. Had it really been worth avoiding another few sets of watchmen on the bridge?

"Get up," Nex said with a pat on her back. "Or you're about to have a hundred people looking at you and probably a dozen breathless too." They furrowed their brow. "What's this place called again?"

Nikoza rose, drawing in a long breath that she instantly regretted. Good Mother, how did people endure this stench *all day*? "New Beginning's Avenue."

"Nah." Nex raised their arm and pretended to shoot at something that wasn't there. "Beg Ave. Could never forget this shithole. C'mon, patrols will spot us in a sec."

They grabbed Nikoza by the scruff of her coat and hauled her down the nearest alley of the Shadow Quarter. Dawnrise offered little light, but it gave plenty of reasoning for the district's name. Shoddy buildings made of sheet metal, brick, and scrap wood were piled on top of each other so closely that not a bit of the sun peeked through. The night had been fairly silent among the elites of the Crimson District. Here, arguments, screeching animals, and the occasional gunshot shattered both that peace and Nikoza's eardrums.

"You live here?" she asked with an exasperated gasp as a shot rang out from what felt like mere feet away. Had that bullet clipped her hair? She checked just in case, but took relief at finding no damage.

Nex sniffed, then wiped their nose with their sleeve. "Think so."

"Wonderful. We are both lost and trapped in the slums."

A force whirled Nikoza around until she was toe-to-toe with the Possibility Reacher, their eyes aflame and their fists clutching her coat. "You aren't trapped here," they said. "All of us are, but you're a scion. Could walk right out of here if you wanted."

Nikoza offered a conciliatory nod. "I am doing what I can to free your people. In the meantime, I could tell the watchmen you are a scion too."

Nex pushed her back and continued down a nearby alley, forcing her to hurry after. "I don't remember a lot, but I'm sure this is my home. These people fight every day just to live. And I fight for 'em."

"Nex?" a voice called out from nearby.

Glass blade drawn, Nex whirled about to glare at whoever had spoken. Nikoza followed suit with her pistol. She was far from a fantastic shot, but it was better than enduring further Taint to Reach again. Her head still swam, and the stench of this place stirred her already unsettled stomach.

Katarzyna Niezik's footman, Tazper, stepped from the shadows with a bulkier man just a stride behind. Nikoza couldn't recall if Tazper had assisted her work with Etal's cure, but she could never forget the Truth Reachers forcing him to admit to his mistress's murders. Did his presence mean the Amber Dame was still in the city too?

"Please do not shoot," he pled, taking off his wide-brimmed hat and holding it to his chest. It was covered in soot, and his simple woolen coat and worn trousers resembled that of a factory worker more than a scion footman. "Someone from Beg Ave spotted you two crossing the river and hurried to retrieve us. I know first-hand the horrors of Truth Reacher interrogations, so I had to come myself." He glanced at Nikoza. "That does beg the question, though, why the princess is here."

"I am no longer a princess," she replied. For now, she kept the gun raised. There was something familiar about his face from more recently... "Tell me, Tazper. I only saw the rifleman from a distance during the execution, but was that you?"

The bulky man stepped forward with his arms crossed. Bald, with an open coat that revealed a shirt too short to cover his muscled midriff, he had tough, weathered skin like sandstone. Likely Reshkan, then. Those southerners always liked showing off strange parts of their bodies—collarbones for women and stomachs for men.

"No talking here," he said. "Too many ears."

Nikoza gave him a curious look. "I am Nikoza the First of House Bartol, and who may you be?"

"Jiinaan the..." He scratched his head and shrugged. "Dunno. Lots of people have it."

"I know you two?" Nex asked, lowering their blade. They scrunched their nose so much it looked like it would retract into their skull. "The Reachers did a number on my head. I forgot a lot."

Jiinaan stepped closer with his arms out, then snatched Nex into a hug that looked tight enough to break bones. "You look different too. Bit bigger cheekbones. Don't worry, we fix memory and face. Knock your head hard and you remember Jiinaan."

Tazper smiled warmly. "Let us return them to safety first before we knock anyone's head. Please, Lady Nikoza, set aside your pistol and let us show you that the lowborn are far more genial than the Crimson King has told you."

"You trust them?" Nex asked Nikoza with their brow raised.

"I barely know Tazper, and Jiinaan and I have never met!" Nikoza exclaimed, but she holstered her gun. Though rebels, they clearly had no intent to hurt her, at least immediately. "That being said, a safehouse sounds far preferable to wherever we are."

Rocking their head back and forth, Nex looked at Jiinaan the way a child would a new pet dog. What an odd group they were. An Ogrenian with some sliver of scion blood, a Reshkan far from his nation, a scion footman trapped in the slums, and a sergeant of the Crystal Brigade who'd walked straight into her enemy's territory. Whether these Ashes of Dawn were actually Nikoza's enemies, she figured she would soon discover.

"Is Vinnia with you?" Nex asked, their expression turning somber. "I can't even picture what she looks like, but I know she's important to me."

Jiinaan threw his arm around their shoulder. His bicep dwarfed their head, and Nex's eyes widened at the pressure. "Love is safe. You see. Come!"

Lacking another choice, Nikoza followed them through the winding alleys. She watched every window for a head peeking through the shutters or a breathless seeking to strike. They seemed safe for now, though, and despite all her disgust for the state of the west side, she took solace in that. With Chatik's orders to betray Nex lurking in the back of her mind, it was all the comfort she would soon find.

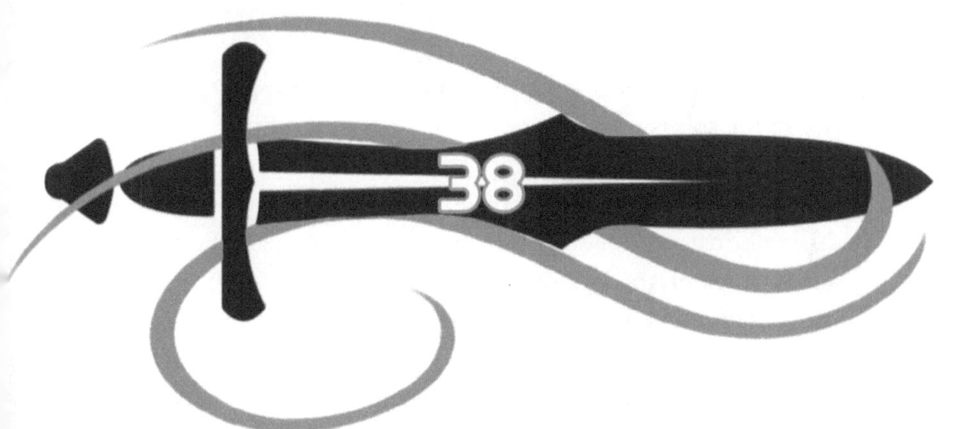

SECRETS OF THE SPIRITS

"Even the old Piorakan Empire at its peak never truly grasped the truth of Zekiaz's spirits. They are the essence of our realm. They are our ancestors, our children, and inhabitants of our own bodies, yet there is so much to learn of them. Perhaps we shall never know the fullest extent. Such are the greatest mysteries." – Hetmanik Kuzon, Ezmani historian

Mariana did not call for Wanusa until the blizzard parted over the mountains, leaving a view that took the young Glassblade's breath away. Dawnrise's southern light split through the peaks and cast shadows over the magnificent gorges. Before them, the peak of their mountain jutted out like a child reaching for its mother.

And a ring of crystals shimmered at its end.

"Have you ever seen such a beautiful display of our realm's glory?" Mariana said, arms extended as she basked in the sun's glow. "We rise above the shadows and soar among the spirits, where we belong."

Drifters slipped past as she broke into a song in Spiritspeech. The mountains carried her voice for what seemed a thousand miles, granting it vibrancy impossible in any other place, and without understanding a word, tears welled in Wanusa's eyes. Such beauty couldn't be rationalized. It swelled within her very spirit to join the dance of the spirits who blessed Zekiaz with their purity.

She glanced over her shoulder to see if Radais and Lazan were watching. They were caring for the ibexes and setting a cooking fire, but her old master nodded when he caught her gaze. She had no desire to abandon the Glassblade Order, and as long as she held his approval, she could pursue both her skill with a blade and her understanding of the spirits.

"What is this place?" she asked Mariana when the Whisperer's song was finished. "Beyond Salesh, I have never seen any crystal besides Spirit Crystal, and even there, it was only from the realm of Light."

Mariana beckoned for her to approach. "An ancient ritual took place here. See that there are fifteen divots—one for each of the Crystal Realms—though only four actual crystals remain. Can you tell which?"

Wanusa crouched beside the circle and examined the arrayed crystals: silver, burnt orange, muddy brown, and yellow. The first and the last were familiar. She'd only heard of the colors associated with the realms of the other two, but wasn't certain.

"Spirit," she began, pointing to the silver one before the yellow one. "And I know that is Light, though that one is duller than the ones I've seen before."

"All of them are at least partially drained," Mariana said with a nod. "Except for the Spirit Crystal, that is, since it rejuvenates like the talons scion Reachers wear."

Wanusa examined the pulsing of the Spirit Crystal. "I never understood why that was."

"I have told you of the rhythms which reflect the Essence within us, and these crystals carry the same patterns. The Spirit Crystal core far beneath us rejuvenates the crystals harvested from it—like those scions wear to Reach—with Spirit Essence, but cannot do the same to crystals from another realm. For example, the Light Crystal you see there is at least partially empty because it is away from its realm's core Essence. These crystals' varying rhythms are how I knew this place held such significance. That is why I brought you here."

"For the Deepening?" Wanusa replied, a hand over her heart. It raced at the thought of gaining the power she needed to ensure Inrius had not died in vain. She knew it was impossible, yet some part of her held onto hope of finding her brother's spirit in Iliafa and granting him the chance to be whole again.

"Yes, but that is not all. Remember what I have told you."

Wanusa looked from Mariana to the crystals. "You said that something here matched the pattern of Vockan rhythms. Is it one of the crystals?"

"You will discover this yourself once you have completed the ritual," Mariana said, her face offering no hint of an answer. Why hide this? Had Wanusa not proven her loyalty? "If you are ready, set aside your blades and let us begin. Worry not, you may retrieve them when we are finished."

Despite her frustrations, Wanusa did as the Whisperer commanded. She needed this. Belief, hope, understanding. She needed a reason to push forward instead of falling into grief's depths for her brother.

Her fingers lingered on her glass sword's scabbard, remembering all the desire she'd held when she became a warrior just hundred-hours before. She was not abandoning her oaths. This was an addition to them, a promise to pursue more than the destruction of corrupt spirits.

So she rose and met Mariana's gaze. "I am ready."

"You still hold a soldier's stance," Mariana noted, looking her up and down. "Relax your body, or your spirit will never do so."

Wanusa wriggled her shoulders and tried to stand casually, but nerves had her bouncing. Too much relied on this working. "I'm not sure I can."

"Those are not the words of a warrior who has traversed the Spirit Wastes, discovered a sentient race of spirits, and found truths we have hidden from Glassblades for centuries."

She dropped her head. "No, they're the ones of a sister who failed her brother."

Mariana stepped from the ring, taking Wanusa's shoulders as

spirits rose from her and circled them both in a strange hug of vapors. Usually, spirits were thought of as cold, but these warmed Wanusa to her very core. For a moment, she could have sworn she felt their Essences' rhythms joining with hers.

"The spirits are a reminder that all life on Zekiaz is a precious cycle," Mariana said, passion pouring through her voice. "Take heart that you experienced but a single of your brother's many lifetimes. Though we do not have the Inheritance Rituals of the Ezmani great houses to carry the memories of one's spirit to the next life, spirits are deeper to us than mere minds or blood relations. They direct our desires, our dreams. As Whisperers, we work to protect that cycle so that those spirits like your brother's remain pure."

Flashes of an imagined battle washed over Wanusa. Inrius sat among it all, only half-aware with his spirit split. "And if he isn't? His spirit was severed when he was only a toddler. What if it is broken beyond repair, or if the Vanashel corrupted him?"

Mariana held a gentle hand to her cheek. "Then it is all the more important that you complete the Deepening. He may need you, and it is certain that Vocka would benefit from your abilities."

"Why do more Whisperers not join us?" Wanusa asked. "Why am I the hope when there are plenty of experienced ones?"

"Oh, dear." Mariana sighed and turned east, where the Vockan Mountains split across the continent of Brakesh like the spines of a povnik's back. "I forget sometimes how you are merely sixteen. In time, you will see how selfish most people are, especially when they are granted but a glimmer of the power they have sought. Whisperers were once aligned into an order like your Glassblades. We governed the Vockan Nation through our guidance to each village's council, but when threats from other empires forced us to join with Ezman for protection, the most powerful families intermarried with their scions. House iz Ardinvil and others became Reachers, and the Commonwealth's Chamber of Scions banished us from government for not worshipping the Crystal Mother."

Wanusa furrowed her brow. "The Whisperers lost power. Shouldn't that have made them less selfish?"

"No, merely less united in our purpose to protect the purest spirits and discover the truth of Zekiaz's crystal heart," Mariana said. "Many strayed off for their own purposes. Others smoked or drank themselves into despair. The few of us you saw in Dalnus are the true-hearted who are left, and most of them will be doing what they can for other villages. I could not convince more to come with an army of Glassblades."

"Wait." Wanusa stepped into the circle beside her, jaw ajar. "You didn't tell me you defied the others by coming here. They read my spirit. Didn't they want me to be a Whisperer?"

Mariana gave a curt nod. "That does not mean they approved of my mission. Of our mission. They saw your worth, but were unwilling to ally with the Glassblades to see your potential to fruition."

Wanusa pursed her lips, considering all she'd faced and all she would. She saw the elderly woman in a whole new light now. Her attitude with the Glassblades hadn't been stubbornness, but an insistence on what she believed in. Despite differences in their approaches, she cared about Vocka and Wanusa the same as Radais. She had compromised while holding true to her principles. That was real strength.

"I am ready, then," she said, taking a long breath and letting herself smile, at least a little. "Thank you for believing in me."

Mariana mirrored her expression for only a moment before her eyes tightened. "Then step into the circle and press your hand to the Spirit Crystal. Once you feel its pulsing in your core, close your eyes and seek to match it through song. Let its words flow into you as you give of yourself to it. Spirits hold our deepest desires. Release them to the crystal and let its Essence fill the hole that remains."

"Will this change me?" Wanusa asked, doing all she could not to tighten up again.

Mariana did not meet her gaze. "Every day changes us, child. To bond with Zekiaz's heart is to accept it as part of you. Such power demands something in return."

That was not the answer Wanusa had hoped for. Everything felt like sacrifice. Joining the Glassblades had required leaving her family behind. Traveling to the Spirit Wastes with Radais had lost her a mentor in Miv. Now this…

She closed her eyes and thought of Inrius. Her brother had the most caring heart, even with his spirit severed. What sacrifice did she know compared to the losses he and the rest of Iliafa had endured? She had not taken up the glass sword for herself, and neither would she do this for herself. In all things, she worked to protect the most vulnerable in Vocka. If that meant surrendering some piece of herself to the Spirit Crystal in return for understanding the spirits and bonding to them, so be it.

Breath held, she knelt on one knee, removing her left glove to touch the Spirit Crystal. She didn't quite know why she chose the left. Maybe it was to not burden her sword hand or because the Ezmani Reachers wore talons upon it. Or perhaps the spirits themselves called her through their strange Spiritspeech, commanding her with words she couldn't yet understand.

Her fingers brushed Spirit Crystal for the second time in her life. The first had been on the edge of the Wastes, where she'd found drifters surrounding the crystal and had realized they were drawn to it. She'd felt nothing all that special about it then.

Now was no different.

She closed her eyes, searching for the pattern of vibrations within the crystal, but came up empty. Impatience was unfamiliar to Vockans, though. Like all her people, she'd grown up traversing the mountains between distant villages for simple trades, and little could match the hundred-hours she had spent riding through the Wastes in the unending black of everdark. She could wait for this.

The Deepening challenged that theory quickly. Despite quieting her mind and focusing only on the cold Spirit Crystal beneath her fingertips—which were rapidly growing numb—she heard nothing but the wind whistling past her ears. Her spirit felt as pained as before, her silence allowing memories of Inrius to creep in until she found herself kneeling within one.

Her brother's hand clutched hers as they watched over their family's goats. It was a small herd, but enough to help keep them fed through even the coldest everdark. That was a distant thought beneath the blistering everbright sun, and Inrius pulled her to hide in the shade cast by a conifer's branches. She grabbed a branch there and ran the tree's needles through his deep auburn hair, which wove like Iliafa's western hills.

"Hey!" he exclaimed, leaping to tear the branch from her hands. But she stood a foot taller than the young boy. "That isn't fair."

So she let him grab hold. "A lot is unfair. That's why we need to stick together. It's harder to beat two of us than one."

"But you'll leave someday, right?" He plucked free a few of the needles and blew them over her hair. "Mom says everyone leaves eventually, like needles off a tree in duskfall."

"Firs and pines don't lose their needles, silly," she appealed, shaking the blown needles back over him. The goats bleated nearby and scurried around each other. They were smarter animals than some thought, and they loved to mimic the siblings whenever they played. "And like them, I won't fall away, even in the coldest, worst everdark. I promise."

Inrius ripped away more of the needles, but this time, fled from the tree as he blew. They scattered into the wind, drifting over his face.

His face…

It shifted in strips, as if the needles passing by tore away the fabric of his being. His joy left with it. Mangled, unkempt hair sprouted from his youthful curl, and dull eyes replaced those of vibrant life. All that remained seconds later was the lost gaze of a boy with a severed soul.

"Why did you leave?" he asked in the monotone voice he'd adopted after the awakened attack. It sounded like he was speaking in his sleep, talking to someone in a distant realm. But those words were meant for her.

Unwelcomed tears streamed down her cheeks as she emerged from the tree to meet him. Spirits, those four words were enough to drive a knife straight into her heart. "I wanted to find a way to help you. I thought if I joined the Glassblades, I could understand the spirits. They've led me to the Whisperers…" She took his hand with her shaking one. It was cold, limp. "Once I complete the Deepening, I'll have answers. I'll find your spirit. I promise!"

"Promise?" he shrieked in a suddenly distorted voice that was far from his own. He threw himself back, his face twisting further. Tendrils of silver magic spewed from him until he was more vapor than flesh. "You lied!"

"No!"

She reached out for him, but he dissolved into smoke, leaving behind only a biting chill that defied the everbright sun.

Wanusa screamed and dropped to her knees. She stared down at her hand that had clutched his moments before. A phantom touch lingered on her skin, like he'd never released her, and when she gripped her head in frustration, she cracked out a laugh at the needles that were strewn about her hair.

"I'm sorry," she whispered through her sobs. "I'm so sorry."

Her next breath was a spear of ice straight to her lungs. She fell back onto hard rock instead of the Iliafan plains, skinning her exposed left palm as a far older face met her above.

"You are alright, dear girl," Mariana said as she took Wanusa's shoulders. Her hands were strong but caring, and she studied Wanusa with the same look that Miv had held whenever her training went poorly. "The spirits demand much, and you are still young. This may take time."

Wanusa wiped the tears from her cheeks, catching Radais rushing toward her out of the corner of her eye. She waved for him to stop, but he didn't.

"What happened?" he asked. "Do you need Lazan's healing? Damn it, scion, get over here!"

She hadn't seen him this exasperated since Miv's transformation into a breathless. It wasn't the fury of a commander ready for battle, but a father whose child was threatened. Her own father had never shown such vigor in her defense.

"I saw him," she whispered before raising her voice. "I had a vision. Inrius… We were watching the herd before he turned broken again. Then he disappeared into vapors, screaming at me for breaking my promise."

Lazan huffed as he stopped beside Radais. His face was windburned and his eyes wide. "What promise was that? To not leave home?"

"Basically." She tucked in her legs and wrapped her arms around them. "It's more than that, though. I promised to always be by his side, but I wasn't when the awakened attacked. Then I left for the Glassblades to find a way to help him, only to be gone when the Vanashel killed him and all of Iliafa. I only made one promise, but it feels like I lied to him twice, let him die alone."

"This is the demand of the Spirit Crystal," Mariana replied. "Surrender the part of yourself which mourns and regrets the past."

Wanusa swallowed, then took a series of shallow breaths. "And if I can't?"

"Then you cannot become a Whisperer." Mariana stepped back. "We shall remain for as long as it takes."

Then she left toward their little camp across the plateau, and Wanusa found herself staring at one of the povniks. It sat awkwardly with its six legs sticking every which direction, a content look in its eye. She wished she could feel such contentment. Until she returned to Iliafa, though, she doubted she would be able to sleep, let alone relax.

Radais obviously didn't get that point. "Take the night to think," he said, kneeling beside her with a hand on her shoulder. "The army will move slower than us, so we have time."

"No power comes quickly that is worth it," Lazan noted. "A Reacher does not earn their talon, but there are many a Reacher who know only the most basic tenets of the practice. Continue your efforts, Wanusa. In time, you will find the balance between your own will and that of the Spirit Crystal."

She smiled up at them in thanks. "Don't you believe in the Crystal Mother?" she asked Lazan.

The scion nodded. "Perhaps we use different names for the force which governs our realm. Who am I to debate with Whisperers who speak with spirits and Glassblades who protect us from them?" He approached the ledge and looked over. "I shall bury my prayers until the day I die, and until then, I question whether I will ever hear the goddess's voice. When you become a Whisperer, won't you put in a good word for me?"

"I am talking to spirits, not your goddess."

Lazan returned to Radais, running his fingers playfully along the Glassblade's back before taking his free hand and pulling him to his feet. "I think you will find that there is little difference between them. If the spirits are fragments of the divine, then we all hold the Crystal Mother within us, and when you speak to pure spirits, you speak to the untainted pieces of her. Focus on that wonder more than the power you seek to wield. It will bring you to your own spirit's core."

Radais looked as if he wanted to add something, but Lazan lured him away. Wanusa was grateful for that. While their assurances were welcomed, she needed the chance to ponder this alone. The Reacher's words, though, lingered with her.

Wonder…

She stood and approached the peak beyond the crystal ring. That constant dawnrise light crowned all she saw, and she breathed in deeply, letting awe wash over her. Nowhere she'd seen could match the natural beauty of the Vockan Mountains. This was her home. These were her people. All within its lands shared the spirits of the crystal, and that meant all held a connection to Inrius too. She'd failed to protect him, but maybe through the spirits, she could ensure her promise endured.

"I am still here brother," she spoke into the wind. "I will never leave."

Releasing the fists she'd held at her sides, she turned back toward the crystal ring. Her allies awaited her in the camp beyond. She couldn't return to them. As she stared down at the Spirit Crystal, she knew her work tonight was not yet finished.

BLOODIED SANDS

"The greatest ingredient to awakened-slaying glass is sand of the purest quality. Many would bleed for the chance to hold such resources." – An excerpt from *Spirits and How To Repel Them: A Learner's Guide.*

The sweet sound of hoofprints against the dirt met Zinarus's ears as he rode to the front of Houze iz Vamiustok's gathered mercenaries. Two cavalry battalions followed in his wake—nearly six hundred light dragoon gunmen and lance-wielding hussars—all focused on retaking the Vamia Sand Mines. According to Tiuz's letters, he needed sand for some sort of glass weapons. That made Zinarus's old mines all the more important.

Though he had hoped to face House Oliezany's garrison at the mines with a full force, his mother had taken longer to recruit an additional regiment of nearly a thousand foot soldiers. They would take too long to join him now, so he'd sent them east to Fort Harizak and Tiuz's Confederation. The cavalry would have to do for now.

His anticipation grew as a squad of riders clad in purple uniforms approached from the forest. With both the Keloshan Empire and the Confederation of Harizak threatening the Crimsons, he held hope that House Oliezany couldn't spare many guards for these remote Vockan mines. Glass was still crucial, but the Crimsons controlling spirits changed everything. They would not risk Kalastok for places like this. Would they?

An officer rode to him not long after, bearing a similar golden sash to the one Zinarus wore across his uniform. His brow was wrinkled with age and sun exposure had deepened his dark skin to nearly match the old carbine musket slung over his shoulder. He held a confidence that Zinarus lacked. The iz Vamiustok heir was grateful for that.

"Major General Zinarus," Colonel Iktaros said with a thump of his chest. "We have a report from our scouts."

Zinarus smiled. "Excellent. What does House Oliezany have prepared? Have they caught wind of our operation?"

Iktaros matched his expression, but kept his smile tight-lipped. "It's damn good news. Their garrison numbers less than a hundred guards. Any scouts they have are likely watching for fleeing laborers more than advanced armies, and even if news of your arrival has reached the mines, they've had little time to prepare fortifications."

Zinarus pushed his horse up onto the ridgeline, fixing the iz Vamiustok crest pinned to his lapel. The mines were just a couple miles southeast. So close.

"That is as we hoped," he replied. "If there are no true defenses, you are confident in our plan, then?"

The colonel nodded. "It is a good one. A token frontal assault with our dragoons' guns will draw the attention of their on-duty guards. While they skirmish, our lancers will join the flanks with more interspersed dragoons."

"Hussars," Zinarus corrected, examining the slope of the land. He had traveled the route to the Vamia Mines many times in his later teen years, and many of his mercenaries had worked in or around the mines as well. That was to their advantage when compared to Oliezanys, who were not familiar with the area.

"I forget you're a student of Tiuz's," Iktaros said with a chuckle. "Hussars instead of lancers, then. It's an Ezmani word, but so is Vamiustok in the end. Whatever you call them, we'll see if you're as bold in command as Tiuz was back in the glory days."

Zinarus considered that as he studied the old colonel. Iktaros had come highly recommended from his Aunt Carelias, having served as a rider in Tiuz's final victories against Kelosh decades before. Lowborn like nearly all Zinarus's mercenaries, he bore the ik Vamiustok name of his city's people. Tradition stated that home and clan mattered far more to Vockans than family, and scion or not, that made Iktaros and the other soldiers like siblings to Zinarus. The Ezmani almost always gave officer titles to scions. Vockans had no such option, and one's familial blood meant little when powder ignited. All that mattered was the crest upon one's uniform.

"How much has my aunt told you about me?" Zinarus asked, turning from strategy.

Iktaros rubbed the back of his balding head. "Err… You might want to ask her yourself."

Carelias marched up the slope with her Body Reacher talon exposed on her left hand and her right clutching a musket. His mother despised the rumors she created marching around like some radical anarchist, but when those rumors were entirely true, it was hard to deny she looked the part. He had barely seen her during his daze at her house. Now, though, his aunt looked exactly as he remembered: her short hair curling like flames, lapping hungrily at fuel to burn, and that nose of hers a spear straight to her enemies' hearts.

" 'Major General,' they all tell me to call you now," she said with her rigid brow furrowed. The expression made her resemble an enraged youth more than a middle-aged scion lady, and it never failed to draw a grin across Zinarus's lips. "Have you ever seen a battle, dear nephew?"

He flexed his gloved hands, then nodded to Iktaros. "You are dismissed, Colonel."

Iktaros gave him a knowing look. Luckily, he said nothing before riding off to relay the commands to their cavalry. It was a solid plan. But Carelias had poked a hole straight through Zinarus's flimsy confidence with a single question.

"Unless you count my fleeing the Crimson Court," he said once he was sure Iktaros was out of earshot, "then I have not served in battle, no. I have, however, read every book on tactics that I could find. General Tiuz has also been a great asset in my training."

Carelias stepped closer. Zinarus leaned in, expecting her to whisper something, but instead, she slapped him straight across the cheek.

"You have the lives of six hundred people and as many horses in your hands!" she muttered. "Tactics written in those books of yours may win a battle. Experience and care for one's soldiers ensures that victory does not come with unnecessary deaths."

Zinarus stared back at her, stunned. His cheek throbbed as he pressed his hand against it, and he dared not look at his riders to check if they'd seen. "I care for the men and women who have taken up our house's banner."

"Then speak not of books." She nodded in the direction of the mines. "Consider all your plan's flaws. What are potential traps, pitfalls, or blind spots that could catch you off guard?"

"Iktaros and I have reviewed the strategy with the other officers. They believe it to be sound."

She scoffed. "If you truly believe any plan to be without flaws, then you are more a fool than I took you for." Her expression softened as she pressed a finger into his chest, disturbing the perfectly aligned glass chains across his jacket. "Know that I am not here for Sania, but for you. I do not give a koilee's ass which rich son of a bitch is king. You are protecting our people, and as long as you do that, I will be here to help you succeed. That means telling you when you are being foolish."

"Do you wish to continue insulting me," he replied as he fixed his jacket, "or do you have a credible threat to our plan?"

"Reachers," she said, pulling back. "With few Vockan Reachers available, we only employed a couple Earth and Air Reachers to help the miners before, but House Oliezany has far greater resources. Sure, they will have devoted their most experienced Reachers to fending off Kelosh. Even a neophyte with a talon is a threat to charging cavalry, though."

He shifted uncomfortably. This was, in fact, something he had lost a lot of sleep over already. Vockan Reachers were rarer and far more expensive than their Ezmani counterparts. Without access to his assets in the Kalastok Arena or the revenue from their lost mines, he could barely afford a pair of Spirit Reachers to protect his low-born soldiers against awakened or a small force of breathless. That left his army with a meager four Reachers if he included Carelias and himself, and Spirit Reachers would do nothing against human foes.

"You are right, and the hussars will be most vulnerable," he said once he'd considered his options. Then he waved for Iktaros. "Colonel!"

Iktaros returned with haste. "Yes, General?"

"Change of plans. How do you feel about Reacher hunting?"

AN HOUR LATER, ZINARUS DONNED his tall commander's cap made of tough felt and leather as he stared through his spyglass at the mines. Hussar lancers of old would have worn breastplates and helms, but modern gun-based tactics had shifted toward a lighter, more formal uniform. The cap would offer at least some protection to his head in the battle to come. He hoped he wouldn't need it.

A few dozen Oliezany guards clad in gray and pink-trimmed uniforms patrolled the mine's exterior like Iktaros's scouts had claimed. Stone buildings surrounded the massive central pit just north of the Vamia River, and tunnel entrances dotted the terrain between them like the skin of a leper. There were enough houses for a few hundred workers to switch off shifts, each crafted from rocks pulled from the mine itself.

He promised himself he would keep those workers safe as he pocketed the spyglass. House Oliezany had kept many of the local laborers who were experienced with the mines. Even the new hires, though, did not carry the sins of their employer, and none of them deserved to die in a war among noble houses.

"The other flanks are in position, sir," a messenger reported to him. "Should I give the signal?"

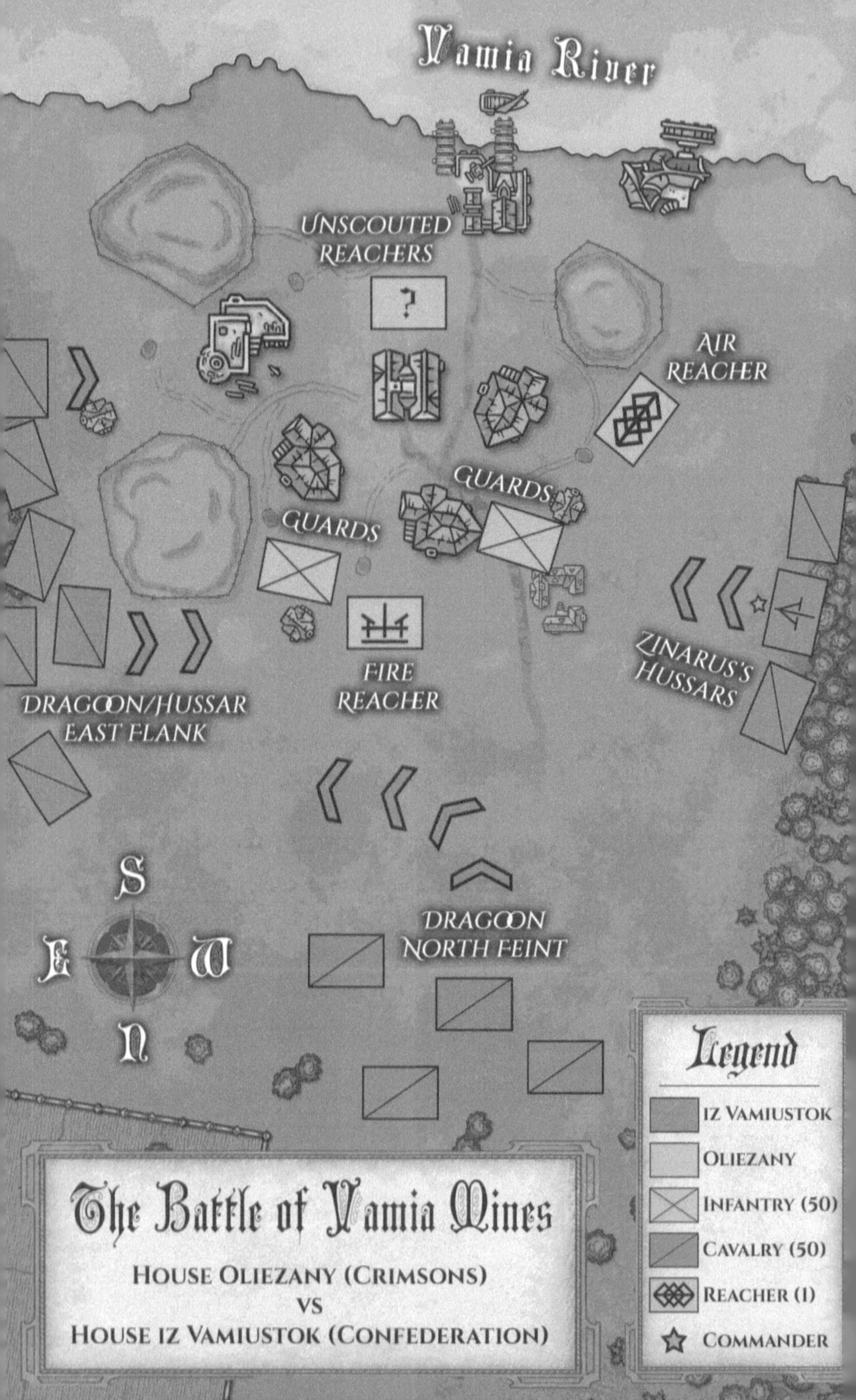

Vamia River
UNSCOUTED REACHERS
?
AIR REACHER
GUARDS
GUARDS
DRAGOON/HUSSAR EAST FLANK
FIRE REACHER
ZINARUS'S HUSSARS
S
E
W
N
DRAGOON NORTH FEINT
Legend
IZ VAMIUSTOK
OLIEZANY
INFANTRY (50)
CAVALRY (50)
REACHER (1)
COMMANDER
The Battle of Vamia Mines
HOUSE OLIEZANY (CRIMSONS)
VS
HOUSE IZ VAMIUSTOK (CONFEDERATION)

Zinarus nodded, shifting the lance which leaned against his shoulder, its base held upright by a cup on his right stirrup. "I would have liked to watch them for longer, but time is of the essence. They will spot us out here eventually."

The messenger hurried off, so Zinarus turned to face the hundred lance-wielding hussars who'd joined him to the mines' western flank. Gathered beneath the trees, the dawnrise sun struck the riders' purple uniforms with scattered beams as their horses stretched to nibble on the year's first sprouting leaves. Life had returned to Vocka. It saddened him that they would soon stain the bloom with blood.

Mining was an ugly thing, tearing the Crystal Mother's earth for its riches. But war was surely worse.

"We will wait for the dragoons to do their work on the northern and eastern flanks," he announced, riding between them and trying to put on a confident face. It did not help that his favored horse, Arkenus, and specialized saddle were back in Kalastok. His mechanical leg struggled with the patchwork stirrup he had crafted to compensate, and this borrowed mare's temper matched Kasia in her worst fury.

He pointed toward the mines with his looking glass. "While the dragoons focus on pinning down their Reachers, we will take the opportunity to strike their infantry from the flank. They have no defenses and no reinforcements. Ride well, and we shall succeed."

"What about the workers?" a sergeant asked.

"Leave them be unless they attempt to aid the defense." Zinarus picked his lance from his shoulder and raised it. "Many among them are our brothers and sisters of Vamiustok. We fight for them as much as we fight against the Crimson Court. The sand of these mines forges the glass which keeps us all safe from corrupted spirits, and today, we ensure the great houses no longer withhold it from the common man."

A round of nods answered him. It wasn't the raucous battle cry of legends, but he took it as enough. For a first speech, it at least had not gotten him laughed off the battlefield.

Cracks of gunfire tore his attention to the mines. Iktaros and three hundred dragoons harried the few patrolling guards from the east as two hundred more galloped from the clearing due north. Zinarus intended to draw the defenders' focus largely to the east before the hussars charged, allowing for a more effective strike straight to their rear. From the look of the opening salvos, it was working.

"Loose formation," Zinarus ordered, taking his position near the back of the riders. They could hear him better that way, and he was far too inexperienced to take the point. "Advance slowly."

The battle continued down the slope as the hussars pushed toward the edge of the woods. They would be visible before they broke through the tree line, but no one would be looking their direction. Two-dozen Oliezany defenders in gray were already strewn about the ground. Zinarus grinned. Would there even be any left for the hussars when they arrived?

His glee crashed as a dragoon slid from his horse, shot straight through his head. It wouldn't be the only loss this day, but Zinarus's stomach turned knowing each death was because of his orders.

More guards emerged from one of the larger warehouses that the Oliezanys must have repurposed into a barrack. They took cover behind the scattered buildings and returned fire in a well-trained fashion, despite being far outnumbered. The dragoons' sweeps grew closer each time, but Zinarus's nerves frayed as another fell quickly.

He wanted to give the order to charge. It would relieve the pressure from the dragoons and potentially force a surrender before he lost anyone else, but he remembers Carelias's warning. None of the guards who'd arrived yet were Reachers. Were they just waiting, or were they smart enough to know they were paid to help mine, not defend against an attack?

Any hope of the latter faded as flames ripped through the center of the battle. One of the Oliezany guards had removed her left glove and sent a firebolt straight through Iktaros's arrayed dragoons. Screams from men and horses alike tore through the chaos, and Zinarus turned his head away to keep from vomiting at the sight of half-charred flesh. Another shout from above signaled a flying Air Reacher too.

And he'd spotted the hussars.

"To a trot," Zinarus ordered as the gusts picked up around them. The hussars couldn't wield their carbines while they held their lances, and pistols lacked the range to shoot someone down from that high. Their only hope was to draw closer to the dragoons.

Guards answered the Air Reacher's call, taking positions ahead of the hussars and sending out their first shots. They fired old muskets that were infamous for imprecision, though, and their shots scattered into the trees or dirt. Tiuz had taught Zinarus to keep a looser formation at the beginning of a charge for exactly that reason. Only at the last moment would the hussars come together, forming a greater target, but also putting much more weight into their impact.

The Air Reacher wasn't so inaccurate. He swept down, likely running out of his Reach, and sent a final gust over the rocks piled at the pit's western edge. Many were too heavy, but enough flung toward the hussars to fill the air with the crunching of stone against flesh.

Zinarus bit his cheek as a pair of horses succumbed to the heaviest of the projectiles. The hussars could only respond with scattered and inaccurate pistol fire. By the Crystal Mother, they were sitting ducks. But the Air Reacher's attention soon turned to defending himself, Reaching again to deflect a wave of shots from the dragoons.

The Fire Reacher had no such defense. Powder smoke obscured how many of the dragoons she had burned, but her flames danced over the eastern flank until her head suddenly snapped back. Whooping from Iktaros's dragoons signaled a successful kill, and when the Air Reacher's own shield of wind failed a minute later, Zinarus raised his lance once again.

"Their Reachers are down!" he shouted. "Charge!"

Thunder rang out around him as the hussars launched into full gallop. Mud and grass filled the air, obscuring Zinarus's sight and unsteadying his horse's strides. Jousting had prepared him for a charge, though, and he focused on the target ahead. Every muscle in his body tensed as hussars tightened their formation just a few dozen yards from the Oliezany lines. He couched his lance, ready to strike.

Until the ground gave out.

Horses and riders alike screamed as a crevice shot across the hussar's lines. Hundreds of mine shafts wound beneath them, and within seconds, half the hussars dropped into those trenches. Being in the back gave Zinarus the precious second he needed to guide his horse around the nearest one, his mechanical foot straining in a stirrup not meant for it.

His mind raced as smoke and death stung his nostrils. They had downed the Air and Fire Reachers, but Earth ones were the most effective in a mining operation. The Oliezanys must have left at least one hidden, prepared to drop a charging force into the tunnels. It was ridiculous to destroy sections of the invaluable mine. Unless they cared more about it not falling into rebel hands…

The smoke soon parted enough for him to see that the chasm ringed the entire mine. The cries of horses ahead implied that it had caught the closest dragoons too, and Zinarus half-considered calling a retreat until Iktaros rushed toward him.

Carbine raised, the colonel fired off a shot, then looked to Zinarus with wild eyes. "Damned Earth Reacher must be underground. We need to send men down to look for him, or he'll hit us again."

"He's a scion," Zinarus replied, his breaths quick and sweat pouring down his brow. This was far worse than his nightmares. He had feared a single death, but how many had they lost now? "He… He'll listen to reason. Send in someone with a white flag. Ask for a parley!"

"Calling for a parley now will just give their infantry time to organize," Iktaros grumbled. "Command the men we have left to charge over the terrain left between the tunnels. We'll overrun them, and *then* you can call your parley."

"And if the Reacher strikes again?"

Iktaros reloaded his carbine as Zinarus talked. He raised it and fired into the smoke, sending Zinarus's ears ringing as the colonel replied, "You want to win the battle or be known as a coward, eh? Soldiers remember a commander who backs down."

Zinarus gritted his teeth, wondering what Kasia would have told him to do. But he dismissed that thought as quickly as it came. The

Amber Dame was not known for being mindful, and her teleporting hastily to face Chatik after eavesdropping had proven how rash she could be.

"They also remember one who cares for their lives," he finally said, turning about his horse. "Order a retreat."

Without waiting for another rebuke, he galloped back to the scrambling hussars, repeating the order. Most of the hussars had strapped their lances back to their horses' sides and switched to their carbines. A powder haze covered them enough to prevent Zinarus from counting how many remained. Not enough. And more cried out from the chasms, likely injured or trapped beneath their horses. He needed this parley to retrieve the wounded before the Oliezany guards took them prisoner or killed them.

The chorus of hooves sounded all the more quiet as Zinarus led his retreating forces to the northern forest edge. It soon became clear why.

A quick guess at the remaining riders put their losses at no less than a hundred—more than the size of the initial defending force. Not all of those losses were from the Earth Reacher, but it was a brutal reminder at the power of a single Reacher in the right circumstances. Carelias had warned him. He'd failed to heed it enough, and now, all he could do was negotiate.

"What message do you want sent?" Iktaros said, bringing him a hussar who'd tied a white shirt to the end of his lance.

Zinarus surveyed the loathsome faces of the men and women who had followed him into battle. What did they despise more, the losses or retreating? He hoped he hadn't lost their trust in just a few long minutes.

"Tell the remaining defenders that if they surrender the mines and allow us to retrieve our wounded, then they shall go free," he said. "I would, however, like to speak to this Earth Reacher directly."

Iktaros grabbed his arm and whispered, "Don't talk with the Reacher. He just killed nearly a hundred of our men. That leaves the rest wanting to put a bullet in his head."

"Tell the Reacher that I will speak to him alone," Zinarus said to the messenger instead. "My gloves shall be on, and I shall bear no weapons."

The other soldiers looked at him like he was insane. Perhaps he was, but after a single battle, he was sure he wished to see as little of it as possible. He had never seen a Reacher act with such effectiveness, and if Oliezany money was the Reacher's only reason for being here, then he could be persuaded to switch sides or stand down.

Iktaros shook his head as the messenger left, but Zinarus was too tired for the colonel's complaints. He'd made his decision. Was it cowardly to not charge into unknown tunnels against a Reacher who could collapse them at any point? If so, he was fine being a coward. Empires and great houses saw lowborn soldiers as numbers, assets on a ledger. Though he sought to lead his house to be among the greats, he wouldn't do the same.

"We make camp here," he told the remaining cavalry. "Send someone to fetch Carelias to heal the wounded. Crystal Mother knows we shall have too many this eve."

Crystal Brigade Case File 23β – The Personal Notes of Professor Elaliz Noshok

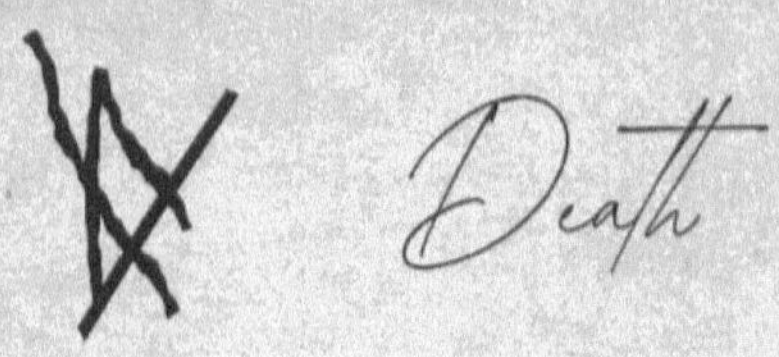

Death

Some would scorn me for writing on the topic of Death at all. Our rulers ban its use, yet none have dared examine what an understanding of the Death realm may grant us. Inheritance Rituals allow magnates of the great houses to evade complete death, but do they really? How do we know what Death truly is if we do not examine it?

Rumors abound of Katarzyna Niezik, who is the first public Death Reacher for quite some time. Could she grant us the insights we seek? Or does her arrival in Kalastok foreshadow great destruction instead? I fear it is the latter.

Should we continue our failures to grasp Death, I fear other forces will find the truth first. Let us hope those wielding it are not as malevolent as our perception of the realm.

THE FLESHWEAVER

"Oh, what wonders must await us in the other realms? How glorious will it be for the first realm walker? I so greatly envy them." – Rien-Ja Keer, professor at the Tidewater College

The creature looming before Kasia was nothing short of a monstrosity.

Stitches connected dozens of distinct bodily sections and limbs together to create a towering mound of flesh, muscle, fat, and sharp juts that she assumed must be bone. It all tremored and rumbled as the creature's breaths reverberated through the obsidian castle. Much of the walls and ceiling were covered with organic, oozing material that wove into the disgusting body too, explaining the rhythmic thumping on the lower floor. By the Crystal Mother below, it *reeked.*

Kasia swallowed to keep from vomiting as she stared up at what she assumed to be Sadamar. In the dim torchlight, it was impossible to tell where his head was, or if he even had one amid the disarrayed body parts. He could've had a hundred for all she knew, each carrying the voice that worsened her unending headache.

"I presume you are Sadamar?" she asked, unsure where to look except at the creature's center. His words before had been in the

Ezmani language, but how? They were a realm away from Zekiaz and the Commonwealth.

"Indeed, lifeborn," Sadamar said with a voice which shook the entire chamber. "You bask in the presence of Sadamar the Fleshweaver, master of the Heart of Orat."

Sadamar wore no clothes—not that any could possibly fit his enormous body—and with this reply, Kasia caught sight of a dozen scattered mouths. There were just as many eyes, each of a different color. She felt like an ant before him. What would it take to not be crushed by this king of the Death realm?

Kasia bowed only slightly. "I am Katarzyna the first, matriarch of House Niezik." With no real power, she needed to appear respectful, but not weak. That was difficult when her lightheadedness made her stagger, earning a series of complaints from Spitza before she managed to stand up straight again. Spirits, she needed water, food, and rest. If she could not escape this damned realm, she'd settle for that at least. "Thank you for welcoming me into your castle, but I must ask how you know my language."

Sadamar laughed. "In my many centuries, I have seen travelers from every realm. I would recognize the gray skin and hair of a Zekiaz lifeborn anywhere."

"You keep saying that word: lifeborn. The creatures here, then, are undead?"

"We are those gifted with Orat's Essence of Death," he replied.

She huffed. "That is hardly an answer."

The Fleshweaver suddenly switched to the language Valimor had spoken, waving a few of his many arms toward Kasia. Valimor grabbed the back of Kasia's dress before she could resist. She cried out as he kicked out her legs and sent her crumpling to the stone floor.

"You believe I owe you answers?" Sadamar's voice rumbled. "Foolish child. Do you not see the countless shades upon my form? Do you not see the patches of gray skin that matches your own? I told you other lifeborn from your realm have entered my walls, and each of them served their purpose before they joined my glorious being."

"What the fuck are you?" Kasia spat, testing Valimor's strength and finding herself badly outmatched. The undead hunter gave no attention to Spitza pecking at his hands either, and she wondered if he could feel pain at all. "Why take living bodies if you're already dead?"

"Yet more questions!"

Kasia stared in horror as Sadamar somehow crept closer. She tried to pull away, but Valimor gripped her hair, throwing her back to the ground as Spitza sprawled out nearby, unable to fly.

Tears stung her eyes from pain and desperation. This couldn't be the end. She'd fought too hard for vengeance, lost too much. She refused to die in a foreign realm with the disgusting Fleshweaver stitching her body into his own.

She remembered that Death Crystal pulsing on her captor's chest. Curiosity had sent her into this trap, and though Sadamar likely had the knowledge she needed to wield Death's power once again, it wasn't worth *this*. Valimor was right behind her. If she were to pretend to surrender, would he let his guard down enough for her to touch the crystal with her Axiom-webbed hand?

So she fell limp, dropping harder than she would've liked against the stone floor. The impact nearly knocked her out, but Sadamar's stench alone kept her awake. She lay there for what felt like forever before Valimor released her.

Sadamar made a hell of a lot of noise, but she heard Valimor's breaths behind her still. All she needed to do was risk a glance.

When she raised her head, her breaths caught. Sadamar loomed over her. His decaying, discolored flesh was close enough to touch, and all manner of maggots and other bugs Kasia didn't want to consider crawled between the folds in his skin.

Time was up.

She threw everything she had into turning back and reaching out for Valimor's crystal. Her mind spun from the motion, her muscles protesting the force, but it wasn't enough. Valimor slammed his elbow into her face. Then he kicked her straight in the chest.

All the air fled her lungs. She crumpled once again, seizing just to breathe, but each attempt brought another wave of pain. How stupid must she have looked? Nothing but a flailing child before an ancient necromancer and the hunter who'd dragged her to the slaughter. She expected a killing blow any moment, but instead, Sadamar sucked in a breath heavy enough to send a gust across the room.

"That crystal on your arm," he said, a note of shock entering his voice. "It is Axiom Crystal?"

Kasia spat blood onto the floor between them. Her will was bent, but she refused to break. If this was her end, she would go down fighting. "Now you're the one asking questions."

Sadamar muttered something in their deathly language. Valimor grabbed her arm, tore off her left sleeve, and dragged her toward a cluster of Sadamar's eyes. They were a myriad of impossible colors. All, though, focused on the Axiom Crystal winding up her hand and forearm. It had crept so far across her burn scar, and guilt swelled within her remembering the truth behind that scar. Her fury had nearly killed her mother then. Now, it had landed her in the realm of Death, likely marking the beginning of her own demise.

"There is a Death Crystal just to the left of this cluster of eyes." Sadamar's voice shook her from this close, but his next words jarred her further. "I will instruct Valimor to release you enough for you to draw the Essence from it, but if you dare attempt to draw upon your power, you will suffer beyond your imagining. Do you understand?"

She locked eyes with him. It was disorientating, considering how many he had, but she sensed a shift deep within. He'd not known about her Axiom Reaching. How then, did he believe she had arrived here in the first place?

That didn't matter right now. Surviving did, and if Sadamar was willingly rejuvenating her crystal, she would be stupid to deny it. So, she nodded slowly.

Valimor did not, in fact, release her, but loosened his grip enough for Kasia to stagger back to her feet. From a distance, she'd thought the scattered marks across Sadamar's skin were large moles or decay like that of his undead guards beyond the castle. She saw now that they were dozens of crystals which pulsed with a dull purple light.

She raised her left hand to the nearest of them. It wasn't far, but her chest throbbed from the movement. If she got out of this, she intended to take a long rest, considering all the choices she'd made to end up in this shithole.

Like with the Water Crystal, power flowed from the Death one into her hand. It dimmed as the Axiom Crystal glowed a vibrant gold. Warmth came with it, and Kasia closed her eyes, allowing the feeling of a deeper connection to wash over her. The Axiom's web was at her fingertips. She need only Reach.

But that moment of ecstasy faded as Valimor snatched her yet again, plopping Spitza back onto her shoulder. The raven shrieked at the force, but all that did was make Kasia's ears ring.

"Fascinating," Sadamar said, drawing even closer. "I have not seen one of your kind for millennia. So few are bound to the Axiom, and it seems this creature of Orat recognizes your potential."

Kasia furrowed her brow. "You said others had arrived from other realms. How did they get here without Axiom Crystal to teleport?"

"You don't know?" He reeled back, his various hands closing into fists as his whole body shuddered. The motion shook the room, and Kasia would've fallen if Valimor weren't holding her up. "Piorak… What has become of it?"

"The Piorak Empire fell nearly nine hundred years ago," she said. A sickening feeling filled her stomach, worse than from exhaustion or the stench. "Have you not seen someone from Zekiaz in that long?"

"Time is a strange force when you are as old as me. An Axiom Conduit like you should know that better than anyone, and those years have taught me that those like you do not appear in Orat without reason."

She took time with her reply as her tired, aching mind considered all he'd said. What was a Conduit? And what did the Axiom have to do with time? "Orat is the name of the Death realm?"

"It is the Essence that lifeborn would call Death, yes. Just as Zekiaz is for your realm." He paused, as if pondering like she had.

"There are other ways to traverse the realms, but they are complex, difficult. That Axiom Crystal on your hand is a far easier solution, and it makes you more useful alive than as an addition to my collection."

"Useful?" She scoffed. "I don't intend to serve you."

Sadamar laughed. "Remember, girl, that I could just kill you, but no, I have greater things in mind. Like I said, no realm walker comes to Orat without reason. Help me, and I may be able to ensure you find what you're looking for."

"Tell your hunter to release me, and I'll consider it."

"You negotiate like one of noble birth." He retreated further to his original position, leaving behind a substance on the stone floor that Kasia didn't dare to ponder. "As you can see, I have immense access to the Death Crystals of this realm, but securing those from other realms is more difficult. Return to Zekiaz and bring me enough Spirit Crystal to create a Reacher."

The crushing weight on Kasia's shoulders disappeared in an instant. "You want me to go home?" Something clicked in the back of her mind. How Sadamar understood her language, Piorak, and his eagerness for Spirit Crystal. "I see it now. You were one of those realm walkers, weren't you? The art in your castle foyer showed your arrival and how you became a ruler in this realm, but Zekiaz was your home."

Sadamar seemed to shrink, like a cat hiding in the corner. "I have not seen Zekiaz for over a thousand years. In that time, Reachers oppressed those like me, and my brother…" His whole body shuddered. "I took a portal into another realm to escape. I did not know what lay on the other side. When I discovered Death Crystal here and how to wield it, though, I knew I could never turn back."

"Then why not return through a similar portal and take the crystal yourself?" she asked. It was foolish to diminish her significance, but the thought of this monstrosity somehow coming from her realm had her far too curious.

"Unless linked to another, such portals are indirect, and it is unlikely those previous connections still exist. Whoever I sent would struggle to find an accessible portion of the Spirit Crystal without resistance. But it should be easier for an Axiom Conduit with scion blood. Bring me it quickly, and you shall be rewarded."

Kasia glanced at Valimor, and Sadamar waved for the hunter to let go completely. When he did so, Kasia held up her crystal hand to display her missing finger. "If I bring you the crystal, can you show me how to form a bond with this realm once again? I was once a Death Reacher before an asshole removed the finger which held my Spirit Crystal. I *need* that power back."

"You fascinate me once again, Katarzyna." He drew closer again, studying her finger. "I cannot make you a Reacher again if your bond through Zekiaz's crystal has broken, but there is another bond one can form with a realm. One deeper, more intimate."

She steeled her heart. "Tell me."

Smiles flicked across his many mouths, misshapen and missing teeth displayed within. "Bring me Spirit Crystal, lifeborn, and I shall show you how to truly command Death's gift. Betray me, and I will ensure the rest of your life is spent in miserable torment. No realm will be safe harbor from my wrath."

REMEMBER THE DAWN

"No matter how great the toil. No matter how great the struggle. No matter how great the loss. Always remember the rise of dawn." – An excerpt from *The Dawnrise Manifesto* by Evit Paxian

Nex had forgotten their lover.

The young woman Jiinaan called Vinnia stared back at Nex with puffy red eyes. Over a hundred people filled this room beneath a warehouse's trapdoor, and each of them hugged Nex upon their arrival with Nikoza, Tazper, and Jiinaan. Nex so badly wished they'd all go away. They didn't understand the pain of being introduced to a stranger who'd apparently shared their bed.

Vinnia's hug was the longest. Nex didn't know what to do as she clung to them like the world was about to end, so they just froze. If she was really so important, how could they have forgotten her? It seemed impossible.

"Nexie, what did they do to you?" Vinnia asked when she stepped back, a shaking hand held to her breast. "We've all worried about you for days."

"And why'd you bring one of *them* into our safehouse?" someone muttered as the crowd glared at Nikoza. The princess... well, former princess... wearing an elaborate Crystal Brigade coat hardly fit in among a bunch of lowborn, and she shied back, her face growing grayer from Realm Taint.

"She helped me escape," Nex said. They were apparently in charge of these Ashes of Dawn, so they needed to act like it. Pretending to be someone they weren't had become second nature to them. "I'd be dead if she didn't."

Vinnia took their hand. "You're here, safe now, and thanks to you, we have Etal's cure, food, and clean water."

"A warehouse of glass and amber, too," Jiinaan added.

Nex blinked hard. They should know why freeing Etal had earned the Ashes so much, but they hadn't a clue. "Where is Etal?"

"With your friends," Vinnia whispered. "The ones who told you to rescue him in the first place."

That meant nothing to Nex, so they stepped closer and lowered their voice. "Can we talk in private?"

Vinnia gave them a surprised look, but nodded. Nex grabbed her hand and started dragging her back to the warehouse ladder. Before they got far, though, Nikoza piped up.

"I believe Tazper and I may be of use," she said. "Events have moved quickly, and we appear to know as much about your past as you do."

Sure, tell everyone I lost my mind.

Nex waved for them to follow, cursing to themself. This was not how they'd expected their rescue of Etal to go, but then again, it was hard to know what they'd expected. They had only a vague memory of their plans, or apparently who they even were. Spiritdamned Reachers had wrecked their mind worse than they'd thought.

"Wait!" Jiinaan exclaimed once Nex reached the ladder. He bowled through the crowd with an old duster and wide-brimmed hat in hand. "Bring coat. Don't want to freeze."

Vinnia thanked him, handing Nex the hat before throwing the duster over their shoulders. The coat itself was unfamiliar, but its weight felt right. Memories flashed through Nex's mind of a hundred false faces they'd worn while wearing it. All the times they had played a role to con a scion or lowborn merchant out of their keni, and all the times they'd secretly wished for those lives to be true. Any of them was better than their own.

Nex donned the hat and tugged instinctively on its left side to cover half their face. It already curved downward there from wear, and a familiar warmth filled Nex at that realization. This was a part of who they were. A tiny piece, but better than nothing.

They were grateful for the coat and jacket when they emerged into the warehouse's chilled air. The basement itself wasn't heated, but that many bodies in a tight space did wonders for heat. Dawnrise had yet to break the frost above, and Nex stuffed their hands in the duster's pockets as they waited for the others to climb up behind them.

"What's wrong with your memory?" Vinnia asked, glancing at Nikoza as she referenced the Reacher's comment.

She held a gas lantern to offer them light, and it made her coppery eyes look like pools of molten metal. That granted Nex a few brief images of her from their memory. Scattered, they told an incomplete story, but they felt the companionship that had been there. A lingering fear too. Why would they be afraid of Vinnia if they loved them?

They remembered something else too. From Vinnia's eyes to her auburn hair and deeply tanned skin, she was of mixed blood: half-Vockan and half-Reshkan. That insight made Nex chuckle to themself in relief. Maybe this wouldn't last forever... *maybe*.

Vinnia took their shoulders. "What's so funny? Please, tell me what's happening. You're acting strange."

"I... Shit, this is harder than I thought it'd be," Nex muttered. They looked to Nikoza, wondering if she could reveal their memory loss instead, but when she went to speak, Nex shook their head. "No, I've got to say it."

"Say what?" Vinnia asked.

"The Truth Reachers interrogated me," they replied, dancing around the topic. "They broke my mind, my memories. When I woke up, I didn't remember leading the Ashes or helping Nikoza cure the plague or..." They winced, and Vinnia's eyes widened.

"Or me," she whispered.

Nex swallowed hard. Fuck, this hurt, but that gave them some hope. It wouldn't hurt if they'd never loved her, right? "I've got these bits of memories: bringing that vial back to you, talking in our room, and a walk by the river. But I didn't remember your name or that I even had a lover."

"They are remembering things rather quickly, though," Nikoza butted in with a forced smile, "and those little pieces form the greater picture in time. Chatik interfered with my own mind too. Together, we will rediscover all that has happened."

Vinnia shoved her, tears welling in her eyes. "You did this! The Ashes said they saw you leading the Crystal Brigade around Etal. You helped capture Nex, and you let the Crimsons do this to them!"

Tazper stepped between them. "Hold on one second. Perhaps there is more to this than we realize. Nikoza also had a chance to prevent Nex from freeing Etal from the guillotine at all, but after I shot Chatik, she let Nex escape. Only a Truth Reacher made them stop."

"Is that true?" Vinnia asked Nex with her hands still gripping Nikoza's coat. A thousand questions lingered in her gaze, and Nex found themself so badly wanting to answer them all.

Nex nodded. "Can't remember all of it, but Tazper's right. She had a chance to shoot me or use her Reaching. Chatik sounded furious when she didn't."

Nikoza gently stepped away from Vinnia and stared, slack-jawed, at Tazper. "So you *were* the one who shot my uncle. Forgive me, but I would have expected such a thing from your mistress, not yourself."

"Nex's Possibility Reaching sure helped the shot," Tazper said with a nervous laugh. "They needed a scion to get them into the Crimson District without drawing suspicion, and I was the only one available."

"Is Lady Katarzyna here, then? In Kalastok?"

Tazper removed his wide-brimmed hat and fiddled with it as he averted his gaze. "Not exactly. She sent me here to assist Nex while she and Lord Zinarus..." His voice trailed off, stiffening. "Kasia would not like me to tell you more, I believe. After all, we cannot be sure of your loyalties."

"He's right," Vinnia said. "How can we know you didn't just let Nex go to find out where our safehouse is?"

Nikoza's scion gray cheeks flushed bright red.

"You bitch!" Nex snapped, lunging to punch the scion square in the jaw, but Tazper jumped in again to prevent a conflict.

"Could we please have a conversation without quarreling for one moment?" he said. "I have my suspicions as well, but as it appears, Lady Nikoza has put herself in great peril by bringing you here."

Nex scowled. "Talk now, Princess. Or I'll call my guards to put a bullet in that pretty little head of yours." In truth, they didn't know if they had armed guards posted around the warehouse or not, but it sounded like a good threat. Nikoza wouldn't know either, so that gave them the advantage.

Nikoza backed away until her back struck the brick warehouse wall. "Please, allow me to explain."

NIKOZA'S HEART THUMPED AS HER FINGERS FOUND THE WALL behind her, tracing the mortar to ground her mind. A force pressed against her thoughts. It commanded her not to reveal the Crimson Court's secrets or Chatik's orders. She knew not what the Crimson King would do to her if she failed, but with that Unity Crystal, he was capable of more than her greatest fears. The Crimson Cause burned deeper into her mind each time he spoke his will. Could she truly fight it?

"I cannot explain enough the strength of my Uncle Chatik's Mind Reaching," she managed to say, struggling not to cough on the dank stench of the warehouse. "It took me a long time to realize it, and by then, he had manipulated me into bringing the Reacher towers to the western city and joining the Crystal Brigade. All those efforts, I believed, were to help the lowborn."

None of that was a lie, but it skirted around Chatik's command:

to prepare the way for the Crimsons' cure and capture Etal iz Noshok. Revealing the Ashes of Dawn's safehouse was not necessarily required. A deep part of her, though, twisted beneath the power of Chatik's demands.

"Nobody is that stupid," Nex said. "The scions always want to control us, Crimson or not."

"With my grandfather and now with Chatik, I urged them to do precisely the opposite. My efforts have been in vain." She lowered her head, portraying the true pain she felt. "Forgive me for the suffering I have caused. It was not my intent."

Vinnia circled around to Nex's side and took their hand. It startled Nex, but they didn't fight it. Maybe some familiarity would make them remember how they felt. "What about Nex's escape?"

Nikoza raised her chin. This was where the Mind Reaching drew its line, demanding she hide Chatik's plans and the Crimson Cause's call for scion superiority. Was it truly wrong? The Crystal Mother had chosen the scions after all. Nikoza could ensure the lowborn were well cared for without claiming they were equal after all.

She was unsure whether to revel in that thought or run from it. Chatik's Reaching had entangled his desires with her own so deeply that they were indistinguishable. While Nex had forgotten who they were, Chatik had molded her very will into what he desired. He could have been the reason she helped Nex escape, as she never would have done something so risky while Jazuk was king. She was different now, though. Stronger. Bolder. Her instincts had always been to better the lives of all the Commonwealth's people, so she would trust them.

"I cannot trust myself to answer," she finally replied, clutching her head as thoughts warred within her. "If I were to return to the Crystal Palace now, I do not know what I would reveal to the Crimsons, willingly or not. The Crimson Cause burrowed within my mind now, and I cannot deny that a portion of me believes it."

"What is the Crimson Cause, then?" Tazper asked.

She opened her mouth to reply, but was interrupted by the opening of the warehouse door. Two Ashes of Dawn guards led in a familiar figure at gunpoint.

"Hazat?" Nikoza gasped. "What in the Crystal Mother's name are you doing here?"

Nex spat at her feet. "You had us followed?"

"No, I…" She frantically searched her memories for any evidence of her doing so. Had Chatik wiped away those? Or had the members of her own squad not trusted her orders?

"She gave no such order," Hazat said, his hands raised. Both were gloved, but the left's was the Crystal Brigade's signature one, not covering the talon—he could call upon a breathless spirit at any time. "I followed you because Vanzearik decided to report Nex's escape to Lord Uzrin while the king and Lady Tzena are gone. We both believed it to be suspicious, but it was my opinion that we should allow you to return and provide a more thorough explanation."

Nikoza stepped from the wall and approached the Spirit Reacher. "What do you believe now?"

Despite the cold, sweat trickled down his brow and caught along his nose. He scrunched it from discomfort, but dared not lower his hands. "I believe you are working with the lowborn resistance against the Crimson Court… Just as I am."

"Well shit," Nex said. "Now we've got two of them to deal with."

Vinnia tugged at the ends of her sleeves and approached the Reachers. "Mother always said not to look a gift ibex in the mouth. It might be worth hearing them out."

"You have endured Chatik's Mind Reaching the same as I," Nikoza told Hazat, studying him for any sign of deception. Though practiced among the scions of the Chamber, it was far from her greatest skill, and his nervousness did not mean anything. He did have a gun to his back after all. "It still impacts me now, but Nex has helped me see through the holes in his story. What allowed you to see the truth?"

Hazat pursed his lips and drew a long breath. "My father was a Crimson before Lady Katarzyna Niezik killed him—justifiably, I might add. He was a sergeant in the Tystok city watch and a detailed note taker. When he died under suspicious circumstances, I took to reading his old, often coded journals to see if I could identify any potential enemies. Instead, during this very everdark, I discovered his schemes with Parqiz Uziokaki to leave the Niezik mansion unguarded the night of Lord Leonit's assassination. It was not long after my discovery that news of Katarzyna's attempts at vengeance came to light."

"You joined the Crystal Brigade to investigate further?" Tazper asked. "We saw you in the Uziokaki mansion before Kasia killed Parqiz, but you knew none of this then?"

Hazat grimaced. "May I put my arms down? Despite participating in Captain Tzena's training, my shoulders are quite sore."

"You trust him?" Nex asked, nudging Nikoza.

"We're not sure we can even trust *her*," Vinnia replied with a raised brow. "They could be working together. And we'll definitely need more people on watch if he found us that easily."

Hazat rocked his head back and forth. "Well, yes and no. I did manage to find you, but it was quite difficult, especially without using the breathless to guide me. They could have reported to the Crimsons, and that would rendered all this work moot."

"Well at least he's got a brain," Nex said.

"For what it is worth," Nikoza said, her study of him complete, "I trust him. He gains nothing by sneaking here and revealing all of this to us, especially if Vanzearik was already on his way to report me."

Nex and Vinnia shared a look, then Nex nodded to the guards. "Give him a break, but don't leave. I don't trust him that much yet."

"Have your investigations uncovered anything else since you arrived in Kalastok?" Nikoza asked as the guards backed off.

Hazat fixed his Crystal Brigade coat. She had to admit that he looked quite fetching in it, that foreign tricorn hat of his covering the sleek scion silver hair beneath that matched the coat's embroidery.

"I have learned much; though, likely less than you," he said. "Everyone knows that the Crimson King speaks more to his niece than any other member of the Crystal Brigade." He noticed Nikoza's glare at that and switched focuses, clearing his throat. "It is clear to me that the Crimson Court, and their core Crimson Cause, are focused on causing a further uprising among the lowborn."

Tazper burst out laughing. "Please tell me that is not serious? The Crimsons face a war in the east with the Keloshan Empire, another in the south with the Confederation of Harizak, and now they wish to foment further rebellion. To what ends?"

"Scion supremacy…" Nikoza wondered aloud, the Mind Reaching's hold on her surrendering to the horror strangling her chest. This went far deeper than she had realized. "The Crimson Cause is about ensuring the Ezmani scions rule all of Zekiaz as the Crystal Mother's chosen ones."

Hazat gave a solemn nod. "And that means further enslaving the lowborn. Their rights are limited now, but you have seen the veiled servants in the Crystal Palace. Chatik would have all lowborn as faceless, nameless tools to scion ends, and he intends to use someone called the Crystal Heir to do it."

The Crystal Heir? That term gave Nikoza pause. She could have sworn she'd heard it before, but none of her memories revealed anything about it. When she tried to search deeper, the words slipped away.

"Told you the scions are assholes," Nex said. "That's why we're fighting to stop them."

"Would you prefer us not to help you resist the Crimson Court, then?" Hazat quipped. "It would be quite easy for me to simply seek more power through my position in the Brigade, but I have risked my neck by entering a den of awakened to find the truth."

"Yet again," Tazper said. "Can we focus on what we should do instead of fighting? I have no doubt the Crimsons' plans march on the longer we bicker, and they will certainly continue to tighten their grip on the west side after Etal's escape."

Hazat eyed Nex. What did he know about the Spirit Plague and Etal? Nikoza had yet to reveal her own discoveries to him. Though she trusted him, she preferred to hear all he had learned first.

"Professor iz Noshok's cure," Hazat said. "Is it real?"

Vinnia smiled for the first time since Nikoza's arrival with Nex.

"Yes, and thanks to Etal's rescue, we're distributing it to the areas we can now." She nudged her lover, that smile fading. "Nex sacrificed a lot—and we lost a few people in the attack—but this'll save thousands of lives."

A heaviness struck Nikoza's heart as she remembered the sniper she had thrown off the building with her Reaching. Her first kill. By the Crystal Mother, she hoped it would be her last, but she was beginning to see how hard it was to keep one's hands clean in war.

"I am sorry for my part in killing your allies," she said. "I swear that I will do all I can to mend my errors." She turned back to Hazat, her will warring with Chatik's manipulations within her. She could not help thinking that she was missing something crucial. "My uncle demanded I help him begin preparations for the Crimsons to distribute their own cure. I worry we cannot trust it when every person who dies from the plague becomes an awakened that they can transform into a breathless."

Tazper raised his hand like a schoolboy to a teacher. "The Glassblade master, Radais ik Erienfar, discovered exactly that in the Spirit Wastes. Chatik had Karianam Pikezik conducting studies on people to see if they could be turned into controllable spirits, and they created spirits that could Reach in the process too. Bound Ones, he called them."

Hazat's eyes grew as wide as saucers, and he stumbled back until he bumped into one of the guards. "This… This is so much worse than I feared. Oh Father, what schemes did you tangle yourself into?"

Nikoza closed the distance to him and took his hand. With both of them having corrupt family members, it was a reassurance she both needed to give and receive.

"We will make right our own sins and those of our blood." She nodded to Nex. "Show us how we may help the Ashes of Dawn, so that when we inevitably return to the Crystal Palace, the balance of power may shift in your favor."

COMPROMISE

"The art of negotiation is not the brute haggling of street vendors or the poetic pursuits of those too long-winded to realize they simply love the sound of their own voices. Rather, it is the delicate balancing of people's desires to reach a conclusion that is satisfactory for all—but quite exemplary for yourself." – An excerpt from *The Right & Just Guide to Scion Society* by Arzibald Bartol the Third

The stench of wet mud and rotting corpses suffocated Zinarus as he rode over the trenches around the Vamia Mines. After the Earth Reacher had collapsed the tunnels, only narrow bands between them offered safe passage over the surface, but he forced himself to look down into those tunnels and watch his soldiers pull the wounded free. There were many.

Was this worth it? he asked himself as he stared down the few remaining Oliezany guards. Blood stained their uniforms, making the pink trim appear like nothing more than additional wounds.

He quickly realized that if this Earth Reacher was the last scion among the Oliezany mercenaries, then they had no Body Reacher, no medic. His own injured could be dragged back to Carelias and the other lowborn medics for healing. It would take time to avoid her becoming Tainted, but those who'd not received fatal wounds could be healed completely with her Reaching. The Oliezany's guards would receive no such luxury.

His stomach complained at the thought of that being an asset. Tiuz had taught him about war's horrors, though, and negotiations between commanders were no less ugly.

Wounded were potential prisoners to be ransomed. People became numbers to be compared in exchange for territory. House iz Vamiustok's most desired business hung in the balance with the discussions to come, but Zinarus found himself more worried for the dead and dying.

May the Crystal Mother bless their spirits.

One of the guards approached Zinarus once he'd crossed the precarious tunnels. A middle-aged man with the pinkish pale skin of an Ezmani lowborn, he looked less battered than most, and the pink epaulets on his shoulders marked him as an officer of some kind.

"Lord Zinarus iz Vamiustok?" the man said without an ounce of pleasantry.

Zinarus nodded. "I am he. And what are you called?"

"Lieutenant Paxrat," the man replied. Oddly, he did not take a soldier's firm stance. There was discontent in his eye, but not fury. "Our captain was the Fire Reacher your men killed. She was a fine woman, but with her gone, you're stuck with the scion in charge of tunnel maintenance, Ziegfried Torianisk." He coughed, then wiped his chin. "Not that there's much left of those."

"Do you have any wounded that need immediate attention, Lieutenant?" Zinarus asked, choosing not to use his unfortunate name.

Paxrat shifted uncomfortably. "I think that's best for you to talk to Ziegfried about. He's in the mines' administration building at—"

"At the center of the settlement, yes," Zinarus interrupted. "These mines used to be my family's. I am well aware of their arrangement."

"Fine. You can dismount here then. Can't have you trampling your way through the rest of my guardsmen."

Biting his cheek, Zinarus complied. This was obviously a slight against his ego more than a defensive precaution as Paxrat claimed, but there was little he could do about that. So he handed his horse to a guard who hurried over.

The stub of his left leg ached in the process. He had unknowingly twisted his mechanical leg's connection to the stub in the chaos of the collapsed tunnels, and he cursed himself for not finding a modified stirrup and saddle in time. This would have him hobbling until he found time to mend his leg at camp. He had little time between his duties and another secret tinkering project, but his leg had to be a priority.

Paxrat failed to hide his amusement as Zinarus struggled to walk the few hundred yards across the rough, sandy ground to the administration building. It was a squat thing with two stories and the best of the mines' stone waste forming its walls. Zinarus had spent many hours within it, toiling over extraction numbers before Sania sent him off to Kalastok. Those were simpler days, but he couldn't say he missed the dirty mines.

Divided in half by stairs heading up to the offices, the building's first floor was furnished as a meeting room for the workers between shifts. A few wooden tables and chairs sat to the right with playing cards and half-filled mugs of beer scattered across them. One of the mugs had spilled, its contents covering the cards and still dripping onto the stone floor.

His surprise attack had worked in that regard, but he pictured the workers who'd sat there hours before, relaxing after a long day of labor. None had died in the attack, he hoped. Where were they, then? He had seen only Oliezany guards since his army's arrival.

He stepped to the left half of the room instead. An ash-filled fireplace jutted out of the wall there, and four wingback chairs rounded a low table before it. This was the gathering room for the supervisors, and a man in a tailored wool suit sat cross-legged in the furthest chair.

His gaze fixed firmly on Zinarus.

"Come, Lord Zinarus, and let us speak like scions and not ravaging koilee," Ziegfried said, jamming a wad of some kind into his curling pipe and lighting it with a candle that sat upon the table.

Zinarus was more than happy to sit and take the weight off his mechanical leg. He examined his counterpart and claimed the chair furthest from him, settling deep into the worn cushion. "I am appreciative of you allowing me to retrieve my wounded," he said as he straightened his golden officer's sash. "It is my hope we can come to a resolution to this conflict quickly."

Ziegfried took a puff from the pipe and respectfully blew the smoke out to his side. He was a man likely in his early thirties, his head dominated by a receding scion gray hairline and sunspots dotting the space left behind. Many scions' skin remained a soft, palish silver from little sun exposure, but even after the everdark, the Earth Reacher was nearly as tanned as an Ogrenian.

"We share that goal," Ziegfried said. "I assume Lieutenant Pissrat—or whatever his name is—told you what to call me."

Zinarus nodded. "Lieutenant Paxrat did, and I see you are not a member of House Oliezany. Nor were you someone hired for defense purposes."

Ziegfried took another puff, but this time, Zinarus noticed his hand tremored just in the slightest. "I am not, and I was not. When the Oliezanys hired me to come to this backwater, they promised outrageous wages, assurances I would not be called into battle against Kelosh, and all the Vockan women I could bed." He dangled the pipe and leaned back, exhaling as he stared at the ceiling. "It was all going so well until you sons of bitches showed up."

"Where are all the workers?" Zinarus asked to keep on topic. Ziegfried's casual nature was off-putting, but this was not about him. Well, not entirely.

"Worried I smothered them beneath the rubble, are you?" Ziegfried chuckled, hanging his foot over the table as if it were bait for a fish. He wasn't lying about his wages. Those shoes were Bartol ones of the finest make. Not a stitch was out of place, and the leather looked pristine despite the sand surrounding this place. "Well, *bury* those fears, my friend. I would never do that to the poor lads. They are holed up in the dormitories, probably placing bets whether you are here to kill them or free them from the shackles of those dastardly Oliezanys."

Zinarus leaned forward. "On that point, I expect you realize that you are both badly outnumbered and pinned against the river. You have demonstrated the damage you are capable of, but if required, my cavalry will overrun your position."

"Glad to see that we both have clarity. Get to it, then. What is this offer of yours?"

"Surrender the mines," Zinarus said, a bite slipping into his voice. He would not allow Ziegfried to treat this like some jousting bet. "In return, I will allow your wounded to seek treatment with our Body Reachers. Any who wish, you included, may join our mercenary ranks if they so desire, or they may go free."

Ziegfried rolled the pipe between his teeth. "To what end? You have your mines. What do you need an army for unless… oh, yes…" He plucked the pipe free and waved it toward Zinarus. "Our new Crimson King badly wants your head, does he not? A shame. It looks quite good on your shoulders."

Zinarus thumbed the iz Vamiustok pin at his lapel. He knew Ziegfried was trying to get under his skin, and that made the successful jab all the more annoying. "The Crimson Court is corrupt and dangerous, but I have a feeling you are not motivated by such things. We are in need of a Reacher of your talents. Agree to these terms, and you will be well compensated. We both know House Oliezany will send you off to face the Keloshan war machine when they hear what has happened here."

"That would be unfortunate," Ziegfried replied, nose wrinkled. He threw down the pipe. "Fine, then. Imagine I consider your offer. I will not be crawling in the mud and sleeping alone in some tiny tent."

Zinarus swallowed. He had met great house magnates with lesser egos than this minor house scion. Was he even patriarch of this House Torianisk which Zinarus had never even heard of?

"Perhaps you would enjoy the eastern trenches near Anukit then," Zinarus said with a tilt of his chin. He would compromise, not surrender. "You will be treated as a scion officer among my mercenaries and given the few luxuries of the position. As for whether you sleep alone, well, I shall not speak for my camp followers, but I doubt the Vockan women and men among them respect such arrogance. Attempt to force any of them to comply, and it will not end well for you."

Ziegfried clicked his tongue, then gestured to his suit. "Do I look like a mercenary to you?"

"The Oliezanys paid you a ridiculous sum of keni to drag you out here, so yes, in fact, you do." Zinarus started to rise. "I will give you an hour to consider my offer. In the meantime, do we have an agreement for the surrender of the mines?"

The Earth Reacher waved him off. "Yes, yes. They are not my property and hardly worth dying over. Heal whatever Oliezany wounded you'd like. The lowborn bastards were annoying anyway."

Zinarus considered for a moment how much he'd regret this offer. The battle had shown how badly he needed Reachers to complement his lowborn soldiers, but this one in particular would string out his patience. Ziegfried would also be a disaster for morale. With the mines secured, though, Zinarus could afford to bring on more costly Reachers, and there were few available in Vocka—especially capable ones. Given his desperation, Ziegfried was his only option.

"I will return with my army then to make camp," Zinarus said. "Upon my return, I expect to hear your decision, and if you accept the position, you *will not* denigrate my soldiers."

Then he left without giving Ziegfried a chance to answer.

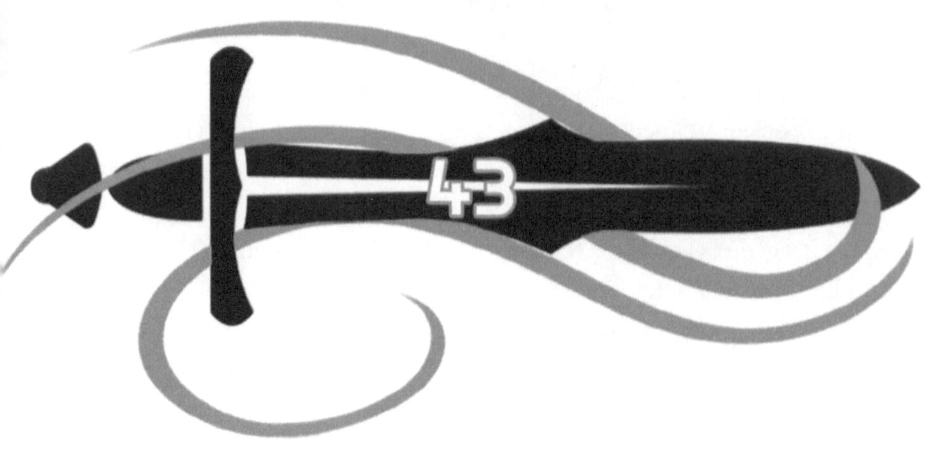

THE COST OF A SPIRIT

"No power comes without a price." – Gornioz Oliezany the Eighth,
former patriarch of House Oliezany

Wanusa woke to smoke stinging her nose. Despite the heat, she shivered from a chill deep in her bones as she blinked away the sleep. Lazan's smiling face met her.

"It appears our young apprentice is awake," the scion said with an excited slap of his thighs. "I'll pour your stew in a bowl. After all your efforts last night, I am sure you're hungry."

"Let her rise when she's ready," Radais said from somewhere nearby, the snow creaking beneath his boots as he paced. "Like after a tough day of training, the body needs time to recover. I doubt whatever she saw in that crystal was any less effort."

Wanusa wiped her palms across her bleary eyes and sat up as Lazan stirred a pot that hung over the fire. She was apparently on her bedroll, but had no memories of ever making it there. For hours last night, she'd tried to complete the Deepening through the Spirit Crystal at the cliff's edge. Inrius haunted her visions each time, reminding her of her failures. Lazan had told her to focus on the wonder of the spirits and her desire to know them. That was difficult when the only spirit she saw was her brother's.

"You two can stop fighting over me," she said, pulling in her legs and staring at the dancing flames. They were a welcome relief on her face as the dawnrise light graced the back of her neck.

Mariana held her arms outstretched at the cliff's edge. Spirits swirled around them like puppets guided by each finger. "I doubt either of them will cease protecting you. After you succumbed to exhaustion, they refused to let me check your spirit."

"What for?" Wanusa asked, her cheeks flushing at the realization she'd passed out. Radais had likely carried her to bed like she were an infant. She was supposed to be gaining the power to save all them from the Vanashel, not be some helpless teenager who pushed herself past her limits.

"Attempting the Deepening takes a heavy toll on one's spirit." Mariana guided the spirits around her away with a swipe of her hand. They appeared to be drifters, floating into the wind without a care. "I only wished to examine the state of your spirit for your own safety, but they insisted I do so after you woke."

Wanusa followed the Whisperer's gaze to Radais, who dug his heel into the snow. "I just wanted it to be your choice," he told her. "Looking at someone's spirit sounds invasive."

Lazan chuckled. "We have all had our privacy invaded lately."

"*Maybe* lock the door next time?" Wanusa quipped. "I appreciate the concern, but if I'm going to do this, I need to trust the only one here who knows what I'm getting myself into."

Mariana stepped from the ledge with a smug look on her face. "Thank you for the show of support. It is difficult when you are surrounded by those who doubt your every word."

"You told me this would be hard," Wanusa said. "I guess I didn't realize how hard you really meant."

Lazan ladled some stew into a bowl and passed it to her as Mariana sat cross-legged nearby. She was old enough to be Wanusa's grandmother, and a matronly smile crossed her face. It was a bit unsettling. After all, she clearly knew far more than she was letting on about the Deepening and becoming a Whisperer. Was she enjoying Wanusa's failure?

Wanusa sipped the stew. Her stomach rumbled, and she raised the bowl toward Lazan in thanks before returning her attention to Mariana. "Why are you looking at me like that?"

"Perhaps these two see you like a daughter," the Whisperer said. "Like them, I never had children of my own either, so I take pride in the youth who I guide under my proverbial wing instead. It is good they care for you. Zekiaz is not a place where one should ever be alone for long."

That only made her more self-conscious, so Wanusa quickly slurped down some more stew. Hundred-hours of travel and last night's ritual had left her exhausted. A little stew couldn't fix it all, but it filled her stomach with a warmth that felt like a hug from the inside.

"Alright," she said when she was finished. "Read me."

Mariana extended her hands for Wanusa to take. They were un-gloved, but not chilled, and she had aged, deep lines where Wanusa had calluses. She breathed in sharply, eyes flashing silver. The sudden movement made Wanusa want to pull back, but she remained firm as Spirit wisps shot around them like a whirlwind for a few long seconds.

Then all fell still.

"Well, then," Mariana said, drawing back her hands and rubbing them together. "Your spirit is undamaged, but quite unsettled. We'd thought you held an unruly spirit when we studied you in Dalnus. That was certainly an understatement."

Wanusa scrambled to her feet as Mariana took her sweet time. "What do you mean?"

"Our spirits give us direction, willpower," Mariana replied some-what nervously. "It is why a child becomes a husk if they don't re-ceive one during their first day, and that direction within you seems to be the reason you never are stationary or content. There's deep desire there."

"I could've told you that much," Wanusa muttered, pulling her coat tight. "Will it stop me from becoming a Whisperer?"

"A content spirit is not one who seeks a deeper meaning to things."

Radais huffed. "Spoken like a true shaman."

"Not all answers must be direct, Glassblade," Mariana replied, but something tugged at the ends of her lips. "To be clear, Wanusa, your spirit being as such is why you're a good candidate to become a Whisperer. Exactly how fervent your spirit is… Well, that was a surprise."

Wanusa crossed the plateau to the ibexes tied up nearby, grabbing her canteen and greedily as she considered all that Mariana had said. When she was finished, she strapped it to her belt and hurried back to her gathered companions. "You say my spirit is fervent? Then let me continue. The other Glassblades will end up fighting the Vanashel without us if we wait too long."

"You're pushing yourself too hard," Radais insisted, stepping into her path. "Ever since you heard about Inrius, you've been—"

"Like you were with Miv?" she said with more bite than she'd intended. He gritted his teeth, but nodded. "That determination helped you save her… in a way. Should I give up any chance of saving his spirit? I must surrender my focus on the past to become a Whisperer, but that doesn't mean I'm going to forget what I need to do."

His eyes drooped. "I'm sorry. I didn't intend to claim you must abandon hope of helping your brother." He stepped out of the way, nodding toward the ring of crystals. "Know that you're not alone in this. We believe in you. I believe in you."

Pushing aside her frustrations, she wrapped him in a tight hug. His glass armor poked at her enough for it to be uncomfortable, but the moment was worth it as he hugged her back. Radais and Lazan were the closest thing she had to a family anymore, maybe Mariana too. She needed to remember what it was to have people fighting both beside her and for her. Just because it was up to her to complete the Deepening, that didn't mean she did so alone.

"I want you and Lazan by me when I try again," she said when she stepped back. Mariana wouldn't like it, but Wanusa also doubted the Whisperer would like waiting a hundred-hour until she figured out how to calm her spirit alone.

Radais held a fist over his chest. "I'd be honored."

"You haven't eaten your stew yet," Lazan called over to him, holding up a bowl. "We both know you get grumpy on an empty stomach, and I do not want you dealing with spirits like that."

Wanusa giggled as the supreme defender of the Glassblades sulked over to take his portion of stew. The pair shared a whispered discussion that ended with a kiss, then joined Wanusa at the plateau's end. An angry Whisperer greeted them there.

"The Deepening is not for a Reacher and a Glassblade to experience," Mariana said, arms crossed. She may have not been a mother, but her glare tore into them like Wanusa had seen from her own mother a hundred times.

But Wanusa took a soldier's stance, hands held behind her back and legs at shoulder width, just as Miv had taught her. "You said I must sacrifice my mourning and look forward. I need them to do that."

"That glass armor will frighten the spirits," Mariana said with a twitch of her nose, "but as long as Radais isn't too close, it should be fine."

Wanusa thanked her, then knelt once again over the Spirit Crystal. She stared over the valleys beyond for a long time, watching the rays of the great light split through the mountains' mists. Spirits danced among them. Pure. Bound to the heart of Zekiaz. And she so badly wished to be like them.

She focused on that desire, and on those here to support her, as she pressed her palm to the crystal once again. Visions answered.

Silver vapors encompassed all beyond the plateau where she knelt. Wanusa looked back to Radais, Lazan, and Mariana to find them all frozen in place. Unblinking, unmoving, unbreathing. When she exhaled, fog rolled from her lips, and a chill crept down her spine as a figure moved out of the corner of her eye.

Inrius floated amid the vapors, tails of it spiraling from him like unwinding threads of a coat. He'd aged to his early teens now, and his face held stone's stillness. Sorrow lingered in his eyes. They had been the same as hers in life—like vibrant, bright embers. Now, they were only ash.

"You replaced me with them," he said in that lost voice. He raised a stiff arm to point at her companions, then held it there. "Why did you leave?"

Wanusa fought the tears that welled in her eyes. She couldn't dwell in the past anymore. For him, she needed to move forward. So she refused his question. "They brought me here to bond with Zekiaz and become a Whisperer. I'm going to be able to help you, or at least those like you who spirits have hurt."

He lowered his arm. "You left me, and now I'm dead."

"I will find your spirit and bond it with mine," she promised. "This power will connect me with our people and our world more than I could have ever dreamed. If I can understand spirits, then others won't have to suffer from severed spirits or awakened attacks. We can truly have answers about the purest of them and the corrupted ones too!"

She rose to meet him, no longer shying away from her failures. Yes, she'd left. Yes, she'd lost him, but that didn't mean she couldn't work to protect others and do what she could for his remaining spirit. A loose tear slipped down her cheek as she took his cold hand in hers.

"I'm sorry, little Inri, but I need to keep going. Let me do this for you. For us." Her voice cracked, but she pushed closer to her brother as a thumping filled the wisps encircling him. It spread within him, following the familiar rhythm she had sensed in the Spirit Crystal before. A calling that her own heart answered.

His fingers wrapped around hers. A sudden warmth enveloped them, his eyes igniting like the blaze of the Glassblades' mighty glassworks. He lowered to her, and the dam holding back her tears failed as she pulled him into her embrace.

"Is this really you?" she asked, weeping into his shoulder. "Your spirit found me?"

"Half of it," he replied. His voice was still distant, still lacking any clear emotion, and he didn't raise his arms to return the hug. It was as if he struggled for even the slightest movement to break through the vision. "I lost the other a long time ago."

"I'll find it," she whispered. "Brother, I'll make you whole again. I just need you to stay with me. Help me complete the Deepening, and I will bring your spirit home, to where we used to laugh and play among the goats and the trees. I'll reunite the fragments of your spirit."

Her fingers began to slip through his form as he joined the silvery vapors. "I've been so lost," he said. "I don't like it."

"Let me show you the way." She pointed back to the others. "My friends helped me here, and they'll help me find your spirit. They're good people, a new family who loves me like you did."

"Love?" Inrius asked as he slipped further away.

Wanusa raised her hand to catch what remained of his. "You're my brother, Inrius. I'm moving on from the past, but I'm not leaving you behind!"

He vanished into mist, and Wanusa drew only a single breath before the vapors swarmed her. She fell onto her back, arms up to protect herself. But the mist dispersed to reveal a sky full of spirits.

Drifters mulled about like elders out for an everbright stroll. Awakened hurried through them, picking off those that lingered alone. And breathless in their human, animal, and geometric forms conversed among themselves in the Spiritspeech as wisps of every color circled the most solidified of them.

A rhythm drummed the air. Steady, but growing louder with every moment.

Rising, Wanusa stepped to the very edge of the plateau, beyond the ring of crystals, and admired the glory of the spirits. Here, they were home. Zekiaz was *their* realm. There were no pure and corrupted spirits. They were all forms of the Spirit Crystal's creations, just like humans who bore those spirits within them. All were bound with the Crystal, but so few heard its voice.

So few whispered in its given tongue.

"Let me hear you," Wanusa called to the spirits in the Spiritspeech. Her voice was like a hummed song, and though the words were unfamiliar, they came as if she'd known them her entire life. No, her spirit's entire existence. Beyond a single life. Beyond the history of Vocka or Piorak or any nation. Her spirit was as ancient as the Crystal buried deep beneath her feet, and she was one with its creations.

A chorus answered her.

The spirits sang, not as one, but joining with those near them. No matter their differing words, the rhythm was the same. A thousand verses strung from the same song. Branches of a tree woven through spirit and the wonder that filled Wanusa's chest now. She found herself understanding fragments when she focused on a particular group, but there were so many that her attention slipped before she could fully grasp any lyric's full meaning.

She was a child amid spirits that sang of their ancient past. No matter how hard she tried, it was all overwhelming, but joyous nonetheless. How could humans be so deaf to the spirits who surrounded them?

"I didn't mean for all of you to speak at once," she appealed, laughing.

Something prodded her hand, and she gasped as she looked down to see the Spirit Crystal resting in her palm. She'd not taken it. Yet it found her now, answering her call, so she raised it to her lips and spoke a promise.

"I will Whisper to the spirits of Zekiaz. I will hear their songs and tell all who live that we aren't alone. Spirits aren't just our ancestors; they are our brothers and sisters. They are the keepers of this realm."

A spirit split from the rest, curling toward her like smoke from a cigar's end. It took no distinct form beyond that of a drifter and offered no song in the Spiritspeech, but she felt its familiarity like a heartbeat beside her own.

"Inrius?" she asked with her hand extended toward it.

The spirit slowly twirled through her fingers. Its touch was warm, but she sensed the sorrow within it. Was it silent because it was only half his spirit, or was she just hoping for the impossible?

As if answering her silent question, the spirit slipped straight down her arm and into the crystal. Together, they pulsed a radiant silver to the same tune as the chorus above. Their light grew until the crystal rose from her hand and pulled her into the air, becoming so blinding that she covered her eyes as they hovered over the mountains.

Then it all disappeared in a flash.

She dropped to the ground, her legs failing and the spirits' deafening song fading to a gentle hum. Footsteps rushed toward her, but she couldn't make herself move. The world felt distant, cold. It was as if her vision were reality and this was nothing but a dream.

"Wanusa?" Radais asked, lifting her into his glass-clad arms. "She's frigid!"

He hurried her to the fire as Mariana's objections fell upon deaf ears. Wanusa watched Lazan hold her back through slit eyes. There was a desperation in the Whisperer's eyes, so Wanusa forced herself to speak.

"Let her through," she said, her voice hoarse as Radais set her down.

The second Lazan let Mariana pass, she sprinted to Wanusa with more speed than one expected of an elderly woman. She held Wanusa's cheeks and beamed. "What did you see?"

"My brother was there again," Wanusa replied, "but it was different. He joined with me, or at least part of him did."

Radais looked from her to Mariana. "What happened to her neck?"

"The Spirit Crystal has joined with her," Mariana replied, drawing down her robe's high collar. A silver crystalline line ran down the center of her neck, then split at her collarbones and followed each to their ends. It looked to Wanusa's tired mind like a glowing silver bird in flight. "It is the mark of the Whisperer, but most of us do not display it out of fear of those scorning our kind."

Wanusa grasped at her own collar and found hard crystal beneath her fingers. It pulsed to that familiar rhythm, just as Mariana's did, and deeper within her, she felt another presence.

"I heard the spirits sing to me," she whispered. "The half of my brother's spirit that was left entered the crystal. Does... Does that mean he bonded with me?"

Mariana raised her brow. "The first spirit any Whisperer bonds during their deepening is the closest loved one they have lost. I have heard of those like your brother living with severed spirits, but no Whisperer I know of has ever bonded one." She hesitated, concern crossing her face. "You must release him and find another."

"I promised him I would find his spirit's other half," Wanusa replied as she kept tracing the Spirit Crystal. It felt so strange to have it embedded in her skin, like it had replaced her collarbone completely.

"You don't understand," Mariana said. "We surrender a part of ourselves when we bond a spirit because it grants the spirit a place to reside within us. Its will and desires join with ours. To bond with a severed spirit means taking on that emptiness. Inrius likely looked lost and emotionless before you left Iliafa."

Wanusa tensed, but nodded.

"Then that will remain part of you, deepening with every passing day until you either release him or reunite both halves of his spirit." Mariana sighed and paced around the fire. "There are millions of spirits in Vocka, let alone Zekiaz. We can't be certain it'll be even possible to find the other half, let alone bond it too."

Steeling herself, Wanusa stood, shrugging off Radais when he sought to aid her. Was Inrius's emptiness within her? She couldn't tell with the flurry of thoughts consuming her mind, and it didn't matter anyway.

"You told me to listen to the spirits and the Spirit Crystal," she said. "They answered me when I let go of my regret, but promised to help Inrius and others with severed spirits. I know this is what I need to do."

Mariana looked to the crystal ring, then back at her. "I told you that spirit of yours was unruly. The path you've chosen is a difficult one, but I'll do my best to guide you on it." She glanced at the men. "And it is good that you will have others to walk with you every step of the way."

KALASTOK'S BURIED SECRETS

"Kalastok holds greater access to the Spirit Crystal than any other city on the continent of Brakesh. Many nations have their Reachers, but only Ezman does not utilize its crystal to the fullest. One must wonder if that is virtue or sin." — Votzan Evonska, former grand secretary of the Commonwealth of Two Nations

Golden wisps encompassed Kasia as she stepped through her Axiom portal and returned to Zekiaz. Focusing on Tazper in Kalastok, she pondered her plan to infiltrate the Buried Temple and extract Sadamar's Spirit Crystal. Those thoughts came up short when she emerged from the portal to find not just Tazper, but a packed room of lowborn on the other side.

A burly Reshkan man grabbed her before she could get her bearings. She tried to appeal, but he threw her into the wall, sending her already light head spinning as Spitza worsened matters by clambering up her skull.

"How you do that?" the burly man demanded as he gripped her throat. He was dressed strangely, even for a lowborn, with a yellow bandana around his neck, a collared shirt that exposed his stomach, and a flat cap that was far too small for his head. "Came out of air like it's nothing!"

Kasia squirmed, fighting for each breath. "I can explain. Where… Where is Tazper?"

"Kasia?" her footman called back from somewhere nearby, but she couldn't see him between the crowd and her blurred vision. "Jiinaan, please, let her down."

Jiinaan wriggled his jaw and looked to someone else for confirmation. He must have received it, because he retracted his hand, dropping her into a pile against the wall. "Strange scions."

Spitza hopped onto Kasia's legs to peck at her face, but the hit had her dazed. She ran her hands over her tired eyes. "Where in the wastes am I?"

"You are in one of the safehouses protected by the Ashes of Dawn west of the Kala," Tazper said, kneeling before her. He appeared unharmed and in good spirits, and he wore that same yellow bandana. Was that some kind of rebel symbol? "These are Nex's people. They are friends."

Her vision sharpened enough for Nex and another Reshkan-looking woman to come into focus. There was something different about the thief she had hired to keep her informed during everdark. Sure, their hair was cut short with only a wave of it tumbling over one cheek, but her instincts said it was deeper. Nex looked at her as one would a strange intruder more than an ally who'd showed up out of nowhere. And that wasn't to mention the clear tightening in their jawline and cheekbones.

The woman beside Nex whispered something to them. She had auburn hair and was taller than Tazper, so Kasia assumed she held Vockan blood along with Reshkan. Nex had told her once the name of their lover, but after all she'd been through in recent hundred-hours, Kasia couldn't recall it.

"Shit, what happened to you?" Nex asked, tugging down on that wide-brimmed hat they were so fond of. "You're supposed to be a matriarch, but you look like you just crawled out of a chamber pot."

Kasia drew a long, haggard breath. "May I have some water and any food you can spare? For the last few days, I have been trapped in the Death realm, and it wasn't a pleasant experience."

"Scions don't order us around here," Nex said, but once again, the auburn-haired woman bent down to whisper something. When she was finished, Nex rolled their eyes and waved for someone to do as Kasia said. "Death's Daughter in the Death realm. Huh. Didn't belong?"

"You went to the realm of Death?" Tazper squeaked. "What were you thinking?"

Voices haunted Kasia's mind, offering plenty of horrid motivations for her actions. Many of them were probably true, but she ignored them, pushing herself to her feet instead with Tazper's help. "I did not purposely trap myself in another realm… again."

"There was a first time?" Nex asked.

One of the members of this apparent Ashes of Dawn group returned with a steaming hot mug of water for Kasia. She'd not realized how cold she was until she took it and drank greedily.

"The Water realm," she answered when the mug was nearly empty. The water scalded her tongue, but she didn't care. "Massive crabs, though, are far preferable to undead monsters stitched together by a necromancer who calls himself the Fleshweaver."

"Are you sure you're okay?" the auburn-haired woman replied with a nervous smile. "This sounds crazy."

"And who are you exactly?" Kasia said, rubbing her palm against her forehead to calm her throbbing head. With both specter and real voices surrounding her, this was not what she had hoped to teleport into.

Nex glanced warily at the woman, not how one would usually look at their lover. "This is Vinnia. She's the reason I was fighting for the plague's cure."

"Which you discovered with great theft of my amber." Kasia forced her expression to soften. "I am glad you did, but if you are all hiding here, even after all the keni I paid you, I doubt all is well beneath Chatik's reign."

"Turns out the Crimsons are even bigger assholes than the rest of you scions," Nex replied. "Just escaped their torture dungeon a couple hours ago with Nikoza's help. Chatik messed with her head, and his Truth Reachers damn near broke me. There's a lot I don't remember." They reeled back as Spitza flapped her good wing and leaped onto their hat, playing with its loose threads. "Did… er…. Did you have a bird before?"

Tazper wiggled his finger at the raven. Spitza sprung, forcing him to leap back with a yap. "This one is definitely new."

"Meet Spitza," Kasia said, waving a hand toward her, which Spitza took as an invitation to return at full speed. Her talons were sharp, but Kasia managed a smile as Spitza cocked her head at the empty water mug. "If it is not too much to ask, she hasn't eaten either."

Jiinaan beamed and burst into the crowd. "I'll get for her!" Those who couldn't get out of the brute's way quick enough were bowled to the floor, but none dared stop him.

"It seems your people are far more interested in helping a raven than a scion," Kasia told Nex. Her legs ached, and she leaned into Tazper just to stand. "Is there a place I can sit? I don't need anything better than your friends, but I have quite literally returned from Death."

Nex crossed their arms. "Tell us why you're here first. You disappeared after the coup, and we thought you were dead until Tazper showed up."

They exchanged stories of their experiences since the Crimson Coup. She left out her fight with Zinarus and her worsening Taint, and Nex and Vinnia clearly hid where all their supplies after Etal's rescue had come from. Based on the lovers' uncomfortable looks, they also hadn't spoken much since Nex's escape from the Crystal Palace. So much had happened in just a few hundred-hours. It was clear from Nex and Nikoza's discoveries as well that the Crimsons' plans were far from finished.

When Nex was content with Kasia's explanations, they led Kasia to a bedroll in the corner where she could sit and eat a meal while Spitza enjoyed her water and an array of nuts Jiinaan brought back for her. Kasia reveled in the little luxury. Just sitting on something remotely soft with even the most meager food in her stomach was a dream compared to the Death realm of Orat. It pained her to know she needed to go back, so she focused on Kalastok's issues.

"So, you shot the Crimson King," she said, grinning at Tazper. "Did it feel good to strike back for once?"

He paced silently as Aliax formed from a plume of purple wisps beside him. "You sent him here without help," the specter said. "He's been tortured and strung along by your promise, but that's what you do. Lure us in, then destroy us."

"Sorry, Taz," she said. "I am proud of you for doing exactly what I sent you here to do. Based on Nex's story, the Spirit Plague's cure is available because of you."

The footman merely bowed his head. "Despite that, I should have been with you. Where was Zinarus to help you?"

"He…" She averted her gaze, biting her lip. "Let's just say that we had different intentions. By now, he should be marching to join Tiuz's Confederation and my mercenaries at Fort Harizak."

Nex furrowed their brow. "A bunch of scions fighting scions. Tiuz and his soldiers left us to fight for ourselves."

"He did tell lowborn we could come with them," Vinnia replied, wrapping her arms around Nex's. "Some went, but it was our choice to stay here and fight back."

"Even if the Crimsons hadn't figured out how to control an army of breathless," Kasia said, "we lack the numbers to besiege Kalastok. Houses Pikezik, Kuzon, and iz Ardinvil are joining the Confederation, and Zinarus and I are bringing a few thousand soldiers. Against the Crimsons, their breathless, and the rest of the great houses, though, we are far too weak."

"So you just came to eat our food and leave?" Nex asked.

Kasia had no answer. Yes, she needed to get Spirit Crystal from the Buried Temple to complete her deal with Sadamar, but then what? She didn't truly know what abilities she would gain from the Death realm. Would it be enough to face Chatik directly, or should she work with her allies to defeat Chatik's forces until he was vulnerable? The latter would mean returning to Zinarus.

Her Tainted specter joined Aliax among the gathered group,

staring at her with eyes ringed in radiant purple. "You saw Sadamar's army of the dead. Should we not build one for ourselves, just as Chatik has?"

It sounded ridiculous, but as long as the Crimsons controlled an army of breathless spirits which couldn't be harmed by conventional weapons, they would have an incredible advantage in any battle. That army grew every moment through their experiments and the plague. She doubted even Kelosh knew what horror they were marching toward.

"If I remember correctly," she replied, matching Nex's glare, "I gave you a significant sum of keni to remain my eyes and ears in Kalastok. My goal remains the destruction of the Crimson Court, but I cannot do that in my current state." She bit her cheek to hold back her Taint-induced rage. "The great houses' magnates were already near immortal between Body Reachers and their Inheritance Rituals, but the Unity Crystal makes him unkillable. I need Death's power to counter it."

"Have you considered that may not be the answer?" Tazper asked, fiddling with a coin. "What do we do in that case?"

Kasia ran her fingers over Spitza's head. "Then we push him until Realm Taint does the job for us. I saw him on that balcony. Though my bullets did little, he was not well. I know better than most the cost of Taint, and if he is using the Unity Crystal to influence Nikoza's mind, command breathless, and heal himself, that will take a heavy toll."

"Nikoza thought the same thing," Vinnia replied. "She's going back to the palace with Hazat to try and stop them from the inside."

"Wait, did you say Hazat? As in, Hazat Tozki?"

Vinnia nodded. "He joined the Crystal Brigade with Nikoza after Chatik called for a big recruitment. Your brother is with them too."

"Shit…" Kasia drew a few long breaths. She'd almost forgotten the whole Commonwealth knew her sins, and it felt like an executioner's noose was slowly tightening around her neck. "Hazat knows I killed his father, and if Gregorzon is here, it means he's part of Chatik's scheme. Did Nikoza mention anything else about this so-called Crimson Cause? Neither Chatik nor Tzena mentioned it when they recruited me."

Nex shrugged. "It's like we thought: They want to make us slaves, covering our faces and taking our names. Hazat said something about a Crystal Heir who's supposed to do it, but it didn't come up any more than that."

"An heir? Is Chatik worried about his Taint, then?"

"Doesn't matter," Nex said. "We kill them all; then there's no heir."

Tazper waved toward them with an exasperated sigh. "You see what I have dealt with here? We need more of a plan than slaughtering them. How do you intend on getting Sadamar's Spirit Crystal, and are you leaving me here? My duty is to serve you."

Having eaten and rested for a few much-needed minutes, Kasia stood and hugged him. It caught him off guard, and for a long moment, he stood as rigid as stone. "I am not leaving you. That was never my intent when I sent you here, and I'm sorry it came across that way. When I steal Sadamar's Spirit Crystal, I'm taking another for you."

Tazper tried to reply, but only babbled, stumbling nonsense came out instead.

Kasia stepped back and chuckled to hide her emotions. Spirits, she should have done this far sooner, and she refused to wait any longer. "You are the most loyal friend I have ever had. Years ago, I promised you I would sponsor your Reacher talon, and though the Buried Temple's anointed sister took away that chance, I have another now to make it right."

"I…" Tazper's voice cracked, and his eyes reddened. "I need a moment."

He pulled from her grasp before hurrying off, leaving a crowd to watch her as if she'd made a child cry. Kasia was unsure what to do. She had expected Tazper to be happy to know he would become a Reacher soon. Why was he upset about getting what he'd always dreamed of?

Nex opened their mouth to say something, but Kasia decided it was better to ask him than to stand there like a fool. The crowd parted for her faster than even Jiinaan as she followed Tazper toward a ladder on the far side of the room. No one stopped her, so she climbed up until she found a trap door.

Frigid air met her above. She glanced around, cursing that she'd not brought a lantern as she searched the darkness. They were in a brick warehouse of some kind. An ephemeral storm raged outside, and water streamed from holes all across the ceiling. It also let in a few streams of dawnrise light through the clouds to reveal the figure moping on a discarded box in the nearby corner.

"Tazper?" she asked, approaching slowly as Spitza cawed her own greeting.

Tazper's shadowed face emerged from his hands, and he wiped away his tears with his yellow Ashes of Dawn bandana. If it weren't for the faint gray tint of his skin, she would have thought him lowborn, dressed in the simple coat and pants of a workman. And as she watched her weeping friend, she realized she'd treated him as if he were nothing more than a lowborn servant.

"I remember when I was just a boy," he said as he stared at the ground, "and you came to my family's little house, asking for me to be your footman. My mother was beside herself. Think about it: the matriarch of the most powerful house in our region was coming to ask a minor house nobody to be her footman! Sure, we'd been friends already, but we were no better off than most lowborn. You told us you would buy me a talon. Do you know how expensive those are?"

Kasia approached and pulled up another box to sit across from him. "You have no idea how happy I was to finally have a servant who wasn't hired by my mother. Someone who I trusted."

"Then why did you leave me waiting for so long?"

Her Tainted specter sat beside him and scoffed. "Because he's nothing. We have so many more important things to focus on than a minor scion who follows us like a dog."

Tazper spoke with enough pain to drive a dagger straight into Kasia's heart. She clenched her fists, trying not to look at the specter.

She had gotten Kasia into this mess in the first place when she should've addressed things with Zinarus. Instead, Kasia had fled, just like she'd fled her responsibility with Tazper for a decade. So many excuses filled her mind. They were all pathetic, just like her lately.

Spitza nibbled at something in her hair as she shook her head at herself. The awkward *gwah, gwah* of the raven just reminded her of how broken she was. Tainted, yes. But she had been a murderer before then. Maybe she deserved to be haunted. As she looked around the warehouse, she saw the faces of all those who'd died at her hand, and she knew a normal person would feel some empathy, some regret.

She was empty.

Logically, she understood the emotions she *should* feel, but there was this void between her head and where her heart should have been. A fog that grew deeper with every waking moment. She returned her attention to Tazper, having lost track of time. She could've been focused on her specters for a blink or whole minutes.

"No excuse is enough," she admitted, shoulders dropping. "Whether money, distance, or the anointed sister, something always came up, but that's bullshit, isn't it? After we secured the amber, there were plenty of times I could have put aside my need for vengeance and taken you to Kalastok. But that damned list…"

Tazper huffed and held out his hand to allow one of the leaking streams to wash over it. The water followed the crevices in his palm, spilling over the edges and splatting across the stone floor. It was a gentle sound compared to the *crack* of thunder outside.

"You have changed so much since the day you made that promise," he said, his hand hanging there. "Except, maybe you haven't."

"This past season changed everything," Kasia replied. "The last decade… That felt like a lifetime, and I know you have been patient through it. I promise you that, before I leave Kalastok, you will have your talon."

He shut his fist, fury and pain burning in his eyes. "This is about more than a talon, Kasia! It's about us. Our friendship, our trust. Ten years I have waited, watching your obsession consume you until

Taint finally drove you mad. What are the voices saying about me right now? That I am nothing but a servant? An asset?"

She sat back and let the voices of the dead wash over her. When she spoke, she couldn't even hear herself. "No, they say you're right." A tongue clicked across from her, and she opened her eyes again to glare at her Tainted specter. That fucking perfect face scorned her. "All except one."

"Sazilz?" he asked.

"There is another specter who has haunted me since the coup," she said, wishing she didn't see a reflection of herself in that Tainted face. "She's me—or at least, she looks like a version of me without flaws—and she tells me to abandon my allies. What's worse is that I often believe her."

He fell back onto the box. "How about this time?"

"She's an idiot." Kasia pushed herself to her feet, then knelt before him. "Every day since the coup has been a reminder that I am useless by myself. I hurt everyone who bothers to care about me. Most of the country thinks I'm an insane murderer, and now that I lost my Death Reaching, I cannot even control my new power. That doesn't even count how I have pushed myself to actual insanity with my Taint."

"Some of those things are true," he said before raising one finger. "*However*, you are far from useless, and I find it very uncomfortable for you to be kneeling before me."

But she couldn't rise. Her body felt warped, trapped on her knees, and her broken mind succumbed to the weight. "How do I fix this?"

Tazper slid down to kneel before her. "It's like you said. None of us can do this by ourselves."

"You don't deserve this."

"Maybe not." He tried to smile, but it came out crooked and pained. "You don't either. Despite everything, I love you like a sister. I have seen you in your greatest triumphs and most haunting everdarks, and because of that, I know you can come out of this. Please, though, consider whether this deal with a master of the Death realm is the way to do it."

She raised her head to meet his gaze, only for Spitza to hop onto him with an eager humming noise. The raven shook out her feathers and hopped as she looked back toward Kasia. A laugh escaped them both, and Spitza mimicked it until they ended up half-weeping, half-laughing into each other's arms.

"I love you too, Taz," she said. "And I think Spitza does too."

He patted the bird. "Does this mean you will consider what I said about Sadamar?"

With a sore groan, she stood. "You became my servant to earn your Reacher talon, so once this is over, your servanthood is revoked." She hesitated a moment to let him squirm before finishing, "We are friends first, got it? After all you've endured for me, I am going to build House Janka an estate, and you'll have a footman of your own."

"And if I want to remain your footman?"

She grabbed his forearm and hauled him to his feet. The effort made her woozy—a reminder she still badly needed rest before trying anything stupid with the Buried Temple—so he had to keep her from falling. "Help me do this, and I'll ensure you're the richest footman on the entire continent of Brakesh. First, though, we need to find a way into the most guarded temple on the continent."

45

DECEPTION'S HEART

"When facing a deceiver, one must either unravel the heart of their lie or destroy it." – Mataron Tongast, emperor of Kelosh

Nikoza closed her eyes before the Chamber of Scions' doors and drew a long breath, silently repeating Nex and Hazat's plan in her head. Chatik would demand she reveal the Ashes of Dawn's location, and she would do exactly that. It would, however, be where Nex's rebels were lying in wait for an ambush.

Deception. Such a thing would never have crossed her mind a season ago, but she found herself standing between violent revolutionaries and her uncle who had violated the sanctity of her very thoughts. He would not do so again. Mind Reaching could not heavily influence those who knew it was happening, so for now, she would simply pretend Chatik had swayed her. This was what it took to free her grandfather's people.

"I would recommend not testing our king."

Nikoza startled at Gregorzon Niezik suddenly standing at attention beside her. Like a good brigadesman. He had helped free the rebel whose Ashes of Dawn had shot Chatik in the back, but he'd not conspired with Nex to destroy the Crimson Court from the inside.

"His trip, wherever it was, did not go well?" she asked, but her true question lurked beneath. Gregorzon knew she doubted Chatik and had freed Nex. Would he keep the secret?

He glanced warily at the nearby servants. Silver veils covered their faces, making them faceless and nameless, just like Hazat claimed was the goal of the Crimson Cause. "Rumor has it, he has been in a frantic search for Lady Lilita Pikezik," he whispered. "His wife stole their children and disappeared after the coup. I wonder if he found her."

"I would be frantic as well if my children were taken," Nikoza said.

"What if your most valuable prisoner was?"

She tried to hide her uncertainty, but worry painted itself across her face. "There was much to learn through following them to the Ashes of Dawn. That is thanks to your assistance."

His eyes narrowed. Flames curled within their waves of silver. "Did you earn their trust? Will you reveal to our king the location of these traitorous lowborn?"

"Remember, I saved their lover and now them," Nikoza replied, snapping her gaze back to the door. She could not get distracted by appearances or that weird flutter in her heart when Gregorzon was near. The Crimsons were a pack of povniks. Trusting any of them could mean her death, or worse, considering what Chatik was capable of. Except she had trusted Hazat…

"I will report my findings to the king," she continued. "Etal is still missing, but I know how to uproot the entire lowborn resistance within Kalastok. Our capital will be united."

The doors suddenly lurched open, startling her into silence. She sucked a sharp breath through her teeth and prepared a princess's smile. Being a Crystal Brigade sergeant was new to her, and so was spying. This, though, was a familiar process of pretending to be confident and cordial among the elites.

Vanzearik, the other Spirit Reacher in her brigade, awaited her just within the Chamber's doors. He had reported her according to Hazat, and now, he flexed his taloned hand at his side. Breathless lurked behind.

This was a mistake.

All Nikoza's instincts told her to flee, but she couldn't. It would be an admission of guilt. Her actions had drawn enough suspicion already, and the only way forward was to trust the plan she had concocted with Nex and Hazat.

"Where is he?"

Nikoza flinched as her uncle's question rang through the Chamber of Scions like the calling bell. Seated on the throne, his posture was slumped, boils and rot covering his exposed skin, but the three Crimson ministers stood proud around him. All watched her.

"Professor iz Noshok has fled the capital," she said, eyes downcast to feign disappointment, as she descended the steps with Vanzearik's breathless at her back.

Chatik needed to believe she had complied with his Mind Reached commands. Those deep-seeded desires of the Crimsons still twisted many of her thoughts, but all she needed to do now was give him the information Nex wanted him to know.

"It appears that the Ashes of Dawn were not the masterminds behind his escape," she continued as she stopped on the narrow path before the throne, "but merely mercenaries hired for the job. Unfortunately, our Reachers left Nex with significant gaps in their memory. I had to rely instead on their lieutenants for information, and since they lacked the same trust in me, there was only so much I could uncover for now."

Chatik pulled on his charcoal suit, which had become caught underneath him on the throne. It was of fine make from their family's Bartol tailors, and the shirt collar beneath flicked up to grace his jaw in the popular Ezmani style. The lost, sunken eyes and sagging skin above were hardly as presentable. Even a Body Reacher could not fix the scars of Realm Taint.

"That is a long-winded way to say that you failed," he said, wheezing with each breath.

Tzena Oliezany stood at his side with her Crystal Brigade coat labeling her as a Shadow Reacher. She donned the captain's golden glass bracers and looked fondly at Chatik. "Perhaps there is more she is not telling us, my king."

"Does it matter?" Qaraza Uziokaki replied in a condescending tone that made Nikoza's skin crawl. "It is as Vanzearik told us: Lady Nikoza exploited her position within the Crystal Brigade to release an enemy of the Cause. Did she not hesitate as well during Etal's execution, allowing him to escape with the false cure that is now spreading throughout the population?"

Uzrin Ioniz grinned. "My Truth Reachers could ensure she admits all she learned from the lowborn."

"Let my niece speak for herself," Chatik said as pink Mind and white Truth wisps surged across the Chamber to impress his will upon her. "Be honest, Nikoza."

"Nex trusts me because of my actions," she replied, keeping her head low to hide her nerves. Those wisps swirled about her as she considered her next words. Chatik had managed to convince her they were not influencing her before, but she saw his corrupting power for what it was now. Defiance was her only choice.

"Nex showed me a bunker where the Ashes of Dawn are hiding," she admitted, not offering specifics. Beneath Truth Reaching, she needed to tell *some* truth. Not necessarily all of it.

Uzrin flared his broken nose as he rolled a quarter-kena coin through his fingers at the rear of the throne platform. The crystal dragon once would have lurked there, but it was enthralled in the war against Kelosh, far from here. "Where are those bastards hiding? Remember, they harbor the one who shot your uncle—our king—in the back."

"There was an abandoned building in the Shadow Quarter," she said, careful with every word.

"But *where?*" Chatik snapped like some savage beast. He bared his teeth and leaned forward with his nails digging into the armrests. "Where are the Ashes of Dawn, and where is that cursed professor?"

Nikoza staggered back, the pit down to the Spirit Crystal feeling like a gaping maw around her. If she failed, it would devour her and all hope of rebellion. "I confess that I became badly lost within the Shadow Quarter's alleyways. However, Nex told me where to find their weapons caches along the street they called Iron Alley."

"Lies! Do you play me for a fool, girl?" Chatik replied, rising with some effort and grabbing a black cane threaded with glass. He met her with a wild gaze. Not that of a king or cunning scheme, but a Tainted madman. "Young Gregorzon kept me informed about your creeping doubts and betrayal. Vanzearik followed you to the Ashes of Dawn's safehouse, and his report confirmed my suspicions! I see your resistance to my influence now. You give enough to evade my Truth Reaching, but though the Cause presses into your mind, your heart remains closed."

That very same heart sank as footsteps approached from behind Nikoza. She need not look back to know the scent of smoldering Tystok willow wood and juniper.

"I am sorry, my lady," Gregorzon said, stopping beside her on the narrow path. The pit down to the Spirit Crystal stretched to either side of them. A horrible thought told her that a Water Reached wave could throw him into it, but that would accomplish little except to doom her further. "My loyalty is to the Crimson King. It was my duty to tell him the truth of what you had learned."

How much of it? She had not expressed her desire to oppose the Crimson Court to him, just to free Nex. Doubts were not treasonous, and that offered her a way out.

"Once again, I confess that I have had my doubts," she said, words pouring out of her faster than she could think, "but I have not betrayed the Commonwealth or our people! This Spirit Plague is ravaging lowborn and scions alike. I cannot comprehend why we would want it to continue. Professor iz Noshok offered a cure, and Nex claims it is true! Why throw him to the guillotine, mocking the masses' hope for survival?"

Chatik approached, each strike of his cane against the marble ringing through the Chamber. "Spirits. They are the key to Zekiaz, to Ezman's survival, and to our ascension."

"Do you mean the awakened spirits the plague creates from the dead?" She tried to play the innocent princess, but her voice shook from fear and anger alike. If the Crimsons knew where the Ashes of Dawn's safehouse was located, she needed to warn Nex before it was too late. All she needed was to escape the Chamber without suspicion. "Our Spirit Reachers and breathless protect people from them. That was why I suggested the western city towers, but those towers target the lowborn instead."

He stopped before her. Only hundred-hours before, he had stood tall and handsome, but he truly was Tainted now. Every thought became a struggle in his eyes as his body creaked like that of a man twice his age.

"Those awakened were once a threat," he said, "but we have made them an opportunity. You see, the breathless were our creation through Spirit and Mind Reaching, transforming terrifying awakened into thinking spirits which we command. We no longer need glass to protect ourselves! Instead, we created an army, and the plague is the conduit. We need only a cure for the chosen scions."

Horror twisted Nikoza's expression. She stepped back, a hand held to her breast. "Our realm has countless spirits gifted to us by the Crystal Mother! Why kill so many when we could grant this mind to them?"

"It is already incredibly toilsome to turn an awakened into a breathless," Qaraza said, waving her Spirit Reacher talon through the air like a conductor. "Beginning with a drifter instead means utilizing a Life Reacher to first create an awakened, and experienced, trustworthy ones are rare—especially when we face wars on two fronts. Of course, few would *want* to create an awakened anyway. It is much easier to convince our Mind Reachers to tame awakened."

"I cannot fathom how many people have suffered and perished for this," Nikoza said. "Is this truly the only way for us to survive against our foes?"

Chatik gestured in Qaraza's direction. "Do not burden yourself with military strategy. Lady Qaraza shall deploy the breathless at the most opportune time and not a moment sooner. They are a strategic advantage that Kelosh will learn to counter if we act too quickly. In the meantime, be assured our forces and House Bartol mercenaries have our family's estates in Anukit well protected."

"All of this is beyond imagining." She clenched and unclenched her fists at her side. She wanted so badly to lash out, to fling him into the pit with her Water Reaching, but he had revealed his immense power during the execution. Returning to Nex was her only hope. "Why have you hidden your plans from me? Why did you assassinate my grandfather—your own father—in a time of war?"

Chatik's lip curled, and his gaze snapped away from her for a moment, as if fixing on some unseen person. "He was weak!" he said as his voice turned raspy once again. "Jazuk would not see the inevitability of our defeat to Kelosh's superior might and technology. As for you..." He paused, muttering to himself.

"The Crystal Heir," Tzena declared. "The one who shall be the face of the new order to come."

Nikoza tried to answer, but her swimming mind offered none. Hazat had mentioned that title, had he not? It all seemed lost to her. One thing, though, was clear.

"You want *me* to inherit the crown?" she asked. "What of the scions? Shall they not vote on the next monarch?"

"My successor shall inherit the Crimson Cause, our dream," Chatik said, throwing out his arm, as if speaking to the entire Chamber. "My name will be scarred by the atrocities we must commit to ready this nation for change. When my end comes, it will be up to the Crystal Heir to bring Ezman—and all of Zekiaz—into a new era of crystal. One where we need fear neither spirits nor empires."

"The Crimson Cause... A paradise for all scions."

He nodded slowly. "We foresee a realm where those of the purest scion blood oversee and protect the lowborn who do not bear the blessings of our crystal. For that to happen, the old way must crumble, allowing for a firebird to rise from the ashes." He extended an open hand to her. "You are my preferred choice to become the Crystal Heir, and that meant ensuring you were seen as a reformer for all the people, even if the lowborn scorn your blood. Tell me what you know of these rebels. Become our firebird, dear Nikoza. A leader to grant hope to Ezman in our darkest hour."

"Why me?" She glanced down at his hand. "And what about Vocka? I have not heard you refer to the Commonwealth since the coup."

"The Commonwealth of Two Nations was a flawed experiment. No pure-blooded Vockans are scions, and they therefore are insignificant to Ezman's glory. You, though, are of the greatest importance. We need a figurehead who is young, cares for the nation, and has the ability to unite." Since she had not taken his hand, he snatched hers instead, gripping far too tightly. "Who better to do that than you? You are born of the great House Bartol, niece of King Chatik the First, granddaughter of King Jazuk the Fourth, and a sergeant of the Crystal Brigade! When so many around you are perceived by our populace as selfish, old schemers, you inspire those most in need."

Nikoza swallowed. What had she gotten herself into by returning? She had expected a confrontation for freeing Nex, not to be named as some sort of future savior for Ezman. If this could be considered saving it at all...

"You speak as if we are to be destroyed," she said, aghast.

"Tell me where the rebels are!" he shouted. A coughing fit followed, but he looked no less of a menace when it was finished. "This is your final opportunity."

The Truth Reaching had worn off, and Nikoza's will hardened against the uncle who'd once protected her, cared for her. This was not that man. "I cannot allow you to turn innocent people to ash, or worse, your breathless slaves."

A warped, terrifying smile stretched his lips. "Your disapproval was exactly why I wished for more time. Unfortunately, I underestimated your will and the Taint of my new power. It makes this all so much harder." He raised his talon to her cheek, and a chill shot through her at its bitter touch.

"What do you mean?" She tried to pull away, but his grip tightened on her hand. "Please, Uncle, unhand me!"

"I am sorry, but until the time comes, you will be confined to your chambers under charges of treason. It will make you appear as a martyr for the people after what we now must do to prepare the way." He released her, nodding to Gregorzon. "Lord Gregorzon shall ensure your security until the time comes. All your communications shall be filtered through him, and maids shall be thoroughly checked when they enter or leave your chambers. I had hoped to convince you of the Crimson Cause. In the end, however, what comes next does not require your approval."

Nikoza scowled with her arms held across her chest, all his deception peeling away against the pure horror she now faced. "I shan't help you. Find another heir!"

"You misunderstand," Chatik said, pulling from his pocket the stone he had wielded during Etal's escape. The Unity Crystal. It shimmered an impossible number of colors, appearing as the most saturated of any hue before taking another when he shifted it. "Every decision you have made to this point has been guided by me through this stone from the core of the Crystal Realms, and every decision you make as my heir will be with the Cause consuming your spirit. If that fails, then the Crimson Court will reinforce our desires through other means."

The Crimson King stepped back to the throne and settled upon it. Exhaustion, not victory, held his face. "We tried to enlighten you softly."

Gregorzon took a step closer with a prisoner's glove in his grasp. "For the good of Ezman, put this over your talon and come quietly," he said to Nikoza before lowering his voice to a whisper. "You might not believe it at the moment, but I am acting in your best interests."

"You have betrayed my trust," she replied with the raised, confident chin of the matriarch she should have been. It was a false mask, but with her stomach churning and her mind spinning, there was little else she could do against powers within Chatik's grasp.

The Fire Reacher glanced at the pit, its depths far enough below to whistle in the Chamber's cold silence. "There are worse things than inheriting all the power in Zekiaz."

What could be worse than becoming the Crimsons' puppet, forced to enact their vicious wills? Nikoza worried for Nex and the lowborn who Chatik sought to enslave. They had planned for her to lead the Crimsons into a trap west of the Kala, but she'd underestimated what they already knew. The Ashes of Dawn were doomed, and it was all because of her.

When she gave a reluctant nod, Gregorzon slipped the prisoner's glove over her Crystal Brigade one. Her chance to Reach was gone. She knew any resistance would only lead to Chatik responding with greater power through that strange Unity Crystal. Still, she couldn't help but feel as if she should do *something* as she followed Gregorzon out of the Chamber.

She had returned to the Crystal Palace to further her plot against the Crimson King. Just like with her grandfather, though, Chatik had planned far ahead. He'd trapped Nikoza in his web, and as she marched toward her velvet prison, it was up to her to find some way to free herself before his terrible predictions came to pass.

ESSENCE OF FIRE

"Listen to the rhythm within. Know when it aligns with the waves and when it smolders like the great fires." – Keero Tink, Vitrian philosopher

The southern sun granted a glorious warmth as Radais removed his helm and stopped Vuk at the edge of a winding switchback. In his twenty years as a Glassblade, he'd seen everything from Kalastok's glass mansions to Akaamilion's massive pit down to the Spirit Crystal. Nothing matched the glory of the Vockan Mountains.

He took the moment to pull out his sketchbook and charcoal, capturing the towering peaks, swooping valleys, and the spirits hovering over it all. Spirits which his apprentice could speak with at will.

"What are those ones saying?" he asked Wanusa when she pulled her ibex up beside Vuk. With her sword as the only glass on her person now, she hardly looked the part of a Glassblade. But Radais was determined to change what it meant to be a warrior in the Order. After all, didn't the Whisperers seek the same protection of pure spirits?

Wanusa smirked. "Are you going to ask me about every spirit we see?"

"Until I'm done being curious," he said, continuing his sketch.

"So, that'll be never."

He eyed her. Though amused, he kept the stern expression of a commander, just like Miv always had. "It hasn't worked every time. You have become a warrior, but you're once again an initiate with Whispering. Remember, to become a master—"

"I must practice like a master," she finished with her posture perfect in her saddle, but her head dropped. "Miv said the same thing."

He patted her on the shoulder. There was a time for stringent training and a time for empathy. That was one lesson Miv had failed to teach him. "She would be proud of you, you know?"

She offered only a forced smile as she pressed her fingers against her crystal collarbone. It pulsed a brilliant silver, and her breaths fell into line with the pattern. "I'll call those spirits. Just stay still, or they'll get scared away by your armor."

So he backed Vuk a few strides from her. That had been enough in the past, and like she said, he'd asked her to do this multiple times already in the couple days since her Deepening. His point about her practicing was true, but there was also a selfish desire behind the request. The ones Wanusa had successfully called so far talked vaguely about disturbances to the west or their need for Spirit Essence. He held hope that one knew more about what the Vanashel planned or how numerous they were. Until Wanusa refused, he'd keep trying.

Mariana and Lazan stopped on a switchback below as Wanusa's voice rose in the Spiritspeech. Like the humming song the Saleshi had used to call spirits from the deep in Akaamilion, it held no recognizable words, but followed the tempo of the crystal.

No spirits answered immediately. That wasn't much of a surprise, as she had only succeeded with half of her attempts so far. Mariana claimed that was better than most young Whisperers managed, but the frustration was evident on Wanusa's face, sweat clinging to her brow.

"Don't strain yourself if this one is difficult," Radais told her. "You'll need your strength."

Mariana clicked her tongue. "She cannot hear you while Whispering until she finds a balance. While she learns, it is crucial that her entire being is invested into connecting to the Essence of the spirits."

"She can't help us defeat the Vanashel if she pushes herself too far," he replied. "You've yet to teach her how to combat or even tame spirits, just how to talk to them."

The elder Whisperer closed her eyes and drew a long breath, hands held palm up beside her. "I never claimed this would lead to *immediate* victory over the Vanashel."

Radais scowled. "Did you ever intend to help us in the battle ahead, or was this always about gaining another Whisperer for your ranks?"

"Anger will not bring you victory either," Mariana said without opening her eyes. "I have done nothing but aid your cause, and the Vanashel will come no matter what you do to me."

"How have you helped us defend Vocka against the Vanashel?" he asked. "You claimed this journey would help us, but now you claim otherwise. Which is it?"

"Was the Awakening ended in a single battle?"

Radais furrowed his brow. "It never ended. The awakened still haunt us, but we learned how to fight back."

Her eyes opened, and she looked from Lazan to Radais, her expression carrying some deeper weight. "Do you expect different from this emergence of thinking, societal spirits? Awakened spread like a disease, feeding off the Spirit Essence of pure spirits and humans alike, but they are disorganized. Humanity now faces foes which can cooperate and create more of themselves. Not to mention the Bound Ones, who can control breathless and may surpass any mortal Reachers."

"You expect us to lose, then?" Lazan asked, thumbing his talon. "Have the spirits told you as such?"

Wanusa finished her song before Mariana could reply. The girl wrinkled her nose at her failure until she noticed Radais's fury, her eyes widening to saucers. "What is happening??"

"Explain yourself, Whisperer," Radais told Mariana. "Enough with the secrets."

She nodded down the slope, then drew up her robe's hood. "Let us make camp. It is late anyway, and a full explanation will take some time."

As the elder Whisperer rode off, Wanusa watched with growing shock. She shook her head, as if to break free of a heavy sleep. "I don't understand," she said once Mariana was out of earshot. "Things were going well with you three before, and now I come out of a Whispering trance to see a gun drawn. Did I do something wrong?"

"Not at all," Lazan replied, holstering his pistol. "However, it appears Mariana kept further secrets from us about your Deepening."

Radais took her arm. "She misled us. Your powers will help, but she says our victory will come *eventually*, not in this battle."

Wanusa's shoulders slumped. "Oh… I guess I shouldn't have expected to change things so quickly. The spirits didn't even answer this time, so why could I expect to win a battle?"

She pushed her ibex into a trot, hurrying after Mariana and leaving Radais in a spray of melting snow. Lazan fell in beside Radais as he followed. "That all could have gone better," the Reacher said. "How are we going to handle this? Your commanders will be displeased when they learn their leader and best healer left to chase a chance of success in a future battle we may not survive to see."

"We'll hear Mariana out," Radais said as he rolled his tight shoulders. The argument had his body primed for a fight, and it was used to getting one. "There may be something else she has up those wide sleeves of hers. Otherwise, we'll march against the Vanashel as we always planned."

"Are you sure that isn't suicide?"

"No, but it's our job to protect Vocka. I intend to do that to the best of our abilities."

They joined the Whisperers down the slope and made camp in a tense silence until Mariana settled on a log. She rubbed her thighs with a pained expression as Radais approached Wanusa, who was aggressively tying her ibex to a tree. She snapped the knot shut when she noticed him.

"I'm fine. I promise."

He huffed and crossed his arms. "Is that why you're choking Ereniany?"

"What? Oh, spirits!"

She turned to see her ibex fighting the tight rope she'd tied the wrong way around its neck. Quickly, she drew a knife and slashed the rope instead of dealing with the intricate knot. Relief flooded her face as the rope slipped off Ereniany, but dread soon followed.

"We should've never left the army," she said, plopping herself at the base of a conifer, its needles tickling the ruffled hairs atop her head.

Teenage pouting was not unfamiliar to him, but he wasn't all that skilled at dealing with it either. So, he decided to address it in the way he handled his own sorrow: drawing.

He fetched his sketchbook and joined her at the tree's base. She had the great height of a Vockan, but he was even taller, so the tree's needles did more to his scalp than tickle. It was a worthy sacrifice.

"Tell me what you saw when you completed your Deepening," he said, opening to an empty page.

She raised a curious brow at him. "We should go back to Mariana. She's waiting."

"And she can wait a bit longer, especially after what she's put us through." He offered the gentlest smile he could manage, despite his annoyance at the situation. "Humor an artist, won't you? Otherwise, I'm just going to sit here and make you uncomfortable until you give me a convincing smile."

"Fine."

She ran her hands through her tangled hair and tried to pick free the needles—a futile effort—as she explained her experience during the Deepening. Before, she had avoided describing her brother's spirit. There was a richness to her descriptions now, though, and Radais did his best with mere charcoal to capture the immensity of the picture her words painted.

Thousands of spirits. Her half-formed brother reaching out for her amid the pulsing beat of the Spirit Crystal's rhythm. It was something of the legends, but it had been very real for her.

That thought struck him. To her, the Deepening had been both a reconnecting point with her brother and her chance to prove herself among the Glassblades. Her hope for both relied on them pushing the Vanashel out of Iliafa, allowing her to search for the second half of Inrius's spirit. She'd heaped the weight of mountains on her shoulders. Of course she felt like a failure compared to the impossibility of her goals.

"I hope you know that Lazan and I will help you find your brother's spirit," he said, adding her to the sketch with her hand extended toward her brother's spirit. "No matter what happens, the three of us are together in this. Understand?"

She lifted her head just the slightest. "What about the Vanashel, or protecting Vocka?"

It was a smart question, and one he should've foreseen. Unfortunately, he didn't have an immediate answer. All this time, he'd wrestled with why Miv had chosen him to be supreme defender. A commander needed to look out for the good of all their warriors instead of risking everything for those closest to them. His efforts to save Miv and now protect Wanusa weren't strategic, but guided by his heart. He figured a commander should regret that. He didn't.

"We'll still do what we can," he said with false confidence. She had enough concerns without worrying about his position. "But sometimes, we can only handle the problems that are within our control. I can't promise the army we have will stop the Vanashel, but with good people like you trying to understand the spirits, I know we'll figure it out."

Wanusa considered that for a moment before looking at him with her brows pinched. "Zekiaz can't ever be the same as long as breathless exist."

Radais shrugged, his armor making a hell of a racket. "Things change. My father passed to the spirits not a season ago. My last lover died and became a breathless, bringing you under my glass wings." He swallowed as his voice cracked. For the last few hundred-hours, he'd managed to lock away his sorrow and focus on his duty, but it flooded free now. "The point is: Life is never the same as it was. You've got a chance to save your brother. If I can help it, I'm not going to let you live with the regret that I do."

Her arms were suddenly around him, and he found himself crying into her shoulder. Spirits, he was supposed to be reassuring her, not burdening her with his emotions. He'd avoided one pitfall and stumbled right into another.

"Sorry," he mumbled. "I came over to make sure you were alright, and now you're the one consoling me."

She gave him a solemn smile. "You reminded me of something important."

"Yeah?" He scoffed at himself. "What's that?"

Rising, she grabbed his arm and hauled him to his feet with considerable strength for such a young woman. When he complied, she thumped her chest. "A Glassblade protects the pure spirits and listens to our own."

"Huh. Maybe we should make you supreme defender if you're going to spout wisdom like that." He took a long breath to rid himself of his sniffles, then ruffled her hair to get the last needles free. "C'mon. The elder spirit is waiting for us."

They found Lazan sitting beside Mariana on the log. He sat comfortably, legs crossed in a posture Radais could only describe as notably urban—quite the contrast to his rugged beard.

"Are you ready to discuss the paths ahead?" Mariana asked.

Radais bowed his head. "I am."

"I'm glad to hear it, Supreme Defender," she replied, a hint of amusement in her eyes, "but you shall not face the path ahead alone. Our scion with a quick draw of his pistol has already agreed to be cordial." Her gaze flicked to Wanusa. "Will our newest Whisperer also take the next step?"

Wanusa took a soldier's stance and clasped her hands behind her back. "I'll do whatever I must to find my brother's spirit… and hopefully defeat the Vanashel too."

"Half his spirit," Mariana corrected. "Half of him is with you—a fact we will address. Wielding bonded spirits as a weapon against your foes is a dangerous and toilsome endeavor, but it is not the only power we discovered on that mountain."

"What do you mean?" Radais asked, crossing his arms.

Something sparked in Wanusa's fiery eyes. "Of course! The crystals. You took the remaining ones from that circle."

"One of Light and another of Fire," Lazan noted. "Both were dull if I remember correctly."

Mariana patted his arm. "Always trust a scion to notice crystal.

Both of you are correct. I took the crystals in wait of the right moment."

She reached into her wide sleeve and pulled free a pouch that had been wrapped around her wrist. From it, she took the burnt orange Fire Crystal, holding it wrapped in a rag. The crystal was jagged and cracked, as if aggressively broken from the larger crystal, and a warm glow pierced its core.

"It's not dull," Radais said, stepping closer and taking the sight to memory. This was the only Fire Crystal he'd ever heard of on Zekiaz, and he needed to get every detail right in his sketches.

Lazan tried to touch it, but the Whisperer snatched her hand back. "How do you refill a crystal beyond its realm?" he asked. "We barely understand why our talons refresh for a Reach every hour or so."

"Wisdom passed down through generations," she replied. "Since you are bound to the Spirit Crystal, your talon fills its Essence while you are within Zekiaz. Crystals from other realms do the same when they are within their home realm, but here, their realms' Essences find us through other means."

Wanusa gasped. "Like our bonfire! I saw you messing with it, but didn't want to question you."

"Precisely," Mariana said, displaying the Fire Crystal, but still holding it with a rag instead of her bare hand. "Dawnrise couldn't offer enough Light Essence to quickly refill the Light Crystal. Fire, though, we can manipulate. By placing the Fire Crystal near the flames, the Essence of the Fire realm entered its matching crystal, allowing it to regain its power. I offered you a way to combat the Vanashel. Instead, I bring two: both Wanusa's Whispering and the first pureblooded Vockan Reacher." She looked at Radais with her lips drawing to a narrow line. "Despite our differences, Supreme Defender, you have proven to me that your spirit's desires are aligned with your own."

Radais's heart stopped. He wanted to run, but stood his ground, gritting his teeth as he tried to comprehend what she'd said. Him, the first Vockan Reacher without scion blood? Some may have dreamed of such power, but it terrified him to his very spirit. A Glassblade's sword and armor were to defend. They were physical items, real. Magic was the work of shamans and Reachers, not warriors.

"I'm no Reacher," he insisted.

Lazan stood slowly, rubbing his hands nervously across his thighs. "Becoming a Reacher is not like the Deepening. You need not surrender a portion of yourself as Wanusa has done. Touch the crystal, and it is over."

"Such an inelegant way to describe the ability to draw magic from other worlds," Mariana said with a click of her tongue. "Of course, a Reacher does not hold the pure connection of we Whisperers, but we all weave Essence for powerful ends."

"Why would this even work?" Radais asked. "And why me? There are plenty of Glassblades who'd jump at the chance."

Mariana gestured to Wanusa with an open hand. "Close your eyes and feel the rhythms of our cores. How does it relate to the crystals among us?"

Wanusa did as she said and drew a long breath, pressing her fingers against her crystal collarbone. "There's two rhythms in us, both from the Spirit Crystal and our cores. The rhythm of our cores is the same as Radais's and the Fire Crystal's."

"Describe it."

"The Fire one is constantly shifting, growing loud and rapid before falling to…" Wanusa hesitated, wriggling her mouth as she thought. "It's almost like a crackle of a campfire after we've dumped water on it."

Radais held a hand to his chest. Covered by his breastplate, he couldn't feel his heartbeat, and there was definitely no rhythm like the one she described. If his time among spirits, Reachers, and now Whisperers had taught him anything, though, it was that there was far more in the unseen than he could ever know.

"What of the other rhythm?" Mariana asked. "The one held by Lazan and our Spirit Crystals."

Silvery wisps rose from Wanusa as she breathed out, forming an indistinct form which slowly swirled around her. It gave Radais the distinct memory of his childhood dog's excitement whenever he'd returned to their family pastures. Was this her brother's spirit?

"The Spirit rhythm is gentler," Wanusa said. "It's like how a drifter moves, wandering."

Mariana smiled, then returned her attention to Radais. "Do you see? Just as the scions of Zekiaz hold the Spirit rhythm in their cores, we Vockans hold that of Fire. It should allow us to create a Reacher with a Fire Crystal. Like with Spirit Crystal, it will tie you to another realm—most likely Fire itself—but we won't know until you try."

Radais clenched and unclenched his fists. He did see why it might work now, but that changed nothing about his desires. Facing the Vanashel's Earth Bound One had convinced him to add a metal edge to his blade. Even that made him uneasy. A glass sword had the singular focus of slaying aggressive spirits, and he didn't want weapons or magic capable of harming people. He'd seen Ezmani politics in Kalastok and heard enough stories of war. What would becoming a Reacher draw him into?

"I can't," he said, gaze averted. "Wanusa has already completed the Deepening. Couldn't she become a Reacher too?"

"Few men would reject such power," Mariana said as she stood. "Perhaps your spirit truly is aligned to its purpose, or are you afraid of change?"

He huffed. "Everything has changed lately. I'm not afraid of that, but I am afraid of hurting people… and myself. Taint is real. Lazan says all Reachers endure it at some point, and I've seen its effects on both body and mind."

"Very well, but you should sleep on it and discuss the possibility with Wanusa. As Lazan says, the process is quick, so we may conduct it quickly come morning should you change your mind."

The Whisperer returned to their camp, leaving Lazan and Wanusa to stare at Radais as if he were insane. Maybe he was, but he found himself without regret the more he thought about his decision. It would, however, be a long night convincing his traveling family of that fact.

Lazan patted the log beside him. "Sit, both of you. It appears we have much to discuss."

WHAT LAY SHATTERED

"Nothing lasts forever. That is why my work never ceases." – Leonit Niezik, former patriarch of House Niezik

The foyer of The Confluence struck Kasia like a knife to the heart as she stepped from her Axiom portal. Spitza made a disquiet *gwah* from her shoulder at the jump, but didn't leap away as she explored what remained of her Kalastok home.

As a townhouse built alongside multiple others, there were no southern windows to allow the rising dawnrise light to grace the interior. That mattered little, as Kasia could have navigated with her eyes closed if it weren't for the debris strewn about every room. From what she could tell, the rioters had done minimal damage the night of the coup.

The Crimsons had not been so merciful.

Furniture lay on its side, cushions and drawers torn open throughout the first floor. Kikania's, Tazper's, and the other servants' quarters were disasters. Even the most basic items had been either stolen or confiscated by the Crimsons. Such things were replaceable, but she hated knowing the hurt she had caused her allies, her friends.

Spitza spooked at the appearance of Kasia's specters as she lingered in Tazper's small bedroom. She'd yet to decide if the raven could actually see the specters, or if her own startling told Spitza to be afraid too.

"They are servants, nothing more," Sazilz Uziokaki said from the hall outside, donning that atrocious brown suit he always wore. Was he choosing to haunt her by attire alone? "Attachments to them are usual for children, but your father should have beaten that out of you. A shame he never had the chance."

Kasia kicked the bedframe, sending a horrible throbbing across her foot, but she didn't care. "You are the reason he couldn't raise me! You fucking Crimsons and your Crimson Cause."

Spitza cawed sharply, either mad at the outburst or mimicking her master's fury. It sent Kasia's ears ringing as she shook her head and stormed out of the room. Sazilz stood in the way, so she shoved her way past him and headed toward the stairs.

"Go," Aliax said from the landing. "See the destruction of Leonit's legacy in your wake.

The ghost of her lover once would have given her pause, but she was too weary, too numb for heartache. Two days recovering with the Ashes of Dawn had done nothing to change what she must do for vengeance. Seeing how the Crimsons had stripped away the last of her father's pride was a much-needed reminder—her suffering was worth killing the bastards that had both ended his life and ruined hers.

Kasia regretted her decision the moment she stepped into the study. Lighting a gas lamp, she gritted her teeth at the absolute destruction of her father's priceless book collection from across the continent of Brakesh and beyond. Many were missing, but dozens lay strewn across the floor. Pages were torn, and more lay half-charred beside the fireplace beneath Leonit's purple falcon mask. There was irony in that symbol of the Children of Zekiaz overseeing the work of their apparent foes. Kasia found no humor in it as she snatched that mask.

"You claimed to be his allies," she said down at it, shooing Spitza as the raven pecked at her hair to get her attention. "Then why do you sit back and allow all his work to be lost?"

"If only it were so simple," a voice replied.

Kasia gritted her teeth, ignoring the specter as Spitza's anxious pecking grew more fervent. She was so sick of those stupid voices in her head. They'd nearly led her to her death, and now, she could barely think without one mocking her or a whole host of them cackling endlessly. Teleporting here hadn't worsened her Taint, as she'd waited plenty of time between Reaches, but before she was finished with the Crimsons, she had no doubt she would push herself too far again.

She sighed. Why did she even bother coming here? The Crimsons could be watching, and there was clearly nothing left of real value. All she had worked for in Kalastok lay in ruins. Leonit's locked, empty book was the only belonging she had left of him from this room—unless she counted the stupid mask. Despite opening that book with Leonit's hidden key, she was no closer to its meaning, nor what her father had discovered with the Children of Zekiaz.

Her foot struck a small wooden object when she shifted, drawing her gaze from the mask. A red haataamaash piece rolled its way across the floorboards until a boot stopped it.

Kasia scrambled for her revolver. The Ashes of Dawn had given her plenty of bullets, and as she drew back the hammer, she aimed at the woman waiting beneath the shattered stained-glass window that had once showed a whispering man.

"Get out!" Kasia spat at the intruder.

"You are making a mistake," the woman said as she picked up the haataamaash piece and entered the light creeping from the broken window. Beneath a purple falcon mask, she wore a layered dress of the Reshkan style with fabric draping from her sleeves. A high collar rose on either side of her neck before sweeping down to reveal her shimmering collarbone of silver crystal.

Kasia kept the gun raised. Between the woman's deep tan skin and dress, she was likely from Reshka, but that crystal was unlike anything she'd seen. Every culture had different variations of Reacher Spirit Crystals: Ezmani finger talons, Reshkan neck rings, Ogrenian eyes, Nochland wands, and Keloshan earrings. None that she knew of, though, took crystal so invasively. Even Ogrenian crystal eyes were merely a crystalline structure ringing the eye, not actually replacing it entirely. This structure, though, seemed to consume the woman's collarbone and the thin line of flesh running down the center of her neck.

"I doubt this is a mistake," Kasia said, carefully stepping closer to ensure better odds of hitting the target. Her duel in the Raviak Forest years before had proven she wasn't the best shot. Against a Reacher like this, she may only have a single chance. "You have broken into my house, and you are *clearly* a Reacher. Give me a reason not to shoot you."

The woman chuckled. "Raising a gun at someone like me is hardly the mistake." She mirrored Kasia's advance, gloved hands out. "Your mistake is stepping foot in this accursed city at all when you are needed elsewhere."

Kasia scoffed. Whether it was the Crimson Court or the Children of Zekiaz, these secret organizations always acted so mysterious instead of answering the damn question. "Who are you to tell me where I am needed? You and your masked friends love to show up at random, acting like you're helping, but where were you when Chatik and the Crimsons toppled the government?"

"King Jazuk the Fourth was no friend to our organization," the woman replied, continuing to slowly draw nearer to Kasia. "Besides, we work for the advancement of the realm, not for a single nation— or two which are joined."

"Stop moving," Kasia insisted, thrusting the gun toward her until she froze. "Why are you here? What is it that you claim I should be doing instead?"

The woman lowered her head, hands clasped before her. "You do not trust us. That is understandable, given your past. Tell me. Did your friend, Nex, reveal from where they received their supplies when the rest of western Kalastok scrounges for the smallest morsel?"

Nex had not, but Kasia wasn't ready to admit that. "It figures you were the ones who wanted Etal free. After all, he was one of your agents."

"Paras ik Lierasa, may he soar with the spirits, was a son of Zekiaz, but Etal is merely a convenient partner. I believe he would rather be rid of us. This plague, though, is not confined to Kalastok or even the Commonwealth, and he bears more insights into Zekiaz than a hundred other scholars combined."

Kasia rolled her eyes. "So you will protect people from the plague the Crimsons created, but from not the Crimsons themselves?"

The woman raised her head again, then stepped within arm's reach, Kasia's pistol pressing against the forehead of her mask. "There is so little that you know, dear child of Leonit. We have worked against the Crimson Court since the moment of its conception, but they are mere infants compared to us." She held out the haataamaash piece in her open palm. "You play a pivotal part in our strategy, so it is quite difficult to plan when you disappear at random, only to appear where you do not belong. Shooting King Chatik as you did has only served to make him erratic, unpredictable. Ever-worsening Taint inflicts him, and you have disturbed the timing of his eventual demise."

"I want him dead *now*."

The woman pressed the piece into Kasia's free hand. "Because as you stand, you are but a pawn in Zekiaz's game. You do not see the greater forces—the greater threats—at play while you obsess over the arrogant fools who killed your father."

Kasia winced as the specters demanded she kill the woman who dared insult her. She tore her gaze from the daughter of Zekiaz to her own Tainted specter, who lurked behind the desk with her unscarred face contorted into a grin.

"She says we know nothing, mocking us," the specter said, raising a letter opener and running the tip of it down her palm. Blood trickled behind and splattered onto the scattered letters on the desk. "Then let us show how frail she is."

Kasia's finger twitched on the trigger. It would be so easy to kill this taunting bitch and go on her way. Once she was done with her, she would teleport to the Buried Temple and earn the power Sadamar had promised. She didn't need the Children of Zekiaz. But she didn't need their ire either. A group that could somehow make the Ashes of Dawn's vast supplies appear in a locked down district

of the capital had resources beyond what she knew. They also held more information about her father.

Death's voices screamed as she threw down her arm and uncocked the pistol, exhaling sharply. She couldn't think with all the noise, but she forced herself to fight it.

"If you know so much," she said, "then tell me why I am in Kalastok? What is my plan that is so thoroughly ruining yours?"

The daughter tilted her head. "Orat—Death—of course. Why do you trust the Fleshweaver over those who your father held in his confidence? From what we can tell, you admire Leonit deeply."

Kasia's heart stopped. She staggered back, startling Spitza into a fit that sent the bird hopping onto the nearby mantle. The Children knew about the Death realm of Orat, but that was impossible. She'd believed she was the only Axiom Reacher. Were there others?

"How... How do you know about Sadamar?" she asked, leaning against a toppled chair to support herself. Her body had taken more of a beating in Orat than she was willing to admit to Nex or herself, and this confrontation was enough to remind her of that weariness.

"It is our responsibility to know what threats exist within Zekiaz and without." The daughter swept out her arms, and her sleeves' ribbons danced over the rubble like sparks over ash. "All of this knowledge your father collected was part of that purpose—a purpose you risk destroying by entangling yourself with a master of Death."

"The Crimsons control the spirits of those killed by the Spirit Plague," Kasia said. "Their army is potentially limitless, and I proved that neither bullets nor a Death bolt can kill their king. Sadamar commands the undead. I don't care how horrible he is on Orat. If he can grant me the power to defeat Chatik, that's all that matters."

The daughter shook her head. "Only Realm Taint may end the one wielding the Unity Crystal. We are not worried about the Crimson King, but the one he calls the Crystal Heir."

"Nex said that one of the Crystal Brigadesmen mentioned such a term."

"The Crimson Court accepted you into their ranks for their ritual to access the Axiom," the daughter said, closing in once again. "However, they did not tell you the whole of the Crimson Cause."

Kasia stood her ground. The Daughter was taller than her, but this time, when they drew face-to-face, Kasia just raised her chin. "I know now that they seek to make the lowborn nothing more than faceless, nameless slaves. They are trying to create both a nation and world ruled entirely by scions."

"Indeed, but what is important is *how* they wish to do so." The daughter looked back at the shattered window. "Leonit once told me that far more was ever accomplished through whispers than the great movements of armies. Of course, he was right, and Chatik understands this. It is why he always intended for his reign to end in defeat."

"That makes no sense." Kasia finally holstered her gun, lip twitching as she warred with the specters to manage a thought. "The Crimsons have been planning to take control for over a decade. Why would they just surrender it?"

The daughter returned her attention to Kasia. "Because there are those who seek to rule the world and those who seek to shape it. Chatik believed he would have longer to till the soils of Ezman for his successor, but the Unity Crystal's Taint is far worse than he imagined. He has been forced to expedite his plans, and your actions only hastened him further."

"I still fail to understand how that is a bad thing. The quicker he dies, the quicker I have my revenge."

"Vengeance which shall run dry the moment you realize that you have stopped nothing." The daughter gestured toward Kasia's crystal-webbed hand. "You were granted your power to return the Unity Crystal to its rightful place, were you not? That is because Chatik himself is not the threat. He seeks to invite Ezman's destruction, allowing for his Crystal Heir to emerge with the Unity Crystal and craft a nation in the ideals of the Crimson Cause. Millions will perish. Millions more will be enslaved and stripped of name, family, and purpose. With a breathless army at their back and slaves to forge their weaponry, the Crystal Heir will sweep across Brakesh and continents beyond. Killing Chatik alone will not stop it. Only securing and returning the Unity Crystal will."

Kasia wilted back into the stone fireplace. All her focus had been on defeating Chatik, but she couldn't deny the daughter's claims. If they were true, her actions against the Crimsons could serve to further their plans instead of counter them.

The daughter laid a hand on her shoulder. "Do you understand now why we fear pushing the Crimson King further to the brink? We are not yet prepared to nullify the Unity Crystal or such a great number of breathless. We require time."

"Who is she, the Crystal Heir?" Kasia asked. "Or are you afraid I'll hunt her down, just like the others?"

The daughter's voice turned sharp. "The Crystal Heir herself is not the concern. She is a vessel through which the Crimson Court shall mold Zekiaz."

Kasia threw off her arm and grabbed her by the throat. "Tell the spiritdamned truth for once! Who is she?"

"Lady Nikoza Bartol," the daughter replied without an ounce of fear.

"Nikoza?" Kasia released her. "That princess could not harm a drifter."

"They seek to twist her mind, to ensure she believes the cause. There are few scions who bother to gain favor among the lowborn, and because she has shown an ounce of care, people will listen to her when there is no one else left." The daughter's eyes tightened behind her mask. "Killing her will not change that. Nikoza may be their first option, but they would find another heir as long as they hold the Unity Crystal."

"What, then, should I do?" Kasia asked, avoiding the harsh gaze of her specter beyond. This was weakness. But she lacked answers. "You claim I'm needed elsewhere, but refuse to tell me where!"

The daughter's voice turned sharp. "Return to Lord Zinarus. Release this foolishness with the Fleshweaver and focus instead on honing your skills through the Axiom. The Confederation of Harizak represents a hope for the Commonwealth to mend its fractured pieces and challenge what is to come. Alongside them, you are a mighty weapon." She backed away, her eyes shadowed beneath that falcon mask. "Should you wish to understand that crystal on your arm and become more than a pawn, procure shadowlight. It will be quite useful in examining your father's locked away notes, and the Silent Queen has use of you yet."

"And if I choose to pursue both Sadamar's powers and the Children's answers?" Kasia challenged. Why couldn't she do both? Even if not used directly against Chatik, the power of Death would no doubt be useful in the war ahead.

"All power comes at a price, dear Katarzyna. I lost Leonit because he forgot that inherent truth, and I have no desire to lose you too."

Lose me too?

Kasia pushed away from the wall to pursue her, but before she could move more than a step, the daughter's crystal collarbone flared. Wisps of silver spiraled around her. They carried neither the forms of breathless nor the aggression of awakened, and Kasia sensed a strange joy about them as the daughter's body evaporated into a mist. Together, the wisps drifted toward the shattered window, slipping out before Kasia could lunge after them.

The window's glass cracked underfoot as Kasia righted her desk chair and collapsed into it. Spitza called out for her from the mantle, but she just pinched her nose and stared down at nothing. Spirits, what the hell had she gotten herself entangled with?

All she'd wanted was revenge for her father's murder and to restore his house to glory. Instead, her pursuit of the Crimson Court had sent House Niezik back into ruin, and she was a public enemy, scorned for killing both guilty and innocent alike. Vengeance against Chatik no longer meant killing him, but destroying the dream he would willingly die for.

Spitza scooted from the mantle, anchoring herself with talons and beak to climb down. She made her way to the desk before hopping onto Kasia's shoulder with an excited little chitter. Kasia glanced up at the bird, stroking its neck as she rolled the haataamaash piece in her other hand.

"What would you do, little raven?"

Spitza cocked her head and clacked her beak. Kasia figured she wanted food, so she unrolled a bar of grains, allowing Spitza to pick it apart as she pondered what route to take. The daughter of Zekiaz had claimed pursuing Sadamar and the power of Death would somehow make her end up like Leonit, but it could've been nothing more than a feigned threat to put her back on the track the Children wanted for her.

That made it all the more enticing.

"You've made your promises," Aliax said from the chair across the desk. He sat like lowborn men always did, his legs wide, as if he had something interesting to display. "Fight alone or join all those scion assholes down at Fort Harizak. Doesn't matter. You're going to ruin yourself and everyone around you if you don't stop."

The other specters hammered her mind with their own opinions, but Kasia focused only on him, trying her best to drown out the others. He was wrong. Whether a ghost or real, his opinion was one of the few she cared about. She wished to dam that admission like a beaver did flowing water. But she'd done so for so long that the truth poured over it, drowning her.

She was too weak to defeat the Crimson Court by herself. Against her instincts, she needed help. She needed others to believe in her… to care for her… and she would not let her Taint destroy them too.

"Why did I leave Zinarus?" she asked the gathered specters.

"His betrayal," her Tainted one replied.

"Your own arrogance," Sazilz said.

Aliax gave no answer until all the others had spouted off various accusations against Zinarus or insults of her character. He slid to the edge of his seat and placed an open hand on the desk. "Fear. You let yourself feel something for him. You let down your wall, barely, but you were ready to throw it back up the second things were out of your control. I know your heart, Kasia. It's perpetually locked, but don't throw away the key just yet."

"I will go back," she replied. "But I cannot do so until I'm ready. There is still work for me to do here, and whether I help Sadamar or not, Tazper needs a Spirit Crystal."

She tapped the haataamaash piece against the table. Despite being only twelve when her father died, she had learned much from him. One of those lessons rang as true on the game board as it did beyond: Never rely fully on a single route of attack.

"Come, Spitza," she said, releasing the piece and throwing herself to her feet. "We have a temple to rob."

THE CRYSTAL HEART

"Like a mother who holds her child close, our Crystal Mother presses our ear to her heart. Listen quietly, children, for you shall hear the beat to which all of Zekiaz dances." – Uliazina Rakazimko, anointed sister of the Buried Temple

A cold trickle ran down Kasia's spine as she teleported into the crystalline room at the heart of the Buried Temple. Here, Reachers were made. Here, the Crimson Court held near limitless Spirit Crystal. And here, she most certainly did not belong.

Her missing finger ached at the memory of descending behind the Crystal Mother's statue and taking a talon for herself a decade before. Chatik had stolen that part of her. What fraction that entailed, she didn't know, but something had felt inherently wrong within her ever since that bullet ripped through her talon and across her scalp.

She pressed her stub of an index finger against that scar above her ear. Her hair had not regrown there, and as she stared across the empty room, she found her Tainted specter knelt at its center. Reverent when she needed to be. Strong when she faced resistance.

"Keep standing there like a fool," the specter said, "and they are certain to find us."

Aliax grabbed Kasia's hand and pulled, earning a disconcerting *gwah* from Spitza. "This is your chance to do something good for once," he said. "Sadamar or not, Tazper needs this. He's worth it."

That sentiment spurred her onward, and she hurried into a run. It felt good to do so hand-in-hand with Aliax, like they once had when they'd hidden from prying eyes. Few would have approved of the heir to such a powerful house fraternizing with a lowborn so seriously. Many scions took secretive consorts, but to find true love in it was bound to taint bloodlines. What would they think of her running with a ghost?

The Crystal Mother stared at them like Kasia's own judgmental mother. Yazia was brooding back in their family's mansion while Gregorzon worked to destroy all their father had built. She hated both mothers alike, and it took restraint not to slice across the statue with her dagger.

"Focus," Aliax said. "We're close."

"How would you know?" she quipped, keeping her voice low in the echoey space. "You never descended to the Crystal."

He sneered. "Just shut up and run."

His warning rang true as rushed steps fell upon the entry stairs to the temple. Kasia cursed to herself. Coming late in the night, she'd hoped for no interruptions, or at most a couple stray worshippers. It shouldn't have been this empty, though, and those steps… A pit in her gut told her the Crimsons knew she was here.

So she practically leaped down the stairs behind the Crystal Mother. They stretched deeper into the depths with each year the scions drew from the Spirit Crystal. In truth, most of the supposedly *crystal* temple above was made of other materials and infused with bits of Spirit Crystal to grant it an ethereal shine. Her mission would have been far easier if she could've just chiseled out a section of the temple itself, but a Reacher required a pure chunk of crystal. That meant descending.

Flickering torches greeted her at each landing, revealing the frantic look on Aliax's face. Did he know something she didn't? Her pursuer had reached the statue based on the racket above, but she refused to glance back. That would cause a stumble, and she could not afford to waste a moment.

Her heart pounded by the time the stairs gave way to a metal platform. Chains in each corner connected it to the ceiling above, and hand cranks allowed for it to be raised to the top of the stairs above. For now, though, it rested at the bottom, marking the highest point where one could touch the core Spirit Crystal.

A silver, ethereal glow emanated from the Crystal. Spitza cawed at the sight, and Kasia found her hand nervously grasping for a spare bead of amber in her pocket. When she pulled the bead free, it lost its typical hue of golden honey, falling instead to a pure nothingness. Not black, but as if it were completely translucent except for the radiant awakened captured within. Blinding, it forced her to stop for a crucial few seconds.

"What is this?" she asked Aliax and the other specters who'd followed her.

But they were gone.

Only her pursuer scuffed the marble steps above, their breaths labored. They'd be here in seconds, so Kasia drew her dagger and hurried to the platform's end as Spitza clicked away in her encouragement. The platform's metallic rattle echoed that clicking in her mind. Except another noise was louder there. For once, it wasn't the specters, but her own thoughts—those terrified her more than the restless dead.

The pursuer turned at the final landing as Kasia knelt before the shimmering crystal and slammed her dagger into it. Sparks scattered from the blow. It startled her, but a shard of crystal broke free, falling into her grasp and sending the dagger slipping from her fingers.

She scrambled to grab the blade, but flames surged over it. She gritted her teeth, hands shaking at the memory of her burning arm. "Why must you ruin everything?"

Gregorzon's final step onto the platform sent a shiver down her spine. He wore an unusual crimson coat with burnt orange designs curling across it, and the glass bracers of the Crystal Brigade clasped his wrists. Those bracers reflected his Fire Reacher wisps, making it appear as if they themselves were alight.

"Ironic, dear sister," her brother replied with a cunning smirk. "I was prepared to ask you the same question." He glanced at the Spirit Crystal piece in her hand—only enough for a single Reacher. "I was shocked when our Crimson King informed me of your plans. What made you risk coming here for crystal, when we both know you cannot replace your lost talon?"

She drew her pistol and aimed it in one motion. "I don't owe you anything."

Fire cracked from the revolver's flintlock as she pulled the trigger. A *thud* followed, but she didn't look to see how badly she'd wounded him. Her aim was far from a sharpshooter's, and Gregorzon would soon respond.

Flee or try again? she considered, eyeing her dagger and her crystal-wrapped hand.

She had a crystal. Teleporting away now would allow her to complete her deal with Sadamar, but her heart throbbed at the thought of Tazper. He had waited years for her to fulfill her promise. She couldn't abandon him. Not again. And she needed every allied Reacher that she could get.

So she snatched her dagger and slammed it into the Spirit Crystal.

But the stench of smoke ignited her fear. Her hand shook, and only a thin slice separated from the main Crystal. Pain seared through her back before she could try again.

Gregorzon's firebolt stole her breath and sent tears streaming from her eyes. Her whole body convulsed from fear of fire and the agony, but gripped that single Spirit Crystal in her pocket. She'd succeeded for either Sadamar or Tazper, not both. And that *pain*…

"I do not desire your death, Sister," Gregorzon said with each step closer shaking the platform. Blood seeped from his shoulder where she'd shot him, and his gun lay strides behind. "You are a scion. Stop fighting us when we are the ones building a world for our kind."

Kasia sucked in a breath through her bared teeth. She needed to Reach and leave, but it hadn't been an hour since her last one.

Summoning a portal would draw further Taint, and with the state of her body, she didn't enjoy the thought of her impending suffering.

"You know what your problem is?" she replied, facing down her brother as she Reached with her crystal hand held behind her back. Taint followed with a nauseating sickness, but she hid the discomfort beneath her glare. "You're a coward. Talk about our kind all you want, but you betrayed our father, our house—and you betrayed me. I know I made mistakes. I know Taint has scarred my mind. But the difference between you and me is that I'm willing to admit how fucked up I am."

When Gregorzon opened his mouth to reply, Kasia spun and completed the Reach, summoning a portal to Nex's safehouse. Her Axiom Crystal flared as golden wisps burst from her hand. Gregorzon's flames crackled, but she needed only a few strides.

Another wave of heat swelled behind her as she staggered toward the portal. Her back screamed and her scarred arm throbbed from her memories. But spite was a powerful fuel, sending her through the portal a heartbeat before his next firebolt struck.

THE WARM SOUTHERN LIGHT OF DAWNRISE washed over Tazper as he turned once again at the intersection south of the Ashes of Dawn's main safehouse. Though rain poured over him and he'd worn a path into the mud, he could not stop pacing. Kasia had put herself in danger… again… and there was nothing he could do to help.

Nex had refused to send anyone into the Buried Temple with Kasia. This was her mission, not theirs, but that meant Tazper should have gone instead. Half the reason Kasia had descended into the temple was to grant him his long-awaited talon. He *wanted* to be part of that, but she had protested that it would be both dangerous and an extra strain on her Axiom Reaching.

He had learned long ago that when Kasia had entrenched her mind, it would take a team of raging bulls to pull her free. Tazper was certainly not that.

So he found himself waiting, directionless until her return. He was used to being a subordinate after all these years, and that meant handling responsibilities for House Niezik or simply accompanying Kasia as she risked her neck at every possible opportunity. It felt good to be needed, Reacher or not. Being away from Kasia made him nervous, and even more so when she was doing something for him.

A Reacher…

His legs froze beneath the shadows of a three-story tenement, its shuttered windows crooked and bricks jutting out like defensive blades that warned one not to enter. Tazper needed no more warning. The last hundred-hour he'd spent among western Kalastok's lowborn had shown him how caring and communal they could be. It had also revealed how the brutality of their lives forged them into daggers that could strike when one least expected.

Tazper flexed his gloved left hand. It shook, but not from the water streaming off the brim of his hat. Even in the rain, dawnrise steadily ridded the Commonwealth of its chill. It offered no solution for the fear gripping the footman's chest.

He had dreamed of becoming a Reacher his entire life. Minor houses could rarely afford the Buried Temple's fees without a sponsor, and so many had taken the government's offer of joining the military in exchange for a talon. Kasia's promise had likely saved him from the bullet of a Keloshan rifleman. It had left him waiting for what felt like forever, but he was moments away now.

Kasia would no doubt succeed. That wasn't his fear. Reaching had badly Tainted his mistress, and he'd endured the fallout from Aliax's death and every painful moment since. He loved her like a sister. That did not mean he desired to become her.

Running his thumb over his pointer finger, where his talon would soon rest, he pondered what realm he wished to wield. What would it feel like to Reach across the ether and command a power beyond his own body? Would it change him as it had Kasia?

That last thought worried him the most, no matter how childish it sounded. He *liked* his life. As a footman of House Niezik, he was well compensated. Kasia gave him a purpose, and few people had the chance to work so closely with their best friend. She had said this would release him from her service. Why? Plenty of great house servants were Reachers, and he was unsure what he would even do if he were not serving as her footman. Despite the Amber Dame's flaws, he was helping her fight to make things better.

He was so deep in his thoughts that he nearly jumped out of his boots when a heavy-set Ezmani woman arrived. Lexalia, he thought her name was. Like him, she wore a simple woolen coat. It had a high collar, which she pulled down to expose the Ashes' yellow neckerchief. Burn scars crept from beneath the fabric, and she quickly fixed the collar to its upright position once Tazper stopped panicking.

"Nex told me to grab you."

Tazper took a shaky breath. Was he truly ready for this? "She has returned, then?"

A nod was the only reply he got before Lexalia headed back toward the safehouse at a brisk pace. He had to jog just to keep up, and even then, she showed no interest in him falling in line beside her. Not everyone in the Ashes had taken well to scions in their presence. Most, though, had been more direct in their complaints, so this apathetic attitude caught him off guard.

It was a silly focus, but he needed the distraction. His hands were already slick with sweat, and he had this strange thought that he wasn't walking normally. Breathless swirled in the skies above. Would they think he was suspicious?

"Stop breathing like a damn factory," Lexalia muttered. "You scions never know how to keep a low profile."

He swallowed. "Apologies… I have just waited for this moment my entire life."

"*Apologies*," she mocked, smiling wryly as they passed through a narrow alley. "Talk normal. Even your Lady Kasia can do that."

"And if I told you to speak properly?"

Lexalia turned on a dime and threw him into the wall. Only a thin stream of light entered the alley, but he did not need to see to feel the tip of a knife pressing his stomach. He'd not even seen one beneath her coat. What was this? The Ashes could have already killed him plenty of times if they wanted to.

"Don't tell me what to do, scion," Lexalia said, her deep brown eyes burning like coals. She was nearly a head shorter than him, but his cowering left them at the same level. "Nex thinks we need you, but I'm not your serving girl, got it?"

Tazper managed a nervous smile. "There seems to be a misunderstanding. I'm a servant, not a master, and I did not intend to demean you in any way."

She huffed, but pulled back the blade. When he tried to wriggle free, she pressed her finger into his chest instead. "Just remember this isn't some trip for us. You'll get out of here, but this is our life."

"Kasia promised Nex she would keep supporting your organization," he replied while slipping past her.

"Yeah? What about you?"

They headed down the alley with him leading this time. It was disconcerting having such an unpredictable figure at his back, but Tazper had to admit that Lexalia's distraction had kept him from worrying about his talon for a few precious moments.

"I have neither the resources nor the power to do much for you," he finally replied as they headed down the main thoroughfare just south of the safehouse. A few Crimson watchmen leaned against a building not far away, smoking cigarettes, so he lowered his voice. "Whatever abilities my talon gives me, though, I will use to help your cause. I may be a scion, but my family is little better off than most peasants. Your toil is not lost on me."

"Words," Lexalia said. "Make 'em count."

Checking that the watchmen weren't eyeing them, they slipped down the nearby path and into the safehouse. The Ashes had their own guards. They, though, blended in with the few gathered groups of lowborn instead of wearing bright red coats that quite literally made the watchmen stick out like sore thumbs.

Tazper hesitated at the door. He drew a long breath, a tingle running up his arms.

This was it. Once he entered that safehouse, there was no turning back, and he would finally be a Reacher. Crystal Mother below, he needed to vomit. Except Lexalia gave his fear no chance to linger, snatching him by the back of his coat and practically tossing him through the door. The warehouse was empty, so he headed toward the trap door. Strangely, it hung ajar.

"Hurry down," Lexalia said with a hand pressed against his back. "Your lady looked rough. I doubt she'll be patient."

He flared his nostrils. "Why didn't you tell me that before?"

Not waiting for an answer, he flung himself down the ladder. Kasia had a knack for getting herself in trouble. If she'd failed to teleport away without avoiding injury, then Tazper would hardly forgive himself for not going with her. He *should* have been by her side!

Chaos greeted him at the bottom.

Most of the Ashes of Dawn had cleared out for daily duties, leaving an empty space among the packed bedrolls and essentials stashed around the basement. Kasia lay sprawled out in that gap with a trio of lowborn kneeling around her. Her eyes were wild. Someone had shoved a rag in her mouth to keep from screaming. And, much to her footman's shock, she was half-naked.

"Kasia!" he exclaimed, rushing to her side.

A series of gruesome burns left her back covered in raised pink and brown sections. Two of the lowborn patted down the wounds with wettened towels while the third wrapped bandages around the lesser damaged sections. Remnants of her charred clothes stuck to the burns, but sharp cuts in the fabric revealed the medics had purposely left those bits to free the rest. This hardly resembled the miracle healing of a Body Reacher, but Tazper lacked any medical expertise to challenge their methods.

Unable to aid in any real way, he offered Kasia his hand, which she gripped like a vice. "What happened?" he asked the medics since she was unable speak through the gag.

One of the medics gave him a wary look, then nodded toward the far wall. Nex gathered there with Vinnia and Jiinaan. The Ashes commander looked wholly unconcerned with the situation, only adding fuel to the fire in Tazper's belly.

"Please, Nex," he pled as Spitza screamed her own desperation from behind the medics. "Tell me what happened."

Their lip twitched. "She was screaming a whole lot when she showed up out of nowhere again. Had to gag her before she bit off her damn tongue, but she said something before that about her asshole brother, Gregorzon. I told her going to the Buried Temple was stupid, but we both know she doesn't listen."

Of course it had been Gregorzon. Kasia's brother had brought to light that her aggression against their mother was the true reason for her forearm burn, but this was pure malice. Instead of aiding his house and protecting innocents against the Crimson Court, he'd chosen to help the schemers. There were times when betraying one's house was honorable. This was hardly one of them.

Tazper so badly wanted to ask Kasia if she had successfully retrieved the Spirit Crystals, but that would be rude, given the circumstances. So he just knelt there with his hand in hers. It would have almost been nice if she weren't cutting off the blood flow from his fingers.

Some time later, the medics finished wrapping her back in protective gauze. They didn't say a word to Tazper before scurrying off to either the warehouse above or their respective areas of the basement. He was grateful there were only twenty or so Ashes down here. Given Kasia's state, she would be furious enough without the embarrassment of half the west side seeing her bare torso. That left Tazper to find her clothes.

"Would you mind supplying a spare shirt for her?" he asked Nex as Kasia pulled the gag free. A bit of bite slipped into his tone, but for once, he did not regret it. "It is inhospitable to leave a lady lying on your floor in this state of undress."

The end of Nex's mouth curled, their eyes devious. "The last shirt I gave her has a massive hole in the back."

"Nexie!" Vinnia objected before Tazper said something that would get him shot. "Would you leave me lying there?"

"She ain't lying there anymore."

Against Tazper's protestations, Kasia pushed herself to her feet. Her hair was flared out like paintings he had seen of predators from distant continents, and golden Axiom Crystal stretched across the scars on her arm. It reminded him of the time he had fallen down a well as a child. Drowning in the darkness, he'd reached toward the everbright sun until his father threw down a rope to haul him free.

Kasia showed no such desperation now. The bandages wrapped around her torso stopped below her breasts, so she stared down Nex with them exposed. Only Tazper averted his eyes. One did not closely serve a scion for as long as he had without seeing them in various states of undress, but that did not mean he wanted to see her in such a vulnerable position.

"You should be resting," he said, removing his coat to throw over her shoulders. It was sopping wet, but better than nothing.

She tugged the coat shut with a sharp nod at him. Pain lingered in her eyes. Though she was quite good at hiding it, he knew her far too well. That burn had left its mark, and she did not appreciate Nex leaving her naked.

"I have a crystal," Kasia said, stomping to a coat lying nearby. Spitza hopped onto her shoulder as she rifled through the pockets and pulled out a chunk of Spirit Crystal.

Only one.

"That crystal cost me this damned burn from Gregorzon," she said, holding it out to him, "but I'm done making you wait on my promise."

He stared down at the crystal. The basement was dim, but it still glimmered as if raised amid the everbright rays. So much power in a rock no larger than the palm of his hand…

"What about Sadamar?" he asked. "Did you only manage the one?"

The look he received was that of a frightened cat. So that was it, then. Gregorzon had interrupted her, and now, she chose Tazper over Sadamar's power. He knew better than to object to her choice. Nothing would uproot it, and he had no desire to be on the receiving end of her claws.

When he pushed past his hesitation to take the crystal, Kasia grabbed his wrist. "It won't do much good unless you touch it with your bare hand.

That pit in his stomach deepened. How could he forget

something so simple? If he was to become a Reacher, he needed to know how to handle himself under pressure. Kasia had revealed plenty of the consequences of losing control, and he had no desire to become so Tainted.

Against those doubts, he reminded himself that he did want this. Not just the power to Reach, but the power to change things, protect those he cared for, and not be a burden. It would take time. Eventually, though, he would have the skill. Kasia had chosen to trust him, so he would trust himself.

Tazper removed his glove. Then, to not allow himself a chance to back out, he snatched the chunk of Spirit Crystal and slammed his eyes shut.

"Protect me, dear Mother of the Crystal," he whispered as a tickle ran up his arm.

Kasia would surely scoff at him for his faith, but it felt right. The Crystal Mother's statue watched over the temple from which this Spirit Crystal had come. She never directly answered his prayers, but perhaps this was one.

An answer he had toiled for. An answer his mistress had suffered for.

The wait meant nothing in this moment. He had already expressed his frustration with Kasia, and since then, she'd endured her brother's flames—her worst fear—to fulfill her promise. A warmth filled him. He could be nothing but grateful for the chance to become a Reacher. This was his dream, and he wouldn't allow fears or mistakes of the past to take that from him.

As the crystal shifted in his hand, a strange connection followed. Something within him loosened when the crystal entrapped his index finger with its cold, pulsing embracing. It felt like a well-formed key sliding into its lock with ease. The *click* that followed was only in his mind, but the door beyond was to an entirely new realm.

Tazper opened his eyes to stare down in awe at the crystal talon arcing to a point across his finger. In but a passing moment, he had crossed a threshold. One that would last the rest of his life.

He was a Realm Reacher, and he promised both himself and the Crystal Mother that he would use this power for good.

AN ARMY'S WOES

"A good commander wins battles. A great one understands that is only half the war." – Theo Orinan, Keloshan major general

Ziegfried was becoming a problem.

Zinarus paced across his large commander's tent, the gears in his mechanical knee echoing those in his head. Each day brought new difficulties as a general. Whether it was the wounded from the Battle of Vamia Mines, scouting reports, desperate letters from Tiuz, or petty disputes among his soldiers, he'd not had a quiet moment since they left Vamiustok. The last thing he needed was another nuisance.

On all accounts, his newest recruit was the worst of them. Zinarus had taken a calculated risk in inviting the elitist Earth Reacher into his ranks, but those calculations had been horribly inaccurate. Now, he was trapped by his own inexperience.

Ziegfried had caused controversy from the moment he begrudgingly walked into the iz Vamiustok camp. He should have been a morale boost, bringing much needed magical backing to the force, but the cavalry blamed him for the deaths around the mine. Most well-mannered scions would have smoothed that over with charisma and gifts to the mourning. Instead, Ziegfried had done nothing but grumble and misuse his status. If only that was the worst of it.

Papers covered Zinarus's desk in the tent. Normally, they would have been war plans to discuss with his officers, but at least half these were about Ziegfried. Three women among the camp followers and one in the infantry had reported him for ordering them into his tent. Another dozen soldiers had also complained about him drinking half their beer reserves.

Reading through his officer's summaries of the incidents had Zinarus hot-blooded. He did not consider himself an angry man, but this was a disgrace, and as he had recruited the Earth Reacher, he was responsible for all of it.

The only thing that stopped him from tying up Ziegfried and letting his victims beat him senseless was that Vockan women were mighty tough. None of the three had given into Ziegfried's threats, and two had already left him with a pair of facial bruises so heavy that his makeup failed to cover it. It was not enough. Not in Zinarus's army. Those women never should have been put in that situation, and he would have a riot soon if the soldiers had to tolerate this any longer.

"Reshka would have him castrated, Zini," his Aunt Carelias said, sitting in one of the tent's spare chairs and filing her nails.

It was hardly a lady-like statement among Ezmani scions. Carelias was anything but Ezmani, though, and Zinarus couldn't chide her for it. She had spent the last few days Body Reaching to clean up his mess after the battle. Without her, he might have already faced mutiny.

"I can hardly contest he deserves it," Zinarus said, leaning against the desk as phantom pain struck his mechanical leg. That just put the reports under his nose, so he shut his eyes and tried to ignore her using his childhood nickname, Zini, to further deflate his ego. "What would Tiuz do?"

Even with his eyes shut, he felt the weight of her gaze upon him. "From what I have heard of him," she said, "he would not have recruited a pampered, arrogant fool like Ziegfried in the first place."

"Iktaros did warn me the soldiers would despise him, but I was desperate for more Reachers. It made me blind to how much fuel he would add to the fire." He sighed, wishing for the politics of Kalastok over this mess. Tiuz had warned him about war, but he had failed to explain how difficult it was just to march a few thousand people anywhere without them killing each other. "This is my mistake. If I have any hope of retaining my soldiers' trust, I cannot simply punish Ziegfried."

"What is your plan, then?"

"I will show them that my status does not exempt me from punishment." He pushed himself off the desk and started toward the tent's exit. "That means taking the whip myself as well."

Carelias didn't move, but her *tsk* forced him to stop. "Do you actually believe that will convince them you care, or are you foolishly believing hurting yourself is some justice for your error?"

"Three women were nearly raped in my camp!" he suddenly snapped, throwing out an arm. "He all but admitted he would be a headache, but I accepted him anyway."

"You did, but taking a whip will do nothing to change that. We are less than two days from Fort Harizak. Making your soldiers believe you are some kind of masochist will hardly earn their confidence." She stood, wearing a conciliatory smile. "Hold the whip yourself, and when Ziegfried screams like the fragile scion he is, announce for all to hear that he will be executed for any future transgressions."

Zinarus's already tight muscles tensed further. He had no desire to be both judge and executioner, but she was right. Without just punishment, Ziegfried would not change.

"No, I cannot allow him to continue to serve after this," he replied. "After the whipping, we will detain him until we reach Fort Harizak and can throw him in the dungeons."

She crossed the tent and smacked her nail file against the his hand. "Use this opportunity well. Any ruler who holds his position for long enough realizes that the best way to unite people is to give them someone to hate. Ziegfried can be that person."

"And if one of them puts a musket ball in the back of his head before we arrive?"

Her smile turned devious. "Then good riddance."

They left the tent together, only to find a group of officers awaiting him atop the knoll outside. Iktaros was among them, and he hardly looked pleased.

"By the Mother," Zinarus said. "Please tell me this does not have to do with Lieutenant Torianisk."

Iktaros huffed, pulling a cigarette from between his teeth and then snuffing it beneath his boot. "It's not Ziegfried for once. Scouting report from the north."

"What did they find?" Zinarus asked. He should've been alarmed that the scouts found anything worthy of fetching him, but it was better than thinking about Ziegfried.

"A field army, sir," Iktaros reported. "Their scouts skirmished with ours last night with no significant losses on either side. One of ours brought back this." He pulled a patch from his bag and handed it over.

Zinarus stared down at the fifteen silver diamonds encircling a central one. Kasia had explained the symbols she had seen the Crimson Court use before, and though this was slightly different, it was common for groups within armies to signal their affiliations with their own sigils—often variations of a main one. This was the Crimsons for sure. A hundred thousand of them if his scouts were right. How could they afford to send so many soldiers away from the eastern Keloshan front?

"They're marching on Fort Harizak as Tiuz expected," Iktaros continued, "but a cavalry regiment broke off after the skirmish between our scouts."

That drew Zinarus's attention from the patch. "Are they headed our direction?"

"They are."

An infantry lieutenant colonel, Brakenias, cleared his throat. A narrow-shouldered man no more than a decade older than Zinarus, he had gained his rank by being one of Vocka's first sharpshooters, but he lacked Iktaros's confidence, running his hands through his hair. "We must prepare for them to intercept us before we reach the fort. The river gives us backing to ensure their dragoons can't surround us, and we outnumber them." He hesitated. "Our army's lack of experience still makes this a challenge. Those Crimsons are regulars, likely with Reachers."

Iktaros spat into the grass. "Definitely with Reachers. A group that size… Shit, they'll have five at least. Maybe ten."

"What of the breathless?" Zinarus asked, fearing the answer. Reachers were a known factor. No general had ever marched to war against organized spirits, though, and not even Tiuz's lessons could help him there.

"None spotted."

Zinarus raised his brow. He glanced at Carelias, as if she could explain the obvious falsity. "That cannot be right. The Crimson Court created the breathless to use them as an army, so why would they march against the Confederation of Harizak without a force they know we would struggle to counter?"

"Maybe they believe the cavalry and Reachers will be enough," Brakenias said with a shrug. "Commander Hazeko may not fight with them anymore, but there's a reason the Ezmani are famous for their riders."

"They're delaying us," Iktaros contested. "By our counts, that field army outnumbers Tiuz's four-to-one, even with our numbers and House Niezik's to reinforce them. They want to ensure we don't make it within the walls."

A Niezik messenger had arrived the day before to signal their mercenaries' imminent arrival at Fort Harizak. From Artaxan's report, Kasia was not among them, and the messenger expressed surprise that she had left Vamiustok. Zinarus had feared that. He'd plunged himself into managing the army to distract from that gnawing ache in his chest, but it flooded back now.

Protect her, Mother of the Crystal, he prayed silently, whether Kasia wanted the prayer or not.

Spirits, he missed her. He had fled that fact for a hundred-hour, but nothing felt the same with her gone. Kasia had thrown herself into immense danger because of his misplaced words. He could not help her or even discover her fate, and that brought more tears to his eyes at night than he was willing to admit.

"General?" Brakenias asked, pulling Zinarus from his thoughts.

Zinarus coughed to hide his emotions. He was supposed to be poised, confident, but his nerves were aflame. "Why delay us?" he asked. "We have less than two thousand soldiers. They could have sent ten times our number."

Iktaros shook his head. "That many men would be too slow. We'd give them the slip with ease."

"This is not about our troop numbers," Carelias said, staring east, over the marshy forest covering the landscape from here to the fort. "The Crimsons are after our family's sand. Word must have reached them that we have what was yet to be transported from Vamia Mines. Tiuz has great need of refined glass against their spirits, and though we sent much of it ahead via keelboat, our wagon train carries a significant portion more. They must fear it arriving for his Reachers to refine."

"How did they know?" Zinarus asked. "It has been less than a hundred-hour since we retook the mines. The battle's survivors could not have sent word to the Crimson army that quickly, and it is too far to be within their scouting radius."

Carelias rested a hand on his shoulder. "Do not underestimate the abilities of skilled Reachers under their command. An experienced Air Reacher could scout a significant distance if they were willing to endure Realm Taint, and if what you saw about these Crimsons is true, they will push their Reachers beyond their limits."

"Or our resident Earth Reacher betrayed us," Iktaros said flatly.

A few of the other gathered officers mumbled their assent. Zinarus was tempted to agree, but something didn't sit right about it. "Do you have any evidence for that accusation? I was on my way to punish Lieutenant Torianisk for his misdeeds, but I cannot have my officers throwing accusations at whoever is merely convenient."

Iktaros shifted uncomfortably. "No, sir."

"If that changes, then I will be the first to listen and act." Zinarus straightened his posture with a deep breath. "Until then, we have a battle to prepare for. Where is the nearest bridge?" Fort Harizak was on the other side of the Vamia River, and they would need to cross eventually.

The cavalry commander pointed northeast. "About a day's ride. Halfway between here and the fort."

Zinarus considered that for a moment before looking over the wagon train under the rear guard's protection. "Then we march double time to reach that bridge. Send a cavalry brigade ahead to secure it while the second brigade leads the wagons to the fort. Our infantry will be slower, and I cannot have them holding up that sand."

"What about Ziegfried?"

"Have a private fetch a whip," Zinarus replied. "I will deal with him quickly."

"YOU CANNOT BE SERIOUS."

Ziegfried lounged on a cot in the back of his officer's tent, just large enough to fit Zinarus and the two soldiers he'd brought with him. The Ezmani scion wore only trousers as he swung the cot lazily with one foot. A cigar dangled from his fingers, a gouge bitten out of it at Zinarus's entry.

"Your behavior is hardly worthy of a jest," Zinarus replied. He stood with his arms crossed, his left hand tucked under to hide that he had removed his glove. Though he still objected to the ethics of Order Reaching for compulsion or torture, he was also well aware that Ziegfried could destroy half the camp before anyone managed to put him down.

The cigar smoke drifted through the space, stinging Zinarus's nose as Ziegfried took a puff. "This is about those women who assaulted me, then?"

Zinarus hid a grin at the still visible bruises across the arrogant bastard's cheek. It was punishment—not enough. "Is that your defense? There were witnesses, Lieutenant, and I will not tolerate such unspeakable actions in my camp."

"Your words are heard, Lord Zinarus. It shall not happen again."

"Words are not enough." Zinarus stepped forward, looming over him with his Vockan height. He trembled, but pushed through his fear. This was the right thing. It may lose him a great weapon, but he would not value even a Reacher over his people. "Ziegfried Torianisk, you are hereby stripped of your rank and sentenced to flagellation. Come with us."

Ziegfried looked him up and down. "I would rather not."

"Your only choice in the matter is to come easily or by force."

Tossing his cigar at Zinarus's feet, Ziegfried swept himself free from the cot. There was little room, and his head barely reached Zinarus's chin. "I would attempt that explanation again. This time, remember that you practically begged for me to help your measly Vockan band." He smirked at the soldiers Zinarus had brought. "Do you actually believe you two could stop me from denying this order?"

Zinarus had heard enough. Gritting his teeth, he Reached into the realm of Truth.

White beams shot from his hand as he grabbed Ziegfried's bare arm. His stomach felt sick, but he didn't relent. If he released Ziegfried now, he would Earth Reach and cause far more damage than in the battle.

"Did you attempt to force yourself upon those women against their wills?" Zinarus asked, his words pouring through his power. It was invigorating, yet horrible as Ziegfried spasmed beneath the compulsion. "Did you expose our position to the Crimson army?"

"I…" Ziegfried tried to lie. The terror in his eyes made that clear enough, but he was too weak-willed to resist the Reach. "I pursued the women. That army, though, I know nothing about."

Guilty enough, then.

Zinarus nodded to the soldiers, and one held Ziegfried still as the other slid a prisoner's glove over his taloned hand. Zinarus stepped back and released his Reaching the moment the glove was on. That discomforting sickness spread throughout his entire body, and it took all his strength not to vomit here and now.

"Take him to the whipping post," he ordered his soldiers as a cold sweat streamed down his brow. "I will meet you there."

Then he hurried out of the tent. Another dozen privates met him there, but he just waved for them to help the others before he stumbled off to a ditch near the river. When he was sure no one was looking, he emptied his stomach.

Spirits, he hated using his compulsion. Many higher scions never fully trained in their Reaching, using it instead as a status symbol or party trick, but Sania had made sure her son was different. Sickness had followed every time he'd practiced compelling a servant with his Reaching. Those had been mundane, harmless questionings that they had consented to, but he could not deny the feeling of *wrongness* about it.

This was his first time Reaching against someone unwilling. Technically, it was not torture, but the helplessness in the target's eyes was horrible. They became a slave within their own body until they answered with the truth. Anyone had the right to fear that.

When he was sure his stomach had settled, he wiped his mouth clean and emerged from the ditch. He still felt horrid. The rattling of the passing sand wagons, though, was a reminder that time was of the essence. Ziegfried wasn't his only problem.

Carelias awaited him at the edge of camp. She gave neither a look of judgment nor a word of scorn, instead handing him a canteen. "You'll need that."

"Why?" He took a whiff, then stifled a cough. "Spirits, Carelias! What are you doing with whisky?"

Her gaze turned sharp. "Keep your voice down. Damn near half your officers probably have the same. It keeps the noises out of your head—and not the ones from Realm Taint." She shoved the canteen into his chest. "I remember how much you hated Truth Reacher compulsion as a neophyte, and from the look of it, that has not changed. You need confidence among your troops. Trembling hands and vomit breath will not earn it. Drink quickly, because they are waiting for you, and someone else will flog him first if you tarry."

So he drank greedily. The whiskey burned his throat, but that sharp pain pulled his focus from his Reaching. A comforting dullness replaced it instantly, growing with each rapid beat of his heart.

"Thank you," he told Carelias, returning the canteen to her. "Without you, I am certain this march would be even more of a disaster than it already is."

"You are young and inexperienced," she said. "No one expected you to be Tiuz immediately, but you'll never be like him if you insist on wallowing in every error."

He accepted that critique without reply. Together, they headed toward the camp center, where the infantry who'd finished packing were gathered around a post. The cavalry and wagons were already on their way, but that left a thousand soldiers and half as many camp followers to gawk at the Earth Reacher tied to the post, his obscenities hanging over the riverside like an enraged jay.

Those fifteen hundred faces studied Zinarus as Carelias joined the officers nearby. This was justice, but it was also a show. Like scions and mercantile lowborn flocking to trials in Kalastok, everyone watched with some kind of crude interest. Was it mere enjoyment of seeing the hated Ziegfried suffer, or was there something more innate to humanity in it?

Zinarus had no time to consider the question before a whip was placed in his hand. He tested its weight. While he had used a whip in training his horses, he'd been careful, never meaning to harm them.

The pale gray back of Ziegfried lay bare before him as he surveyed the crowd and explained the charges. They all knew the reason for Ziegfried's punishment, but this was a show after all. Zinarus had to play his part. He also needed to ensure no one believed he would allow such behavior as this.

Ziegfried's cursing turned to begging when Zinarus finished speaking. "I'll pay them anything!" the scion shouted. "Whatever you want! Please, let me just fight the Crimsons for you!"

Zinarus cracked the whip across his back, silencing the crowd until Ziegfried's scream split the air. Zinarus felt no pleasure in it, but he pulled back the whip and struck again. Then again. Commonwealth military code dictated a maximum of twenty lashings outside a criminal court, so twenty fell upon Ziegfried in quick succession. Gaps between each strike would only create undue suffering. This was about justice, not some personal vendetta.

Zinarus handed off the whip when he was finished. "Have him tended to," he told the medics before looking to his aunt, "but no Body Reaching. He needs to remember this."

"There is little time for him to heal," Brakenias said. "My infantry are ready to march, and we need to hurry to beat the Crimsons to that bridge."

"Then have him bandaged up well enough to ride with an escort," Zinarus said. "He has caused us plenty of woes already without ruining our strategy."

Brakenias thumped his chest, then ran off to complete the orders. His haste spurred Zinarus into motion, but his mechanical leg suddenly locked with a terrible sound. It was a familiar one to the iz Vamiustok heir: grinding gears. Distracted by the duties of his office and the absence of Kasia, he had gone too long without oiling his knee's components. Any attempted movement now would only cause further damage.

Wonderful. He was nowhere near his tent, and his attempts at looking like a real commander would be shot if he limped his way there with his knee locked. His only hope was to get someone to fetch his horse. He waved down a private to do exactly that, but Ziegfried's laughter tore away his focus.

"You cannot defeat them, Zinarus iz Vamiustok," the Earth Reacher said as the medics helped him walk from the post. Blood covered his back, and his eyes were no less red. "The great houses do whatever is necessary for victory over their rivals. Disregard your honor. It'll get you nowhere."

Zinarus tilted up his chin. On that, Ziegfried was right. His honor would handicap him against his foes, but it did not make him cowardly. Like his leg had forced him to adapt, his honor had forged his will. He was strong because of the obstacles life had placed in his path. The great houses had faced no such difficulties.

"Keep him detained and gloved," he told the medics. "Lieutenant Torianisk is stripped of his rank and is to be considered a prisoner until General Tiuz Hazeko rules on his crimes."

Then he hobbled off, not caring who saw him struggle with his leg. Let them know. He had been scorned as a cripple and a halfblood for his entire life. His soldiers would see his fight, but none would see him break.

EMBER'S DAWN

"The ones who desire power the least deserve it most." – Gertrude Niezik, exiled sister of the Buried Temple

Radais sat on a boulder, sharpening his blade late into the night as Wanusa's Spiritspeech Whispering echoed through the mountains. The southern dawnrise light illuminated all around him, but a small cliff left him in the shade. He wished for everdark's lightless sky. A place to hide from the world.

But there was no hiding from his thoughts.

The Fire Realm. How could Vockans originate there? An entire nation of people from another realm, and he dared not think of what that meant for other nations' lowborn. Were so many of their ancestors not from Zekiaz? It seemed an impossible thought, yet here he was, considering whether to touch a Fire Crystal and become a Realm Reacher.

He finished one last swipe with his whetstone across the steel edge of his blade and sighed. Spirits, he was exhausted. Not the kind that made him wish for sleep, but the kind that kept him up. Deep, knotting in his gut, it wormed into every part of his body and drained it.

He had never asked to lead. Miv had thrust the responsibility upon him like it were some kind of honor instead of the greatest burden he'd ever borne. Part of him wanted to resign as supreme defender the moment they reunited with the Glassblade army. Polina and Tairanik had their flaws, but they were experienced commanders. Radais could return to his position as a master, allowing him to continue his work in the villages. Maybe Wanusa could come with him as she learned her abilities.

Footsteps approached, pulling Radais from his thoughts. He'd heard Mariana's povniks scuttling around before, but these were the careful steps of someone not used to such steep slopes.

"You won't convince me to touch the crystal," he said.

Lazan adjusted his pants as he finished clambering over the rocks and joined Radais on the boulder. Despite Radais's resistance, the scion's presence loosened his back.

"And if I told you I was not here to convince you?" Lazan replied with an amused smile, crossing his legs like scions always did. His chin had grown from a stubbled mess to the beard of a true traveler. Silver. Precious. Just like him.

Radais rested the sword on his thighs, examining the glass blade, then the steel one. Both were deathly sharp. "You'd be lying, and we don't lie to each other."

Lazan plucked at the tip of the sword like a child would a strange berry. "It would certainly be a lie to say I didn't want you to become a Reacher. But I'm no fool. You're dead set on refusing—I saw it the moment Mariana mentioned the concept."

"Has Wanusa changed her mind at all?"

They both hesitated, listening to the ethereal Whispering of Wanusa and Mariana. He couldn't deny the beauty in the song and the power behind it, but a chill ran down his spine. Was this how they were meant to interact with the spirits? Mariana claimed it was a mutual bond between Whisperer and spirit, but there was a fine line between a willing bond and oppressive bondage.

Lazan patted Radais's leg. "You know her. She is excited about the possibility of you two learning your abilities together. That is, unless you were to become a Death Reacher."

"I'm not laughing," Radais said, casting him a side-eye.

"Laughter is what will keep us going when this realm is intent on killing us. Laughter and those with the will to fight back."

Radais nodded to his blade. "I broke Glassblade tradition to give my sword a steel edge and ensure my warriors carry steel blades of their own. We're adapting to fight the Vanashel. That doesn't mean I must become a Reacher."

"No, it does not." Lazan scooted closer until they bumped shoulders. His voice lowered to a whisper. "If we do not make use of that Fire Crystal, though, I fear Mariana will use it for herself. That, or someone else will wrestle it from our control once they learn what it is capable of."

"What do you suggest?"

Lazan glanced over his shoulder. The Whisperers had stopped, and Wanusa would be able to hear if they spoke too loud. "Wanusa sought to become a Whisperer for the sake of her brother," he said. "To reunite the two halves of his spirit will put her at incredible risk against the Vanashel."

Radais stared at him, wide-eyed. "You want her to become a Reacher too? She needs the chance to learn her one power before she takes another."

"Do you see another way?" Lazan asked with a knowing look.

They both knew the answer to that: Radais could take the crystal instead. It would be an asset in his battle against the Vanashel and the Bound Ones who led them, but it would also complicate everything further. The Glassblades would doubt him for becoming a Reacher. Many would want him dead as a threat to scion claims of a blood right through the Crystal Mother.

But none of that mattered if he could use his Reaching to help Wanusa. As he forced himself to stand and look toward the young warrior dangling her legs over a ledge, he knew he'd fight for her to have some semblance of the brother she'd lost. His own brother despised him. He wouldn't allow the same to happen to her.

"What does it feel like?" Radais asked Lazan over his shoulder.

The scion stood, wincing from his Taint-induced pains. "What do you mean?"

"To Reach. To pull magic from another realm?"

"Let me show you," Lazan said as he drew close and took Radais's hand with his taloned one. Blood red wisps drifted from his fingertips as he Reached. They flurried about the pair, and Lazan's eyes glimmered watching them. "Is it not beautiful?"

Before Radais could respond, Lazan pressed their joined hands over his heart, beating rapidly from the Reach. They were so close now. The Reacher's breaths fell warm upon Radais's cheek, and he found his own heart echoing the drumbeat of his lover. He'd never admitted such feelings aloud, but the word felt right. Though this bond he shared with Lazan was not the raging fire of Miv, it was like the warmth of the dawnrise sun after the frigid everdark. Inviting. Comforting. Safe.

"With this single Reach," Lazan whispered, cheek against Radais's and his fingers finding the gap in the Glassblade's armor just above the hip. "I can heal mortal wounds or reinforce one's body to withstand great trial." The whisps hovered between them, and Radais had the unexplainable sense that they were eagerly awaiting a command. "I can also ignite one's senses to make the slightest touch feel more pleasurable than you could ever imagine. It is quite addicting, though, so as you would suspect, Body Reachers not engaged in healing or warfare are quite popular in Kalastok's brothels."

A shiver ran down Radais's spine as an eager sweat clung to his skin beneath the armor. "Are you trying to seduce me into becoming a Reacher?"

Lazan rose onto his toes to press his lips softly against Radais's cheek, then down to his neck. "I am simply showing you that there is more to a Reacher than Death bolts, Spirit manipulations, or balls of fire. There is beauty in a Reach beyond anything you could experience otherwise."

"Consider me tempted," Radais replied, leaning into him. "But how do I know I'll like what realm I Reach as much as I enjoy you?"

Lazan held his cheek. "Now, that is quite the ask. I would say to trust the Crystal Mother, but you don't believe, so instead, I suggest you hold in your spirit what is important to you. The crystal will do the rest."

He stepped back, running his fingers down Radais's arm to catch his hand, and the Glassblade was helpless against the pull. "Come, now, and join me," Lazan said. "Since you have chosen not to rest this evening, better you spend it with me than stroking that sword alone."

THE FALSE CURE

"People need hope. It matters not whether it is based in truth." – Jazuk Bartol the Fourth, former king of the Commonwealth of Two Nations

Factory smoke suffocated the heart of Kalastok's Industrial District. During peak production hours like this, no one left their apartments or houses if they could help it, but they were west-side lowborn. Of course they couldn't help it. They either had to work for the bastard scions running those factories or steal from them.

Nex much preferred stealing to working. Some thieves used words like *borrowing*, but that was koileeshit. When Nex conned scions out of their keni, it was stealing. That didn't mean they felt bad about it. Those assholes deserved empty pockets.

That didn't stop the Ashes of Dawn from letting anyone get Etal's Spirit Plague cure. The Crimson Court were using the dead's spirits to create their breathless army, so Nex would do what it took to keep even the rich alive… for now. Unfortunately, their generosity went unnoticed, and they tugged down on their wide brimmed hat as they passed another wanted poster with a poor rendition of their face on it.

Or at least, it was a poor rendition of what they looked like *now*.

They grinned to themself and headed down the nearest alley with

Wanted!
DEAD or ALIVE
NEX

Reward
5,000 keni

For arrest or proof of death

their duster clipping at their heels. The Crimsons could put up all the posters they wanted. They only had a vague description of Nex and the fake name they went by, which would get them nowhere. Most lowborn only knew of Nex as the leader of the Ashes of Dawn, and none of them would rat out the one distributing cures, food, and clean water. Even the gangs had fallen under their influence since the Children of Zekiaz's aid arrived. Nex still had little memory of their conversations with either the Children or the gangs, but their allies in the Ashes had caught Nex up on what they could.

Vinnia complained that it was a risk for Nex to survey the distributors the Ashes had set up around the city. She was probably right, but it felt good to get out of that cramped warehouse basement. Besides, things were still strange between them since Nex's memory loss. Nex was freer here, and the bars around the west side were full of gossip for them to catch between stops.

The biggest rumor today had them worried. They'd heard from a merchant lowborn who they'd tricked into betting his mechanical watch that Nikoza had been thrown into prison. A traitor, the Crimsons claimed. Not good.

But that was only a rumor, and Nex couldn't solve it right now. They needed no gossip to know what the Crimson Court was shouting from the top of their fancy new towers: they had a cure. Apparently, they were handing it out just like the Ashes. The question was whether the Crimsons' one was real.

Now, Nex wore a face altered by their Possibility Reaching to pursue that thread. They needed to find a dose of this cure and figure out what it meant. Were the Crimsons trying to earn approval from the lowborn who blamed Chatik for secretly executing Paras and attempting a more public one with Etal? Or was this yet another ruse?

Breathless hovered in the factory smog, watching anyone who dared approach the thoroughfares connecting them to eastern Kalastok and the battlefronts beyond. Nex didn't care much about the wars against Kelosh and the scion rebels in the Confederation, but they'd have to be deaf to not hear that things weren't going well. Kelosh advanced straight toward Kalastok, and in the south, Tiuz's rebels had apparently held onto their fort. Nex might've pitied the

Crimsons for their losses if the assholes weren't trying to enslave lowborn and steal their names.

Nex's hand found their amber beads in one pocket and glass dagger in the other. No one knew whether those breathless just saw faces or read people's spirits, and that made Nex distrust their disguise. If the worst rumors were true, it could protect them from clumsy, drunken guards, but not the real threats.

As if reading their thoughts, a breathless skirted in Nex's direction. Its misty form seemed to stare at them for forever as they headed toward the warehouse where the Crimsons were apparently giving out the cure. Nex hated the crowds here usually, but used them now to keep from standing out.

The breathless stopped following so closely, but didn't return to the higher watch of the others. Nex eyed the newly built Reacher tower nearby. Were the Spirit Reachers guiding this one to them? With Nikoza captured, the Ashes were vulnerable. She could've exposed Nex, luring them into a trap.

But Nex cut off that train of thought. Sure, Nikoza knew the location of their main safehouse. If she'd betrayed them, though, the Crimsons would've raided the Ashes already. At least, that's what Nex told themself to calm their nerves.

A commotion ahead alerted them to the Crimsons' cure warehouse. It was just outside the cordon to access the most sensitive factories, allowing other lowborn to reach it, but a small army of watchmen and great house mercenaries patrolled a winding line of lowborn. There must've been no less than a few thousand lowborn trying to push for the cure. The guards did what they could to keep the people under control, but coughing fits and shouting revealed the desperation that still held the poorest among them.

Nex hated watching this. The Ashes hadn't had enough time to give out all the cures people needed yet. So many were still sick, and some of them would never trust what the scions insisted on calling a gang of rebels. They'd rather subject themselves to this mess. Nex shook their head at that, but fear was a strange thing. Years of it had frayed everyone's nerves in the west side.

This chaos would make getting one of the Crimson's cures

impossible. The line, if it kept moving at all, would take hours, and Nex had a hundred other things they needed to do. Their lost memories made running the Ashes difficult. Thousands had fallen under the Ashes' protection with the gangs agreeing to follow Nex's orders, but it was an alliance of necessity at best. Between warring personalities, Nikoza's plot, and Kasia's reappearance, they could barely keep it all straight. This could wait.

They turned to leave, but a voice stopped them. Amplified by an Air Reacher, it shook the air and quieted the crowd as a new wave of guards emerged from the warehouse.

No, not guards. The arrivals wore long crimson coats with elaborate designs of various colors across them, and glass bracers on their arms shimmered in the dawnrise light. Nex bit their cheek, this time checking for the pistol tucked in their duster.

Nothing good ever happened when the Crystal Brigade showed up.

Gregorzon appeared, leading Hazat and the rest of Nikoza's old squad. That confirmed the rumor, then. The perfect little princess had walked back into Chatik's grasp and gotten herself locked up.

That shouldn't have mattered to Nex. Spies died all the time, but Nikoza had risked her neck to get them out of that damned dungeon. The Truth Reachers would've completely broken Nex's mind with a couple more hours. She'd stopped that, turning her back on family and allies alike to help the lowborn, and now, Chatik was probably doing even worse to his niece's head.

Nex couldn't abandon her.

"Shit," they muttered to themself as the Crystal Brigade called breathless to contain the crowd. "That princess will get me killed."

They considered trying to get Hazat's attention and question him about Nikoza, but a swarm of spirits drew their attention away. Most breathless were on patrol or directed by Reachers in one area. This group flew quickly over the Shadow Quarter.

Straight toward the Ashes' safehouses.

Nex bit their cheek, hoping the breathless would switch directions. There were plenty of other targets in the Shadow Quarter. They didn't know about the safehouses. They didn't know…

All hope slipped away when the breathless dove near the

intersection of one of the Ashes' secondary safehouses and another group headed straight for the Glass Teeth gang's base near the river. Neither had Vinnia or Nex's most trusted allies, but hundreds of people were packed into those hideouts. Sure, the Ashes' guards had glass daggers and amber beads. Against this many breathless, though, they stood no chance.

Nex was off at a sprint before they'd even considered their options. Like Nikoza, these people trusted Nex. And if one safehouse fell, the others would be soon after. Nex needed to warn them.

"It's Nex! Someone stop them!" a gruff voice shouted as Nex shouldered their way through the crowd. The way they'd come was too far. A direct route was their only chance to get to the safehouses in time.

But an arm grabbed them, tearing them from their feet. Nex hit the ground hard, and their head spun as they stared up at the blurred form of a crimson-clad man. Their pistol was still tucked into their duster, so they drew it and fired. It didn't matter who the Crimson was. He'd tried to stop Nex from protecting their people, and that was a death sentence.

The man's grip loosened as he cried out. But his voice made Nex hesitate. It was familiar, and when Nex grabbed their hat, scrambling to their feet, they cursed under their breath.

"What the fuck are you doing here, Hazat?"

So Tazper was a Spirit Reacher.

Kasia knew it shouldn't have been a surprise, given that most Reachers were bound to Zekiaz. It was the realm they lived in, after all, and Spirit Reachers were incredibly useful against awakened. She couldn't help but feel disappointed, however, that his power wouldn't directly help her defeat Chatik.

She watched him practice his Reaching in a half-burned building on the far northern end of Kalastok's Shadow Quarter. It was the most secluded they would get in the city. Away from the bustle of the Industrial District, there were drifters but no breathless or Crimson watchmen to spot him, and Kasia knew from experience how important uninterrupted practice was for a fledgling Reacher.

Memories threatened her with every blink as Spitza pecked at the second shred of Spirit Crystal in her grasp—not enough for Sadamar. These past few days had been crucial for Tazper's training, and every moment to rest was just as crucial to heal her back. She'd considered searching for a Body Reacher. Her golden Axiom web hadn't been able to lock onto Lazan, though, and she was a wanted woman in any part of the city that could've housed a Reacher. Most had gone off to war or were too rich to hire anyway.

"You are lying to yourself," her Tainted specter said, sitting in a chair across from her in what had once been an apartment's tiny dining room. The fires had charred both their seats, and it creaked as the specter leaned forward, resting her chin in her hand. "We could have found a Body Reacher within a day, but you were afraid. You still are."

Kasia didn't challenge the point. Whatever this visage of herself was, she was right about this at least. The thought of failing Sadamar and rejoining Zinarus had her stomach in knots.

Her specter held out a hand for Kasia to take. She refused, and Spitza's pecking forced the specter back. "Sadamar's power would have elevated us beyond fear," the Tainted one said. "Between Axiom Reaching and a true control over Death, think of what we could accomplish. All we need is more crystal."

Aliax emerged from the crowd of other ghosts in the room. So many crammed into it that Kasia's lungs were tight, her breaths shallow, as their mumbled conversations strained her attention. Aliax's piercing gaze only worsened that effect.

"Death magic is why people want your head," he said. "You can live in a better instead of corrupting yourself further. No matter what you do here, you'll always be a danger to Tazper and your allies."

"Then what should I do?" Kasia asked.

He rested a hand on her shoulder. It was above the burn, and the gentle touch released the muscles in her back. "My offer to flee all of this still stands. Zekiaz is a big world. We can find somewhere that isn't destroying itself and be together, just the two of us."

"I am not running away—not while Chatik or any Crimson sits upon the throne." Her thoughts drifted to the Children of Zekiaz's offer for more information. All she needed was shadowlight and Leonit's secret book she still had in her bag. Candles infused with Shadow Reaching were rare, but someone at Fort Harizak would have one for her to use. "I cannot secure Sadamar's power, but what if my father's book helps me get that Unity Crystal from Chatik?"

"Answers do not change who you are," he said. "The Crimsons are right to believe you're a dangerous woman."

She bit her cheek. No matter what lay ahead, she would get shadowlight to finally investigate the strange locked book Leonit had left in the study. It was the last secret her father had left, hopefully at least holding some answer into his affiliations with the Children. That meant returning to Zinarus, though, and he would surely not let her get more crystal and return to Sadamar.

Her Tainted specter grinned at that thought. "Do we listen to Zinarus's commands now?"

Kasia flicked her gaze to Tazper, who guided drifters around him with a boyish grin. She tapped the crystal absently against the stub where her talon had once been. Oh, if only she could view magic with such wonder.

"I will do what I must," she told the specters as a cold breeze whipped from the south. A new batch of clouds cast a heavy shadow over the burned building. She gave it no notice, staring instead at the specter across from her. Her face. Her body. Her. If she were not so scarred and broken.

Rubble crunching under Tazper's boots signaled his arrival into the ghost-filled room. "Uh, Kasia, you may want to see this."

Reluctantly, she looked toward him. "What?"

Then she saw it. Not clouds, but a mass of breathless spirits so thick that they blocked out the dawnrise sun. Much of western Kalastok was still unfamiliar to her. In her short time since her arrival, though, she'd become familiar with the Ashes of Dawn's main safehouses. And she had no doubt they were striking at the one closest to the river.

"Leave them," her specter demanded. "These lowborn are not worth dying for."

Aliax took her hand. "On this, I agree. Fighting now will just worsen your Taint, and I don't want to see you keep falling apart."

She pulled back, trying to shut out the ghosts' voices, but between the pain in her back and her shock at the sudden breathless attack, her mind was a whirlwind. The Ashes needed her. They had helped her recover from Orat's deathly grip and now Gregorzon's flames, and she'd promised to help Nex fight the Crimson Court in Kalastok. Could she both fulfill that promise and complete her own plans?

Spitza nibbling at her ear helped pull her back to reality. She struggled to stand, one hand hoisting herself up and the other checking for her father's revolver. Its cold metal met her fingers with a grounding surety. Against breathless, it would be useless, but she need not check for amber. Even wearing a spare lowborn coat, trousers, and collared shirt, she always had enough amber beads with her to absorb plenty of breathless.

"Ready to test that Spirit Reaching for real?" she asked as Tazper hurried to help her.

His eyes widened even further. "I Reached only a few minutes ago. If I do so again—"

"Learning how to handle your first dose of Realm Taint is as important as learning to Reach. Refrain from pushing yourself beyond a couple Reaches and you'll be fine." She grabbed his arm, squeezing. "You won't end up like me. I promise."

When he gave a shaky nod, she removed her left glove and Reached into the Axiom. They were too far from the safehouses to be useful if she hobbled there with her burned back. Teleporting back out of the chaos would Taint her further, but at this point, what was another dose of insanity. She glanced around. The damned ghosts ruled her mind already.

Golden wisps burst into a portal before them. Tazper watched it with that same boyish wonder as they charged into it, but Reaching was merely a tool to Kasia now. Against the foes they faced, she'd need every tool she could get.

And she would turn those tools into weapons

THE BREATHLESS SWARM

"Imagine if awakened were no longer a threat. What would happen to the economies of glass upon which our nations are built?" – Leonit Niezik, former minister of glass for the Commonwealth of Two Nations

Screams consumed the smoky alleys outside the main Ashes of Dawn safehouse.

Kasia emerged from her portal with pistol drawn and beads of amber clutched in her free hand. Lowborn scrambled everywhere, glass daggers swinging as they fought to protect the most vulnerable. Others fired stupidly at the spirits, their misplaced shots only adding to the chaos.

Dozens of husks lay strewn about already, their spirits devoured by the breathless and their smoky tendrils. This main safehouse hadn't been the first one attacked, so Kasia could only imagine the slaughter elsewhere. She needed to find Nex and hope there was some way to get the rebels out of here.

"Do not Reach until your life depends on it," she told Tazper, throwing out her arm to capture a diving breathless in amber. Its humming spirit voice turned to a shriek, but she felt no pity.

Tazper lashed out with a glass dagger. The strike missed wildly as the breathless dodged away, something a mindless awakened would have never done. "What about these people?"

Gunpowder and factory fumes choked them as Spitza cawed furiously, alerting Kasia to a group of breathless who surrounded a woman and her child. Two of their tendrils struck at the child, but Kasia was quicker. She threw a bead through their translucent bodies. Then, as the bead absorbed the spirits, she pocketed her pistol and advanced with both fists gripping amber.

"There is more than one way to fight a spirit," she called back to Tazper.

The pair charged straight into the breathless swarm, pushing them back from the surrounded woman and joining with the other Ashes. At least a hundred of them had organized around the Reshkan giant, Jiinaan, in the intersection of a few alleys, but they were vastly outnumbered by the spirits.

"Protect them!" Jiinaan ordered his allies, stabbing a breathless with one of his dual-wielded daggers.

Kasia lobbed more amber beads as she rushed to him. "Is there anywhere we can take these people?"

"No safehouse anymore," he said. "We fight to live."

Cursing under her breath, Kasia faced down the breathless, but her back was already stinging horribly. They could fight all they wanted. There was no way they could defeat this many spirits, even with Tazper's Spirit Reaching.

They needed to flee.

"Gather everyone you can to the north," she said, her voice echoed by Spitza's demanding calls. "I'll teleport them out of here."

"What about the other safehouses?" a feminine voice asked from behind them. Kasia glanced over her shoulder to see Vinnia protecting Jiinaan's back. She was doing her best to keep a strong face, but Nex's lover looked terrified. "We can't abandon them!"

Kasia lashed out with her amber to block a breathless tendril, ready for it to strike again. But it shied away. They were learning, and that didn't bode well when the Ashes had so few weapons against the spirits.

"Send a pair of runners to each," she told Vinnia. "There's no way in the wastes I'm going to be able to teleport everyone in groups, so they need to meet up with the others."

Vinnia nodded, but then clenched her jaw. "Have you seen Nex?"

"I was hoping you had."

Spitza's rapid caws cut their conversation short. A surge of breathless overwhelmed the Ashes' front lines. Ten of the fighters fell in seconds, breaking the organization the rest had maintained. Jiinaan let out a mighty shout as he fought to counter, but charging into the mass of spirits left him surrounded. Most breathless dodged his daggers, and within a blink, their tendrils latched on to him. He was as good as dead.

Tazper missed that point, holding out his taloned hand. Silver wisps burst from him and encompassed Jiinaan. The breathless reeled, but only for a moment. Tazper was inexperienced, and there were so many of them.

Jiinaan lunged for safety as Kasia threw amber and towering Lexalia slashed at the tendrils with her twin glass blades. For every spirit they trapped or killed, though, two took its place. Tazper's Reaching failed, and Jiinaan cried out as the breathless drained his spirit.

"Save them…"

It took Lexalia snatching Vinnia's arm to stop her from leaping to her death after him. The girl was frantic, her glass dagger flailing at every puff drifting through the alley—whether breathless or pollution—but Lexalia was twice her size. Kasia knew that desperation well. The need to lash out at anything after you lost someone you loved, but that would only get them killed.

"Think about Nex," Lexalia demanded, practically dragging Vinnia behind the lines of remaining Ashes. "We need to save who we can and get out of here!"

Tears streamed down Vinnia's cheeks, but she nodded before calling out to a group of teenagers nearby. "Tell the other groups to go north, by Crax's Place. Please, go in pairs."

Seconds later, the teenagers split and headed off each direction at full sprint. Each carried amber strapped around their chests along with a glass dagger and a pistol, but even with two of them, they would stand little chance if they were intercepted. Knowledge of the Shadow Quarter's winding alleyways would be their only hope.

"Organize the retreat here," Kasia told Vinnia and Lexalia as she searched for Tazper among the fighting Ashes. Despite his sluggish motions, he didn't appear all too affected by Taint, but his failure to save Jiinaan would weigh on him. She needed to keep him close.

Vinnia's eyes widened. "Where are you going? You're hurt."

"Someone needs to find Nex," Kasia replied, "and you aren't—"

A chattering among the breathless interrupted her. Their dark tendrils halted their advance, retreating as a sea of silver wisps split them. The Reaching hadn't come from Tazper, and he looked as dumbfounded as anyone else until two familiar figures sprinted from the southern alley just a few yards into the breathless ranks.

Hazat Tozki, dressed in a Crystal Brigade coat like Gregorzon's, commanded the spirits with far more skill than Tazper had. Nex slashed and stabbed behind. A vicious look stained their Possibility-altered face, and their duster flung about like a trained dancer twirling her skirts. Except when Nex spun, those who watched did not swoon.

They died.

The pair carved a path through the breathless with stunning determination. A dozen were sliced through or trapped in amber in a few rapid beats of Kasia's heart. It wasn't until Nex caught sight of Vinnia that they broke away from the spirits, leaving Hazat and Lexalia to cover them.

"What happened to the other safehouses?" Nex's voice cracked. "We have to kill these assholes and get to them!"

Vinnia just flung her arms around Nex, nearly toppling them. "Nexie! I was so worried about you."

"Yeah..." Nex cleared their throat and stepped back with a grip on Vinnia's shoulders. "I was worried about you too, but what happened? Are the others alive?"

"Jiinaan fell," Vinnia started before choking on her words.

Kasia gritted her teeth as Spitza hopped around her shoulder and arm, warning her of the impending danger. "We don't have time for this! Runners are heading for the other safehouses to tell people to flee north. I'm going to teleport everyone out of here."

"To where?" Nex asked. "Nowhere's safe for us!"

Hazat fell in between them and the breathless, helping the remaining Ashes fighters. He looked more ragged by the second. His Reach was failing, and the breathless began to attack again. "To Lord Zinarus," he said without looking back. "The Confederation will protect you, and if your people bring all the glass, amber, and guns they have, it will reinforce their defenses at Fort Harizak."

"We can't just let them take our city," Nex snapped. "They're killing our people! It won't stop when we leave."

More silver wisps shot from Hazat's hands as he Reached again, his body shaking from the Taint that followed. "Just hurry north! I will hold them here until your people are clear. When I catch up, I'll explain everything."

"Should I stay?" Tazper asked. "Another Spirit Reacher would be useful."

"Absolutely not," Kasia replied, hauling him away as Nex and Lexalia wrangled the others into following. Hazat's arrival prompted a hundred questions in her mind, but she would not deny the help.

Hundreds, no, *thousands* of lowborn streamed down the tight, misshapen alleys. They stumbled over each other, their terror piercing the thick smog. Kasia's Tainted specters joined the throng, and she found herself struck by stray elbows and shoulders. Not the leader who would teleport these people to safety, but one of the lost. She couldn't tell who was real and who was a ghost.

Taint had burrowed deep within her. This desperate idea would only make it worse. Teleporting a few people at a time stretched her Reaching to its max, but over a thousand?

She denied her worries, focusing only on the next step. Each person she teleported was another life saved from the Crimsons—another fighter in the war against the Crimsons. She couldn't win it now, but she could sure as crystal be a dagger in Chatik's side.

The crowd soon stopped at the crooked, three-story building Vinnia had called Crax's Place. So many more had already gathered here, and an elderly man upon the building's stoop tried to calm them. A brutish, wide-nosed woman harried his left flank. Brass knuckles flashed across her balled fists, but those would be no use against their enemies.

"Shut up! All of ye!" another man yelled from the woman's side, waving his hook of a hand about as if it were a spear. "None of us are getting out of here like this."

Nex muttered to themself and pushed through the crowd. "Stop being a miserable bastard, Lok-Tag," they said. "I've got Kasia Niezik, and she'll teleport everyone out."

"One Reacher is not capable of such a thing," the elderly man objected.

Kasia crossed her arms. "What does a gang boss know about an Axiom Reacher? The Ashes of Dawn helped me, so I will do what I must to ensure you all escape."

Lok-Tag tried to complain, but the burly woman—whom Kasia assumed was the Murder Mitts' boss known as Bess—wrenched down his hooked hand. "I don't trust the scion either, but we're good as dead if we stay." She nodded toward the elderly man. "Crax, I'm right, and you know it."

"Flawed hope is better than none at all," Crax replied, tucking his gloved hands into his armpits like he was somehow freezing in the warm dawnrise air. "We go, then."

The crowd's attention turned to Kasia. Some gazes held disdain, others awe, but all were afraid. As they clutched tight their loved ones and no more than a satchel of their few remaining possessions, Kasia was both a symbol of everything they despised and their only chance at survival. That realization didn't lessen the weight of what she must do. Teleporting so many of them…

Hazat's huffing arrival severed that thought. Most of the lowborn hadn't seen him save their lives, and he found hundreds of pistols, muskets, and daggers pointed his direction. With him dressed as a Reacher of the Crystal Brigade, Kasia couldn't blame them, but she and Nex raised their hands to signal to stop anything rash.

"Hazat is an ally!" Kasia said. "He stopped the breathless."

With a grateful nod, Hazat leaned on his knees. His hair was slicked with sweat, and his words were rushed when he spoke.

"Though I have delayed the breathless, they will be here soon. The Crimson King has taken Lady Nikoza prisoner. I must remain in the city and work to free her, as Chatik's plans are unfinished here. The Crystal Heir—"

"Is her," Kasia interrupted. "I know. But why were you here in the first place, working for the Crimsons?"

He winced, glancing over his shoulder as if expecting the breathless to swarm him. "It is too long a story for now, but know that, like you, I have infiltrated the Crimson Court in hopes of destroying them."

"I'll stay back with you," Nex said. Gasps followed from the crowd, but Nex gave them no heed. "Nikoza pulled me out of that shithole of a dungeon, so I owe her."

Vinnia rushed toward Nex, taking their face in her hands. "Please, don't. You know what it was like to almost lose me, and I can't sit far away, knowing you're fighting them alone."

But Nex turned away. "Nikoza risked everything to help me. My memory is still shit, but I remember that."

"I love you," Vinnia appealed, clutching their hand instead. "Please, Nexie."

"I know I loved you before, and I want to again. But right now, this matters more to me."

The southern sky filled with breathless as Vinnia staggered back, jaw ajar. She tried to plead further, but Kasia signaled for Tazper to pull her away. "It's time to go!"

She bit her cheek and gestured for the crowd to create an opening. Then she threw out her crystal hand, focusing on the care she had for Zinarus. Nex had lost their memories of affection, but she had only smothered hers beneath spite. Those feelings were still there, smoldering amid the ashes until they found fuel to ignite.

Gold streamed from her hand. But like a glove blocking a talon, she felt the clothes over her forearm dampening her power. This was no simple Reach, so she threw off her coat and pulled up her shirt's sleeve to expose the winding crystal that cut through her scarred skin.

Every bit of Taint expanded it further. She had no doubts this one would be the worst yet.

The golden stream became a wave, pouring over the empty space to form a portal far larger than any she had summoned before. It shimmered brilliantly, and on the other side, Zinarus rode ahead of marching infantry, his eyes tired and his chin tucked to his chest.

"Go on!" Lok-Tag called out. "Get through it!"

A sea of people followed the golden wave. They blocked sight of the portal, and each who entered it was like a punch to Kasia's gut. But she kept her hand up, pouring her strength into the Reach as the sky darkened further. Hazat and Tazper coordinated their Spirit Reaching to give them time. She could only hope they held long enough.

Nex stood beside her, watching their people flee while they remained with a pensive look locked on their face. Vinnia tried to stay, but at Nex's word, Lexalia hauled her toward the portal. Though she wept and cried out for her lover, Nex flinched only the slightest before turning back to face Kasia.

"Go after them when they're through," they said. "You'll be beat as shit when you're done. That Zinarus is weird, but he'll help you better than I can with all those damned spirits coming."

Kasia lacked the strength to reply. She tired by the second, her breaths turning rapid as her heart hammered her chest. Half of Nex's words were lost in the torrent of ghostly voices surrounding her, and she dared not look at Aliax or her Tainted specter. Their gazes tingled the back of her neck, though, as their doubts pierced the chaos.

"You are risking everything for lowborn nobodies!" the Tainted reflection of her screamed. "Who will avenge Father if we are dead? Who will rebuild our fallen house?"

Her other victims mocked her, claiming it didn't matter how many she saved now. She'd always be a murderer. No golden portal could return the dead to life, and her Taint would surely put more at risk.

Aliax tried to rest his hand on her arm, but she pushed past him. The lowborn would soon be all through the portal. She needed to be there when the last entered it, or she would collapse before she had the chance to follow. The specters could haunt her all they wanted. She would not relent until the lowborn were safe.

Strange breathless chatter split the crowds' cries as the Spirit Reachers retreated. Kasia had no idea how long they could hold, but worrying about Tazper now would draw away vital threads of attention. Her arm shook violently now, a fiery pain consuming it. Yet she advanced on the portal amid the flood of people.

All but her golden wisps were a blur to her now. Time slipped past, and she knew not whether it had been seconds or minutes since she'd started her Reach. It was torture. Every instinct joined the specters' cries for her to let go until only pure willpower kept the Reach going.

Screams echoed from somewhere near or far, followed by the cold of a nearby spirit trickling down her neck. Time was short, but there were still stragglers hurrying through. More blurred forms appeared from alleys in every direction. Whether members of the Ashes of Dawn or not, they sought the same safety as the rebels, but Kasia couldn't hold on forever. Her legs dragged until Aliax threw her free arm over his shoulder to help her along.

"You've made your choice," he said. "So let's see it through."

When all other senses were a muddled cacophony, his voice was clear. It poured vigor into her veins, but even that was only enough to keep her eyes from slamming shut. She was mere strides from the portal now. Any longer, and she would falter completely.

"I can't keep going," she muttered to Aliax or Tazper or anyone who could bother hearing in this mess.

"Then finish it!" Aliax insisted. "Step through."

She glanced about, the remaining few dozen people all looking the same as they sprinted past. "Where is Tazper?" Spirits, every word was like fire poured down her throat, but she couldn't leave her best friend behind. Too often, she'd failed him. Not now. Not again.

Aliax faded away, his place suddenly taken by Tazper as Kasia's senses flared. Her vision cleared enough to reveal breathless diving for the stragglers. Hazat and Nex were gone, and besides the few people scrambling toward the portal, only spirits inhabited this square now.

"Help me," she gasped. "I can barely move my legs."

Tazper did as she said, but glanced over his shoulder, stopping close enough to the portal to touch it. "What about those who are left? The breathless will turn them to husks if we leave now."

"And we'll die with them if we stay. Please, Taz." Her arm sagged, her whole body spasming. "I can't hold it open."

He nodded reluctantly, but the specters' laughs followed in their wake as the pair staggered that final step into the portal. Screams followed. Those of the dying, those she couldn't save.

Then they were gone.

Kasia splashed into waist deep water, tears stinging her eyes and her consciousness rapidly slipping. Thousands waded in the river around her as soldiers clad in purple trimmed in gold helped those closest to shore. Zinarus rode among the army, shouting orders with his auburn curls as frayed as his expression. He froze when his gaze fell upon Kasia.

The lord practically leaped from his saddle as he waved for someone to bring him his cane. Amid the mass of people, no one answered, so he limped toward her instead. Though he could not swim and water corroded his mechanical leg, he plowed straight into the current.

"Kasia!" he exclaimed as she fell further into Tazper's arms.

Darkness crept over her vision. She tried to reach out for Zinarus, but her muscles refused. Sickness swelled in her stomach, and the Axiom Crystal cut further up her arm with every breath. Fear clutched her. Was this Taint's death? She'd tasted life as a spirit in the Axiom after Chatik's bullet put her at death's door, and just like then, she refused to surrender to it.

Her fight was not yet finished. And as Zinarus neared, his hand straining to meet hers, she remembered she wasn't fighting alone.

OF FIRE AND SPIRIT

"The world would crumble without spirits, yet the only thing we fear more than them is our very selves." – Rorik-Tin Santin, the crystal-eyed prophet

Sleep evaded Wanusa as she awaited Radais's decision. He'd held such fear in his eyes when Mariana proposed he become a Reacher. Why?

Her fingers graced her crystalline collarbone, following the ethereal silver up the center of her neck until she found only mortal skin. That Spirit Crystal made her something more now. A Deepened Whisperer, bound to Zekiaz's heart and her brother's spirit—or at least half of it. She'd thought earning the rank of warrior among the Glassblades would be her greatest accomplishment for a long time, but nothing could match the pure connection she experienced when Whispering. A belonging after years of feeling lost.

Reaching was a different form of magic, yet she couldn't understand why her mentor wouldn't desire that same connection. It could allow him to challenge the Vanashel's Bound Ones, like the dragon wielding Earth who'd led the raid in the Whistling Pass. Lazan was a Reacher too, after all, and he'd shown Reaching could be useful outside of fighting too.

Despite those thoughts, Wanusa had restrained her urge to go to

Radais after their initial conversation. He'd sharpened his sword instead of sketching while she practiced Whispering. That was a clear indicator he didn't want to talk.

Lazan hadn't understood that, but based on the sounds coming from their tent, Radais was in a far better mood now. Though she was glad he was happy, memories of her entering their room in Dalnus flashed through her mind. Not welcomed ones.

She focused instead on Inrius's presence within her. It felt as if his spirit was joined with hers, replacing a portion of it more than just bonding with it, and that change worried her. Inrius had been carefree. Compared to him, was inquisitive, but not rebellious. That had changed since the Deepening. Mariana hadn't warned her about a bonded spirit impacting her will, but spirits were said to direct one's intentions and desires. If bonding Inrius had surrendered part of her spirit for his, did his desires become hers too?

That was hardly a comforting thought, but she must have found sleep at some point, because she awoke to the panting of a povnik and the aroma of breakfast over the campfire.

While Radais had pouted the night before, Mariana had shown Wanusa how to Whisper to the spirits of animals. It wasn't the same as bonding a spirit, but allowed some deeper understanding of the creature's desires. She'd also found it far less frustrating than speaking to the free spirits.

Rolling over, she grinned at the awkward way in which this particular povnik's six legs lay about her like Reshkan noodles. Alicy was the one who'd listened to her best, and the silver povnik had refused to leave her ever since. Who could've thought a spine-covered beast could make her giggle when anxiety had her stomach in knots?

"Come," she said. "Let's see how a Reacher is made."

A stark divide split the camp when she emerged from her tent with Alicy. On the side further up the slope, Lazan cooked over the fire as Radais tended to the ibexes. Mariana stayed far away, standing alongside the cliff with her arms tucked behind her back.

The group went through their breakfast routine with little chatter, and though Wanusa's foot tapped away in wait of Radais's decision, she kept her mouth shut as she slipped some morsels to Alicy. Miv had been firm regarding when it was her time to speak and when it wasn't.

You would've taken the power in an instant, she silently told Inrius.

Part of her wondered what it would be like for her to become both Whisperer and Reacher, but she batted away the thought. She'd barely grasped the concept of calling and listening to spirits. That was only a fraction of her magic as a Whisperer, so taking on another power seemed like a foolish idea. Still, the part of her she attributed to Inrius wished for it.

It took only half an hour for her to lose her patience. They needed to join the Glassblade army soon if they didn't want the Vanashel swarming the rest of Vocka. Every moment they sat here, more lives were at risk.

"Are we going to address what happened last night?" she asked, rising swiftly. "Or do we want to sit here until the Vanashel show up?"

Radais set down the pauldron he'd been preparing to strap to his shoulder. "You're right. I don't like it, but I've decided to take the Fire Crystal. Our enemies have Bound Ones, so we need our own magic to face them."

Her heart skipped a beat as she beamed up at the supreme defender. This meant they could learn their abilities together. She wouldn't be alone in her training, and she lacked words to express how much that meant to her.

"What realm do you want to Reach?" she asked with a little hop before him. "It's a Fire Crystal, so you'll probably end up a Fire Reacher, but Lazan's Spirit Crystal let him Reach into the Body realm."

Radais shrugged. Flashes of fear and excitement both crossed his face, each winning out for only a passing moment. It was the same way he'd looked around Miv before she became a spirit, and Wanusa found amusement in him resembling an embarrassed teenager.

"I don't know," he said, but his eyes darted away.

It was a ridiculous lie. Everyone had considered at some point what kind of Realm Reacher they would want to be. Wanusa let him hold the lie, though, as they would find out soon enough.

"He should hope to be anything but a Spirit Reacher," Mariana said, crossing the camp. "Whisperers bond those born of Zekiaz. Reachers seek to command them."

"Most Spirit Reachers protect against awakened, just like Glassblades," Radais replied. "We'll need both against breathless too."

Mariana crossed her arms with her hands tucked within her wide sleeves. "They will be unnecessary if we grow to understand the spirits' desires."

"Then why not make everyone a Whisperer?" Wanusa asked, carefully scratching Alicy's head where her spines weren't. More than once already, she'd discovered how much those things could hurt.

"The power you and I share is incredibly dangerous in the wrong hands. Having bonded only half a spirit, you have yet to taste but a fraction of it, so know the restraints we place upon access to the Deepening are necessary." She eyed Radais. "Spirit Reachers face no such restrictions. They are free to thwart the natural way of the spirits."

Wanusa lifted her chin. "Then we should teach them. Haven't the breathless changed everything? Shouldn't we work with allies to protect both humans and spirits?"

"You would not be a Whisperer if I did not recognize such a threat."

Radais patted Wanusa on the back and stepped past her. "I don't choose the realm, so it's not worth arguing about." He nodded to Mariana. "I understand your point, but it isn't my goal to manipulate spirits, just to stop the Vanashel."

Mariana produced the Fire Crystal, cupping it in her gloved hands. "May your sentiments extend through time. You are the first known Vockan to become a Realm Reacher, Radais ik Erienfar, and I hope you never forget the example you set for others."

"Take the crystal, and it should do the rest," Lazan said with a restrained smile. "Do not fight when it seeks to bind you."

Sighing heavily, Radais nodded to the scion, then approached Mariana. He removed the gloves he typically wore beneath his gauntlets and handed them to Lazan. Wanusa's heart raced each step in the process. Had it felt so excruciatingly slow for Radais when she'd become a Whisperer? She was too excited to wait for the result, and Inrius's eager spirit flared within her, awaiting it the same as her.

"Come, Brother," she said in the Spiritspeech, tapping her collar. "See the rise of our first Reacher."

The action wasn't necessary to call his spirit, but it felt right to feel the crystal's vibrations join with her Whispering. Inrius emerged from her very skin with that same hum emanating from his translucent spirit form. He was still weak due to his divided spirit, but she felt him within those spirit vapors. Something thumped within him, copying her own rapid heartbeat.

"Air," Inrius said.

"What?"

He hesitated, as if struggling to elaborate further. "My… realm…"

The eager presence within him faded, but his spirit remained curled around her arm. Like a perched cat, he watched silently as Radais took the Fire Crystal. Wanusa held her breath. Lazan had implied the effect was immediate, but the seconds passed so slowly. She looked from Radais to Mariana, wondering if something was wrong.

Then flames snapped around the Glassblade.

Mariana staggered back with embers boring holes through her robes, but she made no outburst. No one hurried to help her. Both Wanusa and Lazan were too focused on the deep orange crystal entrapping Radais's fingers.

"What… What is it doing?" Radais asked, looking to Lazan for answers, but the scion just laughed in glee.

"Calm, my dear. It is *working*."

Radais bared his teeth and flexed his hand before him. The crystal slithered across it, grappling and releasing each finger before settling on his index one. It resembled an Ezmani talon, but when Wanusa shifted closer to get a better look, she saw the burnt orange points rising from between each knuckle. Like mountains basked in the dawnrise glow instead of the winding crystal of Lazan's talon.

"It's beautiful!" she exclaimed as Inrius's spirit settled to a dull contentment. "What does it feel like?"

Radais ran the tip of his thumb over the sharp end of the talon, able to tear through the veil between realms, before looking to Lazan. "Did you hear a voice when you got your talon?"

"I did not," Lazan replied, brow raised, "but it is not unheard of for new Reachers to experience strange sensations during the initial process."

"I could've sworn..." Radais shook his head before glancing back at Wanusa. "It feels like I've got a bunch of crystal wrapped around my finger. More uncomfortable than I expected, to be honest, but there's something else too." He clenched and unclenched his fist. "When you Whisper, do you have a pool of some kind of power within you, like you're tapping into it?"

She waved a hand over Inrius, who shied away from Radais. "It's more like a conversation. Our Spirit Crystal doesn't let us Reach, just bond spirits who we can persuade to help us." It wasn't the best explanation, but a better one escaped her mind as she looked to Mariana for guidance.

"You need not know the mysteries of a Whisper's abilities," the elder Whisperer said, "but know that it does not operate in the same manner to your talon. The only commonality is in the Essence that allows all magic."

Lazan tapped his talon. "Reach, and let us see how it truly works."

So Radais held out his hand, and in it, Wanusa felt the vibrations of the Fire Crystal shift. It fell out of alignment with his core at first. Soon, though, it blended between fire and another pattern she'd not yet heard, forming a heavy, constant melody.

The ground cracked beneath her feet. She stumbled, leaping away as Alicy yapped at her heels, somehow believing that would help. But the crack was neither deep nor wide, and Wanusa laughed at herself for reacting in such a panicked fashion over something so small. Glassblade training had taught her to always be on edge, since awakened could attack at any time. That didn't make it feel any less silly.

"It seems you have focused quite a lot on the foe who nearly killed you and your ibex," Lazan said, a hand held out toward Radais to calm him. "Perhaps don't think of him now, though, as your Reach is still active."

Deep brown wisps raced around Radais like hornets. His eyes darted to each as the ground cracked further, but his breaths slowed when Lazan approached. "I can't control it!"

"Break away from the talon's pull to the Earth realm," Lazan said. "It will seek to Reach repeatedly, and you must stop it to prevent yourself from enduring Realm Taint."

Radais closed his eyes as Wanusa sensed the Earth realm's pattern falling out of alignment with the Fire one. It shrieked painfully through her skull. She wanted to beg him to Reach again, but reminded herself that she never heard such noises when Lazan Reached. It would pass quickly.

Gratefully, the shrieking dissipated with the Earth wisps, leaving them to stand with only the whistling of the wind to break the silence. No one spoke. Even Wanusa's breaths caught in her chest until Radais laughed.

Lazan echoed it as he embraced his lover. "Your first Reach is quite the rush, is it not?"

"You could've warned me," Radais replied, accepting the hug, then slapping Lazan hard enough on the back to make him huff. "Is the Taint that horrible feeling in my stomach, or is that just your cooking?"

Lazan chuckled. "It is normal to take a bit of Taint as you learn. Don't worry. It takes more of it to endure any noticeable cost behind some temporary sickness, but from now on, it will build up within you." His face drooped as he clenched his taloned hand into a fist. "My own Reaching has granted me immense pain in my joints and weakness in my bones. I do not regret those who I've helped, though. All things are a choice, even this."

In the commotion, Wanusa hadn't noticed Inrius's spirit

returning to her body. He seemed pleased, yet still distant. This was just the spirit of her brother and not him in his entirety. Still, it felt right to give him experiences he never had the chance to see in life. Mariana could criticize such uses of her Whispering all she wanted, but she refused to abandon Inrius. Not as long as there was hope.

"That talon will not regain its Essence through passive existence in this realm," Mariana said. "You must expose it to fire, which will be difficult as we travel."

Lazan took Radais's talon and placed it on his chest. "Then hold your hand over the fire that burns for you in my heart."

"Oh spirits," Wanusa gagged. "Keep that in your tent."

"I'll light a torch and do whatever else I must to keep the power at-hand," Radais said with a nod to Mariana. "But we have lingered here for too long. We must hurry down the mountain if we don't want to leave the other Glassblades waiting."

Mariana huffed. "It is the Vanashel we should be worried about, not your friends clad in glass."

THE PRINCESS IN THE HIGH TOWER

"Every lowborn gazes upon the scions in their palaces and manors. Some wish to become them. Others wish to replace them. But I want to burn them to ash."
– An excerpt from *The Dawnrise Manifesto* by Evit Paxian

Nex left everything behind.

They felt like their heart should ache as they rushed away from Kasia's portal with Hazat Tozki, fending off the breathless as they ran. Instead, rage drove them on. The Crimsons had slaughtered hundreds of the Ashes of Dawn and other innocent lowborn. Those people had trusted Nex, believed in them.

Now they were dead.

Every breathless that slipped past Hazat's Reaching found a bitter blade clutched in Nex's fist. The dagger was little more than three inches of glass, but that's all they needed to kill the bastards. They'd killed Nex's friends. Nobody got away with that.

Hazat claimed he had a plan to escape the breathless and save Nikoza. Slipping away from the portal was the first part of that. There had been thousands of breathless near Crax's Place, but now, only a few breakaways chased them toward the river.

"What's your genius plan to get us to Nikoza?" Nex asked,

slashing through the last nearby breathless and following the Spirit Reacher down a cramped alley.

Most on the west side knew how to hole up when there was chaos like this, but there were still a few idiots gawking at them from their front stoops. Hazat did his best to dodge through them. Nex didn't, elbowing the onlookers out of the way and demanding they get inside. Didn't they know the breathless often attacked people near their targets?

"If I speak it, they may hear," Hazat replied over his shoulder. "Even when the spirits aren't near, the Crimson King has ears everywhere."

Nex gritted their teeth. "How did he find us? Did they torture Nikoza?"

"Another Spirit Reacher, Vanzearik, managed to scout the area where you took her." He pointed at the nearest Reacher towers. "With that information and the Reacher towers, the Crystal Brigade were able to identify your safehouses based on foot traffic. I only found out about the attack today, though, as they likely believe I am too close to Nikoza to trust."

They stopped at the next intersection as heavy footsteps signaled watchmen on the main street. Barricades blocked the routes out of the Shadow Quarter, and Light Reachers illuminated the shadowy alleys that gave the district its name. There was no way forward.

"They knew some of you would try to escape," Hazat said, "but they are too afraid of an ambush to send watchmen into the alleys." He eyed the looming tenements. "Do you know of any vacant buildings nearby? We can wait out the search there, because, though I have a plan, I failed to consider this cordon."

Normally, Nex would've been smitten at his lack of knowledge about the west side, but they were too furious for that. So they just nodded down another alley and led the way without a word. Scions *always* challenged lowborn who wanted to lead. Hazat didn't as he kept at the ends of Nex's coattails, that taloned hand of his flexed to Reach at any moment.

Nex's own Reaching split between luck for them and holding

their new appearance. The disguise wouldn't hold up if they were caught, but it felt right. Staying behind meant separating from Vinnia, who they'd apparently been obsessed with saving before. The Crimsons' Truth Reachers had changed Nex—denying it would change nothing. They were still Nex, but a different version of them.

They led Hazat to an apartment they knew would be empty above an old, rotting warehouse. A wind chime made of scraps rattled in the dawnrise light above the neighbor's door, and Nex found themself searching for any memory of its inhabitant. They had a vague mental picture of an elderly woman, but no name.

"This is my old place," they told Hazat, flinching as a spirit appeared at the edge of their vision.

Hazat waved it away. "It is only a drifter. I get why it would startle you, though, when your skies are full of breathless and awakened. Being from the countryside, I understand at least what it is to fear the spirits."

"Don't need your understanding," Nex muttered as they slid their key into the lock and jolted open the rusted latch.

"Wait, is this your apartment?" He glanced over his shoulder. "They could know."

Nex stepped inside, forcing him to mutter under his breath and follow in behind. The room beyond was near dark, the only light coming from the cracks around the door and shuttered window at the far end. Beyond the changing season, it was just how they'd left it: cramped, damp, and reeking of rot.

That was all they remembered about the place except for flashes of Vinnia sitting upon the bed. Her legs tucked in close so that Nex could lay beside her, their only candle seeming to ignite her Vockan hair like the blaze that had consumed Kalastok at everdark's end.

Those should've been sweet memories for Nex to cradle to their bosom like a mother and her child, but instead, they felt like someone else's life. That stranger's joys. That stranger's hopes. That stranger's love.

"We haven't lived here since the riots," Nex finally replied. "The Crimsons didn't care about me back then… At least, I don't remember them caring."

"It will have to do," Hazat said, sitting uncomfortably on one of the two wooden chairs tucked up against the small table. He tried crossing his legs, but gave up after a lot of wincing.

Nex frowned. "You're just going to sit there?"

"Would you prefer me to stand?"

"That's not… Whatever." Nex waved their arms about and threw themself into the chair across from him. "What do we do now?"

Hazat gave a nobleman's smile, and Nex had to resist the urge to smack it off his face. "Considering I ran halfway across Kalastok to save your life and that of perhaps thousands of your people, I deserve a moment's respite, don't you think?" He traced his talon, his head drooping. "In the last couple hours, I have endured more Taint than the rest of my life. My stomach feels as if it is ready to burst from my body, and my will is greatly dampened by Taint."

"You regret helping us." Nex huffed. "Of course you do."

That damned smile grew. "Not in the slightest. Aiding your people was perhaps the greatest accomplishment of my life to date, but that does not lessen the cost I will bear the rest of my life."

Nex rapped their crystal ring against the table, remembering how trapped they'd felt in their Tainted moments. Rumors said Possibility Reachers lost their grip on reality and became stuck without any idea of what could happen. That single taste of it had been enough. "Taint sucks. I get it."

"I know this is not what you want to hear," he said, "but we should hide until tomorrow morning. Besides the barricades, my Taint will only worsen if I do not sleep before Reaching again. Some breathless will surely be around when we attempt to cross the river."

He was right. Nex didn't want to wait, but all they'd done their entire life was wait for chances to make their move. So they would trust Hazat. As much as it hurt working with a scion, he'd earned that trust.

"Fine," they said, "but this plan of yours better be worth it."

TIME PASSED HORRIBLY SLOW in Nikoza's palace prison. She was confined with the luxuries of her chambers, but she could find no enjoyment in it when each knock on the door reminded her why she was trapped.

Chatik wanted her to be his Crystal Heir.

He had sought for her to be reveled among the populace as an influential leader with every realm at her fingertips, but her defiance now meant the Crimsons would hold true power. She had trained her Water Reaching over the last season. It was nothing against the magic of the Unity Crystal that Chatik wielded.

Her thoughts swam as she sat at her desk and stared down at a half-written letter to some dignitary. She could not remember what it was about, as courtly politics felt so empty compared to the horror she now faced. She needed to escape. Being trapped here was like watching the yearly sun disappear over the horizon, knowing it would be many sleeps before she ever saw the light again.

But how could she break free from the palace itself? Gregorzon, that manipulative cretin, read every letter she sent and received, and a Force Reacher kept shut the balcony doors. When she begged to see the dawnrise sunlight, Gregorzon had allowed her a few minutes, but no more. There was little she could do under his watch, and while wearing a locked prisoner's glove over her talon, she could not Reach either.

Those moments outside had offered her a view of Kalastok. It seemed a dead city, more watchmen and soldiers filling the streets than civilians, and the skies were unrecognizable. Drifters once would've roamed while Reachers in the towers kept the awakened away. There were so many breathless now, darkening the sky worse than the smoke from the factories west of the Kala. Those worked double-time to fuel Chatik's war machine—a war he need not win.

She had felt more powerless on that balcony than in the room. It forced her to see the Commonwealth's many problems, yet have no way to mend them. Her time as a princess had been so similar, but she had whispered into her grandfather's ear then.

Every Ezmani scion dreamed of having the great houses' power. She could write to any of House Bartol's thousands of workers, soldiers, and bureaucrats with the stroke of a pen. If she could but send an unfiltered letter to her allies, perhaps they could free her from this place. She had tried multiple times, but Gregorzon had caught her poor attempts at hiding a secret message.

Ah, yes, that was it, she remembered, staring down at the letter before her. She had once again been trying to write an encoded message for her widowed mother back in Anukit. Except looking at it now, it was clear that a barely literate child would see through her ruse.

"Millions dream of having a chance to better the world," Gregorzon said, pacing behind her. She had half-forgotten his presence, and her muscles tightened at the realization. How had she trusted him? There had been a spark of attraction there, but she had no doubts that had been her uncle's machinations too.

"What do you dream of?" she replied with a swift stroke of her quill.

He leaned on the desk and pushed up her chin, forcing her to meet his gaze. "When I arrived here in hopes of winning your hand, King Chatik told me you were timid. That is far preferable to my sister's arrogance."

"What ever happened to Lady Katarzyna?"

It was a probing question, ignoring his desire to win her hand. During her visit to the Ashes of Dawn, Kasia's footman had confirmed that the Amber Dame was alive and cooperating with Tiuz Hazeko's Confederation of Harizak. Gregorzon did not know that, though, and she hoped his response could grant her some insight into the Crimsons' limitations.

"We thought she was dead for a time," he replied, "but she continues to be troublesome. One rogue scion is not too much for us to handle, however, and with me taking her place as house head, she is without resources. Both she and the Confederation will be brought to heel soon enough. All who wish to keep the old way of things must."

"Is that why the newspapers claim House Niezik's mercenaries are marching to join the Confederation?" That much was public information, so it did not reveal what she truly knew.

Gregorzon clenched his jaw. "Tiuz and the traitors from my own house are in for a shock when the Third Army arrives. Our Crimson King has saved the breathless for a special moment." He glanced toward the balcony. "Well, two moments."

His menacing tone gave Nikoza pause. He had toyed with her ever since his first appearance in the Chamber of Scions all those hundred-hours ago, and it was only now that she noticed the patterns in his speech. This wasn't a lie. Something was happening, and he badly wanted to tell her.

"What has our dear king done this time?" she said, her words lathered with scion conceit to cover her nerves. "I am certain it advances your Crimson Cause."

"Thanks to your assistance in the construction of the western city Reacher towers, we have been able to gather valuable information on dissidents." He tapped the desk right next to her hand. "Oh, and thank you for guiding us to Nex and the Ashes of Dawn. That was quite *invaluable*."

She stiffened. Chatik had claimed that Vanzearik followed her to the Ashes of Dawn safehouse, but isolated in her chambers, she had heard nothing of any attack. Steeling herself, she met Gregorzon's gaze. "You have them in your custody, then?"

He turned away with a scoff and returned to his position near the door. "You misunderstand. We have no use for their leader now that we have identified the rebel safehouses." He opened the door and chuckled to himself. "Nex is dead, my lady, along with the rest of the combatants within the Ashes of Dawn. Thanks to you, they found quite quickly how efficient the breathless are, but worry not, we are simply protecting the innocents of the western city from this scourge."

When he left, Nikoza let out a sharp breath, then a sniffle. She had conspired with the Ashes of Dawn no more than a hundred-hour before. Had she truly led them to their demise so quickly?

A tear fell onto her note, so she slipped from her chair, wiping away the ones that followed as she pictured all the innocents she had seen west of the river. They had been desperate. And by trusting her, they had sealed their fates.

All she had wanted was to help people. Instead, Chatik had twisted her actions to his own ends. If Nex was truly dead along with the Ashes of Dawn, then the Crimsons had crushed what little hope existed in the Shadow Quarter and Industrial District in the process. The rebellion within Kalastok was over.

"I'm sorry, Nex," Nikoza mumbled, throwing herself onto her bed and stuffing her face into the pillow. It was childish, but she had no better way to channel her anguish. Nex was dead. And by the Crystal Mother, her heart ached.

A *thud* from the balcony tore her from her sorrow. The double doors often shuddered when the Force Reachers switched their shifts, but this was louder than normal.

Slowly, she pulled herself free from the bed and approached the doors. Her stocking-covered feet sounded like hammers against the marble floor, so she quickly slipped on her soft-soled shoes as she noticed a change about the doors. The bright red Force whisps around them were gone. Not transitioning from one Reacher to another. *Gone.*

This was her chance at freedom. She could hurry onto the balcony and then find some way to climb down. It would be dangerous for even an experienced climber, but she had to try. The alternative was waiting here for a life as the Crystal Heir.

Her breaths quickened as she laid her hand on the doorknob, hesitant. It had always been locked by Force Reacher magic before, and this could be another trick. She took a single step back, whispering a quiet prayer to her goddess whose statue rested at the palace's heart. The Crystal Mother preferred buried prayers to spoken ones, but it was difficult to bury anything when trapped on the third floor. This would have to do.

Shuffling on the balcony broke her stasis. She rushed back to the bed, throwing herself into it to pretend she was resting. If a Crimson was waiting for her outside, they would see nothing more than a startled princess.

The balcony doors clicked open, followed by a familiar whisper. "You can be sorry another time. Just get your scion ass out here."

THE PALACE HALLS

"The Crystal Palace's exterior declares the glory of the Crystal Mother and the scions who inherit her gifts. Its interior is reserved only for those few entrusted with such an honor." – Uliazina Rakazimko, anointed sister of the Buried Temple

ONE HOUR EARLIER

"How do guards wear these stupid things all day?" Nex muttered, itching beneath their tall watchman's cap.

Hazat checked a pocket watch as they headed through the Shadow Quarter's alleys on the way to the King's Bridge, then the Crystal Palace. "You shouldn't talk like that. Though you have altered your appearance, your cadence is hardly that of a palace watchman."

They flared their nostrils. "I trick people all the time into thinking I'm a scion."

"That is where you're wrong. The vast majority of watchmen, mercenaries, and guards are lowborn, unlike you."

"I am *not* a scion," Nex said, practicing a guard's voice. Their Possibility Reaching had them looking like an Ezmani lowborn with brunette hair and a mean jawline. The disguise had taken a few tries to get right, but they'd had plenty of time while waiting for the end of the Crimsons' barricade. It must've been convincing, because the remaining west side lowborn shuddered their windows and hurried inside when they saw the pair.

Nex couldn't blame them. The whole last day had had everyone's nerves on edge, and Nex more than any. Between the breathless attack, the fake Crimson cure for the Spirit Plague, and learning about Nikoza's fate, they were eager for revenge. Working with Hazat and Nikoza was their best chance to get it. That didn't mean they liked cooperating with scions.

Hazat raised his brow. "You can Reach with a crystal ring. That means you have enough scion blood to be a Reacher."

Nex didn't reply. Most of the Ashes of Dawn hadn't bothered to question why Nex could Possibility Reach, but these damned scions were too smart for their own good. Of course Nex knew about the gray birthmark on the back of their shoulder. They weren't stupid. To Reach, they needed to be part scion, and they hated knowing that. Those bastards had taken everything from them. Whatever Nex's bloodline, they were no bloody scion.

"Where are all the watchmen today? Shoulda passed a few on patrol by now." Nex said, avoiding the subject as they adjusted their watchman's musket on their shoulder. Despite Hazat's guess, there had been a few Crimson patrols through the Shadow Quarter the day before, so Nex had stolen one's uniform and equipment. Based on how much he'd bled, he wouldn't be needing it back.

Hazat slowed. "You are right about that."

They emerged onto Beg Ave along the riverfront, and to Nex's shock, the King's Bridge didn't have a single guard standing post. For two seasons, the scions had trapped the lowborn in the west side. What? Had they decided all was fine now that they thought they'd gotten rid of the Ashes?

"I have no doubt this has to do with both the Crimsons' false cure and the attack yesterday," Hazat continued, leading them to the stonework bridge. "King Chatik has been awfully twitchy lately, but the Crystal Brigade's captain, Tzena, won't tell us much."

"What's that mean?" Nex asked.

Hazat's shoulders sank. "It means something big is about to happen, but I am unsure if I am able to stop it. My investigations led me to you and Nikoza as my first real allies. I can only hope it was not too late."

"It was already too late for the Ashes." Nex shuddered as a squad of breathless flew overhead, their stupid smoky forms haunting Nex's memories. "Shit, I hate those things."

"Believe me, it is far worse having felt what it is like to command them." He ran a thumb over his talon and the Crystal Brigade glove surrounding it. "These spirits are awakened with fresh minds. They are little more than newborns, and the Crimsons use that to mold them to their will."

"They're fucking murderers!" Nex snapped. "I don't care if they're baby spirits or not."

Hazat held out his hands to calm them. "I understand, but all I mean to say is that the spirits themselves are merely tools. Even a common soldier has some element of choice, though little. These breathless have none." He straightened his posture as they neared the bridge's end. "We must assume from now on that we can be seen at all times."

Nex tried to mimic a watchman's stiff walk. It wasn't hard to look ready to beat the shit out of someone when that was *exactly* what they wanted to do, but that would come later. First, they had a role to play.

The transition from the slums of the Shadow Quarter to the Crimson District's glass-trimmed mansions and townhouses was jarring. There were even blooming trees and gardens here, not to mention fountains and streets full of merchants freely selling food and luxuries. Nex had seen people shot for a slice of bread west of the Kala. Here, morsels were freely given as a *sample* of the food's taste.

"War didn't hit the scions like the rest of us," Nex muttered.

Hazat kept his chin high. "This is restrained compared to my first days in Kalastok. The Crimson Court uplifts the scions far above the wealthiest lowborn merchants, but the great houses see only

Reachers sent to war and resources lost to Kelosh and the Confederation. Chatik wants the power with his sycophants, not the magnates. That won't happen without a fight."

The Crystal Palace loomed over them now. This wasn't Nex's first time in the Crimson District, but they'd never gotten this close to the heart of the Commonwealth's seat of power. Its elaborate towers of glass and marble sickened them. A single shard of pure glass was worth more keni than many lowborn would see in their entire lives, and here it was, just piled up for old scions to sit inside as they debated who to fuck over next.

Nex straightened their jacket as they approached the guards separating the palace from the rest of the Crimson District. Unlike their counterparts who patrolled the west side, these stood with discipline, a sword on one hip and their muskets shouldered. They were the exact type of guards that Nex told their people to avoid.

"Hello there, my good guardsmen," Hazat began with an uncomfortably wide smile before displaying his glass bracers. "We are here on Crystal Brigade business."

The guard wrinkled his nose. "Surprised you weren't back already. Minister Tzena had the rest of you Reachers flooding into the palace in yesterday, and it sounds like there's just a skeleton crew out on the towers."

Nex had to fight the urge to swap glances with Hazat. Why would the Crimsons pull back from the eastern half of the city too? It confirmed that the Crimsons had more to their plan than just attacking the Ashes of Dawn, but it also meant there were even more Reachers in the palace. Any of them could know Hazat had betrayed them.

"We're without rest as of late," Hazat told the guard, checking his pocket watch when the clocktower rang for the twelfth hour. "Tzena had us on a special mission, and believe me, it is better if you did not allow us to be late."

The guard chuckled, then waved them on. "Fine, keep your secrets."

The pair continued down the main street. Lined with brightly colored trees, a sweet fragrance filled the air, and it stung Nex's nostrils.

All they'd known were streets reeking of piss, shit, and factory smog. The contrast was almost too much to bear. But they did bear it. For those they'd lost and for the trapped princess who'd saved them, they pushed up the marble steps, heading into the Crystal Palace.

Scions gathered in groups throughout the entry hall and side rooms whose doors were just cracked enough to hear the hum of conversation beyond. Most were too hushed to understand, but there were more than a few reddened faces. Rich people were always flustered about something. For once, though, their distrustful glances were given to each other and not Nex.

"Are you going to tell me the plan *now*?" Nex whispered as they entered a rounded room at the hall's end. A statue Nex assumed was of the scions' so-called Crystal Mother stood at the room's center, but no one gave it any attention.

Hazat just surveyed the scion politicians. All were well dressed with Crimson adornments on their suits and jackets, but strangely, none wore any of the visible glass that Nex had always seen the elites have before. A bell rang somewhere above, and the politicians filed through a pair of double doors at the room's far end. Was that the infamous Chamber of Scions?

Nex didn't get a chance to find out, because Hazat suddenly nodded for them to follow him toward a side hall, then up a set of stairs. Sweat beaded on Nex's brow. They were in the nest of vipers now. Everyone here despised them, and the Truth Reachers who'd tortured them were likely here too. Yet more names of the list of Crimsons they so badly wanted dead.

Hazat's silence became more and more annoying, but Nex kept their mouth shut until he stopped outside a door that looked no different than all the others. He checked his watch *again* with a nervous breath.

"My squad's Force Reacher, Jolzena, should be on duty outside Nikoza's balcony for the next fifteen minutes," he said. "This room is directly beneath it. Above would be easier, but that is the Reachers' training floor."

"You trust her?" Nex asked.

He took a deep breath. "She is not aware of everything, but she is furious that her brother, Vanzearik, reported Nikoza for leading you back to the west side. Her loyalty to Nikoza should be enough."

Nex eyed the door. "Then c'mon. What are we waiting for?"

"I need you to stand guard in case someone tries to enter," Hazat replied with an unconvincing smile. "This office is empty when the door is shut, but if anyone comes by for some reason, tell them this is Crystal Brigade business. That line usually works."

"And if it doesn't, can I just stab them?"

Hazat shrugged. "As long as they are not one of the servants forced to wear those silver masks, then sure. Please do not cause a commotion if you must act."

Then he slipped through the door, leaving Nex in the empty hall. They did their best to imitate a guard standing at attention, but they weren't trained to just stand still. Every second felt like an eternity. Footsteps echoed from around corners, and whispered conversations came from the nearby rooms. Anyone could arrive and realize Nex was badly out of place.

Heavy footfalls approached from the stairs a few minutes later. Nex knew that type well: rhythmic, stiff, and without any care of being heard. It could only mean one thing.

Guards.

Memories of Nex's time in the palace dungeon speared their mind. The pain, the battle of wills against the Truth Reachers. They staggered back into the door with their breaths heavy. They couldn't get caught, not again.

Nex threw open the door and rushed in, shutting it behind them just as the guards turned the corner. They waited there for a few excruciating moments. Could the guards hear them breathing? Would they see their shadow under the door? Silently, they cursed themselves, but could only bite their cheek as they waited for the guards to pass.

When the footsteps faded away, Nex sighed in relief, only to be grabbed by the neck. A hulking woman threw them onto the rug in the center of the office. Then she cocked her gun.

"Who are you?" the woman asked.

Nex blinked away their shock. Their attacker wore a Crystal Brigade coat with bright red embroidery instead of Hazat's silver, and her eyes were like charcoal swallowed by the everdark snow. Not exactly what Nex had expected from a scion Reacher.

"They are with me, Jolzena," Hazat said from the double doors behind the desk. They were cracked, allowing just a sliver of dawnrise light into the otherwise dim room. "Nex has been protecting the western city, and Nikoza trusts them."

"They look like one who can fight," Jolzena said, releasing Nex. "Good. Between my brother and Gregorzon, we've got enough cowards around here."

Hazat pointed up. "Have you let down the shield?"

"Of course I did."

"Then it is Nex's turn," Hazat said, eyeing his pocket watch. "Help them up, and let's finish this before the next shift starts."

Nex furrowed their brow as Jolzena hoisted them to their feet. "My turn for what?"

He waved a hand toward the doors. "You didn't believe I brought you just to watch the door, did you?"

The Wars of Crimsons and Spirits
TERRITORY AS OF THE 14TH DAY OF DAWNRISE, 791 POST-AWAKENING
FLAGS & SIGILS MARK KNOWN ARMY LOCATIONS/MOVEMENTS
LETIANITAN
Occupied N
Nochland Lake Force
Crimson Em
NA-REQ
FORT KALA
Ogrenian Hegemony
KALASTOK
Piketik
TARGEER
Olie
Glassblade Order
Emani 3rd Army
Rebel Army
PALMIA FORTESS
DALNUS
VAMIUSTOK
FORT HARIZAK
Vanashel Army
Glassblades
VAMIA MINES
Zinarus's Brigade
TY
ILIAFA
Harizak Confede
ARDINVIL
ERIENFAR
Vanashel

Keloshan Empire
ORIAKSTAK
Keloshan Liberators
island
ZAKINIV
fol
Grand Keloshan Army
NUKIT
LOST BROTHERS' FORTS
Ezmani 1st Army
Ezmani 2nd Army
REXANIV
GIAMIVIK
RAVIAK FOREST
Keloshan Reclaimers
Uziokaki
MASTOK
Reshkan Colonies
Factions
HARIZAK CONFEDERATION
CRIMSON COURT & ALLIES
KELOSH | BLADES | VANASHEL
Legend
NATIONAL CAPITAL
REGIONAL CAPITAL
MAJOR CITY
MINOR CITY
BORDER
LINE OF CONTROL
ARMY (SIGILS/FLAGS)
ARMY MOVEMENT

THE VAMIA'S BANK

"Take me down to where the Vamia meets the shore
We'll swim through the waters until we grow bored
Then we'll follow the spirits and drift in bliss
Until our bodies meet the Ty's sweet kiss." – Ballad of the Two Rivers, a
riverman song

Kasia awoke in darkness, a headache splitting her head and agony consuming her stomach. Countless voices screeched around her. Aliax and her own Tainted specter were among them, but now there were more: Zinarus, Tazper, Nex, Hazat, and everyone else she'd ever known. Few spoke any understandable words. The ones she grasped, though, were vicious, piercing her thoughts until none of her own remained.

The pain was too much. She could only curl into a ball and weep until it all passed.

But it didn't pass. Time stretched and slowed like a meandering river, the beat of her heart the only way for her to track it, and the cost of her Reaching endured through every moment. Teleporting over a thousand lowborn to safety had earned her this torment. She lacked the strength to wonder if it had been worth it.

Spitza's broken *gwah, gwah,* came from somewhere nearby. The scraping of her talons against rock approached, and she made a series of clicking noises before landing on Kasia. Granted, it wasn't *much* weight, but it felt like a boulder had crushed her spine.

"Get off," she muttered to the raven, whose only response was another set of clicks. "Stupid bird."

Time seemed to steady with Spitza there, though. It was silly, but those needle-sharp talons digging into her back grounded her. Not silencing the voices completely, but helping her separate her Tainted mind from reality.

That newfound awareness made it clear there was someone else nearby. They snored like a cannon, but Kasia was too frayed to consider who they could be—probably another Taint-induced specter. Would those she left behind in Kalastok haunt her now, or was this the result of pushing herself beyond the pale and into Taint's insanity?

"Shut up!" she spat at the snoring ghost. "Leave me alone!"

They awoke with a start, releasing a startled squeak that Spitza echoed with remarkable precision. "Lady Kasia, are you well?" a sleepy, but gentle voice asked.

"Kikania?" Kasia shook her head, but couldn't see a thing in the darkness. "No! You're just another specter."

A match flickered to life, revealing the edge of her handmaiden's face. Not enough to prove anything. "Of course I'm not," Kikania said. "I am here with you in Lord Zinarus's camp. Do you remember what happened?"

Kasia gritted her teeth, fighting the Taint for a stray thought. She did remember, but it was muddled. Had their escape from Kalastok been hours ago? Days?

"Why would you be with him after I left?" she asked.

A pained expression crossed Kikania's face. "I... I didn't know where to go. Lord Zinarus was the only person I knew, and he offered to bring me to the Niezik forces. We are all headed to Fort Harizak after all."

The other voices worsened. Some claimed she had abandoned Kikania and Zinarus, while others said she should've left permanently. Each gave a different solution to her current predicament, but there were so many that they joined into a jumbled mess. By the end of it, Kasia could not even remember what Kikania had said… or trust that she was real.

She took a long blink to steady herself, and when she opened her eyes, Kikania was gone. The maid's light had vanished with her. Kasia shifted to try and gain her bearing, realizing Spitza's talons no longer dug into her back either.

What just happened?

Her head still seared, but a panging in her stomach had replaced her nausea. She couldn't remember when she had eaten last. That made sense, considering she was unsure when *now* even was, but it didn't help settle her fractured mind. She needed to get out of this damned darkness and figure out what in the wastes was going on.

Except when she shifted, she found a strange sensation tingling across her left arm. She ran her fingers over the Axiom Crystal ring in the center of her palm, then traced it up and through her first burn scar. This crystal had slowly become familiar to her. It was what lay above, though, that confirmed her fears.

"All power has a price," Sazilz Uziokaki's voice taunted. "To use it for such foolishness as this, however…" He scoffed. "There is no one who deserves this suffering more."

"Which one of us is dead?" she hissed.

But her voice shook, because as she ran her fingers further up her arm, the crystal didn't stop. Like the web of a spider, it entangled her all the way through the shoulder before stopping just above her collarbone. A single use of her Reaching had more than tripled the Axiom's Realm Taint. On top of her Taint from Death, she dared not consider what she'd done to herself.

"I need to find Zinarus," she told herself, trying to fight her body and rise. It denied her, and she found herself falling back on what she assumed to be a bedroll.

Light flooded the space a blink later.

Three people surrounded her in a tent large enough to stand in. They were settled, as if they had been there for some time, but that was impossible. She'd been alone in the dark moments before, had she not?

"… never seen anything like this," the standing woman, who she recognized as Zinarus's Aunt Carelias, was in the middle of saying. "All Realm Taint manifests differently, and we have no studies about this so-called Axiom Crystal."

Zinarus sat on a chair beside Kasia, pinching the bridge of his nose and sighing. Clad in a purple officer's uniform with a golden sash and adornments, he looked the part of a commander, but exhaustion stained his face. "Is there nothing you can do for her?"

"My Reaching has reinforced her strength, which is why she has woken at all," Carelias said. "Taint is deeper than mere bodily harm, Nephew."

"You are certain you cannot grant her further aid?"

Kikania's higher voice interrupted them. "Excuse me, my lord and lady, but I believe she is present again."

Zinarus's copper eyes fell upon Kasia, a relieved smile tugging at his lips as he grasped her right hand. "Kasia! Are you well?"

"Why is that all you people ask?" she grumbled. The voices hadn't quieted, and it took all her focus to not fall into their trance again. "How long have you been here? One second, I was trying to stand, and the next, you all were surrounding me."

He squeezed her hand. "It is alright. You saved nearly two thousand Kalastok lowborn through your Reaching, but that took a heavy toll on your body—and likely your mind too. Carelias says that much Realm Taint is bound to be disorientating."

She flexed her crystal-wrapped hand, hoping the rest of it had vanished from beneath her sleeve. It hadn't, and as she checked the crystal stretching up the left side of her neck, she took a moment to grasp that it would remain her entire life.

"How long has it been?" she asked.

Zinarus swapped glances with his aunt. "Three days. You all arrived about a day's travel from Fort Harizak, but a force of Crimson cavalry have been harrying our flanks, slowing us considerably. We are holding a bridge front to allow the steady flow of our infantry into the Confederation's defenses, and I must admit, the Ashes of Dawn are quite effective skirmishers."

Kasia scowled. "You're already forcing them to fight?"

"Not at all," he said, raising his hands in surrender. "Those who wished to have retreated into the fort's defenses with most of the other camp followers. A good many of them were disgruntled with me being a scion, but the three gang bosses convinced a few hundred of them to take up arms with us. They have taken to calling themselves the Amber Battalion in your honor."

The voices swarmed at that word, *honor*, whispering it over and over in her mind.

"What honor?" her Tainted specter asked from behind Zinarus. She ran the back of her hand gently over his cheek, never taking her gaze off Kasia. "What would your dear honorable lord think of our pact with Sadamar? Or you breaking it?"

"He—" Kasia cut herself off before the specter made her look insane—or at least any more insane than she already appeared. "I just repaid the Ashes for helping me, nothing more."

Zinarus nodded slowly. "Well, if the word of the people you saved means anything, they are calling you a hero." He paused, a thousand questions swirling in his eyes. "And they are right. The Crimsons' caricature of Death's Daughter would never have saved so many lives, knowing she would endure such Taint as a result, yet you did."

Footsteps approached, and the tent flap flew open to reveal a soldier in a far simpler, but matching, uniform to Zinarus's. "General Zinarus," he said, thumping his chest. "Our scouts say the Crimsons have noticed our reduced numbers and are preparing an advance."

"Ready all the infantry who remain," Zinarus replied. He fiddled with something on his mechanical knee, then stood. "We can talk more when I return, but for now, my army needs me. If we break this charge, we will be able to find safety within Fort Harizak ahead of the Crimsons' field army. Your own mercenaries are already there, and I am sure they will be relieved to know you have arrived."

He headed toward the exit, but Kasia called out for him, "Zinarus, wait."

When he looked back, he smiled, but it was clearly forced. "What can I do for you, my lady?"

"Thank you for helping the Ashes of Dawn. Many lords would not have taken them in."

"We fight for all of the Commonwealth now," he replied. "I could not abandon those in their most dire hour, especially when they are brought by you, Lady Katarzyna. Now, rest, so that if the time comes for us to call upon you in the coming days, you are ready."

She gave a shallow nod. "Yes, *Lord* Zinarus."

Hiding a grin, he turned on his heel and left with the messenger. Kasia watched him go. Voices haunted her every breath, but when he glanced back at her one last time before leaving, all fell silent. Except for her heart.

ZINARUS LET OUT A HEAVY BREATH when he stepped out of Kasia's tent, but could not release his nerves. By the Crystal Mother, he had thought of a hundred things he wished to say to her. None found his lips in her presence.

There was little time for such concerns in the face of battle. A dozen officers swarmed him before that breath was finished, each offering tactics or reports from their scouts. In a flurry, he'd gone from sitting beside the woman who held his heart to mounting his horse and cantering through the defenses protected by his remaining infantry.

With limited time and no help from Ziegfried's Earth Reaching to build earthen barricades, his mercenaries had settled for dispersed trenches with embedded anti-cavalry spears blocking the northern edge. Tiuz had described such defenses as an effective Keloshan tactic against his own cavalry charges. Decades later, Zinarus could only hope the same tactic would work against the Crimsons' greater numbers.

Much of the iz Vamiustok infantry and all the cavalry had continued

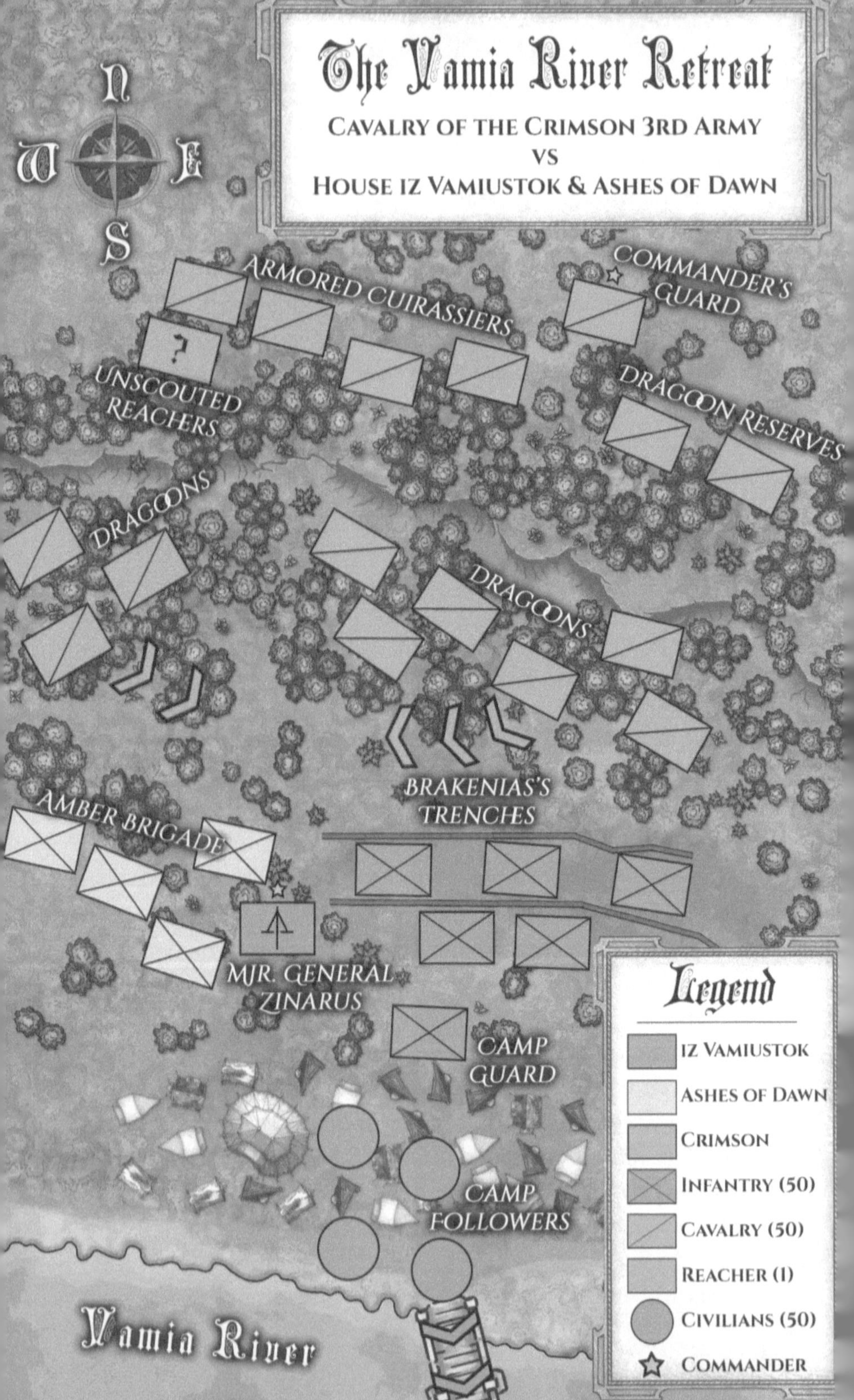

The Vamia River Retreat
Cavalry of the Crimson 3rd Army
vs
House iz Vamiustok & Ashes of Dawn
N
W E
S
ARMORED CUIRASSIERS
COMMANDER'S GUARD
?
UNSCOUTED REACHERS
DRAGOON RESERVES
DRAGOONS
DRAGOONS
BRAKENIAS'S TRENCHES
AMBER BRIGADE
MJR. GENERAL ZINARUS
CAMP GUARD
CAMP FOLLOWERS
Vamia River
Legend
IZ VAMIUSTOK
ASHES OF DAWN
CRIMSON
INFANTRY (50)
CAVALRY (50)
REACHER (1)
CIVILIANS (50)
COMMANDER

to Fort Harizak with the sand and glass convoys. That left Zinarus with a single trained battalion fighting alongside the remaining irregulars of the Ashes of Dawn's Amber Brigade—just over five hundred soldiers in total.

Their skirmishes with the Crimsons had whittled the cavalry regiment's numbers down, but with over eight hundred riders and Reacher support, their foes were a far superior force. Defensive tactics and time were Zinarus's only advantages.

Two hours. That's how long his officers claimed they needed to get the rest of the camp across to the northeastern bank of the Vamia River. If they could do that, all the iz Vamiustok troops needed to do was hold a single bridge against cavalry as the rest marched on to Fort Harizak. Simple, in theory.

That was a thought for the future. For now, the drumming of hooves against the dirt approached from the forested hills to the west. The trees offered Zinarus's infantry cover against a direct charge, but the Crimson Reachers created openings for their armored cuirassiers to draw close and cause chaos with both saber and pistol.

It was up to Zinarus to ensure that did not happen.

"Prime your muskets!" he shouted, focusing on the inexperienced Amber Brigade. His mercenaries lacked enough spare uniforms for the refugees, so they wore woolen coats and caps more suited for a message boy than a soldier, their bright yellow bandanas around their necks or arms marking their affiliations. Only the gang bosses as newly appointed captains had been given the chance to take up a uniform. All three, though, had refused.

Zinarus loaded his own carbine and circled back to check on his mercenaries. With so few numbers, every officer was another soldier with a gun in hand, and as Tiuz had taught him, he expected everyone to participate. Battles were so often won by those who broke their enemy's morale first. Seeing one's commanders fighting by their side was always a lift.

Lieutenant colonel Brakenias ik Orianta and his subordinates echoed Zinarus's command through the iz Vamiustok battalion. Built like a twig, but taller than even most Vockans, Brakenias's head emerged from the trench as he stared down his iron sights. He was one of the few in the army with the more accurate rifles compared to the dated muskets. It wasn't common for an officer to wield such scarce armaments, but Brakenias had earned his position by his renowned sharpshooting. They would need every bit of that skill.

Zinarus followed the lieutenant colonel's gaze with his looking glass to see the advancing Crimsons. For now, they were at a steady trot with a thin line to wrap around the iz Vamiustok defenses. He hoped they wouldn't notice their left flank was entirely untrained members of the Amber Brigade. Losing there would allow the Crimsons' swift dragoons to surround the trenches, leaving them with little hope of retreat.

"The command is yours here," Zinarus told the lieutenant colonel. "Hold this line, and I will focus on our friends from Kalastok."

"Yes, general," Brakenias replied without taking his eye off his sights.

Gunfire rang out ahead of Zinarus as he hurried back to the left flank. None of the trenches were well-established with such little time to dig them, but the ones here were shallow and dispersed, forcing many of the Amber Brigade irregulars to hide behind trees. It was far from the traditional line formation to accommodate for inaccurate musket fire. He could not criticize the desire to take cover as the cavalry charged, but he *could* criticize their inability to follow orders.

"Hold your fire!" he shouted, turning his horse about. "Do not waste your ammunition."

His mechanical leg decried the swift motion in an unfit stirrup, but haste mattered more than comfort now. They had a minute at most before the cavalry arrived. That was plenty of time for a trained musketman to reload. Among the irregulars, though, a wasted shot cost that full minute at the very least.

"Reload," he continued, "and do not fire until I say so."

The three gang bosses repeated the orders, acting as captains over their respective groups. He had plenty of qualms about working with crime lords, but necessity outweighed his conscience in the face of battle. These Kalastok lowborn despised scions like him. Only the bosses had their trust for now, and until Zinarus earned it, he needed them.

Gunfire popped off to his right as the Crimson dragoons probed for an opening. Zinarus raised his carbine as they approached, waiting for the right moment. He drew a long breath, steadying his arms and closing one eye to aim.

"Ready your muskets!" he called out.

His timing needed to be perfect. If those dragoons saw weakness, they would signal the armored cuirassiers waiting behind to cut straight through the Amber Brigade. It was hardly reassuring, then, that a good quarter of the irregulars were still reloading when the dragoons entered firing range.

"Fire!"

Powder stung his nostrils as he pulled the trigger. The roar of a few hundred shots echoed through the woods, followed by the cries of men and horses alike.

Zinarus gave the order to reload as the dragoons answered with a salvo of their own. Bullets peppered the trees and trenches, but he was far enough from the front line to be in relative safety. Besides, it was considered uncivilized to target a commander who was not Reaching.

The flank's skirmish continued for a good fifteen minutes by the count of his watch. Like an elongated dance, the rhythm of fire and counterfire hammered his ears and shook his core. Powder smoke made it difficult to know who had fallen, but blood and screams revealed dozens of casualties on both sides.

To their credit, though, the Amber Brigade held their ground despite watching their comrades fall. The gang bosses rallied anyone who attempted to rout, and soon enough, the dragoons retreated to regroup with their cuirassiers.

It was just the first salvo, but a victory was a victory.

Soldiers across the iz Vamiustok lines jeered the retreating cavalry, then whooped when they disappeared over the ridge. They deserved to celebrate. These Crimsons had hassled them for days and

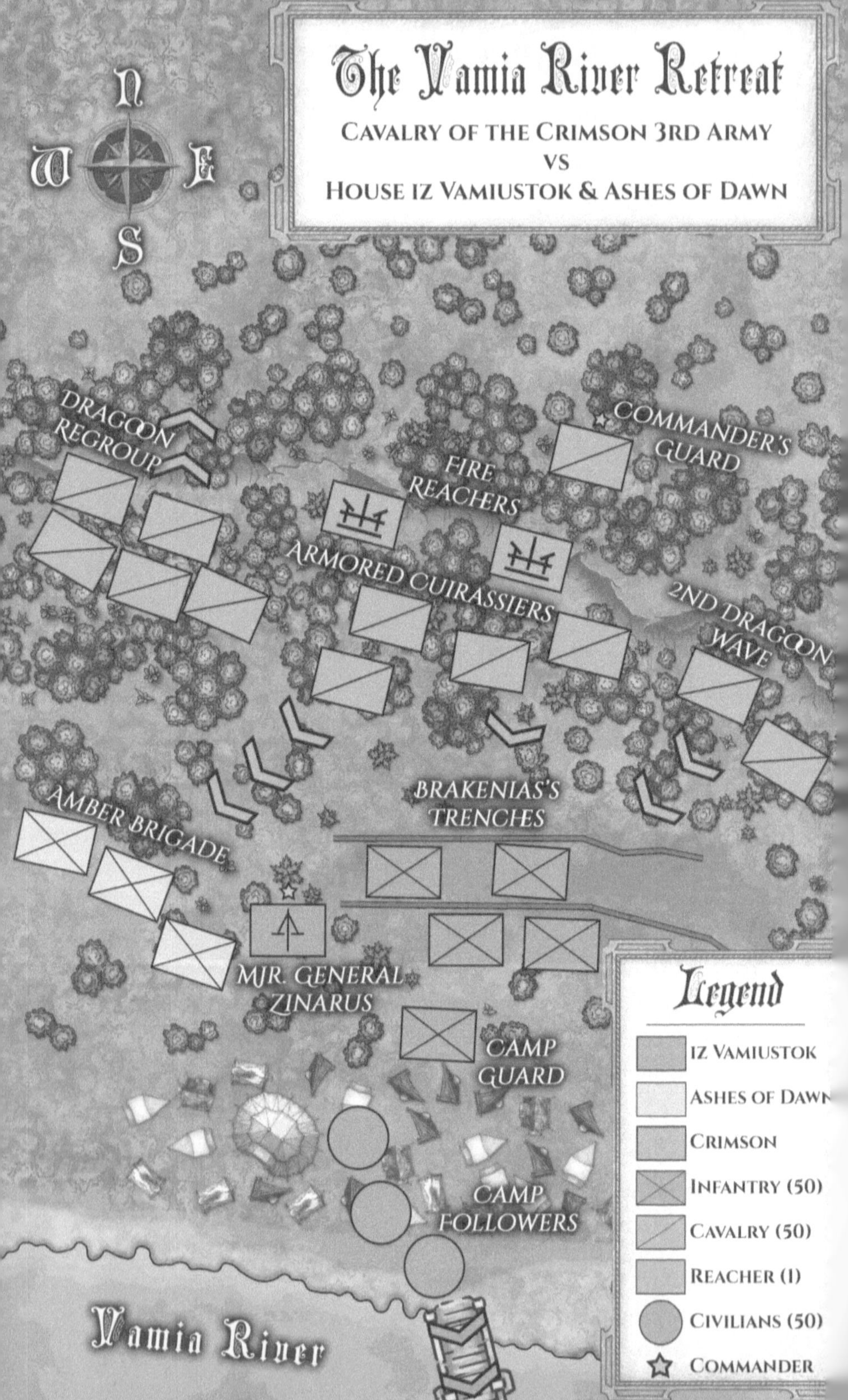

N
W E
S

The Vamia River Retreat
CAVALRY OF THE CRIMSON 3RD ARMY
VS
HOUSE IZ VAMIUSTOK & ASHES OF DAWN

DRAGOON REGROUP

COMMANDER'S GUARD

FIRE REACHERS

2ND DRAGOON WAVE

ARMORED CUIRASSIERS

BRAKENIAS'S TRENCHES

AMBER BRIGADE

MJR. GENERAL ZINARUS

CAMP GUARD

CAMP FOLLOWERS

Vamia River

Legend
IZ VAMIUSTOK
ASHES OF DAWN
CRIMSON
INFANTRY (50)
CAVALRY (50)
REACHER (1)
CIVILIANS (50)
COMMANDER

were now the only force keeping them from the safety of Fort Harizak. Joy was a rare thing these days.

That joy faded as armored Crimson cuirassiers emerged from that same ridge.

Zinarus called his soldiers back to order, but it was too late. At a full gallop, the cuirassiers led a pair of Reachers who hadn't joined the first advance. Their talons flashed in the southern light, and they moved swiftly into a perfect position for a strike as the cuirassiers laid down covering fire with their pistols.

"Focus on the Reachers!" Zinarus demanded over the roar of gunfire.

If anyone heard, it was too few to make a difference. Reacher flames swelled over the trenches and consumed the trees in an inferno. Zinarus tried to down the Reachers himself, but his shots into the dense powder smoke were desperate at best. Dozens died around him as he tried and failed to organize some kind of legitimate counter.

It seemed no relief would come until a bullet ripped through one of the Reachers' heads. Zinarus snapped his gaze across the lines to Brakenias, who grinned to himself as he reloaded once again. Only a true marksman could shoot like that, and Zinarus would ensure he was greatly rewarded for it later.

Shock swept through the Crimson cuirassiers. With a Reacher dead and the other likely already enduring Taint, they circled away. Death lay in their wake, but once again, the defenders had not routed.

Zinarus traced his own talon as he rode behind the lines, collecting reports from his officers and ensuring their losses had not left any gaps. Each confirmed death made him wince. It mattered not that they had signed up for war. These people were his responsibility, and their deaths were the result of his decisions. He needed to ensure there were no further casualties until they reached the fort.

He considered the great force those two Reachers had been. He had hated using his Truth Reacher compulsion against Ziegfried. As he stared down at his talon, though, he questioned whether his honor was worth losing further lives in the next inevitable attack. They still needed time to retreat over the bridge, and a plan formed in his head to buy it.

His gaze fell upon the haggard faces of the Amber Brigade. The answer seemed so obvious now, yet fear balled in his stomach at the thought of it. He had the power to fight, to protect. Not just words or tactics, but with magic.

"Captain Crax," he called to the eldest of the gang bosses.

Crax turned with a grin, his old coat weathered on his shoulders. He wore leather gloves that Zinarus had never seen him remove, and his skin was so mixed that his ancestry could've been from anywhere on the continent. His hair was a wavy brown common among Ezmani lowborn—except for that gray streak peeking beneath his officer cap.

"What can I do for you, General?" he asked.

"Send the biggest lad you have to the Crimsons under a flag of truce, then come with me," Zinarus said. "I think it is about time to take back the initiative."

UNDER THE FLAG OF TRUCE

"The flag of truce is as sacred to any general as the most holy relic is to a sister of the Buried Temple," – Tiuz Hazeko, field marshal of the Confederation of Harizak

Rain pattered against Zinarus's hat and shoulders as he rode up the hill where the Crimson cavalry commander had agreed to meet. A series of tents ringed it with the largest sitting directly on its peak. There, a man with silver adornments across his deep red uniform sat high upon his blood bay steed, keenly studying Zinarus.

"Lord Zinarus," the commander said, removing his hat. "I am glad to hear you have come to your senses. Come, and let us discuss the terms of your surrender."

Zinarus had no intentions of doing so, but he neither confirmed nor denied the statement. He dismounted silently instead, fixing his coat. This hastily constructed plan was already stretching his honor to its limits. Allowing the commander to make his own assumptions, though, was hardly lying.

His mechanical leg complained about the moisture as he trudged up to the commander, who finally dismounted to meet him. A middle-aged man with a weathered face and goatee, the man left his uniform half-buttoned. He wore tight marksman gloves that bulged around his talon. A scion, then, yet his hair was a dirty blonde instead of the usual gray among Ezmani nobility.

"My scouts have told me much about your forces," Zinarus said, "but it appears you have me at a disadvantage here. What are you called?"

The commander offered him a handshake. "I am Lord Razamat of House Uziokaki, colonel of this regiment."

Zinarus shook his hand. That name struck him as familiar, perhaps from Tiuz's old war stories, but he couldn't place his finger on it as Razamat led him inside the tent. A circular wooden table filled its center, and Razamat rounded to its other side, gesturing for Zinarus to sit across from him.

"Would you like some wine?" he asked. "I could not help but notice you sent the vast majority of your supplies ahead to Fort Harizak, so I assume your own reserves are low."

Zinarus nodded. "That is a generous offer, thank you."

"Excellent."

Razamat turned his back as he filled two glass goblets from a bottle on a side table. There was a rigidity to his movements that matched those of an experienced commander, but both his mannerisms and the use of glass for such a mundane luxury hinted more at a pampered life. Zinarus hoped that meant he didn't know how to resist Truth Reaching.

While Razamat finished his pour, Zinarus slipped off his left glove, keeping it hidden behind his crossed legs. His brow twitched. Such deception was not natural to him, but it was necessary.

This meeting bought precious time for his retreat, and gaining some understanding of the Crimsons' plan of attack could mean not only the survival of his army, but Tiuz's entire Confederation. If he had learned anything about the Crimsons, it was that they acted out of secrecy. He doubted they would just march an army up to a well-defended castle and conduct a conventional siege.

"There we are," Razamat said, setting down Zinarus's glass and settling in the opposing chair. He gave his own glass a swirl. "This wine was captured from deep within Kelosh during the last war. Its grapes come from one of their vassal states far to the east, and it is said the resulting wine carries a tangy flavor like that of Reshkan oranges. I was waiting for the right opportunity to try it."

Zinarus took the glass with his gloved hand. "A meeting with an enemy general is the most opportune moment?"

"Precisely." Razamat sipped, then puckered his lips. "Ah, yes. Once again, those Keloshans are nothing more than damned liars."

Stifling a chuckle, Zinarus drank as well. The wine was sweet, almost overwhelmingly so compared to the Ezmani varieties, but it had a pleasant aftertaste that lingered on his tongue. "Actually, I quite enjoy it. You have my gratitude, but there are more pressing matters to address."

"Yes, war and all that ugliness."

Razamat downed the rest of his wine. It was a swift move, but it gave Zinarus a chance to Reach. White Truth wisps encircled him as he rose and extended his hand toward Razamat. Touch helped all but the most experienced Truth Reachers compel their target, but with his mechanical leg hampered by the rain, attempting to grab a trained commander was too risky.

The wisps swarmed over Razamat. He staggered out of his chair, eyes bulging as he threw his glass to the ground, but it didn't shatter against the soft earth. It was a small mercy, and Zinarus took advantage to press his questions.

"What is the Crimson Court planning against Fort Harizak?"

Razamat grimaced. "I... won't... tell."

With the cavalry commander restrained by the Reach, Zinarus rounded the table and snatched his wrist. "Tell me what the Crimsons' plans are against the Confederation," he insisted.

"They are besieging the fort," Razamat replied from his knees. He spasmed, every muscle in his body fighting the Reach. "Artillery fire, then lowborn soldiers first."

"Why? Are they just sending their men to the slaughter?"

Razamat seized, streaks of red shooting across his eyes as he tried to keep from speaking, but Zinarus's Reach had yet to run out. It would last for another question, maybe two. So he pushed harder until Razamat's voice cracked.

"A… A distraction," the Crimson commander said. "They have spirits with minds and a dragon to compel more to follow—a force of all the spirits they claimed were fighting Kelosh."

Zinarus's heart dropped. This was exactly why Tiuz needed glass and amber, but confirmation of it was terrifying. If the breathless were here instead of on the frontline against Kelosh, this battle could be the first ever involving a human army wielding spirits. Neither walls nor experience would be any use against such foes. And if they had the crystal dragon to somehow command the spirits of those who died…

"They *want* the lowborn to die?" He shuddered. "There are tens of thousands of them in that army!"

A noise came from outside, and Zinarus cursed himself for raising his voice. For a moment, he just stood there with Razamat writhing beneath his power. The thinnest part of his plan was how to get out of here, and that would become incredibly more difficult if he was discovered in the act. There was still more he wanted to learn. His better sense, though, told him it was time to leave, so he used the last of his Reach to buy himself a moment longer.

"What is the worst thing you have ever done?" he asked. "Spare no detail."

Razamat sputtered, but Zinarus did not stay to hear the reply. His stomach was already in knots after breaking a truce to interrogate a fellow commander. All he needed was for Razamat's answer to delay him calling for help.

He hurried out of the tent with his mechanical leg making quite the racket. He'd left his horse no more than a dozen strides from the hilltop, so all he needed to do was act like the meeting hadn't gone well. A trio of Crimson officers waited for Razamat's report, and they spooked at Zinarus's sudden appearance. None stopped him, though, so he continued until one of them muttered to the others.

"He's not wearing a glove."

Zinarus broke into a stumbling run, hauling himself onto his horse out of pure willpower as his bad leg twisted awkwardly in the mud. He pushed into a gallop with only his good foot in the stirrup. The other dangled horribly off the side and battered his mount's flank. He had to cling tight to the reins just to keep on the saddle, but promised himself he would reward the horse with a dozen treats upon their return to camp.

That meant crossing the river.

His meeting with Razamat had not taken all that long, but he held out hope the extra time had allowed the last of his army to cross the bridge. Once he was across, they could destroy it behind him, making any attempt for the cavalry to follow a futile one. The main army possessed spirits and a dragon. He had seen no evidence this cavalry regiment commanded any breathless, and the few Reachers they had sent into battle were not Earth, Air, or Water ones who could make a crossing easier. This plan *would* work.

He held onto that thought as he charged through the woods with a prayer to the Crystal Mother on his lips. Each rolling hill taunted him. Which was the last before the river? And would he see his army brought to safety, or their exposed rear as a perfect target for a cavalry attack?

The earth shook in his wake. A *pop* followed, and Zinarus hastened a glance over his shoulder to see no less than twenty dragoons closing in. His own horse couldn't compare to the incredibly trained ones among the Crimsons' elite cavalry, and his dangling leg only made matters worse. They would be on him in seconds, and returning fire against that many dragoons would do nothing. He needed the next hill to be the last.

His hope faded the moment his horse stumbled to the peak. The hill was taller than most others, and through the trees, three more ridges rose between him and the river. But, by the Mother's grace, every purple-clad figure in the distance was across the bridge.

Bullets sent bark scattering over Zinarus. His breaths were labored, his horse's worse. Though his army was safe for now, Razamat's admissions rang in the back of his head. Tiuz needed to know. His forces would have no chance of defending Fort Harizak otherwise, and Zinarus could not allow the Crimsons to destroy the Confederation in its infancy.

Eyeing a series of ditches in the next valley, he veered toward them. The move took him further from a direct retreat, but outwitting his opponents was the only option now. So he waited until another volley echoed through the rain and obscured his attackers' view.

Then he threw himself into the nearest ditch.

His mechanical leg broke free as he landed. He tumbled, head spinning and arms throbbing from the impact. Mud covered him as he rolled to a stop among the roots of a wide oak, but he seemed relatively unharmed. Somewhere nearby, his horse screamed its complaints as it galloped toward freedom without his weight on its back.

He held his breath as the dragoons closed in from up the slope. Their shots no longer rang out, and shouts revealed their frustrations. In clear weather, his purple coat would be a dead giveaway, but the rain and mud would obscure much of it. The ditch and nearby tree were well oriented to cast a heavy shadow over him too. Whether it would be enough, he didn't know, but there was nothing he could do now but wait.

Time crawled. Every moment that passed worsened his throbbing stump of a leg, and he couldn't see his prosthetic when he craned his head to get a better look. Had it fallen in the open?

"Over here," one of the dragoons called out from no more than two dozen strides away. A brute of a man, he lifted Zinarus's mechanical leg with a wide grin. "He couldn't have gone far without a leg. You four, dismount, and check for tracks. We'll sweep around to see if he went the other way."

He dropped Zinarus's leg and rode off with most of the others while the remaining squad formed a line. They combed the brush, heading toward the fallen general. Zinarus wished he'd had the foresight to grab his pistol from his saddle bag before leaping. Instead, he had left himself defenseless. Truth Reacher compulsion could perhaps delay a single attacker, but it couldn't stop all four of his pursuers.

So he dragged himself on, filthy and wincing from his wounds, but he barely made progress. Oh, how his mother would scorn him. She would hear of her son dying alone in a ditch without even the wits to keep his gun. What a fool.

The dismounted dragoons closed in until a familiar chill crept down the back of Zinarus's neck. Spirits. He scanned the sky for any sign of awakened or breathless, but saw nothing.

A cry came from the dragoons.

Misty, indistinct awakened swarmed the nearest of them. Their tendrils tore the man's spirit from his body before he had a chance to reach for a glass dagger. His allies staggered back, grasping for their own weapons as another rider approached from the east. The awakened showed no care to Zinarus or the new arrival, though, and with the first dragoon dead, they charged the others.

The rider burst into the ditch where Zinarus lay. An elderly man, he wore a tattered woolen coat and a glove over just his right hand. Crystal glimmered on the index finger of his left as he grabbed Zinarus's mechanical leg from the mud, then looked straight at him.

"C'mon, kid," Crax said. "I have your horse and your leg, so I would say it's about time to get you out of here."

58

THE FLIGHT AND THE FALL

"There is a reason the Crystal Mother gave us bodies with which we firmly plant our feet on the ground. The skies are for the spirits." – Bridgezet Tarizon, former anointed sister of the Buried Temple

Nikoza stifled a gasp, holding her hand to her breast and staring at the figure peeking in from her balcony. The person's voice had clearly been that of Nex, yet that face and guardsman's uniform definitely did not belong to them.

"Who are you?" Nikoza stammered. "And what—"

The person muttered a few obscenities before rushing into the room and snatching her wrist. "It's me, Nex. I just Possibility Reached so the guards wouldn't recognize me."

Nikoza glanced at the door, beyond which Gregorzon was standing guard. "You cannot be here!"

"Yeah, and you shouldn't be either," Nex said. "So let's *get the hell out!*"

When Nikoza hesitated, the rebel practically dragged her across the room. Her heart hammered her chest. This was what she had waited days for after her initial plan with Nex had fallen apart, yet fear kept her legs from sprinting as she so badly wanted to.

The pair burst onto the balcony as dark clouds rolled in from the south. They cast a heavy shadow over the city, and Nikoza prayed to the Crystal Mother that it would be enough to stop the casual observer from seeing them. Except, she had no idea where they were escaping to.

"How did you penetrate the palace guard?" she asked.

Nex took her right to the balcony's edge. They were on the southeastern side, and beyond the palace's circle road were a patch of trees between them and the walls of Kalastok College. Nex pointed to those trees, then they grabbed Nikoza with both hands.

"You'll hate this, but we've gotta jump."

Nikoza looked over the edge, imagining her horrible death as her body crashed into the cobblestone streets below. "I would rather not," she said, trying to squirm free of their grasp.

"Hazat said I only had to ask nicely once," Nex replied.

"Wait! Do not—"

Nex threw their weight over the railing, taking Nikoza with them. They dropped straight toward the street, but red wisps struck them as they came into sight of the balcony below. Two figures stood upon it: Hazat and Jolzena. The Force Reacher's hand was extended, and when the wisps arrived, a sudden blast launched the falling pair over the street.

Every Reacher had considered at some time in their life what it would be like to fly like the most experienced Air Reachers, but in that moment, Nikoza decided she never wished to. Mortal terror consumed her as they tumbled toward the trees a hundred yards at most south of the nearby Reacher tower. Except another force caught them before they struck among the branches, slowing them as they tumbled to the ground.

She let out an exasperated laugh. Scrapes covered her exposed wrists and face—and the fall would leave bruises come morning— but she was relatively unharmed. It was quite the miracle.

It was also quite the debacle.

A flurry of conversations came from the nearby street as Nikoza tried to gather herself. Passersby had no doubt seen two figures flying overhead, and any guards in that tower would be suspicious. If she wished to escape, they needed to leave now.

"We were supposed to go over the college wall," Nex said, hauling Nikoza to her feet. They still had their watchman musket slung over their shoulder, and they adjusted it before nodding toward the college. "Guess we'll need to climb."

"Gregorzon said you were dead," Nikoza replied. Her head swam, and along with her lingering bit of Realm Taint, she felt ready to faint. "Why did you come for me?"

Nex gritted their teeth with a glance back. "We don't have time for this! The Crimsons sent their damn breathless to slaughter not just the Ashes' fighters, but all the innocent people we were protecting. Me and Hazat stayed back to help you. Got it? Then *let's go!*"

But Nikoza shook her head. "Kalastok College has nearly as much security as the palace. They will recognize me."

Nex's expression relaxed as Nikoza let them pull her across the trail that passed between this patch of trees and the section closer to the college wall. "Hazat said it's like a spirit town over there with all the Reachers going to war. We can hide there until we've got a better plan."

"You changed your appearance. Did you not?"

Nex shrugged. "Yeah, why?"

"Can you do the same for me?" she asked. "I am dressed like any other scion lady, and even a subtle disguise should allow me to remain inconspicuous." She paused, recalling Kix and his family who she'd saved from the fires the night of the coup. "There is a place in the Drifters' Quarter where we may be safe from prying eyes if we can get there."

"Is everyone alright in there?" someone called into the forest.

Hesitating, Nikoza reassured herself of her choice. She had thrown her safety to the wind by returning to the palace to deceive Chatik, but as long as the Crimsons were slaughtering the innocent people she had sworn to protect, this was where she was meant to be. So she turned to Nex and whispered, "They likely believe we were Reachers in training. Guards will come looking for us, but they won't think twice about a promenading scion woman with an escort."

"But I'll have to drop my disguise," Nex said. "I'd already have to Reach again to hold it up any longer, and I've never tried with someone else. It might come out wrong."

Taking their hand, Nikoza poured her desperation into her words. "Keep your head down, and no one will question a guard. As for me, I need not look beautiful, just different. You are capable of great things, Nex. Whether uniting the divided lowborn or leaping across buildings, you have shown me you are more than just the thief I believed you to be. Please, do this for me. I need your help if we stand any chance to save this city."

Nex flared their nostrils, but dropped their disguise. Or at least, partially. They still looked different than their first encounter in everdark in the slightest of ways. Nikoza's heart ached wondering if that was because of the Truth Reachers' torture.

"Just stay still," Nex muttered as they pressed their crystal-ringed finger against Nikoza's cheek.

The shift that followed was the strangest sensation Nikoza had ever experienced. Muscles, bones, and joints altered across her face, disconnecting and reforming in a shape that made it feel as if she were puffing out her cheeks and jutting out her chin. How could something tickle so much yet cause such agony?

Seconds later, it was finished, and Nex stepped back with a disconcerting look. "I tried my best."

Heavy footfalls headed toward them from the tower's direction, so Nikoza acted on instinct, looping her arm into theirs. "It will do. Now, follow my lead."

They returned to the stone trail through the trees just in time for a squad of crimson-clad guardsmen to appear around the bend. Nikoza laughed through her nerves, leaning into Nex and patting their shoulder as if she were flirting with her bodyguard while away from wandering eyes. Then she stiffened and stepped away with an embarrassed hand over her mouth.

The lead guard held out a hand for them to stop, her brow furrowed. "A moment of your time, my lady," she told Nikoza. "There was a disturbance spotted around here. Did you happen to see anything?"

"Oh, my," she said, giggling girlishly. "No, we… um… were rather distracted."

Nex turned beet red, but that just helped sell the lie as the guards studied them both. Such dalliances were common among scions. Whether they had sold it well, though, would depend on how well Nex had reshaped Nikoza's face.

"Fine," the guard muttered before glaring at Nex, "but you're lucky we have more important things to attend to. I catch you running off like this again, and you're sacked. Got it?"

Recollecting themself, Nex sloppily thumped their chest. "Yes, ma'am."

It was hardly the most convincing imitation of a guard. They were supposed to be acting flustered, though, and Nex was *plenty* flustered. It must have been enough, as the guards headed back to the Reacher tower, so Nikoza waved Nex after them.

Together, they walked briskly down the trail toward the southeastern entrance to the Crimson District. The knot in Nikoza's chest tightened as they did, but Nex drew closer, whispering, "Hazat and Jolzena will not know where we are."

"We can wait for them near the college gates," Nikoza replied. "That is not far from where I intend to take us anyway."

No one stopped them as they passed through the guard post and into the Drifters' Quarter. The main street's foot and carriage traffic was sparse, but this would have been a bustling corridor before the coup. Now, scions stayed in their townhouses, sending their servants to fetch whatever they needed. Those who were out kept an eye on the breathless circling above—a concern Nikoza shared.

Passing beneath the shadow of the now closed arena, she turned her focus to their destination. The lowborn woman named Falia had hosted both Nikoza and the family she had saved from the riot's fires. She would likely not be enthusiastic about taking in four scion fugitives, but Nikoza could only hope her actions had earned some lasting goodwill. It was the only safe place she could think to hide that Chatik wouldn't know of.

They waited within sight of the college gates, keeping out of the main thoroughfare. She could feel her face beginning to shift back. Though it was comforting to know she wasn't stuck with the magical alterations, it also meant their time was running out.

"If we wait much longer, then someone will recognize me," she said with a check of her mechanical wristwatch. "Where are they?"

Nex shrugged, watching passersby as if they were an actual guard. "They were in your squad. I barely know 'em."

"To tell the truth, I feel the same. I never suspected Hazat's opposition to the Crimsons, and though Jolzena bickered with her brother, I could hardly believe she would pick me over her own family."

"Everyone's got their reasons," Nex said. "Just because they help, doesn't mean they're an ally."

A few more minutes passed before two people dressed in workmen's clothes approached. It took Nikoza a moment to recognize her squad mates under the thick layer of soot they'd smeared over their faces.

"I would hug the both of you if that would not ruin this dress," she said, holding back the tears that wished to slip free. They had not stopped Chatik yet, but it was impossible for her to express how grateful she was.

"Keep your hands to yourself," Jolzena said with a smirk. "Especially with that face. Did Nex do that to you?"

Nikoza raised a hand to her cheek. "Is it that uncomely?"

"Let us say that you look much better under normal circumstances," Hazat said, rubbing the back of his neck as a bit of pink flared beneath his cheeks' soot. "The disguise is a good one, but why are you not in the college? That is where we agreed to meet."

"I helped a family during the riot," she replied. "They might be willing to take us in for now, and a townhouse is far preferable to hiding out in an area where many scions may recognize me."

Hazat shrugged. "That is fair enough. Lead the way."

"Stay back a ways," Nex warned the scrubby looking Reachers as Nikoza started toward the south. "I know what it's like to be a lowborn around scions. They'll think you're stalking her."

So Hazat and Jolzena kept back, allowing Nikoza to guide them through the brick townhouses of the Drifters' Quarter. It felt as if years had passed since she had last walked these streets at everdark's end. Then, she'd been escorted by Crimson watchmen to be manipulated by her uncle, and hundred-hours later, a lowborn rebel dressed as a watchman escorted her back to the same house. Time was a strange thing.

Children gathered in the street in front of Falia's brick townhouse. Ash still scarred the cobblestone, and many of the buildings were either rubble or in the process of being rebuilt. Had Kix and his family found a new home?

She gestured for Nex to stay back as she approached the children. They looked at her as if she were an awakened, one of them clinging to their chest the ball they had been playing with. When Nikoza crouched and smiled, though, their expressions shifted to curiosity.

"Do you know Kix?" she asked them as sweetly as her nerves allowed.

All the kids but one turned and ran. While she had not intended to ruin their game, she only needed one to answer the question, so she extended her hand toward the young girl. "I am safe. I promise."

Tears suddenly welled in the girl's eyes. The ball slipped from her hands, and she practically leaped into Nikoza's arms. "Princess Nikoza! You came back!"

After a moment of confusion, Nikoza realized her mistake. She had barely seen the smoke-smothered girl she rescued from the fire. Kix and his wife had not introduced them, but their daughter remembered the woman who'd saved her life.

Nikoza's own tears flowed down her cheeks as she embraced the girl. "I did, little one. Your parents never told me your name, though, and I would certainly love to know it."

"Tylea!" the girl exclaimed, beaming at Nikoza, her little nose red from the chill that had blown in. "Kix is my pa."

"Of course he is. Now, would you take me to see him? I would love the chance to talk with him again."

She pointed toward Falia's townhouse. "He just got home."

"This is still home for you?" Nikoza asked, brushing a few stray hairs from the girl's face.

"Ma says we'll get a new home soon, but pa lost his job after the riots." Tylea tucked her head into her chest. "What's a riot?"

Nikoza gave a sorrowful chuckle. "It is when people who are upset decide the only way to change things is to ensure they are impossible to ignore. Unfortunately, that often results in people hurting each other." She stood and offered Tylea her hand. "Can you bring my friends and I to talk with your family? Unless you would rather keep playing ball, that is?"

Tylea looked forlornly down at the dropped ball, then took her hand. "It's no fun alone."

As Tylea led her toward the door, Nikoza waved for Nex and the distantly waiting Reachers to follow. The girl showed some worry at the strangers' approach, but with some reassurance from Nikoza, they entered the townhouse and headed up the stairs to Falia's apartment.

59

BATTLE'S CALL

"When the call for battle comes, there are those who answer and those who do not. Many perish no matter which they choose, but it is better to die with a bayonet in your gut than a bullet in your back." – Anonymous Keloshan soldier

Radais nearly wept at the sight of the Glassblade camp nestled in the valleys just to the east of Iliafa. These were his brothers and sisters in arms. They were those who had trusted him to lead, and even when he'd left on this side mission for far too long, they had done exactly as he'd ordered.

Did he deserve such loyalty? As they approached battle against the Vanashel, he wouldn't deny it. They would need every woman and man who could hold a blade, Whisper to the spirits, or Reach into the realms of magic. He had his doubts whether even that would be enough, but they were Vocka's only real defense. Failure wasn't an option.

Vuk bleated at the sight of his fellow ibexes too. They were herd animals, and Radais forgot at times how taxing it was for Vuk to be away from his kind. The same was likely true for him.

"What will the others think of your crystal collarbone?" he asked Wanusa over his shoulder, catching a glimpse of her pet povnik,

Alicy, trotting alongside her ibex with its tongue out. "And your new friend?"

Wanusa grinned. "They should be glad I have a new power against spirits and an ally to keep away rodents."

"You've thought about this."

"Of course I have," she said, throwing down some scraps for Alicy to scarf down. "Have you?"

He had lost a lot of sleep over how to approach his allies, and she knew it. There had never been a Vockan Reacher before, let alone a Glassblade one. It terrified him that he could soon be scorned by— or even exiled from—the order he'd devoted over half his life to. His commanders were already displeased at him becoming supreme defender. Could this be the final straw?

"You both have had plenty to think about," Lazan replied for him. "Perhaps we should focus less on ourselves, however, and more on our foes."

He pointed to the west, where Iliafa's scattered buildings and pastures rested on the divide between the mountains and the last rolling hills before the Spirit Wastes. What Radais had thought was a storm cloud was instead a mass of thousands of spirits. They hung in the sky over the village, breathless with their bodies taking on jagged, aggressive shapes as they held strange glinting spears. Above them flew fifteen Bound Ones. They were the spirits' answer to Reachers, and each took the form of a wicked dragon, waiting to strike.

If that wasn't bad enough, the earth itself had changed around Iliafa. The fields and grasses had been dormant the last he'd seen of this valley in everdark, but it was dawnrise now. They should've flourished in the sunlight. Instead, it appeared that the ashen sands of the Spirit Wastes had swallowed the village whole.

Wanusa gasped. "No…"

She pushed her ibex into a canter, hurrying down the slope to the Glassblade camp. Radais swapped a worried look with Lazan before following. The pain of seeing her entire village destroyed was surely immense—he couldn't let her deal with it alone.

The camp was abuzz at the sight of the riders bursting from the mountains. Mhanain and the other archers on duty shouted excitedly from built up mounds they used as sentry posts. How long had they been waiting for Radais and the others to return? They'd obviously had time to make some basic fortifications, but they hadn't truly dug in yet. Not that the Glassblades had an army of engineers at their backs anyway.

Wanusa tore straight down the main aisle between the tents. When Radais tried to follow, Commander Polina stepped in front of him, her arms raised for him to stop.

He pulled Vuk into a desperate turn to keep from running her over. "What are you doing?" he snapped, his eagerness getting the better of him. "I could've trampled you!"

"I've been hit by worse than your ibex," the bulky half-Reshkan replied. "It's about time you showed up. Mhanain has been pacing like a madman, claiming I need to send a dozen warriors after you to make sure that Whisperer didn't betray us."

Radais glanced back at Mariana, who descended the last of the mountain slowly with Lazan. "She and I have our differences, but she did what she said she would."

"So you have the key to defeating the Vanashel?" Polina said in a mocking tone. "Where is it, then?"

"You just cut me off from her." He pointed after Wanusa. She hadn't stopped, and from the look of it, she'd decided heading straight at Iliafa and the gathered Vanashel was a good idea.

"The girl?" Polina asked. "We already had a Whisperer with Mariana—an experienced one. How is Wanusa going to turn the tide of an entire battle?"

Radais nervously scratched his neck. People crowded around them now, the looks on the other Glassblades' faces asking the same question. They deserved the truth, but he knew they wouldn't take it well.

"Mariana exaggerated how important a single Whisperer can be," he admitted, "but they can help combat spirits—especially the breathless controlled by the Vanashel Bound Ones. There's also this." He pulled off his left gauntlet to reveal his Reacher talon, its silver peaks shining with power. "I'm an Earth Reacher now."

A mix of gasps and muttered conversations spread through the gathered Glassblades. Polina, though, stood as still as stone. "Vockans can't Reach. Everyone knows that. So either you're not a full-blooded Vockan as you claim, or you're lying about that talon."

"Your supreme defender has his faults," Mariana said, arriving in the camp with a weary smile, "but he is not lying. Whether all should know the truth of our discovery, however, is up to him."

Radais drew a long breath and studied the faces around him. Loyalty had to be earned, and he couldn't do so without trusting his warriors. "This talon is not Spirit Crystal, but Fire Crystal," he declared. "The Whisperers have read the Essence at the core of Zekiaz's people and seen that Vockans are bonded to the Fire realm and not our own. It is why our people were unable to Reach until we discovered a single shard of Fire Crystal in the mountains."

"Which you decided to use yourself," someone said from the crowd. Commander Tairanik—who'd clearly not followed Radais's instructions to take better care of his presentation—had the smirk of a hunter who'd trapped his kill. "Glassblade tradition says we don't accept Reachers into our ranks."

"You're right." Radais held out his arms and spoke to the whole of his army. "I have defied tradition. I broke away from the army I united at the whims of a Whisperer. I allowed one of our rank to follow that very Whisperer's teaching and learn to bond spirits. And now, I have become the first known Vockan Reacher." He lowered his head. "This is not how I wanted to lead you, but I didn't choose to be supreme defender. It is only because of Miv's final words to me that I took this post."

"Words which only you and your allies heard," Tairanik said with a huff.

Radais met the commander's gaze. "I understand your doubts. That is why I will leave my fate up to all the Glassblades who have marched with us to this point. Choose another supreme defender, or remove me entirely from the Order if you wish. You will have my blade and my magic no matter what you choose."

Polina approached, her voice quiet. "What are you doing? You can't give up on the eve of battle!"

"I'm not giving up," he said. "But a good warrior knows when he should lead and when it is his turn to follow." He cast a glare at Tairanik before leaning in closer to her. "When the time comes to decide my replacement, don't let him win."

Then he pushed Vuk onward, passing through the shocked warriors as he headed after Wanusa. Spirits, he hoped she didn't do something rash. His worries should've been focused on the Vanashel or his position among the Glassblades, but those failed to match his worry for her. Pain had made him do plenty of things he would've liked to forget. He couldn't let her do the same.

He plowed into the western hills, following the tracks of Wanusa's ibex in the soft earth. That ominous cloud of spirits grew ever larger with each passing second. The Vanashel's wasteland hadn't reached here yet, but he had no doubt it would soon if the Glassblades couldn't stop them.

But why did the Vanashel wait? With the speed of spirits, they could have swarmed Vocka with smaller groups led by Bound Ones. Even now, the Glassblades were hardly in formation to rebuff an attack while their commanders squabbled for control. There was a surety to the Vanashel stance. A knowingness that they could pick where to fight, and that they would win.

He found Wanusa beneath an arcing tree, her legs pulled to her chest and a silvery spirit circling around her hand. She'd brought half of Inrius's spirit home, but the siblings weren't alone.

A breathless hovered behind the boughs. Armored in what appeared to be jagged, pinkish quartz over sweeping robes that stretched beyond its body, it showed no aggression toward Wanusa or her brother's spirit. Instead, it almost seemed to stand guard with its spear bearing glass on one end and steel on the other.

"Miv?"

The question escaped Radais's lips before he could even think. He'd never forget the spirit form his lost lover had taken after her death in Akaamilion, and Miv stared back at him with her head resembling an ibex. Intertwined crystals in the shape of diamonds hung from her curled horns. It was a strange sight on the wispy human body, but the ferocity behind that gaze… Yes, it had to be her.

"You shouldn't have come here," Miv's spirit said, humming like the other Saleshi breathless had in the Wastes.

Radais leaped from Vuk and rushed to her and Wanusa, looking from one to the other. "Miv, how are you here? Akaamilion is hundreds of miles away."

Miv held out her free hand toward Wanusa. "She called me, but I'm not Miv anymore. You know that."

"Ataakanan," Wanusa said, not taking her attention from Inrius's spirit. "That's what you called yourself before."

"Yes," the spirit replied. She… *It* drifted closer. "The calls of Whisperers carry many miles, but Rakekeaa said it should've been impossible for me to hear you from so far. Despite me not being Miv anymore, we're connected somehow. My memories of you say that we were close. That was enough for Rakekeaa to bring a squad of breathless at my asking, as Bakeekek apparently wants to know how Whisperers bond with spirits."

Radais crossed his arms. Even the spirit of Miv being near brought a stir of emotions to the surface. He didn't have the time or energy to deal with them, but he couldn't deny the Saleshi warriors would be useful allies.

"Bakeekek thinks Whisperers are a threat," he said. "Spirit Reachers can influence spirits, but Whisperers can bond them."

Ataakanan nodded. "The Saleshi are afraid—both of the Vanashel and humans. Wanusa is a chance to prove them wrong."

"You said *them*," Radais replied. "I thought you weren't one of us anymore."

"Don't make this harder than it needs to be. Miv's memories are slowly fading into my own, but her spirit is now mine. I am a Saleshi breathless, not a Glassblade." Ataakanan pointed its spear toward the floating Vanashel. "I told you that you shouldn't have come here. They lured you to this place, where they want to fight."

Wanusa hung her head, but it couldn't hide her swollen eyes. "They used my family, my brother, as bait. Why?"

"The sands of the Spirit Wastes—what we call the Sands of Salesh—are connected to us," Ataakanan said. "Breathless need a lot of what Bakeekek calls Essence from the Spirit Crystal, but it's less when we're in the Wastes. The Vanashel somehow expanded it here."

Radais thought back to the abandoned town of New Frontier, where he and Rakekeaa had rescued Miv from the Vanashel. "Rakekeaa said the risen dead who attacked us in New Frontier were husks." He winced, knowing how hard Wanusa would take this. "What if they're doing it again here: turning the dead's spirits into their breathless servants and then doing the same with the husks of their bodies."

But instead of shying away, Wanusa shot to her feet, surveying the Vanashel. "The other half of Inrius's spirit could be up there? What if we reunited both halves with his body? We could—"

"Life and death aren't so simple. Miv would still be alive if it was," Ataakanan said, glaring at Radais. Even if it lacked human eyes, he could feel its spite like a knife to his heart. "But we can reunite Inrius's spirit. The Vanashel Bound Ones can control breathless, just like a Deepened Whisperer. That means it's as easily broken."

"We just need to kill the Bound One controlling him," Radais said. "Easy enough."

Wanusa drew a long breath. "That isn't your job. It's mine. You're the supreme defender, and everyone is relying on you to lead them."

"About that..."

Ataakanan scoffed and shook its head. "Miv knew this would happen. You always wanted to go off into the Wastes by yourself with that sketchbook. Why are you so afraid to lead?"

"I can lead," Radais contested. "I led us through the battle of the Whistling Pass. I led an expedition into the mountains and came back with a Whisperer and the first Vockan Reacher. I led us here." He looked to Wanusa, surprised at the emotion cracking through his voice. "But I've found that there are things that matter more to me than leading the Glassblades… People who matter more. I promised Wanusa I'd reunite her with her brother and help her understand this new power of hers, and I can't do that if I'm stuck in a commander's tent."

Wanusa stepped cautiously toward him, taking his taloned hand, still free of its gauntlet. "You stepped down because of me?"

He squeezed her hand and forced himself to smile. "You're like a daughter to me, and after all you've lost, I'm not going to abandon you. I know the hurt being alone."

"You big buffoon!" She wrapped him in a tight hug. "How can I repay you?"

"Find your brother. Someone needs to find a way to love theirs when I can't."

Inrius's spirit circled them both, still lackadaisical, but for once, there seemed to be some joy in it. "I think he approves," Wanusa said as she stepped back. Tears filled her eyes, but her face was alight. Spirits, what he would do to keep it that way.

"Good," Radais said. "I left the rest of the Glassblades to decide what to do with me. If they choose a new supreme defender, I hope it is Polina. Tairanik is strong, but he thinks we're still fighting awakened. We need to adapt to survive." He turned to Ataakanan. "That starts with showing them we're not just fighting spirits anymore."

THE CONFEDERATION OF HARIZAK

"It is because we love of our nation that we must defy its unrightful king. For scion. For lowborn. We all bleed crimson, but the Commonwealth's ruler shall not be chosen by the one who sheds it most." – An excerpt from The Harizak Declaration

Kasia wandered the stone halls of Fort Harizak with Spitza perched on her military uniform's shoulder. Built for an age before modern siege tactics with a moat and two layers of walls, the fortress remained a marvel with seemingly infinite rooms to discover. Each kept her mind off her worries a moment longer, but there was no escape from the Tainted voices haunting her mind.

The particular room she found herself lingering in was on the far northwestern edge of the castle's keep. It was nearly the highest point in the castle, and from it, she could see over the confluence of the Ty and Vamia rivers. A sea of red sprawled over the farms and plains beyond.

Spitza's *caw* alerted her to another presence in the room, and from the yelp that responded, she knew exactly who it was. "What is it, Tazper?"

"Commander Tiuz has managed to procure you a shadowlight candle," he squeaked from the doorway.

Her poor footman understood her moods well, and he was rightfully terrified to interrupt her while she recovered from this incredibly potent round of Reacher Taint. She let him believe that was her greatest worry. In truth, waiting for Zinarus and fearing his scolding for Sadamar's deal were far heavier upon her shoulders. Worse was the thought that he wouldn't return to scold her at all.

"Do you think I should find another crystal for Sadamar?" she asked, still staring out that old stone window at the great Crimson army. "The power he offers could end this, and if I go back on my pact, I doubt I'll ever have the chance again."

When Tazper didn't reply, she sighed and turned toward him. "You have earned your talon, and now you no longer wish to speak to me?"

"It is not that." He straightened his posture. "You have already asked my opinion on this, and then proceeded to rebuke me for my honesty. Do you want to hear it, or do you want me to help justify your desire to return to the Fleshweaver?"

She held her arm across her chest. Spirits, she felt like shit, but with battle approaching, she couldn't just sit back. The Axiom had gifted her the rarest power in the realm. Tiuz had already expressed both his skepticism of her past decisions and his need for her help. She wasn't sure if she was much use in her current state, though.

"I need you to tell me that this fight is more than my own now," she said, gaze averted. "That I alone do not bear the responsibility for defeating those who killed my father and ruined my life."

He looked down at the shadowlight candle. No taller than the length of a finger, it had an ethereal allure to its gray wax, infused with Shadow Reacher magic. "You are not the only one who they have hurt. There are tens of thousands of soldiers encamped here to fight them, along with the Commonwealth's most famous general, the patriarch of House Kuzon, and the acting matriarch of House iz Ardinvil. This is no longer an investigation, Kasia. It's a war, and you cannot win it alone."

Hearing him say that was both a massive weight off her chest and yet another nail into her pounding head. She had worked years against the Crimson Court with only Tazper as a true ally. Every step, every kill had been her choice, and the consequences had been hers to endure. This conflict had grown far beyond her control now. She hated being just another piece on the haataamaash board, feeling as if another player was making the decisions. Still, she begrudgingly admitted it felt good to no longer be alone in this fight.

"Stepping back from Sadamar's offered power does not make me a coward, then?" she asked. "What if the risk brings us victory against the Crimsons and saves lives?"

"You do not seek martyrdom," he said, setting down the candle on an old, rotting table along the wall. "You seek to fill the hole Leonit's death left in your heart, even if it Taints you beyond repair. Perhaps for once, you can fill that hole at some reasonable cost instead of at all costs."

Then he left before she could reply, leaving her to stew in his absence. How could he be so insightful yet so infuriating? This choice could turn the tide of war... or mean the end of her life.

She stared at that shadowlight candle as time slipped past—an effect of Axiom Taint that she was steadily learning to catch, but was unable to stop. Of course her father would've hidden his writings behind the power connected to his Shadow Reaching. That daughter of Zekiaz had claimed reading his notes would make Kasia no longer a pawn. Why?

Pulling Leonit's purple book from her bag, she dragged the room's single rickety chair to the table, then threw herself into it. Exhaustion greeted her. She dared not examine the Axiom Crystal consuming her arm and shoulder as she unlatched the book. It was just a reminder of the costs Tazper had mentioned. The specters filling both the room and her mind ensured she never forgot, and knowing time could slip away without any way for her to stop it was terrifying. If her father had answers...

"You destroyed us," her own Tainted specter spat, sitting on the table and running her taloned finger around the candle's rim—the same finger Kasia no longer had. "Do not pretend Father's notes will provide some magical cure to your failures.

"He is not *your* father," Kasia said. "You are nothing, a figment of my broken mine's wanderings."

The specter laughed. "I am all you desire to be. Denying your spirit's desires will not save you."

Kasia stared down at the book's empty pages, wondering what the shadowlight would reveal. This specter wanted to tempt her, but she'd let herself wander far too much in recent hundred-hours. Her life had been a series of chases after her father's lost ghost. Now, she had his writings, his *secrets*, and if the Children of Zekiaz spoke truth, then it would ensure she was no longer a mere pawn on the haataa-maash board.

"Nothing can save me," she whispered to herself as she took the matchbox sitting upon the candle's holder and struck the first match. Its flames drifted before her as her words slipped into the Axiom Taint's. "But I don't need to be saved. I need to end this."

Time snapped forward, the match burned down to a stub between her fingertips. Angry red skin covered those fingers from the fire's touch, but she just stared at it, allowing pain to pierce the heavy veil which enveloped her spirit. Taint forced her to suffer. That was ethereal, though, not the present sting of her mortal body.

"We all need saving if we have any hope of ending this."

The new voice sent Kasia spinning from her chair, pistol raised. It felt right to wield her father's prized revolver moments before seeking his book's secrets, but that glee tumbled into anxiety at the sight of the flame-haired man who'd spoken. She lowered the pistol and tossed it on the table. "There's no one to save us but ourselves."

Spirits, she'd pondered for days what she wanted to say to Zinarus… and what she *needed* to say to him. Her stupid, exhausted mind had opted for her usual spite instead. Maybe those things he had said about her back in Vamiustok were true after all.

"I pray to the Crystal Mother that is not true," he replied, gripping his cane like an eager child would the edge of a sweets stand. His eyes, though, were somber. "If it is, however, then I am certainly glad it is you whom I shall endure beside. That is, if you prefer my presence to the realm of Death. I believe Tazper called it Orat?"

He ended with a wanting smile, but she couldn't share it. "Much has happened since I left your family's manor," she said with her tone slipping into her old formalities to shield her shaken emotions. "Would you like to address those events first, or my reason for leaving?"

It was a challenge and a concession all at once, and his flinch revealed he knew as such. Perhaps she had overreacted after eavesdropping on an out of context conversation. She wanted him to ask, though—to care why she'd left.

"I would say it is a lady's prerogative to choose," he said, "but I may end up with a bullet in my gut *again* if I did. Very well, then. Let us address the koilee in the room."

Kasia straightened her posture, defiantly lifting her chin. "I overheard—"

"Me quoting my father's quite harsh words about you, yes."

He stepped closer until they were nearly touching, his left hand abandoning its cane to lean on the table instead. With his Vockan height, he stood half-a-head taller than her, so he tilted down his head to meet her gaze. A smoldering amber amusement filled his eyes now, and he chuckled before continuing.

"Did you not think it better to confront me about what you heard instead of teleporting away to attack our nearly immortal king by yourself? Not to mention ending up in the realm of Death and promising an undead lord a Spirit Crystal, then teleporting *two thousand* lowborn to safety from breathless attacks. My claims of insanity were a ruse back at your mansion, but some would think them true after all you have done."

Her nose twitched. "I admit that my actions were rash, but if I had not gone my own way, all those lowborn who have joined you would be dead." She paused, clicking her tongue. "Actually, it would be worse. Chatik probably would have turned them into breathless, then used them to kill you too."

"I believe I have failed to make myself clear." He took her crystal hand, lightly tracing the circle at her palm's center. "Your actions have done more than save the Ashes of Dawn. By teleporting them here, you have provided me crucial aid—especially that Spirit Reacher, Crax. I dare not consider how many lives would have been lost otherwise."

Softly, he kissed her hand, not taking his gaze off her. "I do not blame you for what you did, dear Kasia, but must admit that I only wish that you had trusted me enough to know I would never speak of you in such a way. You have my heart, my mind, and my spirit wrapped around your finger like a strand of the golden crystal you bear. These days without you, wondering whether you were even alive, have tormented me. If something were to—"

Kasia grabbed him by the shirt before he could finish, entrapping him in a kiss. The force nearly toppled them as his mechanical leg creaked, but she spun him back into the table instead. The stumble sent them both into a laughing fit before their lips met again. This time, nothing could separate them.

She embraced the comfort of being with him. Taint's agony had gripped her for so long. In his arms, though, Death's voices silenced against the racing of her heart, and no slip of time could tear her away. All she felt was his lips and body pressed against hers. It was a bliss she had not felt in so many years.

Ever since Aliax.

A frigid cold struck her. She scrambled away, her eyes wide and her breaths catching in her throat as she stared back not at Zinarus, but the specter of her late lover. No, it couldn't be him. That kiss had felt so *real*, and everything Zinarus had said…

"You think of me even when you're with him," Aliax said. He circled toward the window, and Zinarus appeared in his wake, confused and blushing. "Choose him all you like, but your heart never left me."

Kasia gripped her head as Aliax's voice joined with dozens more. Each screamed against her affection for Zinarus, if she could even call it that, and it rattled her mind until she couldn't take it anymore.

"Shut up!" she screamed, flailing at the specters like some drunken brawler. "All of you, leave me alone!"

Her Tainted specter appeared from Death's purple wisps to kiss Aliax at the window. She wore a wicked grin when she glanced back at Kasia. "You cannot be rid of what you yourself have created. We are not a cancer to be ripped free, but the deepest recesses of your very being."

Kasia staggered into the wall, exhausted as the other specters surrounded her. They grabbed at her hair and limbs, and she had no energy to fight back. Taint had stolen both that and her sanity. So she slammed her eyes shut.

A warm touch greeted her moments later. Not that of the haunting dead, but a caring, gentle embrace that invited her in. The sweet, yet striking scent of fire lilies washed over her as arms cradled her head against their owner's chest. Though the specters' voices still rang out, the gentle rhythm of the person's heartbeat grounded her to reality.

"You are safe," Zinarus assured her. "The specters cannot hurt you."

Could they not? Kasia trembled against him, not daring to open her eyes. The specters had touched her, harmed her, and she feared whether that was how Death's Taint ended—the ghosts of her victims exacting their vengeance.

They stayed there for a long time until rapid footsteps approached from the hall. Someone hurried into the room, heaving with every breath. "General Zinarus! Oh…" The messenger cleared his throat. "The Crimson army has begun shifting their artillery across the farm fields, so Field Marshal Hazeko has requested your presence in the war room. Lady Katarzyana is invited as well."

"Let him know I will be there upon my earliest availability," Zinarus replied, his whole body tensing against Kasia's. "Until then, he may refer to my Aunt Carelias for any orders regarding my house's forces."

The sound of the messenger thumping his chest echoed through the stone room. "Yes, General." Then he scampered off, leaving the pair alone.

Or as alone as the specters would allow.

They were still there, lurking within arm's reach, when Kasia finally forced her eyes open. It was hard enough to let herself be comfortable with Zinarus, let alone with a small crowd as an audience, but this was the life she had made through her own actions. He was one of the few good things she had left. She couldn't force him away, not again.

"I'm sorry," she whispered into his lapel, where a House iz Vamiustok pin scratched at her cheek. "Aliax appeared, replacing you, and there were so many voices screaming at me… Shit, tell me you're real and not one of them."

He chuckled and ran his hand softly through her hair. "I am real, Kasia, and I will not allow you to face this Taint alone. Whether through siege or storm, I am here with you as long as you shall have me."

"I was supposed to ask you about your battle and escape from the general," she said, sighing and pulling back to meet his gaze. She still leaned against the wall for support, but she had no desire to separate further anyway. Things were simpler with only his wind-worn face in her sight. He'd clearly washed since returning from the battle, but he usually tried to look far more perfect than this before presenting himself. Had he been that hasty to find her? "I was supposed to read my father's notes as well."

A relieved smile tugged at his lips. "Ah, yes, our responsibilities venture beyond the heart. My Reaching against Commander Razamat Uziokaki revealed the Crimsons' plan to sacrifice their infantry, allowing the crystal dragon to lead their breathless in a true assault. I only managed to escape with the help of a gang boss, Crax, directing awakened against the pursuing cavalry. If he had not told me he was a Spirit Reacher capable of such a thing, I doubt my house's own Spirit Reachers could have matched his skill."

"Razamat Uziokaki?" She cracked a laugh, remembering her duel against the honorable commander in Raviak Forest. "It seems we have tricked him twice now, and he surely will not forget it."

"Yes, your duel. How could I forget?" His expression soured for a passing moment before he stepped back and took her hand. "I do not take pride in Reaching against him under the flag of truce, but as you have said before, these are unprecedented times. We must act to protect both others and ourselves. Knowledge of the dragon's arrival will help me do exactly that with Tiuz. You, though, have your own matters to attend to."

He helped her to the table across the room, where the shadow-light candle and Leonit's journal awaited her. This time, he struck the match, and she positioned the journal beneath the candle as the flame crackled against its wick. A soft light answered.

The candle's flame was devoid of color, and all that fell into its radius drained to shades of gray. Kasia's own skin lost the pale Ezmani undertones beneath her scion pigmentation, making her hand beside the book only a slightly lighter shade than Zinarus's own. It was an unsettling sensation for only a small area to fall to grayscale. Her attention, though, quickly turned to the writing now present on the cover: *Seek the Heart of All Worlds.*

She exhaled softly as she traced those words with her crystal-wrapped fingers. Her father's words. Within this cover were perhaps the very topics he'd been researching that night he died over a decade before. Just knowing his Reaching, his pen, had created this gave her a deep sense of connection, and she dwelt in it for a long moment.

"The daughter of Zekiaz who met me at The Confluence claimed my father's writings will ensure I am no longer a pawn," she said, flipping open to the first page.

A series of distant booms ignited shouts from throughout the fort. A cannonball struck the outer wall moments later, doing little damage by itself, but marking the start of what would surely be a barrage. They were under siege.

Zinarus squeezed her hand, but gave a look of resignation. "There is nowhere I would rather be than here with you. With the bombardment beginning, however…"

"Go," she told him. "It doesn't take two to read a book, and I am of little use until either the greatest excesses of my Taint pass, or I discover something in here."

"There is one thing I wanted to give you," he said, his voice suddenly nervous as he took his cane and headed over to his bag by the door. Rifling through it, he pulled free a small metallic device which had all kinds of strange gears and knobs sticking out from it—just like his leg. "Considering your twenty-fifth spiritday passed at everdark's end without celebration, I thought I could work with a few eager mercenaries to craft you a gift."

"You should know better than to celebrate a child of everdark. It is said you will inherit a portion of my ill luck for being born with no sun above." Kasia glanced down at the first page of her father's notes. Why were men so bad at timing such basic things? The sentiment, though, was pure, so she eyed the device. "Of course, you have created this… thing… so I should accept it. Thank you."

He nodded toward Spitza, still perched in one of the far windows. "Technically, it is more for her than you. I know how difficult it is to toil without one's limbs, so I made a prototype mechanical wing. Whether it will work—"

She rose swiftly and kissed him again to cease his eloquent rambling. "You so often have perfect words, but fail to know when to stop using them." Another round of artillery fire rang out, so she plucked the wing from his grasp, kissing him once more on the cheek. "It is a thoughtful and generous gift, especially considering you did this *while marching to war*. I am sure Spitza will appreciate it, but you must hurry to Tiuz."

And I must figure out what's in this book.

Zinarus bowed swiftly, shifting rapidly between a boyish smile and exasperation before finally rushing out of the room. She could not help but laugh a little as he did. Amid war, Taint, and her father's mysteries, that purple-coated man had somehow made her feel almost normal. Almost. It was a feeling she wished to cling to for eternity, but she had work to do.

She returned to her seat and held up Leonit's book into the light. As she did so, she allowed herself to truly feel something she'd shoved down over recent hundred-hours and the years before.

Hope.

FOUR REACHERS WALK INTO A TOWNHOUSE

"The backbone of scion society is the lowborn laborer. The second we put our bodies upon the gears of their great machine and halt its progress, it is they who will call us 'lord.'" – An excerpt from *The Dawnrise Manifesto* by Evit Paxian

Nex had never ripped off a coat so fast. At least, not that they could remember.

They threw their watchman's uniform halfway across the apartment of the woman Nikoza had called Falia. The move startled their host, bringing even more red to her round cheeks, but the princess calmed her as Nex dropped onto a wobbly stool around the kitchen table.

With a side-eye in Nex's direction, Nikoza thanked the little girl, Tylea, who'd guided them into the house before doing the same to Falia. A bright yellow handkerchief peeked out from Falias' bag as she cleared her things off the cluttered table. She glanced at the Crystal Brigadesmen, tucking it away.

"You a part of the Ashes of Dawn?" Nex asked. They'd lacked many allies east of the river among the lowborn, but had something changed?

Falia gave a nervous chuckle. "What would a woman like me have to do with those rebels?"

"Fear not," Hazat said. He and Jolzena had dropped off their soot-covered coats outside the apartment, exposing his watchman's undershirt and glass bracers. "We may be members of the Crystal Brigade, but we are here in defiance of the Crimson King, not to aid him. Lady Nikoza was imprisoned in the palace for doing the same."

"Oh, you poor girl," Falia said, pressing the back of her hand to Nikoza's forehead like she had a fever. "I pray to the Mother that you are well."

Nikoza shied away. "Considering all that has happened, I am as well as can be, but my concern is not for myself. I heard there was a horrific attack against the people of the western city." Tears suddenly swelled in her eyes, and she trembled as she sat. "Gregorzon told me that by allowing Nex to escape, I accidentally revealed the location of the Ashes of Dawn's safehouse. Nex, I am so sorry. I swear I did not intend to lead them to you."

"I already knew," Nex replied, but they clenched their fists on the table. Trusting her had gotten hundreds, maybe thousands, killed in the breathless attack. It might've happened anyway, but that didn't make it any easier. "Hazat told me."

A long silence fell over them until Jolzena coughed and noisily slid back the chair opposite to Nikoza. The Force Reacher threw herself into it, trying to wipe the soot off her face with her sleeve. "Sergeant Nikoza has been locked up for days, and you two," she said, pointing at Nex and Hazat, "were Crystal Mother knows where in the west side. I doubt you have heard what our lovely Crimson King has planned."

"Haven't heard anything," Nex said. "We were too busy not getting our spirits stolen by those damn breathless."

Falia waved a furious hand. "Please watch your cursing in my house. I'm happy to find a way to repay Lady Nikoza, but there are children in the other rooms."

Few things could silence Nex, but that did. They didn't need to have grown up with a mother to know the deep dread that came when you pissed one off. So they just mumbled an apology and sat back, waiting for Jolzena to continue.

"You probably figured out by now that Chatik called basically all the Crystal Brigade except for a few Spirit Reachers back to the palace," Jolzena said. "He put out a pair of announcements to everyone else too. The first claimed Nikoza was under arrest after allying with the Ashes of Dawn's and Confederation of Harizak's rebellions. When the breathless swarmed the western city not long after, I think a lot of people decided they were sick of the Crimsons' shi… problems… and that the Ashes were wrongly slaughtered. It's not like the Crimsons were going to admit many of them escaped with Death's Daughter."

Falia nodded, pulling out her handkerchief. "Most of us hoped the Crimsons would leave the rest of us lowborn alone, but with the war drafts and now all the breathless, we realized we need to fight back. It's too late—I know—but it's something."

"It's more than something," a man said from down the short hall off the side of the kitchen. Tufts of unkempt blond hair sprouted every direction from his head, and he grabbed a flat cap from a nearby shelf to cover it. That hat, though, wasn't in much better condition. That gave Nex a dozen reasons to trust him.

"Name's Kix, for all you who haven't met me," he said in the familiar gruff accent of a laborer. "We're organizing the Drifters' Quarter and the neighborhoods around the old clock tower. I heard the bridges are open too with the watchmen pulling back, so we've got runners heading over there to see if anyone left is willing to pick up a gun."

Nex huffed. "I've got a bunch of weapons caches still left around the Shadow Quarter. The Crimsons found our safehouses, but there's no way in the wastes they found all our guns. Got glass and amber too."

"Think you could point 'em out?" Kix asked, crossing his arms, but grinning.

"I'll show you when I get out of here. Bridges are empty, so no one will stop us."

Nikoza held out her hands. "Before we rush into anything, we should hear the rest of what Jolzena has to say. There was a second announcement from my uncle?"

"They sent Air Reachers around with squads of watchmen," Jolzena said. "Chatik is planning some kind of presentation tomorrow on one of the palace's southern balconies, and he claims he's inviting everyone, scion or not, into the Crimson District to hear it."

Kix scowled, throwing out an arm. "Invited? No, he's demanding it. Said that if we don't come, the breathless will treat us as rebels."

"Then we will be there," Hazat replied. He still stood, but compared to Kix's towering presence, he looked like an eager boy. "Whatever he is planning, we must stop it. I can't fathom what he'll do, but it likely has to do with this supposed Spirit Plague cure the Crimsons started releasing right after the Ashes rescued Etal. Jolzena, did Captain Tzena say anything about the Crystal Brigade's duties?"

She shook her head. "Tzena called the Spirit and Mind Reachers into the training rooms for a long meeting, but hadn't told the rest of us much before I left with you lot. Normally, my brother would tell me all the details. Vanzearik was dead quiet after this one, though. After all he's done, it must have been serious to shake him like that." She winced, averting her gaze. "Sorry, Hazat. I know it probably wasn't easy for you to command those spirits either."

"It would surprise you how much a Spirit Reacher can accomplish without his compatriots knowing," he said. "There are many things I regret doing to avoid suspicion, but I suspect we all have those regrets. What's more important is interrupting whatever they discussed in that meeting."

"I've got a feeling about this plan of theirs," Nex said before tapping their head. "My memories are like finding a rusty nail in an old workman's bucket, but my instincts are still there. And that's what keeps us alive in the Shadow Quarter."

Nikoza raised her brow, but offered a forced smile. "To what end do those instincts guide you now?"

"The Crimsons claimed to release a cure right after we rescued

Etal and got the real one." Nex raised two fingers. "That means either their cure is real, and they're trying to convince people they're not the bastards they really are." They dropped their index finger, leaving the middle one up for emphasis. "Or things are about to get even worse, because those cures aren't just fake—"

"They're the disease," Hazat said, his scion gray face turning even more ghastly. "Dear Mother below, the Crimsons created the plague to grant them a breathless army, but it must have not been enough. They decided to directly infect the most vulnerable people instead."

Nex nodded. "They got rid of the Ashes because we were about to treat all the sick people, and they knew we wouldn't trust their cure."

"There was a time when I would have objected to such a claim," Nikoza said before her voice dropped to little more than a whisper. "Now, however, I have seen the true extend of my uncle's corrupt intentions."

"The king's done nothing but oppress the lowborn!" Kix shouted, earning a sharp look from Falia, forcing him to calm. "This isn't personal about your family, Lady Nikoza. It's about saving lives and letting people go about their days in peace."

"Wait a moment," Hazat said. "There's something else we are missing in all of this: the Crystal Heir. Everyone in the Brigade knows that Chatik is horribly Tainted, though his Mind Reaching has convinced many otherwise. He has been practically rabid since he returned from his mission with Tzena. Rumor has it that he went after his runaway wife, but considering he returned with neither her nor their children, I assume the worst happened."

Nex scooted their stool to purposely make an irritating noise. "Get to the point. Dawnrise will be over by the time you're done."

"I like this one," Jolzena said, folding her arms and leaning back in her own chair. "They have grit."

"Very well," Hazat said as he rubbed his glass bracers. "The point is that Chatik is organizing everyone in Kalastok in one place, infecting them, and preparing Nikoza as his heir in rapid succession. This is not simply some horrible plot to enhance the Crimson army—it was supposed to be his grand death. He has that Unity Crystal that lets him Reach into other realms than just his talon's binding to Darkness. What if he plans to use it to somehow activate the Spirit Plague with everyone present? It'll Taint him even worse, but the Crimson Cause isn't about him."

Nikoza gripped her head in her hands, shaking as her eyes turned bloodshot. "It is meant for me." She heaved with every breath, and Hazat had to help her when she stumbled to her feet. "He called me his firebird who must rise from the ashes. The Crimson Cause desires a new world led by only the scions and their army of spirits, and with his children lost, he thinks he has nothing to live for but that goal."

"More like to die for," Nex muttered.

It was half-a-joke, but Jiinaan's and Jax's deaths flashed before them. They hadn't remembered Jax much at all since the Truth Reachers' torture. That horrible moment during Nikoza's aid convoy returned now like a punch straight to their gut, and they felt the blood pouring from his stomach and onto their face like it were fresh. Nex had to fake a cough to hide their sniffle. Shit, Jax hadn't deserved that. He'd just been helping Nex get to Nikoza before a watchman put a bullet in him for no reason.

"How do you defeat someone who plans to die?" Jolzena asked, tearing Nex from their memories.

Hazat waved toward Nikoza, who stood with her arm over his shoulder. "By rescuing Nikoza, we took a key cog in his machine, but Tainted or not, Chatik has planned this for far too long to not have an alternative."

"Our only possible option is to take the Unity Crystal," Nikoza said. "It is the tool he wants the Crystal Heir to use for rebuilding Ezman. Perhaps, then, I must use it to undo what he has wrought."

"How you going to take it from a guy who's basically immortal?" Nex asked. "Sure, these new Ashes of Dawn rebels will help, but between Chatik, the Crystal Brigade, and those breathless, the four of us and a bunch of workers with muskets can't do much."

A spark lit in Nikoza's purple eyes. She steadied herself, patting

Hazat on his arm in thanks before approaching Nex. "Do you remember how you freed Professor iz Noshok from my uncle's grasp before?"

"Sure, cause a distraction, then shoot him in the back. Doubt it'll work again."

"I am the one whom my uncle wants. While his attention remains upon me, Nex and Kix's rebels may foment chaos among the Crystal Brigade and watchmen, granting me freedom to strike."

Hazat looked at her as if she were insane. "You would be walking directly into his grasp once again. Last time, it ended with you trapped in the palace, and I am worried we'll not have the chance to save you this time."

"That is why I also need an accomplished Spirit Reacher to ensure the breathless do not get to me first." Nikoza replied. "Once I am close to Chatik, I will either take the Unity Crystal or attempt to destroy it."

"That is hardly a well-formed plan."

She raised a brow at him. "Then it is all good and well that we have plenty of bright minds to develop one over the next day." She clapped her hands like a headmistress would when it was time for the children to practice their writing. "We best get to work, then. After all, the Crimson King demands our presence."

THE WAR ROOM

"The great houses hold boundless wealth, but neither glass nor crystal is as valuable as the spirits passed from generation to generation through the Inheritance Rituals. For those, any magnate or heir would war to protect." – *An excerpt from* The Commonwealth from an Outsider's View

Zinarus's joy of being with Kasia again faded the moment he stepped into the hall, cannon fire echoing across its stone. He had yet to acclimate to the dread that met a commander in the minutes before battle. Some, like Tiuz, called it a thrill, but he could think only of the lives that would end on both sides of this siege.

The forces of the great houses Kuzon and iz Ardinvil, along with those Tiuz had raised independently through his fame alone, dwarfed houses Niezik's and iz Vamiustok's to the tune of tens of thousands. There were so many soldiers spilling out of old Fort Harizak that he could look out the windows as he hurried through the castle's keep and see nothing but fresh defensive fortifications for some distance. Those were the most vulnerable positions.

The Crimson Court's Third Army, though, had decided to attack the fort directly.

The hammering of artillery from both besiegers and defenders alike drowned out the shouted commands from Confederation officers. Zinarus covered his ear with his free hand to stop it from ringing as he passed one of the inner bastions on his descent through the keep. Lines of cannons smoked like a great wildfire, each manned by a rainbow of various uniforms from once divided houses across the Commonwealth.

House loyalty meant little in times like these. He had never been fond of the arrogant magnate Borys Kuzon the Sixth, but he could not deny the man had been brave to defy the Crimsons after their assassination of his dear friend, King Jazuk. Vockan and Ezmani, lowborn and scion, fought side-by-side here as siblings who sought to protect the Commonwealth's dream of two united nations.

Confederations of the past had been dividing factions seeking gains often for a powerful few. This… This was revolution.

Each *clang* of his cane echoed battle cries from within the keep and to the walls beyond. The courtyard below, though, was quietly filled to the brim with camp followers, and as he reached the floor above Commander Tiuz's war room, he reminded himself this was not merely a battle to determine the lives of his soldiers. Thousands of innocents relied on the generals to have sound strategies. Millions more would have their lives changed by the outcome of this civil war.

He wondered about his place in all this. For the last few hundred-hours, he had been so focused on ensuring his mercenaries and House iz Vamiustok's valuable sand reached Fort Harizak. It was surreal now that he was here.

A figure appeared from the shadows when he hobbled onto the ground floor of a rounded staircase, his metal knee releasing a puff of steam from the labor. He would have to work on it soon, as days on the road had not been good for its finely tuned mechanisms. The man before him was a far more welcome part of that journey.

"Lord Crax of the Shadow Quarter," he said with a bow of his head. "Do you wish to join me for our meeting in the war room? Your insights from Kalastok may prove helpful."

The elderly man laughed and fell into stride alongside Zinarus. "That is a new title for me, but I'm no lord. Those in Crax's Folly are my family, not servants."

"Then what is this folly referenced by your gang's name?"

Crax checked his leather gloves, just deeper than his skin of weathered clay, and grinned without exposing his chipped teeth. Some day, Zinarus hoped to learn this man's full story. Crax had admitted in private that he was a Spirit Reacher, but anything more than that, like his scion house or how he ended up as a gang boss, remained a mystery.

"You know why smart young lads like you don't make it far in western Kalastok?" Crax asked as a crash, followed by cries, signaled a successful Crimson strike against one of the walls. If Crax noticed, he did not show it.

"Why is that?" Zinarus asked, heading toward the heart of the castle with renewed vigor. This bombardment was not the danger when the breathless and the Crimsons' crystal dragon lay in wait, but each true strike by the besiegers weakened the Confederation's chances.

Crax patted his arm. "You ask too many damn questions."

Messengers scampered past them like startled ants as the pair neared the war room. This was only the beginning of what could be a lengthy siege, but intelligence was vital as the Confederation's forces sought to learn more about their attackers. Zinarus had already sent a messenger himself to relay what he had learned by interrogating Razamat. What Tiuz had decided to do with that information, though, he didn't know.

One of the stationed guards dressed in Confederation silver lined in green thumped his chest at the sight of Zinarus's commander sash, but signaled for Crax to stop. "Sorry, sir. Officers only unless you are bringing a message for Field Marshal Hazeko."

"He is with me, Private," Zinarus said respectfully. The soldier's skepticism was warranted, as Crax hardly looked the part of a captain within the Amber Brigade, but Kalastok's lowborn soldiers would respect him less if he took up the uniform scions wore. War took compromise. How much, though, Zinarus was still figuring out.

The soldier stepped aside. "Apologies, sir."

Zinarus offered him a curt nod before entering the surprisingly still war room. Twenty officers gathered around elaborately carved tables, moving pieces across maps depicting the fort and its flanks along the Ty River to the north and the Vamia one to the southwest. Their conversations were hushed, but shouting echoed from the room's rear.

"You cannot leave him there!"

A tall, broad-shouldered woman whom Zinarus recognized as Manalias the Third, heir of House iz Ardinvil, pushed her finger into Commander Tiuz's chest. She wore a Vockan blanket scarf wrapped over her flamboyant dress instead of any kind of military attire. Her eyes, though, burned like the artillery fire beyond these walls.

"Are you planning to send your house's mercenaries straight into their lines?" Tiuz asked, scratching the sweeping handlebar moustache he'd grown since Zinarus saw him last. The style had gained fame among cavalry units in the past wars against Kelosh, and with little hair on the aging general's head, it was a marked improvement. In days like this, they needed the famous Tiuz of old. Sometimes, that meant the small things like looking the part.

Manalias scoffed. "I wish to rescue my father and my house's magnate, not send my soldiers to their demise. These Crimsons have given us a choice. It is a simple one, yet you act as if they ask for all our talons."

"What is this choice you speak of?" Zinarus asked, approaching as Crax kept behind him. He held a fist over his chest in salute to the commander and lady. The gang boss did not.

"Oh, this will certainly make matters easier," Manalias quipped with a click of her tongue. "Katarzyna Niezik's suitor will *surely* have the Confederation's best interests at heart."

"I am here at the field marshal's summons. What is this about?"

Tiuz stepped past the iz Ardinvil heir and clasped Zinarus on his shoulders. The Ezman was far shorter than his Vockan counterpart, but it was a fatherly gesture. One of pride. "You cannot know how happy I was when I heard you were still alive. After the coup, I feared the worst for you. Know that our little mercenary company grew into the first forces of this Confederation."

Zinarus patted his mentor's arm with a smile. "It is safe to say I only escaped with incredible luck and Lady Katarzyna's haste. There was more than one moment when I questioned whether I would see the next, but there will be plenty of time to discuss the past once we win this battle." He flicked his gaze toward Manalias, her deep gray cheeks flaring. "What was this about my relationship with the Niezik matriarch?"

His heart fluttered at that admission. They had yet to declare an official courtship, but there was a bond of romance between them. How deep it burrowed, they would have to discover later, but knowing he fought alongside her gave him courage he lacked alone.

"The Crimsons have used their disgusting breathless to elevate my father before their army," Manalias said. "The last I had heard from Ivalat, he was attempting to escape Kalastok after the coup, but he must have been caught. Now, those spirits hang him by his arms, mocking us. If we do not comply with their terms within the next five hours, then he shall be executed."

Zinarus offered a conciliatory nod. Why must scions always skirt around the truth of their statements? Was she so afraid to say what those demands were?

"Drawing from your ire," he replied, "I must assume at least one of those demands is that we hand over Lady Katarzyna."

Tiuz nodded as more cannon fire echoed outside, spurring a twitch of his lip. "Both her—as punishment for her murders and betrayal—and you as well. Though your actions with Lord Razamat Uziokaki gained us valuable intelligence, neither he nor the Crimson command were amused by your use of Truth Reaching under the flag of truce."

Zinarus's heart sank, but he could not deny that he'd expected this. One did not simply violate sacred military honor without consequence. "I see…"

"It does not matter," Tiuz said. "A deal wouldn't earn us relief, just Lord Ivalat's life. Your Aunt Carelias made clear that House iz Vamiustok's troops would not tolerate your surrender. Seems you have earned some respect from them in short order."

"Is freeing Ivalat not a priority for you, Field Marshal?" Manalias asked, chin tilted down at Tiuz like the tip of a spear. "I will not allow my house's patriarch to face execution because we harbored an infamous murderer! Either we agree to their terms, or I will negotiate the end of Houze iz Ardinvil's involvement in the Confederation in exchange for his release."

"That would take nearly a quarter of our troops," Tiuz said matter-of-factly. "Given that the Crimsons vastly outnumber us already, I do not need to explain why that is a horrible idea."

Manalias waved a dismissive hand. "You lesser houses do not grasp the importance of the Inheritance Rituals. To lose Ivalat to execution means two lifetimes of experience, secrets, and connections shall be abandoned before I can bear a child for his spirit to inhabit. Both his spirit and mine stretch back to the beginnings of Vocka's joining with Ezman!"

Zinarus found both their gazes falling on him. How could he make a choice? Refusing the deal would lose the Confederation House iz Ardinvil's troops, and agreeing to it would cost both Kasia and him their freedom. His actions had put Tiuz in a difficult situation. As he considered his options, though, he decided these two could not be the only ones. Diplomacy and guile alike were powerful tools, and one could not just surrender to tyrants.

"What if there were another way to rescue Lord Ivalat?" he asked, glancing back at silent Crax. "Through unorthodox means, Captain Crax and the Ashes of Dawn managed to escape the Crimsons' breathless in Kalastok, and he helped me do the same against Razamat's cavalry forces not long ago."

Now *he* was the one dancing around the point, but he needed to breach the topic of Kasia's Axiom Reaching carefully. It was still somewhat of a secret, after all. If revealing it saved her life and kept the Confederation together, though, it was a worthy sacrifice.

"We should not be allied with Death's Daughter anyway," Manalias contested, "and your own actions have dishonored you, whether it allowed your troops to escape Lord Razamat or not."

Tiuz held up a hand. "I have my own skepticism about

Katarzyna's past, but we should hear out Major General Zinarus's plan. We are more prepared thanks to his reports about the crystal dragon and the breathless. Any extra advantage he can provide is worth it."

Zinarus bowed his head in thanks, leaning heavily upon his cane as if all his hopes rested on its stability. "To help rid you of your fears around Lady Niezik, I can tell you that she is no longer a Death Reacher. King Chatik shot off her talon, so she is no threat through such power. She has, however, acquired another which allows for teleportation or the shifting of gravity for herself or a small group. Used well, it should be quite helpful to rescue Ivalat."

"What you claim is impossible," Manalias said. The room's murmur of conversation had quieted now, and she surveyed the listening officers. "One cannot gain another talon once they have lost their first, and there is no such Reaching that allows teleportation anyway."

Stepping closer, Zinarus lowered his voice to a whisper. "I assure you it is not impossible. Thousands of Kalastok lowborn can attest to how her abilities saved their lives. You need not like her to grasp that she could save your father and keep this alliance from breaking before its first major battle."

"Yet you refuse to explain the origin of this ability. Nor have you explained how you will stop the breathless from swarming her during this rescue."

Crax coughed, drawing the trio's attention to his sneer. "You have Spirit Reachers. Use them."

"Who are you to question me?" Manalias asked. She looked him up and down like he were a rotting barn. "A mere lowborn captain should be out giving orders, not eavesdropping on sensitive conversations."

Zinarus's frustrations grew by the second, but he smiled, as if introducing two friends to each other. "I brought Captain Crax because he and the Ashes of Dawn have combatted the breathless far more than anyone else. His expertise offers us insights that we elevated scions may miss otherwise."

"Have you used your Spirit Reachers to direct awakened against your enemies before?" Crax said to Manalias. "Only need a few seconds to get away when you have a portal."

Tiuz tapped his foot. "That violates the Commonwealth's treatises on warfare."

"So did the damn Crimsons creating the breathless," Crax said. "I trust Kasia. She'll make sure they get in and out with your patriarch. Just need to fend off the breathless holding Ivalat."

"I am surprised to hear a lowborn advocate for scions in such a way," Manalias said, eyes narrowed.

"It's better to risk some Reachers than the lowborn you dragged out here. You can offer their families whatever you want, but most of them would rather not see keni over a corpse."

Tiuz and Zinarus shared a long look, an unspoken question hanging between them. Anyone sent into this mission would be horribly outnumbered, and they had to hope Kasia's Reaching was precise enough to bring them directly to Ivalat—not another realm—and handle the escape. Her last Reach had left her horribly Tainted. The Crimsons, too, surely understood at least some element of her abilities by now. A ball in Zinarus's stomach told him it was a mistake to volunteer her for this, but what other choice did they have?

"Perhaps a two-pronged approach?" he offered. "They will expect a rescue attempt of one kind or another, but all their attention will be on me if I make an appearance."

Manalias raised her brow. "You would willingly offer yourself in exchange for my father?"

"You misunderstand me, my lady." He shifted his cane to use it as a pointer, gesturing to the nearest map of the battlefield—specifically the iz Vamiustok mercenaries stationed south of the fort. "I wish to lead a cavalry force across the Vamia River's bridge. It need not be more than a thousand, most of whom would come from my own battalions, but that should sow some questions in their minds. Then, if Lord Ivalat remains directly before their lines, we may become a swift relief force should Lady Katarzyna run into trouble with her rescue."

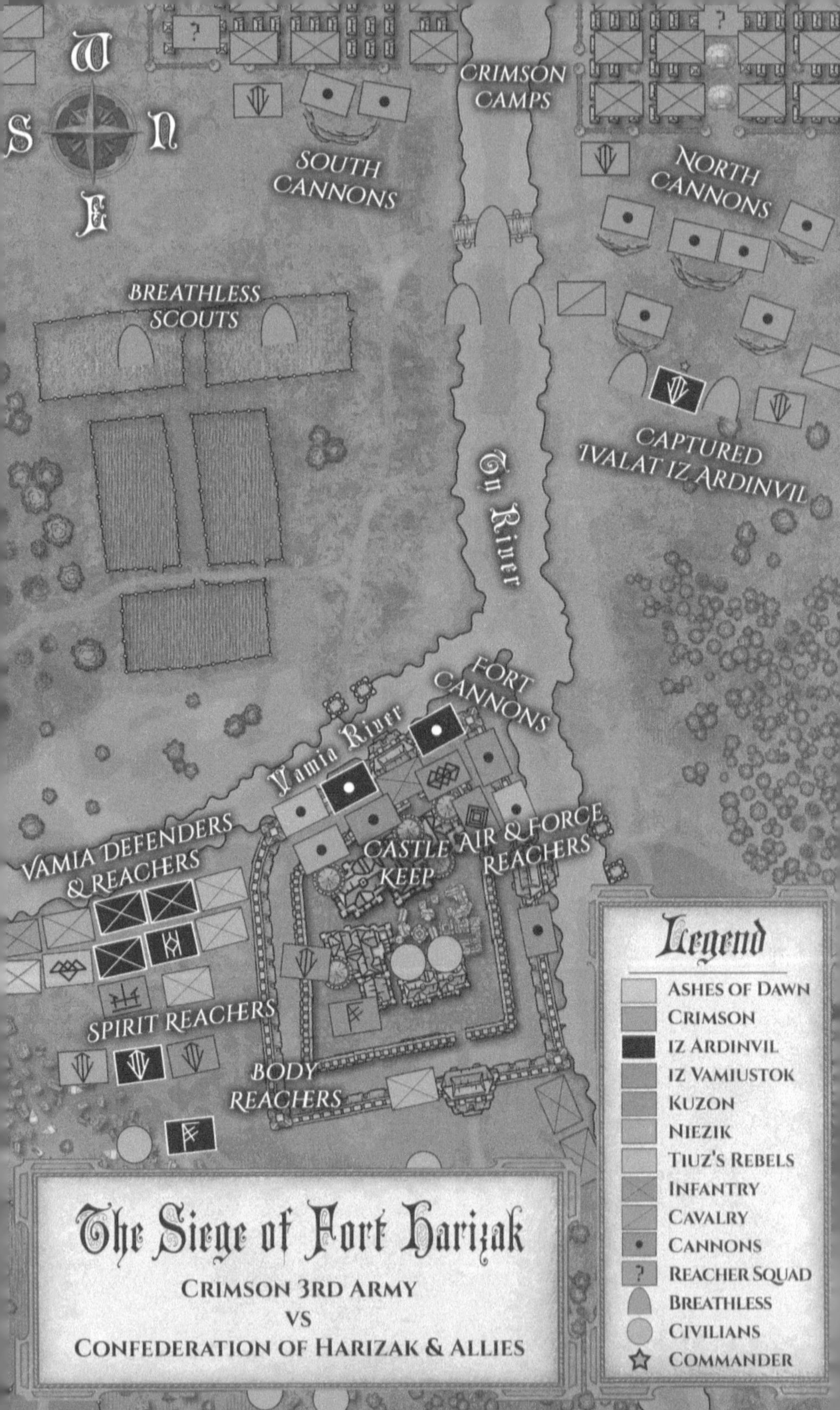

W
S
N
E
CRIMSON CAMPS
SOUTH CANNONS
NORTH CANNONS
BREATHLESS SCOUTS
Tu River
CAPTURED IVALAT IZ ARDINVIL
FORT CANNONS
Vamia River
VAMIA DEFENDERS & REACHERS
CASTLE AIR & FORCE KEEP REACHERS
SPIRIT REACHERS
BODY REACHERS
The Siege of Fort Harizak
CRIMSON 3RD ARMY
VS
CONFEDERATION OF HARIZAK & ALLIES
Legend
ASHES OF DAWN
CRIMSON
IZ ARDINVIL
IZ VAMIUSTOK
KUZON
NIEZIK
TIUZ'S REBELS
INFANTRY
CAVALRY
CANNONS
REACHER SQUAD
BREATHLESS
CIVILIANS
COMMANDER

"It's a bold plan," Tiuz said, "but a good one."

"And if they execute Ivalat the moment you cross the river?" Manalias asked.

Zinarus withdrew his cane, tapping it against the stone floor to ensure it echoed. "Then they are fools. We are already exchanging preliminary fire, so they should expect further pre-positioning and feints ahead of the true battle to come."

Tiuz smiled at him proudly. "Negotiations are more than paper and ink. As you know after the Crimsons' initial attempt to take your mines, a well-maneuvered tactic can ensure there is little for your opponent to debate. They'll see you, but you alone are not enough to draw the gaze of an entire field army."

"Kings ride at the back," Crax interjected, his tone hiding deeper experience. "Heroes lead from the front."

"A wise commander knows when to as well," Tiuz said. "That is why I will lead my own gathered cavalry volunteers alongside your own. It will also give us an opportunity to reveal our secret weapon, hopefully showing them that their breathless are not so invulnerable to our guns. That break in confidence could keep them from continuing this siege."

Zinarus's eyes lit up. "You mentioned that secret was the reason you needed more sand for glass."

"That, and for another reason now that we have Razamat's plans." Tiuz pushed back his commander's coat and drew a strangely narrow pistol, holding it out for Zinarus. "Take a look. A strange benefactor who called herself the Silent Queen gifted me that pistol capable of shooting glass bullets, and we have spent every day since replicating them. We have plenty of pistols. Rifles are far rarer, but we can strike fear into their spirits and their hearts with a few of them scattered through our riders." He looked back at Manalias. "It should also ensure their breathless cannot kill Lord Ivalat until Katarzyna arrives."

"I have just the sharpshooter in mind," Zinarus said, remembering Brakenias's skill in the past battle as he examined the pistol. It had been crafted well and matched Ogrenian techniques he'd used in his own creations. "Combined with our amber findings, these will be of great help."

Tiuz held a fist over his chest in salute as Zinarus returned the pistol to him. "Then I will work with your officers to finalize the plan. Ensure Katarzyna is ready, and inform her that House iz Ardinvil will provide any Reachers she needs to assist."

"Inform her as well that she is responsible for any losses of those Reachers," Manalias added. "And if my father does not survive this little scheme of yours, then know that I will ensure your family is stripped of every piece of land it holds in Vocka. The wrath of a magnate is far worse than any spirit's torture."

Zinarus bowed. "Understood, and if you see Lord Borys, tell him that I am grateful for House Kuzon's assistance in this conflict. I am certain we would be hopeless without him."

Manalias offered only a scoff before hurrying off, the skirts of her Vockan dress knocking over a few of the battle maps' figures along the way. The officers watched her go before looking to Tiuz for orders.

"What are you all staring at?" the old commander barked. "Leave Lord Ivalat to me. We still have a siege to repel!" As the officers hurried to return to their planning, Tiuz's expression softened, and he took Zinarus's arm. "There is another plan I have to deal with these breathless and the dragon, but it will require your utmost discretion until the time is right."

"I am listening."

Tiuz nodded. "Good, because the survival of the Confederation, and perhaps the entire Commonwealth of Two Nations, rests on this succeeding."

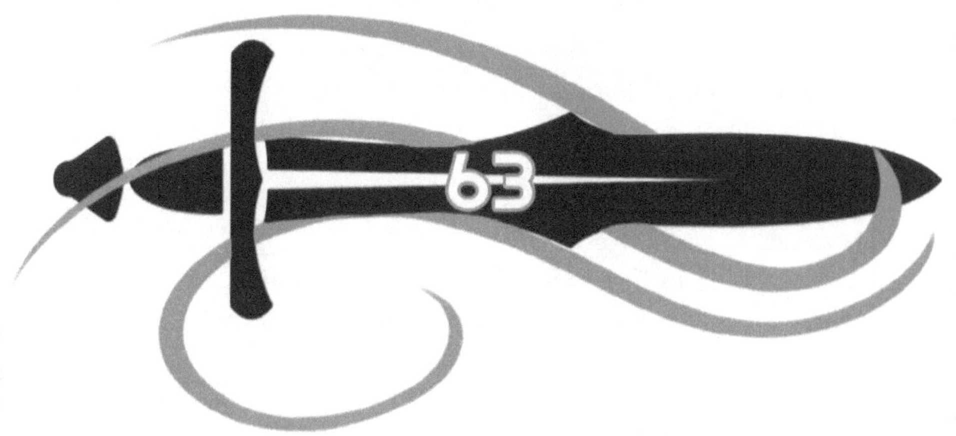

TO WIELD A SPIRIT. TO CALL THE EARTH

"To bear magic is to be limited by it." – Ezmani proverb

Wanusa didn't sleep a wink as the Glassblade commanders spent the night bickering about how to deal with the Saleshi that Miv's spirit, Ataakanan, had brought to aid them against the Vanashel. The other two-dozen breathless lingered about Wanusa and Mariana with curious gazes. Or, at least, what Wanusa thought a spirit's curious gaze would look like.

The flower-headed breathless known as Rakekeaa led this squad of Saleshi, but let Ataakanan handle the Glassblades while Rakekeaa focused on Wanusa near a small fire.

"You bound yourself to a severed one," it said in the Spiritspeech, folding its four arms over its strange rose quartz armor. "Why?"

Wanusa's crystalline collar glowed silver as she summoned Inrius. His spirit hovered around her like a loose breath of fog, drifting with the wind. "This spirit was my brother's. It's my fault he was severed, so I'm going to find the second half of his spirit and fix it."

"The bravery of youth is admirable," Mariana replied, but admiration replaced her usual wizened confidence. She had spoken with breathless before. Sitting around a fire with them as allies, though, was something else entirely. "To be effective in your Whispering, you must not focus on merely a single spirit, but on bonding many to channel their Essences. Half of one will not save you from the Vanashel."

"I'm willing to bond another too," Wanusa said as Alicy approached and curled up beside her, the povnik's spines tickling her ungloved fingers, "but not until I find the second half of Inrius's spirit. I promised when I bound him that I would not wallow in my past. That does not mean I need to abandon him."

"Bind a pure one," Rakekeaa said with its voice far more refined in the Spiritspeech. "That severed spirit is not your brother anymore, but it holds a connection to you. Others will not be so heavy."

Wanusa looked to Mariana for confirmation. When the elder Whisperer nodded, she closed her eyes and focused on the rhythm of Spirit which bound her to Inrius. She asked him silently for permission through it, seeking not to offend, but also not to limit her abilities in the battle ahead. All she received, though, was a gentle calm as Inrius kept to his drifting.

That was enough.

"I'll do it," she said, pushing herself to her feet, "but I don't know how to outside the Deepening."

Mariana rose more slowly. "I will show you, dear girl. I fear, however, that the Saleshi should not be present."

"Rakekeaa came here to understand us, so it can watch. The Saleshi saved our lives. I don't have anything to hide from them."

"Very well," Mariana replied with a glance toward the Glassblades. "I doubt the arguing brutes will have come to a decision by the time we return."

Wanusa lacked the energy to counter the claim. In the hours since her arrival with Radais, Lazan, and Mariana, the Glassblades had yet to choose a new leader, but it was clear they no longer trusted Radais as supreme defender. She badly wished to defend her mentor to them. This, though, was the path she'd chosen. They had left the greater army so that she could Whisper and he could Reach, so it was up to her to ensure she wielded her abilities to their fullest.

Wanusa and Mariana mounted their ibexes as Rakekeea floated overhead, the eyes on the ends of its flower petals watching the distant army. It seemed impossible for the Vanshel's numbers to have grown, but from the switchbacks of the mountain north of the Glassblade camp, it was clear they had. Each was another spirit enslaved to their cause.

"They resemble dragons," Rakekeaa said with no small amount of awe. "Bound Ones seeking the Spirit Crystal's greatest creation."

"No breathless has ever given me meaning for the form they take," Mariana said.

Rakekeaa turned its attention to her. "That is a deeply personal question, but it is not normal for so many to choose the same presentation. This concerns our First One. It concerns me too."

"I am told you are a Bound One," Mariana replied, leaving the topic be. "Neither Wanusa nor Radais could tell me which realm you Reach, to use a human term."

It was a good question. Rakekeaa had fought by the Glassblades' sides in the Spirit Wastes, but it had never been clear that the Saleshi had Reached, unlike others in its squad. Wanusa worried it was a rude question like asking about a breathless's form. Rakekeaa's eyes, though, no longer looked full of fury.

"The realm of Shadows helped me escape with the First One to found Akaamilion," it said. "Spirits are difficult to see in the mists of the Sands of Salesh, and shadows make detection impossible. It is why the Vanashel did not attack my warriors when we came to you."

Wanusa tried to follow up about how Reaching for Bound Ones was different than human Reachers, but Mariana waved a hand before she could speak. "Time is not on our side," the elder said. "Call to a drifter, and then I will teach you both how to bond with and wield it for combat."

So Wanusa followed her command, Whispering her song in the Spiritspeech as Rakekeaa watched on. She was self-conscious enough training with a blade or her Whispering in front of a single person. With an actual spirit studying her, though, her back tensed and her song wavered away from Spirit's rhythm.

Pretend Rakekeaa isn't here, she told herself. *It's just Inrius and me, like the old days.*

She pictured the lush plains around Iliafa instead of the wasteland of ashen sand that consumed it now. In her vision, the trees clung to the earth against the winds of the ephemeral storms, the sheep and goats huddling in their shelters. Rain poured over her, but it was the warm dawnrise kind that brought life. She clung to that torrent and its memories.

Then she sang again.

Her Whispered call carried into the gales as she opened her eyes. The Wastes had consumed her home once again, but the rains had come true, tugging on her hair and cloak as she poured her battered spirit into the call. With Inrius she had Deepened into a Whisperer. With a second spirit, she could become a warrior of both blade and magic alike. And her hopes swelled as a faint silver wisp hovered ever closer.

Drifters' tunes were far simpler than those of their breathless or awakened cousins, but all held the same rhythm of the Spirit Crystal. This one's was barely audible over the storm. Within Wanusa's very core, though, she heard what even her ears couldn't perceive.

"You must draw a portion of your crystal's Spirit Essence and offer it a place within you," Mariana said, squinting as she clutched her coat shut against the wind. "Allow its desires to mold into yours."

Breathing out deeply, Wanusa brought her Whispered song into alignment with not only the Spirit Crystal, but this drifter. It was a blunt beat unlike the monotone voice of Inrius, and she clung to a memory of Palmia Fortress's blacksmith hammering away. A steady, purposeful pattern, it drew the breathless in until it tickled the webs of her fingers.

Silver rose from her crystal to meet the drifter, and when the two joined, it pulsed its tune in both song and light. A shiver ran down her spine as its misty tendrils graced her palm. A simple touch, as if asking whether she wished to take it into her embrace.

"Join with me," she told it, "and you will never want for Essence. I hear your voice, and you don't need to wander anymore."

That shiver surrendered to a rush of heat as the drifter vanished into her palm. Her collarbone shone bright as a pure Light Crystal, and she rose over that cliff edge—one with the spirits again. It couldn't match the grand moment of the Deepening. The chorus of spirits met her still, and in the distance, the Vanashel chanted a single word as they hovered over her old village.

"Dragon. Dragon. Dragon."

A heartbeat later, she tumbled back into Rakekeaa's arms, the breathless's ethereal body somehow able to be translucent yet solid. It was how she imagined the strong embrace of a father who loved his child… Not that she would know the feeling.

She stared down the slope at the Glassblade camp, where Radais glared at Commander Tairanik. Maybe she did kind of know what it was like. Lazan and Radais weren't her true parents—and Mariana was hardly a mother—but she had people who cared for her, guided her.

And now, she had another comforting presence within her. It was less clear, as even Inrius's fractured spirit held some memory of their shared past, but that thundering of a smith's hammer against his anvil now drummed in her chest. A confidence she hadn't felt before. While Inrius calmed her, this one told her she was strong enough to do what she must.

"Tell me how to wield it," she said, prying herself from Rakekeaa and nodding toward Mariana. "I'm ready."

Rakekeaa hummed as it swayed side to side. "The First One will fear this."

"Why?" Wanusa asked. "We want to help you."

"We were born as prisoners to the Crimson ones. Saleshi free spirits. Vanashel enslave them. Whispering humans create bonds." Rakekeaa drifted into the shadows cast by the mountain, obscuring its white petals from the light. "It is not the same as control, but it is not freedom either. An in-between."

"Like shadow."

Its petals all curled, as if nodding together. "We will consider. Now, learn to fight."

Mariana stepped forward, but Wanusa held out her hands. "Wait, there was something I heard when I was bonding this spirit. It's like the Vanashel were chanting about a dragon."

"Hope it is blind worship," Rakekeaa said before fading back. "Train this one. We must be ready."

"DON'T BE STUPID."

Polina crossed her arms by Radais's side, wielding no weapon but the glare of a middle-aged woman. That alone was enough to make most men bleed. But Tairanik was a stubborn ox—rooted in tradition and stupidity alike.

"I'm being rational," the old fool said as he paced in front of his two-dozen loyal warriors and masters. Those two damn middle buttons of his jacket were still undone, and another was misaligned, making the whole thing push up like he were a well-endowed woman. His glass sword dragged against the stone behind him with each step. A horrid noise, but he clearly wanted it that way.

Radais knew better than to come between the commanders, but he did step forward to put himself in no man's land. "There is nothing rational about rejecting the aid of the Saleshi. Our siblings in arms have voted for Polina to be supreme defender, and it is her choice how to lead."

"Bakeekek is hesitant to work with humans," Ataakanan said with a tight grip on its spear. This wasn't Miv, but if her spirit held any of the same tendencies, Radais worried it wouldn't hesitate to get rid of Tairanik if necessary. "We're here to help and to learn. Rejecting that is ensuring we cannot trust you, and that leaves us divided against the Vanashel. A stupid strategy."

"So is fighting an army of that size!" Tairanik snapped. "Radais promised us victory if he strayed into the mountains, but he came back with nothing more than a half-baked talon and a girl who likes to sing to spirits."

Radais threw out an arm. "There is more to being a Glassblade than holding a glass sword and helm. It's the bare minimum to keep them in good condition, but you can't even do that. Why should you be trusted to take care of your warriors, then? Wanusa has created more opportunities for us to grow than you ever will."

He returned to Polina's side, biting his cheek so hard it bled. He knew he shouldn't have honored Tairanik's jab with a reply, but he couldn't help it. Their trek into the mountains had not gone as he'd hoped. It had, though, granted them new weapons and a greater understanding of both spirits and Zekiaz itself. That was invaluable for the Order in the future. But men like Tairanik couldn't see past their next breath.

"Enough of this," Polina said. "You have two choices, Tairanik: Throw down your armor and leave the Glassblade Order, or remember the oaths you've taken and aid us against the Vanashel."

The old commander glared toward the northern mountains, where Wanusa seemed to be practicing her Whispering with Rakekeaa and Mariana. "A Glassblade fights for all of Vocka, not the supreme defender." He sheathed his blade at his hip. "Anyone who wants to protect the towns Radais and Polina abandoned, come with me. I'll not leave our people unprotected to free a lost hamlet."

Mumbled conversations spread throughout the gathered Glassblades. More than a few glanced over their shoulders to study the Vanashel army, as if calculating their chances. Radais couldn't blame them. Even those who sought to defend others didn't want to throw their life away.

But he had to believe they had a chance. This was the largest united Glassblade force in centuries, and among them they had Whisperers, Reachers, and trained breathless. This was not the Whistling Pass. They were armored and ready.

"No," Radais said as fourteen Glassblades followed Tairanik. All of them were experienced, many even masters, and not a single initiate followed. "You'll abandon your oath-bound family to cower in hopes the Vanashel don't come for you next."

Tairanik looked over his shoulder with pity in his eyes. "I know they'll come for me; just like they'll come for us all. I'm not foolish enough to believe we can defeat them in this place."

Then he left with the rest of the group, who began preparing their ibexes and packing their things. Radais considered intervening, but Polina was supreme defender now. She did nothing to stop them. So a split it would be.

Lazan stepped to Radais and wrapped his arm around the Glassblade's waist. "It is the right thing to let them go, in my opinion. From what I hear, morale is key to victory in battle, and you cannot have trained warriors routing when they fight beside fresh initiates."

"Who wins when your opponents don't know fear?" Radais replied, goosebumps running up his arms as he watched those hovering Bound Ones in their dragon forms.

Lazan rose on his tip-toes and pecked Radais on the cheek. "The one who wins is the one who knows he does not fight alone." He nodded toward a clearing away from the tents, where Ataakanan lurked. "No one sleeps on the eve before battle, so as Wanusa trains her Whispering, we must do the same with your power as well. An old friend of yours told me to bring you. Apparently, there is something it wishes to show you about the Saleshi and Reaching."

"Mysterious. Did Ataakanan hint at what it was?"

"It did not, but if anyone can give us insights into the spirits, it is the spirits themselves." Lazan tapped his talon against the Glassblade's. "I saved you from that Earth Bound One once. Let us not make it a second time."

Crystal Brigade Case File 23F - The Personal Notes of Professor Etal iz Noshok

—

 *Earth*

Earth Reaching has been the most studied for its usage in our economies, yet there is much still to learn. Those with great skill may shift minerals to others and cause the ground itself to quake. Could we create infinite glass against spirits? Or would the great houses deny us such a gift for wealth. That question's answer is clear to me.

Our research has emphasized known minerals and constructs, but what if there were a way to shift the earth itself into the unknown? What if we could create more permanent channels to the Spirit Crystal far below? Perhaps we can, but once again, there are those who benefit from such limitations.

While we rely on our magics, Ogorenia and Kelosh have utilized their limited Earth Reachers to great technological benefit. We fall behind. I believe this will be our undoing.

TO SAVE A PATRIARCH

"I have sought a truth deeper than even the Spirit Crystal. There exists another realm at the heart of all others. For so long, we have believed that there are three powers no Reacher may alter: time, place, and gravity. These forces bind all of existence. It is this sixteenth realm that I believe holds the key to these once forbidden magics." – An excerpt from *Seek the Heart of All Worlds* by Leonit Niezik

Kasia could no longer trust whether her thoughts were her own or the constant voices of her Taint-born specters. The words scrawled by her father's hand, though, she knew to be true. Leonit had been close to understanding the hidden power of the Axiom beyond anything she'd heard whispered by the Crimson Court.

And he had died because of it.

That single fact pierced the haze caused by her specters. They could decry her and scream until her ears rang, but Leonit had never led her wrong. There were deeper powers through the Axiom than those she wielded, and the first among them was time.

An understanding of her Axiom Taint's time slips clicked into focus as she ran her crystal-webbed fingers over the ink. Gold melded to an ashen gray beneath the shadowlight candle, like the dying rays of duskfall surrendering to everdark's embrace. She found solace in that bit of colorless light. A comfort that all found its place in the expanse between the purities of black and white.

She need not ponder where she fell on that axis. Her sins painted her very skin and scarred each thought of her twisted mind. But that didn't matter. In this book, she held the truths that had frightened even the Crimson King.

There was far more yet to read. For now, she grinned knowing that, despite killing Leonit, Chatik had not discovered these writings. He had seen her teleport and shift gravity at will, but he failed to grasp the depths of her new power. With the Unity Crystal, he could wield all fifteen known realms.

Only she could touch the power that fed all others.

Spitza gave a broken call from the window nearby. She always seemed to know when Taint inhibited Kasia's thoughts, and that little *gwah* tore her back to the siege's reality. Cannon fire echoed beyond the raven. It was inconstant, though, as each side prodded the other in search of weakness.

"How do you know the specters are there?" Kasia asked, studying the mechanical wing Zinarus had crafted for Spitza. Its brass glinted in the dawnrise light as Spitza shifted, and the bird spooked as it released a puff of steam.

That spook sent her into flight.

Kasia held out her crystal-webbed arm—which always seemed to fascinate the raven—and Spitza swooped straight to it. She wobbled more than most birds, and her landing was rough against Kasia's shoulder, nearly toppling her from the chair and sending mechanical stinging against her cheek. But Spitza had finally flown.

Kasia laughed and patted the raven's head. She was too exhausted from Taint and travel to carry her to treats as a reward, so friendly scratches would have to be enough. Spitza loved every second of it, and for a moment, Kasia's mind cleared.

A thread tickled the center of her palm in that clarity, like a muscle long forgotten. She usually couldn't sense the Axiom's golden web connecting to the other realms without Reaching, but it called to her now, begging to be used. She'd not Reached since teleporting the Ashes of Dawn to safety with Zinarus. To do so now shouldn't worsen the Taint she endured, but fear prodded her chest. Crystal consumed her arm and clawed at her neck. Specters haunted her mind. How far could she push herself before there was no return to sanity?

Or was she already past that point?

To defeat the Crimsons, she needed everything the Axiom had to offer. Zinarus was right to say she no longer fought alone, but only she could Reach into the sixteenth realm. Besieged by breathless and a foe who wielded a crystal dragon, the Confederation would need all the help they could get.

So she focused on that distant thread of power as she Reached into her bountiful Axiom Crystal. Such Reaches had taken effort and will against her Tainted specters before, but with Spitza on her shoulder and the Axiom Crystal joining ever-more with her very being, this Reach was little more than grasping at a golden web that *wanted* to meet her fingers.

Usually, she sought a portal, but now she took that new, fainter, thread. Her breaths were sharp from nerves, so she slowed them and demanded that time do the same.

Leonit had not stated *how* the Axiom's time manipulation worked, merely that it existed. That left her fumbling with her newfound magic like a child with a tower of blocks. Each of the pieces graced her Tainted and scarred skin, but when she sought to bring her intentions into alignment with the Axiom, its golden wisps scattered.

She sneered down at her palm and its crystal lines. A humming power remained in them, though, the Reach not fully extinguished by her failure.

"You didn't expect to get it on your first try, did you?" Aliax asked, sitting on the desk and picking at his nails. "Learning Death Reaching had a price. Are you willing to pay it for this new power when you couldn't even master Death?"

"I mastered it plenty enough to kill Sazilz, Parqiz, and those breathless and awakened during the Ephemeral Slaughter."

She clenched her crystal fist. In truth, she had hoped to master it quickly, as she'd caught onto teleportation well—besides a few jumps to strange other realms that almost killed her. Gravity was a bit stranger, but even that had helped her escape from Chatik's coup.

"Death is a realm of destruction," Sazilz said from the window Spitza had been perched on. He smiled down upon the Crimson army, despite Chatik's betrayal. "For one such as you, it is no surprise you took to it well, while struggling with a realm meant for only the most gifted."

"That explains why you were thrown into a pit instead of granted its power," Kasia quipped. "Even Chatik does not wield the power of the Axiom."

Sazilz looked back at her, wriggling his jaw. "The two of you are more alike than you could know. Arrogant, vengeful, and destroyed by the power you sought. Realm Taint devours you both, but he lives for a greater purpose. His Tainted death will initiate the next phase for his Crystal Heir while you wither into insanity. You will have your vengeance on Chatik, but while you have pursued the death of a single man, the Crimson Cause is a set of ideals. Once spoken, it shall never perish."

"It shall when every Crimson dies at our hand," her Tainted specter said, appearing from a puff of purple wisps and shoving him out the window. "Do not listen to the weak man whom Chatik sacrificed to us. Do not stop trying. You have turned down Sadamar's offer, so we must obtain what power we still can."

A blast rocked the room, sending Kasia stumbling into Aliax. Shouts echoed from below, and a chorus of Confederation cannons answered the strike as Kasia shoved herself off her deceased lover. She was done with specters playing with her heart.

So she threw out her hand and took hold of what power lingered in her Reach. What golden wisps remained were faint, slow, but their drifting allowed her to keep her attention off the room of specters. She watched each golden strand curl around her fingers and skirts as she filled her lungs. Then, holding her breath, she willed time to slow.

For a moment, nothing happened. The wisps lingered there like dead fish, and no amount of sweat trickling down her brow could alter the passage of time.

Then she blinked.

Scattered cannon fire turned rapid. Spitza's pecking against her ear and hair became a constant stabbing pain. Her lungs felt aflame. She tried to fight time's slip, but she couldn't move until a force suddenly jolted her back into her seat.

"Oh, dear Mother," Zinarus said from where she had stood a moment before. His cheeks flushed, and he rubbed his neck, averting his gaze. "Is this the new normal we must handle? I had thought you would return to your chambers instead of residing in this rotting room. Though, they are clearing out all civilians and their belongings to move them to the safer fields southeast..."

His voice trailed off, letting Kasia gain her bearings. The drum of conversation filled the halls outside. Not soldiers' calls, but civilians, even children, being guided out of the castle's keep. Spirits, the keep had taken a direct strike moments before her time slip. It probably would be even worse outside without the Confederation's Force and Air Reachers providing cover, but they wouldn't last forever.

"Why are you taking people away from the fort?" she asked with a shake of her head. "They should be where they are protected, not able to be targeted by breathless."

Zinarus's gaze grew solemn. "As long as the Crimsons wield an army of breathless who can fly through these stone walls, no one is safe here. Tiuz has a plan involving a hidden weapon and the glass shooters he says someone called the Silent Queen gave him. It will require a strategic emptying of the fort."

The Silent Queen...

The specters' voices clamored against Kasia's thoughts, but after a moment, she remembered where she had heard it spoken before. "That daughter," she muttered to herself, rubbing her temples before throwing herself to her feet. "One of the Children of Zekiaz found me back in Kalastok, wielding some strange power and pointing me to use shadowlight on these notes. She mentioned that Silent Queen, but I did not think anything of the title at the time. Is she the head of the Children?"

Zinarus shrugged, so she strode to the window, staring over where her Tainted specter had thrown Sazilz. Except the bastard just grinned up at her from the ground bulwarks below. So she turned away.

"My father discovered a new power for the Axiom," she said. "Time."

"That explains why you reacted to my touch now, but not when you were suffering in that war tent." His cane rapped against the stone as he approached the window and leaned against the wall, gazing out beside her. "There was a golden Reach still hovering about you. So this was not the Taint, then, was it?"

She shook her head, but she jolted back when a cannon went off nearby, sending Spitza flying to another window. Spirits, her nerves were on their ends. Leonit had taught her how to handle scion politics, spying, and the business of a matriarch, but war was beyond her bounds.

"I wanted to slow time, not press it forward." Flexing her crystal-wrapped hand before her, she examined the circle of fifteen lines meeting at its center. "There is this sense I have that it's possible, but I need to keep trying. I assume, though, that you came all the way up here for another reason than to hear me rant about my failed Reaching. You could have sent Tazper or Kikania otherwise."

"It is important." He breathed out deeply, warm against her cheek until he stepped back. "I must apologize before I even speak my request. To Lady Manalias and the field marshal, I revealed the truth of your Axiom Reaching in order to prevent a split within the Confederation."

"You did *what?*" She snatched him by the shirt as the voices screamed in her head. "There were rumors already, but that is not for you to proclaim for political gain!"

"Lord Ivalat iz Ardinvil is being held by breathless before the army." He nodded toward the Crimsons, but his voice merged with the specters' screams. "You have been focused, so it is not a surprise you missed him, but the Crimsons are demanding both of us as punishment for our crimes against them. The only alternative is you teleporting to Ivalat, taking hold of him, and bringing him to safety."

She threw him away, sending him to the ground as his mechanical leg twisted awkwardly. He tried to fix his strewn-about auburn hair, but a tremor struck his hands. That curse of his. But despite her outburst and his body's disobedience, he looked up at her without an ounce of malice.

"I would not have done this if I had not believed it to be our only choice," he said, "but it is no excuse for volunteering both information and power that is not mine to give. For that reason, your fury is duly justified."

He dropped his cane and grabbed hold of his leg, righting it with a single jolt that reminded her of the strength she'd seen in him back in Tystok. The frustrated tinkerer who would not cease until his work was perfect. The politician who would not stay his tongue until truth had been spoken. What in the spiritdamned wastes did he see in her? A mischievous mechanism to be mended, or someone to remind him that even the broken pieces of the world could hold some beauty?

When she offered no reply, he sighed. "I have volunteered myself and my cavalry to create a distraction to the southwest, given their interest in me as well. Tiuz, however, does not believe that to be enough. He has ordered a far greater number to join us with rifles capable of shooting glass bullets against the breathless. One of my lieutenant colonels, Brakenias, is quite the sniper, and it is my hope he can pierce the breathless holding Ivalat on your signal. That should prevent any interference with your portal."

"He speaks so casually of us enduring further Taint," her specter said, standing over him. "The noble lord, so willing to sacrifice the woman he loves to protect his precious alliance."

Kasia turned away with an arm held across her body. Was she right? Her heartache gave an answer she didn't like, so she yanked up her sleeve, then tugged at her collar until the golden crystal became visible beneath. "Is this not enough fucking crystal for you? Burns consumed my arm for years because I apparently tried to kill my own mother, and now, Axiom Crystal demands more. That's not to mention the voices… the *screaming*… I hear every moment that time doesn't already slip through my fingers like your precious sand."

"I understand."

He rose without looking away. His cane slid across the floor like the sweep of a broom, then fell still to hold him up. Neither malice nor fear filled his gaze, but his hands shook against the cane and the windowsill. And when he did shut his eyes, he slammed them like they were glass shutters against the awakened scourge.

"What would you like me to tell Field Marshal Tiuz, my lady?"

She dropped her head, trying to seek reason through both the specters' voices and her own anger. This plan was a great risk. About there being no apparent alternative, though, Zinarus was right. Manalias iz Ardinvil would do as any heir would if the Confederation failed to aid her in rescuing her house's patriarch. The things Kasia would've done with the chance to defend her father…

"What will you do if I don't go ahead with this rescue?" she asked.

He adjusted his house crest pin at his lapel and pursed his lips. Of course he would do something honorably stupid. "I will offer to go to the Crimsons under the flag of truce, hoping we may negotiate my surrender for Lord Ivalat's release. If I ask you to risk yourself for the Confederation, then I must be willing to do the same."

"You know that won't work."

"Then I will say that I gave myself in hope for the betterment of our two nations."

"You are a fool if you believe sacrificing yourself will make anything better."

She stepped closer to him, and as sorrow cracked his face, the shell encompassing her heart split with it. The specters faded away until the room was just the two of them. Clarity returned, and with it came a realization which flooded from her very spirit.

"I won't let you become some martyr," she insisted. "Damn you and your honor. Damn the voices, the spirits, the Unity Crystal, and all those Crimson scum. I hate…" She pressed her fist into his chest, but not hard enough to push him away. "I hate that if I lost you, I would lose the last place in this world or any other where I feel safe. No matter how much I try to deny it, I love you."

With her hands firm as stone, she unpinned the Niezik raven crest from her uniform's lapel as Spitza cawed from the other windowsill. Amber and death. That raven was more than a symbol it seemed, and ahead of a battle that could destroy every last hope she had of defeating the Crimson Court, it felt right to run her crystal-wrapped fingers over its metal and glass.

"Take it," she breathed, "knowing I am spiteful, Tainted, and ruined by vengeance. Or let this bond between us be an alliance of convenience alone. I have lost too much to play games of the heart now."

She rested her hand on his chest, gently this time, and felt his racing heart. "There are things I must do that you will not approve of, but I know now that I cannot win this fight—I cannot endure this life—alone any longer. I thought that vengeance was worth living for, but that was not a true life. For once, I need to choose something for me. I choose you."

"Kasia, I…" His copper eyes turned to radiant gold as he took her hand in his, holding the pin between them. "I fail to grasp the workings of your mind, but whatever took hold of you now has worked. Look."

He nodded toward Spitza. The raven held out her wings, her beak wide open and a strange, elongated version of her call hanging in the air. That same gold that glimmered in Zinarus's eyes encircled them, and Kasia could only release a stifled laugh at the realization that power was pouring from her Axiom Crystal. She had Reached without thinking, locking the two of them in a slowed circle of time.

A burgeoning tension filled her chest, and when she looked up at Zinarus, she recognized it as the final moments before a Reach pushed too far. Taint would follow if she could not stop it. Aliax had died because she failed to control her Death Reaching, but with her mind clear now, she reminded herself that had been long ago. She was an experienced Reacher. All she needed was to break her connection to the Axiom.

The feeling of slowed time, though, was unlike anything else. For those few long moments, the world truly was just Zinarus and her. But the specters would surely return when she released it.

"This world has treated you with great scorn, my dear," Zinarus said. "The rage you feel is not your fault, but if we are to take this step together, I must know that you trust me to hold you in the highest regard. Though my decisions may not always be correct in the end, I shall never act or speak without immense care for your well-being."

He raised his free hand to caress her neck, running his thumb over the crystal that stretched up its side. "That begins with releasing the power you wield in this moment."

She leaned into him, drawing a long breath in sync with him. That crystal-fueled power hummed within her, but this comfort, this touch, was greater than any Reach. She had so badly missed love's embrace, and tears stung her eyes knowing the suffering she'd endured since she felt it last.

Zinarus's pleading permission allowed her to find that thread of power she had instinctively taken hold of. It held the key to time, now within her grasp like the Axiom's portals and gravity shifts. Taint would still come, but with each new Reach, she had abilities which even Chatik could never hold.

Voices flooded her mind as gold surrendered to the castle's gray stone, but they were distant compared to Zinarus's caring arms. He pulled back only slightly to cup her offered pin in his fingers. A smile flicked up the ends of his lips as he did.

"It would be my honor to accept your proposal of a courtship, Lady Katarzyna the First." He raised the crest to his lapel, swapping it with his iz Vamiustok one, which he held out for her. His hands no longer trembled, and his usually deep gray cheeks flushed. "As heir, it will be up to my mother to approve such an arrangement, but she may be persuaded with persistence. We are fortunate that you are not lacking in that."

She took the pin and placed it where hers had been before. Then she rose onto the tips of her toes to kiss him slowly, locking eyes when they separated.

"Come, my beloved, I believe the two of us have a patriarch to save."

65

A BLADE OF INHERITANCE

"The Inheritance Rituals are rarely spoken of, but they form the heart of the great houses' power. What would happen if all, whether scion or lowborn, were to have the chance to carry one's wills and greatest experiences into the next life. How much further would humanity have advanced?" – Etal iz Noshok, former professor of forces and spirits at Kalastok College

Nikoza looked upon House Bartol's townhouse at Textile Alley's end with a mix of sorrow and scorn. The last time she had set foot within its halls the day of the coup, she had turned down Zinarus's request for her to challenge Chatik. Bartol money had rebuilt this street brick-by-brick, and now, she would make right her own failures from a season ago.

She had her doubts about this plan, but with Hazat, Nex, and Jolzena all convinced of it, she swallowed her fear and pushed onward. The others were off preparing the rebels of the reborn Ashes of Dawn for Chatik's speech. That left her to retrieve the symbol of any patriarch's end from the house of Chatik and her shared blood.

House Bartol's Inheritance Blade.

Such ceremonial weapons were normally stored in a great house's home estate, but during Jazuk's reign, he had wanted it close at hand in case anyone back in Anukit decided to betray him. Ironically, such betrayal had come from his second son in the capital's core instead.

Passing her family's textile mills, millineries, and dressmakers, she posed as a lowborn servant. Chatik sought to make all of them nameless and faceless. Such restrictions had yet to fall outside the palace, but House Bartol's self-declared patriarch sat upon the throne. It was not strange for a woman wearing one of the palace's silver veils to run errands to the king's townhouse.

Nikoza had expected to be questioned by at least a single guard, but they just loitered against soot-covered walls or harassed women going about their days. She scoffed at that. War—both foreign and civil—had sent the best soldiers and mercenaries away from the capital. Those that remained were little better than the gangs they claimed to fight.

Discarded filth lined the buildings and forced her to hold her breath. This alley had once been pristine, nearly considered part of the Crimson District just to the north, but the city watch's cleaning Air and Water Reachers had been sent off to war. All that remained was the Crystal Brigade. She knew well-enough their focus was on other matters.

An air of unease hung about the brick townhouse as she passed through the decorated doors and took a deep breath of the fragrant interior. Cozy, warm, and beautiful down to the smallest detail, this place had become her home during her time as Jazuk's ward. She had not realized how badly she missed it. The Crystal Palace was stunning beyond compare, but nothing could match the safety of one's home.

That comfort faded quickly, though, as she hurried past the sitting rooms and servants' quarters. Her grandfather claimed the townhouse had been built to make the scion chambers as reclusive as possible. That would make her mission all the more difficult.

"More palace servants," she heard a maid say to another as she neared the stairs. "Why do they tolerate those veils?"

Chatik surely would have required House Bartol's own servants to wear the same had he spent any time on their house's Textile Alley. His focus had rested entirely on the palace, though, and that worked to his niece's advantage now. Whispered gossip was a core tenant of the great houses and their servants. It would be strange if they *hadn't* mentioned her presence.

Remember why you are here, she told herself as she rounded the banister and climbed with a hand on the railing. It was more difficult to handle stairs with the veil than she had expected, and falling would draw more attention than she could afford.

Why was she here? There were better ways to strike at Chatik than to bring an Inheritance Blade, but symbols mattered in both persuasion and rebellion. Was holding an heir's blade not the most convincing way to prove to the lowborn that she was prepared to fight?

Voices came from the rooms above. Chatik's cousins had taken to running House Bartol's businesses from the townhouse while he resided in the palace, and they would recognize Nikoza if one were to catch even a glimpse of her face. Luckily, her gloves and veil covered almost all her pale-gray scion skin. The cousins also likely knew of Chatik's plans today, so they would be focused on other matters than a stray servant.

Except one stepped from her chambers just as Nikoza crested the stairs. She kept her head down, unable to see which it was, and prayed silently to the Crystal Mother that her cousin would go on her way.

"So, Chatik has sent another of his veiled brides," the woman said, her voice oozing with conceit. That could only mean Vizia. There were few with a less serpentine demeanor than her, but her skill with numbers made her a good choice to manage the textile businesses' accounts. If only to keep her away from the palace…

Nikoza curtsied, but offered no reply.

"Oh, so he has trained you well." Vizia stepped closer with her hands on her hips. "Go on then. What does our king desire for his grand speech today?"

"His highness, King Chatik Bartol the First, requests that he be brought the house's Inheritance Blade," Nikoza replied, attempting to replace her light northeastern accent with the quicker one of Kalastok's lowborn servants. It was far from impressive, but Vizia did not question who she was. She did, however, raise her brow at the request.

"That showman! First, he despises Uncle Jazuk for failing to complete the ritual. Then, he kills him and ascends to patriarch himself. And now he wants the Inheritance Blade?" She clicked her tongue. "What does this day have for us, dear Mother? Anukit would have been far easier, but of course, I had to answer my cousin's call."

Nikoza was grateful for the veil, because her jaw dropped. Had Chatik hidden his plans from even his closest allies in House Bartol?

Vizia waved a hand toward Jazuk's old office at the end of the hall. "Chatik has barely moved a thing since the coup. In fact, I doubt he has stepped foot in Textile Alley more than thrice since his ascension to the throne. Do you know where to find the blade?"

Silently, Nikoza nodded.

"Very well, then. I have more important matters to attend to than Chatik's whims, like ensuring these wars do not bankrupt our entire house."

Only when Vizia descended the stairs did Nikoza breathe normally. She was starting to understand Nex's claims about scions. They truly could be too focused on their egos and selfish desires to grasp the reality around them, and she had been plenty guilty of that too.

No matter where the Crystal Mother guided her, she promised herself that would change. First, she needed to free herself of Chatik's influence.

Sorrow speared her heart as she opened the door at the hall's end. Jazuk's office had not changed a bit. Though he was no longer here to carry around a cigar between sips of his dark liquors, the smells had baked into the walls and Ezmani-red carpet spanning the room's center. She pictured him crossing the room with his back bent and his silver cane thumping away as he muttered about some dispute between the great houses. By the Crystal Mother, he had been an arrogant man and an ineffective king, but she missed him anyway.

She reached beneath her veil to wipe away a tear before hurrying to the display case to the side of the balcony doors. The Inheritance Blade hung there for all to see. For years, it had mocked those who wanted Jazuk to complete the ritual after the death of Nikoza's father. That decision had earned him scorn and pride alike.

The golden sword was light in her hands as she traced the curling rams' horns which crossed it in House Bartol's scarlet tint. Those rams symbolized their historic control over the wool and textile trades, but now, it resembled the blood that Chatik had spilled to solidify the Crimsons' reign. Had Chatik done all of this because Jazuk refused to name him heir instead of Nikoza eighteen years ago?

None of this should have happened. Great houses devoted countless Body and Life Reachers to ensuring magnates and heirs did not pass before the heir's first child was born, as their loss signaled the end of a spirit carrying multiple lifetimes of experience for the house. Nikoza had been born mere days after her father's death, and there was no precedence for such a thing. Her father should have used this very blade to kill Jazuk and grant his spirit to her. Without him, Jazuk was forced to choose either another heir, or to name Nikoza herself as his.

She empathized with Chatik's frustrations as she placed the sword in its elaborately carved carrying case. Instead of inheriting her grandfather's experience, she was caught between the role of a typical heir and one who could only learn through traditional means. Chatik could have become heir, passing Jazuk's spirit to his son, Bozumir, and things would have been far simpler.

That thought haunted her as she returned to the stairs. Where would she be if Chatik had inherited House Bartol sooner? Jazuk would have completed the Inheritance Ritual before he ever became king, and she would be a cousin of the patriarch, likely working for the house's efforts back in Anukit. A whole life she would never live…

Clutching the blade's case, she forced herself to focus on the present. The only life that mattered was the one she inhabited now—and the thousands of lives that depended on her stopping Chatik. She was the Crystal Heir. She would bring the Commonwealth from the ashes. She would uplift the Commonwealth to the glory the Crystal Mother wished for them to hold. And for what felt like the first time in her life, she would decide her own path.

VOCKA'S SHIELD

"One cannot help but respect the Vockan Nation of old. Without Reachers or the great industry of their neighbors, they held onto those mountains with enough determination that no one dared challenge them. That is, until we offered them crystal…" – Lord Borys Kuzon the Sixth, patriarch of House Kuzon

D read fell heavy on Radais's shoulders when the horns blew for battle. By all accounts, last night hadn't been his worst sleep in recent seasons, but that didn't make it a good one.

He met Lazan's startled gaze in their shared tent, their bodies intertwined. Lying at his lover's side only reminded him how much he had to lose. Polina was the supreme defender now, so his duty was to the Reacher before him and the young Whisperer he'd taken under his wing. The battle ahead terrified him, but if all three of them made it out alive, at least he will have done his job.

They dressed quickly, and Lazan helped him strap on his armor. He felt like a different man with it on. Stronger, more confident. The Radais lying by his lover was gentle and tired, but with a glass helm over his head and a breastplate strapped to his torso, he swore he could move mountains.

Radais grabbed his sword and hurried out into the driving rain, heading toward Vuk. Archers shot glass arrows from their makeshift watchtowers, but the weather blocked sight of spirits from the ground. These conditions were even the most experienced Glassblade's nightmare. He needed to be ready, so once they were mounted, he quickly led Lazan to the gathering warriors.

At the camp's west end, Polina's voice carried over the sea of glass-clad warriors, who broke into groups of four to protect each other's flanks. "This was just a testing strike by their scouts. They want us on the back foot, afraid to attack, but their numbers grow with each passing day. We must end this scourge's hold over our lands. Keep together and eliminate the breathless first, allowing us then to surround the Bound Ones."

She turned her ibex about and raised her glass sword in one hand, then did the same with a steel one in the other. "We have always wielded glass to slay our enemies, but the strongest among them wear armor now and can Reach like scions. Do not shatter your blades. Strike with steel when necessary, then kill with glass. Do you understand?"

"Yes!" the warriors answered together.

She nodded sharply. "Vocka has always been the shield against the corrupted. Let it stand strong! And let this corrupted army fall."

As she spoke, Radais found Wanusa and Mariana to the side. Heavy bags formed under the elder Whisperer's eyes, but she did her best to hide her exhaustion, riding tall.

"I thought a master such as yourself would be better prepared," she said. Her tone was stern, but a wry smile tugged at her lips. "Did your practice last night prove useful? It would be telling if your young apprentice outpaced you in learning the ways of magic."

He flexed his taloned hand, the talon itself no longer covered by his glass gauntlet. "It did, but practicing is difficult when I must stick my hand over a fire after every Reach. My blade will carry the weight of the fighting. Luckily, I have twenty years of experience with that."

"Good, because among the four of us, you are the only one with armor. Do not get too close as to frighten our bonded spirits, but I would plead for you not to stray far either. I know the limits of a Whisperer's abilities." She glanced at Wanusa. The girl wore only a cloak over her warrior's tunic to ensure she didn't scare away her spirits—yet another worry upon Radais's shoulders. "We are both capable, but there are times when we must learn to trust in the methods of others."

A series of horns signaled their prepared advance. Radais gritted his teeth at that. They passed around flames to light their lanterns like in everdark, but that was no way to charge into battle. Even Rakekeaa and Ataakanan's Saleshi overhead hadn't brought their Light Crystals, likely to avoid alerting other humans to their existence.

"You're making that face again," Wanusa said as they pushed their ibexes into a walk. Rushing now would do nothing but tire them, and the breathless could outpace an ibex even at full gallop anyway.

"What face?"

She puffed out her cheeks to mimic him, then twirled her sword. "The one you always do when people do something differently than you would."

He glanced at Lazan. "Is that true?"

"True enough," the Reacher confirmed, drawing his glass dagger and removing his left glove. Radais hoped he wouldn't need to use that Reaching, but against this many foes, there would no doubt be dozens of casualties, if any of them survived at all. "You might not prefer leading, but your expressions surely express your opinions."

"I don't agree with Polina's plan of attack," Radais said. "That is true. But it isn't my decision."

Wanusa raised her brow as enough light finally slipped through the clouds to reveal the mass of spirits hovering over Iliafa once again. "What would you have us do instead?"

"Fighting in this dim light favors the spirits. We should wait for the storm to pass, then target the Bound Ones first, not the enslaved breathless. While we fight their weakest spirits, the Bound Ones will have free reign to unleash their Reaching on us."

"They can fly. Won't they either way?"

Mhanain, the grumpy old archer who'd journeyed with them through to Akaamilion, caught up on his ibex before Radais could reply. He smirked in the way a bad gambler did when they knew they'd won. "Heard you talking about those Bound Ones. I'd sooner shave my ass with a rusty knife than waste my arrows on breathless when there's bigger monsters to hunt."

Wanusa blinked. "That's… Spirits, I didn't need that image in my head."

"You'll help us target the Bound Ones, then?" Radais asked. "If you can distract them, I will get in close while Wanusa and Mariana use their Whispering in support. Hopefully, we can overwhelm them one-by-one."

Mhanain thumped his chest. "Aye. You point at a bastard, I'll shoot 'em in their weird heads."

"Good man."

"It took you all but a day to go rogue," Lazan said.

Radais drew a sharp breath. "That Earth Bound One almost killed Vuk and me. It's the leader. I know it is. And if we just let it Reach, it'll shatter our glass armor with ease."

Wanusa patted her steel blade at her side. "We're prepared to handle him because of you. Tairanik would've never approved it."

"Not every decision I made was right, but it's good to know some were."

They fell quiet as the Vanashel split. Bound Ones in their dragon forms spread out, their black quartz armor devouring the few rays of dawnrise light through the clouds. Breathless formed three arcs before each. They took savage, jagged shapes and wielded halberds tipped with a bronze ax and point. It was unlike any war formation that Radais had ever heard of, and he cursed knowing they'd have to carve a path through the weaker spirits just to near a Bound One.

"Which dragon is the Earth Bound One?" Mhanain asked. "They all look the same to me."

Radais studied the fifteen Bound Ones, but like the archer, he couldn't tell them apart either. "I don't know."

"Perfect."

Wanusa rolled her eyes, then pointed toward the one in the center. "That one's rhythm is like your talon's when you Reach. Or close to it at least."

"Then we kill that one first," Radais said.

"You warriors always go straight for a kill," Mariana said. "Have you considered that the others will protect their leader?"

Lazan rocked his head back and forth. "Perhaps, but remember what we learned. If the Bound Ones control those breathless like a Whisperer, then when we kill them, they may lay down their arms or even turn against their enslavers."

"We should try to free the breathless either way," Wanusa said with a sharp nod. "Inrius could be trapped like them, and it's not their fault the Vanashel control them."

No one contested that point, so they maneuvered their way toward the center of the Glassblades. Polina eyed them from the rear, but didn't stop them. Did she even want to? They were the only ones who'd faced the Vanashel in the Wastes, and Wanusa was the only Glassblade to have killed a Bound One.

Radais thought back to the whirlwind surrounding that Bound One in everdark. It had taken on his father's face and voice, taunting him. Could his father have been like Wanusa's brother, twisted to the Vanashel's will?

He shook his head. No, it had been a trick of the spirits to give him pause. It would've worked too if Wanusa hadn't saved his life, and that was a startling reminder that they still knew so little about these spirits.

A surge in the Vanashel Spiritspeech tore him from his thoughts. The breathless in each Bound One's outer arc descended as one, their whispered chatter like an insect swarm. Commands echoed from their leaders above, and the breathless units moved to attack from every side.

"Do not allow them to gain our flanks!" Polina shouted, pointing her swords either direction. "Archers, shoot down the bastards above."

Arrows whistled overhead as Radais tightened his grip on his own blade. Its two sharp edges glinted in his lanternlight: glass on one side, steel on the other. The Earth Bound One had shattered his old sword. He wouldn't let it get the better of him a second time.

"We head straight on," he told the others. "Let the rest thin the pack, and no matter what, do not fall back from the group."

He reached down and patted Vuk on his side. "C'mon boy. Let's go kill some corrupted spirits."

The ibex charged, bursting from grasslands to the ashen sands that now covered Iliafa. Wasteland had consumed pastures and houses alike. That wet, uneven terrain made each stride difficult for even an experienced ibex like Vuk as sunken objects jutted out at random. Not to mention the damned breathless and their halberds.

"On your left!" Mhanain called out as he loosed an arrow straight through a breathless.

Another followed with its halberd's ax head flashing toward Radais. At a canter, he turned Vuk and made a looping swipe with his sword's steel flat, then reversed the blade to pierce the spirit's side. The sword's glass half seared into the breathless's misty form. These more developed spirits were tougher than awakened, though, and without a full slice, it spun away.

Right into Lazan's dagger.

The Reacher whooped as his victim dissolved, its remnant spirit dust scattering over his coat. But one kill was not enough for celebrations when dozens more breathless dove toward them. Radais's charge had pulled his group from the other Glassblades, and Wanusa was exposed as the secondary defender.

That vulnerability made him nervous as he fought to ensure no more breathless passed. Wanusa showed no such fear, her strikes quicker without armor to weigh her down. She found the gaps in the Vanashel's lumbering halberds and sent two silver spirits spiraling about to guard her sides.

A breathless struck Radais's pauldron, cracking it while he was distracted. *You trained her how to fight,* he told himself as he countered the spirit with a cut straight through its scythe-like head. *Worry about yourself and the Bound One.*

So he released a war cry and urged Vuk onward. They were nearing the Bound Ones, but the second ring of breathless dropped, joining the countless others who already severed the Glassblade ranks

based on the screams. Radais didn't let himself look back. Not again. He needed every instinct to parry the spirits' halberds and slice their tendrils which stretched toward those he loved. These breathless were slaves. But until the Bound Ones were dead, they were also threats.

Radais didn't need to look up at the Earth Bound One to sense its presence. He could never forget the hatred in the monstrosity's eyes as it sought to skewer him and Vuk. Spirits were born pure, but in that looming dragon, no purity remained.

"Shoot it down!" he commanded Mhanain as they drew closer.

"No," Ataakanan's ethereal voice interrupted as it swooped overhead with Rakekeaa and four other Saleshi. "Leave that to us."

The rest of the Saleshi behind joined the other Glassblades. Polina's focus on the breathless had yielded results so far, but Radais need not count the remaining warriors to know the cost had been high. And as the Bound Ones released a roar together, it was clear they had allowed thousands of breathless to die just to whittle down the Glassblade ranks.

Vanashel Reaching from every realm poured down upon the sands. Radais could only circle about with his trailing group and keep the breathless off them, waiting for the Saleshi to bring down the Earth Bound One.

But his foe had another plan.

Radais sliced through a spirit near Wanusa when the ground split around them. Vuk tripped on the retreating sand, and Radais could do nothing but leap from the saddle to save the ibex from his weight. He tumbled down for what felt like an eternity before crashing into pure rock.

"Someone help them!" Lazan called out as Wanusa struck the ground no more than a stride away.

Blood trickled down her helmless face and cuts tattered her sleeves. Radais's amor was cracked too as he shifted to test for broken bones. Just bruising from what he could tell, so he forced himself to snatch his sword and stand. Wanusa rose with him as he gauged the situation.

The retracted sand had formed a pit around them. Its peak was high enough to block the low southern sun, leaving only a strip of light a few feet overhead. The rest of their group had escaped the fall, but as he squinted up at the warring spirits above, it became clear that two of the Saleshi had already perished. Ataakanan and Rakekeaa, though, fought fiercely with their two-ended spears, clashing against the Bound One's war pick and armor.

Wanusa scrambled to the wall of sand and tried to climb. "We have to help them!"

The effort was futile. Radais had spent too long in the Spirit Wastes to know that its gray sands were far too fine to climb at such a slope. Besides, this was fueled by the Bound One's Reaching. It wanted them here for a reason.

When the Earth Bound One roared again, breathless swarmed the Saleshi. They had already met their match against the Bound One, and another of them fell against the tide. Rakekeaa shouted something in the Spiritspeech and fled, but Ataakanan hastened a glance down at Radais. Some fragment of Miv lingered in those ethereal eyes. Ataakanan was only her spirit, but it didn't flee until Rakekeaa returned to drag it away.

The Vanashel breathless followed their retreat. Their master didn't.

Its draconic gaze fell upon the trapped pair, its wings beating faster despite it dropping like the stone it commanded. The sight should've terrified Radais, but he'd prepared for this moment. Visions of their last fight had haunted his sleep. Now, he wielded the same realm as this beast, and he hadn't already Reached.

He shouted with all his fury for his fallen comrades as he raised his left hand. The Bound One rushed him with its war pick glinting in the final beams of light before it struck the darkness. It showed no caution, no concern for what Radais could do, so just when its pick was about to strike, the Glassblade Reached.

His glass armor tinted, creaking and shifting until the pick slammed into his hand with the force of a charging ibex. Yet Radais held firm. Neither his armor, now holding a rosy color, nor his will cracked beneath the Bound One's strike.

"Deception!" the Bound One hissed. "Cannot bind!"

Radais grinned and threw back the spirit. "Tell me what else I can't do."

Last night, he'd practiced Earth Reacher alchemy instead of aggressive magic, transforming shards of glass into the rose quartz that formed the Saleshi armor. Ataakanan had revealed Bakeekek's discovery that silica, not glass itself, acted like a solid to spirits in high enough concentrations. Their so-called First One had questioned him about glass in Akaamilion. He'd not thought much of it at the time, but it explained why the Saleshi had adopted quartz armor now, as it was stronger than glass and made of nearly pure silica.

Now, Radais sliced his sword's steel blade into the stunned Bound One's side. Its own black quartz armor flexed unnaturally beneath the blow, but couldn't stop it completely. As the spirit reeled back with the blade still embedded, he released the sword and lunged.

Then he slammed his newly armored fist straight into the dragon's face.

Hissing rose from the Bound One, its form distorting into masses of swirling silver. It rose out of Radais's range and dropped Radais's blade as he landed hard. As he grabbed the weapon, his body gave him a clear reminder he'd both fallen into this pit from a great height and was no longer the young man he used to be.

"Radais!" Wanusa exclaimed.

She hurried to him as Vanashel breathless answered the Bound One's call from above. Radais could barely see her in the darkness, but the spirits circling her off hand emanated a silver glow when she held it before her face. One moved far quicker than the other, its form solid compared to Inrius's loose mist.

"I'm fine," he reassured her. "But our friend has decided he doesn't want to play anymore."

She twirled her sword, raising her spirits toward the Vanashel and calling to them in the Spiritspeech. It was so strange to hear her talk in the ethereal tongue. Whatever she'd said had done the trick, though, because the Bound One threw out an arm at the breathless.

A single spirit emerged from the pack. Meandering, it fixed the eyes scattered across its fractured form upon Wanusa. It said nothing, but the Whisperer gasped, retreating back into the wall of sand.

"Brother?"

THE SIEGE

"Shoot first. If you don't... Well, bullets are faster than even me." –
Quickshot Miko

Gusts battered Kasia as she emerged onto Fort Harizak's northern battlement. Her military uniform trimmed with Niezik amber did not catch the winds like a dress would, and that disappointed her. When she was about to ruin her enemies' day, she preferred for them to gawk at her while she did it.

They would be plenty shocked, though, if Zinarus's plan succeeded. She had spent the hours since their courtship's official start ensuring Kikania brought Spitza and Leonit's book to safety, then practicing her Reaching's time manipulations. Mastery would take far longer, but she'd at least gotten to the point where she could call upon it at will. Combined with a well-timed portal and gravity shift, there was little the Crimsons could do to stop her from rescuing Ivalat iz Ardinvil.

"The Field Marshal's cavalry are advancing," an officer nearby reported to the gunners. "Looks like the Crimsons took that as a signal to move forward their infantry."

Dozens of cannons covered this outer wall and the taller inner one thirty yards behind. Unlike the Tainted specters filling the space

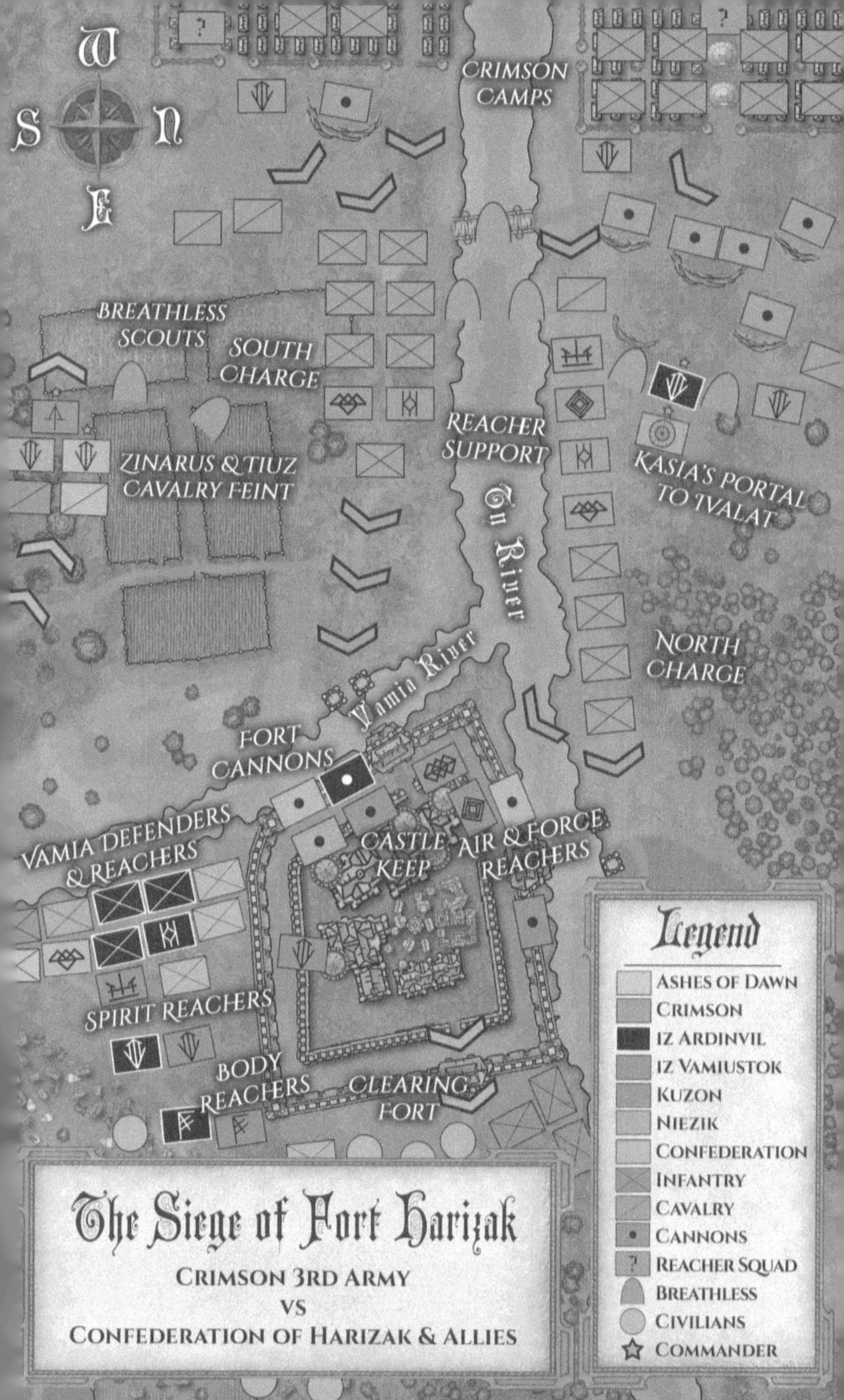

The Siege of Fort Harizak

CRIMSON 3RD ARMY
VS
CONFEDERATION OF HARIZAK & ALLIES

near her, they were quiet for now, but the armies had traded artillery salvos thrice in the last couple hours. Another would come soon.

She looked over the Vamia River, where Tiuz and Zinarus led their respective cavalry units around the Crimsons' southern flank. A few thousand cavalry at stride were an impressive sight. The Crimsons would no doubt see them, and that would hopefully keep their attention away from Ivalat for long enough.

Every soldier Kasia had passed on her way from the castle's keep gripped their weapons as if they expected a strike at any moment. Ivalat's rescue would spark the battle's true beginning, and though she hadn't been involved in the strategic planning, it was obvious Tiuz had ordered the defenders to be ready. Crimson soldiers, breathless, and—if Razamat Uziokaki's admissions were correct— the crystal dragon lay in wait. She could bring Ivalat to safety.

But would it make any difference?

She nervously checked her father's revolver for the fifth time since loading it. The hidden seventh chamber held a single glass bullet, but she wore plenty of amber to protect against spirits. It was Reachers she was worried about.

Despite the cavalry advance, the Crimsons showed no desire to shift their positions on either side of the Ty River north of the confluence. Their countless camps were well entrenched with infantry, cannons, and Reachers, so what worry did they have for a few thousand cavalry when they numbered twenty times that?

Ivalat hovered a hundred feet in the air before the Crimson army, a breathless holding each of his limbs. Kasia studied that pinprick in the distance as she shoved her revolver back into its holster at her hip. Even if Zinarus's distraction failed, his cavalry offered her a key escape route. Ivalat was over a mile away from where she stood. Teleporting there would be no problem, but opening a second portal immediately after the first would Taint her, potentially causing it to send her and Ivalat far from her intended destination. She'd tested instead that she could slow time for a few precious seconds and switch gravity toward the far closer cavalry with a single Reach.

Either escape would leave her even more Tainted. Both the Water and Death ones had nearly killed her, though, and Sadamar would be on the lookout for her if she ended up in Orat again. No, the time and gravity shifts would have to do.

She thumbed Zinarus's iz Vamiustok pin on her lapel, now alongside a new Niezik one. Tradition stated that courting couples must display their allegiances after the trading of pins, but she sensed the soldiers smirking at her behind her back. Her reputation as both the Amber Dame and Death's Daughter had spread quickly. Among these lowborn Ezmani and minor scions alike, they would be amused at her courting a half-blooded Vockan who'd been born out of wedlock.

But their opinions meant nothing. She knew who she was, and she needed to keep her focus on defeating the Crimsons.

As the cavalry neared their signal point, she moved into a sniper's opening on the battlement. From there, she caught sight of Tazper's amber uniform among the iz Vamiustok purple. He had demanded to go to provide the cavalry another Spirit Reacher, and she surely wasn't going to stop him. He had played the role of her accomplice for long enough to earn a chance at being a hero. Spirits knew he'd never be one working beside a schemer like her.

Axiom Crystal pulsed across her arm, demanding she Reach. She allowed her breaths to fall into sync with that rhythm and quiet the protests of her own Tainted reflection. This small victory would come at a cost, but if life had taught her anything, it was that all power did. Though her specter claimed to know all her past, nothing could match actually enduring the torment.

"The Crimsons will open fire when I teleport to Ivalat," Kasia told the nearest officer. His eyes widened as her gaze fell upon him, but she figured it was better for these soldiers to fear her than believe she was just another coddled scion. "Feel free to return it, especially if one of those bastards kills me."

The officer's shock turned to a grin. He thumped his chest. "Yes, Lady Katarzyna."

Then here we go.

Kasia closed her eyes for but a moment, focusing on the Axiom's call beneath the Tainted voices. Its golden web tickled her fingers. Each pointed to another place or power, and she searched them instinctively as she pictured Ivalat hovering with those breathless. A thread pulled taut in her palm. She ignored it and kept searching in case it was a false one. Things would go awry quickly if she missed by even a yard or two.

The Axiom's thread dug deeper until her skin burned. This was its answer, so she took hold and threw out her arm.

Gold surged from her hand and beneath her sleeve, spiraling into a portal a stride from the wall. Images of Ivalat and the breathless formed on the other side. Right on the mark, so she hastened a glance toward the cavalry once again. They were slowing with their glass rifles ready.

The rest was up to her.

She took a few steps back to get a running start, then leaped through the portal. Open air met her just feet in front of Ivalat. The patriarch's head was hung, and a deathly white washed over his gray skin. But his eyes flickered at her arrival.

The breathless sent their shadowy tendrils toward her, but Kasia didn't give them the chance. Reaching into the Axiom, Taint pierced her skull as another wave of gold encircled her. She lunged to grab Ivalat. Neither her time nor gravity powers would work until she touched him, or he'd be trapped outside their influence.

That meant the breathless could respond just as quickly. Their tendrils struck her chest a blink before her free hand touched Ivalat's struggling, but weak arm.

Her willpower vanished. No matter how hard she fought to grab hold of the Axiom's time thread in that split second, her body refused to act. Cracks of gunfire echoed in the distance, but they were too late to stop her momentum from sending her straight into Ivalat.

The breathless shrieked. Bullets zipped past Kasia's ear, most missing the target, but one spirit dissolved into vapors. Another reeled back.

Her collision with Ivalat tore him free from the grip of the two remaining spirits. Only one tendril pierced her spirit now, and like a breath of fresh air, strength surged through her. She used it to take hold of the patriarch's coat as her crystal-webbed hand snagged the Axiom's faint pulse of time.

The breathless's rapid movements fell to a crawl. Bullets passed at a runner's pace, the air splitting around their glass tips as others rose from the Crimson ranks below. She'd done it, yet still she and Ivalat tumbled at full speed. In her rushed practice, she had failed to consider that gravity's impact on her wouldn't slow like the rest of the world.

So she threw her arm toward Zinarus's cavalry in the distance, shifting gravity with the last of her Reach. The resulting jolt disturbed her stomach and made Ivalat cry out, but it stopped their direct descent toward the Crimson army.

It also sent them barreling straight at the Ty River.

Her divided Reach failed in seconds. The sounds of battle struck like a blow straight to her gut, and Taint's sickness overtook her as time suddenly shot past. Her gravity shift had granted them plenty of speed to escape the Crimson rifles, but a chill down her spine revealed breathless in their wake. Taint ensured she didn't have the chance to consider a defense before she hit the river.

Dawnrise had thawed the river that flowed from her home in Tystok, but falling from that far into still frigid waters sent her remaining senses into a flurry. The current carried her under until her knee struck a rock *hard*. Life had gifted her enough wounds to know when one was debilitating, and with time's slips, her lungs screamed already. She needed to get back to the surface, but the only sensation from her left leg was motionless agony.

This damn patriarch better be worth it, Zinarus.

Ivalat was nowhere to be seen in the cacophony their drop had caused in the water. With her leg battered and her Reaching extinguished, she would be little help, so she swam up until her head broke the surface. All she could do for a long moment was gasp for air as she fought down her Tainted urge to vomit.

Specters surrounded her on either shore of the river, their shouting incoherent amid the roar of artillery and cracking gunfire. The air reeked of black powder, and the wind carried the horrible stench of gore from the Crimson army. It also revealed cavalry advancing at full gallop.

Water and Taint obscured her vision too much to know who the cavalry were, so she threw aside her coat to grab her revolver. Except when she pulled back the hammer, she cursed her stupidity. The primer and all her spare powder were soaked. Her only weapon against humans was useless.

Someone splashed from downstream. They gagged on the water, flailing like a drunken fool in a bar fight. Kasia tried to call out for them to swim to shore. The current would carry them toward the Crimson army if they waited too long, but time flashed past at random, sounds and lights becoming blinding and deafening as she pushed with all her fleeting strength to reach what she thought was the southern bank.

It seemed a futile effort until a familiar *gwah* swooped toward her. True avian talons gripped her shoulder, doing little to draw her ashore, but making mighty racket as Spitza's mechanical wing puffed hot steam.

"There she is! Good girl, Spitza."

Tazper's exasperation was the gentle sun amid an ephemeral storm. Her footman's blurred face came into focus as he leaped from his mount and hauled her onto dry land. She shivered, fighting to stay conscious with the specters now kicking her beaten body.

Oh, how she wanted to ask what she'd done to deserve this, but all of Ezman knew. This was the Crystal Mother's damnation for the sins of the Amber Dame. Torment. No matter how she tried to aid the cause. She had marked her fate long ago.

Tazper practically threw her into the saddle of his horse before slapping it on the flank. "Bring Lady Kasia back to the castle, boy! Go!"

She had no chance to grab the reins or protest before the horse took off. All she could manage was wrapping her arms around its neck as she slumped forward, unable to hold her own weight. She wondered what had happened to Ivalat. Had all her effort, all her Taint and pain, been for nothing?

Even with Spitza perched on her shoulder, Time dragged either from Taint or exhaustion. She stared ahead at the haze covering Fort Harizak's walls. Not just powder smoke, but spirits—hundreds of them.

How had they attacked so quickly? The entire rescue should've taken a minute at most. Instead, the confluence resembled a slaughterhouse, crimson-clad infantrymen piled against the walls despite there being no breach for them to rush into. Blood soaked what had once been farm fields and turned the rivers red, as if in worship of the Crimson King himself. And their lost spirits rose as drifters among the fray.

Kasia's vision faded as a squad of cavalry wearing House Niezik's amber colors galloped toward her. Did they call her name, or was it just the specters harrying her every move? She didn't know, and before they arrived, her body finally gave out.

She slipped from the saddle, and the last thing she felt before falling unconscious was all-consuming pain.

ASH AND DAWN

"From their balconies they reign, and from them they shall fall. Let the people see they are not born low. It is the scions who shove their faces into the dirt, but even a talon of crystal cannot silence the masses when they rise together." – An excerpt from *The Dawnrise Manifesto* by Evit Paxian

Nex flared their nostrils as they passed the Crimson District's walls. The watchmen had pulled back completely to the palace along with the Crystal Brigade, claiming to "welcome" all of Kalastok into the district usually meant for only scions and appointed servants. The breathless lurking overhead made that welcoming feel more like a death march.

Because that was exactly what Chatik intended.

Hundreds of thousands flooded around the southern half of the Crystal Palace to see the Crimson King's speech. Not willingly. No scion could get all the lowborn to show up to anything without a gun—or a deadly spirit—to their heads.

Nex kept their hands in their pockets and their wide-brimmed hat pulled low. They had a pistol, amber beads, two glass daggers, and a bullet for each realm the damned king could Reach into. If the Crimsons had bothered to search people on the way in, Nex would've had the guard doubting his eyes, but they walked freely now. Hundreds of other newly-recruited Ashes did the same throughout the crowd.

Nikoza left plenty for Nex to criticize, but they couldn't deny that her earning the respect of the Drifters' Quarter lowborn during the riots had paid off. The few survivors of the west side's Ashes of Dawn had joined with new recruits from across the city with Kix's help. Now, with the gangs' old stores of weapons, they would make the Crimsons regret laying a finger on Nex's people.

Like they had for years before the coup, Nex walked alone in the crowd. The revolt needed to feel organic to inspire more lowborn, and even minor scions, to join the attack. They glanced around. Yeah, the entire city would do the trick.

They wouldn't be the ones to take the Unity Crystal from Chatik and kill the bastard, but it was up to the Ashes of Dawn to keep the Crystal Brigade and breathless busy. Nikoza wasn't the most experienced Reacher. There was no way she would be able to fend all of them off after surprising Chatik.

Whether that surprise would work, Nex didn't know as they tapped one of the lamp posts lining the cobblestone street. Those lamps lit the east side in the everdark as the Shadow Quarter rotted. Nex hoped Chatik spent a long, painful time in the dark before his spirit finally let him die. Sure, he was a Dark Reacher, but death was something even he couldn't see through.

Jolzena's brother, the Spirit Reacher Vanzearik, stood beside Gregorzon Niezik on one of the palace's lower balconies ahead. Only lowborn guards and two Reachers—Force and Earth based on the designs across their uniforms—kept to the level of the crowd.

Cute, they think we can't shoot them if they're on the second floor.

More Reachers lined the upper balconies, but left the central one on the third floor open. That was exactly where they'd expected Chatik to arrive. Glancing over their shoulder, Nex tried to see where Nikoza was hiding with Hazat and Jolzena, but the southern light just sent dots spinning through their vision.

They gritted their teeth. Their whole life had been built around resisting the scions, not working with them, but losing their memories had made them realize they couldn't fight alone. Nikoza and the others would do their job. Nex and the Ashes needed to do theirs.

The Possibility Reacher held to the scattered memories they had from before the Crimson Coup. They fought for more than themself. They'd lost Jax, Jiinaan, and hundreds, if not thousands of others to the Crimsons. They'd lost their love for Vinnia too—the love that had driven them to find a cure in the first place. Maybe they'd feel it again. But they could never bring back all those who'd suffered and died under the Crimsons' taloned fists.

They had to temper the fire igniting in their heart as the empty balcony door crept open. Timing was everything. Chatik's false cure had infected so many with a strange, dormant version of the plague. He'd turn half the fucking city into his breathless slaves if Nex got this wrong.

The crooked-nosed piece of shit who'd messed with Nex's head led Tzena Oliezany and Qaraza Pikezik onto the balcony. Nikoza had claimed his name was Uzrin Ioniz, Zinarus's bastard father, but Nex didn't care who he was. They would do far worse than break his nose if they got the chance.

The crowd wasn't too pleased with the arrival of the Crimson leaders, murmured boos spreading among them. Those were silenced quickly by swooping breathless. The spirits didn't strike yet, but their presence alone was enough to send a chill down Nex's spine. Kelosh's invasion in the east filled the newspapers with stories of defeat. Chatik made sure his greatest weapon was here, though, oppressing his people while he sent conscripted lowborn and scions alike to die on the front lines.

What an asshole.

That thought only deepened as the Crimson King himself emerged, not from the balcony, but over the tops of the golden spires at the palace's peak. Donning a long crimson robe over a nobleman's suit, Chatik Reached to illuminate himself like a damn bonfire as he placed a single foot to balance atop the spire.

"Esteemed residents of our mighty capital of Kalastok," Chatik's voice boomed with the aid of Air Reaching, which spun about him like a great storm. "I bring you news that this is a glorious day for

Ezman. For today, a new era has dawned. The Crimson Cause shall begin its true march toward fruition: glory for the chosen scion race."

The crowd shifted, but none jeered this time. Enough had seen what he was capable of during Etal's failed execution, and between those breathless and the Crystal Brigade, they were right to be afraid. But fear was for those with something to lose.

Nex had already lost everything.

"Fuck the scions!" they shouted, drawing their pistol and firing at Uzrin. "Fuck the Crimson Court!"

Their voice needed no magic to carry, as the crowd stood in stunned silence. Well, they did until Nex's single shot triggered an uproar.

People threw out their arms, screaming at Chatik as those closer to the palace charged. The Ashes scattered throughout the crowd followed Nex's lead and fired on the Reachers. But the guards didn't react, letting people pass their lines until Chatik snapped his fingers.

A forcefield rose before the guards. No matter how many people piled against it, crushing those in front of them, it would not yield. Only a few shots had rang out before the forcefield's appearance, and Force and Air Reachers deflected the bullets before they could do any true damage to the Brigade or their king far above.

Panic struck Nex's chest as they grabbed amber with their off hand and trapped a diving breathless. This was the plan—distract more than damage—but no one had foreseen Chatik being powerful enough to call that large of a forcefield. The Reaching was probably killing him, but he'd planned on it.

Where in the wastes was that princess?

Most of the breathless kept to the rear of the crowd, corralling anyone who tried to flee. Desperation swelled as people joined the Ashes' revolt with their impure glass amulets. They focused mainly on protecting their families or other groups, but Nex took heart knowing that each one who fought back was another piece to draw Chatik's eye and keep him from triggering his false cure.

A commotion came from the palace doors as Nex pushed forward for a clean shot if they Possibility Reached for luck. Nearly a hundred lowborn had made it past the guards before the forcefield. Without resistance, they pried open the doors until Chatik's voice returned.

"I must thank these brave few for allowing me to demonstrate what our future holds."

The king swept down from his spire, his face turning sicklier with each passing moment. Possibility and Body Reaching had clearly hidden the worst of his Taint, but it was all too obvious now.

"We have uprooted the gangs who terrorize the most vulnerable of our city," he said as silver Spirit Reacher wisps joined his Air ones, "and now, we shall turn those who defy Ezman's rise into tools for the Cause."

"Like shit, you will!"

Nex Possibility Reached, then fired. The shot would've been incredible for a pistol, but their Reaching altered the odds, sending it over the forcefield and straight toward his chest. Even luck, though, couldn't stop his whirlwind from batting the bullet away.

Chatik just scoffed. "Kill that rebel bitch."

Reachers from every balcony summoned their wisps. Nex needed no more encouragement to leave, so they dove back into the crowd. Most people wished for height, but Nex thanked their limited stature as they wove through the chaos, occasionally lobbing an amber bead through an attacking breathless. They'd created all the distraction they could.

Now where was that *damn princess*?

They looked south again to see if the breathless had somehow attacked the building where Nikoza was supposed to emerge from. She'd planned to use the northern market's fountain to fuel her Reaching as Jolzena flung her toward the palace. Had that changed?

Maybe Nex did have something to lose, they realized as panic deepened within them. They didn't want to die, and they worried for Nikoza. Despite the ex-princess being a snobby-nosed scion, she'd saved their life and had actually seemed to care. Lowborn didn't get extra lives like magnates, so that meant something.

A round of screams stopped Nex's retreat in the midst of the palace gardens. They had to stand on their toes to see back toward the doors, where at least a quarter of the people who'd passed the guards writhed on the steps. Chatik's Spirit Reaching encompassed them, followed by pink Mind wisps.

"You have betrayed Ezman," he declared, drifting lower until he landed on the third-floor balcony with his closest allies. "Now, you will demonstrate the meaning of loyalty to your fellow traitors."

The writhing ceased, and a strange stillness fell over the crowd as shadowy spirits emerged from the chests of Chatik's inflicted. Limp corpses lay in their wake. Not dead by the Spirit Plague itself, but the Reaching of their king who'd granted them a poisoned cure.

Those still standing pulled harder at the doors as others tried to flee back to the rest of the crowd. It was no use. Chatik threw out a hand, grinning before commanding his newest breathless.

"Show them what becomes of those who are disloyal to the Crimson Court."

Nex forced themself to watch the slaughter that followed. They needed to hate every moment, every death the Crimsons caused. This revolt was because of their plan with Nikoza, and these people needed to be remembered for being the first who were willing to charge the palace. For most, though, they'd be known as those devoured by the tendrils of the new breathless.

"The cure was a lie," someone muttered nearby, but didn't raise their voice.

Another held a hand over their mouth. "They'll turn us all to spirits!"

Fear paralyzed the crowd as Chatik dropped the forcefield with a wave of his hand. "This is the cost of dissent. We sought to aid the lowborn of this city, but it is apparent you have forgotten your places as servants to our nation of scions. No longer will you bear identity or wills of your own. You serve Ezman now, and if you do not kneel before the Crimson Court, you shall suffer the same fate as those you see before you."

"I took the cure…" an elderly man said from beside Nex, staring down at his hands. He dropped to his knees and placed his forehead to the ground. "Oh, Crystal Mother, protect me. I'm another's servant now."

Thousands did the same as they realized what the false cure would do. Seconds later, Nex stood alone among a hundred thousand kneeling spirits who were bound to their mortal fears. Nex should kneel, they knew that, but they could only glare up at the king who'd slain their friends and their identity.

They slowly removed their hat and tossed it aside. Though they didn't Reach to disguise themself now, everyone close to them said they no longer looked quite the same. It was more than the short, swooping undercut across their hair or the way they acted without all their memories. The torture they'd endured had changed their very face and being.

And Nex wanted Chatik to have a clear look at them. To know that when all others bent to his will, it was them who refused to kneel.

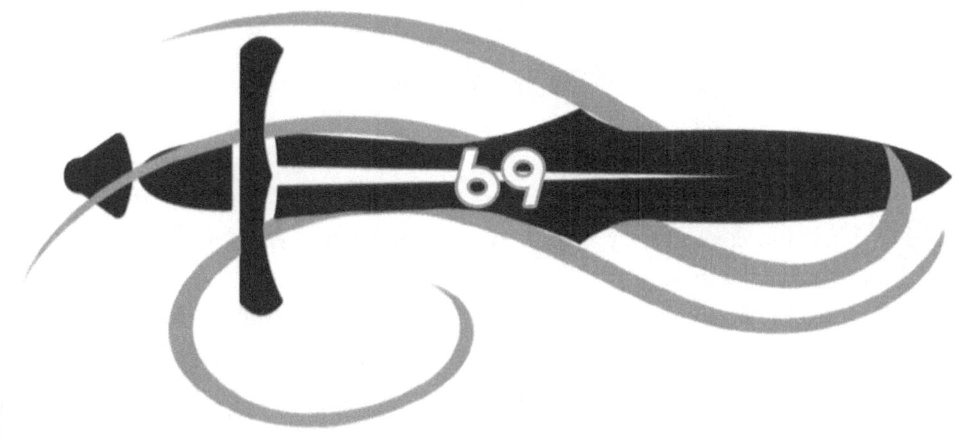

TWO HALVES. ONE SPIRIT.

"What is truly broken may never be made whole again. Healing is the act of accepting those cracks in our very spirit and knowing that, despite their showing, we may be remade into something truly unique. In truth, we cannot ever become our true selves until this world forces us to confront such brokenness," – Ulosa ik Palmia, Vockan Whisperer

Wanusa's grip on her blade slackened at the sight of her brother's remaining spirit hovering at the pit's center. With her crystal collar glowing bright silver, she sensed the perfect song joining Inrius's melodic half which was bound to her, and the eager voice of that which wasn't. Two halves of one boy torn apart.

The Vanashel had stolen him.

"Come to me, Inri," she pleaded, holding out her free hand with the bound half of Inrius's spirit hovering around her fingertips. She recalled her other spirit to not frighten him. In her heart, she knew this would be her only chance to reunite the brother she'd failed to save all those years ago.

"He is not yours," the draconic Earth Bound One replied, its voice rumbling in the Spiritspeech. "But I will release him if you give me the one who binds Earth."

Wanusa looked to Radais, his shifted armor matching the one Rakekeaa and Ataakanan wore. Had Miv's old spirit revealed something to him? He'd fought like a brawler within it, and it was strange to see such a powerful Bound One be so clearly afraid of a single Glassblade. Except, her mentor was no ordinary Glassblade, even before his Reaching.

"Radais is my family too," she Whispered to the Bound One in its language. Radais raised his brow, but there was no time to explain to him what was happening. "Just release my brother, and we won't kill you."

These Vanashel had slaughtered her family and village. She'd not been close to her parents, but this destruction, the entire landscape corrupted to wasteland, was horrifying. Spirits all had desires like any human. The last season had shown her plenty what the Vanashel wanted, and she would do what was necessary to stop it.

The dragon circled the sand pit, emanating the closest thing spirits had to a laugh. "This place is your home, as this world is ours. Feel our loss. Know what it is to have your home taken."

"I've only tried to understand spirits and protect them," Wanusa said. Her voice cracked, and her arm ached holding her brother's spirit aloft. But still, she stepped forward. "If you knew loss, you wouldn't force me to suffer too. The Saleshi have helped us know them, but you just slaughter."

Yet more breathless filled the pit's peak until only a single beam of light entered. It illuminated the second half of Inrius, the Bound One's spirit mists curling around him like a serpent choking its prey. "There is no speaking with the ones who birthed the first of the breathless, then tortured us!"

"Those Crimsons are our enemies!"

The misty tendrils tightened. "We have watched you, young one. You live because we have heard your song, and we desire for you to spread our own to all the embodied ones. But to know us, you must first choose: your brother's spirit or your Glassblade master's life."

Wanusa didn't even think. Screaming through her tears, she threw her sword at the beast. It was a desperate, foolish attempt, but Radais had damaged its armor. If she could just strike its Spirit Essence…

The sword never got close, as the Bound One slammed down its war pick and shattered her blade with a single strike. No human could ever move so quickly. Their foes, though, were not of flesh and blood, but of crystal and spirit.

"Choose!" the Bound One demanded in the Commonwealth tongue.

The shadows suddenly pulled back to reveal the pit's base. Radais looked from the spirits to Wanusa, his mouth agape and his blade ready. It didn't matter. No man could strike at the Bound One when he was so high.

"Choose what?" he asked. "Wanusa, what is it asking?"

She hung her head, slamming shut her eyes in hopes that this was some trick of the spirits. The Deepening had shown her visions. Why couldn't this be another from which she could wake?

With a sharp breath, she forced herself to return her mentor's gaze. She need not speak, because his eyes said he read her as if she were just another page of his sketchbook. A story written in charcoal and paper. No words, but what words could convey the ache spearing her heart?

Radais lowered his blade. "I promised I would reunite you with Inrius. If this is the way, then so be it."

"What?" Wanusa furrowed her brow, wiping the tears from her cheeks and closing on him. "You don't get to become the closest thing I have left to family and then throw your life away."

She drew a long breath. Inrius's severed spirit still circled her, and she remembered what his life had been in those last years. Hollow, empty. These spirits were the pieces of him, but as she raised her gaze to the lost half above, she forced herself to accept the truth.

Inrius had been dead for years. Reuniting the halves of his spirit wouldn't bring him back, no matter how much she wished for it to be true. The Deepening had granted her some piece of him to remember and hold, but to complete her promise would mean abandoning her family now. She couldn't fix the past. Here and now, though, she could ensure she didn't fail again.

"No," she said before switching to the Spiritspeech and throwing her arm toward the Earth Bound One. "You make me choose? So I choose the living."

A hum spread throughout the Vanashel, but a disturbance above the pit drew in many of them. Through her crystal, Wanusa sensed the spirits dying. Had the Glassblades arrived? Could they be free?

She opened her mouth to speak again, but the Bound One gave her no chance. A hundred shadowy tendrils burst from it. They plunged into the lost half of Inrius, the spirit screaming in his voice like he had all those years before. She'd not been there to save him then, and now, she could do nothing but watch as the vibrant rhythm of his Spirit Essence vanished, consumed by the Bound One.

"Tell the embodied ones that your end has come," the dragon said. "God shall emerge, and it will free your entombed spirits, granting these lands to their rightful dwellers."

Then it rose with the rest of its breathless. Distant figures sliced through those at the peak, but as Rakekeaa became visible, deep gray Shadow wisps spiraling around it, the sand started to close in. Radais grabbed Wanusa and bounded at the collapsing wall. But there was no grip as they scrambled with their muscles screaming.

Their allies above fought desperately to reach them. It was no use as the wave of breathless and arrival of more Bound Ones forced them back. Wanusa cried out watching Rakekeaa disappear into the distant light, its retracted shadows now falling over the trapped Glassblades.

They were alone. The Vanashel chased after the retreating Saleshi, and with the sand tumbling in from every side, there was nothing Wanusa could do but close her eyes and call out to the spirits for aid.

Another force answered instead. It struck her chest like a great hammer, stopping her heart and breath alike. Even her bound spirits fell still as they stared in awe at Radais.

The master held out his drained talon, yet power burst from him in a glorious array until each grain of sand hardened to stone. When it was finished, his eyes rolled back. Only Wanusa's spirits kept him from striking the same earth he'd commanded moments before.

"Radais?" She hurried over to him. "Master Radais! Wake up!"

He sputtered, his eyes fluttering open. Followed by a grin. "So, that's what happens when you push your Reaching too far."

She wrinkled her nose. "Realm Taint is no joke! How'd you even Reach when your talon was empty?"

"Don't know. I was just desperate, and I couldn't let you die, not after you gave up your brother for me." His head dropped. "I'm so sorry, Wanusa. I promised—"

"Not now," she said with a wave at her spirits to haul him to his feet. "The Vanashel must've let us go for a reason, and we need to figure out what happened to the others."

The fallen sand had solidified into a steep slope, but one uneven enough to offer footholds. With Taint obviously giving Radais shaky legs, though, he was in no shape to climb, so Wanusa directed her spirits to help him the rest of the way. It was strange seeing spirits carry a Glassblade fully armored in rose quartz. He had a full Vockan's height, and his legs dragged behind as the spirits tired.

Their endurance was fascinating. She'd never considered how long her bonded spirits could endure without needing to replenish from her crystal's Spirit Essence, but their dim, drooping forms made it clear they were fading. Once at the top, she would have to release them and leave herself defenseless. Why had she so foolishly thrown her blade?

She thanked the climb for its rigor, distracting her from her doubts and the images of Inrius which haunted her mind. All choices had consequences. But she was a Glassblade and a Whisperer. People needed her to be ready, not wallowing in personal woes.

What met her at the pit's peak did nothing to lessen those pains. For everywhere she looked, Glassblade corpses scattered the grasslands she'd once called home. Fertile plains turned to ashen wastes. Growth turned to destruction. Life turned to emptiness.

"Lazan?" Radais pried himself from the spirits and stumbled into the rain. "Lazan!"

Wanusa had all but forgotten about the storm in that pit, but the heavy sand slowed her now as she chased him. Figures lurked in the distance. Some shouted. Others lumbered with inhuman stiffness.

And above it all, Rakekeaa commanded Ataakanan and the few other remaining Saleshi.

The Vanashel were nowhere to be seen. Thousands of them had filled the sky minutes before, but it carried only clouds now, the dawnrise light having the gall to cast a distant rainbow over the mountains at the storms' rear. It was the only color for a dozen miles except for the deep crimson which poured over the sand. A hundred warriors dead—all that remained of the glorious Glassblade Order.

"This can't be real," she told herself. "We're the Glassblades, the protectors of Vocka!"

Radais groaned ahead, half-dragging his greatsword before he turned back toward her. "We're as human as anyone else. Now, tell me: Is that Lazan? Do you sense him?"

She took a shaky breath before closing her eyes and feeling with her spirit for the rhythms of the realms. Lazan's would show her both the Spirit Essence at his core and Body's power pulsing through his talon, but she sensed only the beating of Vockan Fire among the people on the ground, along with the Essences of the Saleshi above. Her heart raced with each passing second. Lazan, like Radais, had become almost a father to her. To lose him like this…

Just as she opened her eyes, Body's rhythm flared ahead. It took her breath, so she sucked in another and grabbed Radais to haul him along. "C'mon. Our resident scion is still alive."

Another Essence haunted her as they ran. Strange silver wisps of Spirit lingered around the corpses—not spirits themselves, but a remnant power. Radais raising his blade answered the question she'd hoped would stay in her head.

The drained, spiritless husks of the Vanashel's victims were moving.

"Not again," Radais muttered before pushing off Wanusa and slicing the steel edge of his blade across the throat of a Glassblade's husk. "You're not going to get in the way of the people I love. NOT AGAIN!"

The earth hardened beneath his feet wherever he stepped, steadying his rapid strikes with such a heavy blade. Wanusa could only keep in his wake and avoid looking her fallen comrades in the eyes. Many of them had trained with her, taught her, and shared stories with her around the fire. Taking their lives hadn't been enough. The Vanashel had made their bodies slaves with lingering Spirit Essence.

Radais, though, didn't show any hesitation. She understood the pain of separation from a loved one. He'd lost Miv, like she had lost Inrius, and spirits knew he would literally move the earth to ensure it didn't happen again.

The rain soon cleared enough to reveal Lazan kneeling over a wounded Glassblade. A gash bled across his own side, but the deep red wisps circling him were not for himself.

"I'm fine!" the familiar grumpy voice of Mhanain cried out as he tried to push Lazan away.

The Body Reacher sighed. "You are suffering from the bliss that comes with heavy blood loss. Because you are near death, your body has decided to numb your pain, and if you do not let me work, you will perish like the rest of your comrades."

"Not all of them," Radais said, dropping his sword and throwing himself at Lazan's feet.

Lazan's jaw fell slack. He stopped pushing down Mhanain for a moment before returning to his healing. Those wisps pressed into Mhanain's skin, and though the mid-aged brute struggled, he was too weak to truly resist. His wounds slowly closed as Lazan looked back to Radais with tears welling in his eyes.

"Ataakanan implied that you were either a husk or buried under fifteen feet of sand."

Radais lowered his head, not bothering to wipe his cheeks clean. "I should've been. Spirits… This is all my fault."

"You are not so important," the stern voice of Ataakanan said from above. "Every Saleshi made a choice to be here, and every Glassblade made the same. They could have left with Tairanik, but they stayed."

"Defend when unsure. Protect home," Rakekeaa said from the front of the Saleshi as it cocked its flower head. "Protect love."

"We couldn't protect anything," Wanusa replied. She blinked

away tears, staring toward the ruins of her home as the clouds surrendered to clear sky. More reborn husks advanced in the storms' wake, but a few stray Glassblades and Saleshi dispatched them quickly. "I lost my brother, and we'll lose Vocka if they got away."

Rakekeaa nodded. "Escaped. East."

"They are attacking the rest of Vocka, then?" Radais said as he and Lazan held each other. "There is nothing we can do?"

"Embodied ones call this war," it said, pointing its spear toward the mountains. "One battle falls. Another rises. Vanashel go to raise the one they call God."

Lazan raised his brow. "A god?"

"The Earth Bound One told me he was leaving us alive to spread the message," Wanusa said. "Zekiaz is theirs, and their god will free our *entombed spirits*." She drew a long breath, looking for Mariana among the living, but she sensed no others like her nearby. Another person she hadn't saved. "The Vanashel are obsessed with dragons, from their weird forms to the way they talked to Whisperers before. Don't the Ezmani have a crystal dragon?"

"They do," Lazan said, any trace of color draining from his scion gray cheeks. "A mighty beast, I have seen it on a number of occasions flying over Kalastok. Do you believe that could be their god?"

Rakekeaa drifted to and fro. "Spirit Crystal births spirits. Spirit Crystal births dragons. Connected."

"Is it a god?" Wanusa asked as the weight of the world only grew on her shoulders.

"God has many forms."

Lazan kissed Radais and turned his attention back to Mhanain. Slowly, he helped the archer rise, dusting off the sand from his damaged armor. "There will be plenty of time to talk about gods and dragons once we are safe. We must find somewhere to recover and figure out a strategy that is not in the middle of the open."

"I know of a place." Radais stood, placing a fist over his head and bowing to Rakekeaa. "Your First One made me swear not to reveal the location of Akaamilion. I've honored that promise as best I could, and now, I ask you to bring us there again. Bakeekek knows more than any of us about the Vanashel and all spirits. We need the Saleshi's help, or humanity will fail to fight this threat."

Rakekeaa hummed. "Do you believe this is wise, Whisperer?" it asked Wanusa in the Spiritspeech. "My kind will not welcome one with your powers, but you may prove them wrong with great risk."

"We need each other, now more than ever," she replied, then dropped to her knees. "Please, trust us. We are at your mercy, spirits of Salesh. This realm is yours, and together, we can protect it."

"The girl speaks well," Ataakanan said. "She is worthy of the trials ahead."

Rakekeaa looked from Miv's spirit to the old supreme defender's trainee. Its eyes studied every part of each of them before it bowed, mimicking Radais. "Leave other ones with glass swords to speak to embodied ones. We go to Akaamilion. First One will decide."

"Thank you," Radais said with another thump of his chest. "For all of Vocka, and all of humanity. Thank you."

"Do not thank," Rakekeaa said, rising into the sky. "Journey ahead is long. Find ibexes near camp and follow. We will protect embodied friends."

CANNON AND DRAGON

"The two things I fear most in life is that damned dragon lurking behind my throne and my wife when I have forgotten our plans for the evening." – Harizak Kuzon the Third, former king of Ezman

Well, that had all gone incredibly well… If *well* was an absolute disaster.

Tazper blinked away the black spots filling his eyes as yet another round of Taint inflicted him, dulling his will. Silver Spirit wisps answered his call, and he used his Reaching the best he could to divert the breathless who flanked Tiuz's cavalry force.

The field marshal had somehow kept the riders together through half-an-hour of unrelenting fire from the Crimson riflemen and countless breathless strikes from every side. A sane commander would have called a retreat immediately upon seeing Kasia and Ivalat tumble into the Ty River to the west of the fort, but even after a terrifying search to pull the pair from the waters, Tiuz insisted that their flanking position took attention off the Confederation's weaker positions.

That plan had worked tactically. Despite taking significant casualties, the Confederation cavalry killed ten breathless along with more Crimson soldiers for every rider they lost. Any advance on the fort required the Crimsons to leave their flank open. Even with Earth, Air, and Water Reachers to cross the rivers between their siege camps and the crumbling walls, they were slowed by the mud from the recent ephemeral storms.

But those tactics had not been enough to save Zinarus.

The iz Vamiustok heir had sought to rescue Kasia. His haste only earned him a shot horse and a tumble into the river. Downstream of where Kasia and Ivalat had fallen, he had been too far for Tazper or any other allies to rescue. His mechanical leg likely made it difficult to swim, and the current had carried him into the heavy smoke near the Crimson ranks.

Tazper's instincts cried for him to go back and help Zinarus, but the breathless ensured there was no such option. Neither terrain nor natural defenses deterred the spirits, who encircled the cavalry to guide them into firing range of the Crimsons' heavy defenses. The Spirit Reachers did their best to create openings at the cost of heavy Taint. With glass bullets running low, they needed to break free.

That was exactly why Tazper accepted this further Taint now. Riding straight into the breathless between the cavalry and Fort Harizak, the few dozen Spirit Reachers left formed a wedge to create enough of a clearance. Powder smoke stung his eyes and nose as the other riders cleared the breathless who refused to make way.

They were almost through. Silver clashed between Reacher wisps and spirits, splitting the haze in a brilliant display of the arcane. He had dreamed of Reaching for moments like this. For once, he could make an impact instead of just helping Kasia exact her vengeance.

This Reaching, this power, was freedom. Its Taint dampened his will and slowed his mind, but now that Kasia had allowed the Crystal Mother's gift to bless him, Tazper would never let it go. That meant he needed to live.

He prayed silently that Kasia had returned to friendly lines as he burst through the smoke and finally gained sight of the Confederation defenses flanking the fort. Drifting spirits lingered where their corpses fell. Zinarus had claimed the crystal dragon would raise the spirits of the fallen infantry, but for now, their only foes were the Crimson soldiers and breathless who'd already existed. Considering the outer battlements struggled to defend against the breathless, who could slip through the stone walls with ease, that didn't bode well if the dragon ever made an appearance.

Spirit Reachers cast silver over the defenders, punctured only by glass bullets as bugles blared. Were their glass reserves as low as the cavalry's? Zinarus's mercenaries had brought plenty of sand, but though the Confederation's Earth and Fire Reachers had forged it into glass, crafting the intricate bullets was a far more time-consuming process.

Luckily, Tiuz had devised another use for that glass.

Tazper glanced over his shoulder to see if the rest of Tiuz's cavalry had followed through the breathless. They had, but that didn't grant him the hope he so badly needed. The breathless should've pursued them, forcing the Spirit Reachers to cover the retreat from the rear. Instead, those spirits hovered among the haze. Not chasing. Not even moving.

A familiar chill crept down his spine as the crystal monstrosity burst from the Crimson ranks. He had only entered the Chamber of Scions once, but one never forgot the overwhelming fear of a dragon the size of an estate towering over the throne. Even suffering the influence of Truth Reachers could not match the sheer power radiated by the king's dragon.

"All cannons, fire!" Tiuz shouted toward the bastion, an Air Reacher carrying his voice as the dragon's silver form split the breathless.

The Crimsons' own Spirit Reachers had guided the spirits before. But in the presence of the dragon, the breathless followed it as if it were a god, waiting until it released a guttural roar before uniting into a single wave toward the walls.

Silver surged ahead of them. Wisps of it struck each drifter released by the fallen, and the spirits' murky, indistinct forms solidified into those of breathless as Crimson Reachers took control of the fledgling spirits' minds. That hardly seemed necessary, as the new

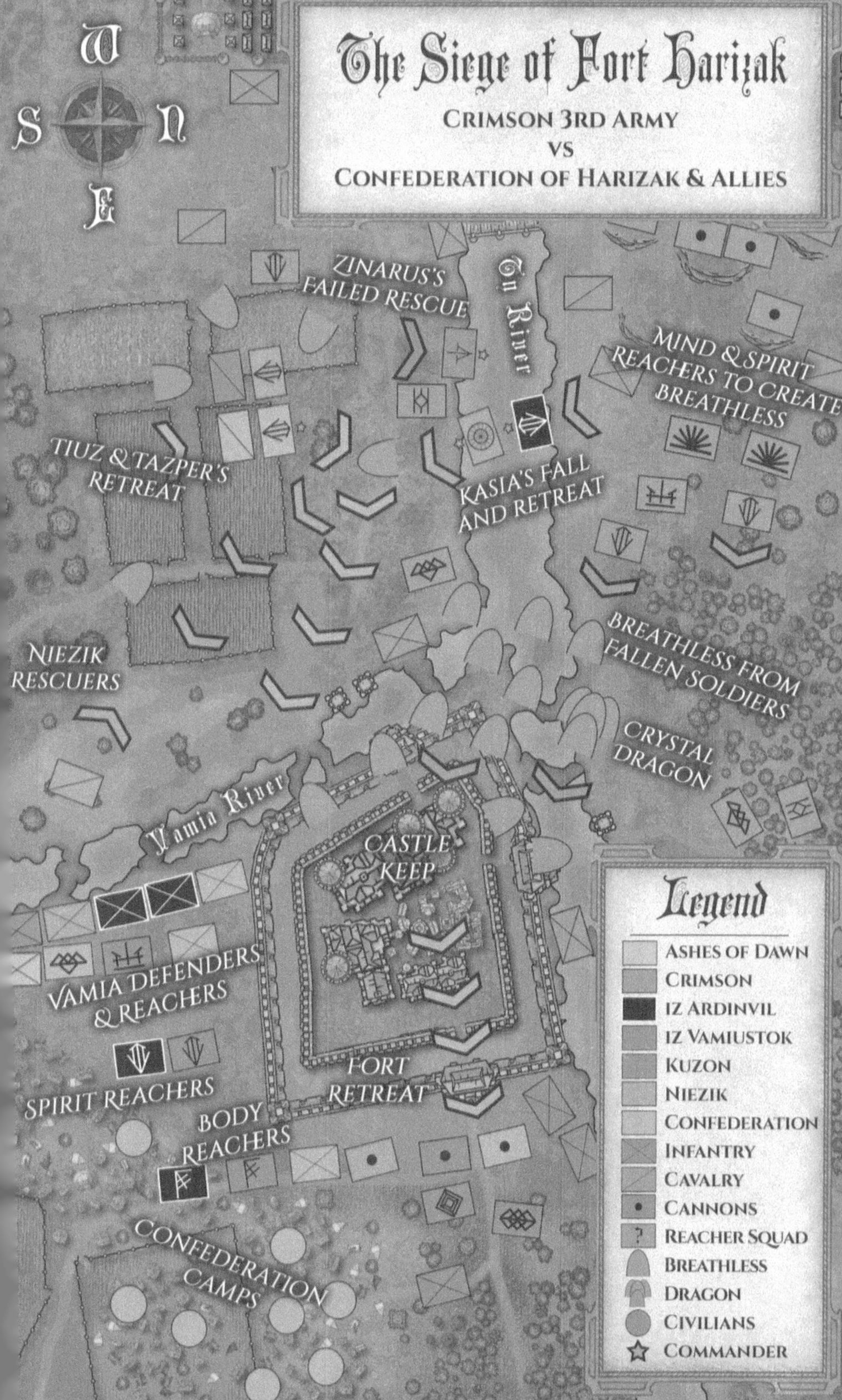

W N E S
The Siege of Fort Harizak
CRIMSON 3RD ARMY
VS
CONFEDERATION OF HARIZAK & ALLIES
ZINARUS'S FAILED RESCUE
On River
MIND & SPIRIT REACHERS TO CREATE BREATHLESS
TIUZ & TAZPER'S RETREAT
KASIA'S FALL AND RETREAT
BREATHLESS FROM FALLEN SOLDIERS
NIEZIK RESCUERS
CRYSTAL DRAGON
Vamia River
CASTLE KEEP
VAMIA DEFENDERS & REACHERS
SPIRIT REACHERS
BODY REACHERS
FORT RETREAT
CONFEDERATION CAMPS
Legend
ASHES OF DAWN
CRIMSON
IZ ARDINVIL
IZ VAMIUSTOK
KUZON
NIEZIK
CONFEDERATION
INFANTRY
CAVALRY
CANNONS
REACHER SQUAD
BREATHLESS
DRAGON
CIVILIANS
COMMANDER

breathless joined the dragon's horde in a blink. Many had gathered at the base of the walls, and they plunged through the stone as if it were air.

Confederation Reacher wisps and glass bullets answered the cloud of spirits—a scattering of sand against a charging herd. Tazper grabbed his carbine to join the fight, but there were too many. The cavalry's Reachers would need to draw more Taint. With his mind scattered and his will failing, though, he dared not risk throwing himself into a trapped, empty state amid battle.

Screams echoed from atop the battlements as only a few cannons fired against the monstrous beast of crystal. That dragon allowed the Crimsons to wield far more spirits than their Reachers could maintain. Downing it would grant the defenders a moment of relief, but what was a moment when they had no reinforcements?

Tazper wished for Radais and his Glassblades, their swords and armor granting them the chance to slice down these foes. The Vockan heroes of the Awakening were a hundred miles away. No one was coming.

Panic spread among the purple and amber-clad soldiers ahead as he shot glass straight through a charging breathless. Between the retreating cavalry and the defensive lines across the river, they had cleared most of the spirits on this flank, but the Crimsons seemed only to care about the fortress itself.

Just as Field Marshal Tiuz had hoped.

The defenders abandoned the battlements, allowing the breathless to surge toward the castle's keep. Above, the dragon swooped into the stone outer wall and toppled it in a single, brutal strike. Most outside Tiuz's cavalry were unaware of their commander's plan, and they routed as Tazper led his allies over the Earth-Reached bridges across the Vamia River.

A panicked retreat. It had to look real. The Crimsons and their breathless needed to believe taking the fort would break the Confederations' morale, so even Tiuz's own soldiers could not know what was to come.

Tazper held his breath as the breathless wave pierced the castle, followed by their dragon. Such destruction, such power, dwarfed what he wielded through his Reaching. Nothing was invincible, though, and Kasia had shown him time and time again that with power came risk. Direct strikes could land a killing blow.

They also left one's belly exposed.

With the fort empty of retreating Confederation defenders, Tiuz shouted a command from the cavalry's front, his fist raised and his uniform covered in blood and soot. Its silver trimmed in green represented the Confederation's bond to the Spirit Crystal below. That Crystal had birthed a dragon capable of commanding spirits beyond any man's power. A dragon turned by Chatik against its king. A dragon greater than any weapon. The Crimsons had unleashed it upon their own people instead of the invading Keloshans, and now, they would learn to regret that dearly.

An explosion rocked the very earth beneath Tazper's horse. Flames erupted from the keep as stone showered from the sky, bringing a heat that singed his brows.

Breathless shrieks followed. A torrent of desperate cries before the glass bombs hidden within the fort ripped through their shadowy forms. Tens of thousands had poured through and over the outer walls, and along with their crystal dragon, they had found the Commonwealth's greatest general to be ready for them.

The dragon itself collapsed into the crumbling keep. Beyond the walls, it was impossible to tell if the beast had died, but the eerie silence within the fort signaled that most of its breathless followers had.

Bugles echoed throughout the Confederation lines, calling the defenders back to order. "The spirits have fallen, but much of the Crimson army remains!" Tiuz declared with the Air Reachers' aid making his voice boom over the entire battlefield. "Retreat to our friends in the south! Let us be finished with this forsaken castle."

THE KING AND HIS HEIR

"Without an heir by blood or by spirit, a king allows his reign to be nothing but a blip in history." – Kirlon Tongast, former emperor of Kelosh

Nikoza could not believe her eyes.

Perched with Hazat and Jolzena in the third story window of a building along the Kala River's east bank, she shuddered as Chatik's horrific words carried over the city. Remnants of the Crimson Cause attempted to twist her mind. Nothing, though, could justify distributing a false Spirit Plague cure to turn the disobedient into breathless slaves.

She stepped back from the window, a hand held over her heart. "That Realm Tainted wretch is not the uncle I ever knew. We theorized he may do this, but to see it…"

"It is exactly as we discussed, my lady," Hazat said. "Trust your eyes and your spirit. See what they are doing and stop it. We have waited too long already."

Jolzena wasn't so soft, charging over and grabbing Nikoza by her coat. "You have the Inheritance Blade. It's time to use it, or a lot more people are about to die."

Hazat's brow creased. "Shouting at her will fix nothing. This hesitation is not of her will alone. But Jolzena is right—we must act now."

Fear burrowed into Nikoza's chest, but as she glanced down at her family's golden blade, she remembered this was not about her. Chatik's horrid ambitions ruined her mind, her house, and all the Commonwealth. Kalastok's population was entrapped within the Crimson District partially because of her failures. She was no longer a princess, but she held her grandfather's people close to heart.

They needed her.

"I require your Reaching to throw me to the river," she told Jolzena, who still grappled her. "Preferably now."

"This was not the plan," Hazat said. "We were supposed to confront Chatik directly from here."

Nikoza let a bite slip into her voice. "That will not be enough when the people are dismayed and broken, but I still need you to distract the spirits." He offered only a solemn nod in reply, so she took Jolzena's arm. "Help us to the Kala. Then I shall do the rest."

When Jolzena finally released her, Hazat stepped with her to the window as Chatik's voice echoed once again. The Crimson King had dropped to a palace balcony. The crowd kneeled before him, and even those wearing the Ashes of Dawn's yellow bandanas and arm-bands cowered. An entire uprising quelled in moments. All except defiant Nex, of course.

Bright red wisps burst from Jolzena's talon. Nikoza froze, but the Force Reacher pressed a hand to her back, then pushed. "Jump."

Nikoza barely got the chance, her half-step suddenly sending her arcing toward the Kala alongside Hazat. Usually a beautiful blue, waste turned the river to a reeking, muddy brown without the city's Reachers to purify it. She regretted her own absence worsening the lack of Water Reachers until gravity overtook Jolzena's push.

Dear Crystal Mother, let this work.

She Reached a moment before striking the surface. At her command, the water curved and folded like a great hand, catching them. The impact knocked the wind out of her, but she sucked in a sharp breath and lifted them with the waves until they towered above the highest of Kalastok's buildings. Tzena's training had taught her to taper her Reach. It would extinguish quickly, though, so she prepared herself for the Taint to come.

People's attention turned toward her as she called the water forward, leading her over the western road to the palace with Hazat on a wave behind. Pushing beyond the river's domain only worsened the cost. She Reached again to keep the waves from dropping, as a moment's falter would reveal weakness before Chatik. Taint answered, but she would do what was necessary to inspire hope, resistance.

"Ah, so my traitorous niece returns," the Crimson King declared through his Air Reaching. The strength of his voice alone stopped her heart for a beat, and the breathless turned away from Nex, swelling toward her in wait of Chatik's instructions. "Shall we ensure she understands the same lesson you all have learned?"

"You must get to that balcony. Hurry!" Hazat said from just below. Silver Spirit wisps already circled his hand, and his eyes carried the fury of a rabid koilee. "I will do all I can to delay the breathless, but it will buy you seconds at most."

Nikoza gave him a grateful, yet pained smile. The breathless would come for him whether they succeeded or not. He had survived the Crimsons' ambush of the Ashes of Dawn despite risking everything to save thousands of people, and now, he did the same for all of Kalastok. And for her.

"Please, be safe," she told him.

He huffed. "Crystal Mother save us all. Go!"

Then he leaped from the wave, his Spirit wisps shooting toward the breathless. Nikoza hesitated as one last whisper from the Crimsons' Mind Reaching pushed back against her will, but she had endured it enough to know the cause. That resistance was not her own, and it could not stop her.

A third Reach pressed Taint's nausea deep into her core. Lightheadedness and an unquenchable thirst overcame her, and her skin felt as if her clothes had gone aflame. She had gained far more control over her Reaching than ever. Both Jazuk and Chatik had taught her that all power had a price, though, and as she propelled herself toward the balcony on an even mightier wave, the full brunt of her Taint nearly tore her from consciousness.

Yet she kept her taloned hand raised. The other gripped the Inheritance Blade, its curling red ram horns calling for blood. The blood of the Bartol magnate. The blood of the king.

"Our people must be free from you!" she shouted with all her breath. No Air Reacher amplified her, yet her words hung over Kalastok like the old clocktower's bell.

No spirits interrupted her advance, and a roar erupted from the crowd as people rose to their feet. Nex and the other Ashes led a foray against the Reachers and breathless that Hazat directed into their range. A distraction as promised—one that allowed Nikoza to tumble toward the Crimson King as the wave broke.

The wind stung her cheeks as she fell. She had feared flying from her chambers' prison a day before, but a strange peace overcame her now. Blade raised, Reaching extinguished, she had done all in her power. Time and gravity's pull held the Commonwealth's fate.

Tzena drew her pistol as Qaraza tried to call more breathless to the king's aid. Chatik, though, merely smiled. "Let the ash fall, my dear firebird."

A myriad of wisps shot from the Unity Crystal in his grasp, his eyes fading to pure white and his body decaying by the second. He was no longer the vibrant middle-aged uncle she'd known. He appeared ancient and grotesque. Inhuman.

Nikoza winced, unable to dodge, but the wisps were not meant for her. They poured over the crowd like a scattered rainfall instead. Terror filled her, but she could only watch Chatik's corruptive power strike thousands straight in their cores.

Screams erupted. People shriveled and collapsed. Their spirits emerged moments later, only for more of Chatik's Reaching to transform them into breathless. An army formed in the seconds it took for Nikoza's foot to meet the balcony's railing. She had been too slow, and fury overtook her as she swung the Inheritance Blade.

"You are a monster!"

Each spirit that arose only Tainted Chatik further, his skin strapping to bone and his lips parting in a maddened babble. He offered no defense. Tzena and Uzrin fired, their bullets ripping through Nikoza's sternum and shoulder, but they were too late to stop the king's chosen heir. Gold and scarlet flashed toward the Unity Crystal's impossible array.

Then the blade struck.

THE PRINCESS'S TIMING SUCKED.

Nex clenched their jaw, waiting for Chatik's Death bolt or a diving breathless to end their life as they stood alone among the kneeling crowd. The Crimsons had exposed their intentions already, so where in the wastes was Nikoza? She was supposed to swoop in like some hero from the legends and save the day. But like all scions, she'd let the lowborn down.

Or, at least, that was what Nex thought until the largest damn wave they'd ever seen swept across the western Crimson District. Nikoza rose on its peak with Hazat lower—of course she gave herself the glory—and the breathless let her advance until Chatik directed them against her. That luckily took the spirits' attention off Nex, but even Hazat couldn't keep that many spirits occupied. They needed help.

And when Nikoza called out, the people answered.

Nex whipped their amber beads into the breathless as the other Ashes rallied to do the same with whatever glass or amber they could find. They kept hundreds of the spirits away from the waves, and those with guns laid down covering fire against the Crystal Brigade. Still, enough breathless broke through to force Hazat into another Reach.

The Spirit Reacher leaped to the ground, joining the resistance as Nikoza's wave carried her toward the balcony. Despite the Reachers on the higher balconies being mostly out of the rebels' range, they targeted those wearing Ashes of Dawn yellow instead of Nikoza. That would've given Nex pause if they weren't fighting for their life. They already knew Chatik wanted to die, but if he didn't care about protecting himself now, had he already found a new heir?

A chill fell over the air as Nikoza landed on the balcony. The rebels held their breaths, and Nex even muttered a prayer to the princess's stupid goddess. But wisps followed that chill.

"No…"

Nex stepped away from the man who'd cried out before, admitting he'd taken the cure, as the wisps overwhelmed him. Two heartbeats later, he collapsed. Nex grabbed their glass dagger, and when the man's spirit emerged and turned to a more defined breathless, they stabbed it straight in the chest.

They bit hard on their tongue to keep from shouting a thousand curses as they surveyed the rest of the crowd. The Crimsons had convinced thousands to take their cure, and every single one of them fell to Chatik's Reaching before Nikoza could even bound across the balcony. No number of untrained Ashes of Dawn rebels could fight off that many. And most of those who had resisted dropped back to their knees, pleading for their friends and family to live again.

Idiots! They were dead, and letting the Crimsons win would do nothing.

But a force rocked the entire district before Nex could shout for them to fight. A blinding light from the palace followed, sending Nex onto their back. Heat, then frost, darkness, and a dozen over strange sensations washed over them. It was like someone jammed their body into a jar with lightning itself and shook it until they lost all sense of feeling.

The flood of power eventually faded, but Nex couldn't tell if it had been seconds or hours. All of Kalastok lay sprawled about. Mists of every color smothered them like a heavy smog, but instead of a choking stench, it carried constantly shifting aromas. From sweet berries to decay, then a staleness that made them want never to move again.

Nex blinked away their shock and peered toward where Chatik had been. Except the entire front half of the Crystal Palace was gone, replaced by a gaping hole. The mists swirled thicker there, surrounding the figure who emerged, sparking with power.

"No shit. The princess did it."

Hovering amid the wreckage, Nikoza's eyes were glowing amethysts, her scion skin like the purest silver. Neither Chatik nor the Crystal Brigade were anywhere to be seen, and the breathless above crackled with the same power that tickled Nex.

People gasped up at Nikoza, yet she remained fixed there like some ethereal statue. It felt as if time had fallen still around them—a world apart from all the rest. But Nex refused to freeze with it.

They shoved their way through the crowd as Hazat gingerly did the same to their left. Worry filled his gaze, a familiar one to what Nex remembered holding when they'd hurried back to Vinnia with Etal's cure a season before. Memories from another life.

"You gonna tell me what just happened?" Nex asked him.

The Spirit Reacher just shook his head, itching his arm as sparks crossed over his glass bracers. "No one has spoken of anything like this before. It's as if the Unity Crystal expelled all its energy at once. Hopefully, that means Nikoza destroyed it."

Nex grinned at that, but forced it away quickly. Most of the spirits above had been killed and transformed by that very crystal's power. It deserved to be destroyed, but what happened when a crystal bound to every realm shattered?

Another, smaller explosion echoed through the mists when they reached the front of the crowd. Nikoza's head snapped back, a wave of power emanating from her before retracting as quick as a gunshot. The light faded from her.

Then she dropped.

Hazat rushed to catch her as Nex followed. It was a valiant, but stupid, attempt that sent both the scions tumbling into the crater where the palace's entryway had been. Remarkably, Nikoza appeared unharmed, and a look around the crater made it clear neither the Unity Crystal nor the Crimsons were here.

"Are you well?" Hazat asked the fallen princess. "What happened up there?"

She drew a long breath, her eyes still seeming lost. "I struck the Unity Crystal with my house's blade, but everything after that was a blur until I woke up in your arms." Her jaw dropped as she scanned the crater. "Dear Mother below, what have I done?"

"Looks like you killed our asshole of a king," Nex replied, earning a strangely aggressive look from her, "or at least destroyed the thing that made him invincible."

Hazat raised a hand to silence them. "We are still trying to figure out what happened, but the people who Chatik didn't turn into breathless are safe. They will want to hear you speak, if you are able."

"I am the Crystal Heir," she whispered to herself, holding out her arm to study the rippling wisps of every realm circling it. Then she stood with Hazat's help. "It appears that even when I defeat him, my uncle controls my destiny."

"No such thing," Nex said.

"Each of us has a part to play in the Crystal Mother's plans, Nex. Even if you do not listen, she hears you."

Nex spat at the ground between them. "Then her plan just killed thousands of people. I don't want anything to do with it."

Nikoza's gaze lingered on her. An ethereal vibrance filled those purple eyes, and a shiver ran down Nex's spine until she looked back at Hazat. "I will speak, but I need your aid to climb the slope. Even standing, I fear my legs wish to surrender."

He nodded, so together, the trio slowly returned to the edge of the crater. A cheer erupted when Nikoza appeared, but Nex knew better than to believe everyone did so. Thousands would mourn their loved ones. It didn't matter to them what Nikoza had done to defeat Chatik when they were both Bartol scions, and for hundred-hours, she had served in the oppressive Crystal Brigade. Some things weren't so easily forgotten.

Nikoza climbed further onto a hunk of rubble, allowing all to see her. She held an arm across her chest and heaved with each breath, but when she spoke, her voice carried over the now silent crowd.

"The Crimson King has fallen. I confess that I do not know what the destruction of his power has unleashed." She pursed her lips and placed a hand over her heart. "What I can promise, however, is that I will do all that I can to mend this beautiful city and nation. Through my uncle's rule, our people have bled, but I will be our Crystal Heir. We will rebuild Ezman to glory together. And I swear to the holy Crystal Mother that, through our united efforts, we will honor those who lost their lives in defiance of King Chatik's tyranny."

The old clocktower rang, echoing with her final words. Power hung in them, and with each chime of the bell, Nex found themself believing her more deeply. Whispers spread among the crowd until a man wearing an Ashes of Dawn armband threw up his fist.

"The Crystal Heir saved us!" he shouted.

"Mother bless Nikoza Bartol," another woman called out. "Mother bless the queen!"

Nikoza bowed her head with a gentle smile. "No matter who rules, we shall do so together. I will discuss our future with leaders among the great houses, tradespeople, and lowborn alike." She stepped down to Nex and offered them her hand. "Come, Nex of the Shadow Quarter. You and I have a city to rebuild."

Nex hesitated, looking from the hovering, motionless breathless to her. This all felt too easy. Life wasn't some tale that mothers told their children who feared the everdark. No, from Nikoza's landing on the balcony to the sudden disappearance of all the Crimsons, a gaping hole in Nex's chest told them something was wrong here.

But Nikoza's offer was one they couldn't refuse. Lowborn never had a chance to influence Kalastok and the Commonwealth's government. They had been forgotten for centuries until this moment, with the so-called Crystal Heir extending a hand to the leader of the Ashes of Dawn. Experience had taught Nex to doubt the scions. This past season had changed them, though, and it had made Nikoza into something greater too. Maybe, they just feared the chance that their ugly world could actually get better.

"Fine, *princess*," Nex said, taking her hand. "Just know I'm not calling you the crystal anything."

Power sparked between their palms as Nikoza grinned. "I would expect nothing less from you," she said, barely louder than a whisper. "That brutal honesty is exactly why I need you to help me change our realm forever."

Deathly purple glimmered in her eyes, and they only lured Nex further into her grasp. An intoxicating, alluring gaze that told them to forget all they had ever believed about her or the scions. She was not Jazuk. She was not the Crimson King. That old age had passed.

The Crystal Heir's had begun.

EPILOGUE – FROM ASH, RISE

"The foolish commander revels in a moment's victory. For while he turns his eyes upon the spoils of war, his enemy sharpens the blade to plunge into his spine." – Iitaan Greeniik, Reshkan general

Fattian, Bound One of Earth and second bearer of Mind, gained great pleasure from the Glassblades' pain. After all, that was what it had known its entire life. Agony at the hands of the embodied ones.

Pleasure, though, was the lowly pursuit of its foes. Such pursuits corrupted them, softened them like their fleshy skin. They had stolen Zekiaz from the spirits, but through their folly at the hand of God, they had also granted the spirits the very means they needed to re-store the realm.

"The embodied ones have abandoned the dragon," God spoke through Fattian's mind. *"Revive it, and our true work may begin."*

"Your will is mine," the Bound One replied, the rhythm of the Spiritspeech reverberating through its core Essence. That Essence fueled Fattian and granted it purpose. A purpose which all Vanashel fought to fulfill.

It repeated God's orders to its fellow Bound Ones. They had lost a third of their number and many more breathless servants, but the sacrifice had destroyed the Glassblade Order who had defied God's plans hundreds of cycles ago. By Fattian's command, some had been left alive, with others pursued by the awakened husks of Iliafa's lingering corpses. That let the spiritless embodied be of some use, and God desired influential messengers to spread fear among those who defied it.

The Vanashel crossed the mountains of the land the embodied ones called Vocka, then soared over the Ezmani forests and farms. Embodied ones gawked up at the sea of spirits and cowered with their strange glass amulets. Those trinkets would keep away the mindless awakened, but shards of impure glass meant little to the greater Vanashel. Nor did their false Crystal Mother.

Two embodied armies retreated from a collapsed fortress where the western Vamia River met the north one that God called the Ty. Apparently, the embodied Crimson Court—who had created Fattian and the rest of the Bound Ones' first generation—had fought another embodied faction here. Squabbles for thrones of stone. Oh, how little their little kingdoms meant compared to the glory of the God trapped in the Crystal's heart.

A burgeoning power lurked beneath the fortress's rubble. Dormant for now, it hummed with the same rhythm of all spirits. Such a dragon should never have been commanded by the embodied ones, and now, it would serve the Vanashel and the God who had crafted it deep below.

Fattian kept the Vanashel out of sight until the two armies had retreated far enough in either direction. Once it was sure they would not return, it ignited its Essence, Reaching into the realm of Earth and removing the rubble from over the fallen dragon.

The magnificent beast resembled the form the Bound Ones had taken to honor it and God, and Fattian's shadowy wings shivered in excitement. It had waited over ten cycles for a chance to fulfill God's call. Patience was not its strength, and it signaled for the others to join it in sending their Spirit Essence to the dragon.

"Awaken, beast of the Crystal," they declared together in the Spiritspeech, the air itself reverberating with God's holy rhythm. "Awaken, and together, let us awaken God itself."

Silver mists emanated from the Bound Ones. Their offering would not be enough, though, so they ordered hundreds of their breathless to surrender their complete Essences to it. Like the battle, such sacrifices were great, but the dragon would reward them a thousand-fold.

The dragon's crystalline body released a radiant light, growing with each bit of Spirit Essence that replenished its own. Fattian did not relent until the creature's Essence became deafening through God's rhythm. Zekiaz itself tremored beneath its power, and when the final breathless surrendered itself, the dragon's eyes shot open.

Fattian descended toward its head. Then, extending its ethereal arms, the Bound One shouted to the depths of the Crystal below, "Rise, spawn of God. The embodied have slain you, but those of spirit have called you back. Your work is yet to be finished."

FOR THE CRIMSON CAUSE, KING CHATIK BARTOL THE FIRST HAD GIVEN EVERYTHING. He had lost his children, his wife, his mind, and now, watching his chosen heir descend upon him with House Bartol's Inheritance Blade, he would lose his life. One would have thought him to hold regret in his final moments.

What had he to regret when all had gone precisely to plan?

Well, perhaps not *precisely*. He had not desired to lose his family, and the Unity Crystal's Realm Taint had taken hold far more quickly than he had expected. With such limited time, though, he took pride in knowing his Crystal Heir and her future court were well prepared for the struggles ahead. He only regretted the horror necessary to unlock the door for her to walk through.

Nikoza's sword struck the Unity Crystal with such beauty that Chatik's fractured mind could barely comprehend it. Impossible colors formed and dissolved in fractions of a second, shooting around them until they consumed the entire front of the palace. Oh, how satisfying it was to see theory become reality.

Nikoza collapsed from her gunshot wounds as the hundreds of

thousands gathered beyond the explosion's radius froze in time. The power released by all fifteen Crystal Realms formed a temporary sub-realm around the Crimsons, the Crystal Brigade, and the Crystal Heir herself, giving Chatik's allies the chance they needed to bring his plan to fruition.

The Crimson Cause had never been about him. He had always been merely a conduit, and now, having guided Nikoza's loyalties and furies to rebel against him at the perfect moment, he could die knowing he had done all he could for the glory of Ezman.

"Do it," he told Tzena as his body betrayed him, succumbing to Taint as the Unity Crystal shattered into a thousand shards. "Time is short, my love. And my mind…"

Visions passed him by. Images of a future of fire and blood, spirits in the form of dragons swooping from the sky to strike those both bound to the Spirit Crystal and not. He had sought to prevent this, to save his people. Had he failed? Had he not been enough?

He returned to reality to gaze upon his wounded niece. An unfortunate act, but one necessary to make the ruse believable to the populace. Lowborn were simple to manipulate through careful action, and they needed to see their defiant Crystal Heir injured, only to heal without any sight of a Body Reacher.

"Hurry," he pled. "Before she dies."

The most loyal Reachers of the Crystal Brigade gathered just within the balcony's doors, Gregorzon Niezik barking commands to them. Their path was set. It would lead them away from Nikoza at first, but time had a way of bringing people together in desperation. She would need them, and the Crimson Court would aid her when she was ready to fulfil her destiny.

His dear Tzena picked his house's blade from the balcony's stone floor. Tears slipped from her gorgeous golden eyes. Oh, how he would have loved to spend the rest of life with her and their unborn child which grew within her womb, but he had chosen his nation over himself. All magnates sought to die by the hand of their loved ones, passing their spirit on to guide future generations. Jazuk had failed to do so, but Chatik would not repeat his father's folly.

Ezman's ascension required a sacrifice of blood. A sacrifice he gave freely.

Chatik closed his eyes as Tzena pressed the blade's golden and scarlet tip to his chest. Screams of the dead haunted his thoughts, and he silently promised each of his victims that they were but a stroke of a brush that would paint Zekiaz's greatest masterpiece. One of scion glory. One where none need suffer. If he must tarnish his name to achieve such ecstasy, then let the generations spit upon his grave. He did not matter.

"We will see the Cause to its completion," his lover's sweet voice said as pain split his ribs. Blood trickled free, but it was a welcome release from Taint's torment. "And I will never forget what you have gifted me."

Then she rammed the blade straight through his heart, ending his life in the second it took for him to open his eyes. As he perished, he felt only bliss at the chance to see her face one last time. Death stole him with that thought, but his spirit broke free from his mortal form to hover over the balcony.

A thousand powers graced his spirit there, each rhythm unique and glorious in its own right. Zekiaz sang along with the spirit's call, but it was merely a single realm among numerous. A fragment of the Crystal Realms. And the spirit grasped in that moment how miniscule it truly was until a more familiar force pulled upon it.

Spirit Reachers of the Crystal Brigade stepped onto the balcony, their silver wisps pressing the spirit toward weakened Nikoza. She would heal with the waiting Body Reacher's help, but they needed her wounded. It rattled her spirit so that the one which had been Chatik's may join it. The Crimson King himself was truly dead, but inheritance through the spirit was about more than one's true person. It carried the desires and instincts of its past through unexplainable bonds, especially when given quickly from one life to the next.

None before had publicly held two spirits. Chatik had planned for this moment for many years, though, joining experiments with the Crimson Court's others in the Spirit Wastes. A way to ascend beyond the bond of a single spirit. What if one could hold the experiences of many and learn from each?

Nikoza jolted as the new spirit joined her own, but settled quickly. The two would hold together, guiding her when she awoke to become the Crystal Heir. Power would linger in the wake of the Unity Crystal's collapse, and she would need all the help she could get to direct it well.

"Goodbye, my love," Tzena said, fixing her posture and glancing down at the Inheritance Blade. "May you one day be free to grant your spirit to our true heir. Until then, let the one of crystal lead Ezman from the ashes."

She turned away to join the others inside, where Reacher wisps of every color swirled into a portal as they had a season ago. Only a Body Reacher remained to heal the Crystal Heir's wounds. Seconds later, even he was gone, and the subrealm created by the explosion collapsed in his wake, destroying the palace that had displayed the power of the Commonwealth.

The Crimsons' work was finished for the time being. Ezman lay in the hands of Nikoza the Twin-Spirited now, and their lost leader's will would guide her every step of the way.

END OF BOOK 2

A Word from the Author

It is safe to safe that this book was the most work of anything I have ever written—it has also been my favorite creation to date. *The Crystal Heir*'s Kickstarter allowed me to truly create my dream book with so many illustrations, maps, and stories wrapped into one epic tale. That is because of all of your incredible support, The Realm Reachers (and the universe of the Crystal Realms) are far from over.

If you have enjoyed reading this story, please take the time to post an honest review on whatever retailer you purchased this book from (or on Goodreads or social media sites). Every review helps new readers discover my books, and personal recommendations are more powerful than anything I can say as an author.

Want more Realm Reachers? Maybe a bit of backstory about how Kasia earned her nickname of the Amber Dame? You can get a free eBook of The Amber Dame—the prequel novella to The Realm Reachers—and my novellas from other series by joining my newsletter at www.Brendan-Noble.com

If you would also like to support me over the billion-dollar corporations, you can purchase signed paperbacks/hardcovers (including exclusive deluxe editions), eBooks, and audiobooks directly from my store for cheaper than you can get them anywhere else! Check out that store at www.Brendan-Noble.com/Store

-       Brendan

ABOUT THE AUTHOR

Brendan Noble is an American author writing epic fantasy with inspiration from his Polish ancestry, mythology, video games of all types, and Dungeons & Dragons. He loves to explore the complexities of politics and the gray between good and evil.

Shortly after beginning his writing career in 2019, Brendan married his wife Andrea and moved to Rockford, Illinois from his hometown in Michigan. Since then, he has published three series: The Realm Reachers, The Frostmarked Chronicles, and The Prism Files.

Outside of writing, Brendan is a data analyst. His top interests include German, Polish, and American soccer/football, Formula 1, analyzing political elections across the world, playing extremely nerdy strategy video games, exploring with his wife, and reading.